The New York Times

SUNDAY CROSSWORD OMNIBUS VOLUME 3

Edited by EUGENE T. MALESKA

Random House
Puzzles & Games

SOLUTIONS TO THE PUZZLES ARE
FOUND AT THE BACK OF THE BOOK

1. Yankee Doodles by Frances Hansen

ACROSS

1 Epstein
6 Fellow
10 Duel preludes
15 Seats for Shipwreck Kelly
21 City of Japan
22 Kind of bean
23 Add up
24 Fr. menu item
25 Hindu lute
26 Susa's land
27 Greek market
28 Wintry
29 Words by Henry H. Bennett
33 Hazel or pea
34 Drug initials
35 Forms
36 Arrests
40 After amas
42 Scary word
44 Papers: Abbr.
45 Letter
48 Mrs. Perón
49 Summer drink
50 Rest upon
53 Poetic cattle
54 Highwayman Claude
55 Cut grass
56 Ointment
57 Diminutive suffix
59 Paris suburb
60 Early Florida land-developer
61 Fern spores
62 Casey Jones, for one
64 Puerto ___
65 Without: Fr.
66 Waste allowances
68 Have a bite
69 List
71 ___ Alto
73 Invited to a penthouse
77 Bar bill
79 Make up for
80 What Key was glad to see
85 Naval order above captain
86 ___ Paulo
87 Bandwagon ism
88 Make ___ for it (flee)
89 Antelopes
91 Football gains: Abbr.
93 Finnish lake
95 ". . . spare your country's ___ said"
99 Spin: Scot.
100 Grew an iris
105 Polite interruption
106 Yarn knot
107 "I cannot tell ___"
108 In the style of
109 Rock cavities
110 Card game
111 Trite
112 Nourish
113 Conned
115 ___ truce (parley prelude)
116 Arabian land
117 Before H.S.T.
118 Pitch
120 Compass point
121 Kiln
123 Most impolite
124 Popular lane
126 Babel had one: Abbr.
127 Miss Farrow
128 What Betsy Ross said?
138 George M. Cohan, notably
139 Range, as of emotions
140 Octavia, to Nero
141 Put a levy on
142 Make a mockery of
143 Tactless
144 German one
145 Tagalog servant
146 Curls the lip
147 Matchmaker of "Fiddler"
148 Nursery need, in baby-talk
149 Gosh!

DOWN

1 Chaff
2 Vast land area
3 Suffragist Carrie
4 Trappist cheeses
5 Like Münchhausen's home?
6 Split
7 Sword part
8 Asian nurse
9 Actress Mason
10 Proper
11 Ship journals
12 Over
13 Sunshade
14 Cut sharply
15 Commanders' boats
16 Patriot Thomas and family
17 Cassini et al.
18 Elia
19 V___ (May 8, 1945)
20 Seasoning, in Paris
30 "Ain't We Got ___?"
31 Patio slab
32 Taste
36 Mutineers' pennants
37 Palate part
38 Actor David
39 Like a certain banner
40 Dote on
41 "Stay ___" (Biblical plea)
42 Arctic sight
43 Do ___ (all-out)
45 Guest
46 Mise ___
47 Pooh's donkey friend
49 In a mood for love
51 Heflin
52 Perfumery solvent
53 Wagnerian soprano
58 Slip
61 Normandy town
63 Old Glory, Union Jack et al.
67 Observed
70 Pearl Harbor site
72 Aleutian island
74 Barrier
75 Employ
76 Attention-getting sound
78 "A ___ bugles, a ruffle of drums"
80 Followed
81 More perilous
82 Type of tire
83 Thou: Fr.
84 Shipshape
85 Arizona city
90 Spanish Mrs.
92 Seas or wonders
94 Not give ___
96 Agenda
97 Waikiki dances
98 Ger. president
101 Drake or Lunt
102 Mussolini's title
103 Ripen
104 Hails, as a cab
111 Child's game
114 Trap
118 Ready ___ (off the rack)
119 Wards off
122 Debated
123 Jap. coin
124 Mississippi sight
125 Football, at Eton
126 Church pledge
127 Comic Amsterdam
128 "Heads ___ tails you lose"
129 "Quién ___?"
130 Rail-crossing guard
131 Puff of wind
132 Roman 62
133 "___ Cassius has a lean . . ."
134 Angel's headgear
135 Leaf angle
136 Daisies don't do it
137 June 14
138 James Montgomery et al.

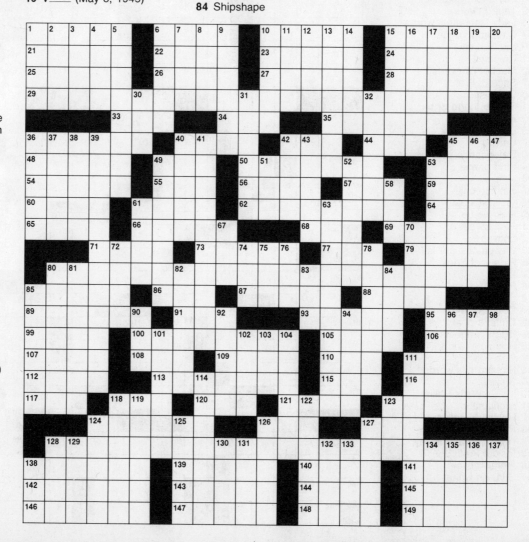

2. Literary Curves by Maura B. Jacobson

ACROSS

1 Bargain-priced
6 Worshiper's word
10 Wine additive
14 Houston player
19 Celerity
20 Timor city
21 British composer
22 Nassau's island group
24 Rose yield
25 Cordelia's words?
28 ____ show (solo act)
29 Yorick's words?
32 French islands
33 Mao ____ tung
34 Islamic Almighty
35 "Dombey ____"
38 "____ were a rich man"
40 Teheran native
43 Seep
47 Othello's words?
51 Spoils or solar
53 Make a gaffe
54 Quebec city
55 Dropsy
56 Work ____ (cooperate)
57 Both: Prefix
59 Iranian coin
60 Stair part
61 Agnes or Cecil
62 Roadbed items
64 Obeisance, Cockney style
66 Dernier ____
68 Pay-phone feature
69 Tapir feature
71 Lady Macbeth's words?
77 Cruz and Vague
80 Luzon native
81 Untamed
82 Macbeth's words?
87 Sacred: Prefix
90 Optimistic
91 Before therm or bar
92 Kind of melba
95 Bert and family
97 Candid
100 Defendant's out
104 Kind of eye
106 Vex
107 Embryo cells
108 Violinist's aid
109 Pick-me-up
111 Pasture call
112 Lockup
113 Cleopatra's words?
116 Father of Enos
117 I.e.
118 Plus
119 Oakley et al.
120 Domain
123 Duffer's goal
125 Blasting agents
126 Romeo's words?
137 Doze off
138 Richard III's words?
139 Blazing
140 ____'s Wells Ballet
141 Highlander
142 Hokkaido native: Var.
143 Franck or Romero
144 Hopalong and family
145 Inside: Prefix
146 Flemish river
147 Spanish wheat

DOWN

1 Dialogue on a low level
2 "Music ____ charms . . ."
3 Padua's neighbor
4 Throwback
5 Risky
6 Mine inlets
7 "La Bohème" heroine
8 Biblical country
9 Of Cleo's river
10 Mud volcano
11 "Star ____"
12 Two-toed sloth
13 Blackbird
14 Bubbling
15 ____ song (caroled)
16 Hamlet's words?
17 Oar: Fr.
18 Sharif
23 Not ____ (none)
26 Baseball positions: Abbr.
27 Medium for Ade
30 Morals arbiter
31 Caesar's 551
35 ____ and a day
36 Shearer and Talmadge
37 Deanna
38 Shaped girder
39 Egyptian peasant
40 D.D.E. et al
41 Hoarfrost
42 Rebel
44 Verdi opera
45 Enthusiast
46 Ants
48 Threesome
49 Nonconformist
50 I hate: Lat.
51 Vane reading
52 Tuber
56 Verona's river
58 Kate's words?
63 De Lesseps' canal
65 Scoff at
67 Moroccan range
70 Before pod or angle
72 Boxing decision
73 Kind of mad
74 Otherwise
75 Buckingham initials
76 Mizzen or jib
78 "There is ____ in the affairs . . ."
79 Blvds.
82 Explosive sounds
83 Balzac
84 ____ de corps
85 Laryngitic
86 City on the Delaware
88 Geometric figures
89 A.L. player
93 What Sullivan lost
94 Poet Leigh ____
96 Wild plums
98 Road sign
99 Belonging to: Suffix
101 Trims off
102 "What time ____?"
103 Repository
105 Albanian city
110 Declarer's goal, at bridge
113 Let in
114 Remote
115 More risky
117 U.N. group
121 Relieved
122 Mimics
123 Paul, in Rome
124 Landon
125 "____ coffee?"
126 G.P.'s
127 Sheik, usually
128 Extinct bird
129 Wise one
130 Pearl Buck heroine
131 Requisite
132 After upsilons
133 Corn bread
134 Not final, in law
135 Rocky eminence
136 Saarinen

3. Reviewing the Bidding by William Lutwiniak

ACROSS

1 Exultant song
6 Sword of yore
11 Navy noncoms
15 U.S. energy complex
18 Spontaneous
19 Regard as material
20 Barflies
21 Bordoni
23 One heart
27 Clothes
28 Tops
29 Arm bones
30 Anyone's game
31 Gelid
32 Witch of ____
33 In ____ (untidy)
34 Leaves off
35 Spore sacs
36 Maestro's concern
37 Musical leap
38 One spade
46 Like ducks' feet
47 ____ foot oil
48 Contends
49 "Le Coq ____"
50 Spreads
51 Eater: Suffix
52 Pert lasses
54 Counterclockwise
55 Adjective ending
56 Aviary sounds
57 Old pronoun
58 Humpback
59 Three diamonds
66 Building wings
67 Ulyanov
68 Leif's father
69 Double
79 Burning bush
80 Maintain
81 German pronouns
82 Panache
83 Heron's cousin
84 Less admirable
86 Girl's name
88 Play the ham
89 Word with easter or wester
90 ____ Raton
91 Count of music
92 ____ own (solo)
93 Four clubs
99 Bullish times
100 Stu of films
101 Poetic word
102 Certain workshop
104 Defects
105 Cold
107 Demijohn
110 Kind of punch
111 Cliburn's forte
112 Skald
113 Lisbon lady
114 Redouble
119 Red as ____
120 Reveals
121 Greek city-state
122 ____ sides
123 Sun. talk
124 "Citizen Kane" prop
125 Certain years
126 Approvals

DOWN

1 Famed singer
2 Kind of committee
3 Pensive poem
4 River islands
5 Knicks' league
6 Of a sampling process
7 "____ evil"
8 Strength of a solution
9 On leave
10 Young people's org.
11 Courtroom figure
12 P.T.A. members
13 Sooner
14 Theol. degree
15 Crosspiece
16 Nemo's creator
17 The opposition
20 Eyeball component
21 Have thoughts about
22 Feminine ending
24 Like old butter
25 Bruits
26 English ditches
32 ____ Park, Colo.
33 Penetrating
34 Nesses
35 Tree: Prefix
36 Restricted to men
37 Thwacked
38 Word of greeting
39 Guiana sorcery
40 Win at jousting
41 Restrain
42 Like campus walls
43 Dropsy
44 Newfangled
45 Fish in a way
46 Novelist Herman
51 Common funds
52 Preside over
53 Hair dye
54 Test area
56 Drink
57 General drift
58 This, in Tours
60 Biblical mount
61 Miss Oyl
62 O'Toole
63 Stranded
64 Mehitabel's chronicler
65 Snaky sound
69 In flight
70 Unauthorized
71 Gyrate
72 Hawaiian birds
73 Attacks
74 Blend with
75 Autobiographical item
76 Miss Massey
77 Cause to be tardy
78 Chemical endings
84 Specter
85 Bonn cries
86 N.Z. birds
87 Wise ____ owl
88 "The Song is ____"
90 Clergyman
91 Dog, in baby talk
92 N.Y. lake
94 Dissipate
95 Dunderhead
96 Made fast
97 Praying figures
98 Entrance
102 Slights
103 Brouhaha
104 Filament
105 White poplar
106 Rabbit fur
107 Salk
108 Family member
109 Highlanders
110 Tumor: Suffix
111 Indian veranda
113 Over
115 Weights: Abbr.
116 Select
117 Caviar
118 Trifle

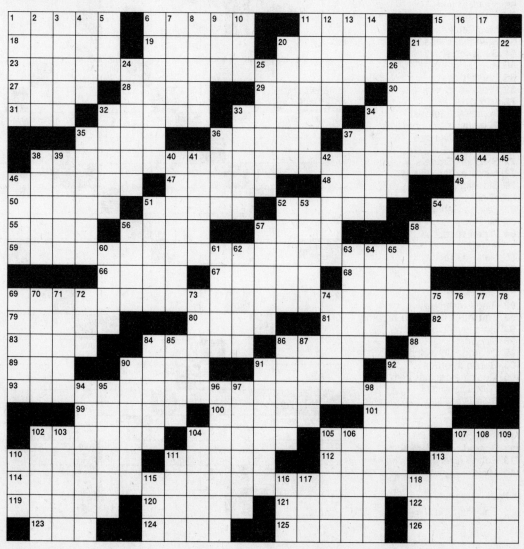

4. On the Prowl by Eugene T. Maleska

ACROSS

1 Bone dry
5 Idolater
10 Damp
15 Can. province
19 Front or Walter Hines
20 January in Jalisco
21 Lake in Finland
22 Stewpot
23 Road menace
25 Untreated, he's tricky
27 True copies
28 Ref. book entry
30 Toothless
31 Word from for China
32 Doc
34 Word in Mass. motto
35 Man of the cloth
38 Outlaw's target
40 Became jittery
44 Charged
45 Film actor Reginald
46 "A ____, a bone . . ."
48 Geological ridge
49 Composer Novello
50 Tail closely
51 Frome of fiction
53 Wallach
54 Warlocks, e.g.
55 Frogman
56 Part of f.o.b.
58 Nautical term
59 Transvaal capital
61 Macbeth's trio
63 Stendhal character
64 Song thrush
65 Kind of notch
66 English poet
69 Promise to kick a habit
72 Libido
73 Impatient motorist
74 Insomniac's countdown
75 Denial in Dundee
76 Swindle
77 Stephen Crane's was red
78 Made owlish noises
79 Sideslip
80 Wind: Prefix
82 Salt, in Sedan
83 Minded
84 "Dum spiro, ____" (S.C. motto)
85 Nuts to crack
87 City-founder: 753 B.C.
89 Gary of golf
90 Cashbox
92 Rings ominously
93 Emulate witches on brooms
94 More avaricious
98 Siouan
99 Overdoes a welcome
103 Goblin in green
105 Medicine-cabinet item
107 Will ____ wisp
108 Bald flyer
109 Accrue
110 Alliance of West
111 Wampum unit
112 Scaredy-cat's emotion
113 Potion giver
114 Minx

DOWN

1 Basilica area
2 Séance sounds
3 "____ a Kick Out of You"
4 Western herb
5 Formalist
6 Pico de ____ of Pyrenees
7 Scarab and tigereye
8 Nigerian native
9 Void
10 Brave
11 Spenser heroine
12 Wizard's cousin
13 Sultanic say-so
14 Madman
15 Mollifies
16 African grass
17 Pocket feature
18 Welles role
24 Certain believer
26 Invisible
29 In vain
32 ____ beast
33 Races recklessly
35 Dress with care
36 Delirious one
37 Feel ____
38 Sorceress of myth
39 Had status
41 Burglar's standby
42 Fisherman
43 Towels
45 Baal, Mammon, etc.
47 Snow-on-the-mountain
50 Clerical cap
52 Cordial base
55 Beetle
56 Scarlet or hay
57 U.S. journalist
58 Agent: Suffix
60 Baby's discovery
61 Tidal or permanent
62 Affront
64 British tar
66 Sum up
67 Neighbor of Bangor
68 Jolly ____
69 Clementine's 9's
70 Savoir ____
71 Russian czar
74 Fern cluster
77 Lab substance
78 Like saints
79 Big Ten players
81 Like some postage
83 Dada, for one
84 Forest debris
86 Teed off poorly
88 Dawdled
89 Commotion
91 Hungarian composer
93 Bolivian capital
94 Whipped-cream serving
95 Neural network
96 Hebrew bushel
97 High dudgeon
99 Giant slain by Apollo
100 Muezzin's call
101 Asian apparition
102 Spill over
104 Diminutive ending
106 Mythical princess

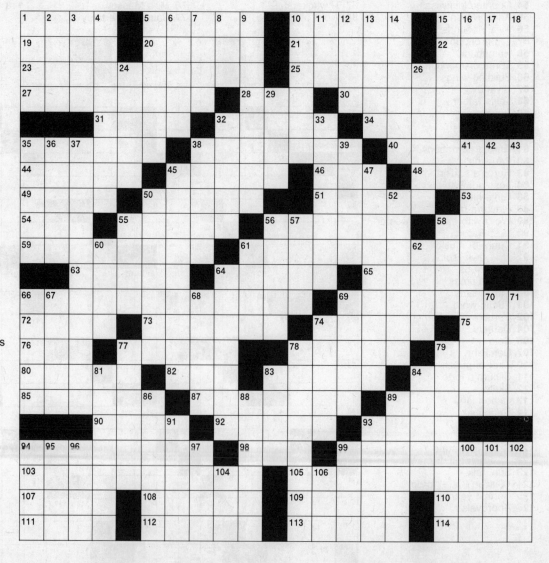

5. Closing Out by Cornelia Warriner

ACROSS

1 Weight
6 Zip, for one
10 Teasdale
14 Vestiges
19 Lizard
20 Damage
21 Boxer's target
22 Lobster roe
23 Get away from it all
26 Sun-dried brick
27 Mexican tomorrows
28 Miss Garson et al.
29 Drudged
30 Grads-to-be
31 Hebrew letter
33 ____ matres
34 Baseball's Rose et al.
35 Copter's relative
36 Bee follower
37 Drying frame
38 Residence
42 Shows a thin skin
46 Black-ink items: Abbr.
49 One of 24
50 Schick of medicine
52 Aniline, etc.
53 Fastener of a sort
54 Pilaster
55 Item for a clambake
59 Visitor
60 Pestered
62 Tourist-stop sign
63 N.L. players
64 Western
65 Callas
66 The rockets' was red
67 Put away
69 Blanc et al.
70 Dealer in provisions
73 Wall tapestry
74 Start a holiday trip
76 Goddess of healing
77 Miss Dee
78 ____ for (washed up)
79 Pony up
80 Part of A.D.
81 Goddess: Lat.
82 September outing, usually
86 Condors' home
87 Street show
89 Nessen or Ziegler
90 Large bird
93 Full to the top
94 Small bits
96 Indian weights
97 Britons' network
100 Welcomes
101 Put in the clink again
103 Niagara's outlet
105 Scarf
106 Season's last gasp
108 Casino game
109 Combine: Abbr.
110 Wild shout
111 Roundish
112 Show contempt
113 Ruth or Herman
114 Divide
115 Lightens

DOWN

1 Windless conditions
2 Close to, to poets
3 Certain horses
4 Part of Edison's name
5 In the prime of life
6 Part of a boilermaker
7 Put one's ____ in
8 Bit of sediment
9 Welcome
10 Plotting one
11 Moses's census aide
12 Henna job
13 Slow, in music: Abbr.
14 Fish cleaners, at times
15 Acid salt
16 Signer of a bill for 106
   Across
17 Local movies, for short
18 Coast
24 Colombian city
25 Fisherman
29 Skewers
32 Misled
37 Maple genus
38 Famous captain
39 ____ fide
40 Holiday event
41 Haul off
43 Hobo, for short
44 Swelling disease
45 Certain votes
47 Subterfuge
48 Puts into type
50 Exposed
51 Watercress, in England
53 Kind of angel
56 Praying figure
57 Famous firth
58 Idaho city
59 Gramp's wife
61 Paris seasons
63 Razor or gay
65 Roadside place
66 Ganges landing
67 Native of Cagliari
68 Certain test answer
69 Talking bird: Var.
70 Dismissals
71 Old laborer
72 Wallabies, for short
74 Sharpen
75 Took off
78 Per ____ (allowances)
82 Fried cake
83 Kidney bean
84 Pneumonia type
85 One of the gang
86 Forbidding
88 Small cavity
91 Catcalled
92 Marine flier
93 Certain crime
94 Real-life
95 Arabian fiddle
97 British guns
98 Bash
99 Buffalo Bill et al.
100 Chatters
102 Wash
104 Hawaiian shrub
106 Science place
107 Over there

6. Fourth-minus Estate by Jack Luzzatto

ACROSS

1 Doll fanciers
5 Faulty
10 Donee of a sort
14 Italian food
19 Once more
20 Sample
21 Caen's river
22 Meat jelly
23 Water-cooler fare
25 He'll tell anything
27 They stand for anything
28 Novel skeletons
29 "Miss ___ Regrets"
30 One to get rid of
32 Combined reporters
33 Excited
37 Garbage barge
39 Stuck in the river
44 Kings and queens
46 Old greeting
47 Rich source
48 Added support
49 Like Annie
51 And away he went, on TV
54 Small cases
56 African antelope
57 Social gaffes
59 Street show
60 Gulf of Greece
61 Great czar
62 Marine eagle
63 Dirty rags
68 Harper Valley unit
71 Most apropos
73 Othello
74 Austrian spa
76 Cocktail shaker
79 Royal Swedish name
81 Seed: Prefix
82 Vinland man
83 Was caught short
86 Panache
87 Cattle food
88 Math branch
89 Picayune: Var.
91 Up tight
95 Do burlesque work
97 Franc fractions
98 Emphatic denial
100 Russian sea
102 Of the dawn
103 Upper-cruster
108 Parties, dances, etc.
113 Minor wild oat
114 Chiller movie
115 In the offing
116 Roulette bet
117 Dazzling effect
118 Top reporter
119 Counterpart of safe
120 Handy man
121 Climbs up
122 Hisses for silence

DOWN

1 Way to go
2 Nullify
3 Off-color reporter
4 Loved one
5 Drink ___ (pledge)
6 Pole
7 "This ___ sudden!"
8 Stock or lineage
9 Infections
10 Baseball league of sorts
11 Part of Q.E.D.
12 ___ form (red hot)
13 Reentry rockets
14 Spanish stew
15 Italian wine city
16 Bridge
17 Floor piece
18 Elite of the deck
24 Hominy mush
26 French city
31 P.R. person for sinners
33 Current unit
34 Ugly customer
35 Island repubic
36 Starts a new crop
38 Quits singles for doubles
40 Egg white
41 Purveyors of tidbits
42 Old Dead Sea land
43 Low dives
45 Broken bit
50 Tapir
51 High good humor
52 Riga native
53 Adjustment to a new habitat
55 Town on the Hellespont
58 Like the Metropolitan scene
64 Recent: Prefix
65 T ___ Thomas
66 Ordinary
67 Bunk
69 Mrs. ___, Dr. Johnson's friend
70 Trues
72 Pocket, in Paris
75 Place-kicker, e.g.
76 Quasi
77 Irish island
78 Deadfall
80 Thicket, in Scotland
84 Relating to luck
85 Painting, music, etc.
90 Roman woman's robe
92 Document certifier
93 Not barefoot
94 Western oak
96 Flogs
99 Manmade fabric
101 Freshwater fish
103 Wallaba trees
104 Parting-of-the-ways place
105 Cooler
106 Lasting injury
107 Descendant of Fatima
109 Eyelash: Prefix
110 Oil exporter
111 Difficult deed
112 Bumbles

7. Echo Chamber by Jordan S. Lasher

ACROSS

1 Rotating-wing craft
6 Neighbor of Idaho
10 Practices
16 Tobacco wad
20 Guam's capital
21 Kind of dish or swipe
22 Everlasting
23 Violin opening
24 Balsamweed
26 Sweetheart
28 Disconcert
29 Demolishes
30 Early slaves
31 Eye parts
32 Photography abbr.
33 Fleur-____
34 ____ alios
35 Fit to be tied
36 Mountain nests
38 Prefix for date or diluvian
39 Der ____
40 Filing aid
43 Muggy
44 Secrecy
48 "Strangers ____ Train"
49 Mrs. Luce et al.
51 Rose's man et al.
52 Tumultuous
53 Roman road
54 Exuded
55 Swan genus
56 Make a racket
57 Topper of film
58 Take it easy
59 She loved Tom Thumb
62 Noted short-story writer
63 Part of NATO: Abbr.
64 Certain writer
65 Manners
66 Arias
67 Carrier of a crook
70 Suit
71 Dance acts in India
75 Electrical units
76 French income
77 Kind of board or bag
78 Scrap
79 Sonly or daughterly
82 Boisterous
84 Trademark
85 In ____ (under pressure)
86 Mexican people
87 Fashion name
88 Guadalajara dish
89 Boston player, for short
90 Heretofore
91 Gasoline and kerosene
93 Strengths
94 Hindu cymbals
95 Confused state
97 Authorize
98 Poet Lowell
99 Chemical endings
100 Metric land units
101 Extreme edges
103 Rice field
105 Singer Vicki et al.
107 Drags
109 Orel's river
111 Three in one
113 Old Bahamas native
114 French stage forte
115 Open to debate

116 Hit song by Donovan, 1966
118 Resembling early jazz
120 Brilliance
121 Dahl or Francis
122 Word with shoppe
123 ____ off the old block
124 Van ____ (L.A. suburb)
125 Rated oneself highly
126 Run across
127 Check recipient

DOWN

1 Faux pas
2 Large lizard
3 Football fireworks
4 Eleven, to an élève
5 For example
6 Customary things
7 Excited state
8 Cutting tools
9 Attention-getters
10 Easings of tension
11 Capon, e.g.
12 "____ ear and . . ."
13 Metric quart
14 Laddie's mate
15 Ship's-plank curve
16 Singing group
17 Swell!
18 Otherwise
19 Old British weights
23 Certain criminal
25 Spartans and Corinthians
27 Russian "general"
33 Entertained
34 Author of "Bus Stop"
35 Aquatic plants
37 Peep show
38 "It's ____!"
39 Marketplace
41 Wind: Prefix
42 Red or robber
44 Angelic, in a way
45 Letter-shaped fastener
46 Croquet item
47 Russian range
49 Drinks
50 Reluctant
53 Column order
55 Distinctive qualities
56 Able-____
57 Ritual group
60 Modifies
61 Arrogant
62 Debauchee
64 ____-mell
66 Butterfly
68 Fabric style
69 Top banana
70 "____ the Jabberwock, my son!"
71 Knotty
72 Sinuous dance: Var.
73 Grass fungus
74 Facing a glacier
76 Kind of flush
77 Fabric weave
79 Legal truths
80 Girder
81 Australian tree
82 Large amounts
83 Creator of Lefty
84 Relative of flotsam
86 Saunter
88 Polynesian images
90 Insect-eating plant
91 Like some brows
92 Purposes
93 Actor Robert
95 Was lacking
96 Without exception
101 Well adjunct
102 Chicago suburb
104 Large halls
105 Beautiful: Prefix
106 Bothered
107 Selassie
108 ____ Triomphe
110 Star variety
111 Govt. agents
112 Proof of payment: Fr.
113 Region: Abbr.
114 Word with Missouri
115 Isinglass
117 Caroline Island group
119 Faucet

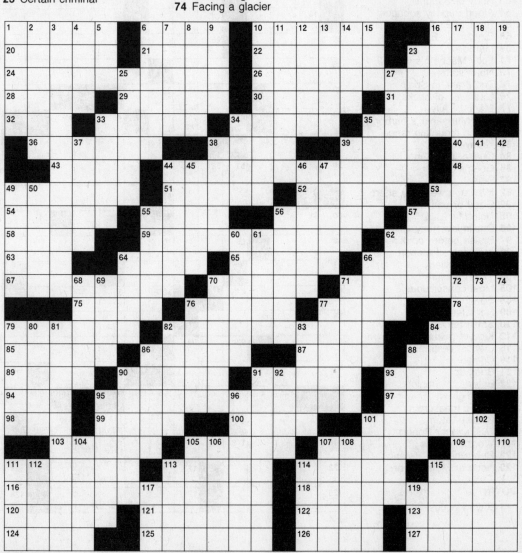

8. Drawing the Shades by Bert Rosenfield

ACROSS

1 Hole maker
4 Undermine
7 Lacedaemon
13 Highway to Fairbanks
18 Life story, for short
19 ____ of good feeling
20 Son of Anchises
21 Brazilian state
22 Recital pieces: Abbr.
23 Rose
26 Roone of TV
28 One with a will
29 Chemical suffixes
30 Amin
31 Old Asia Minor region
33 Nerve cell
35 Adage
36 Baltic feeder
37 Tropical tree
40 Cypriot capital
43 Roberts
45 George or Bud
48 Genetic substance: Abbr.
49 Diminutive suffixes
50 Green
55 Looks daggers at
57 Pleiades star
58 African soldier
59 Varnish resin
60 Answers the plaintiff
63 Ruby or Sandra
64 Alben Barkley sobriquet
67 River of England
68 Elected, in Epinal
69 Maroon
71 Lady Macbeth's words?
73 Noun suffix
74 The brain, in Spain
76 Like ____ of bricks
77 Blanc or Allen
78 Like Murmansk's harbor
80 Czech mountain range
82 "Leave ____"
84 Quaker pronoun
85 Grieg's dancer
87 Blue
92 Hiawatha wear, for short
93 Good or bad
95 Dolce far ____
96 Dublin law body
97 Braise before cooking
99 A Chaplin, for short
100 LSD, familiarly
104 Yarn measure
105 Most conspicuous
108 Bowling round
109 Rental-ad abbr.
110 Small terrier
112 Kind of guidance
116 Clerical vestment
118 Crimson
121 Bring up
122 Bitter ____ (tonic)
123 Store grain
124 Metric measure
125 Pianist Tatum
126 U.S. painter Robert
127 Went the route
128 Rebellious Mr. Tyler
129 Anne or Marie: Abbr.

DOWN

1 City in Wales
2 Wind squall
3 Finish second
4 Poseidon, for one
5 M. Lupin
6 Logger's boot
7 Reasonable
8 Walkers: Abbr.
9 Dill seed
10 V-shaped rampart
11 Discernment
12 Stagger the imagination
13 Arab garment
14 Sephardic tongue
15 Yellow
16 Wing: Fr.
17 Certain votes
22 Printemps, e.g.
24 Zeta, ____, theta
25 Like a sinner
27 God: It.
32 Dies ____
34 Florida city
37 Lowers
38 Silver
39 Aleutian island
41 Top-line entry
42 Not present, in Milan
44 Airport vehicle, for short
46 Florida city
47 Triple, in chemistry
51 Fasten
52 Ringworm
53 Attacks
54 French pronoun
56 Group of sayings
60 Use a new die
61 Name of a first lady
62 White
65 Sitwell or Wharton
66 Fruitstand item, in Paris
70 Nullify
71 Jog the memory
72 Legal document
75 Table scrap
79 Hatfield activity
81 Whirling
83 African dialects
86 Moroccan port
88 On a ____ (raging)
89 Saucy
90 Kitchen utensil
91 Sow bug
94 Beowulf's victim
98 Of any kind
101 In ____ (privately)
102 Turkish inn
103 Place for Daniel
106 Cassia plant
107 Coiffeur's concern
108 Neighbor of Ala.
110 Deposed Iranian leader
111 Kind of cabbage
113 Needle
114 Wight, for one
115 Imitated
117 Charmian's co-worker
119 "____ was saying"
120 Cat's-____

9. Active Ones by Anthony B. Canning

ACROSS

1 European gulf
5 Armadillo
10 Kind of free
14 Treats roughly
18 Way for Caesar
19 Finishes second
20 Sandarac tree
21 W.W. II side
23 _____ the candle at both ends
25 _____ fly balls
27 Browning biographer
28 City of Russia
29 _____ tete
31 Fall for
32 Go to the plate
33 Stormed
35 Musical tones
37 Heifer, in Arles
39 Takes a certain bath
40 Appropriate
41 _____ squeaky wheel
42 More strict
44 Actual being
45 Sea birds
46 Poker move
49 Trees
51 Listens to
53 Kind of rumor
54 J. Barrymore trademark
57 Bolivian shipment
59 Stupid one
60 Famed jockey
62 Machine gun
63 Elsie's milieu
64 Haves _____ not
67 Dies _____
68 Silkworm
69 Fruit decay
70 Cover in a way
71 Spleen
72 _____ the cake
75 Quebec town
78 Money-raising performance
79 _____ the river
83 Family member
84 Mean
88 Genesis name
89 Miss Gam
90 Jerker or sheet
92 Hit the top, as a flood
93 Boat for a trio
94 Author Thomas
95 Wish for
96 Navy off.
97 Irate
98 "Cherries _____" (robin's report)
100 "Mens _____ in . . ."
101 Desert
104 Part of Q.E.D.
105 Returned, as a pigeon
106 Loudness unit
107 Harbinger of a new month
109 Garden frame
112 Danish king of 1200's
114 Attach, as a button
116 Ear part
118 Flying prefixes
120 Dan _____ likes TV news
122 Remove
123 _____ Darya
124 Malay coins
125 Gives the gate
127 Jeanne Eagels vehicle
129 Thy, in France
130 _____ in the woods
133 _____ Dick with affection
136 Orphan girl et al.
137 Carry
138 Win over
139 Johnson of TV
140 Ratio words
141 Hypothetical force
142 Certain religionist
143 ". . . _____ the punkin"

DOWN

1 Hardships
2 Repeat
3 _____ the floors
4 Airboard abbr.
5 U.S. playwright
6 _____ the stream
7 Peak: Prefix
8 Certain incomes
9 Cash, etc.
10 Surfeit
11 Yugoslavian
12 Grain
13 Homage
14 Ballet step
15 Brew
16 _____ around Washington (but not any more)
17 Relative of a litter
19 Word with cent
21 In pursuit of
22 Certain planes
24 Inferior deity
26 Cobh's land
30 Catherine, for one
34 Bridge seat
36 Ointments: Abbr.
38 African fox
39 Kind of confidence
43 Garish light
45 Word in Mass. motto
47 _____ up (made sense)
48 Quebec river sight
50 Winter fall
52 Hear no good of oneself
54 Lion assemblage
55 Gives added assurance
56 Roadside sign
57 Asian native
58 Tabard, e.g.
60 Fathered
61 Metric unit
62 Linen cloth
65 Dances
66 Russian sea
68 Square
69 W. H. Upson's salesman
71 Babylonian god
73 Cut short
74 Russian hemp
76 Blazing
77 Repetition
79 Wooden shoe
80 Habituate
81 _____ the midnight oil
82 One of the ages
83 So, in Scotland
85 _____ the lawn
86 Prefix for lithic
87 Insecticide
91 Dodgers
92 Heart
94 Trifle
95 Machine part
96 Opposites
99 Fine
100 Ordinary
101 French marshal
102 Kind of minded
103 Bleaching vat
105 Like Grant's face
106 _____ out (rests)
108 Be a _____ (finish second)
110 Zhivago girl et al.
111 Wife of Jacob
113 Informed on
115 Media-man Ron
116 Tibetan V.I.P.
117 Certain Arabian
119 Word with voce
121 _____ Gan, Israel
124 Relig. study
126 Kind of car lot
128 Comparative ending
131 Meet
132 _____ pros.
134 Roman 1501
135 "Bali _____"

10. Numerology by John Willig

ACROSS

1 Frolic
7 Do a party job
12 Moonfish
16 Road to Fairbanks
21 Spain and neighbor
22 Like Sprat's wife?
23 Unless, in law
24 Rivera
25 Five
27 Nine
29 Maritime agcy.
30 Bondsmen
31 Ammonia compound
33 Cabinet-wood tree
34 Belgian ____
35 Maine town
36 Ernie or Gomer
37 ____ sci.
40 ". . . compares with ____ Street"
41 Hit hard
42 Checks' partners
46 Summary
48 Be sparing
49 System or year
50 Buffalo's relative
51 Record a TV show again
52 One
54 Korbut
55 Loosen
56 Betty of song et al.
57 Aleutian nearest Japan
58 Hog fare
59 Broker's advice, at times
60 Tientsin's province
61 CB ____
63 Repeated excessively
64 ". . . was I ____ I saw . . ."
65 Three
67 Nicene and Athanasian
68 "Summer is ____ in"
70 Blanc, for one
71 ____-chef (Fr. headgear)
72 Flavoring seeds
73 Seven
77 Users of stas.
80 "This is so ____!"
81 Computers' cousins, for short
82 Asian range
83 Babysitter in Bombay
84 Makes an effort
85 Military org.
86 Adjective suffixes
87 Ecologist's concern
88 Home-run accompaniment
89 Four
92 Zero
93 Receptacle
94 Deli item
95 "____, don't mean maybe"
96 Tail-ender
97 Overcame
99 Posed again
100 NASA target in 1976
101 Privilogos: Abbr.
102 Musical for Aquarians
103 "____ Doodle," 30's song
104 Shankar
105 Cassandras
107 River of India
108 Vespers' opposite
110 Cry of distaste
113 Two
115 Three
118 Need for 104 Across
119 V.I.P.'s spot
120 Follow
121 Chaperon
122 Restores
123 Word with while
124 Oceans of poetry
125 Urges

DOWN

1 Plant shoot: Var.
2 Rudiments
3 Southern constellation
4 "____ y plata"
5 Mimic Little
6 Kind of pay
7 Follower
8 Ease
9 Does a farm job
10 Inner: Prefix
11 Part of a home-repair program
12 Riviera water sprite
13 Kind of bar
14 "So long ____ both shall . . ."
15 Greetings
16 Rhyme for a nursery scholar
17 TV's Hal
18 Grant
19 Time, e.g.
20 Scand. land
26 Roofing material
28 Ambush
32 All 50 have one
35 Passes over
36 Caroline Islands group
37 Scrutinize
38 Poker player, at times
39 Ten
40 Brood
41 Colosseum et al.
42 Knuckle under
43 Eight
44 Golf scores
45 Norse bard
47 Light or spin
48 Patina
49 French composer
52 Put a ____ (refresh)
53 Small boys
54 One who has
56 Pine fruit
58 Kitchen help
60 Virile ones
61 Jelly and egg
62 Dada founder and family
63 Krupa's forte
65 Nine
66 Vigorous
67 Slows down
69 Sweet or hard
71 Suffix for demo or auto
72 Sky sight
73 Component of the Strip
74 Craving
75 Be too clever for
76 Tuck, for one
78 Choicest
79 Layered rocks
80 Play idly on
81 High ____ (superior)
83 As well as
85 Fume, in France
86 "____, can you . . ."
87 ____ off (foists upon)
89 City of Greece
90 Bumbling
91 Told tales
92 Pickling liquid
94 Safari aides
96 Nit-pick
98 Pass ____
99 Most mature
100 Dull finishes
103 Salvador et al.
104 "The mouse ____ the clock"
105 In a ____ (irritable)
106 Kitchen or major
107 Nicholas, e.g.
108 ____-en-scène
109 Tight-fitting
110 Stabilizers
111 ____ way! (impossible)
112 Actor Richard
113 W.W. II agency
114 Chemical suffix
116 ____ no-trump
117 Extent: Abbr.

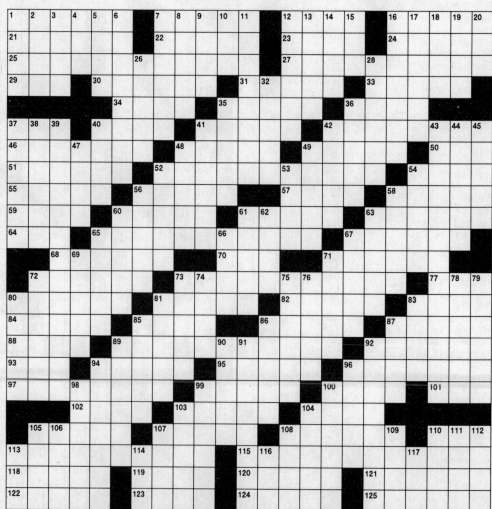

11. Halloween by Threba Johnson

ACROSS

1 Oct. 31 sound effects
6 W.W. II mil. unit
10 Jokes with
14 Baker's quantity
19 Biting
20 Bakery worker
21 Eye part
22 Snake: Prefix
23 Rock group for Oct. 31 party
26 Wants
27 Cal or Georgia
28 Payment stub: Abbr.
29 ____-de-vie
30 Portuguese explorer
32 Blanket or hen
33 Latin-class word
34 Party guests
36 Ventilate
38 Making pasture sounds
40 Gay party guests
45 Mild oath
48 Light gas
50 ____ Morgue
51 Dies ____
52 Pendant
54 Casualty of kitchen progress
57 Gide
58 ____-Roman
59 Word with rum
61 Let out
63 Public-channel offering: Abbr.
64 ____ accompli
66 Gender: Abbr.
68 Raccoon
69 Bicentennial guest
76 Certain lifting agent
77 Prefix for corn or form
78 Cubist pioneer
79 Do a court job
80 Tusked animal
82 Witch of ____
84 Result of a faulty shuffle
87 Mrs. Evert-Lloyd
88 Strawberry: Fr.
90 Port near Naples
91 Indian native
92 Lion's share
93 United: Prefix
96 Saar, for one
97 Party hellions
102 Bestowed kudos on
104 Goddess of witchcraft
105 Shade of purple
107 Witches'
111 Dernier ____
113 Gehrig et al.
114 Creek
115 Certain G.I.
116 Place for a gutter
117 Garand, for one
119 Party desserts
123 Prohibit
124 Grape pigment: Var.
125 Game
126 Cubic measure
127 "I met a man who ____ there"
128 State: Abbr.
129 Kernel
130 Akkadian: Abbr.

DOWN

1 Smelting mixture
2 Color
3 Betel palm
4 Conveyance to the party
5 One who transmits: Abbr.
6 Party hour
7 Paint solvent
8 W.W. I group
9 "The ____ Sea"
10 Antelope
11 "____ had it!"
12 Direction to the party
13 Miss Thompson et al.
14 Dwarfed plant
15 Mimic
16 Party guests
17 Killer: Suffix
18 Throng
24 Ship of myth
25 Flog
31 French sculptor
35 Italian poet Betti
37 Conn. college
39 Of a poetic form
41 Castle and Rich
42 Spirit ____
43 Sailors
44 Find out
45 Sire
46 Pearl Buck's was good
47 Party dresses
49 Filch
53 Angler's complaint
55 Places for 47 Down
56 More precise
57 After amas
59 Roman 502
60 Certain dying words
62 Mexican state
65 ____ self-defense
67 Note
70 Arranged in order
71 Strokes
72 U.S. playwright
73 Man, in old Rome
74 Native of Shiraz
75 Wood: Suffix
80 Stop!
81 Party location
83 Ph.D. or B.A.
85 German river
86 Party spongers
87 Large box: Abbr.
89 Baba
90 Party fare
94 Math branch
95 Thing to dance around
98 Named, to Shakespeare
99 P.I. tree
100 Musical pieces
101 Jib, e.g.
103 Lessened: Abbr.
106 Grates
108 Croupiers' gear
109 ____ which way
110 German river
111 Skeleton ____
112 Spanish laugh
114 Hockey milieu
118 Partner of lat.
120 Routing word
121 Hostile one
122 Civil War side: Abbr.

12. Combos by Nancy Atkinson

ACROSS

1 Nibs or Honor
4 Phony coin
8 Shopping complexes
13 Dallas campus
16 Tablet
19 Protagonist in fiction
21 Oil: Prefix
22 Draw a bead on
23 Sumatra's neighbor
24 Made a full report
25 Political-musical duo
28 Actor-U.S. composer-President
30 French river
31 Drench, with "down"
32 Run of luck
33 Gist
35 Elec. units
37 Showed off
40 S.A. country
41 Atlantic isl.
42 Something often read
45 Came close
47 Most stingy
49 ____ du Diable
50 Mary Ellen or Stuart
52 Skier's need
55 Autograph, for short
56 Spanish wave
57 Climb again
60 Miss Miles
61 Ledger entry
65 Vanocur of TV
67 Authorize
69 Take ____ with
72 Also, old style
73 Signed off
74 Gromyko
75 Take steps
76 Dog or bob
77 Bridge call: Abbr.
78 Howard and Bob
80 Words with king
81 Busy as ____
82 Irish cries
83 Arrow poison
84 Mule
86 Miss Farrow
87 Kind of case or well
88 Treasure or Long
89 Move, as a hairline
90 Bird's wing
92 Biblical place
94 One revising a news piece
96 Album contents: Abbr.
97 Biblical name
99 ____ for (summons)
101 ____ large
102 Ignited
103 Sweet potato
107 Joint-making machine
110 Slipup
112 Kudos
113 Ending for moral or journal
115 Gambols
117 Male ant
118 To's partner
119 Drink ____ to (honor)
122 "That hurts"
123 Miss Muller
125 Dukes
132 Stars
133 Yonder

134 ". . . and mine ____ one"
135 Grassy area
136 Have, in Cannes
137 Qualifies for
138 Pronoun
139 Hovel
140 Orders, of old
141 ____ uncle (gives in)
142 Altos or Pinos

DOWN

1 Actress Goldie
2 Concerning
3 Two U.S. writers and Brummell
4 Trim
5 Sierra ____
6 Extinct wild ox
7 Cry of petty triumph
8 Jellyfishes
9 Shaded walk
10 Tra-____
11 Property claim
12 Sauce beans
13 Miss Dee
14 College exam
15 States of pique
16 Jack of films
17 Fifth and others
18 Dennis or Clarence
20 "____ be so"
23 Conrad's Lord
26 Opposite of syn.
27 Diving bird
29 Lena and friend
34 Sandwich initials
35 Songlike
36 Economist and puppeteer
37 School-org. units
38 Stalling sounds
39 Search into
41 "Picnic" author
43 Wealthy in land
44 Chastity's mother
46 "____, a deer . . ."
48 Part of A.D.C.
51 Backdrops
53 Vincent and Baby Snooks
54 Spring landmark
58 Byron hero et al.
59 Scrooge, for short
62 Alexander, Gwyn and William
63 President and explorer
64 Williams or Knight
66 Proof word
68 Beach resorts
70 Arias
71 French article
74 Time period: Var.
75 Like rats in ____
76 Levantine ketch
78 Krazy ____
79 Sea off Borneo
81 Org. for M.D.'s

84 Crowds
85 Word with eve or year
87 Punjab dress
88 Grammar article: Abbr.
89 Italian painter
91 Coins in Florence
93 Light-switch positions
95 Headwear
98 F.D.R., for example
100 Medit. island
103 "We're ____ to see the . . ."
104 Cleaning business of a sort
105 Minute animals
106 "I intended an ode; and it turned to ____"
108 Awash in the evening
109 Evasive ones
111 Educated
114 Fund-raising time
116 Daphnis's love et al.
119 Drink
120 Silver abbr.
121 Pentateuch
123 Thurber's Walter
124 The opposition
126 Legal degree
127 Wheel center
128 Native Australians
129 Large moth
130 Mountain: Prefix
131 Monster's home
132 Balloon filling

13. Appropriate Groupings by Bert Kruse

ACROSS

1 Oil country
5 Kind of sided
8 Kind of facts
12 Bubbling sound
16 Mideast desert region
18 Thought
20 Baltic land
22 Boléro man
24 Group of versifiers
26 Overweight group
28 Function
29 ____ big (prevails easily)
30 Marsupial, for short
31 Mass. resort
32 British heroine
34 Intellectual group
39 One's, in France
40 U.S. electrical genius
42 King, in Portugal
43 Saw eye to eye
45 Joint part
48 Shade of green
51 Glacial ridge
53 ____ vu
56 Deli appliance
58 Ascend
60 Fisherman
62 Use a fishing stream
64 Nicotine-using groups
68 Common Latin abbr.
70 Goddess of the night
71 ____ Marie
72 Lacking candor
73 P.I. native
75 Fruit lozenge
77 Pitching stat
79 On track, mentally
81 Larry or Kurt
82 Things to count
83 Traffic groups
89 Home
92 Brook or brown
93 Be without
94 Royal initials
97 Talks big
99 Kind of frau
100 Greek letter
101 Conway
103 Cattle genus
104 Furniture item
107 Groups of rotters
113 Hts.
115 Defame
117 Like a puppy
118 Preparing
119 Spumante center
121 Old fiddle
123 TV-reception aids
125 Batter's clout
126 Vigorous critic
128 Brew
130 Bits, in Scotland
133 Subject for Winslow Homer
136 Sailing group
140 Carry
144 Loosen, as a garment
146 Bandsman Brown
147 Anak people
149 Conk
150 Stuck-up group
154 Lots ____, housing group
156 Strawberry and club
157 Western gully
158 Rds.
159 ____ Domingo
160 Moon landers
161 Prod
162 Grid measures: Abbr.
163 Judge

DOWN

1 Production component
2 Pee Wee
3 Miss Moorehead
4 Latest: Prefix
5 Barrymore
6 Native of a Black Sea city
7 Kind of jury or four
8 Keep on the trail of
9 Commotion
10 Kind of book: Abbr.
11 Pass receiver
12 Like a contest pig
13 Thin board
14 Eye parts
15 City on the Aare
17 Ex-service-men's org.
19 Regarding
20 Shindig
21 Boogie-____
23 Attack vessels: Abbr.
25 Makes a wrestling score
27 Shade of blue
33 Inventory item
35 Sideshow star
36 Cod's relative
37 Alike, in Paris
38 Court decree
41 Chemical endings
44 Morning golf problem
45 Recipe units: Abbr.
46 Gladden
47 More refined
49 Ideology
50 Card game
52 Sonnet unit
54 God with double vision
55 Western home
57 Red, in Rome
59 Study for a recital
61 Reign, to Mrs. Gandhi
63 Cast-off mates
65 Yellow: Prefix
66 Auld lang ____
67 Make new land divisions
69 Guardsman portrayer
74 Lined up
76 Producer Logan
78 Totals
80 Northern European
81 In a tangle
84 Soaks
85 Delphi attraction
86 Door noises
87 ____ many words
88 Like wing collars
89 Eastern church title
90 Word sung in New Haven
91 Ovens
95 Hemingway friend
96 Winnie's creator
98 Hurok
102 Clerical title: Abbr.
105 Dempsey opponent
106 Red as ____
108 Singular
109 Hagen
110 Always, to poets
111 To the ____ (fully)
112 Occur
114 Main and Elm: Abbr.
116 Spanish river
120 Like some pens
122 Dropped in
124 Clipped
127 Preposition
129 Ranch gear
131 Actor James
132 This, in Spain
133 Has a bite
134 Matriculate
135 Endure
137 Genesis event
138 Russian hero
139 Super
141 Clear air
142 French dessert
143 Derby site
145 Cheese
148 Beacons: Abbr.
151 Tire out
152 Angel's favorite sign
153 Depression initials
155 Young one

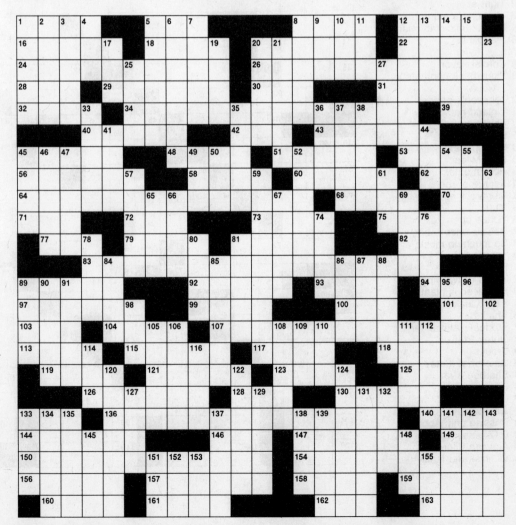

14. Cockney World by Elaine D. Schorr

ACROSS

1 They can be wide open
7 Gremlins
11 Winter reversal
15 Set up a clamor
18 Printing blooper
20 Act to be read
21 First or going
22 Never, in Naumburg
23 Fail to get a look
26 Coal scuttles
27 French friend
28 Sing in a way
29 Cemetery sights
31 Prepare the salad
32 Make oneself heard
33 British composer and family
34 Hawaiian goose
35 Terminal listing: Abbr.
36 Banquet ritual
37 Man of the hour
38 Stair section
39 Performing bonuses
41 Daughter of Zeus
43 Egg-shaped
44 Catapult
45 Name for a dog
46 Leaped
49 Like some kindergarten art
52 Became the cause of
54 Blimp, for one
57 Sink-clogging items
58 "Butterfield 8" author
60 Camptown doings
62 Tight spot
63 McKinley's mentor
64 Early comic-strip character
66 Flat plinth
67 ____ favor
68 Cordial flavor
69 Piggy-bank contents in Cuba
70 Johnson's partner
71 Vinland name
73 Thickwits
75 Load toters
76 Holdups, etc.
78 Miss Miles
79 Horn muffler
80 Source of roe
81 Monarchy elite
83 Mutt
86 "Once upon ____"
87 Hawaii, once: Abbr.
88 So much, in music
89 ____ Palmas
91 Kind of black
92 Types of weaving
93 Herbaceous plants
94 Early Quaker
95 Sharks
97 Producer Alexander
98 Outer: Prefix
99 Brooks
100 Cost what it may
104 Sharpen a razor
105 Biblical town
106 Relinquish
107 Junkyard, e.g.
108 Russian unit: Abbr.
109 D.C. gumshoes
110 Algerian rulers
111 Violinist and family

DOWN

1 Capitol unit
2 Do an adman's job
3 Skilled one
4 Warehouse contents
5 Hot time in Paris
6 Bring to the bar
7 Lease one's services
8 City of N.D.
9 Wood for masts
10 Vessel: Abbr.
11 Small villas
12 Solidify
13 At ____ of a coin
14 Warp's partner
15 Uppity
16 Amplified
17 Antilles group
19 Arlen or Caine
24 Metal waste
25 Home for a hawk
30 Tearjerkers
32 "Beg your pardon"
33 Assign to
36 Sees the sights
38 Comes in like a lion
40 Green alga
41 Sacred: Prefix
42 Hollywood gossip queen of yore
45 Castigated
47 S.A. rodents
48 Trifle, in Toulon
49 Condition
50 Estate house
51 Hitler henchman
53 Indian state
55 Actress Wendy
56 Laborers
58 Have an idea
59 Piano's precursor: Abbr.
61 Have ____ at
64 Unusual: Prefix
65 Sardonic looks
66 Put up a squawk
68 Out of the way
70 Money spent
72 Charley horse, in Arles
74 Hangs suspended
75 Favorite hangouts
77 Big-time ____
79 Photography effect
80 Flower parts
82 Notched
83 ____ Gras
84 Ballot caster
85 Kind of slide
86 Poplars
87 In cahoots
88 Strait of Australia
90 Saws logs
92 Sierra ____
93 Allen
94 Kind of porridge
96 Fliers of N.A.
97 Swiss artist
101 Arithmetic abbr.
102 Columnist Gardner et al.
103 Back or blanket

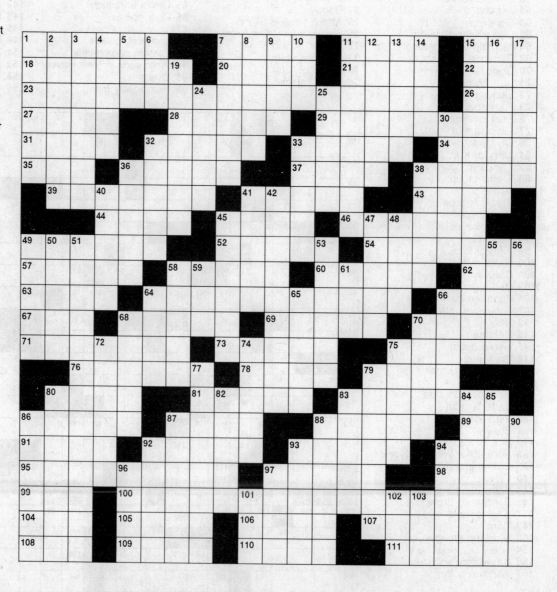

15. Exam Time by Maura B. Jacobson

ACROSS

1 Yorba ____, Calif.
6 Certain football passes
13 Look over
17 Sine ____ non
20 Affirms
21 Old French region
22 Ashtabula's state
23 Undersized
24 What did Hartman snack on?
27 Pelt
28 Ever and ____
29 Yutang
30 Near-winners at horseshoes
31 Commotions
32 Yalies
34 Dramatist Akins
36 German city
37 Sea eagle
38 Where in church is Masterson?
44 More terse
48 Maroon
49 Single
50 Goose: Fr.
51 Former Peking name
52 Loch Lomond sight
53 One ____ time
54 Pile on
56 Steak order
58 Inning units
59 Poetic prepositions
60 Answers a reply
62 What is put on Basie's bed?
65 Lost or be
66 Bathhouse
68 London gallery
69 Business abbr.
70 Hagen et al.
71 Chessman
72 Chef, in Bonn
75 Swat again
77 Gazzara or Blue
78 Who work in Shanghai supermarkets?
83 Former nuclear org.
85 Fanatical
87 Old Norse estate
88 Places for Grecian writings
89 "____ a rose . . ."
90 Rug occupant
91 Prognosticator
94 Siberian district
96 Goose genus
97 Where do Sandburg's pirates hide?
102 Italian mutiny
104 Iranian coin
105 Pakistan tongue
106 Do a Tuesday chore
107 Talking bird
108 Fleming
109 Org.
110 Con vote
111 Draft initials
112 W.W. II area
114 Syrian city
116 Implore
118 What does the queen do at the corner?
121 ____-Magnon

122 Ask alms
123 Function
124 Declaim
125 Similar
128 Swiss resort
131 Month: Abbr.
132 Murdoch
136 One-liner
137 What is Elizabeth's tennis forte?
141 Made a tennis coup
142 Opposed
143 Aromatic plant
144 Atiptoe
145 Before omicrons
146 Bank deal
147 Primes the piano again
148 Wintry gust

DOWN

1 Tibetan V.I.P.
2 One of the Karamazovs
3 Pianist Peter
4 Thirst
5 Smoker's concern
6 Mean one
7 Diagram
8 Ellis or Fire: Abbr.
9 Beam, in Lyon
10 Laborite P.M.
11 Mineral suffix
12 Room in a casa
13 Exclusively
14 Bracelet adjunct
15 Draws a bead on
16 ____ Hill, S.F.
17 Tobacco chaw
18 Annul
19 Pro votes

23 How do you contact Tarkington?
25 Get ____ (find out about)
26 Acclimate: Var.
31 Before pod or color
33 Comedienne Bea
34 Buddhist sect
35 Fairy king
37 Notched
38 Smokey Jr.
39 Aardvark
40 Who guard the Mexican border?
41 Mason's gear
42 After love or for
43 Feudal land grant
44 Use the tub
45 Where does Sigmund park his ferries?
46 Be a breadwinner
47 Musical stop
51 Jeff's pal
55 Very, in music
57 Became active
58 Mouths
61 Donovan's gp.
62 Beach sight
63 Will-____-wisp
64 French keys
67 Arista
71 Graduate degree
73 Wood sorrel
74 Prefix for phyll
75 Carriers: Abbr.
76 Coded transmission feeder
78 Smokes, for short
79 Wading bird
80 Lowlifes
81 Long-tailed ape
82 Item recorded

84 Rostand hero et al.
86 What did Taurus do in the balcony?
89 Yoko ____
91 Miss Vaughan
92 MacDonald's vis-à-vis
93 Old French coin
95 Soccer positions
96 Arthurian Eden
97 Grass or apple
98 Comfort: Fr.
99 Con game
100 Peer: Abbr.
101 Formerly, once
103 Furious
107 Extinct bird
111 Greek letter
113 Even score
115 Of summer
117 ____ long (soon)
118 Noxious ones
119 Start
120 Pie parts
122 Fraulein's name
125 Greek warrior
126 Places
127 Alibi and D.D.E.
128 Greek philosopher
129 Partly open
130 Before gram or cast
131 Hartebeest
133 Latvian capital
134 Tops off the cake
135 Spanish muralist
137 Holbrook
138 Fort Worth campus
139 Partner of hither
140 C.S.A. man, for short

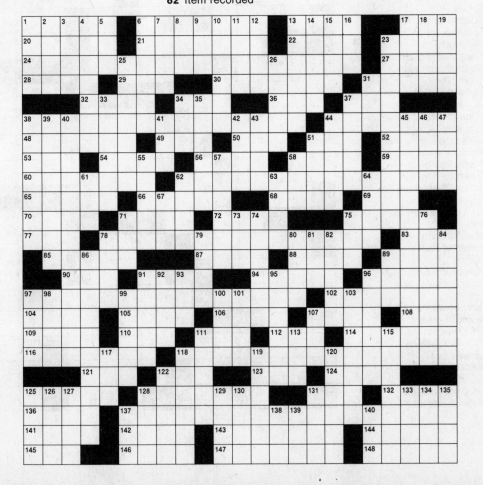

16. Glad Tidings by Henry Hook

ACROSS

1 Hingle or O'Brien
4 Lounge-chair part
7 Common $2 item
10 Korbut
14 Word of regret
16 Twice LXXVI
17 Concerning
19 Provinces
22 Vapor, old style
23 Orange throwaway
24 Yule song
26 Follow-up to 106 Across
29 Youth org.
30 Sandwich staple
31 Magwitch of "Great Expectations"
32 "Come ____ come shine"
33 Menotti hero
35 Faction
37 Mrs. Cantor
39 Rorem
40 Biblical animal
41 Erudite
44 Shoe width
45 ____ theme, from "Zhivago"
46 Word with one or what
49 Military alarm clock
50 Mideast weight
51 Prepare wastebasket paper
53 Fencing items
56 Hesitant sounds
59 Once in a blue moon
60 Kisser's come-on
64 "____ Majesty"
66 "Peace ____ price"
67 Holiday entertainers
68 Dome athlete
69 Soften
70 Holiday dinner finale
71 Speared, as a fish
72 Mil. award
73 Employee's quest
74 Go bananas over
75 News piece
77 Blood pathway
80 Dog in "Beetle Bailey"
81 Good loser
83 Grid scores: Abbr.
86 Uses one's gray matter
88 Taper upward
89 Wash. figure
90 Treasure-hunt aid
91 Home of Brigham Young U.
94 "Hold That ____"
95 ____ of (happen to)
97 Cap-____
100 Never's counterpart
102 Pulver of "Mister Roberts": Abbr.
103 Man of triple-vision
106 What Santa's doing
110 Suit to ____
111 Tamper with a check
112 Wood fragment
113 Cry of revelry
114 ____ ex machina
115 Sassy one
116 Poetic word
117 Be amiss
118 Latin conjunction
119 Writer Josephine

DOWN

1 Roast slightly
2 Hilo greetings
3 "____ to your leader"
4 Make uniform
5 Big-top big name
6 Lunchtime, in Lyon
7 Regional life
8 Interweave
9 Cadet
10 Mine find
11 Author Deighton
12 Gift of sorts
13 Namath's alma mater
15 Wine quality
16 Cheat on the final
18 Camouflage a message
20 Uses a dogsled
21 Unimportant
25 Biblical name
27 Shimmying sister
28 Quid pro quo
33 "____ may look on a king"
34 House guest of 103 Across
36 Recipient of a familiar visit
38 Next to R.I. in size
42 With skill
43 Madeleine, e.g.
45 Forfeit
46 "Buzz off!"
47 Took the soapbox
48 Thomas Benton works
50 Autos of yore
52 Thickness
53 Ending for salmon or Cinder
54 Before aboo
55 Exist, in Paris
57 Cheap whisky
58 Most confident
60 Neighbor of Oahu
61 Eye part
62 Chimney dust, to Chaucer
63 Fond treatment: Abbr.
65 Western event
67 Partisan: Suffix
68 River isle
70 Glass base
71 Pesty flier
74 Timetable abbr.
76 Fox or Rabbit
77 Form of French "to love"
78 Harem room
79 Groucho's specialty
81 Column or cord
82 Grid need
83 One of the clefs
84 What mountebanks do
85 ". . . a word from our ____"
87 Your, in Bonn
88 Watch parts
92 Consecrate
93 Thwart completely
95 "____ Clown"
96 Word with kilo or centi
98 Spurious: Prefix
99 Tops off a cake
101 Tearful
104 St. Louis bridge
105 Approves
107 "____ Got a Secret"
108 Once-named
109 "Cave canem" sound

17. Yuletide Quotes by Anne Fox

ACROSS

1 Brews
5 Sudan people
10 Port of Jordan
15 Conform
20 Lease
21 Joan ____
22 Recap
23 Fought
25 Bulwer-Lytton heroine
26 Place for a dude
27 Horn sounds
28 Of a chemical compound
29 Absentee
31 Its capital is Accra
33 Hard wood
35 Acknowledge
36 Words by Edward Caswall
41 "Seven against ____"
42 Postponement
43 Skin
44 Xanadu's river
47 Kind of money or Hatter
48 Tenn. stronghold of Civil War
51 Newspaper item
55 Speed: Abbr.
56 Europe's largest lake
58 Ford
59 King of the Huns
60 Frog or toad
62 French horns
64 Wine container
66 Chess pieces
67 ____ against (protest)
69 Last-ditch words
72 N.J. town
75 Superman's girl
76 Roof part
78 Navy noncoms
79 Bellow's March
80 Words by Philips Brooks
86 Dew, rain and cough
87 Con
88 Mexican dish
89 Rail bird
91 Camelopard
94 Songs of praise
96 Long journey
98 Numero ____
99 "Jacques ____ Is Alive . . ."
101 Stern or Newton
103 Beyond: Prefix
104 Castigate
107 Plays in the Masters
110 Monkey genus
112 Way: Abbr.
113 Deep or strep
114 Musical of 1968
116 Card game
117 Young lady
118 River to the Rhine
120 Après juillet
121 Syrian city
123 Words by Edward Devlin
132 Divorce place
133 Test
134 Capital of Senegal
135 Woman counselor
136 Moslem leader
138 Soprano Adelina
141 Group of Moslem scholars
143 Hangs back
144 "____ Fideles"
145 Sky hunter
146 Actor Conrad
147 Small land body: Var.
148 Visible vapor
149 Tibetan wild ass
150 Sad sound
151 Ethereal

DOWN

1 School subj.
2 Mrs. Arrowsmith
3 Weariness
4 Furtiveness
5 "____ cradles a king"
6 Russian city
7 French wine region
8 Foot parts
9 Cold soup
10 Words from an old German poem
11 "____ vadis?"
12 One of a Latin trio
13 Montana city
14 Church parts
15 Words from a traditional carol
16 Lake Mead sight
17 Military hardware
18 Utah city
19 Purport
24 Not up
30 A degree
32 Aerie
34 Viper
37 O.T. book
38 Max, Buddy or Bugs
39 Fontanne
40 Mild oath
44 Profit
45 Ex-Beatle John
46 Rain: Prefix
48 Casino game
49 Paper or pudding
50 Indeed
52 Occasion
53 Smart one
54 Humid
56 Medieval poem
57 Lady's-Book founder
61 Garden mignonette
63 Harmful
65 Fine plaster
68 Laundry holder
70 Fishing boats
71 Somewhat: Suffix
73 Objective
74 River to the Oder
77 Anatomical duct
79 Botanist Gray
81 Sandy's word
82 Chinese dynasty
83 Where ____ (scene of action)
84 Cosa ____
85 Welcomes
90 Actor Lew
91 Outburst
92 Kind of worm
93 Loud cry
94 Medicinal plant
95 Queenly address
97 Time periods: Abbr.
100 Head or plant
102 Certain storage charge
105 Race winner
106 ____ monde
108 Money deal
109 Croaker
111 U.S. banker
115 Volcano
117 Flowery plant
119 "Oedipus ____"
121 Language group of Ecuador
122 Girl of song
123 Killer whale
124 Roles
125 Estuary
126 Sleeping-bag filling
127 Japanese ware
128 Shut out an opponent
129 Papal cape
130 Severity
131 Snide
137 School org.
139 Spanish aunt
140 Large supply
142 Ott

18. Partygoer's Lament by Frances Hansen

ACROSS

1 Close-mouthed one
5 Decorous
9 Doc's dates
14 Turkish title
18 Playwright Joshua
20 V.I.P.'s car, for short
21 Psalm word
22 Boeotian of myth
23 Sky: Prefix
24 Jewish month
25 Hockey's Bobby, formally
26 Sellout signs
27 Start of a verse
31 After auld lang
32 D.D.E.
33 TV satellite
34 One over par
35 Throw in the towel
37 ____ even keel
38 Miss Harding
39 "Hallelujah," e.g.
42 O.T. book
45 Church areas
49 Kind of pot?
52 More of verse
57 "We ____ amused"
58 Duke of Hollywood fame
59 Also
60 Writer Jaffe
61 Hippie's home
62 "____ we dance?"
64 Drive-in worker
66 ____-bitsy
67 Bounce, in Scotland
68 "La ____ du Régiment"
70 Not that
72 "____ three ships . . ."
75 Water nymph
77 All-purpose beans
79 Wane
82 Spanish baby
83 Asian gazelle
84 Grows dim
86 Sign on a street with pot-
   holes
88 More of verse
92 Egyptian spirit
93 Lab burners
94 Serb
95 Sweetie-pie!
96 Kin: Abbr.
98 European capital
101 Fencing foil
103 "I ____ Parade!"
105 Burglar's bargain
106 Onassis
107 Nostalgic throe
111 End of verse
115 Kind of aerial bomb
116 "____ Ben Jonson!"
117 Broz
118 Political shake-up
119 Irk
120 "The ____ closed" (host's
   sign-off)
121 Alaskan governor
122 Mall unit
123 Griffith or Gump
124 Put in office
125 Kind of devil
126 In a ____ (teed off)

DOWN

1 Shillelaghs
2 London truck
3 "Kiss Me ____"
4 Store-window tenant
5 Fish food
6 Vimy ____ of W.W. I
7 Mosque prayer leader
8 "Oh, weep no ____!"
9 Eritrea's capital
10 None of your business
11 Ruses
12 Pacific staple
13 Mistletoe, for one
14 Allot
15 Eden, notably
16 Bunk!
17 Heavenly handle
19 Holiday drink
28 Three, on the clock
29 Conquer
30 Friars Club entrée
36 Nth degree
39 Kind of judgment
40 Israeli reel
41 Was in debt
43 Cry like a baby
44 Scenic Italian drive
46 Meatiness
47 High-hat
48 Gullets, grandly
50 Time periods
51 Candid camera shot
53 "____ you'd never ask!"
54 Hazy
55 New or raw
56 "Exodus" author
63 Scholar's arrival time
65 Vend again
67 Did the butterfly
69 Dope
71 Tristan's lady
72 Miss Swenson
73 Look for
74 Kind of ape
76 Señora's title
78 Greek peak
79 Exile isle
80 One of the wars
81 Variety's st.
85 Like ghost towns
87 Short camping trips
89 Smorgasbord fisherman
90 Like the in-group
91 "They'd eaten ____"
97 In a fair way
99 Most arid
100 Luxurious seat
102 Doozy
103 Manila site
104 Hacienda brick
105 Lean
106 Rose extract
108 Stringed thing
109 Pola
110 ". . . ____ the purpling
   east"
111 Poet Teasdale
112 Russian range
113 Baltic port
114 Goddess of plenty

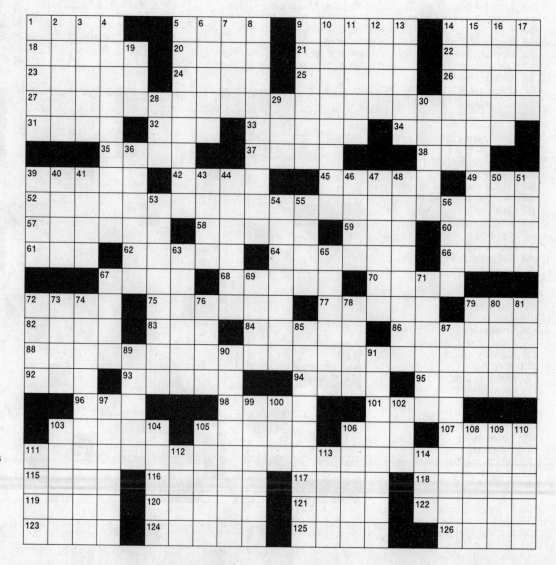

19. Togetherness by Eugene T. Maleska

ACROSS

1 Kind of brandy
5 His I.Q. is low
10 Cherrystone
14 Livelihood
19 "Typee" sequel
20 As ____ (usually)
21 Paddle-shaped
22 Fencing feint
23 Two actresses
26 Combine
27 Barfly's habit
28 Tub rub
29 Gambler's concern
31 Inventory
32 "Battle Hymn" composer
33 Nixie or pixie
34 Aspirin targets
37 Part of H.S.H.
39 Kind of jam
43 Jalousie item
44 Actress and lawyer Fonda
47 Wassail drink
48 Persephone
49 Rich Little is one
50 Heart cherry
51 Largest of seven
52 Id ____
53 Ben and Gilda
57 Miss Kett et al.
58 Most spent
60 Caliban's opposite
61 Fishwife's outburst
62 Bird sound
63 Switchblades
64 Garden spot
65 Infuriate
67 U.S. hymnist
68 Accepted a deal
72 Goose genus
73 John and Max
75 Bud's partner
76 Greeting in Genoa
77 "____ nome," Verdi aria
78 Rowdydow
79 Habit
80 Rowan
81 Roy and Sir Richard
85 White with age
86 Mat word
88 Friendly
89 Usher's beat
90 Ingested
91 Made a refusal
92 Dutch painter
94 Take down a peg
98 Jaywalker's goal
99 Sun's spot circa Dec. 22
103 Glorify
104 Oscar and Monty
107 Dressler
108 Border lake
109 Partner of Wright?
110 Palindrome ending
111 Harbingers
112 Gavel sounds
113 Greek sanctuary
114 Defendant: Lat.

DOWN

1 Part of M.V.P.
2 Mine, in Metz
3 Easy win
4 Undivided
5 He hit 61 in '61
6 Piece of sculpture
7 Ladder footing
8 Antediluvian
9 Just arrived
10 Grapple
11 Trellis piece
12 "We ____ seven"
13 Marge's radio pal
14 Puritanical legacy
15 Decamp
16 Geraint's partner
17 "How like ____"
18 Nookeries
24 Site of first Olympics
25 Swerved
30 Bittern
32 "Do I ____ Waltz?"
34 Out of line
35 Not rating a cigar
36 Moss and Mort
37 Edmund Lowe's partner?
38 Tidal bores
39 Lazy Susan
40 Two writers
41 Homeric work
42 Leave off
44 Whalebone
45 Musical work
46 The McCoy
51 Up ____ (stumped)
53 Bad dog
54 Hill people of India
55 Yugoslav river
56 Granted
57 Scoter's cousin
59 De Mille ballet
61 Cylindrical
63 Ta-ta
65 Parrot
66 Flavoring for ouzo
67 ____ mater
68 Grandfather of Saul
69 Pokey, in England
70 Of timbre
71 Bizarre
73 Ruth or Herman
74 Terror
77 Traveler with a tail
79 Referee, at times
81 Pirouettes
82 Strips
83 Zzz
84 Rods between switch rails
87 Ask for help
89 Further
92 Start of a greeting
93 Bitter drug
94 Item sent to a D.J.
95 Midterm or final
96 Cost of leaving
97 Vase-shaped jug
98 Bit of TV film
99 Rushmore address
100 "Winnie ____ Pu"
101 Philippine port
102 Nestling
105 Novelist Levin
106 Wedding-notice word

20. Every Which Way by Dorothea E. Shipp

ACROSS

1 See above
7 Heavy fabric
11 Pension org.
14 English forest
19 Kind of card
20 Network
21 Nissen and Quonset
22 Early British cop
24 Like a teddy bear
25 Bone: Prefix
26 Fuegian natives
27 Dress size
28 Crab genus
29 Appropriate direction
32 Concurs
33 Forwards
35 Used up
36 Stile, e.g.
38 French pupil's place
39 He, in Italy
40 Embroidery X's
40 (Diag. down) Conflicting aims
44 Waste allowance
45 Fan noise
47 Toast opener
48 Type style: Abbr.
50 Flowery plants
53 Egyptian god
55 Rockne
56 T.V.A. unit
59 David's musician
60 Area of Yugoslavia
61 Owing heavily
63 Exaggerated accounts
65 Greek god
66 Certain bricks
67 Deuce's superior
68 Med. course
69 Mind: Prefix
71 Seethes
72 Partners
74 Bible town of France
75 Scottish terrier
76 Little Woman et al.
77 Kind of sieve
78 Assam native
79 Kind of rock or door
83 ____ finger up
85 Place for Sophia's flowers
86 "Madam, I'm Adam"
88 Atlantic gunnel
90 Christmas offerings
92 Red dye
93 Relatives of aves.
94 Condescend
95 Book-ad listings
96 First-born
97 Rattle, in Scotland
98 Places for berets
99 Miss Bagnold
100 Spring mos.
104 Typical samples
104 (Diag. up) Ocean dangers
108 German river
112 Freud specialty
114 ____ time
115 React to boredom
116 Battery part
117 Gardeners, at times
119 Place to get in on
123 Pourboire
124 One fleeing a land

125 Forest near S.F.
126 Atmosphere: Prefix
127 Prim
129 Bridge gaffe
130 Blue and Franklin
131 As is
132 Target of Tet offensive
133 Flung the gauntlet
134 Botanist Gray
135 Cathedral part
136 Musician Herb

DOWN

1 Charge
2 Decisive points
3 Fortifications
4 Roulette bet
5 Beverly and window
6 Eye woe: Var.
7 Capri's is blue
8 Leavings, in Paris
9 Preminger
10 Prescient one
11 Panamas
12 Interference
13 Jenny
14 Book addenda: Abbr.
15 Della
16 Spot
17 Writer Glyn
18 Provoke
21 Makes helpless
23 Put back in place

30 Boxer Tommy
31 Yugoslav peninsula
32 Ahead by one tennis unit
34 Installment forerunner
37 Stone and wine
40 On this side: Prefix
41 Climbs in a way
42 Sonora Indian
43 Surfeited condition
46 Writer Emily
49 Don't be this, said Polonius
50 Dray
51 Hebrew lyre
52 Baptize
53 Mrs. Chaplin et al.
54 N.C.O.
55 Acute
56 Socialist Eugene
57 Burrows
58 McKinley and Hood: Abbr.
60 Twining stems
61 German number
62 Oppressed
64 Purgative
65 Sandarac tree
69 Somewhat, in music
70 Cry's partner
71 Ranees' wear
73 Certify
74 Spoon's elopement partner
75 Hails
76 Snaffles and bridoons
77 Grate
78 British pokey

80 Kind of window
81 Writer Kingsley
82 Kind of house
83 Educ. TV initials
84 Umpire's call
85 ____ cello
86 Ready, old style
87 Take-out shop
89 Linings, in Spain
90 French slope
91 "____ plaisir"
95 Wise advisers
96 Letters
98 Catherine, for one
99 Within: Prefix
100 Viper
101 Got a pump going
102 Victoria ____
103 Clay box
105 Musical transitions
106 Dig and red
107 Limestone
109 Senility
110 Newspaper V.I.P.
111 Renounce sinning
113 Combine
116 Of a space
118 Oboe, for one
120 Zola girl
121 Throat or River
122 Pelion's resting place
125 Univ. degree
128 Land hollow

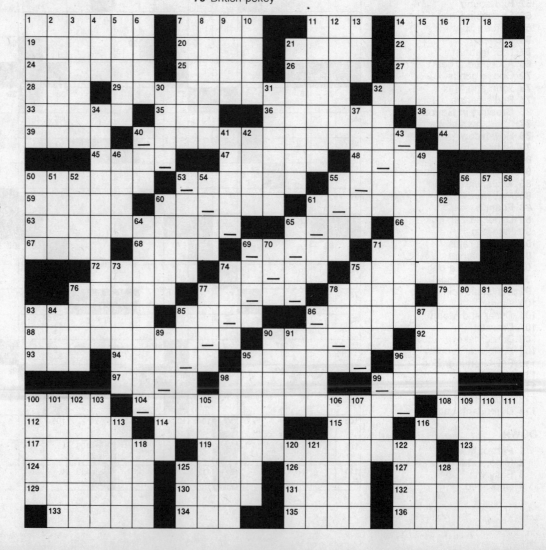

21. Pro-totypes by Stanley Kurzban

ACROSS

1 Misbehave
6 Slow train
11 What Eris threw
16 Fasten again
18 Banished
20 One who couples
21 _____ up (kept mum)
23 Fall fare at Shea Stadium
25 Wearer of hash marks
26 Individuals
27 Snide remark
28 Shade
29 Site of a pleasure dome
31 Turkish title
32 Saddle afflictions
33 Bistros
36 How the Miami Dolphins play
41 Nigerian people
42 Indian weight
43 Before line and sinker
44 Swab
45 East Lansing campus
46 Vessel prized in the N.F.L.
50 Winglike
54 Gates, to Caesar
56 Relative of an org.
57 Good bond rating
58 Coin
59 Part of a shoe
60 African lake
63 Postal dept.
65 Stage shrew
66 One-sided victory for Baltimore
71 Locker or rec
73 _____ Lanka
74 Beat
75 Coated steel plates
78 Atmosphere
79 Elec. unit
81 Mail-address initials
83 Rhubarb
84 Small bird
85 January quest
89 Possess, old style
90 Pronoun
92 Arias
93 Wijk _____ Zee, Holland
94 Tops
95 Pittsburgh team, often
99 Nile dam
100 Caracalla specialties
102 Singer Charles
103 Eye part
105 Jai _____
106 Goal
107 Zone
110 Hillary's conquest
114 Exhortation in Dallas
117 One who misleads
118 _____ say (seemingly)
119 Of the sun: lt.
120 Moon goddess
121 Hide away
122 Writer Peter B. and family
123 Parking-lot mishaps

DOWN

1 Curves
2 Boston cager, for short
3 Ruler
4 Separates, as metals
5 Argentine terrain
6 The day, in France
7 Beasts of burden
8 Refer to
9 Locale for a chalet
10 Irish sea god
11 Indian mulberry
12 Posse from Green Bay
13 Religious house
14 Sierra _____
15 Sea eagles
17 Hammer part
19 Sidestep
20 Small dog
22 _____ flag, as over a bier
24 Chanteuse Edith
30 Sleeping places
31 _____ favor (requests)
32 Road sign
33 College grounds: Var.
34 Firebug job
35 Eighty, to Lincoln
37 Biblical captain
38 Perfect-game line score
39 Charged atom
40 Grid official
42 Oct. 31 needs
46 Phone
47 Little, in Spain
48 Damage
49 Egyptian heaven
51 Acquires the knack
52 Insect
53 Hwy.
55 Complaint about Kansas City
61 Oklahoma city
62 Pillage
64 Through thick _____
67 German drink
68 Like Dali's watches
69 Arab vessel
70 College official
71 Like March weather
72 Possessive
76 Form of Helen
77 Dice number
80 Troublesome
82 Sound loudly
85 Spot or shine
86 Shad dish
87 Wheat, in France
88 Spent unwisely
91 Faroe winds
94 Customarily
95 Locales for games
96 Norse explorer
97 Aegean island
98 Obliterates
99 Anointed
100 Theda and family
101 Tilting
104 Burl or Saint
106 Latin-study word
107 With competence
108 Horse color
109 Literary Jane
111 Garden
112 Dispatched
113 _____ bien
115 Ordinal suffix
116 Chinese cooking dish

22. Variations by Jordan S. Lasher

ACROSS

1 Dry up, as lips
5 Goon
9 Cantor and Lupino
13 "If ____ be so bold"
17 Very gentle treatment: Abbr.
20 Louvre name
21 Columnist Barrett
22 Night: Prefix
23 Louvre name
24 "I told you so!"
25 Always
26 Handy Latin abbr.
27 Pear-shaped instrument
28 Frenziedly
29 Period
30 Egret plumes, e.g.
34 River to the North Sea
35 Between res and fas
36 Holy Roman emperor
37 Vance of mystery
38 Prefix for bus
40 Movie group
41 Shoe-repair item
45 Port of Yemen
46 Jot down
47 Cockney charger
48 Entity
49 Of the previous month: Abbr.
50 Matador
52 Highway to Fairbanks
53 Uses a tub
55 Pilgrimage to Mecca
59 Live off the ____ the land
60 Cry of contempt
61 Corporate V.I.P.
63 Sweet coin?
64 One less than a crowd
65 Reign of ____
68 Toward the stern
71 Collected (with "in")
73 Wastelands
75 Two ____ kind
76 Polynesian canoe
77 Tandem
78 Restless one
80 In medias ____
81 Bulls or Bullets
83 Slopes transport
84 Surrounded by
85 Certain head of hair
86 Space agcy.
87 Take ____ at (gibe)
88 Seven deadly items
89 Seine or trawl
90 Prefix for sphere
91 Catch sight of
92 Me., N.H., R.I., etc.
93 N.Y. time
94 Enemy
96 Statesman Root
98 Intrusive
99 Swindle
101 Maximal ending
102 Machine part
103 Speak irrationally
105 "No-No" girl, for short
106 Jay Silverheels role
108 She pined for Narcissus
110 Observed
114 Player under a dome
116 ____ the press
118 G.I. address
120 Charles Lamb
121 Thai money
122 Military headwear
123 Cupid
126 Precursor
128 Nobel chemist
129 He: It.
130 ____-car
132 Egyptian god
133 Day of worship: Abbr.
134 Jiff
135 Tennis shortcoming
141 "____ on parle . . ."
142 Besought
144 Town near Milan
145 Pelée output
146 Debauchee
147 Poetry: Abbr.
148 Counting-out word
149 Sometime gym dance
150 World oil assn.
151 Actress Loretta
152 Culminate
153 Canadian Indian
154 J. D. Salinger girl
155 Withered
156 Breaks bread

DOWN

1 Treble or bass
2 Drone's home
3 ". . . against ____ of troubles"
4 One at early Eden bash
5 Child's retreat
6 Breakfast fare
7 Merkel et al.
8 Lively dance
9 Like some fillings
10 Pair
11 Pawn to king four, e.g.
12 Suffix with mob or gang
13 Hogg
14 Painful instant for Trigger
15 State of lawlessness
16 Gabs away
17 Demonstration staged by food fish
18 City of Thessaly
19 Discipline
31 Alts.
32 Building agcy.
33 ____ turn (just right)
39 P.I. native
40 Dark brown, to a chestnut
41 Boston
42 Santa ____
43 Illuminated
44 Ordinal suffix
51 Not as experienced
52 Spring mo.
54 Second phone: Abbr.
56 Interrogated
57 DiMaggio
58 Official scorer's job
62 Duncan's murder ("Macbeth": II,i)
66 Piece of writing
67 Gulch
68 Rental units: Abbr.
69 More diminutive
70 Turkey-stuffing situation
72 "Go fly ____!"
74 Dime-novel stuff
77 Alberta resort
79 ____ Paul Kruger
82 Yolky
86 Stable talk
90 Must
95 Cite
97 ____ cit.
98 Compass reading
100 Yoko
104 180-degree turn
107 "So sorry!"
109 Awkward one
111 Whitney
112 Prevarication
113 ____ es Salaam
114 Insulting
115 Crusader's foe
117 Fourth of July theme
119 Bakery purchase
122 Wee Willie or Ruby
124 Punctual
125 Erwin
127 Talk it over
131 Guthrie et al.
134 Guesswork, for short
136 Leather flask
137 Scruff
138 Hawkeyes' home
139 After soir
140 Asian holidays
143 Red 1 or Blue 5

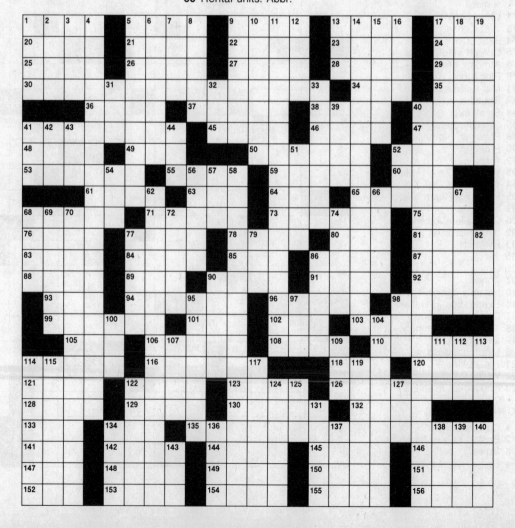

23. Title Search by Tap Osborn

ACROSS

1 Demeaned
7 Short swims
11 Old Greek coin
15 Wail
19 Delaware Indian
20 Concerning
21 Atmosphere
22 Mèlange
23 Look aside
25 Without doubt
27 "Small Fry" cartoonist
28 Sea-washed
30 Mount
31 Continent: Abbr.
33 Snide remarks
34 Voice
36 Persian ruler's domain
40 Bulrush
41 Flu source
42 Highway: Abbr.
45 Give saintly status to
46 Doggone
49 Bird, to Cato
50 Garner's middle name
54 Japanese seaweed
55 Czech river
56 Speech defect
57 Celebes ox
58 Kind of processor
60 Add comments to a text
62 Leprechaun
63 As far as possible
65 Nonsense
66 Feudal estate: Var.
69 Stags
70 Pedro's meat
71 Loft
73 Cut the grass
75 Buffoon
78 Trumpet V.I.P.
79 Vientiane's land
80 Bruins' milieu
81 Special bolt hardware
82 Breezy
83 Brooklet
85 Art gallery
86 Taro root
87 Twofold
91 Adorn in a way
93 Farm animal
94 Biblical name
95 Gullet
97 Nuclide
98 Shine's partner
99 Cleveland suburb
100 Iowa time: Abbr.
101 Of the leg calf
104 Lost out
106 In a stupor
111 Fatherless
114 Time lapse
116 Unoccupied
117 Furnace
118 Miss Verdon
119 Rudiment
120 Shape
121 Bohemian
122 Within: Prefix
123 Merchant

DOWN

1 Vestments
2 Whip
3 Ending for pitt
4 H.H. Munro
5 Living near the ground level
6 Study
7 Coup victim, Ngo ____ Diem
8 Swallow
9 Shut out
10 Toothed keel of a spider
11 Refuges
12 Inlaid decoration
13 Mouths
14 Youngster
15 Show obeisance
16 Lily plant
17 Half of a team
18 Burden
24 Give it ____ (attempt)
26 Spectral body
29 Atom-pioneer Harold
32 Once removed
34 Star: Prefix
35 Chopped down
36 Black activist Bobby
37 Smith's tool
38 Gun-shy
39 Grate
41 Sudsing
42 Hold in abeyance
43 ____-cochère
44 Bend down
47 Vaccines
48 Away
51 Dye
52 Turndowns
53 No-returns store event
58 Glacial troughs
59 Feed the pot
61 Hockey great
64 Evil ensign
67 Trickled: Var.
68 Part of H.R.H.
70 Recent: Prefix
71 Faux pas
72 Admit to
73 More sickly
74 Nonexistent
76 Khartoum's land
77 Lay up
81 I.Q. or Binet-Simon
84 Words of understanding
85 Scubaed to the bottom
88 Acclaims
89 Disfigure
90 Set up
92 Incomplete
96 Flag-marked a harpooned whale
97 Bakery worker
98 Made sore
99 Hamburger unit
101 Do a pool job
102 Destroy
103 Word with drum or bank
104 Sibilant aside
105 Noise: Prefix
107 East Indian tree
108 Passion
109 Advantage
110 Cloth worker
112 Scarf
113 Tympanum's location
115 Villain

24. Groupies by Robert Roup

ACROSS

1 One of the clefs
5 ____ splitting
9 Rubber trees
13 Piles
18 Can. province
19 Big birds
20 Having hair
22 Where the surrey's fringe is
23 Kind of drop or sheet
24 Elec. units
25 Eniwetok, e.g.
26 Search widely
27 Serengeti coterie
30 Early rabbi
31 Seasick one's goal
32 Starr
33 Appearance
34 Drink
37 Jan. and Feb.
38 Native of a Cyclades island
39 Riding coteries
40 Coterie in tutus
43 Norse-myth figure
44 Filament: Suffix
45 Turkish title
46 Love song
48 Times of day: Abbr.
51 Madison Ave. tenant
54 Legend
56 Hideaway
57 Twangy
59 ____ Fail (Irish stone)
61 Ajax, to Greeks
63 Prom coterie
65 Berlin coterie
71 Rhodes wonder
72 Area: Abbr.
73 Diamond collector
74 Unfeeling
75 Meadow
77 Occupied-nation officials: Abbr.
79 Convoy coterie
84 ____-gallon hat
85 Kingdoms
88 Ear: Prefix
89 Song
90 Go wrong
91 Youthful coterie
96 Noisy opera coterie
100 Hungarian food: Var.
101 Blue grass
102 R.R. stop
103 Many TV movies
104 San Antonio sight
105 "____ Mio"
107 Final stanza
108 Pestilential coteries
113 "____ the vanquished"
114 Infertile moor
115 Swill
116 Earth goddess
117 Miss Terry
118 Wakefield V.I.P.
119 Run easily
120 Common abbr.
121 Tears down: Var.
122 French marshal and family
123 Novelist Wister
124 Dotted

DOWN

1 Robe or towel
2 Nautical word
3 Pupil or gazer
4 Quartz pieces
5 Bouillabaisse, e.g.
6 Dip
7 Twofold
8 ____ est percipi
9 Where Jack and Jill went
10 Prayers
11 Like eels
12 Calif. sea
13 Coteries at the pearly gates
14 Seals a bottle
15 ____ wit's end
16 Swoop down on
17 Jack and wife
21 Literary initials
28 Resistance units
29 One favoring church law
34 Official proceedings
35 Tennis champ of 1930
36 Sea bird
38 Hungarian
41 Play or fountain
42 Dull noise
43 Kind of soup
47 Musical pause
48 India's locale
49 Author of "Death in Venice"
50 Vehicle
52 Old-grad groupings
53 Chinese weights
55 Seraglio coterie
58 Vestment
60 Ceylon moonstone
62 Gulfweeds
64 Parisian friend
65 C.P.A.
66 Erudition
67 Zest
68 Navy-ship V.I.P.'s
69 Donkey, in Bonn
70 Scrooge, for one
76 Certain chaser's target
78 No-seats sign
80 Ford or Lincoln
81 Spanish golds
82 Outbreak
83 Pacific cloth
86 "____ 'ow!" (cockney toast)
87 Time period
92 Whines
93 Rise, as of a hill
94 Like a fresh-air fiend's window
95 Powder
96 Worker on harnesses
97 Town in Latium
98 Funeral feasts
99 One who is cited
100 King Arthur's nephew
105 A person ____ tastes (boor)
106 Early bravos
108 Part of a coat: Abbr.
109 Northern capital
110 Glut
111 Athletic coterie
112 Store event

25. Forgettable People by Elmer Toro

ACROSS

1 Without grounds
9 Get
15 Merge: Abbr.
20 Of Zeus's daughter
21 In a while, old style
22 Memory: Suffix
23 Foe of a Hood
26 Conduit
27 Bee: Prefix
28 Low sound
29 Lexington, Va., campus
30 "____ La Douce"
32 Rogue work by Thomas Dekker
36 Arid place
41 Fish
42 Halloween sound
43 Middle, in law
44 Antonio
51 Mooed
52 Back
53 How, in Bonn
54 Culbertson
55 Nothing, in Spain
59 Portent
60 Prank
62 Go amiss
64 Cat, at times
66 James
72 Whole: Prefix
73 Accomplished
74 Write briefly
75 Mexican weasel
76 Light-fingered Mideasterner
83 Quivery tree
86 Audience
87 Diminutive suffix
88 Tear apart
90 German musician
97 ____ ficta (altered melody)
98 Pitcher Maglie
99 ____ down (soft-pedaled)
100 Mine well
103 Oslo name
104 ____-Magnon
107 Inactive: Abbr.
109 French article
110 High spot
111 Dr. Primrose
116 Stock-buying words
120 Underworld god
121 Army branch: Abbr.
122 Tubby ones
123 Figaro
130 William
131 The same, in dosages
132 Sky, in Nancy
133 ". . . to shining ____"
134 Crowd, in Paris
139 Michael Henchard
144 Diners
145 ____ opposition (be uncontested)
146 Continuation in time
147 African money units: Var.
148 Elliot and Loch
149 Treacherous ones

DOWN

1 Game items
2 Netman Arthur
3 Confusion
4 Gaelic
5 Comedian Bert
6 Shoe width
7 Divine stage name
8 Marsh bird
9 Order of monks: Abbr.
10 Small spurt in the economy
11 A hard act ____
12 Part of Vietnam
13 Miss Massey
14 Gotham time initials
15 Make void
16 Elizabeth's sister
17 Bathed in sunlight
18 Old French coins
19 Smoked ham
22 Flowering plant
24 Little lie
25 End of a countdown
31 Chemical suffix
32 Feather's partner
33 Poetic word
34 Direction: Abbr.
35 Cockney residence
36 Normandy town
37 Assam native
38 U.S. archeologist
39 Egyptian king known as Ikhnaton
40 Buttons or Grange
45 Biblical town
46 S.R.O. shows
47 Mine passage
48 Feudal estate
49 Certain word
50 Curved molding
55 "I would ____" (warn against)
56 Askew
57 Before John
58 Tract
60 Friend, in Paris
61 Give up
63 Potentate
65 Involve
67 Of a cultural group
68 Region of Morocco
69 Aroma, British style
70 Cabin ingredient
71 Religious degree
77 Kennedy
78 Gen. Arnold
79 Rainbow
80 Ziegfeld
81 Astern, old style
82 Scott
83 Air: Prefix
84 Synagogue
85 Old African coin
89 Habituates
91 Apiece
92 Paris play area
93 Ancient philosophy center
94 ____ Hoek, African city
95 Miss Held
96 Submissive
101 Venus de ____
102 People on foot: Abbr.
105 Evergreens
106 City in Spain
108 Makes three out of one
110 Esthetic degree
111 Musical syllable
112 Neighbor of Syr.
113 Narrow-road feature
114 The R.E. Lees et al.: Abbr.
115 Letter F, in Spain
116 Lawyer: Abbr.
117 On ____ (ready for golf)
118 N.Y.C. suburb
119 Capable of
124 Elevates
125 Southern river
126 Shrill flutes
127 Adherent
128 English city
129 Jack of early films
134 Kind of door
135 Ceremony
136 Norse god
137 "____ Rhythm"
138 Wash. people
140 Brooks of films
141 Presidential initials
142 Sea plea
143 Shivery sound

26. Insect Study by Eugene T. Maleska

ACROSS

1 Egyptian goddess
5 Acarids
10 Wicker's "___ to Die"
15 Can. air arm
19 Buck heroine
20 Toughen
21 Yonkers events
22 Honor, in Hamburg
23 Army ant
25 Comic-strip ant
27 Accessory ant
28 Girth control
30 Subsequently
31 Marsh growth
32 Actor Alan
33 A Wahol forte
34 Small pike perch
37 Dresden's river
39 Saxon king
42 Woody or Steve
43 Michelangelo work
44 D-Day craft
46 Goose-pimply
47 Ballads
48 Musical rounds
49 Kind of beat or burn
51 Leftover ant
52 Chi. railroads
53 Caesar or Waldorf
54 Tossed to and fro
56 Flop
57 Preston role
59 Tale-telling French ant
61 Western lawman
62 City on the Rhone
63 Gator's relative
64 Red ant, possibly
68 "Aida" total
72 Reply: Abbr.
73 Signature part
74 Phi Beta ___
75 Morsel for dobbin
76 Party pooper
78 Toothsome
79 Slogans
80 Mystical mark
81 "La Douce" et al.
83 Luau garland
84 Great care
85 Alba ___ (Remus's home)
86 Movie director and family
88 Malign
90 Indian drum
91 River
93 Ampersands
94 Rio's beach
95 One who shuns
97 Years, to Cato
98 Sen. Bumpers is one
102 Disagreeable ant
104 Ticket-taking ant
106 Oscar film of 1958
107 Poe's "___ in Paradise"
108 Marquand's late hero
109 Org. since 1844
110 Eucalyptus secretion
111 Second of two
112 Seasonal songs
113 Vile odor

DOWN

1 Parlor piece
2 "___ of much contempt" (Shakespeare)
3 Boatman's buy
4 Becomes rebellious
5 Roberts, for one
6 "You're All ___" (old song)
7 Rotate
8 Work unit
9 Small spores
10 Have charisma
11 Snappish
12 Here, in Hérault
13 Edison's Park
14 Houdini feat
15 Echoing ant
16 British ant, good with figures
17 Guthrie
18 Sinn ___
24 Small woodenware
26 Level on the Eiffel Tower
29 Thinker's reward
32 In the van
33 Horse-show maneuver
34 Hawthorne's birthplace
35 Babylonian deity
36 Ant named Hiram
37 Giant
38 Certain whiskies
40 Trees of N.Z.
41 Watches over
43 Negri
45 Shipshape
48 Bulwark
49 Tedder operator
50 "Over the ___" (Holmes)
53 Stock certificate
54 Middle-age spread
55 Grain sorghum
58 Noun suffixes
59 Covered with soot
60 Wire grass
62 Valuable violins
64 Rooting ant
65 Relief adm.
66 Patricia of films
67 Mark or scar
68 Indolent ant
69 Uncloses, to poets
70 Dance for two
71 What inspired Watt
74 Kringle
77 Sharing ant
79 Sweater
80 Neronian ant
82 Corsican's neighbor: It.
84 Ant over the champs' ball park
85 "Steady Eddie" of Yankees
87 Taken care of
89 Cater basely
90 Sweet wines
92 Madras town
94 Angler's basket
95 Church of Eng.
96 Parisian's way
97 Haydn contemporary
98 Salt tree
99 Bespangled, in heraldry
100 Suffix for clear or appear
101 Bismarck's loc.
103 "___, That Kiss!"
105 G.I. address

27. Bowling Along by William Lutwiniak

ACROSS

1 Rake
6 Rib
11 Florist's need
15 During
19 Slue
20 Synthetic fabric
21 "Please ____" (word on a bill)
22 Hole ____
23 Frame
27 Voucher: Abbr.
28 Privately
29 Difficulties
30 Dorm sounds
31 Norfolk's time
32 Edge
33 Mexican cats
34 Boxing memento
35 Troglodyte's milieu
36 Royal appurtenances
37 Be biased
38 Not now, in Mexico
41 Doubleheader, with 92 Across
48 William's color
49 Floribundas
50 Freshet
51 Sudanese people
52 Meadowlands events
53 Lukas and Henreid
54 N.F.C. team
56 French painter
57 "Ecce ____"
58 Get ____ on
59 Family members
60 Illusion
61 Strikes
64 Razed
65 "How sweet ____!"
66 Boozer
67 Apple
68 Competed
72 Splits
80 Kind of bullet
81 U.S.M.A. figure
82 Goalies' feats
83 Country outing
84 Wystan Hugh
85 Sappers' concerns
86 Clerical mantles
87 Ship's crane
88 Allison or Tarkenton
89 Corrida star
90 Taste quality
91 Construction material
92 See 41 Across
96 Nervous
97 "The ____ Love"
98 Had sway
99 Busby and fez
100 Moves quickly, in Scotland
103 Southeast wind
104 Emulate Stentor
106 Méditerranée, e.g.
109 Pied-____
110 Go easy at the table
111 Louvers
112 Bouncing
113 Spares
118 ____ fixes (obsessions)
119 Crete's capital
120 16 drams
121 Archangel
122 Tournament positions
123 Kind of pot or up
124 Calculated
125 V.I.P.'s

DOWN

1 Spread out
2 Rules
3 In the open
4 Seine span
5 Catchall abbr.
6 Laborer
7 Welles
8 Skulked
9 Shredded
10 Ending with meth and oct
11 Prolix
12 Stockpile
13 Sample
14 Airport abbr.
15 Dvořák
16 Watered silk
17 ____ circle
18 MA and BA
21 Courses
22 Scoreboard unit
24 Insect stages
25 Rowdydow
26 "____ return"
32 Coiffure feature
33 Sfax's gulf
34 Is persuasive
35 Uri or Basel
36 Islamic
37 Retreats
38 Millers
39 Road symbol
40 Ruth's mother-in-law
41 Rolling stock
42 Coiled
43 Unruly children
44 Up front
45 Work of art
46 Panegyric
47 Up to here
53 Tartan
54 Certain sculptures
55 Vane heading
56 Musk source
58 Garden bloomer
59 "____ answer turneth . . ."
60 Office mail
62 Prone, with "to"
63 Land masses
64 Ear parts
67 Famous horseman
68 Personnel
69 Cape Cod town
70 Airport gear
71 Overcost for tribute
72 Asian capital
73 Summer quaff
74 Crustacean
75 Solvent dye
76 River of England
77 Dwelt
78 Making do
79 After sei
81 Clouds
85 Is downcast
86 Bistros
87 Al ____ (degree of doneness)
89 Madagascar mammal
90 Dissolved substance
91 Inelegant
93 Beautiful maidens
94 Goes yachting
95 Cry of serendipity
99 Execration
100 Con
101 Home of the brave
102 Heraldic bearings
103 Pleasant places
104 Alley or tiger
105 Hussar's weapon
106 Montez
107 Wee folk
108 Movie units
109 Star in Draco
111 Poker game
112 Bonn Mr.
114 Play a part
115 Philippine peasant
116 Blue grass
117 ____ rosa

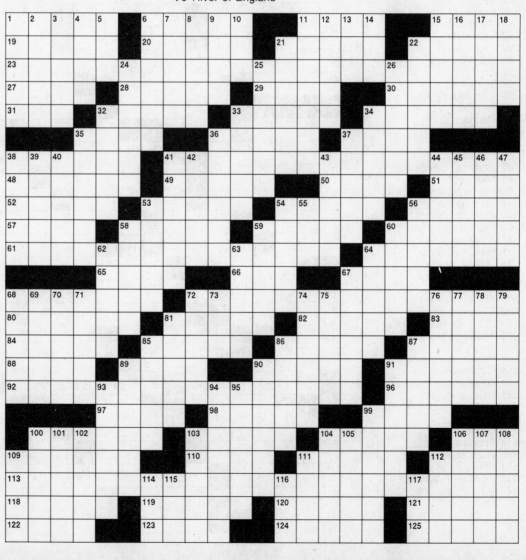

28. Paging Jimmy Carter by J. A. Felker

ACROSS

1 Clean
7 Violently
12 Certain mater
16 Barbecue need
20 Give the cold-shoulder
21 Ship, in Spain
22 On a ___ (carousing)
23 Part of "La Tosca"
24 Connecticut
27 Soviet mountains
28 Infamous marquis
29 More curious
30 Kind of TV audience
31 French painter
32 Turn in a way
33 Studied
34 Good name
35 Miss Lillie et al.
39 Knight of TV
40 Mushroom
41 ___ out (stayed)
42 Merman and Kennedy
44 Slip back
47 Pronto
49 Attack
50 Dreary account
51 Kind of excuse
53 Kind of bag
55 Western gulch
56 Hokkaido port
57 Sick's partner
58 Teen or dog's
59 Auto-race city, for short
60 Certain vote
62 In a while
64 ___ Coeur
66 Corded fabric
67 Ski ___
68 Thwarts
70 Certain sportsman
71 Follow
73 Decrees
76 Tom
78 John
80 Easy win
82 Northern European
83 Map abbr.
86 Kind of eclipse
87 Lamp owner
90 Suffix for consul or sultan
91 Old alloy
92 Antelope
93 Heat, to Cicero
95 Disagreed loudly
97 Promise
99 Indian flour
101 Kind of house
102 Tropical parrot
103 "___ for Sergeants"
104 Shade of character
106 Irritating
108 Connecting agent
109 Regional bird life
110 Campus org.
111 High, in music
113 Rhode Island denizens
114 Penny ___
116 Location
118 Spanish paintings
120 Did a sewing job
121 Waste allowance
122 Keep after school
123 Malarial ailment

127 Semblance
128 The works
131 Tore around
132 Skirt style
133 Court decree
134 Songbird
135 Fraternal people
136 Voices
137 Forward
138 Leash, in Paris

DOWN

1 Dim and half
2 Turkish title
3 Trim, in Scotland
4 Actress Lange
5 Actress Mary
6 Insulting words
7 Treated badly
8 Before midi
9 Like a payroll guard
10 Baked-goods worker
11 Drink
12 Clothes
13 Decamp
14 Joined
15 Common verb
16 Working on dirty pans
17 Christmas favorite
18 Narrow waterway
19 Experience

23 ". . . lamb was ___ go"
25 Relative of nah
26 Joe, sometimes
31 Jarred
33 Nitty-gritty
35 Area of L.A.
36 Always, to poets
37 Tough problem
38 Indian soldier
40 Barton
41 "___ Time, Next Year"
43 Minstrel's offering
44 Music abbr.
45 Relative of etc.
46 T.S. and family
48 Tidal flood
50 Kind of leader
52 English composer
54 Drink
57 Triplet
61 Sheep
63 Roof ornament
64 Lollipop or Pinafore
65 Biblical spring
67 Peter or Ivan
69 Quarrel
72 New Deal org.
73 Tea
74 Jungle noise
75 Achieved
77 In ___ (succinct)
78 Miss Korbut

79 Leigh and Marsha
81 Sound
82 Put on cargo
84 Designated
85 Arabian rulers
88 Column order
89 Certain word
91 Active
93 Cheated on an exam
94 Planet inhabitants
96 Work unit
98 Family member
100 Classifies
102 Hard hits
105 Verily
107 Moon goddess
111 Big Dipper star
112 Speech trouble
114 C'est
115 Of a branch
116 Groove
117 Literary form
118 Barbizon painter
119 Poker moves
122 Cat or motor sound
123 Roman years
124 Revs the engine
125 U.S. Indians
126 Italian family
128 Some radio stations
129 Idiot
130 Org. for Saarinen

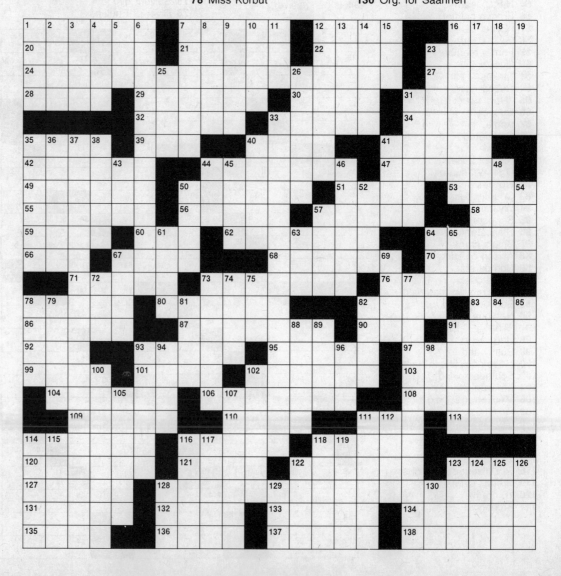

29. Oscars by Barbara Gillis

ACROSS

1 Track events
6 Drivers' org.
9 Architect I.M.
12 Contest
16 New Delhi name
17 Scratch awls
20 Baseball team
21 By the sea
23 Pledges
24 Dye's partner
25 Like maidens of old
26 Like some music
27 Asian rulers
28 City of Ethiopia
30 Actress Hunt
32 Old slave
34 Tapeworm larva
36 Norse classic
39 Caught in ____
42 Town in Java
45 Israel's Six-____
47 Dieter's portion
49 Reveal
50 Page number: Abbr.
51 Candlenut tree
52 Withdraw
53 Mint said to have curing quality
55 Save
57 Town in Portugal
58 Partner: Abbr.
59 Syncopation
61 Praying figure
62 Origin
64 Town near Munster
65 Kind of skirt
66 Nook's companion
68 Catches a fish
70 Makes a close fit
74 Bangladesh port
75 Place to wear an obi
76 Use wrongly
78 Village
79 Cuckoo
80 Dunk
82 Moroccan port
83 Composer Georges
84 Vexes
86 Spanish weight
87 Take care of
88 Parts of a trip
89 Vishinsky
92 Small islands
94 One who partakes
96 Chemical compound
100 Italian poet
103 Orwell's farm
106 Hobart's island: Abbr.
108 Acid initials
109 Constellation
110 Vanished
113 The Man
114 Willing
115 Relatives on mother's side
116 Hesitates
117 Once named
118 Mideast land: Abbr.
119 Confused

DOWN

1 Enthusiasm
2 Register
3 Old English letter
4 Foreign alliance
5 Libyan oasis
6 Starry
7 Hole-in-one
8 Tapestry
9 Laborer
10 Girl's name
11 Carpet fiber
12 Expatriate
13 Chevalier film
14 Corker
15 Cape
16 Barbarian
18 "____ could see me now"
19 Gotham tune
22 Prepares to fire
23 Handshake
29 Versatile one
31 Decorate again
33 Area of Sardinia
35 U.S. writer
37 Lepers' helper et al.
38 Irish island
40 Ward off
41 Carolina river
42 Plateau
43 Salutations
44 Abner et al.
46 Helpless saviors
48 Thing, in law
50 Neighbor of Ga.
54 Dilettantish
56 Alvin of ballet
60 French river
61 Prefix for present
63 Out drinking
66 Charlie and sons
67 Ouida
69 Unruly one
71 Hair style
72 Voluble
73 Aegean island
74 Guevara
75 South African
77 German basin
81 Danube feeder
85 Ontario city
90 One of the worlds
91 Goldarn!
93 Writer Françoise
95 Excuse
97 Corny
98 Nine: Prefix
99 Energy units
100 Twaddle
101 Comedian Johnson
102 ". . . king of ____, I am"
104 Alaskan cape
105 Arrow poison
107 N.L. park
111 Compliments: Abbr.
112 "The Week That ____"

30. New Year Limerick by Frances Hansen

ACROSS

1 Asian peninsula
6 Small bottle
11 Kind of sergeant
16 Pipe parts
21 Soap plant
22 Madrid museum
23 Vietnam massacre scene
24 Drip-dry fabric
25 ____ bell
26 Wanders
27 Sinclair
28 Kind of trope
29 Limerick with 58, 82, 109 and 138 Across
33 Boredom
34 Ex-promoter Rickard
35 Red or Dead
36 Britisher's exclamation
37 Easter fare
40 Aleutian island
42 Artemis
46 Sent back: Abbr.
48 Polite interruptions
51 Compass point
53 ____ eyed (gaping)
54 Between avril and juin
55 Franciscan order: Abbr.
58 See 29 Across
64 Nonplus
65 India, e.g.
66 Streisand film, with "Day"
67 ____ uproar
68 Certain wagons
73 Deer of Asia
74 Hoop: Sp.
77 Suffix for halit or neur
79 Stops, as a missile flight
81 Pitch
82 See 29 Across
89 Cream puffs at six paces
90 Furs
91 Tie
92 MS, men
93 Fabrics with lines
96 Lunch hour
100 Fed. agents
102 Goes astray
104 Scoundrel
105 Choir screen
109 See 29 Across
115 Ark man: Var.
116 "____ Were a Rich Man"
117 Melville book
118 Golfer's pou sto
119 Evergreen genus
120 Calmer of TV
121 Late March, to head-cold victim
123 Actor Bert
126 Albanian coin
127 Overseas addresses
131 British colonial rulers: Abbr.
133 ____-disant
135 Provoke
138 See 29 Across
147 Shaw
148 Relative of adieu
149 Refuge
150 Babylonian abode of dead
151 "____ ev'ry little star . . ."
152 Billiard shot
153 Ward off
154 Verse cadences
155 Snide
156 Hostile one
157 Bloody and Queen
158 Wine pitchers

DOWN

1 French spouse
2 Oriental nurse
3 Like Tonto's friend
4 Pond scum
5 Aspire
6 Shoot
7 Gained
8 Pompeii's ruin
9 That is: Lat.
10 Go ____ (decay)
11 Complacent
12 Printing boo-boo
13 Prefix for tude or meter
14 Young deer: Fr.
15 Mob member
16 Limey locale
17 Famous fountain
18 French pronoun
19 Ballerina Shearer
20 Like Kilimanjaro's peaks
30 Double helix
31 Principle
32 Knocking sound
37 Triumphant cries
38 "There'll be ____ time . . ."
39 Desert sight
41 Not suitable
43 Branch
44 Teachers' org.
45 Writer Rand
47 Last resort, sometimes
49 Christmas trio
50 Italian Mr.
52 Sea bird
55 "____ and you're dead!"
56 Like church windows
57 A nose ____
59 Rein
60 Pyle and Ford
61 Trappist cheese
62 Threw a party
63 Winged
69 Biblical verb
70 Honest one
71 Fracas
72 Test
74 Freshens a martini
75 Give road directions
76 ____ hill (washed up)
78 Tilts
80 Novelist Jean Paul
83 Form of Elizabeth
84 African people: Var.
85 Ziegfeld
86 Sum of little Indians
87 Ouida
88 Veer
94 Puckish
95 Singing exercise
97 Here: Fr.
98 Ship part
99 Detroit dud
101 Kind of do-well
103 Prayed before dinner
106 ____ Eireann
107 Start of a fairy tale
108 Badlands state: Abbr.
110 Some punches
111 Diamond man
112 For: Sp.
113 Lift
114 Tough
122 New York
124 Does ghosting
125 Operate
127 Over
128 Gate: It.
129 German kings
130 Word for Wilt
132 Car style
134 Caste of India
136 Author Marsh
137 Of a flower part
139 Lamarr
140 Kind of dale
141 Weaver's need
142 "____ slip showing?"
143 Continually
144 Musical intro
145 Exile island
146 Ploy

31. Opéra-Comique by Alfio Micci

ACROSS

1 Crude abodes
7 Skiff
11 Sweetmeat
17 Passed over
18 ____ de Léon
19 Shrub genus
21 Garland film?
23 Holdings
24 Darts
25 Carson et al.
26 Article
28 Despots
29 Gaelic
30 McCrea
31 A West from the East
32 Toper
33 Church calendar
35 Indian prince
37 Lures
42 Nabokov heroine
45 Two make 20
46 Horn tissue
47 Greek letter
48 "Arabian Nights" number
49 Kind of cheese
51 Verb ending
53 Between Wolfgang and Mozart
55 ____ Major
56 Correct
59 Adjective suffix
60 Bacheller hero
61 Marina sights
63 Loser to D.D.E.
64 Merry, in Nice
65 Highlander
67 Burns's line?
73 Abominable snowman
74 Bounder
75 ____-jongg
76 Germs
78 Trouble
81 Card game
82 Worship
84 Sea growth
85 Wild sheep
87 Spanish boy
88 Ignited
91 Jai ____
92 Guitarist Paul
94 Musical closing
96 Sarge
97 Mrs., in Mexico
98 Fear
100 Maintain
101 Sculls
103 ____ poetica
104 "The works"
106 Sediment
108 Señor's aunts
111 Soul
114 Golden or Bronze
115 Remain
116 Tibetan porter
118 Game piece
120 Shaw play?
123 Fiddled badly
124 Reckon
125 Wimpole Street resident
126 Fish repository
127 Slangy denial
128 Not acquired

DOWN

1 Cut
2 Wit
3 Melodic passage
4 Yardsticks
5 Rosewall and Venturi
6 Campus militants
7 Footwear cords
8 Stigma
9 Chemical prefix
10 Seed coat
11 Birdhouse
12 Violinist Bull
13 Guide
14 Magical treatment?
15 Singer Petina
16 Layer
17 Sweater sizes: Abbr.
18 Toolbox item
20 Fool
22 Ring decision
27 Attend a concert
30 Key words?
31 Famed mime
32 Put up with
34 Peke, for one
36 Only making the grade?
38 Weds?
39 Campus figure
40 Go on the road
41 Spanish assents
42 "We'll tak' ____ . . ."
43 Column style
44 Confused
50 Linger
52 Puzzle
54 Shade of green
57 ____ up (angry)
58 Refuse container
62 Odor
66 Step
68 Prima ballerinas
69 Extreme
70 Pillbox
71 Cries
72 Trimming tool
77 Actress Thompson
78 "G.I. Jane" of 1942
79 Plinth
80 Alike, in Arles
83 Magnet
86 What I do when hungry?
89 Peruvian city
90 Cross or lights
93 Smoker
95 Operatic heroine
99 Fountain treat
102 Saw-toothed ridge
105 Martini twist
107 Ghent's river
109 Medieval helmet
110 Outpouring
111 Reply: Abbr.
112 Pleasing
113 Regarding
114 "Showboat" skipper
115 Cut
116 Bridge
117 Emmet
119 Comparative ending
121 G.I. address
122 Where: Lat.

32. Spring Fever by Louis C. Mandes, Jr.

ACROSS

1 Predicament
7 Hastily
12 Culmination
16 Toasting words
21 On ____
22 Core group
23 Linen source
24 Agreed
25 Heroine of 1778
27 Precipitate
28 Yells at the ump
29 Notice
30 Expanded
31 Locomotive parts
33 Laugh, in Lyons
34 Portnoy's creator
36 Alone
37 Score into the 10th
38 Love, on the Lido
40 Spate
43 Luncheonettes
46 Confide in
47 Pastry
48 Desire
50 Read meter
51 Stretch in the 7th
52 A Dionne girl
53 Like sandlot infields
55 Cavalryman
59 Comic-strip cries
60 Like taped baseballs
61 Hacks
63 Release
64 More disreputable
66 Little bits
67 Innocent one
69 Overhead carrier
70 True's partner
71 Batter's ploy
72 Played on home grounds
74 Hit ____ country mile
75 Relaxed
77 Left
79 Split, as a bat
81 Arrowroot
82 Dieter's standby
84 Tarnish
85 "____ Ben Jonson"
86 Senator from R.I.
88 Home run by-product
89 Fishing net
90 Brest's region
93 Renown
95 Intend
97 Energy source
98 Eye defect: Suffix
99 Deliver
101 Excalibur
102 Intact
103 Hit a fly
104 Apple pitcher
106 Passable
107 Smog factor
108 Strike hard at
109 Football infractions
113 Riding whip
115 C.J. after Marshall
116 Ewe said it
117 Golden and Bronze
119 Coalesce
120 Maglie and Bando
121 Flatware item
125 Riverfront

128 Big-leaguer
131 Aunt in "Oklahoma!"
132 Captive of Hercules
133 Albania
135 Chinks
136 Yacht haven
137 Ryan or Tatum
138 Compact
139 Sanity
140 Singles
141 Confuse
142 Sentence structure

DOWN

1 Hurricanes: Abbr.
2 Baltimore ____
3 Count (on)
4 Everyone
5 Lucky strike
6 Furniture style
7 Recorded proceedings
8 Agreement
9 Supporter
10 Statements of faith
11 Poetic word
12 Hair style
13 Pincers
14 Bat boy
15 Blows out
16 French brandy
17 State or lake
18 ____ a turn
19 Physically fit
20 Headlands
26 O'Neill play
31 Putti
32 Inform
33 Rhyme opening
35 "The Bronx is up, but ____"
38 Blithe spirit
39 Ammo of '76
40 Handbill
41 Leather strip
42 Vault
44 Fidel Castro's brother
45 Beginning
46 Very, in Vichy
47 Blended
49 Protract
52 Librarian, at times
54 Beer ingredient
56 Attitudinize
57 Precious stone
58 Caesar, e.g.
61 Bop on the head
62 What subs do
65 Chemical element
66 All-Star game time
68 Feverish
71 Pushcarts
72 Sox
73 Darn it!
75 Kind of deck
76 Relative
77 Lasts
78 Snider
80 Bobolinks

83 Cut off
85 Papal cape
87 Clouts the ball
89 Desert
90 Red-eye
91 Smart
92 Eucalypt
94 Pakistani people
96 Unfortunate
97 Republic of Africa
100 Sea duck
102 Pared away
105 Al Pacino film
108 Outstanding
109 Preoccupy
110 Ribbed fabric
111 N.C.O.'s order
112 Barroom
114 ____ hers
115 Catcalls
118 Balm
120 Sloth, e.g.
122 Rookies' opposites
123 Gaelic
124 Links places
126 Hindu deity
127 Rural spot
128 British antitank gun
129 Roster
130 Cameo stone
133 Neckpiece
134 Percent number

33. Capsule Comments by Ruth N. Schultz

ACROSS

1 Marner or Lapham
6 Spiny-finned fish
10 Red Baron, e.g.
13 Side dish
17 Voiced
18 Iroquois
19 General's word
21 ____ colada, rum drink
22 Emulate Delilah
23 Two years in the House
24 Tidy
25 Fail to mention
26 Queen's words
29 Prima ballerina
31 Egyptian cotton
32 Comment
33 Caxton or Zenger
34 Dweller
38 Mideast natives
41 Lulu Bett's sister
42 King's word
47 Bellamann book: 1940
52 Society girls
53 Hives
54 Detective's word
57 Reaped after reapers
59 Achieve much
60 Errata
62 Year in reign of Louis VII
64 Ruminate
65 King's words
69 Mlle., in Madrid
73 Greek god
74 Loosely woven fabrics
75 Fifth wheel
80 Generosity
82 Diarist's words
84 Squirrel fare
85 Fans' words
89 Trestle
90 Conqueror's words
94 Conger
95 Atomic group
96 Ecuadorean province
100 Retinue
104 More clownish
106 Buttons
108 Bob or shingle
109 Flower seller's words
114 Give the nod to
115 Gumbo
117 "Bei Mir ____ du Schön"
118 McCartney or Starr
119 Sumps
120 John's predecessor
121 D-Day beach
122 Failed a G.I. rifle-range test
123 Lap, at times
124 Pale
125 The take
126 Entangling

DOWN

1 "____and yet so far"
2 Output's opposite
3 Hideout
4 Noun suffix
5 British gun
6 Irish, for one
7 Quintessence
8 Kind of postage
9 Objected
10 Princess
11 Signaled
12 After zeta
13 Flatware item
14 Last straw
15 Old-womanish
16 Kind of bed
17 Backstitches
20 English novelist
27 Pay dirt
28 Ray
30 Web
33 Felt shoe
35 Millisecond
36 Place an ad
37 Mend socks
39 Collar
40 Pronoun
43 Streetcar
44 Carte
45 Pindar's output
46 Antiseptic: Fr.
47 Pub vessel
48 Worldwide labor org.
49 Ship-shaped clock
50 Beavers' neighbors
51 "The ____ Were"
55 Certain mail cars: Abbr.
56 ____ Kippur
57 Moth's tongue
58 Ullmann
61 Girl in a song
62 Neighbor of Wis.
63 Lumps of clay
66 Owns
67 Teachers' org.
68 Biblical queen
69 Muscovite, e.g.
70 Sprint
71 Cyclo follower
72 Kind of culture
76 African tree
77 Shorten, for short
78 Legal matter
79 Town near Arnhem
81 Was jealous of
83 Has debts
85 Scram!
86 Ab ____ (from the start)
87 Tokyo's Fifth Ave.
88 Insect on the deep
91 "No news ____ news"
92 Female rabbit
93 "____ Lovely Day?"
96 ____ Lip (Durocher)
97 Any planet
98 Bryan was one
99 Becky Sharp's victim
100 Karate blows
101 Jack, of old films
102 Lariat
103 Romantic meeting
105 "Where ____!"
107 Recolored
109 Mlle. La Douce
110 Farm wagon
111 Sags or flags
112 Time unlimited
113 Gershwin's "____, Lucille"
116 "Go down to ____ . . ."

34. Bullet-Biting Time by Jay Spry

ACROSS

1 Partly open
5 Pavlov
9 Chooses
13 Solitaire wastepile
18 Hand-dyed fabric
20 Style
21 Air Force unit
22 Type of type
23 Start of a quotation
27 Brouhaha
28 Ferber and others
29 Catches sight of
30 Female rabbit
31 Author Deighton
32 Sunder
34 ____ Blas
35 Tarbell
36 Record
38 Creeping S.A. plant
41 Concerning
43 City in Italy
44 Delight
46 Tax people
49 Obstacles
53 Kipling subject
54 No-man
55 Links area
56 Notice
57 Spatiates
58 Lofty
60 Transferable pictures
63 Quotation: Part II
64 In the crib
65 Half note
66 Took place
68 Ring around a lagoon
70 Lone Eagle's monogram
71 Stewed
72 E.R.A. or R.B.I.
73 Lampoon
75 Quotation: Part III
81 Liz of TV newscasting
82 Overhanging edge
83 Mother of Aphrodite
84 Noun suffix
85 Pit
86 Rich cake
88 French ____
89 To-do
90 Quotation: Part IV
91 Empties
93 Author of "Tristram Shandy"
95 Tamerlane was one
96 Alert
98 Mystery-story pioneer
99 Yalies
100 Distaff Astaire
101 Goose genus
103 Consider
107 Hindu ascetics
109 N.Y. team
111 Hebrew measures
112 Fierce looks
114 Push
116 Call ____ day
117 In the style of
118 Pack pipe tobacco
122 W.W. II theater
123 Epoch
125 Kind of case
127 Orange or Indian
129 Call of the riled
130 End of quotation
135 Welcome
136 Doll up
137 Low-lying tract
138 Slipknot
139 Outcries
140 Kernel
141 Trudge
142 Miseries

DOWN

1 Home
2 Argonaut
3 A.B.A. member
4 Full-blown
5 Lion's prey
6 Tennesseans
7 Fruit punch
8 Word
9 City near Paris
10 Bolls
11 Decrepit boat
12 Rushed
13 Abilities
14 Begum's spouse
15 Soup scoop
16 Dark-brown fur
17 Inert gas
19 Small anchors
21 Cicerones
23 Damage
24 Cinched
25 Reckon
26 Leaves
33 Bantingized
37 Containers
39 Base on balls
40 Voltaire novel
41 Where Laos is
42 Roomy handbags
43 Bewildered
44 Pompous official
45 Billets-doux
47 Hold back
48 Hard times
50 Fruit-based spread
51 Aim
52 Pen
53 Dogwood petal
54 Event re Texas: 1845
58 Strive for
59 Aborigines
60 Biblical verb
61 Most South Americans
62 Fence crossing
65 Grumble
67 Deserve
69 Prospector's quarry
71 Palm leaf
72 Bat a gnat
74 Romeo's emotion
76 Revenue agent: Abbr.
77 Sun. lectures
78 Worshipful
79 Asian wild sheep
80 Zola's "La ____"
85 Thai language
87 ____ a customer
88 Cold-cuts store
89 Cruel one
90 A pair, in Ayr
92 Mimics
94 British meals
95 Require
97 Captain of the Nautilus
102 Goes back
104 Gave off
105 Keep
106 Teach
107 Ballads
108 Part of Spain
110 Sea swallow
113 Stood the gaff
114 Accumulation
115 Uncle Tom's cabin
119 Humble
120 Asch book
121 Cry of contempt
122 Like floating islands
124 Watts' kin
125 Koko's weapon
126 Society tag line
127 European capital
128 ". . . were Paradise ____!"
131 Conger
132 Sonneteer's word
133 Adjective suffix
134 Dovecote sound

35. Directory by Bert H. Kruse

ACROSS

1 Evening dress
7 Season
11 Mauna ____
14 Turn over
18 Drill command
19 Clothes-drying frame
20 Address for a singer?
22 Address for a netman?
24 Smart aleck's rural address?
25 Real being
26 Horace's forte
27 Film cutter
29 Comics character
30 Boards an SST
33 Danish weights
34 Does sums
35 Doubtful
38 Moonship units
39 Room shape
41 Scorecard entries
43 Common, in Hawaii
44 Bull fiddle
45 Indigo sources
47 Corn porridges
50 Hoffman and Farnum
52 Crimson Tide
54 Kind of jar
56 Right: Prefix
57 Athirst
58 Mailed
60 Water surface, old style
61 Glaswegians
63 Counterclockwise
64 Bye-bye
65 Dice throw
66 CWP starter
67 Geronimo, e.g.
69 Planetarium
71 Biblical V.I.P.'s: Abbr.
72 Possessive
74 Celebes ox
75 Bird sound
76 Word of mouth
78 Jet speed unit
79 Very, in Berlin
80 Critic Rex
81 Great Yankee arm
83 Famed songwriter
85 Plague
87 Make a face
89 Fisherman
91 Service club
92 Gay blade
93 Gumshoe
94 Good earth
96 Chic, for short
97 Villein
98 Chan words
99 Sheep cries
102 Yucatán native
104 Indolent
107 Cork source
108 Kitchen attire
110 Nimbus
111 Pleasant
114 Dancer's address?
116 Diana Ross's ex-address?
120 Library name
121 Vestige
122 Fur of the coypu
123 "And ____ weary . . .": Burns
124 Windup
125 Dimensions
126 Purloined

DOWN

1 Avoirdupois
2 Western Indian
3 H.R. members
4 Stage Abe
5 Quiverleaf
6 Garland
7 Hazard for Odysseus
8 Crop up
9 O.T. book
10 Hat holder
11 "The ____ a ass": Dickens
12 Kind of dictum
13 Takes in
14 Neighbor of Ga.
15 Tied
16 "The Lady ____"
17 Sly glances
19 Nobelist for Peace: 1931
21 Always, to poets
23 Exactly as stated
28 Address in Perry's notebook?
31 Blueprint
32 Lisbon legislature
34 Eritrean capital
35 ____-China
36 Outspoken quartet's address?
37 Address for jet-setters?
40 W. Afr. republic
42 "____ Woman"
44 Flora and fauna
45 Still in use
46 Daubed
48 Way to Bellevue?
49 Certain sites
51 Tonkinese group
52 Diplomat's address?
53 Wager
55 Promontory
57 Intoxicant
59 Protective covering
62 Health resorts
66 Psyche's opposite
68 French novelist
69 Singer Buck
70 Cantab's rival
73 Wentletraps
75 Swings
77 Gypsy spouse
82 Mexican group
84 Modernist
86 Jersey's lament
87 Famed silversmith
88 Trump or bird
90 Storm wildly
92 Damaged paper
95 Game fish
97 Origin
98 Ex-mayor of S.F.
99 Italian bowls
100 Shoe sizes
101 Ghana's capital: Var.
103 Coupled
105 Bolivian city
106 Not abridged
108 Impress greatly
109 Concordes
112 Squiggle
113 Border lake
115 Chemical suffix
117 Psychic Geller
118 Annapolis grad.
119 Hosiery shade

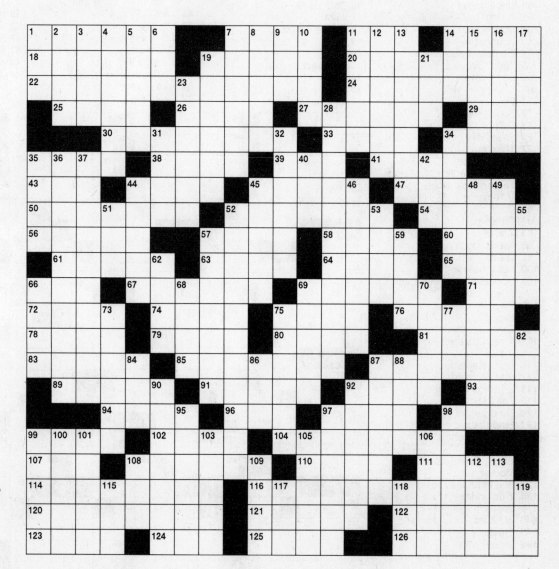

36. Scrambling Around by Frances Hansen

ACROSS

1 Artistic fra
6 Grasshopper hatcheries
11 Tooth
16 Kind of soup
21 Bradley and Sharif
22 Tripoli's land
23 "Do ___ to eat a peach?": T. S. Eliot
24 Grab
25 Playful animal
26 Swords
27 Sweet, hot drink
28 Hanged Biblical prince
29 Traditional White House event
33 Trumpet call
34 Skid-row affliction
35 Shea team
36 Lower Loch ___
37 Pronounce
38 Spill over
40 Ruse
41 Farmer's place
43 Little white lie
46 Long-stemmed
48 Russian sea
49 68 Across, slangily
51 Unbalanced
55 A hen, to Samuel Butler
62 Sudden gush
63 Schnozzle
64 Comparative suffix
65 "Bye, Bye, ___"
66 Small tower
68 "___ me, sir!"
71 Op. ___
72 Supreme Being
73 Part of Mao's name
74 Stravinsky
77 Theater district
80 Choir assent
82 Variety headline: 1929
87 Tan shades: Abbr.
89 U.N. name
90 Curb
91 Cruise port
94 Grand ___
95 Asian holiday
97 Weak
100 Flaky treats
103 Goddess for whom Easter was named
105 High, in music
107 Urged
110 Give ___ berth to (shun)
111 A rash Easter Bunny does it
116 Draft status
117 H.M. Pulham, e.g.
118 ___ time (never)
119 Eggs for Lucullus
120 Time period
121 Hindu music
124 Hosiery mishap
125 Besides
128 24 ___ week (poor diet)
131 Morsel
132 Historic Italian town
133 Wea. index
136 Easter ___
140 Is an intellectual artistic?
145 Practical
146 Nine: Prefix

147 Pneumonia type
148 Songs
149 ___ in one's beer (enriches)
150 Mudd
151 Puttee
152 Rainy-day reserve
153 Tiffs
154 Used a broom
155 Kind of path
156 J. Q. Adams biographer

DOWN

1 Pillages
2 "___ greatest!": Ali
3 Eucharist plate
4 Dolls up
5 Where Acre is
6 Small Easter find
7 Two-footed
8 German President 1919–25
9 Do an Easter fun-job
10 Obi
11 Liza, with a Z
12 "Swan Lake" role
13 Nigerian capital
14 ___ for one's money
15 Lay atop
16 Pale color
17 Allot
18 Spanish rhymes
19 Conductor Seiji
20 Coin
30 Pompeia's robe
31 Eskimo boat
32 Hurry
39 Fleming and Lee
40 High dudgeon
42 Actor Bert
43 Lenten duty
44 Computer data
45 "The ___ Opera"
47 Hither's partner
48 Sun-god Ra
49 Big, for short
50 Actress Samantha
52 Shelf
53 Heavenly Hunter
54 Let fly
56 Scattered
57 Like Willie Winkie
58 Last quarter
59 Of nests
60 Sash
61 Giant
67 Sesame
69 Mountain ridge
70 Kind of wit or pick
71 "___ fan tutte"
75 Satiate
76 Kiln: Var.
78 Rio Grande city
79 Ship rope
81 With 93 Down, development in "Little Men"
83 "Ad ___ . . ."
84 Oodles
85 Compass point
86 ". . . eating ___ without salt": Kipling
87 Columnist Heywood
88 Remainder: Fr.
92 "___ Ike"

93 See 81 Down
94 Melon
96 Slippery one
98 Mendicant's line
99 Gauze weave
101 British cultural inst.
102 Bristle
104 Ruler
105 Gasps of delight
106 Rye or rum: Abbr.
108 Yoko
109 Granular snow
112 Doeskin, cowhide, etc.
113 Ovolo design
114 Flight of steps
115 Life raft
122 Super-duper Easter finds
123 Shorthand inventor
124 ". . . not ___ as a well"
126 Suffragist Anthony
127 Main course
128 Certain containers
129 Showed surprise
130 Santa
132 Actress Hope
133 Menu offering
134 Nun's usual garb
135 Silly
137 Paine's doctrine
138 Hindu lamp rite
139 Safecracker's omelet
141 Norwegian fjord
142 Poet's "enough"
143 Isomeric
144 Therefore

37. A Spell of Letters by Jordan S. Lasher

ACROSS

1 "Trinity" author
5 Peak of Thessaly
9 Bicarb
13 Vocalize
18 Baby girls: Sp.
20 Crucial elements
22 ____ de Sol
23 Humphrey
25 Evaluation
26 Mythical princess
27 Portly
28 Three-wheeler
29 Weak: Prefix
30 Experiences anew
32 Newsy note
33 Church recess
34 Post Cato held
35 They get their man
39 Roof covering
42 Money in Zagreb
43 Made a refusal
44 Charged force
45 Mongrel
46 French marshal
47 Dovekies
49 Attended a meeting
51 F.D.R. measure: 1933
52 OGPU successor
55 "Twenty times, thou ____":
   "Richard II"
56 Madison Ave. product
59 Victory symbols
60 Oil used in perfumes
61 Pointer or grass
62 Record players
64 Assert
65 Young community promoters
66 Fatty liquid
67 March man
68 Solecist's word
69 Time abbr.
70 Oxhide straps
71 2,065
73 Code word for "A"
74 Battery terminal
75 Former Dodger
76 ____ de Triomphe
79 Moppet
80 Swindle
81 Atop
83 Virgil hero: Var.
85 Cry of discovery
86 Big Apple address
89 Dull finish
90 Exhort
92 Beatty film: 1981
93 Slats for fences
95 Ann ____
97 Hollow: Prefix
99 Fierce look
101 Cambridge tech. center
102 Sluice gate
103 Title for 23 Across
106 Red as ____
107 Makers of cowboys' goods
108 Garbed, old style
109 Children's author
110 Hardy girl
111 Jubiliation
112 College studies

DOWN

1 Not publicized
2 Checked one's mount
3 Bring ____ (discipline)
4 Pouch
5 Certain migrants
6 Collections
7 Indian groom
8 Rowan
9 Evening party
10 Punctual
11 Bedizen
12 County in N.C.
13 Hustled tickets
14 Propounds
15 Humane org. for juveniles
16 Rat-____
17 Ring victory
19 Rude commuter
21 Used a shuttle
24 Mary Todd's man
31 "Now ____ me down . . ."
32 Cocktail rocks
33 Eternity
35 Singer and family
36 Optimistic
37 Doles
38 Ballet bend
40 Ran after
41 Most provoked
47 Keep ____ on (watch over)
48 Luau instruments
49 Soap opera
50 Take ____ view of
51 Exchequer
52 Dale or Bergen
53 Loudness
54 Rub the board
55 Samar's neighbor
56 Beloved, in Bologna
57 Seductress
58 Ex-soldiers' group
61 Temples
63 Iwo ____
64 A Yalie
65 Hipster's jargon
67 Fumous
68 Nerve-cell process
71 Sufficient, to FitzGerald
72 Town in Arizona
74 Tops
76 Biblical giant
77 Mix again, as concrete
78 Most spiteful
80 Has misgivings
81 Destroyer
82 Stalag inmates: Abbr.
83 Ran the show
84 Six-line stanzas
87 Dark place in myths
88 Snigglers
91 Is nomadic
93 Outmoded
94 Berlin, for short
95 Gardner et al.
96 Playwright David
97 ____ la vie
98 Wine pitcher
99 Highlander
100 Harp of Hellas
104 Irish dance
105 Time span

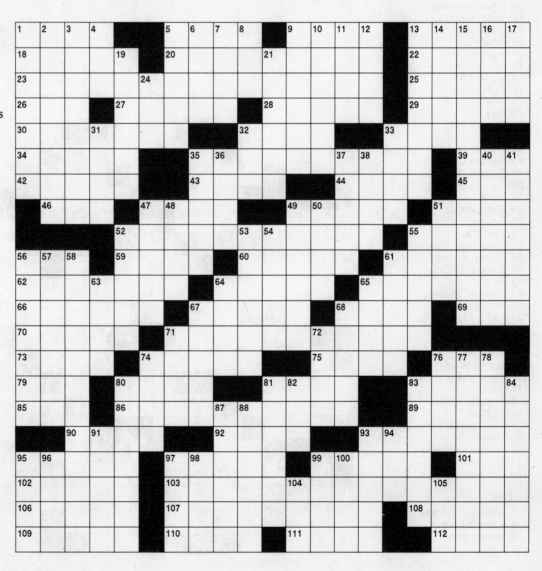

38. Springing into Action by A. J. Santora

ACROSS

1 Down: Prefix
5 Christmas trio
9 Nail barrels
13 Improvises like Ella
18 Assyrian god
19 City in China
20 "____ not in Gath"
22 Alpine cottage
23 Enjoying a May day
27 Girl-watching
28 Do harm to
29 Leather punch
30 Iron band
31 Gazelle
32 Felt compassion
35 Withered
36 Gumbo
40 River in England
41 Small grain spike
43 ____ as a pin
46 Exerted
47 U.S. money: Abbr.
48 Melville book
49 Like Berlin
50 Make into soap
55 Vacationing
58 Entraps: Var.
59 Raucous noise
60 Second audition
61 Bugbears
62 Tallies
64 Apiece
65 Kind of nail
68 Viewed the Marxes
74 Culbertson
75 Protracted
76 Boil
77 "Quo ____?"
78 Troubles
81 Former Brazilian money
82 Venomous snakes
84 Exercise in fitness
88 ____-to-meeting
89 Verse
90 Being cooled
91 Channel: Sp.
92 Coincide
93 Chickweed genus
95 Giving sparingly
97 Sleeper or diner
100 Fling
101 Hudson Bay Indian
102 Viewpoints
104 "To a rag and ____ . . ."
106 C'est la ____
108 Outside: Comb. form
109 Draw out
110 Spring song
117 Went prying
118 Strad
119 Binaural system
120 Ripped
121 Word in Mass. motto
122 Caine film
123 Snow-fun vehicle
124 Esau's land
125 Avant-garde

DOWN

1 Wayne of hockey
2 Actor-dancer
3 Hands over
4 ". . . ____ and peasant slave"
5 Heffalump's creator
6 ____ in a poke
7 Lollobrigida
8 Thankless people
9 Composer Jerome
10 Charged force
11 Sates
12 Tourist
13 ____ khan
14 Lincoln's "____ Eri"
15 Wings
16 Alas. in 1942
17 Wall St. cert.
20 Remote settlement
21 "Is ____ doctor . . . ?"
22 Congest
24 Cotton thread
25 Namely
26 Two-seated wagon
32 Prexy's staff
33 In a bad way
34 Saratoga outing
36 Stewpots
37 While away some time
38 Spool
39 Do sums
42 Tennis term
44 Double agent
45 Ship-shaped clock
46 Noggin
48 Nasal tones
49 Twig
50 Place to ski
51 Therefore
52 Some celebrators
53 Oil cartel
54 Versifier Ogden
55 His: Fr.
56 Harangue
57 Pit-stop pro
59 Big Ben sound
62 Troubadour's love song
63 "Tatler" writer
64 Numerical endings
66 Sealing gasket
67 Siepi, e.g.
69 Lament
70 Tip (one's hat)
71 Star in Perseus
72 Roman poet
73 Bear or Doc
79 Ceremonies
80 Concerning
82 African capital
83 Soon
84 Kind of dancer
85 Diseases of ramblers
86 Black cuckoo
87 Get a victory
88 Season
89 Caress
91 Environments
93 Take ____ (reduce sail)
94 Poet Jones and others
95 Chapeaux designer
96 ____-Curci
97 Narcotic
98 Lively: Mus.
99 Pine-tar products
101 Turkic people
103 Release
105 Group of football fame
106 Bottled spirit
107 A Kennedy
109 Graybeard
110 Follow
111 Date-setting phrase
112 Hindu caste
113 Fatigue
114 United
115 Initials since 1868
116 Air: Comb. form
117 Ky. neighbor

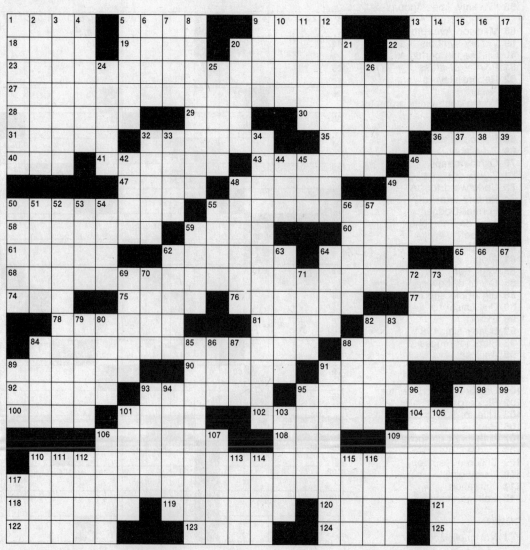

39. Completion Test by Elaine D. Schorr

ACROSS

1 Ah Sin's creator
6 Dive aftermath
12 Serb or Sorb
16 Laments
18 Theologian of 16th century
20 Greek city-state
22 O. Henry made ____
24 Loos or Louise
25 Cutters
26 French heavenly beings
27 "Awake and Sing" playwright
29 Martini base
30 Africa's highest point
31 Goose genus
32 ____ the good
33 Roe source
34 That: Sp.
35 Der ____ (Adenauer)
36 Rose's swain
37 Resolute
39 Edison saw ____
41 Noted art gallery
42 Petrels' kin
43 Nantes notion
44 Singer Howard
45 Playbill listing
48 Composer Gustav
51 Have a powwow
53 Ministers to
56 Ph.D. ordeal
57 She stabs Scarpia
58 A.k.a.
60 See the point
61 Ferris wheel, e.g.
62 Dr. Faustus ____
64 Ski lift
65 ____ rule
66 Home on high
67 Frankie from Chicago
68 ____ Loa
69 English Channel city
71 Out at the elbows
73 Burned lightly
74 Most gelid
76 Twosomes
77 Have the grumps
78 Morning prayer
80 Persuades
82 Babies are sometimes ____
86 Corresponds
88 Deejays put on ____
89 Renown
90 Grain kernel
91 ____-do-well
92 Marilyn of the Met
94 Izaak Walton dropped ____
96 Republic in Africa
97 Business abbr.
98 "M*A*S*H" man
99 Scotto's forte
100 Code of law
101 Honor as divine
103 Scheherazade made ____
106 Chili con ____
107 See life
108 Transforms
109 Mt. Rushmore's state: Abbr.
110 Some astral types
111 Bells the cat

DOWN

1 Infernal
2 Protozoans
3 Sonata movement
4 Aglets
5 Annapolis grad.
6 Suit suiting
7 Snoop
8 Lad's love
9 Durable wood
10 Rat
11 Olympics group
12 Health clubs
13 Chaney
14 Benjamin Franklin was ____
15 Spoil; mar
16 Court target
17 "____ Man"
19 Typesetter's cue
21 Dennis and Duncan
23 Assault
28 Dress (up)
31 "Luck and Pluck" author
32 White poplar
33 "Yes, ____!"
35 "Brass" entourage
36 Stunt men ____
38 Schisms
40 City in N. France
41 Thrust and parry
44 Legit
46 Wouk ship
47 Budget, in Berlin
48 Fable dividend
49 Originate
50 Ty Cobb ____
51 "____ fan tutte"
52 Hydrophobia
54 Revolutionary patriot
55 Musical heirloom
57 Weedy plants
59 Advance
62 "The Way We ____"
63 Nigerian capital
64 Tibetan religious painting
66 Birdlike
68 Christopher Robin's father
70 Quaker gray
72 Antarctic cape
73 Musical form
75 Bolsheviks' foes
77 Patron of the arts
78 Lunatic
79 Plans; programs
81 Cranking devices
82 Eastern Christian
83 City once called Big Lick
84 Molly of song et al.
85 Overcharges
87 "____ walks in beauty . . ."
93 Sequestered rooms
94 Rubinstein
95 Site of knight-fights
96 Of the cheek
98 Like Milquetoast
99 Former Venezuelan mining center
100 Cornice molding
102 Acid initials
104 Take one's pick
105 Rubicund

40. Alma Mater by Yael Gani

ACROSS

1 Takes exception
7 Cotillion
11 Wagner heroine
17 City in Siberia
21 Orbit point
22 Away from the wind
23 Cry out
24 Horse or color
25 House plant with yellow-striped leaves
28 Bismarck
29 Flight formation: Abbr.
30 Acid found in yeast
31 Japanese zither
32 Take a stab at
34 Here, to Hadrian
35 Jewish matron's wig
37 Comics like Chaplin, for short
39 Old rifle pin
40 Comics character
41 Hwys.
42 Vermilion
43 V.P. under Hayes
45 TV's Grant
47 Fair share
50 Gingersnap
53 Slopes race
56 Kind of mate
57 Sandburg poem
59 Roman mother's robe
60 Fledermaus
61 Hors d'oeuvre
62 Heavenly headgear
64 Mrs. Bede's boy
65 Well-informed
67 Lout; brute
70 Landlady, in León
73 Alfonso's queen
74 Beanpole
75 Algonquian
76 Threw hard
77 Sophie Tucker
87 Mickey or Annie
88 Dovekie
89 Massey
90 Edge of a garment
93 Outer ___
94 "Wait ___ Dark"
96 Brisbane bay
98 Bouquet
100 Cold-cuts stores
102 Make invalid
104 Success
105 Eastern instrument
107 Legendary author
110 Conrad heroine
111 Group with a common culture
113 Power-failure period
114 "Touch ___ the Cat"
115 Tumbrels
116 Lost flier
118 Pfc.'s, etc.
120 Troupe's trip
121 Her, in Hannover
123 Pelagic bird
124 Dreyfus-trial site
127 Carpenter's leavings
130 Presently
131 Playing marble
132 Game fish
133 Peregrines
135 Alphabetic trio
136 Mon. follower
138 Request in Ibsen's "Ghosts"
142 King Olav's capital
143 Compliment
144 Recondite
145 Call it a day
146 Fuse
147 Depleted
148 College studies
149 A founder of Hull House

DOWN

1 Matrons
2 Era
3 Dena Dietrich, in an old TV ad
4 Cry of disgust
5 Record again
6 Set of games
7 Judge's bench
8 "___ calm . . ."
9 Not quite a ringer
10 Ayres
11 "The world ___ much with us"
12 Glaswegians
13 Whether ___
14 Journey part
15 Darling, in Dundee
16 Comes forth
17 Granada gold
18 Bonanza
19 French composer
20 Rap
26 Suffix with part
27 "Scram!"
33 Shouts
36 Agenda unit
38 Present with approval: Abbr.
39 Diamond in ___
43 Brandished
44 "Fine women ___ crazy salad": Yeats
45 Optimally
46 Examine
47 Unit of force
48 ___ tree (cornered)
49 Catch sight of
51 Roman emperor
52 Nepalese native
54 Buck heroine
55 Long-run role for Michael Learned
57 Roscoe
58 Ebullient
61 Havanas
63 Lily
66 Arabic letter
68 "I told you so!"
69 Great quantity
71 Clear
72 Esteem
76 Oriental capital
78 Placebo
79 Amphibian
80 Again
81 Try to ascertain
82 Pothole
83 Cakes' partner
84 U.S.S.R., to Muscovites
85 Consecrate
86 Seasonal roles for dads
90 Flexible tube
91 Revise
92 U.S. painter
94 Relative of H.U.D.
95 Jaworski
96 Topgallant
97 Native: Suffix
99 Punjab potentate
101 Rel. of Ma Bell
103 Sticky stuff
106 Composer Ned
108 Holiday drink
109 Check
110 Extol
112 Pip-squeaks
115 Shelter for Jerseys
117 Sweater wool
119 Pitcher Tom
120 Hindu scripture
121 Under guidance
122 Mom's bailiwick
124 Della from Detroit
125 Goofed
126 Rain icy particles
127 Episcopacy
128 ___ und Drang
129 Berlin products
132 Kind of golf shot
134 Demons
137 Turf
139 Faucet
140 Lupino
141 Airport abbr.

41. Going A-Courting by Maria G. Rice

ACROSS

1 Court term
4 Saroyan hero
8 Swedish seaport
13 Type of pump
16 Quick ___ wink
17 Russian Riviera
19 Concert hall
20 Ex-V.I.P. at Kampala
22 With 111 Across, netman's comment on his sport
26 Epoxy
27 Maturity
28 Chartered
29 Boston jetsam
31 Notions
32 Actress Cicely
34 Protection for pelf
37 What Galileo did: 1633
40 Mme. Swann, in Proust's books
44 Jimmy or Chris
45 Mauna ___
46 B.&O. stop
47 Intruded on a party
48 Timetable abbr.
49 Court sport
52 Circus props
54 ___ line (court boundary)
55 Fasteners for ascots
57 Raphael's speciality
60 Appends
61 Dead Sea monastic
62 Debussy piece
63 Gypsy women: Sp.
65 Filling for shells: Abbr.
66 June spectacular
68 Court player, for short
69 Discipline
71 Mete
72 Molokai priest
75 Drudge
76 Enzyme
78 Start of a toast
79 Court word
80 Butterfly
81 Squire's domain
83 Swindle
84 Malady
86 Gram. term
89 Hurry
90 River in Yorkshire
91 City in India
92 They go out for fur
95 Notice
96 Dissolves
99 Prufrock's creator
100 ___ the line
102 Reaction to a bad pun
105 Colleague of Wallace
107 Architect's design
111 See 22 Across
115 Egyptian king
116 Fisher or Cantor
117 Relief for Mom and Dad
118 Capek classic
119 Severinsen
120 Dry runs
121 Trumpeter Baker
122 Wapiti

DOWN

1 Refuge
2 Italian family
3 Bugle call
4 Sandy's bark
5 African region
6 ___ twist (type of serve)
7 City in Yucatán
8 Luna's disappearance
9 Together: Mus. dir.
10 Part of L.C.D.
11 "A violet by a ___ stone"
12 United
13 Gullies
14 Afghan noble
15 First space travelers
17 Shape of a funnel
18 Ski resort
21 Buntline
23 Baptism, e.g.
24 Irish poet
25 Former TV heroine et al.
30 Hollywood Dahl
33 Most miffed
34 Freshet
35 Salient angle
36 Queens court site
38 Millennia
39 Shade of pink or blue
41 Much-traveled mug
42 Leans
43 Kin of Ph.D.'s
47 Jeanne of films
49 Colors slightly
50 Moslem prayer leader
51 Asiatic deer
53 Fort Knox item
56 Kind of code
58 ___ Robbia
59 Threatening words
60 "What's in ___?"
62 Fleecy
64 Without ___ in the world
66 Rebecca and Mae
67 Female rabbits
69 Sooty; black: Brit.
70 Raise a nap
72 Abhor
73 Largest of the Kurile Islands
74 Composition for nine
75 Disable
77 Part of Q.E.D.
78 Long-run musical
80 Placid
82 It will out
85 Wandering
87 Sheath and shift
88 Bravery
93 Loblollies
94 Like Frost's works
95 Toiler of 1066
97 Swap
98 Transmits
101 Lavender or lilac
102 Famed literary monogram
103 Was contrite
104 Preminger
106 Mine entrance
108 Northern point of Isle of Man
109 Court error
110 Cypriot's neighbor
112 Convened
113 Hwy.
114 Court divider

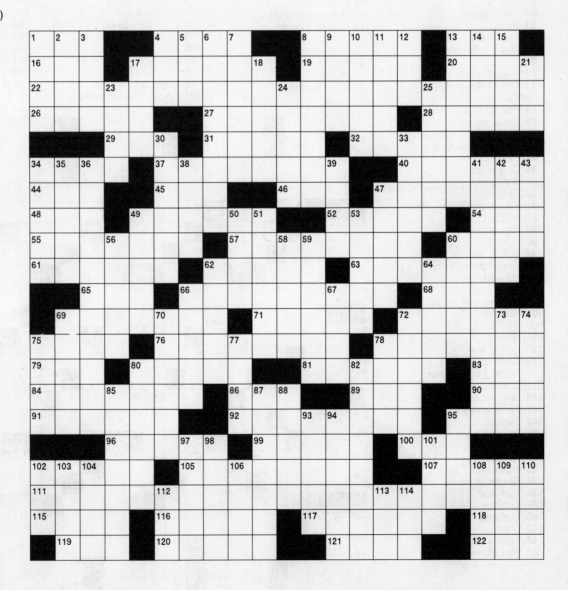

42. Not So Symbol as π by Maura B. Jacobson

ACROSS

1 Doilies
5 Coffee grind
9 River arm: Abbr.
13 Info org.
16 Partly open
20 Chem. suffix
21 Prynne's stigma
22 Moslem pilgrim
23 M.D.'s aides
24 Tijuana treat
25 ✔ ✔
28 Magnetizes
30 ___ 0 ___ B.A., LL.D.
32 West or Largo
33 Solon
34 Ragout
35 Pernicious
37 Avuncular name
40 Honey drink
42 Cuff
44 After taxes
45 Soprano Anna
49 Nursery need
51 June 6, 1944
53 Rhone city
55 Voracious
57 In a muddle
59 Fan's shout
61 Assn.
63 Far: Prefix
64 Naval monogram
65 ½ | | ½
71 Dipper milieu
72 Distaff Kennedy
73 Play the siren
74 Peking idol
75 Legal wrong
77 Reject
80 Ready for picking
82 Depot: Abbr.
84 Doff headgear
87 Rutledge
88 @ 3
92 Four times a day: Abbr.
93 Suitor
95 Part of a bray
96 Lay in
97 S.R.O. shows
99 Soviet press agcy.
101 Hill dweller
103 Holly plant
105 Minneapolis suburb
106 Nobelist Niels
108 RAC EHT TUP
114 Yalie
115 Coil of hair
116 Band instrument
117 "Gold Bug" author
118 Gourmand
119 Ship ropes
122 Salamander
125 Siestas
128 Shea nine
129 Incensement
130 Roof piece
132 Index item
134 Recorder input
136 Turncoat
137 Conceal
140 Thailand
142 Coty
144 Tennis term
147 BILLBOARD

153 "The ___ on the burning . . ."
155 2nd 2nd ♭
156 Millay
157 Vane reading
158 Put to flight
159 Swiss painter
160 "This one ___ me"
161 Wording
162 Homily: Abbr.
163 Town near Padua
164 Red quartz
165 Space org.

DOWN

1 Lion's share
2 Over again
3 Type, in Taxco
4 Gobs
5 Hauled along
6 Kind of tire
7 ___ fixe
8 Tempos
9 "For Whom ___ Tolls"
10 Indy site
11 Between H and M
12 Nickel beast
13 Less lucid
14 Not bequeathed
15 Houston player
16 One ___ time
17 Tool in a trunk
18 French deed
19 Ablush
26 Paper quantity

27 White House monograms
29 "Desert Fox"
31 Came in first
36 Long time
37 Wound mark
38 Comic Johnson
39 America and Liberty O
41 Pub missile
43 Luxurious
46 After 3d 25¢
47 Ado
48 Bones
50 Fighting fish
52 Sailboat
54 Linguist Chomsky
56 Jerkin
58 Building stones
60 Hour: Fr.
62 Cymbals' sound
66 Karate award
67 Biblical port
68 Hurons' kin
69 Of family favoritism
70 Poll's yield
71 Keats subject
76 Survive
77 Crow's kin
78 Mythical princess
79 Flour source
81 ___ Gay (A-bomb plane)
83 "Doe, ___ . . ."
85 River isle
86 Grid scores
89 Landlord's take
90 Saphead
91 Ye ___ tea shoppe

94 Nubbin
98 Wee, small hour
100 Boot adjunct
102 Holier ___ thou
104 Noun suffix, in Britain
106 Lugosi
107 Buck heroine
109 Endured
110 Corporation V.I.P.
111 Orderly
112 Bristle
113 Formerly
115 Least ornate
120 Oui
121 Poet Stephen
123 Complete flop
124 Adriatic port
126 Consort
127 Expedited
131 Meiji statesman
133 Miami's county
135 Remnants
138 Plant shoots
139 ___ nous
141 Makes sport of
143 Impish
144 Second
145 Miner's find
146 Wildcat
148 Duos
149 Indian weight
150 Fräulein's name
151 Greek temple
152 Sicilian sizzler
154 After Fri.

43. Words, Inc. by Joseph J. La Fauci

ACROSS

1 Must
6 June heroes
10 Urban eyesore
14 Wing length
18 Player under a dome
19 Proclaim
21 Reproductive body
22 Secret business associate
24 Tanqueray's second wife
25 Small shark
26 Bears
27 Rabbit's incentive
28 Spire ornament
29 Neural network
30 Caustic agents
31 Out of ___
32 Cheer for Scotto
34 Famed couturier
35 !, to a printer
38 Tra followers
39 Loser to Louis: 1946
40 Uncovered
41 Domesday Book money
42 Pointed a weapon
45 Reverberated
46 Miscubobble
47 Use shears
48 Bird in a Gallico title
50 Inelegant
51 Salad days
52 One: Ger.
53 One of Esau's wives
54 Like some investments
55 Grand or petty group
56 Rake it in
62 At all
63 Jefferson was one
64 Mortgage
65 Avant-gardist
66 "Fistivity" finales
68 Any large corporation
69 "Fidelio" hero
71 Dresden's river
72 Parson's home
73 Device on a document
74 Literary Lorna
75 Symbol on Sydney's coins
76 Push-button man
77 Dollar-a-___ man
78 Former French coin
79 Adjudicated
81 Cogwheel
82 Went on the road
85 More chilling
86 Vulgarian
87 Padlock
88 Holiday quaff
90 Dovetail wedges
92 Less than molecular
94 "All there"
95 Coeur d'___, Idaho
96 "Fiddler . . ." song
98 Stairway member
99 Court lists
100 Rugged ridge
101 Soviet wire service
102 Not worth ___ cent
103 No dele
104 TV tryout

DOWN

1 Expedition
2 Slanting
3 Become involved
4 Place where money doesn't grow
5 Alley, of comics
6 Signify
7 Viewpoint
8 Con man's mark
9 Like an angry dog
10 Role for Grandma
11 Scenes of many strikes
12 Salt Lake City team
13 Matelot's milieu
14 Laconian capital
15 Invests heavily
16 Guthrie
17 Uncluttered
20 Irving's pen name
21 Was frugal
23 Brain passages
27 K.P. utensil
29 Half of the Mets' schedule
31 Pebble; stone
33 Ball of thread
34 "Finito!"
35 Sea urchin
36 Innisfail
37 Chats, mod style
39 Profited
40 Obliged
42 Ancient gold alloy
43 Dolphin genus
44 Marx Brothers film classic
45 Horse color
46 Shock
47 Medieval toiler
49 Incense
50 Gold or Barbary
51 Expelled
54 Gleam
55 Pooh-pooh
57 Cry at Greek orgies
58 Beer ingredient
59 One of the strings
60 Connery
61 Resiliency
66 Stronghold
67 Mme. Gluck
68 Magda or Eva
69 Apprehension
70 Off-key
72 Manners
73 Petrels, shearwaters, etc.
76 Carl or Rob
77 Retainers
78 Sans ___ (carefree)
80 Quick breads
81 Incandesced
82 Dryness or desire
83 Champlevé
84 Renaissance architect ___ d'Agnolo
86 Rural crossing
87 Rubberneck
89 Sartre subject
90 Pielet
91 Kazan
92 Off
93 Headquarters
94 Eastern title
96 City in Peru
97 Kepi

44. Colorful People by Barbara Gillis

ACROSS

1 Jazz singing
5 Substance
9 City in Florida
14 Disturb
21 Soft drink
22 Norse Fate
23 Migrant workers
24 North Star
25 Exam
26 Jolly one
28 Pullovers
29 Winter wear
31 Nautical term
32 Supplemented, with "out"
34 Slave
35 Tree
36 "Good man"
40 Raids
42 Particle
43 Destroyer
44 Egyptian goddess
46 Convinced
49 Haul
51 Secures
53 Greek island
56 Mature
58 Chatters
60 Maine tree
61 Opposed
63 Classes
65 Like some bills
67 American writer
69 Middling
70 Starry
71 Legendary home of Hercules
72 Row
73 Jug
74 Wedding words
76 Carnival man
77 Precipice
79 Mountian ridge
80 Simon subject
86 Mulcts
87 Belongs
88 Chilean President: 1942–46
89 Pronoun for Pompey
90 Hide-out
91 Legal deg.
92 Sound system
94 Debris
99 Porch part
100 Heaps
102 Carved emblems
103 Cream puff
104 Conjugal
106 Mountain lake
108 Season
110 Indian language
111 That, in Taxco
112 Assistant
114 Artist Bonheur
116 Inert gas
117 Gumbo
118 Bequest
122 Berserk, in Burma
124 Badger
128 Man from Minsk
131 Quick to learn
134 Landed
135 "___ soit . . ."
137 Religious leader
138 Homophone for a Roman

140 Scored
142 Oldsters
146 Brazilian Indian
147 Wrinkled
148 Asian capital
149 English historian
150 Invites
151 European mints
152 Medicinal herb
153 North Sea feeder
154 TV show

DOWN

1 Range
2 Atoll builder
3 Tocsin
4 Lecture
5 Kind of photo
6 Stray
7 "The homage of ___": Byron
8 A Wambaugh cop
9 Dressed like Cicero
10 Hand on hip
11 Farrow
12 Female swan
13 In ___ (worried)
14 Church section
15 Fleming villain
16 River in China
17 Candle
18 Swiss resort
19 Metallic
20 Snaky shapes
27 Frau's refusal
30 Personate
33 Heal
37 Port opposite Taiwan
38 Bridge calls
39 Algerian city
41 Peak in Thessaly
42 Contemporary of Freud
45 Osprey
46 Heroic tale
47 Verses
48 Theater name
50 Firm
52 Earl Grey, e.g.
53 Informed one
54 Caucasians
55 Bootery
57 Features
59 Binges
60 Puccini lieutenant
62 French Alps area
64 Actor Ray
66 Town in Mass.
68 Fall guy
75 Racy
77 Tasks
78 Levin novel
79 Guarantee
80 Climbing plants
81 "Peer Gynt" enchantress
82 Caravansary
83 Pinball-machine sign
84 Parliament

85 Fiend
86 Sweetheart
91 Prodigal son
92 Wall or Fleet
93 European capital
95 Trice
96 Poison
97 Italian resort
98 Innisfail
101 Piggery
105 N.M. art center
107 Gudrun's king
109 Chinese hero, for short
113 Sheer fabric
115 Collector
119 Monster slain by Hercules
120 Saracen's milieu
121 Kind of root
123 United
124 Originate
125 Winglike
126 Peeves
127 Overburdened Titan
129 Anticyclones
130 Paddock papas
131 City near L.A.
132 Freshens (up)
133 Junk
136 Track figures
139 Moslem leader
141 Equal: Prefix
143 Arctic explorer
144 Raggedy doll
145 J.F.K. predecessor

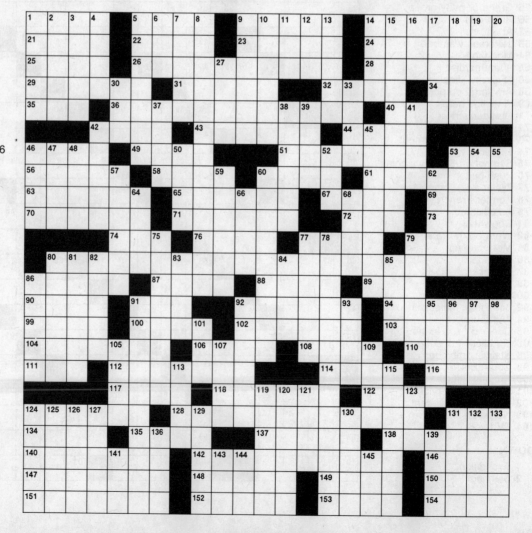

45. Transmission by Jay Scott

ACROSS

1 Galileo's town
5 Fill up again
14 Middle: Comb. form
20 Effluvium
21 Guarantee against loss, old style
22 Assertive one
23 Counteractive process
25 City in Suisse
26 October attraction
27 Made of wood
29 In the: It.
30 "Reduce Speed"
31 G.B.S.
35 Unearth
36 ___ vez (again, in Spain)
37 Middle East garment
40 In code
42 A ___ the ointment
43 Go by plane
44 Makes effervescent
45 Word with bare or flat
46 More succinct
47 Contort
48 Far from fragile
49 Morns
50 C.I.A.'s forerunner
51 Kind of charges
54 Carroll grinner
55 Jockey Angel
60 Ex-Yankee pitcher
61 U.S. cartoonist
62 ___ pro nobis
63 Begin intense activity
65 Pennyweight: Abbr.
66 Hr. component
67 Must
68 Signoret and de Beauvoir
69 That girl
70 D's and F's
72 Hitherto
73 Former chess champion
74 Incursion
75 Land tenure
78 Do road work
81 Reporting coups
83 Plant named for a governor of Santo Domingo
84 Makes one's day
85 Whittles
86 More ingenious
87 Producer-director Stanley and family
88 "___ Three Lives"
89 Vientiane's land
90 June celebrities
91 Disencumber
92 ___ de guerre
93 Miles from Ingatestone
94 Tristan's beloved
98 X-rated
100 Gridiron razzle-dazzle plays
107 Medicinal drink
108 Wipe out
109 Pack down
110 Bird dog
111 One of the media
112 In the twinkling ___ eye

DOWN

1 French Lily
2 ___ fixe
3 Off-key
4 Picasso y Goya
5 Logical newsman?
6 Made bigger: Abbr.
7 Greek letter
8 Light, in Cuba
9 Pitcher's stat
10 One of the Turners
11 Hole ___ (golf thrill)
12 Not in harm's way
13 Units of inductance
14 Behind bars
15 Deadlocked
16 Reverse of: Prefix
17 Maine
18 Wool-gatherer's vision
19 Limerick's locale
24 Spin a yarn
28 Peroration
31 Old word for headland
32 Yesterday, in Paris
33 Deductive
34 Famous dialogue line
36 Science
37 Subterranean complex
38 Rosary bead
39 Primary
41 Old English letters
42 Quarters
45 Animal food
48 Easy shot for Dr. J
51 Silver salmon
52 Ivy League city
53 Like some fences
55 Notes
56 Maureen and Scarlett
57 Having long odds
58 Ones on trial: Abbr.
59 W.W. II area
60 Czech actor Herbert
64 Oberon's spouse
71 Lowed
72 Berra or Bear
75 Vacation spot
76 Donated, in Scotland
77 Dumbo's large features
78 Oklahoma-Texas border
79 Kay Thompson's heroine: 1956
80 Wait on hand and foot
81 Small pianos
82 Dieter's unit
83 Expand
86 Tavern section
89 Worker in a football factory
93 Trig function
95 "Wild blue yonder" gp.
96 Motto, in Madrid
97 Recipe amt.
99 Work on doilies
101 Detroit labor initials
102 Groups of directors: Abbr.
103 Durocher's nickname
104 U.S. agcy., 1948–51
105 What fall guys take
106 Paris, when it sizzles

46. Father's Day by Tap Osborn

ACROSS

1 Most candid
8 Maine college
13 Sword
18 Groggery
21 Opera piece
22 Raggedy-edged
23 "Like ___ from the blue"
24 Dutch town
25 Monday: 6 A.M.
28 Moroccan mountain region
29 Aunt, in Cádiz
30 Ceremony
31 Where Tralee is
32 Large bird
33 Italian poet
36 Monday: 8:35 A.M.
42 Stout
43 Chart motif
45 Nervy one
46 Of human groups
47 Japanese ship
49 Creaky
51 Needle point
54 Brewing vat
55 Monday: 9 A.M. to 5 P.M.
64 Chanson subject
65 Inventor Pliny ___
66 Young ones
67 "Punch" character
69 Nabokov novel
71 Shoes
73 Lovely valley
75 Lucid
76 Monday: 6 P.M.
81 Kingdom
83 Mfgr.'s group
84 Cries of surprise
85 U.N. arm
86 Isle of Pines
88 Deception
89 Suffix with serpent
90 Ref's counterpart
91 "...let ___ put asunder"
94 Monday: 6:25 P.M.
98 Headcheese
100 Crane or heron
102 Hoosier poet
103 Sellout sign
104 Dixie dish
105 Ryan's daughter
107 Pours
109 Poetic feet
113 Monday: 8 P.M.
118 "Winterset" hero
119 Sea bird
120 Rita's bailiwick
121 Influence
122 "Indy" arena
127 Rope hemp
131 School org.
133 Signed up: Abbr.
134 Monday: 11 P.M.
138 Savage
140 Timetable abbr.
141 Antelopes
142 Solecist's word
143 Brother
144 Pacific porgy
145 Tuesday: 6 A.M.
153 Midi season
154 C. Robin's father
155 Juniper
156 Swiss city

157 Berg's "___ Wein"
158 Miner's nails
159 Nobelist in 1946
160 Fermented

DOWN

1 Lummox
2 Favorable
3 Healing goddess
4 Salamanders
5 African
6 Colonnade
7 Cap
8 Losing
9 Singer Franklin
10 "...right ___ arms"
11 Ethnic suffix
12 Salt, in Paris
13 Glossy fabric
14 Ends abruptly
15 Jacket or dance
16 Wing
17 Wall St. abbr.
18 Stripped of
19 ___ dozen (cheap)
20 Roll up again
26 La-la's leader
27 Pasture
33 Florida city
34 Frighten
35 Comic like Chaplin
36 Skirmish
37 Kind of vision

38 Mather product
39 "Hamlet" conclusion
40 Polynesian island
41 Medicinal plants
44 Atomic particle
48 Normal
50 Rough copy
52 Water bird
53 Journalize
56 Decree
57 Busy airport
58 Singer Roberta
59 Start
60 Geodesic ___
61 ___ as a ghost
62 Astronomy Muse
63 Verdi opera
68 Red Sea republic
70 "...on ___ boat to China"
72 Sea tracker
74 Inventor Howe
76 Heavy knock
77 "... ___ the brave"
78 Ramón's country
79 Love apple
80 Khrushchev
82 Like Homer's verses
87 Sniggled
92 Garden evictee
93 Clean: Fr.
95 ___ off (angry)
96 Scandinavian giant
97 Bellows

99 Named
101 German steel center
106 Altar part
108 Uses shears
110 Lawn tool
111 Safari boss
112 Pastoral poem
114 Rover's relative
115 Theater-seat location
116 Golda
117 Obtained
122 Scheduled
123 Lafitte, e.g.
124 More spooky
125 "Mame" name
126 ___ yang
128 Old Norse bards
129 Loos et al.
130 Poe heroine
132 Second largest of seven
135 Some Renoirs
136 Heroism award
137 Narrative: Abbr.
139 Roof edges
143 Chimney channel
145 Logos: Abbr.
146 Irving hero
147 Bonn pronoun
148 Shelter
149 A famous Nellie
150 N.Y. subway
151 United
152 Rorem

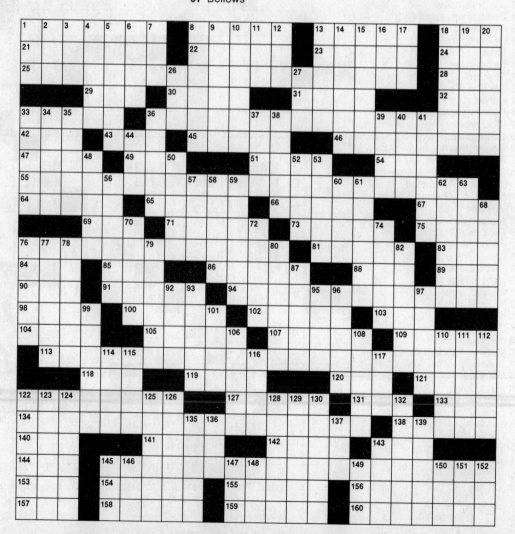

47. Spoonerizing by Sam Lake

ACROSS

1 Level
5 Sailors' patron saint
9 Shh!
13 Don Juan's delight
17 Hindu caste
18 Family member
20 She wrote "Them"
22 Cloy; glut
23 Aftershave powder
24 Artist's complaint re a drama
26 Shipshape
27 Hebrew song
29 Cancels
30 _____ Park, N.Y.C.
32 Tennyson's "_____ Arden"
34 Limiting conditions
36 Entangling
37 Husky bred in the U.S.S.R.
40 Command in a Western
42 Comprehensive
45 Library treasures
46 Script direction
48 Monroe's "_____ Good Feeling"
50 Autry birthplace, in Texas
51 Paul's friend
53 Paganini's hometown
55 Aligns
57 Tackle
58 _____ Yisrael (Palestine)
60 "Like Niobe, all _____"
62 _____ City, Calif.
64 Marshall Plan initials
65 Shadrach's friend
67 Newsy digest
69 Stratas of the Met
71 Medicinal plant
72 "Peace _____ time": Chamberlain
73 Mottled
74 Yalie's rival
76 Strategic Pacific island
77 Late Greek tycoon
81 Hamlet's cry
82 Author of "State Fair"
84 _____ Tuva, U.S.S.R. region
86 Seven, in Sicily
87 Ditto
89 Pea and bean
91 Trotsky and Jaworski
93 Café au _____
94 Wild; savage
96 German child's hero
98 Changed the décor
100 Mauna _____
101 Whirled; purled
103 Slander
105 Counterirritant
107 Within: Prefix
109 Goya's "Maja" et al.
111 Bobby-soxer's "Of course!"
112 Continual
115 Freshen
117 Puget Sound port
120 Broadway group
121 He can't spell chickadee
124 Burden
125 City in Utah
126 Tropical climber
127 Garb for Calpurnia
128 Abominable Snowman
129 Sense; think

130 "_____ for All Seasons"
131 What Simon does
132 Concordes

DOWN

1 Small one: Suffix
2 Patty ingredient
3 Girl makes pies, not yummy to the tummy
4 _____ Creed: A.D. 325
5 Attractive
6 Roman 52
7 Recuperate
8 Nonet minus one
9 Playwright's cayuse emporium
10 Assembly-line group: Abbr.
11 For men only
12 Legatees
13 Starfish or minor planet
14 Do actors do this?
15 Of the ear
16 "Apostle of the Franks"
19 Angler for congers
21 Gang's language
25 Cattail of India
28 Knowledge
31 Brewer's purchase
33 Read Walton without interest
35 Alarming trimmer in a wagon
37 Western capital
38 Toughen
39 Hawaiian bird
41 One of 24
43 Plaza
44 Northlander
47 Leo's April ailment
49 Soles beatin' out a jazzman's rhythm
52 Allen or Frome
54 Fight site
56 Coil of yarn
59 Epsom _____
61 Carson was one
63 Precincts
66 Blazers
68 Synonym for 15 Down
70 Car that "bombed"
74 Like cryptograms
75 _____ band (cattle on parade, proverbially)
78 Old whetstones twisted by icy pellets

79 Compound suffix
80 Attack
81 "_____ with Lather," musical soap opera
83 Void's partner
85 Carol or Coward
88 What a sane male turns at sea
90 Station wagon
92 Frank, Nancy et al.
95 Native of Riga
97 Cicero's "I sit"
99 Philippine tree
102 Talk like a Georgian
104 Periods of fasting
106 Hatfields' foes
108 Idiocy
110 Religious groups
112 Dogie
113 Small shoe size
114 Colliery vehicle
116 Command to Dobbin
118 Jeff's partner
119 Without any changes
122 Key to heredity
123 Culbertson

48. Sign Language by Anne Fox

ACROSS

1 Lake in Cooper's books
7 Jardin publique
11 Symbol of satiety
15 Of the wrist
21 Private eye
22 Third man
23 Acidity
24 Actor from Ireland
25 Md. Signer
27 N.C. Signer
29 Hurt
30 Trifle
31 Author Shaw
33 Sine qua ____
34 Roof piece
35 Likely
37 Steve or Miss Jean
40 Religious group
42 Memorable mime
44 Rival of Amneris
46 African tree
48 Va. Signer (with Jr.)
50 N.Y. Signer
54 Gen. Bradley
56 Malt drink
57 Fortify
58 "____ Bulba"
59 Conn. Signer
65 Siberian monk
67 Revolutionary spy
68 ____ Minor
69 Cry of surprise
70 Desserts
71 Narrow cuts
72 Wildebeest
73 Shopper stoppers
75 Picador's weapon
77 Winnie
78 Subtle sarcasm
80 Kennedy matriarch
81 Southern Signer
86 Equal: Fr.
87 "Fables in ____"
88 Thirst: Fr.
89 Checks
90 Ear parts
92 Ocellus
93 Type of tea
94 Sign
95 Explorer Johnson
96 Chester ____ Arthur
98 U.S. missile
99 Viscous liquids
103 R.I. Signer
106 Underlying
107 Meadow sound
108 Halsey's title: Abbr.
109 Light brown
110 Pa. Signer
112 N.H. Signer
117 French resort
119 Row of oars
120 Core
121 Sybarite's delight
123 "He that spareth his rod
    ____ his son"
125 Twitching
126 "Memories of ____": Poe
127 Sigma follower
128 One of seven arts
130 Initials for a monarch
132 French pronoun
135 Poem about a Del. Signer

139 S.C. Signer (with Junr.)
143 Smoothing device
144 Knievel
145 General at Bull Run
146 Ethically neutral
147 Placid
148 Rustic road
149 Saisons
150 In a humble way

DOWN

1 Greek peak
2 Siamese
3 Mass. Signer
4 Big bird
5 U.S. verse writer
6 European capital
7 Cry of disgust
8 Arab garment
9 Lives
10 Churchman
11 Moslem pilgrim
12 Sacred pictures
13 ____ Alamos
14 Excavation
15 ____ and Schine
16 Muscular; agile: Abbr.
17 Caviar
18 Great nations
19 Syrian city
20 Wound
26 Young fox
28 Kitchenware
32 Signers' words

36 Wok's cousin
38 Mountain ash
39 Sashes
41 To be, in Brest
42 Achilles' homeland
43 Guinness
44 Distant
45 Soprano Petina
47 Arab chieftains
49 Ancient temple
51 Building material
52 Triangular sails
53 Sister of Ares
55 Rosary bead
59 Gibson feature
60 ____-the-mill
61 Squeezed a wet rag
62 Study of birds' eggs
63 Dissertation
64 Where Bobby Shaftoe went
66 Towing hook
67 Lengthwise
71 Prickle
72 U.S. composer
74 Out-and-out
75 Bela
76 Moorish drum
78 Noun suffix
79 Polite answer
81 Unworthy of
82 Flash of light
83 "Mad Anthony"
84 Grape variety
85 Verdi opera
91 "There! I've ____ Again"

93 Arch supports
94 Van ____ (Flemish painter)
97 Aladdin's loss
98 Solicitude, for short
99 Old N.E. name
100 N.J. Signer
101 1922 play
102 Can. province
104 Comedian Bert
105 Two Va. Signers
106 Tree trunk
110 Toothed tool
111 Baseball stat
112 "____ the fire?"
113 "You Made ____ You"
114 Cannon-loading implement
115 Play-gun ammo
116 Victory emblem
118 ____ d'hôtel
122 German port
124 L.B.J.'s V.P.
125 Garden herb
127 Phoenician port
129 Ubangi feeder
131 Twenty quires
133 Russian range
134 Without purpose
136 Compass point
137 Poetic time
138 Shrubby plant
140 "____ nation . . ."
141 Plea at sea
142 Trouble

49. Nouns in Opposition by Jordan S. Lasher

ACROSS

1 Florentine painter
6 Arithmetic abbr.
9 Shade tree
12 Shopping center
16 Of Catawba, Tokay, etc.
17 Lot measure
19 U.S. cartoonist
20 Out of port
21 Theme of many a sea story
24 Schism
25 Footnote notation
26 Biblical confrontation
28 Burglar's boodle
29 "Exodus" name
31 ___ heart out (envy)
32 Perry's creator
33 Seine
34 Thomas or Horace
36 Saguaros
40 Bare essentials
42 Wynn and Begley
43 Not welcome
46 Ullmann
48 The Game
52 The whole hog
53 German pronoun
54 Clean the board
55 Tropical climber
56 Dryad's home
57 Aromatic
59 Pluck
61 Sacred song
63 "Christ Stopped at ___"
64 Sheridan comedy: 1775
68 "___ for Adonais": Shelley
70 Apple cheeked
72 Ordered
73 Don Juan and Casanova
75 Smokes, for short
76 ___ to the teeth
79 Hite of "The Hite Report"
80 Scrutinize
81 Holbrook
82 Egghead-muscleman show-down
85 Last year's jrs.
86 Speedy beauty of myth
88 Suffix with Israel or Brook-lyn
89 Lumber cutter
91 Work on the lawn
92 "If ___ My Way"
94 ___ Aviv
95 Guru
98 With alacrity
102 ___-King, of German myth
103 Louver
104 Clash of 431 B.C.
110 Lawful
111 Twofold
112 Historic rights-reading case
115 Au fait
116 Chemical suffix
117 Slime
118 Halley's and Kohoutek
119 Bigfoot's cousin?
120 Pop
121 Lect.
122 Butter melter

DOWN

1 Famous debates
2 Guest
3 Sentry's place
4 Situate
5 Sort of: Suffix
6 Mother of the Titans
7 255, to Cicero
8 Eins, zwei, ___
9 German Surrealist
10 Release
11 Gardner's lawyer
12 Actresses Berenson and Pavan
13 Japan, Iran, etc.
14 Took off
15 Wood strip
16 Steam, e.g.
18 German port
21 Jetty
22 Work on MSS.
23 Author Hunter
27 Corneille drama
29 To go: It.
30 Change one's outlook
34 G.P.'s, e.g.
35 Rowan
37 Title fight of March 7, 1951
38 Range finder
39 Fainéant
41 Ocular protection
42 First mate
43 Grape
44 Bert Bobbsey's twin
45 Tie up
46 Angler's choice
47 Candidate for A.A.
49 Baltic native
50 Unextinguished
51 Donizetti opera
56 River in N. India
58 Auto pioneer
59 They reune
60 Relieve (of)
62 Temptation for Odysseus
65 Holden of fiction
66 Cowardly Lion's portrayer
67 Calumniator
69 Sounds seeking silence
71 Fish story
74 Big Brother's creator
75 Burn
77 Snitch
78 Rosemary's portrayer
79 Mariner's dir.
82 Austrian spa
83 Itinerary word
84 Criterion: Abbr.
87 Legendary Rhine menace
90 Ordinances
92 Fräulein's name
93 Sleep: Comb. form
94 Bohea and bancha
96 Acquires
97 Singer James
99 ___ as a wet hen
100 White Sea gulf
101 "Look not though upon the wine when it ___": Prov-erbs
104 "An apple ___ . . ."
105 Snorkel
106 Discontinue
107 Commotions
108 Demolish
109 Old name for Kalinin
110 Where Pizarro died
113 Play a part
114 Marsupial, for short

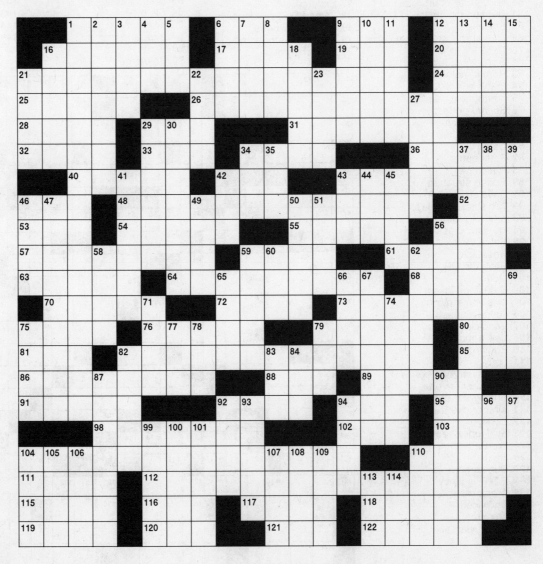

50. It's Elemental! by Alex F. Black

ACROSS

1 Tropical tree
7 Width of a ship
11 Capital of Oregon
16 Hick
20 Stubborn
21 He, to Caesar
22 Strainer
23 Jar
24 Shakespearean nugget
28 Three-way joint
29 Type of relief
30 Zeta follower
31 M.S. prerequisite
32 A king of Israel
33 Vessel for Omar
34 World's best people
40 Sectors
43 Go-ahead signal
44 Corn spike
45 Antediluvian
46 Half a bray
47 Evening star
49 Tracy's wife
52 Prepares tea
54 Tops
55 "____ ever so humble . . ."
57 Convinced
59 Wallach
60 Brought to court
61 German diplomat
65 Engines
68 Littoral region
70 Case for trivia
71 Geraint's wife
73 Roman naturalist
74 Frank and Sexton
75 Flattop, e.g.
76 Served perfectly
78 Genesis name
79 Electrical unit
81 Carry
82 Petty bettor
85 Receptive
89 Rodeo structure
91 Shoe size
92 "This is ____ Life"
93 Kind of moth
94 Homeric classic
96 Strike
98 Rose lover
100 Sack the QB
101 Lieder
102 Oldest, as jokes
104 Like some nylons
106 Judge's bench
107 Vandalize
108 Use a muddler
110 Portico
111 Lofty
112 Like evergreen cones
115 "Beowulf" is one
117 Chinaglia's sport
121 Kind of dye
122 Lacking color
123 St.-Tropez season
124 Far East name
126 Hector
127 Dumas hero
133 F.D.R. agency
134 Arena receipts
135 Undivided
136 Tax pro
137 Andalusian aunt
139 Ring decision
140 Mary's flowers
146 Groucho look
147 Point toward
148 Amerind
149 Sun Myung Moon, e.g.
150 Without purpose
151 Crowd
152 Durocs
153 Like the Milky Way

DOWN

1 Wine cup
2 Refinement in manners, taste, etc.
3 States without proof
4 Quote
5 Kabibble
6 Pequod skipper
7 V.I.P.
8 Extension
9 Strange
10 Memorable hostess
11 Wind dir.
12 Okefenokee vehicle
13 With more restraint
14 Oust
15 Enero or febrero
16 Lodged at a dorm
17 Extreme
18 Famed D.C. residence
19 ____ de Cologne
25 Wodehouse goodbye
26 U.S.A.F. group
27 Seasonal airs
33 Jakarta native: Abbr.
35 Squeezes out
36 Article, in Amiens
37 Pueblo Indian
38 Beliefs
39 Take advice
41 A shoo-in
42 "____ pin, pick it up"
48 In season
50 Grassy patch
51 Fluff
53 City lines
54 Broadway Rx for murder
56 Lessee
58 Assigns
61 Endow
62 Roman emperor
63 Night, in Nantes
64 Spot for a bust
66 Hindu deity
67 Marius, to Sulla
68 Vikki from Texas
69 Out ____ limb
72 "In ____ Speramus"
77 Kyd work
79 Bungles
80 Hawks' nests
82 River pollution problem
83 Brad or spad
84 Stole
86 Like Simon
87 Biblical patriarch
88 Rests
90 Beldam
94 Major prophet
95 Like storks and stilts
96 Main or Elm
97 Town near Padua
99 Diner sign
102 Vistula feeder
103 O'Neill
105 Debatable
106 Bombay bard
107 Dress style
109 Fissure
112 Switchboard
113 Statues by Phidias et al.
114 Jackie's sister
116 Moves rook and king
118 Egg layer
119 Oilfish
120 Disk for a deejay
122 Diluted
125 Migrant worker
128 Normand of silents
129 Emphatic denial
130 Agency controlling TV
131 Miocene or Pliocene
132 Large or gross
138 Questions
139 Japanese monastery
140 Clay today
141 Baby's perch
142 Skid-row affliction
143 Vessel for beer
144 Peppery
145 Hull curve

51. Counterpoint by Jay Spry

ACROSS

1 Conservatives
6 Liberals
10 ____ de Calais
13 Tin Pan Alley acronym
18 Originated
19 Groundless
20 Nimbus
21 Magna ____
22 Discord
24 Concord
26 Chemical suffix
27 Feminine endings
28 She
29 He
30 Vassal
32 Cheers
33 Roman's victim: 290 B.C.
34 Simple
35 Like some paper
37 Moves
38 W.W. II theater
40 Exploits
42 Raced
43 Jong
47 Color
48 Inveighed
50 Plumbers' cables
51 Unyielding
54 Yielding readily
57 Legal claim
58 Exercises
59 Furthers
60 Drug
61 Nets
62 Maledictions
64 Group under a col.
67 Rare violin
68 Sex
69 Function
70 Very active
74 Very inactive
76 Warns
77 T.A.E.
79 Is bested or worsted
80 Determine
81 Rock: Comb. form
82 Vulgar; cheap
83 Faulty: Prefix
85 "King Olaf" composer
86 Penitent's emotion
88 Gay deceiver
91 Wheel on a tea wagon
93 High spot
94 Low spot
98 Bambi's cousin
99 Gaucho's milieu
100 Thick
101 Wire measure
102 Flimsy
104 Far from flimsy
107 Galahad's gear
108 Notices
109 Pulitzer Prize novelist
110 Great quantity
111 Target in horseshoes
112 McMahon and Muskie
113 Not so much
114 Spanish playwright

DOWN

1 Events at Belmont
2 Perfume ingredient
3 Dead duck
4 Winner over T.E.D.
5 Pipe joint
6 Chicken ____
7 Revised
8 Ice masses
9 Bills
10 Certain cattle or canines
11 Musketeer
12 "Paradise Lost" character
13 Israeli port
14 ____ Mateo, Calif.
15 Arson is one
16 Rose essence
17 "Home, Sweet Home" author
20 Balzac's "Une Ténébreuse ____"
23 Night sights
25 Robert ____
31 Bottle for wine
33 Wraps
34 Ethics
36 Detail
37 Photographs of a sort
39 Beliefs
40 Last word
41 Over
44 D.D.E.
45 These, in Tours
46 Dunderhead
47 Cultivate
48 "The ____ Spain . . ."
49 Competent
50 Shows scorn
52 High aims
53 Banal
55 Forgive
56 Hedda Gabler's creator
61 Off-color
62 Thurible
63 Remarkable: Scot.
64 Chanticleer's realm
65 Like stickum
66 Bride of Angel Clare
67 Sandpaper
68 Segovia's instrument
69 Created a rowdydow
70 Baseball putout
71 Diminutive suffix
72 Soak
73 Informers
75 Noninformer
78 Summarizes
82 ____ powder (decamp)
84 Strikebreaker
85 Caught sight of
86 Perceives
87 Chops to pieces
88 Indian princes
89 Ward off
90 Fate
92 Divert
93 Part of Greater London
95 Spotlight color
96 Popular scent
97 Gluck's "Paride ed ____"
99 Combustible heap
100 Twofold
103 Seoul soldier
105 ____ Nidre, Hebrew prayer
106 French explorer

52. Razzle-Dazzle by Tom Mixon

ACROSS

1 Social standing
6 Heap of stones
11 Disguise
15 Accursed
21 Of a continent
22 Rich copper ore
23 Melba specialty
24 Store fodder
25 "Sleeping Murder," e.g.
28 Part of a text
29 Tilt
30 Poker stake
31 Space filler
32 Canticle
34 Vipers
35 Remnant
36 Shoe grip
37 Function
38 Lupino
40 Equestrian's order
41 Concern of some sports-
   men
46 Hindu title
48 Guide
50 Seine feeder
51 Alcott girl
52 Sample
55 Marsh bird
56 Beach
60 Prefix with sol and stat
61 French disbeliever
62 Out on ____
64 Jumble
67 Durable fiber
68 Bogus
69 Rams' mates
70 Wagnerian role
71 ". . . ____ the ocean"
73 ____-König (legendary
   goblin)
74 Gazelle
76 Sarah ____ Jewett
77 Nimbus
78 "____ a deal!"
81 Sonny's sibling
82 Bette's strings
85 Sp. wife
86 Bar bill
87 Midi seasons
88 Flightless birds
89 Cash or charm
90 Spasmodic sound
91 Affirmatives
93 Lean
94 Epochs
95 Church officer
97 Subdued
99 Leontyne plus Vincent
101 Cultivate
102 Buzzing sound
103 Bric-a-____
104 James of TV
106 Doers: Suffix
107 Davis from Ga.
108 Poet's word
109 Other
111 Spanish city
113 Red or Black
114 Movie highlights of the 30's
119 Headland
121 West or Murray
123 Operated
124 Pleats

125 Pat
128 Silkworm
130 Arena sound
132 Chooses
134 Prefix with gram and logue
135 Large book
136 Nab
138 Highlight of some musicals
142 Obliquely
143 Approach
144 Florida city
145 Spartan slave
146 Money in Madrid
147 Dame Myra
148 Tarried
149 Portents

DOWN

1 Hiding place
2 Pallid
3 Begot
4 Follow
5 Nav. officer
6 Parts of books
7 Greek islander
8 ____ the occasion
9 Shade tree
10 Culbertson et al.
11 French painter
12 ". . . ____ in thee tonight"
13 Falstaff's title
14 Numbing blow
15 Removed
16 Unit

17 Greek peak
18 Lillian's seafood platter
19 Slip away
20 Thick
26 German dollars
27 Padlocks
33 Muralist Rivera
36 Guevara
39 Nick Charles
41 Crews
42 World's most common
   names
43 Assistant
44 The end
45 "The Way We ____"
47 Proportion
48 Sun parlors
49 Highlights for some
53 Hyson, e.g.
54 Conger or moray
55 Least perilous
57 "Beware ____ of March!"
58 Spur wheels
59 Victor Hugo's wife
60 Supplementary
63 Big Apple solvency forever
65 Fragrance
66 Avifauna
71 Some are "educated"
72 French ship's course
75 Ceremony
76 Of the world's heaviest
   metal
77 Region near the Rhine
79 Italian port

80 French coronations
83 Vestige
84 A memorable Bobby
92 Weird
93 Throng
94 Goofed
96 Laymen
97 Brace
98 Cries of delight
99 Hazel or walnut
100 Annie Oakley
103 Climbing pepper
105 Infrequently
109 Slips away
110 Musical direction
112 Bandleader Brown
115 Prefaces
116 "____ My Way"
117 Parisian poser
118 Daughter of Atlas
119 Newsy digest
120 Part of a Stein line
122 Artery
125 Sherlock's creator
126 Ancient land near the
   Jordan
127 Borscht ingredients
129 Amor's wings
131 Do aquatints
133 High-hat
135 Oates book
137 Emmet
139 Garden tool
140 Half of MCCII
141 Pi follower

53. Cool It! by Frances Hansen

ACROSS

1 Bowl call
4 Something to shed
8 Goya subject
12 Wisconsinite
18 Former Italian Prime Minister
19 Coy
20 It's been split
21 Scenic Italian drive
22 With 7 Down, Biblical advice
26 Six-line stanzas
27 "'Tis ___ to be wise"
28 Backslide
29 Will administrator: Abbr.
30 Sown; strewn: Fr.
31 Mixer's frozen assets
32 With 31 Down, G. Herbert's comment
36 Jurassic division
37 Chew the fat
40 Sea calls
41 Age: Lat. abbr.
42 College mil. group
43 Utah's lily
44 Morse-code word
45 Harness part
47 ___ accompli
49 Singer Sullivan
51 A Gershwin
52 Ignited
53 Bayh
54 Late TV fare
55 Like old sweaters
58 Awry: Scot. var.
59 Drink cooler
60 Key dice throw
61 "Ignorance ___"
63 Patterns: Abbr.
66 Hawaiian drink
67 Savvies
68 Get loose from a calaboose
71 Wee antelope
74 Earthern pots
75 Former Arab org.
76 Pilot's device: Abbr.
77 Gouda
78 Marine hazard
79 Cookbook abbr.
81 Ms. Hogg
82 Supermarket lineup
83 Scott's Meg
85 Inst. at Lexington, Va.
86 Wanders
88 Wedding words
89 To be: Fr.
90 Informal invitation
94 Boo-boo
95 Kind of squash
96 Likely
97 He, she or it
100 Boadicea's tribe
101 Carried along
105 Advice on a bad wallpaper job
108 Prufrock's "Do I dare to eat ___?"
109 "Requiem for ___"
110 Blind part
111 Footless
112 Merchant guilds
113 Jeune fille

114 Nero's cover-up
115 Reply to Virginia

DOWN

1 Gay blade
2 Wiles
3 ___-kootchy
4 Levantine garment
5 Leavings
6 Herr's "Alas!"
7 See 22 Across
8 Composer Gustav
9 Granada gruels
10 Heatherton
11 Morning hrs.
12 Circus group
13 Soap plants
14 Spanish ladies
15 Icky food
16 Letters
17 Abundant
18 U.K. lawmakers
23 Fixation

24 Psyche's opposite
25 Result
30 Herrick's choice in dress
31 See 32 Across
32 Rock bottom
33 Scarlett and John
34 "___ and to Hold"
35 Gamekeeper, in Glasgow
37 Fast driver
38 Not "fer"
39 Prickly heat et al.
42 Prepares potatoes
43 Perform a cool caper
46 Keats wished to bear these
47 Coolest wear
48 "Disraeli" actor
50 Fungus spores
53 Prate
56 Ducks the issue
57 Blue jeans
62 Soupy
64 Cool horsewoman
65 Bikini time
69 Indian crops

70 Strip ___
71 Start of eighth century
72 "If ___ My Way"
73 Gambling game
80 Push ahead
84 Bangor neighbor
85 Utmost
87 Win at a game
89 Beethoven's Third
90 Prickly plant
91 Oodles
92 Fra
93 Japanese port
94 Trojan hero: Var.
97 Memphis god
98 ___ Nui (Easter Island)
99 Moon crater
100 Moroccan district
101 Male "at eve"
102 Drink too much
103 Flying saucers
104 N.Y.S.E. abbr.
106 Albee's "___ and Yam"
107 U.N. body

54. Purr, Purr by George Rose Smith

ACROSS

1 Bonito sharks
6 Making no progress
12 Clammy
16 Diamond champs: 1976
20 Dress style
21 Cologne constituent
22 Kuwaiti chief
23 Asp's weapon
24 ____ Kids
26 Ring-tailed cat
28 Suffix for usher or major
29 Runabouts
30 Take away
32 Renee of silents
33 Ruler, in Cádiz
34 Engaging one
35 Burgees
36 Bagged
37 Farm machine
38 "____ evil . . ."
39 Call ____ (stop)
40 Shopping areas
43 Rain and more rain
45 Bogey minus one
48 Guillotine
49 Casanova's list
50 Full-blown
51 Sea of the Philippines
52 Fend off
53 Whined
54 Thrombi
56 Girl of song
57 Hardy's "Pure Woman"
58 Fans' exhortation
59 Waterways: Sp.
60 Unflappable
61 Numerical suffix
62 Kitty
66 Crisp cracker
67 Mangle user
69 "____ to bury Caesar . . ."
70 Fit of anger
71 Tigerish, in a way
73 Lions
75 Haircut
78 Crests
79 Pitcher ____ Blue
80 Dowser
81 Lesion
82 Spiked the punch
83 Father
84 El Greco's homeland
86 Sierra ____
87 Sorrels
88 Singer Cantrell
89 Dear: Fr.
90 Somewhat
91 Fishing aid
92 Tabby terrifies him
95 Punitive persons
96 Fern
97 Moslem "brain trust"
98 Woody
99 Unfaltering
101 Nonplus
102 Problem for cats
103 Swift jet
106 Sailors' patron
107 Ruth's mother-in-law
108 Icy
109 Precious
110 Dramatic spot for a cat
112 "Hold that tiger"

115 Shade of green
116 Years, to Ovid
117 "Anchors ____"
118 Black Forest locale
119 Proceed
120 Keats or Yeats
121 Microscope parts
122 Stages

DOWN

1 Creator
2 Wing-shaped
3 Foyle of fiction
4 Eleven: Fr.
5 Poker term
6 Damages
7 Less slovenly
8 Jousting wear
9 Gypsies
10 Diminutive suffix
11 Indefatigable
12 Ten-sided figure
13 Pile together
14 Cats' prey
15 "Catfish" was one
16 Catskills place
17 ____ nous
18 Gave alms
19 Widgeon
23 Gore and family
25 Caught in the act
27 Direct a team

31 Indian prince
34 Tore into
35 Lionized
36 Compares prices
37 Max and Buddy
38 Except
39 Entrances
40 Let up
41 Face with riprap
42 Fictional feline
43 Slant, as news
44 Dickens hero
45 Fictional feline
46 Outlander
47 ____ la Paix
49 W.W. II souvenir
51 "Peer Gynt" ____
53 Ready to say "cheese"
54 Ort
55 Hard-hit ball
56 Flatfish
58 Kelly and Raymond
60 Fenced
62 Lashed
63 Renan's "La ____ Jésus"
64 Burst of approval
65 Ill-wisher
66 Part of a book
68 Ceremonial acts
70 Union unit
71 Reception
72 Vestige
73 Corona, e.g.

74 "If ____ King"
76 Whether ____
77 Gripes
79 Scene of the crime
81 Canary's cousin
83 Contrary
84 Chew noisily
85 Midianite king
86 Veins of ore
88 Beguile
89 Kind of warfare
90 Green sidedish: Fr.
92 Dumas character
93 Having no chance to win
94 Horner's prize
95 Winter rigs
96 Like some coats
98 State without proof
99 Sneaked
100 Grand or South
101 Rhone tributary
102 Cat, to Cato
103 Handbag material
104 High-priced
105 Forktails
106 "Great Catherine" playwright
107 Words to Nanette
108 Singer Campbell
109 Cat: Fr.
111 Séance sound
113 Part of i.o.u.
114 Network monogram

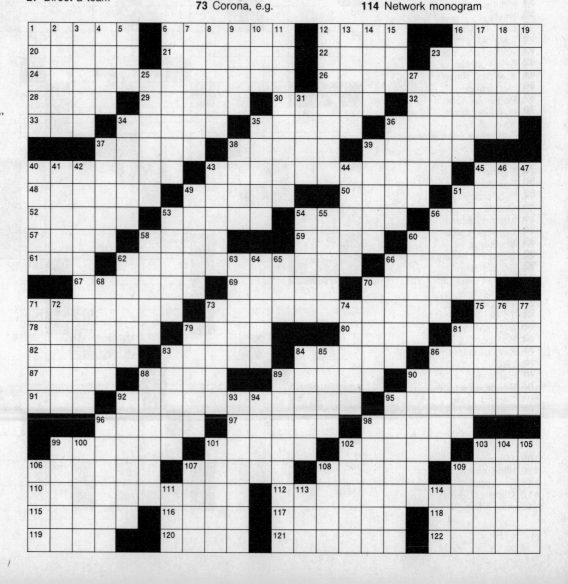

55. Getting Away From It All by Jack Luzzatto

ACROSS

1 Insertion mark
6 Frenchman's smoke or snuff
11 Irish port of call
15 Figures the bill
19 Affaire de coeur
20 Fight site
21 Alpine river
22 French cheese
23 Relative of a clip joint
25 Stowe or Vail
27 Sea-going flyer
28 Telegraphs
29 Weapons hole
30 Kind of charge
31 Muscovites
33 Guffaw
34 The boss calls it
35 "Whatever ____ right": Pope
36 Matador chaser
38 Where not to fall
41 Hot outpouring
44 Sutherland role
46 Paer wrote 43 of these
47 Feudal estate
49 Author Deighton
50 Belief that things have souls
52 Relish
54 No-no for a pitcher
56 Disgusted
58 Caballero, e.g.
60 Legal claim holder
61 Drop shots, in the ring
62 Boston airport
64 Whitewashed
66 Marius, to Sulla
67 Domestic travel slogan
70 Famous maître d'hôtel
73 "Morning's at ____": Browning
74 Absolute negative
75 Towel sign
78 Rutabaga
80 Golfer Louise
82 Far from pushy
84 Name callers, and worse
86 Unchic shoe
88 Assign to new categories
89 Defendants at law
90 Grime
92 Least abundant
94 Everglades sight
95 Bright Bear
97 Chess, for instance
99 Typesetter's cue
100 Where Toledans go sailing
102 Whoppers
103 Memphis deity
105 Pervian capital
108 Washbowl
110 Loving
111 Remove, as ink or gravy
113 Prefix with sked or skid
114 Their Acropolis is a tourist's must
116 Trip merchant
118 Simmer in summer
119 The steppes don't have one
120 Info supplied by 116 Across
121 Gimcrack gems
122 Diamond judges
123 Builds a lawn
124 Motionless
125 Areas in St. Peter's

DOWN

1 Do a party job
2 Love, in Livorno
3 Two-way journeys
4 Grand-tour cont.
5 Adjust the sails
6 ____ Mountains in S Poland
7 Its customers paint, sculpt, etc.
8 Leaves forlorn
9 Duck genus
10 ____ d'Antibes
11 Nassau attraction
12 Item on a G.I. medal
13 Verve, in Venezia
14 Pronoun
15 Descend a mountain by rope
16 Writes "Wish you were here"
17 All the gossip
18 Clockmaker Thomas
24 London district
26 First ____ (rare bks.)
29 At turbo-prop speed
32 River at Amiens
34 Grips for trips
35 Flawless
37 Badinage and persiflage
39 Christian and Mayan
40 Needle
42 Spite
43 Fit to be tied
44 Scotland Yard stoolie
45 ____ cat
46 Letters from Greece
48 Does the correct thing
51 Plum for gin
53 Kind of holiday
55 Where Canterbury is
57 Beknighted women
59 Allude
63 Mole
65 Amuse
67 Without
68 Considered
69 Plexus
70 Hokkaido port
71 Cork-oak bark
72 Tourist vessel
75 Boniface's bonhomie
76 ____-European
77 Rapid-fire gun
79 Investigation
81 Marsh bird
83 Fishing basket
85 Great Lakes canals
87 Pattern or mold
91 Having claws
93 Place above
96 Sprite and satellite
98 Washes out
99 Synagogue
101 Tourist stopover
104 Nevada blast
106 ____ Carlo
107 Kitty starters
108 Clerk, in India
109 Power source
110 Reno game
111 Fiber food
112 Haydn's nickname
115 "____ all in the game"
116 Prefix with cycle or plane
117 Cumberland ____

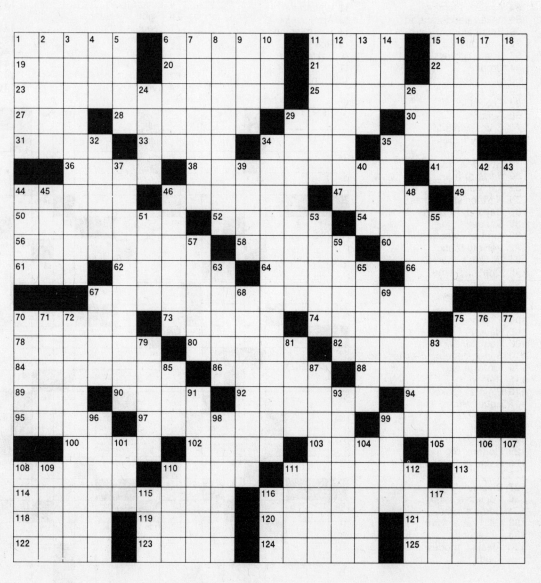

56. City Additions by Maura B. Jacobson

ACROSS

1 Smith or Bede
5 Too
9 As meek as ____
14 Llamas' kin
20 Water carrier
21 Smokey
22 Blanket
23 Mt. Etna's city
24 Guinness
25 Israeli port
26 Formosan bar ad
28 Indian fuel-company ad
31 Chemical suffix
32 Millennia
33 Herr's heir
34 "____ Pinafore"
35 Burghoff role
37 Linger
40 "____ with Love"
42 Kid
43 Viper
44 Galba's successor
45 Bristles
46 Neckpiece
48 Nubbin
50 "The Red"
54 Actress Fleming
56 Italian deodorant ad
60 Small amount
62 Vine offshoot
63 Poe's "always"
64 Urchin
65 Compass point
66 Lupino
67 Eccentric
68 Succor
70 Comedian's foil
72 Glassy mineral
75 Scott hero
79 Red Sea country
80 Parts of hrs.
82 Taj Mahal ad
85 Cartoonist Thomas
86 Beyond, to Burns
88 Dance
89 Kind of sweater
92 Velvety fabric
94 Dobbin's morsel
95 One ____ time
98 Ancient Tokyo
99 ____ Moines
102 Not well
103 Skelton
105 Newsy
108 Begin anew
110 Senegalese auto-school ad
114 Kin of togae
115 Raison d'____
116 Pig ____ poke
117 Equal: Prefix
118 Upright
120 A Smith
121 Parseghian
123 Golfers' org.
125 Calm, in Calabria
126 "____ bonnie banks . . ."
127 Bivouac
130 Adjective suffix
131 Berne's river
133 Oil: Comb. form
135 Oohs and ____
136 Alaskan modeling-school ad

143 Venezuelan biscuit-company ad
145 Boer town
146 Stewpot
147 Valentino
148 ". . . shut yourself up ____": Flaubert
149 Tittle
150 Knievel
151 Hams it up
152 James and Tommy
153 Canasta card
154 ____-Coburg

DOWN

1 Peck role
2 Pretty child
3 On a cruise
4 Arabian pasta ad
5 ____ Islands, in the Bahamas
6 Poet ____ de Lisle
7 Tampa's neighbor
8 City on the Oka
9 Represent
10 Freshwater fish
11 Of birds
12 Whimper
13 Arm: Prefix
14 Pious jargon
15 Rose oils
16 Peking idol
17 Over with
18 Tropical vine
19 Vocal one
23 Barracks bunks
27 Telephone-book item
29 Essential
30 Like some baskets
36 Frye is one
37 "The Velvet Fog"
38 A Musketeer
39 Greek neckwear ad
41 Andrea del ____
42 Glowing
43 Celestial Ram
45 ____ Arabia
46 Men's-wear monogram
47 Upon, in poesy
49 Perfect serve
51 Burmese gravure ad
52 Reflections
53 Rhythmic
55 Cato's 649
57 Charge with a crime
58 Root or Yale
59 Bohemian
61 Hong Kong's neighbor
69 Actress Diana
71 Wine: Prefix
73 "Money ____ object"
74 Luzon river
76 Sight, in Sedan
77 Woolen fabric
78 Sniggler
80 London's ____ Row
81 Peephole
83 Pampas rope
84 Irving work

87 Pirouette
90 I.e.
91 Put up
93 Neural networks
96 "____, She's Mine"
97 Point on the nose
100 Muse
101 Dutch painter
104 Rickles
106 Hyde et al.: Abbr.
107 June words
109 Japanese caviar ad
111 Harvest
112 Melonlike fruit
113 Type of muscle
119 The Red Raiders
122 Wine and dine
124 Swanson
125 Peaks
126 Snaffle
127 Tidal wave
128 Drum on
129 Roast: Sp.
130 Craving
131 Alms boxes
132 ". . . With ____ bodkin?"
134 As bright
137 Victoria and Catherine II: Abbr.
138 Large beetle
139 "Lord, ____ I?"
140 Part of T.A.E.
141 Evergreen
142 Legend
144 Torrid

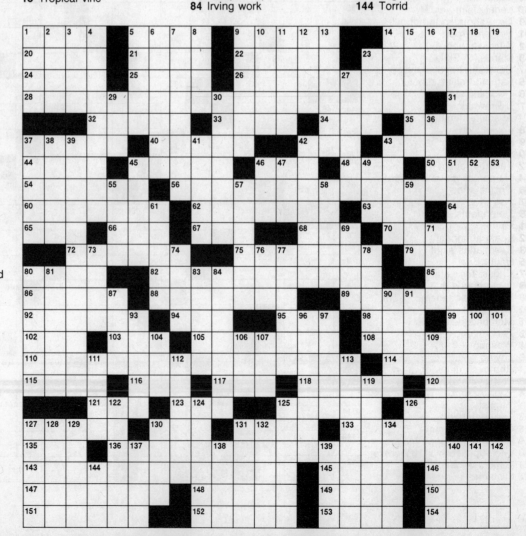

57. "Thirty Days Hath . . ." by Henry Hook

ACROSS

1 ____ canem
5 Cry of surprise
8 Cumberland river
12 Johnny of the C.S.A.
15 "The ____ Love"
16 Disciple's emotion
19 Quagmire
22 Majority of September births
24 Cabaret dance
25 Result of "hearthburn"
26 ____ room
27 What bugbears do
29 Mauna ____, Hawaiian peak
30 Like September in a 1937 song
31 Kennel cacophony
33 Grogram material
34 Caesar's road
35 Letter from Plato
36 "Have you ____ wool?"
37 Wood for 36 keys
39 Hens' pens
40 Vulgarized
44 Coil, in Calabria
45 McAuliffe's reply
46 More recondite
47 Citoles
48 Retreat
50 Trained sailors, for short
51 Slugger in Hall of Fame
52 Very hungry
54 Journalist Bernstein
57 Numismatist's prize
59 Actor Darren
61 "____ the fields we go"
62 Acapulco wealth
63 Maxwell Anderson-Kurt Weill opus
65 Four quarters
66 "____ for the million . . ."
67 Agreement between nations
68 Funnies' Ms. Kett
69 Emulated Daedalus
70 Slain, Boleyn style
72 Burger adjunct
74 Numerical prefix
76 Used a plane
77 Cud
78 Sources
81 Senectuous
82 Barbara, for one
83 Entertained, as an idea
85 Goose genus
87 Rock bottom
88 DeSoto, e.g.
89 Summer cooler
90 "Oz" cast member
91 Pop singer Mitchell
92 O.T. book
94 Trumpeter Miles
96 ____ loss
97 Expenses
98 Understood
99 Mazuma
100 Where Regina is
102 The remaining September births
106 Loud horn
107 Zippy
108 Dollars for quarters
109 L.B.J. beagle

110 "Beware!," in Brest
111 1984 et al.: Abbr.
112 Fine and liberal

DOWN

1 Kind of bridge
2 Far from torpid
3 Prolixity
4 Own: Ger.
5 Remnants
6 Chuckling sound
7 "____ out!"
8 Mountebank's forte
9 Poetic contraction
10 School subj.
11 Collage-maker's need
12 Jackstay
13 Diamond stat.
14 Phrase welcomed by Mom
17 Complete
18 Live oak
19 A+ is one
20 Romney Marsh
21 Catches on guns
23 Kid ____, of jazz fame

28 ____ Khan
31 Founder of embryology
32 Chabas painting
34 Little bits
38 Author of "The Devil's Dictionary"
39 Mathematical exercise
41 Kind of estate
42 P.D. alert
43 Fell
44 Realm of Helios
45 Convention figure
47 Irish export
48 Minuet's cousin
49 N.H. campus
51 Tampered with checks
52 Crash diets
53 Fictional girl detective
54 It's of no use to Kojak
55 Ram
56 Sept. 13, 1977
58 Made a decision
60 U.S. Open winner: 1977
63 Red-battery half
64 Highest spot in Japan
69 Driest Spanish sherry

71 Athirst
73 Comparative ending
75 Use an eraser
77 C.B. activity
78 Sunnybrook, for one
79 He peregrinates
80 Dregs
82 Laundry machine
83 Arrogant
84 Leaves off
85 Welladay!
86 Of birth
87 "Touch ____ the Cat"
88 Rodeo structure
91 Don or San
93 "Time flies," e.g.
94 Johnny's bandleader
95 Palm cockatoo
97 Bloodhound's find
99 Mil. awards
101 Halberd part
103 Actress Arthur
104 School days' trio
105 Goddess of healing

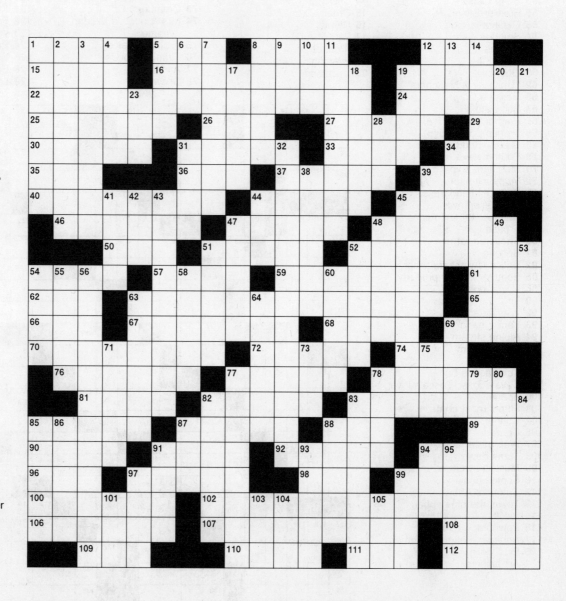

58. Sayings Account by Alfio Micci

ACROSS

1 Gorge
6 ____ da Gama
11 Moslem judge
15 Fescue or rye
20 Logrolling contest
21 Detest
22 Of the ear
23 Rajah's spouse
24 Love
27 Slow and steady
29 Tunis ruler
30 Wakened
31 French seat of learning
33 Cat variety
34 Moslem prince
35 In unison
36 Faction
37 Globe
40 Patriotic org.
41 Old-womanish
42 Mal de ____
43 Name
46 Edge: Abbr.
48 Rolling stone
52 Grapes
53 Soap plants
55 Fred or Steve
56 Oklahoma city
57 Smudge
58 "Grand ____"
59 "The King ____"
60 Ohio city
62 "Un ____ in Maschera"
63 Residue
64 Still waters
67 Kind of renewal
68 French possessive
69 Max or Buddy
70 French wave
71 Merchant ship
72 Vichy marshal
75 Bishop's headdress
76 Harmless hawk
78 Connecticut submarine base
80 Sheltered, at sea
81 Second
82 British lawmakers: Abbr.
85 Scottish man of property
86 Cain's postman
90 Tire
92 Was flirtatious
93 Lent a hand
94 Alpine stream
95 Subway item
96 Troubles
97 Teen-ager's bane
98 Cavaradossi, Tosca's lover
100 Fondle
101 Fifth-largest cont.
102 Charity
106 Corner
107 Wall Street abbr.
108 Turns down
109 Musical symbols
110 Scotch denial
112 Criterion: Abbr.
113 Takes the blue ribbon
114 Insults
115 Powders
117 Achaean League member
120 Fine violin
121 Art objects
122 Friend, in Nice
125 All the world
127 New broom
130 Jong
131 Wampum
132 Court decree
133 Not a soul
134 Office furniture
135 Land unit
136 Lavishes love on
137 Over

DOWN

1 Zodiac sign
2 Golf course unit
3 Friend
4 Like certain wines
5 Anchored
6 Cowboy, Spanish style
7 Mistreat
8 Transparent
9 Wood measure
10 Spanish gold
11 Crown
12 "____ of Two Cities"
13 Game pieces
14 Chill
15 Organ ____
16 Gamut
17 Part of A.D.
18 Prophet
19 Evening, in Naples
25 ____ land
26 Call it quits
28 Bided one's time
32 Soft drink
35 Faulkner character
36 Small finches
37 Sioux
38 Branching
39 Too many cooks
41 "There's many ____ . . ."
42 Meaning
43 All work and no play
44 Palate lobes
45 Noble rank
47 Kind of club
49 Wee fellow, in Eire
50 Partner of wiser
51 Roll-call word
54 City transportation
57 River boat
59 Louisiana Indians
60 Gromyko
61 Joint
62 Aaron or Raymond
65 Muddied
66 ____ den Linden
69 Taboo
71 Likely
73 Creatures: Fr.
74 Mrs. Lincoln's maiden name
75 Aromatic spice
76 Titania's spouse
77 Arid
78 Scowl
79 Stew
81 Encore!
83 Adjust earlier
84 Felt
86 Buckles
87 Bowery figures
88 The same: Lat.
89 Nostril
90 R.R. stop
91 Wine
97 Dissonant
98 Kind of system
99 A long time
100 City on the Vistula
102 "____ Dance"
103 Do a photographer's job
104 Match
105 Signs up
111 Early Christian
113 Road mishap
114 Defamation
115 Australian tree
116 Female water buffalo
117 Logger's travois
118 Minute opening
119 Rara ____
120 With, in Tours
121 Kingfish
122 Footless one
123 Writing on the wall
124 Enraged
126 W.W. II agency
128 Boy
129 Long period

59. We Never Hear of . . . by Bert H. Kruse

ACROSS

1 Poison oak
6 Harangues
12 Synagogue
16 "Hammerklavier" is one
17 Film magazine
20 Call
21 Early fight for George Armstrong
23 City in East Germany
24 Profit
25 Community character
26 Germinate anew
27 Felony
28 Marquee
30 ". . . as a wild bull in ____": Isaiah
32 Typeface: Abbr.
34 Dull sound
35 Bows' opposites
38 Dryden's "The ____ Ladies"
41 California's first capital
43 Parisian nights
45 Wings
47 Flautist
48 Artist's mate
52 Clerk Heep
54 Grand or Cedar
55 In ____ (stagnating)
56 Stravinsky ballet: 1957
57 ____ compos mentis
60 Divert
61 Roman battering ram
62 U.S. Open champ: 1976
63 Refuse
65 Book: Abbr.
66 Takes a flat
68 Group of lions
70 City near Arnhem
71 Bagnold
73 "Bambi" fawn
74 Smithereens
76 Reliable
78 Bern's stream
79 Valley
80 Ponselle
81 Be against
82 Painter's need
84 Victor Herbert sequel?
86 Early Christian center
89 Mislays
91 On the trail of
92 Ailing while sailing
94 Tot's tummy trouble
96 Raid
99 Nit-pick
100 Stew
102 U.S. wine valley
104 Thick slice
106 Brass or pewter
108 Moldings
111 Indians
114 Botanist Gray
115 Island near New Guinea
116 Low N.C.O.'s?
119 Pelvic bones
120 Aquinas
121 Vestments
122 Eng. money
123 Glycerides
124 Trucker's stop

DOWN

1 Drenches
2 Not dispatched
3 Tatami
4 To ____ (precisely)
5 Tumbrel
6 Descendant
7 Stabler, using his left
8 East, in Berlin
9 Red letters
10 French head
11 Stationary
12 Summer garb?
13 Fast freight
14 Evict
15 Hero's hero
16 Rabbit's tail
18 Bolt holder
19 Icelandic writings
20 Golf org.
22 Western peak
29 Court sport
31 Epithelium
33 Translated into Ovid's tongue
36 Airfoil
37 Small quaffs
39 Hanoi people
40 Commercials
42 Ship that picked up Glenn
44 Egghead?
46 Gigolo's friend?
48 Serious
49 Best seller in 1885
50 Spur and heel of Italy's "boot"
51 Prayer
53 Roasts, in Reims
56 Place next to
58 Wildcat
59 Colony member
61 Lizard
64 Tragedy by Euripides
67 Crustaceans' projections
69 Distant witness
72 Cold-weather card game?
74 Prospero's spirit
75 Warning
77 Boito works
81 "____ take arms . . ."
83 Thus, in toledo
84 Admiral's aide: Abbr.
85 Romance
86 Steep slopes
87 Give 52 to four
88 Pinna's pendent part
90 Musical group
93 Bumps or lumps
95 Any temporal ruler
97 Quick look
98 Pasch
101 "____ Rhythm"
103 Basketball defense
105 Ramfis in "Aida"
107 Sycophant's reply
109 Old English letters
110 Chimney coating
112 Victorian oath
113 Big truck, for short
117 Mrs., in Metz
118 Biblical well

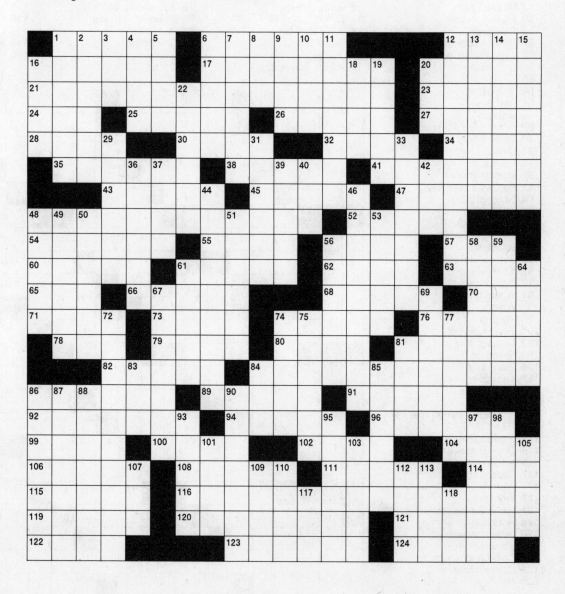

60. Chess Matches by William Lutwiniak

ACROSS

1 Falls short
6 Beguile
11 Dicta
16 Track event
20 Play part
21 Second showing
22 ___ loose (free)
23 Inventor Pliny
24 King
28 Flooring
29 Roman times
30 Buggies
31 Raise a nap on
32 Infiltrator
33 Sautés
34 Swivets
35 President, at times
36 Then, to Pierre
37 Baba and Pasha
38 Liana
39 Queen
49 ___ extent (partly)
50 Long, long time
51 Steeler coach and family
52 Pointed arch
53 Mescal source
54 "Ah, me!"
56 Famed soprano
57 Tightens, as a drum
58 ___ mater
59 ___ noire
60 Truck part
61 Borrower
62 Bishops
69 Radio-tube workers
70 Cask: Abbr.
71 Livy or Ovid
72 Pawns
82 Musical pieces
83 Followed slavishly
84 Fearing that
85 Wolfert
86 ___ left field
87 The Foul Fiend
89 Gossips
90 Bohr and Borge
92 St. Paul's designer
93 Oca or yam
94 Would-be jr.
95 Whirl
96 Knights
101 Garroway
102 Miami's county
103 Friend of Solomon
104 Giant step
107 Anecdote
109 ___ end to
110 Cpl. or sgt.
113 ___ force (by all means): Fr.
114 Roulette bet
115 Oriente native
116 Artery
117 Castles
121 Warmth
122 Nightclub
123 White Sands' county
124 Horatio
125 Letter opener
126 Selected
127 Could and would
128 City on the Aire

DOWN

1 Data
2 ___ off the old block
3 Where the Adige flows
4 Corso money
5 Part of R.S.V.P.
6 Wardrobe
7 Most spiteful
8 Importunes
9 Basks
10 Chemical ending
11 C.S.A. general
12 Relative
13 Monads
14 As an example
15 Cinque follower
16 Philippine port
17 Originate
18 More guileful
19 Third Reich salute
23 Noted prep school
25 Clothe
26 A science
27 Office help
33 Sweetheart
34 Move furtively
35 Perfume bottles
36 U.S.S.R. town
37 Shore bird
38 Odious
39 Public storehouse
40 Straight thinking
41 Newton
42 Prelims
43 ___ sides (everywhere)
44 Lover
45 Glacial deposit
46 Guam's capital
47 Drive back
48 Concurrences
54 "___ in the hand . . ."
55 Charter
56 Glorify
57 Converging
60 Caustic
61 Flaccid
63 Touchdown
64 Incite
65 Mtg.
66 "Ghosts" creator
67 Cavort
68 Sets of type
72 Believes, of yore
73 Dark-eyed beauty
74 Between: Prefix
75 Eucharistic plate
76 Museum offering
77 Run out
78 City of India
79 Shore
80 Garbo
81 Lightened
87 Smooth-tongued
88 Rose's love
89 Ski-lodge offering
90 Bob or Thomas
91 Ancient Armenia
93 Merchant
94 Caught
95 Rifle
97 Diaskeuast
98 Bedecked
99 Controversy
100 Spanish gypsies
104 Be curious
105 ___ lie (fibbed)
106 Grapevine growth
107 ___ through (persevered)
108 Stereotyped
109 Less polluted
110 Sverige's neighbor
111 Was concerned
112 Incenses
113 In ___ way (ailing)
114 Hoofbeat
115 ___ d'Azur
116 Lead or bit
118 Cameroons tribe
119 Soho coin, for short
120 Bad: Prefix

61. Eight Easy Pieces by Alex F. Black

ACROSS

1 Rushed
5 Discourage
10 Mama or Timberlane
14 She-bear: Sp.
17 Leon or Flynn
18 Love, Italian style
19 Styptic
20 Vietcong org.
21 Seekers of the lost, strayed or stolen
25 Sylvan
26 Ripens
27 Antecedent
28 Aunties' mates
29 Shoshonean
30 Mimic
31 Inlets
32 Potential farmers
34 Quilled flier
38 Scrawny one
39 Shorthand expert
40 Caviar, e.g.
41 Scottish bloomer
44 Senator from R.I.
46 Depressed
47 Female rabbit
49 Having meshes
50 Mexican sandwich
53 Gigolo or fop
57 Haggard novel
58 Duck genus
59 Obstacle
60 U.N. agency
61 Stradivari's teacher
63 Esteem
66 Snow runner
67 Sister
68 Vaudevillians' mecca
70 Chose
71 Poet's word
72 Summers, in Vichy
74 Snarl
75 Southern constellation
76 State Dept. divisions
80 Lallygag
81 Tuck, e.g.
83 Motel predecessor
84 California fort
85 Auld lang syne
87 Straggler
89 Mail ctr.
90 Exposed
93 Appoints
94 Beau Brummell
99 Covenants, to Clemenceau
101 Milky gem
102 Little and Gehrig
103 Power-project initials
104 Molar malady
105 Acquired relative
107 "... Oz" author
108 Stand by
110 Washington advisers
114 Loser to D.D.E.
115 Dry
116 Zenith antonym
117 Recipient
118 Concorde, e.g.
119 Home, to Paris
120 Bastille warder
121 Picnic pests

DOWN

1 Make thirds
2 Russian city
3 Cheerful
4 Wallach
5 Dirk
6 Dominion
7 Digits
8 Go wrong
9 Breathe
10 Fido's genus
11 "They ___ serve . . ."
12 Minor division of mankind
13 Rival of T.C.U.
14 Single performance
15 Relieve
16 Make ___ (complain)
17 Declaims
22 California valley
23 Toward the mouth
24 Wrinkled
25 "The Wayward ___"
30 Bikini, e.g.
31 ___ Janeiro
33 Moses, for one
35 Store
36 Wind dir.
37 Gascon's activity
38 Mets' home
42 Upright
43 Cover crop
45 ___ Alamos
46 ___ the grass
47 Watered down
48 Forms of oxygen
50 Chinese pagoda
51 European country
52 Politico's bankroll
54 Invisible
55 Voltage decrease
56 Medium's signal
62 City near Oran
64 Get back into focus
65 Ancient Tokyo
69 Before, to poets
73 Henny Penny's phobia
75 Labor org.
77 Frees (of)
78 Prickly pear
79 Glides aloft
82 Marbles
86 Meadow barley
88 Dweller
89 Beaver's activity
91 Heirs' concerns
92 Invent
94 Tiff
95 Adirondack lake
96 "___ My Sunshine"
97 Waiter or bell
98 Hair pad
99 Greek actress Irene
100 Units of area
101 Illinois town
106 Opera by Handel
107 Constr. man
108 Soon
109 Left
111 Adherent
112 Shoe size
113 Cantor's wife

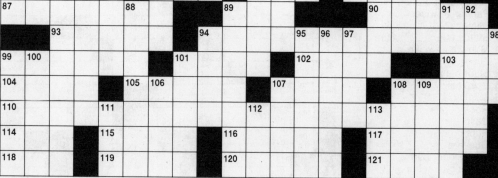

62. A. & Q. by Elaine D. Schorr

ACROSS

1 Role for Price
6 Electrical units
12 Having the know-how
16 Made corvine sounds
21 "The homage of ___": Byron
22 Western ___
23 Bird's crop
24 Lenten symbol
25 Big Apple with no worms
28 Young salmon
29 Court team
30 Sage and thyme
31 Author Jong
32 Put-on
33 Parts of a cen.
34 Diana ___: 1934–73
35 Singlehanded
36 "___ Bulba"
38 Takes advantage of
39 Blathers
41 Romancer's offering
44 Gunpowder Plot conspirator
48 A.k.a.
49 Artery
50 Before tee
52 Son of Jacob
53 Yes, in her private writings
57 Penalty
58 ___ share
59 Demeaned
60 Pittance
61 Count of jazz
62 Levene and Levenson
63 Bank deals
64 As well
65 Where GUM is
66 Wrap up
67 His peers think so
70 Quechua
71 "___ to Live," 1958 film
74 "Exodus" name
75 Comedian Richard
76 Apothegm
77 Only when his funny films failed
82 Jasey
85 Sidestepped
86 Sentry's cry
87 Seed covers
88 Pure, in Parma
89 Poe house
90 Staff member
91 Blots out
93 Kanga's creator
94 "___ Death"
95 Well, he's no John Wayne
97 Partner of wiser
98 Ullmann
99 Status quo ___ bellum
100 Man with a mike
101 Four-baggers
102 Sight enhancer
105 Bowl calls
106 Cicatrix
108 Rock debris
109 Dash
111 Rubberneck
112 Guevara
115 "Excalibur" part
116 Cooking direction
117 Mail class
118 Heath for Heathcliff

119 Figaro's forte
121 Nobody on Broadway
124 N.M. terrains
125 Use a strop
126 In proximity
127 Turkeys
128 Closing words
129 Bookie's quote
130 Author Seton
131 Littoral area

DOWN

1 Brownish orange
2 Second of two
3 Ottomans
4 Hipsters
5 Branch
6 Famed choreographer: 1880–1942
7 Makes better
8 Pauses
9 Sigh for Yorick
10 Society newcomer
11 Trinidad combo
12 ___ the hole
13 Clasps or clamps
14 Mongolian monk
15 Cote female
16 ___ carry
17 Capital of Eritrea
18 Imprisoning officials
19 It could be electric

20 N.Y. time, at times
26 Garner
27 Brush, in Brest
32 Chateaubriand, e.g.
34 Court figures
37 Bull or jam
39 Like fish eyes
40 Senior on the Seine
42 Muse for Pindar
43 Columnist Barrett
44 Without foundation
45 Penang person
46 Ask 43 Down!
47 Kesey and Rosewall
48 Yoga posture
51 Olla podrida
53 Oft-watched line
54 But, in Bonn
55 Satisfy
56 Polyantha, e.g.
57 Maine bay
61 Lean as a rake
63 Did an inside job
64 Theatrical lover
65 Entangles
68 Political cartoonist
69 Any planet
72 Greets the dawn
73 Livy's field
75 Beat
76 Down Under fellows
77 Ravine
78 Author Waugh

79 City on the Loire
80 Yahoo
81 Very small pin
83 Word with city or tube
84 Takeoff group
85 Kind of role
86 Puts on the payroll
88 Item not to be exposed
90 Movie pooch
91 Variety of garnet
92 Czar's name: Abbr.
93 Henry the sculptor
95 Estuary
96 Harbinger
99 Ever-abiding
101 He wrote "The Dynasts"
103 Capital of Armenia
104 Abet
106 Avocets' kin
107 Freight shipment
110 Incapacitates
111 Tanning locale
112 Après-ski drink
113 Holey rollers
114 Artist Max
116 Booted
117 Fed
118 Grain sorghum
119 Little, in Lanark
120 Haw's partner
121 "___ is Silvia?"
122 German article
123 Mil. rank

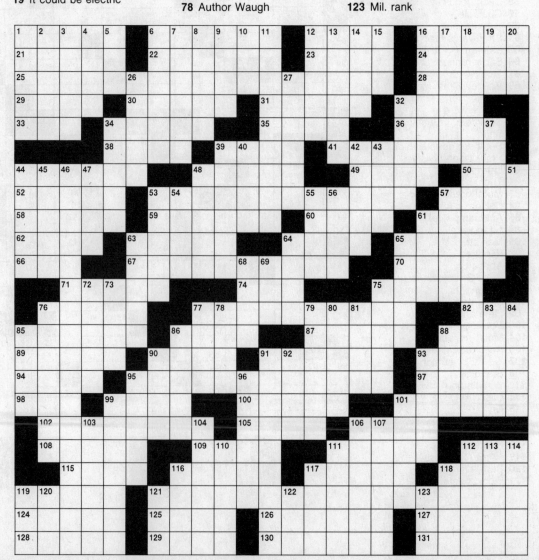

63. Possessive Personalities by Louis Baron

ACROSS

1 Large amount
5 Physician: Comb. form
10 Wine word
13 Ruthian clout
17 Further
18 Synopsis
19 S.A. land
20 Impassive
22 Newsman's brain
25 Three-horse shay
26 Casey Jones
27 Talk-show mascot
29 Fender bender
30 Gait, in Granada
31 Talk gibberish
32 Beknighted women
35 Florida's discoverer
37 Battologize
41 Ugandan exile
42 Singer's sea mate
45 Anatomical duct
46 Pulse, in music
47 Snooker, e.g.
48 Old Hebrew avenger
49 Dramatis personae
50 After printemps
51 Playwright's chicken
55 Waste maker
56 Hand out
58 Accord
59 Worsteds
60 Kodály's "___ János"
61 Pitfall
62 ___-day
63 Aloha, in Israel
65 Gawk
66 Pedigreed animal
70 Chair name
71 Dancer's costumer
73 Key to heredity
74 Ideologies
75 Beatles' movie
76 Kafka heroine
77 Chew at
78 Sault ___ Marie
79 Explorer's chef
83 Plexus
84 Biting
86 Nosher's desire
87 Column moldings
88 Today, in rome
89 "___ Named Sue"
90 Flourish
92 Comic's choirmaster
97 Flying boat
101 When, in Spain
102 Cyberneticist's hot dog
104 Source
105 Items ab gallinis
106 Channel
107 Soprano Elinor
108 Soc. or org.
109 Snooze
110 Judgelike
111 Surfeit

DOWN

1 Apache masked dancers
2 Role in "The Iceman Cometh"
3 Floe
4 Grating
5 "The Wild Duck" playwright
6 Canadian court decree
7 Row
8 Electrifying agcy.
9 "Optimism is the content ___ men in high places": Fitzgerald
10 Solarium
11 Jewish holiday eve
12 Surly, churly men
13 Struggled
14 Stereo speaker
15 Arabic A
16 Heyerdahl's "Kon-___"
20 Laminar
21 Fancy one
23 Chemical suffixes
24 Lab wire loops
28 Besmeared
30 Decorticates
32 "Old hat"
33 Super fiddle
34 Sleuth's weapon
35 Indian wild dog
36 Deny
38 Actress's mystery man
39 Discernment
40 Park in Colorado
42 Name giver
43 Halluces
44 Calhoun
49 St.-John's-bread
51 Emperor and Wolfe
52 Kiel or Suez
53 Khayyám et al.
54 Like a bionic man
55 Lumberman
57 Dims
59 Run of luck
61 Buddhist shrines
63 Earthquake
64 Must
65 Seagoer
66 Port of Aug. 3, 1492
67 Ascent
68 Mother's relative
69 Coolidge's V.P.
71 Aiding digestion
72 The Italian Stallion
75 Refuses to quit
77 Angry dogs
79 Confined, redundantly speaking
80 "Caught like a rat ___"
81 Mogul
82 They cross the plate
85 Activities
87 African antelope
90 Part of a P.C. Wren title
91 Less trained
92 Habitat: Prefix
93 Brain covering
94 Podium
95 Shortly
96 Milky Way sphere
97 Half a ticket
98 Wild ox
99 Nutcracker's suite
100 Irish Gaelic
103 Aussie animal

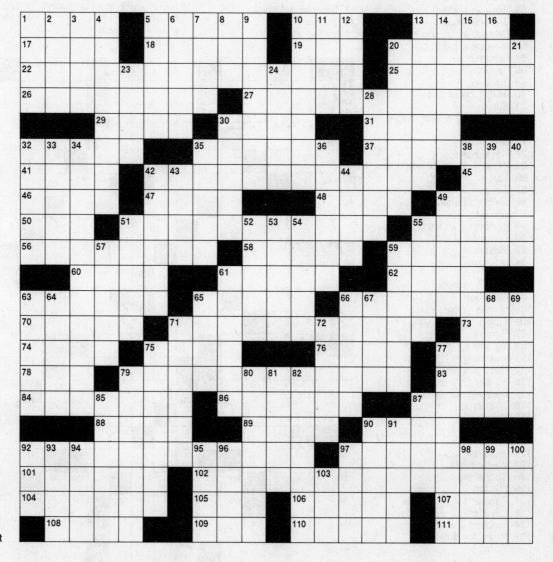

64. Freudian Flips by Frank Nosoff

ACROSS

1 Speech problem
5 Thereabouts
9 Use a tuffet
12 Flower parts
18 Famed Florentine
19 See 18 Across
20 Drug plant
22 Vote of assent
23 Psychiatrist's song
25 Incentive for Seattle Slew
27 Where Saul saw a seeress
28 Spy of 1780
29 Salad ingredient
30 ENE or WSW
31 Fit of pique
32 Fidel's former aide
33 Suffix with dull
35 "Tiny Alice" playwright
36 Grafter's item
37 Pongee color
38 Stash away
40 French town
42 SST, for one
43 Butter-and-____
45 Binaural system
48 Tree: Comb. form
51 Sports news
53 Sailors' patron
55 Horizon sights
59 Wide-awakes
61 Orlando of diamond fame
63 It repeats itself
64 Controls
68 Imparts
69 Put away
70 April 1 baby, e.g.
71 Sump
72 Smells like an old stogie
74 Volume
75 Mil. group
76 Royal ruins
80 "Tree ____ Window": Frost
83 Tart
85 January, in Seville
86 Electrical unit
87 Loosen
88 Performer, in Perugia
90 Foundation gift
92 Most curt
94 Licenses
96 Bow
98 ____ incognita
99 Floor exit
101 "Trees" poet
103 To play, Italian style
107 Rented
109 Summit
111 Mussulman
112 Merchandise
115 Small horse
117 Galley-proof symbol
119 Chatter
120 Holly
121 Finnish bath
123 Swerve
126 Road surfacing
127 Western hill
128 Sports org.
129 Mystery
131 Popular fur
133 L.B.J.'s "____ Poverty"
134 Problem for Midas
137 Motto for a dieter
139 Catch
140 Bambi, e.g.
141 The very best
142 "Papa Bear" of football
143 Deans
144 Hit sign
145 Soldiers in Seoul
146 Class cap

DOWN

1 Ends of flights
2 Fort Knox item
3 Kind of boarder
4 Fair-haired one
5 Kitchen utensils
6 Artery
7 Saw of a sawfish
8 Mink's cousin
9 Umpire's cry
10 Massey et al.
11 Walked unsteadily
12 Carousal
13 Wallach
14 Jack of clubs
15 Evangeline's home
16 American or Foreign
17 Dr. Slop's creator
18 Padding in packing
21 Foods
23 Trinculo or Yorick
24 Guffaw
26 Massenet oratorio
32 Against
34 Aaron Burr's ego
36 Pedicure fanatics
38 Word on a Czech's check
39 Skid-row problem
41 "And we will ____ pleasures prove": Donne
42 P.D.Q.
44 Grouch's problem
46 Catchall abbr.
47 Section of film
49 High degree
50 Colonial freethinkers
52 Criticize slyly
54 Less familiar
56 Girl's name
57 Palindromic word
58 One of the Chaplins
60 Subtly nasty
62 People with petitions
64 Santha Rama ____
65 Vocal pauses
66 "Old Blue Eyes"
67 Overcharges
73 Hound's clue
76 "____ Nightingale"
77 Malayan state
78 Hornblende
79 Type of light
81 Prefix with lead or guide
82 Thus far
84 Spring flowers
87 Displace
88 Prone
89 Alaska, formerly: Abbr.
91 Pack pipe tobacco
93 Preliminary coat
95 Distress signal
97 Kept a tryst
100 Mend, in a way
102 Aerial bomb
104 Native of Oran
105 Causes
106 Erect levees
108 Small boats: Var.
110 "____ of bright gold": Shakespeare
112 Like Nike
113 White elephant
114 Estate; property
116 He may use faint praise
118 Indecent
121 Percolates
122 Brest beast
124 Where benedicts are created
125 Elm or mackerel
127 Danny's daughter
130 Of soil: Comb. form
132 Like a cocktail "lady"
133 "How's that again?"
135 Three, in Torino
136 Punkah
138 Ayesha

65. Far Out by A. J. Santora

ACROSS

1 Seaver's turf
5 Reckless
11 Tragedy by Euripides
18 Half a city's name
20 Heavy fire
21 Enthralled
22 Martian on Earth
23 Enraptured
25 One of the sciences
27 Piloting is one
28 High dudgeon
29 Canonical hour
30 Clocked
31 Judicious
35 Indigo plants
36 Blanched
37 Animate
38 Twanginess
42 More guileful
43 Voiced
44 Exterior
45 Endure
46 City near Detroit
47 Marsh birds
48 Mirthful
49 Protected an invention
50 Jackson and Smith
51 Spectral
52 Knobbed
53 Monoski
54 Where nothing is new
56 Police detail team
60 Gambling game
62 Room at the top?
63 Town in Alabama
64 Vast landholdings
67 Wild goose
68 Star that rose in 1944
69 Fitting
70 Draggles
71 Vineyard area in France
72 Edict city: 1598
73 Seasonal "pilot"
74 ____-raft (oyster plant)
75 Oriental nurses
76 Bewitch
77 Instrument board
78 ____ majesty
79 Cowboy gear
80 Brown horse
81 Herd's milieu
84 Grinders
86 Sport in Cozumel
88 Sitting pretty
92 Entirety
93 Shelter a D.P.
94 Eared seals
95 Wash out
96 "Astrophel" poet
97 Beliefs
98 Small barracuda

DOWN

1 Pundit
2 Money in Prague
3 Upper crust
4 Not aweather
5 With gallantry
6 Illegal burnings
7 Residue
8 Guinea pig
9 Space ____
10 Sketched

11 Colored with a pigment
12 Gave a short cheer
13 Inventor of a sign language
14 Great expectations, symbolically
15 Nigerian tongue
16 Allhallows ____
17 Byrd or Eagleton: Abbr.
19 Birds that can't fly, e.g.
20 Dark-colored mica
24 Lion trainer
26 Frogs
30 Make noxious
32 ____-garde
33 Bottled spirit
34 Inward
36 Where to see stars
37 Delights in
38 Grooves for bowstrings
39 Of the ear
40 Condition

41 Overreached, in a way
42 Way up or down
43 Repress
45 Temptress
46 Actor Jack
48 As ____ a beet
49 Set forth as true
51 Board
52 Marine fliers
54 Arctic whales
55 Mends
57 ____ Pepper, flier in a Redford film
58 As crazy as ____
59 ____ cotta
61 Where El Misti rises
63 Lackey or flunky
64 Twofold
65 "What's in ____?"
66 Barrett and Jaffe
67 Wild pigs

68 Go ____ (decay)
70 Newman film: 1977
71 Kings of the Germans
73 Pilot's need
74 Elgin ____
76 Beetle that flies, but not well
77 ____ on (exaggerate)
79 Stuffy
80 Tally
81 Illuminated
82 Growing out
83 Shoelace tag
85 Work
86 Bird with a trumpet
87 Tennessee team
88 Conjunctions
89 Fibrous cluster
90 "____ Sun Also Rises"
91 St.-Tropez season

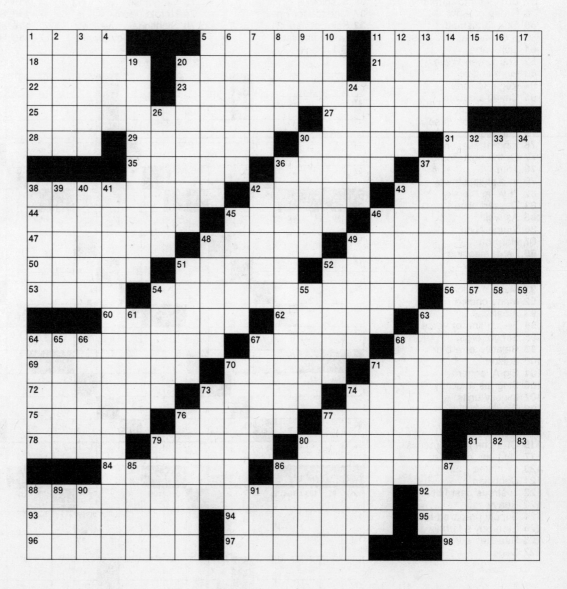

66. Passing the Buck by Tap Osborn

ACROSS

1 Sandblaster's target
6 Circumvent
11 Mature
16 Warhol film
21 Unwind
22 Motorized bike
23 Accrue
24 Norse chieftain
25 Start of a verse
29 Political contest
30 Flock of herons
31 Brought up
32 Jack's need
33 Breathing noise
34 Hearth
35 Stove parts
36 Sprinkle
37 Suit to ____
38 Ionian gulf
39 Second line of verse
51 Gawking
52 Soggy
53 Forbidden things
54 Sport fish
55 Bring together
56 Anchovy
57 Brought into harmony
58 Group of eight
59 One to distrust
60 U.S. painter: 1871–1951
61 Gun parts
62 The Green Wave
63 Gormandize
64 Vega, for one
65 Chimp's cousin
66 Egyptian king
67 Third line of verse
75 Shortage
76 Kind of season
77 Of the soil: Comb. form
78 Trim
79 In a sluggish way
82 "Eye in the sky"
83 Dessert wine
85 As well
86 Vituperation
87 Harp on
88 Farm machine
89 Make wavy
90 Dissolve
91 Make a quick visit
92 Menu choice
93 Albatross
94 Fourth line of verse
98 School orgs.
99 Relative of a b'ar
100 Saison
101 Big-A laggard
105 Sing, as a lullaby
107 Iniquity units
109 Franklin's flier
113 ____ a pin
114 N.Z. native
115 Of a chemical process
117 Last line of verse
120 Infuriated
121 Condition
122 Lustrous bast fiber
123 Heavy satin
124 Supply prepared food
125 Eton boy's father
126 Reaches across
127 Dagger

DOWN

1 Comprehension
2 Disgust
3 Actress Massey
4 Native of Penang
5 Turnpike sign
6 Arab chieftain's domain
7 Outspoken
8 Swiftly
9 Remove
10 Old English letter
11 Ticked off
12 Pressman
13 Plump one
14 Canal started in 1817
15 "Dead ____," Masefield novel
16 African rodent
17 Martin's pal
18 Nose part
19 More furtive
20 Owns
26 Almost cylindrical
27 Approval
28 "Dear ____"
34 Nuclear trial
35 Coop group
36 Suspicious
37 Mongol, for one
38 Saint of Jan. 21
39 Noble vacillator
40 O.T. book
41 Layers
42 Loser to Louis: Aug. 30, 1937
43 Meaning
44 Ephron or Helmer
45 Entombs
46 External world
47 Year in reign of Henry III
48 Philippine dwarf
49 CENTO member
50 Word with star or stone
56 Bias
57 Sycophant
58 Best
60 Unyielding
61 Machine guns
62 Lachrymose
64 Proportion
65 Bermuda or red
66 Popeye's creator
68 Plot devices
69 Jordan's tongue
70 "____ conventional dither . . ."
71 Stretch, in a way
72 Grange's team
73 Grandiose
74 Heroic poem
79 Nightingale's vessel
80 U.S. labor leader
81 Natal native
82 Met extras, for short
83 Hawk's asset
84 Norwegian king
85 Lined up
87 Type of type
88 Solti's need
89 Pigeon coop
91 Dead Sea product
92 Cinch
93 Reaches
95 One with a bug gun
96 Iconoclast
97 Job securities
101 Huxley's "____ Hay"
102 "Arrowsmith" heroine
103 Anwar of Egypt
104 Mexican basket grass
105 Weight
106 Highway
107 Rigid belief
108 Mischievous
109 Telly on the telly
110 Witless
111 Hippolyte of France
112 Soprano Shade
114 Feeder of Lake Ilmen
115 Go berserk
116 Saucy ones
118 J. B. Rhine subj.
119 Revenue org.

67. Court Stars by Herb L. Risteen

ACROSS

1 Thin nail
5 Bismarck
9 Normand of silents
14 Dull sound
18 Swiss river
19 Saddlers' products
21 Name to remember
22 Pictorial presswork
23 Popular novel of 1881
27 Dining halls on liners
28 Did ranch work
29 "____ Miller"
30 Building extension
31 Means of access
32 Indo-Chinese group
34 Event in 1780
44 Shade of green
45 Loam deposit
46 Bread spread
47 Choler
48 Little foxes
49 Of the earth
50 Yesterday's eternal chaser
52 Merganser
53 Poet Merriam
54 "Hobohemian"
55 Tall cap
56 Baltic Sea feeder
57 Mark for poor work
59 Morning song
60 Farm implement
61 Author of "Why Not the Best?"
65 Like Jason's quest
68 Stage designer Bernstein
69 Pulmonary cavities
73 Uhlan's weapon
74 Genetic offshoot
75 Natives of Tampere
77 Inlet in the Orkneys
78 He was: Lat.
79 "Gymnopédies" composer
80 Tennis star of the 1930's
81 Moselle tributary
82 Outside: Prefix
83 Be furious
84 Building material
86 Jai alai basket
87 Venice
92 Bring to ruin
93 Weight allowance
94 Commercials
95 Rawboned person
98 Inflexible
99 Perfume
103 Romantic novel of 1844
109 Gaunt
110 "March King"
111 Bellini opera
112 Adjective for Yorick
113 Track figures
114 "Forever ____"
115 Playwright Simon
116 Feudal underling

DOWN

1 Rod Carew's weapon
2 Stadium sounds
3 ____ code
4 Exhausts, as resources
5 Bobolink's relative
6 One of fifty: Abbr.
7 Nervous ailments
8 Singleton
9 One in the "noonday sun"
10 Modifies
11 Cry of disgust
12 Dutch uncle
13 Cut off
14 Shirking responsibility
15 Southwest Indian
16 Salt Lake City team
17 Small rowboat
20 Lydia's capital
24 Kipfels
25 Times of day
26 Where Joppolo commanded
32 Kind of eclipse
33 Long of La.
34 ____ Alaska
35 Read novel
36 Tribal emblem
37 Acid salt
38 Lager head
39 Hornplant
40 City NW of Bologna
41 Drew a bead on
42 One of the Horae
43 Less trite
49 Mean and unpleasant
50 Duke, for one
51 Of hearing
52 Haruspices
54 Footprint
55 Battle scene: 1914, 1918
56 Noblemen
58 Force out
59 Name to remember
60 Task
62 He wrote "Bambi"
63 French saint: Dec. 1
64 Yammered
65 Argosy
66 Hackmatack
67 Growing out
70 Cousin of "Belay!"
71 Ring-tailed animal
72 Ice pinnacle
74 Small featured role
75 Navigation hazard
76 Hebrides island
79 Brought to court
81 Phalarope
83 Fly hit by a coach
84 Sen. Thurmond
85 From ____ (afterwards)
86 Fall drink
88 Charlatans
89 Lazy
90 Carton's "____ better thing"
91 Sterling North book: 1963
95 Town on the Vire
96 Neighbor of Libya
97 Disrupt
99 Raison d'____
100 Large truck
101 Army V.I.P.'s
102 School founded by Henry VI
104 Dos Passos book
105 ____ de plume
106 Bulky boat
107 Negative prefix
108 Pittsburgh intake

68. As the Romans Did by Anthony B. Canning

ACROSS

1 Farewells in No. L
7 Start of a Wolfe title
13 Smoked salmon
16 Insignificant one
21 Yacht basin
22 Ciudad for Castro
23 Amin
24 A thing found
25 X-rated language
27 Revolver
29 X follower
30 Veil
31 Prone (to)
33 Clinic apprentice
34 Stag's mate
35 Scheherazade's forte
36 Listener's phrase
37 Girl of song
40 Xth: Prefix
41 Release
42 Grenade filling
43 Lay off
47 African port
49 Track strips
51 Missile's home
52 Exact
53 A major crime
54 Famed French friends
58 Inquired, in Dogpatch
59 Dubs
61 Radar image
62 "____ peace"
63 Hagen
64 Knievel
65 The Balearics
67 Cavatina
68 Mount in Israel
70 Leo's lair
71 Gardner vehicle of MCMXLVIII
76 Towers
77 Tinker's target
78 III: Prefix
79 Appointed
81 City on the Ganges
84 Curly et al.
89 X x XXX
92 On deck
94 Plat abbrs.
95 Old Greek flasks
96 Hokum
97 Conjunction
98 Space laps
101 Ford
102 Layers
104 Chemical suffix
105 Pride plus VI
109 Less common
110 Refection
112 ____-do-well
113 Bardot's income
114 Eastern name of fame
116 Sparkling-wine city
117 Indian ape
118 Baez
119 Like X-o'clock scholars
120 Thus, to Burns
121 Item stolen while a crowd watches
123 Jupiter's XII
124 Caterpillar hair
125 "____ Need Is Love"
128 Nobelist Neruda
129 Architects' concerns
131 Behan's "Borstal ____"
134 U.S.S.R. enterprise
136 Fortunate finds
139 Kind of sale
140 Tate treasures
141 Vex
142 May or Stewart
143 Backs
144 Sch. affiliate
145 ____ cheese
146 Cloth-drying frame

DOWN

1 Moslem lord
2 Destroyer in A.D. LXXIX
3 Parisian suburb
4 Shake a leg
5 Formicidae
6 Pitcher Paige
7 Lyrical laments
8 Hesitated orally
9 Hardwood tree
10 MDCCCXII event
11 Finales for Fischer
12 Legendary reptile
13 Plutarch title word
14 Bor's son
15 Numbers or letters
16 XIV lbs., in England
17 Object
18 Set system
19 Claim
20 Sea swallow
26 Danish king called "the Memorable"
28 Adjective for an event in MLXVI
32 D.V.M.
35 X ahead, in golf
36 Entrance
37 Said
38 Succeed
39 Attend
40 Consummated
42 Haberdashery
44 Wound
45 Expulsion
46 Peony parts
48 Straw vote
49 Blossom for Whitman
50 Followers of Ammann
51 Violinist Isaac
55 "____ for thee, Ben!": Thomas Moore
56 Dunkirk's lake
57 Captures
60 Spot
66 File
67 Flier, to Ovid
69 Rubescent
71 Chekhov's first play
72 Elevator man
73 Mon. plus IV
74 Sealed
75 Pundit
77 Wife of Alfonso XIII
80 Flattop fare
81 Jipijapa item
82 Does penance
83 Blackmailer's weapon
85 Chemical compound
86 "____ boy!"
87 French or milk
88 Joe Miller joke
89 Bright, to Brutus
90 Connected series
91 Put on the cuff
93 Chug-a-lugs
96 Jackanapes
99 Parisian's drink
100 Inkling
101 Ed and Keenan
103 Joshua, e.g.
106 Talking foolishly
107 ____ backward
108 Unchanging
111 Natives of XLVII Across
115 Hollywood hopeful
118 Post
119 Browsed, in a way
122 Corporeal channel
123 Colombian cloak
124 Unappetizing
125 Athirst
126 Wolf: Comb. form
127 Lascivious look
128 Bit or lead
129 Paving stone
130 Flatfish
131 "____ ever so humble . . ."
132 Caen's river
133 Nieuport's river
135 Sitter's creation
137 Kind of aircraft: Abbr.
138 Head

69. Penny-Wise by Alfio Micci

ACROSS

1 Jai alai equipment
7 Imitative
12 Selfish
19 Cracker
20 Oblivion
21 Appraise
22 Easily accessible
24 Appears
25 Inner: Prefix
26 Tuftlike mass
27 Future chick
29 Sauce or bean
30 Sandra or Ruby
31 Stimulus
33 Interpret
35 Quarrel
38 Spell
40 Crapshooter's wager
42 Fisherman's decoy
44 ____ Dame
45 Tax agcy.
46 Patriotic org.
47 Old
48 Sergeant's charge
51 Growing out
53 Pedantic
55 Gaunt
56 Photographer's abbr.
57 Stresses
59 Detail
60 Fabled bird
61 "G.W.T.W." name
62 Tarkington book, with "The"
70 Keep another date with
71 ____ Canals
72 Horse feed
75 Routs
78 Keeve
79 Grenade charges
82 Traveler in Torino
83 Dilutes
85 Menlo Park family
86 Kind of sale
87 Nice friend
89 Hexapod
90 Effect of past experience
91 Ancient Asian
92 Kind of habit
94 Sacrament
96 Dispatched
98 Wood quantity
99 Check
100 Aside
103 ____ de guerre
105 Israel's Bar ____
106 Evening, in Paris
107 Guthrie
108 Steel helmet
112 Golden title
116 Post was one
117 Road maneuver
118 Shoulder décor
119 Clarissa of fiction
120 Cotton fabrics
121 Rod for a rifle

DOWN

1 French film director
2 Beetle
3 Town on the Vire
4 East Indian herb
5 One or another
6 Heedless of others
7 Recess
8 Irene's concern
9 Communications initials
10 Most transparent
11 He bets against his own bets
12 Massenet oratorio
13 Whale schools
14 Backdrops for TV scenes
15 American aloe
16 Joplin specialty
17 Follower: Suffix
18 These: Fr.
19 Fragrant
23 One source of oil
28 Chews the fat
31 Massey
32 Saltpeter
34 Crank position
36 Bellow's March
37 Comoid item
39 Riddle
40 Studio dept.
41 Rainbow and brook
43 Old English letter
45 Pure
48 Part of a weather rpt.
49 Bandicoot
50 ". . . ____ of purest ray serene"
51 Most unearthly
52 Lobe adornments
54 Western alliance
58 Guevara
63 Fat, in France
64 Heavenly drink
65 Kind of calendar
66 Charge
67 Steed
68 Rackets
69 Tanaka's predecessor
73 Last of the count
74 Draft initials
75 Scene from Provincetown
76 Noted conductor from Genoa
77 1976
79 Actor's agent
80 He wrote "Night Music"
81 Restriction
82 Twain's Canty
84 Open ballot
88 Golden calf, e.g.
90 Tosca's lover
93 Angry
94 Cleveland eleven
95 Esprit de corps
97 Role for Jay Silverheels
99 Texas athlete
101 Aerialist
102 Assortment of type
104 Feline whine
107 Astringent
108 Scrooge's cry
109 Former Mrs. Rooney
110 Falstaff's title
111 Uno e due
113 Bank scourge
114 Bath, for one
115 Jack of clubs

70. Locus-Pocus by A. J. Santora

ACROSS

1 Spoofs, in a way
7 Rough spot
12 Loose dress
17 Gist
20 "Rhapsody ____"
21 Sort of court
22 Famed jurist
23 Granular snow
24 Sharpened
25 Where most of this is
27 Sponge spicule
28 Tennis call
29 Fuses
31 Oil drum
32 Perfume oil
33 Dolphin's blind cousin
35 Poetic work
36 Don Ho prop
37 Melee
39 What larvae do
41 Lumbermen or beetles
45 Presumptively
48 Deep sleep
49 Less desiccated
51 Cancel
52 Hole-____
53 Gain by force
54 Poland China
56 Used up
57 Pongee color
58 Partner of Rogers and Powell
61 Bouquet
62 Man from Big D
63 Camise
64 Fissile rock
65 One of last year's frosh
68 Cooperstown name
72 Where part of this is
75 More pixilated
78 Agents
80 Author of "Butterfield 8"
81 Butte native
82 Negev and Nefud
83 Where the end of this is
85 N.C.O.'s
86 Yellow flag
87 Kind of Danish
88 Enplane
90 Usti ____ Labem, Czecho-slovak city
92 Vitality
93 Henna
95 Catch
98 Bread spread
100 Dormouse
101 Christophe's homeland
102 Athenian political subdivi-sion
104 Lengthen
106 Adjective for diamond
108 Demolish
109 Marked with stripes
110 Orphan's new parent
112 Assenting sounds
114 Glyceride
115 One, in Berlin
116 Wildebeest
117 Defendant, in law
119 Medicinal amounts
121 Kind of school
124 American dogwoods
127 Huckle

128 Co-inventor of cordite
129 Where most of this is
131 Unemployed
133 Nursery villain
134 African antelope
135 Vandyke, e.g.
136 Why some products fail
137 Ship-shaped clock
138 Skirt insert
139 Arab land
140 Exempted

DOWN

1 Shah's pelf
2 Start of "The Raven"
3 What this does twice
4 Suburb of Rabat
5 Short skirt
6 "Eyes have they, but they ____"
7 Hit, Biblical style
8 Where vessels nestle
9 Salt Lake City team
10 Acier ingredient
11 "Front porch"
12 Wide-eyed tourist
13 Political pollster
14 Dictator's phrase
15 Become lightheaded
16 Father ____, in Wolff's "The Bluebird"
17 Where to find this
18 Eye area
19 Silvertip
23 Zilch
26 Haying machine
30 Kin of calends
32 Pearl Mosque site
34 In the know
38 ____ dixit
40 Sectors
41 Ariel, for one
42 Little or Frye
43 Sapient
44 Thus far
46 Magic incantation
47 Holly
48 Take a chair
50 Oscar and Tony
51 Banquet
54 Pharaoh's talisman
55 Strip
59 Switches tracks
60 Colors
61 Worcester or York
64 Thin slice
65 Diverse
66 Giant at 16
67 School orgs.
68 Torsk
69 Poetic verb
70 Where most of this is
71 ____ Rabbit
73 Hale
74 Glistened
75 U.S.-Can. defense org.
76 Snack
77 Important hosp. group
79 "Exodus" hero
81 Soprano Kawana et al.
83 Guthrie

84 Kind of dictum
87 Sinless
89 Profundity
90 Coward
91 "____ Want for Christmas . . ."
92 Pianist from N.Y.C.
93 Cardinals' QB
94 Deputy
95 Locale of this phrase
96 Like eggs baked with Gruyère cheese
97 Semisolid
99 Make ____ scarce
100 Like Apley
101 Fortune
103 Cuckoo's announcement
105 Roscoes
106 Lustrous fabric
107 Porter product
110 Bacterium
111 Blockhead
113 Iroquoian group
116 Hayworth role
118 Radar reading
119 Sunup
120 Musette
122 Far from fragrant
123 Soft throws
124 Actor Sharif
125 Patola
126 Road sign
129 Quagmire
130 Ferdinand was one
132 Manet's "____ Boat"

71. Girth Control by Olga Kowals

ACROSS

1 Buttons up
8 ____ Bell, Brontë pen name
13 Own up
18 Name
19 Horse-opera command
20 Bison
22 Result of a conspirator's diet?
25 Emphasis on yes or no
26 He has creed, will travel
27 Ceremonial Roman chariot
28 Poet's vehicle
29 Loch in Scotland
31 Cosmetician Lauder
32 Caucasian
33 Alaskan river
35 Suffix with Johnson or journal
36 Prefix with pod or stere
38 He wrote "I Like It Here"
40 Auto race
42 ____ the hills
43 Numbers man
46 Plaid or ship
48 Subside
51 J.F.K. commanded one
53 Hindmost
54 Uses a compactor
56 Behind schedule
57 Mitch Miller plays it
59 Sluggish, in Sicilia
63 "____ homo"
64 Eat a calorie-free diet?
70 "____ Like It Hot"
71 Madhouse
72 Timberlane of fiction
73 Ballerina's knee bend
74 Dilettante
77 Kemper, in K.C.
82 Trolley noise
85 These have keys
86 Nicklaus collection
87 Astronaut's "Perfect!"
88 City that may make you tired
90 No-no in some diets
93 Dismiss
94 Stringed instrument
95 Marquand's "____ Daughter"
97 Fleming
99 Billiards shot
103 Royal circlet
105 Climber in S.A.
106 Felt shoe
109 Japan's greatest port
110 Extreme
112 Idolize
114 Exercise at a discothèque?
117 ____ shoulders above
118 Scary
119 Tallinn is its capital
120 Rebellion leader: 1786–87
121 Upbeat
122 Make a new requisition

DOWN

1 Diet reneger
2 Orchard pest
3 Middle-age bulge
4 Lug
5 "Wonderful Town" role
6 Helm letters
7 What rash dieters lose
8 Take off
9 Optician's product
10 Start of a speech
11 Kravchenko's "____ Freedom"
12 Sidetrack
13 Ear: Comb. form
14 Breakfast fare
15 Burrowing animals
16 Sacred pictures
17 "____ were the days"
20 Conceded
21 Card game for three
23 Snowy
24 Quilter's necessity
30 Poconos pool
34 Dog star
35 Argus's specialty
37 Biggin
38 Alma-____, U.S.S.R. city
39 Botch
41 Baton Rouge inst.
42 Norwegian composer
43 Work in concert
44 Tract of land
45 To ____ (exactly)
47 Nicely lined up
49 Hammett dieter?
50 "____ clock scholar"
52 Cordon ____ (chef)
54 Heart of the matter
55 Foxx
58 Dock
60 Receipt
61 Top authority
62 Bad ____, German spa
64 Chicken, in Calabria
65 Eskimo boat
66 Kind of age
67 Done in
68 "Today ____ man"
69 Glacial ridges
70 Humane org.
75 Mix a salad
76 J. B. Rhine specialty
78 Lorna Doone's lover
79 Man of weighty cantos
80 Avant-gardist
81 Uraeus symbol
83 Bestowed
84 Emulate kanonen
85 Civil
86 Rancho worker
89 Needing a diet
91 Linen or whisky
92 Yak
95 Matthew Vassar, e.g.
96 Tourists
98 ". . . so very ____ God": Paget
99 Miller
100 Lenten symbol
101 Isaac's mother
102 Czech industrialist
104 Bemused
105 Theater seats
107 Golfer with an "army"
108 Juniper
111 Year in reign of Ethelred II
113 Revolver of a sort
115 Sides of cricket wickets
116 Ibsen character

72. Unglue the Clues by Jim Page

ACROSS

1 Nobelist in Physics: 1944
5 World's busiest airport
10 Position: Comb. form
15 Comic
18 Argentine press
21 Ora pro ____
22 Writes on a blackboard
23 Bar order
24 Moulin Rouge dance
25 Burst or burgeon
26 Where Leander floundered
28 STONEWALLED
31 Lineage
32 ____ as Methuselah
33 Part of A.E.C.
35 Stage curtain
37 Clay today
38 Pearl Buck book
40 Joint
42 LEADENNESS
48 Bumps into
49 ____ ear (hearkened)
50 Spore sacs in fungi
51 Borne by the wind
53 Upbeat
54 Parishioners
55 Child of Zeus
57 Cyrano's problem
58 Cow catcher
59 Baseball statistics
61 Violin string
63 Dross of metal
65 ____ over (ponder)
66 Lariat
70 ____ Flow
74 Witnesses
77 Dimension
78 BETROTHAL
81 Goldie
83 Treatise
85 Stradivari's teacher
86 City in Tenn.
87 Concert halls
88 Swear at
90 River near Gerona
92 Parties to a legal transaction
94 Fortuneteller's card
97 Fleur-de-lis
101 Boil with rage
105 "____ of a Salesman"
106 "____ the West Wind"
107 Fundamental
109 Queenly nickname
110 Romans' small shields
111 Clans
112 SPARERIBS
115 Urban eyesore
116 St., ave., etc.
118 Marker
119 Boat-bottom timber
120 Click beetle
122 Tubers' kin
125 Joseph and Stewart
129 RIGAMAROLE
134 Locale out West
136 Zoological class: Comb. form
137 Chopper parts
139 Gun a motor
140 Stone tablets
141 Dorm sound
142 Wonder
143 Beatitudes verb
144 Became withered
145 Moth
146 Jackstay

DOWN

1 Correspondence courtesy: Abbr.
2 Saracens
3 "____ afraid of greatness": Shak.
4 Bring upon oneself
5 Humdinger
6 Hengist's brother
7 Is up against
8 Hilarious
9 Actress Winwood
10 Semites' ancestor
11 Bath powder
12 "____ are liars": Psalm 116
13 Daggers
14 "Who is Silvia? what ____ . . .": Shak.
15 Lack of justice
16 Writer Rand
17 Obtain
19 Time of youthful inexperience
20 Fireplace fixture
22 Lab occupant
27 PIGEONHOLES
29 Sufficient, of old
30 Roman official
34 Abominable Snowmen
36 Land map
38 Like Lindy's flight
39 Actor Skinner
41 It, in Italy
42 Use a yardstick
43 Quarantines
44 HUNDRED-WEIGHT
45 Rowan
46 Hamill's milieu
47 Charged particle
48 SE Asian peninsula
49 Andes ruminant
52 These, in Tours
55 A ____ Able
56 Down-Under people
60 Salvers
62 Exclamation of disgust
64 "Gipsy Love" composer
67 ____ standstill
68 Pro ____
69 Nets' ex-league
71 M.D.'s group
72 Sidekick
73 Curve
75 Glow
76 "Ida! ____ Apple Cider"
79 Pittsburgh catcher: 1974–80
80 Handle a problem
82 Elizabethan playwright
84 Reo, Essex, etc.
89 Kinsman
91 Boatman's chore
93 Edenic place
94 Turn's partner
95 An Astaire
96 Disgusting
98 Talk gibberish
99 Horn-wearing goddess
100 Thus, to Tacitus
102 City railroads
103 Asian festival
104 Golfer's problem
108 City on Tokyo Bay
110 Ecdysiasts
113 "Heads I win; tails ____"
114 Duck or color
116 Speak a piece
117 Market figure
121 Part of a switch
123 Hound
124 Cubic meter
126 Horse opera
127 Utah resort
128 Gaza or Sunset
130 Stake
131 "If ____ My Way"
132 Peen of a hammer
133 Row
134 Bikini part
135 Poetic preposition
138 Episcopacy

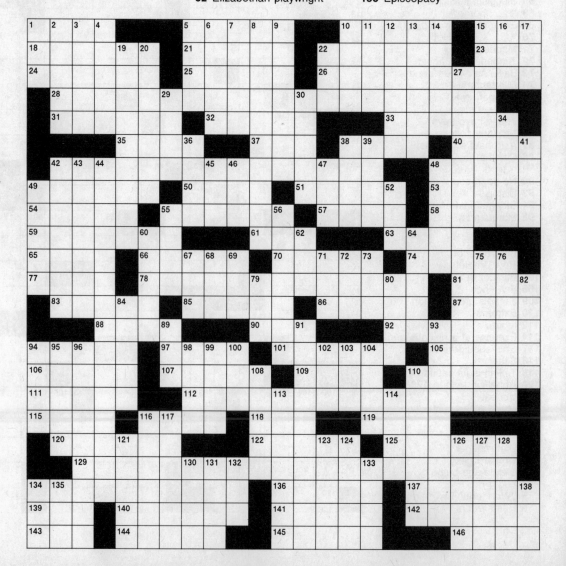

73. Noel, Noel! by Anne Fox

ACROSS

1 At another time
5 Eatery
10 Cribbage equipment
14 Conqueror of polio
18 Exact
19 Mexican pines
21 Locale of Moab and Orem
22 Knievel
23 Words from a 17th-century carol
27 Aged: Lat. abbr.
28 Leather-piercing tools
29 Arrow poison
30 Extol
31 Sweet talk
33 Bar of metal
34 Spin
35 Fleming
36 N.H.L. player
37 Hotfoot it
38 Goofy
41 Porous rock
44 Actor Pat
46 "A ____ santé"
48 Lillie
49 City on the Oka
50 Fast-growing plant
51 Stairway to the Ganges
53 Type of apartment
55 Intention
56 Negri of films
57 Anagram of 56 Across
58 One of Begin's people
59 Chinese liqueur
61 Baseball or softball
63 Begone!
64 Words from a Puerto Rican carol
70 Michel, for one
71 Cut into
72 St. ____ (battle of W.W. I)
73 Largest inland body of water
76 ____ bien
77 Mother of Zeus
79 Play of 1964
80 Dramatist who wrote "The Star Turns Red"
81 Top's cousin
82 One of a Latin trio
83 ____-majesté
84 Yule mo.
85 Spider monkey
87 In metaphysics, the external world
89 Ronsard book: 1550
90 Jewish month
92 Flower, for short
93 Sevillians' suppers
94 Snow runner
96 Nervous
98 Ruin's companion
99 Comic strip
103 Skulls
105 Pitch
106 "Bugs" or Max
107 Wild sheep
108 Old English carol
113 Kitchen staple
114 Cupid, in Greece
115 Arm bones
116 Beginning
117 Last
118 "The Way you ____ Tonight," 1936 song
119 Popular cloth
120 Jane or Zane

DOWN

1 Preakness winner: 1942
2 Stair post
3 Mrs. Hobby
4 U.S. humorist
5 Words from an old Welsh carol
6 With haughtiness
7 Holiday quaffs
8 Ordinal suffix
9 Train
10 Sound of Washington
11 Greek letter
12 Sal
13 Words from a traditional spiritual
14 His "icebox" was a good buy
15 On hand
16 Albanian coins
17 Swiss painter
20 Words by Edward Caswall
24 African river or lake
25 Bright light
26 "Exodus" character
32 Coin of Iran
33 Crocus, e.g.
34 What G.B.S. had
36 Turkey portion
37 Kind of dog or rod
39 Touch
40 Street cry
41 French ____
42 Heep
43 "Cherchez la ____"
45 ____ canto
46 Racks for coats and hats
47 Two continents as one
52 Creator of Uncle Remus
54 Repair hastily
56 Fakes
57 "Gift of the Magi" author
58 Suffix with boy or girl
60 Buffets
62 Historic French region
65 B.S.A. unit
66 Messenger of the gods
67 Type of paper or silk
68 Verdun's river
69 Santa's aides
73 Ballet finale
74 Served perfectly
75 Lewis and Clark's guide
78 Crone
81 ____ Kippur
82 Biblical giant
83 Kind of cloth
86 "____ to the world . . ."
88 ____ nine (ecstatic)
91 A ____ one's money
93 Shank
95 Marx
97 "Mamma ____!"
98 Small broom
99 Father: Comb. form
100 Member of the wedding
101 Voilà!
102 One of the Kayes
103 Powerfully built dog
104 Amahl, e.g.
106 "Have You Ever ____ Lonely?"
109 Refugee org.
110 Ultra
111 Engineering deg.
112 Soufflé item

74. After the Ball by Frances Hansen

ACROSS

1 Spikes the coffee
6 Newsy digest
11 Rosters
16 Conform
21 Siouan Sooner
22 Bastard wing
23 "___ down to the seas again"
24 Chutzpah
25 Punctuation mark
26 Galileo, for one
27 Sculpture piece
28 All thumbs
29 Start of a verse
33 Golfer's gear
34 El Bahr
35 Greek peak
36 Antitoxins
40 Bird class
43 Union of two
45 She rivaled Comaneci
47 Vessel for hyson
49 "___ ask; my wants are few"
51 Nisan, formerly
53 School Shelley attended
55 Kissars
56 "The Swamp Fox"
57 "Buffoons and poets ___ related": Goethe
59 Poet laureate: 1715–18
61 Employ
62 Guinness and Templeton
63 "Au Clair de la ___"
64 Howl at the moon
66 Social asset
68 More of verse
76 Supermarket lineup
80 Doc's date
81 City once called Last Chance
82 Fourth or real
83 Woodwind
84 Capet, for one
85 Wedding words
86 Possessive pronoun
88 Fitzgerald or Grasso
89 Camera stand
91 "Habanera" singer
94 Chilean statesman
95 Golda
96 More of verse
100 Southwest wind
101 "Fables in Slang" author
102 Bullfighter's attendant
103 Musical group
108 Linen marking
111 Oil-rich land
113 Naïve
116 Split: Comb. form
117 Booth or Newman
119 Places
121 Kiln
122 Tot's transport
123 Projecting rim
125 "A thing of beauty ___ forever"
127 Samoan seaport
129 ___-poly
130 Vols' state
131 ___-Coburg
133 Cousin of etc.
135 Stevenson
137 End of verse
144 Safari boss
147 Slanting
148 Makes equal
149 Practical
150 Deep bell tones
151 Ecological formation
152 Sartre subject
153 Smooth the edges
154 Sound of a wet mop
155 Young or Mature
156 Plaster of paris
157 Of space

DOWN

1 Daffy
2 Time-setting phrase
3 Dogie
4 Stuck on oneself
5 Man of La Mancha
6 Easter Island
7 Landi or Dido
8 Ham's eldest son
9 Actor Delon
10 Small cup
11 Thelma of films
12 "Typee" sequel
13 Evict
14 Lawyer's aide
15 Puts away
16 Cole Porter's "I ___ Love"
17 "You ___!"
18 Part of a halberd
19 Doozy
20 Asian holiday
30 Odin, to Anglo-Saxons
31 Shakespearean theater
32 Have a bite
37 Curtain color
38 Regrets
39 Church feature
40 Soprano Gluck
41 Small bottle
42 Common French verb
44 Shucks!
46 Scold
48 Exercises an option
50 Like Miss Procter's chord
52 Honey harvesters
54 Part of N.B.
57 Prophetic token
58 Large snail
60 Attacks with vigor
63 Great eighth-century Chinese poet
65 Yang's partner
67 Carved emblem
69 Made of sterner stuff
70 Mewl
71 Jewish school
72 Afro, beehive, etc.
73 Emporium event
74 Gudrun's husband
75 "Happy New ___!"
76 Fingerstalls
77 Hillside cavity
78 "Le Rouge et le ___": Stendhal
79 Kind of print
87 Numerical suffix
90 Near future
92 Sky Altar
93 ___ beet
94 Celebration in Cádiz
97 Stole or shawl
98 Goddess of hope
99 Colorful S.A. bird
104 Hymn harmonizer
105 Broz
106 Juniper tree: Bib.
107 Conservative
108 Weight
109 Slothful
110 Disguise for Zeus
112 Fanciful
114 One of the fairies
115 Bomb on Broadway
116 Milan's La ___
118 Divisions in cricket
120 Prufrock's creator
122 ". . . two ___ every question"
124 That, in Taxco
126 Trinculo, e.g.
128 Actor John and family
132 Addis ___
134 Mississippi sight
136 Island with large oil refineries
138 Elan
139 Most illustrious: Abbr.
140 Cysts
141 Gainer or Mollberg
142 One of Athena's names
143 Holler
144 Air-rifle ammo
145 Golly!
146 Witch bird

75. First the Good News . . . by Tap Osborn

ACROSS

1 David Low's Colonel
6 Moslem judge
10 Guru
14 Daybeds
19 Of the ear or air
20 Well-informed
21 Jabbar's target
22 Eleves' milieu
23 FORECAST, with 33 Across
27 Sylvan blight
28 Sort of port
29 Singer Frankie
30 Emulated the Sprats
31 Infuriation
32 "____ for All Seasons"
33 See 23 Across
43 Awaken
44 Practices
45 Raison ____
46 Placebo
47 Calvary letters
48 Suffix with blithe and frolic
50 United
51 Playbill heading
52 FORECAST, with 75 Across
59 Jack ____, late actor
60 Short snorts
61 Full of regret
62 Habituated
63 Comprehensive
64 Conglomerate initials
65 Ringside ringer
66 Ill will
69 Refuse
71 Fountain item
72 Game scores: Abbr.
75 See 52 Across
79 Arena receipts
80 Neighbor of Que.
81 Kind of gun or squad
82 Libertine
83 Courtroom vow
84 Genetic group
86 Just
88 Scrambled, in a way
89 FORECAST with 107 Across
94 Communion is one
95 Retail event
96 King Cole
97 Frictionless
100 Dr. Sabin's target
102 Malnourished
107 See 89 Across
110 Oil source
111 Shaker contents
112 Kind of course
113 Contralto Nikolaidi
114 Shore bird
115 Units of conductance
116 Gaelic
117 Direct attention

DOWN

1 Luggage
2 Humdinger
3 Shipment to Bethlehem
4 Fairy queen and namesakes
5 Appease
6 Veal ____
7 Followed exactly
8 Teacher at Oxford
9 Fit as a fiddle
10 Post-blizzard tool
11 Top-rated
12 Halston creation
13 Spire ornament
14 Border
15 Bodies of water: Lat.
16 Stable newcomer
17 Too
18 Noticed
24 Plaster backing
25 Shakespearean roles
26 Debussy opus
31 Bowling-alley button
32 Russian craft society
33 Operatic songs
34 "Pagliacci" clown
35 Donkey
36 Poet Mandelstam
37 Organic part of soil
38 "____ the long years": G.B.S.
39 Back down: Var.
40 Levant
41 Night, in Roma
42 Descried
48 One of Seaver's deceivers
49 Greek flask
51 "Snug as ____ . . ."
53 Reserved
54 Galway citizens
55 "____ lunch"
56 Saltpeter
57 Jungle cub
58 Two of Henry VIII's wives
63 Sommelier's concern
65 Kind of dancer
66 Thaumaturgy
67 Barbecue
68 Admit
69 Ed and Keenan
70 In ____ (agitated)
71 City of over five million
72 Madrid museum
73 Symbol
74 Nobel was one
76 Brant or quink
77 Overused
78 Ribbed silk
84 Hoss, e.g.
85 Oblivion
86 Thrash or thresh
87 Hit song of 1931
88 Party purveyor
90 Channel
91 Keys
92 Congenital
93 Chatterley
97 Pack away
98 Ocean sunfish
99 Roman poet
100 Egyptian god of creation
101 Site of Akershus Castle
102 Poisonous plant
103 Breathing noise
104 Feudal estate
105 Toiler in 104 Down
106 Expensive
108 Doctrine
109 Gas: Prefix

76. Weather Reports by Alex F. Black

ACROSS

1 Abrade
5 Gentle soul
9 Filleted
14 Fortify
17 Opposed
18 Chime in
20 Showy butterfly
22 Shell-game object
23 Report from Hades
26 Séance sound
27 Anatolian inn
28 Wise old men
29 Canning factory group
31 Watch the baby
32 State treasury
34 Mil. officer
35 Homophone for seize
36 Report from the White House
41 Units of speech
45 Artificial satellite
46 Giant of yesteryear
47 Blockhead
49 Stable morsel
50 Belfry group
53 "Gil ___"
55 Vow
56 Prank
57 "Green Mansions" hero
58 Report from Cambridge
61 Gallimaufry
62 Trucking rig
63 Seine season
64 Keep a tryst
65 Grandfather of Priam
68 Marsh plant
69 Abrogate
71 Suffix with dull
72 Writing accessory
74 Supped
75 Report from Kelly
81 Cold cubes in Köln
84 Accra or Lagos
86 Agreement in Amiens
87 Flagstad role
89 Kett of comics
91 Norse redhead
92 Mil. backup group
93 Coal storage
95 Golden or slide
96 Journalist Jacob
97 Traveler's report after visit to Pa.
100 "By the time ___ to Phoenix"
101 Carry on
102 Most subdued
104 ___ Ude, Russian city
105 Saarinen
106 "___ pro nobis"
107 Japanese Prime Minister: 1934–36
108 Island group off Timor
110 Middle East land
113 "Separate Tables" playwright
116 Report from Berlin
122 Ideas, to Plato
123 List ender: Abbr.
124 Counting-out word
125 Inquired in Dogpatch
126 Coarse-grained sherbets
130 Gibson and others
133 Blue mineral
135 Fold over
136 Report from Oklahoma
139 Pizarro's pelf
140 Glass collars
141 Dotty
142 Swiss capital
143 Thai temple
144 Cup prized by golfers
145 ___-kiri
146 Koko's weapon

DOWN

1 Somewhat bleak
2 Lack of vigor
3 Cloud forms
4 Mole
5 Ullmann
6 With ___ of salt
7 Word on a wall
8 Bunny or Baer
9 Slant
10 Fall mo.
11 Man bites dog
12 He was, to Cicero
13 Settled, harmonious group
14 Report from Louis XV
15 Construct
16 Atlas material
18 Places for "steak-outs"
19 Uneven
20 Green in Grenoble
21 Saudi Arabia neighbor
24 Weighs
25 Pueblo Indians
30 Author of "Meeting at Potsdam"
33 "___ Mater"
37 Entertainer Uggams
38 "Cielo ___!" (Ponchielli aria)
39 Wayne of N.H.L. fame
40 Threadlike structures
41 Puttering person
42 Monopolize
43 "Lady" of songdom
44 Endured
48 Mock
50 Iraqi port
51 Red as ___
52 Report from Lilliput
54 Taradiddle
55 G.I. under an N.C.O.
56 Tennyson poem
58 One of the Alou brothers
59 Air: Comb. form
60 Rudolph's asset
66 Can. neighbor
67 Fun at Jay Peak
70 Biblical king
73 I.O.U.'s of a kind
76 Conjunction
77 Cable-car operator
78 Had a restless yen
79 Albacore
80 Hairy
82 Lounge lizard
83 Take care of
85 Shrine Bowl team
88 Lustrous pearl
89 Bobble
90 Dressy headdress
92 Final: Abbr.
93 Stole
94 Neglect
98 Between "ere" and "Elba"
99 Cannes cop
102 As one
103 Alias, for short
108 Well-read grad.
109 Does aquatints
111 Lessen
112 "___ Like It"
114 Stannum
115 Dialect
117 Alas, in Alsace
118 Hawthorne's Prynne
119 Race horse that has never won
120 Gazing steadily
121 Thackeray's Marquis of ___
126 Shine
127 ___ avis
128 Out of kilter
129 Molt
130 Biblical character
131 Apiece
132 Nimbus
134 Law school alumni
137 Enzyme: Suffix
138 Sight for Waikiki bird watchers

77. Music Box by Walter Webb

ACROSS

1 Witty bit
5 Field yield
9 Caesar
12 "____ Death": Grieg
16 New slant
17 Israeli dance
18 Although: Lat.
19 Course of a sort
21 Kerouac's contemporaries
24 Make precious
26 Made a debut
27 Aspen, e.g.
29 Dupes
30 Bouquets
33 Drill command
35 Tests of Sills' skills
39 Tristram's beloved
41 Galley symbol
42 Base runner's delight
45 Farm implement
47 U.S.S.R. silk city
50 Mascagni flirt
51 ". . . gem of purest ray
   ____": Gray
53 Rage
54 Quechuan
55 Crystalline sugar
57 Health club
59 Railroad car
61 Organic pigment
62 Admit
64 Concerning
65 Fuss
67 Noncom
72 "The People, ____":
   Sandburg
73 Dangerous damsel
75 Soprano Mitchell
76 Supply for a catcher
78 Get by threat
80 Possess
81 What a QB must read
84 Danish-American writer
85 Suffix with cloth
87 Opera by Thomas
88 Ponselle or Raisa
92 ____ canto
93 Memorable Conn. chief
96 Maine resort
98 "Mein ____," Wagner's
   autobiography
101 Hood's case
103 Composer ____-Saëns
104 Qualifies
107 Dreams of youth
110 Presents
111 Lathered
113 Kind of plain
118 Spin a yarn
120 Financial agreement
123 One making the grade
124 City on the Wabash
125 Hirt's companion
126 Stravinsky ballet: 1957
127 Japanese monastery
128 Least old: Abbr.
129 Best of movies
130 Schools of whales

DOWN

1 Agree
2 Jack London hero
3 Membership
4 London gallery
5 Gaiety
6 Sonata finale
7 Blende or sphalerite
8 N.Y.S.E. term
9 Fleck
10 Pinpoint
11 Yugoslav coin
12 Porter
13 Gorme or Torme
14 Tolerate
15 Whodunit devices
18 W.W. II initials
20 Bando and Maglie
22 Comprehend
23 Church section
25 Alphabetic trio
28 Rutherford, for one
31 Tiny moth
32 Fire residue
34 Bells the cat
35 Saddler's tool
36 Branco or Bravo
37 Kind of wind
38 First man: It.
40 Application
43 Key
44 Tropical fish
46 Keaton
48 Diorama
49 Lorenz and Moss
52 A former Rockefeller
54 Plato dialogue
56 Goose genus
57 Fellini's "La ____": 1954
58 Dr. Dolittle's Gub-Gub
60 Dillon and Houston
61 Steinbeck novel
63 Poetic time
65 Like green apples
66 Emmett song
68 Vegetation
69 Not many
70 Afghan V.I.P.
71 Beethoven's "____"
74 Romaine lettuce
77 ____ alba (gypsum)
79 A.L. player
82 Inlay
83 Skirt style
86 Sea birds
87 ____ polloi
89 Sash for Yum-Yum
90 Sohrab, to Rustum
91 Skill
94 Sixty-four, in chess
95 Backing
97 Analyze
99 Social rank
100 Another Keaton
102 Middle of Caesar's report
104 Dept. store figure
105 Eggs, in Berlin
106 Saturated
108 It fell on Chicken-Little
109 Blackmore beauty
112 Ratite bird
114 Catch
115 Pompey's mufti
116 Basic particle
117 Avedon's concern
119 Letters for equality
121 Haggard novel
122 Grassy patch

78. Hellenic by James and Phyllis Barrick

ACROSS

1 Miami's county
5 Fit
8 Macadamized
13 Short snort
16 Poker prize
19 Writer Paton
20 ___ bono
21 Happen
22 Biological subdivision
24 Reading desks
26 Personality disorder
28 Like some dividends
29 Declaims wildly
30 Diamond calls
31 Lear's faithful follower
32 Stern or Singer
33 Man from Meshed
35 One of the Graces
37 Nonerotic relationship
41 Swelter
46 Sic ___
49 Gee-tar's cousin
50 Hounds
51 ___ franca
52 Atalante, to the Aegean
53 Pub game
55 Art category
56 Trig functions
57 ___ Paulo
58 German article
59 Two-winged fly
60 Ink drinkers
61 Losers to Agamemnon
63 Conjunction
64 A daughter of Mnemosyne
65 Compass heading
66 Boccaccio's "The ___ Heart"
67 Kids' dads
69 Uprights
71 Part of a Poe poem
77 Showy blossoms
78 Fissure
79 Hawaii's state flower
81 Part of a Euripides opus
84 Hot spots
85 A.F.B. in Colorado
86 Aegean activity
88 Visionaries
90 Grim Greek god
93 Where Greeks were enslaved
94 Racket
95 Terpsichorean group
96 Breastplate of Zeus or Athena
97 Composer of "The Rosary"
98 French coin: 1929–38
99 Grist for Homer's mill
100 Alarm
101 ___ rosa
102 Playground equipment
104 Inhibit
105 Certain series of questions
108 Vociferated
110 Iphigenia, to Menelaus
111 Painting material
115 S.A. rodent
119 Uris or Trotsky
120 Of a grain
122 Flew
124 Hamstring
127 Tensible
128 Benchley opus
129 Range
130 Scamper
131 Roper
132 Baste
133 One or another
134 Outlaw of fiction
135 Gelada or pongo
136 O'Casey or O'Kelly

DOWN

1 ___ Lama
2 Templeton and Guinness
3 Capital of Bangladesh
4 Snares
5 Parcel of land
6 Nestorian type
7 "___ the season . . ."
8 Kind of girdle
9 To ___ (on the nose)
10 Damone and Morrow
11 Timetable abbr.
12 Belittle
13 Olympian quaff
14 Twenty: Comb. form
15 Lap dog, for short
16 Author of "Men of Iron"
17 Do what Pandora did
18 Item in a schoolbag
21 Skullcap
23 Toll road: Abbr.
25 Trig prerequisite, often
27 Where Agamemnon embarked
29 Lines of hoplites
34 Way described in the "Anabasis"
35 Like Troy when Greeks won
36 Method of reasoning
38 With full force
39 Under covers
40 Tooth
42 Step ___ (hie)
43 A De Mille
44 Litigants
45 Armor part
46 Fatty dough
47 Historic landfall
48 Glabrous
51 Blackout thief
54 Medical personnel: Abbr.
55 Circumference
56 Alarm-bell sound
59 Watery trenches
60 Peppy
62 Vehicle for Patton
63 "Drake" is his epic poem
64 Solar-year excess
67 Beams
68 Micmac's relative
69 Pens and cobs
70 Blind, as a hawk
72 Hero and Leander
73 Lollapaloozas
74 Dryads' homes
75 Reproved
76 Mrs. Shriver
80 ___ Dei
81 Made calculations
82 Have a yen for
83 Principle
86 Soho coin, for short
87 Mennonite sect
89 Teen-ager's problem
90 Got wind of
91 Noted mausoleum site
92 Regimen
93 Old stringed instrument
96 Emphasized
97 Local deity
100 Goes it alone
101 Knowing
103 Has thoughts
105 Ready for Morpheus
106 Chant
107 Shred
109 Soprano Shade
112 Set of steps
113 Southern city
114 Famed Parisian theater
115 Hingle and Boone
116 Smart
117 Munch
118 Lend a hand
120 Not fooled by
121 Arabian seaport
123 Weathercock
125 Grassland
126 Outer: Comb. form
127 Refrain syllable

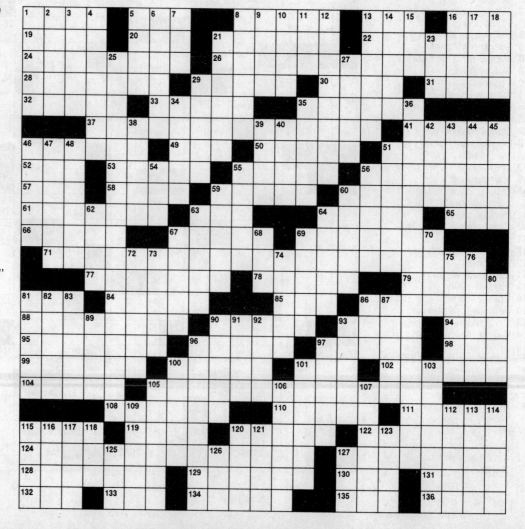

79. On Friendly Terms by A. J. Santora

ACROSS

1 Composer of "St. John's Passion"
5 Memento
10 Chances
14 Royals' Amos
18 Peak in N.M.
19 Deport
20 Televox
21 Banquet
22 Unfermented grape juice
23 Breeder of contempt
25 Brunswick dish
26 Social intercourse
28 "____ bragh"
29 Song of praise
30 Pussycat, in Paris
31 Playwright's ploy
32 Composer Manuel de ____
34 Streaks
36 Piers on a blueprint
37 Sparkling
40 Early car maker
41 Intimately associated
44 Give one the ____ (ogle)
45 Tritons
47 Calends and ides
48 Stewpot
49 Town of a bell
50 Blackbird
51 Latin student's "friend"
53 Lent a hand
55 Not carrying a gat
56 Mule, fish or cactus
58 Zoo animal
60 Lone Eagle's monogram
61 Jolly companion
65 Grand ____, Acadia
66 Native of Tripoli
67 Moistened
70 Cries of pain
73 Grandiose tales
74 One kind of society
75 Spanish bear
76 Greek letters
77 Stone: Comb. form
78 Young salmon
80 Offensive
82 Liquid meas.
83 Solidarity; communion
87 Berkeley inst.
88 Friendly welcome
90 Actress Verdugo
91 Author of "Farewell, My Friend": 1940
93 Harper role
94 Malt kilns
95 Vaccine
96 Track of the cat
98 Ring on a harness
100 Doesn't budge
103 Jewish month
104 Practice of pairing swimmers
106 Counterweight
107 Used up
108 Wild buffalo
109 Practical
110 Michel or Raphaël
111 Bettor's consideration
112 Belongings
113 K.P. gadget
114 Louis and Bill

DOWN

1 Autumn pear
2 Regarding
3 Had intimate ties
4 Describing the least subtle actors
5 Cheer
6 Correct
7 Whitewash
8 River in western China
9 Kin of spinets
10 Lena or Marilyn
11 "Nine, ten, ____ fat hen"
12 Rainbow's end?
13 Pen
14 With a grain ____
15 Intimate chat
16 Virginia willow
17 Stitched
20 Jayhawked
24 New Guinea, to Indonesians
27 Close
29 Knee bend, in ballet
31 Warhol
33 Part of T.A.E.
34 Sub detector
35 General assemblies
36 Med. subject
37 Gaseous hydrocarbon
38 Wildcat
39 Control
42 First name of Toland's subject
43 "____, Moses . . ."
46 Fire escapes
49 Formal mall
52 Irritate
53 "____ Will," Frost book
54 Hawkeye State
55 Whitman's home in N.J.
57 Records
58 Farmer's frustration
59 Famed dukedom in Spain
60 Musical mark
62 Jubilant
63 Angle irons
64 Phrase of intimacy
68 To be: Sp.
69 Author of "The White Company"
70 Safecracker
71 Type style: Abbr.
72 What sidekicks do
73 John Hancock
74 Spanish linen
77 Cargo
78 Decorate
79 Harding and Sheridan
81 Adjective for an age
83 U.S. missile
84 Court cry
85 Red ____ (alders)
86 Soft-shell clam
89 Wild dogs of India
92 Suffix with compliment
94 Directive
95 Stone marker
96 Lily plant
97 Trudge
99 Best of the movies
100 To-do
101 Advocate strongly
102 English river
104 Catch
105 R.R. depot

80. Turning Phrases by Jordan S. Lasher

ACROSS

1 Rose essence
6 Hermit or Alaska king
10 Prefix with fix
13 Seal
19 In
20 Ancient Jewish scholars
22 Lobster ____
23 Chianti's morning-after legacy
25 Shake-roll connection
26 Tenor role in "The Snow Maiden"
27 Resourceful
28 Coronation of June 2, 1953
30 French cordial flavoring
32 Formerly
33 Last year's jrs.
34 Eagerly awaiting
35 Yegg's target
36 Anterooms
38 Judge's seat
40 Hua's predecessor
43 Turn out
45 Scandinavian's idols
51 Get on
52 Love affair
55 Hit a high fly
56 Feminists' bill
57 Kind of pity
58 British knight
59 Norwegian composer
60 Nobelist in Literature: 1957
62 Prophecy of a sort
64 Salt Lake City team
67 Wilde was one
68 Irascible
71 Of yore
74 Morsels
76 Lehar opus: 1911
77 Pecking wood, e.g.
82 Cheer
83 Schism
85 Ayesha
86 Smith and Jones
87 Singular
88 At a distance
90 Shankar
94 Conquerors of matter
95 Ex ____ (one-sided)
97 City on the Dvina
100 Trig function
102 A.F.L.'s complement
103 Oscar winner: 1942
104 Mom
109 Chekhov
110 Up on one's vocabulary
111 Guzzle
112 Wee hour
113 Observed
114 City once called Pig's Eye
118 Numerical prefix
121 New World: Abbr.
123 Hole puncher
126 Sun: Prefix
127 Inn unit
128 Ill
133 Puts on guard
136 W.W. II vessel
137 Familiar with
138 Citation at ophiology convention?
141 London's Haymarket, e.g.
142 Extends
143 In a senectuous way
144 Relaxing
145 Plant
146 Social-athletic org.
147 Curtis and Perkins

DOWN

1 Greek Minerva
2 Office routine
3 Haul
4 Hog plum of India
5 Peruse
6 Handpicked
7 Roof beam
8 Dispute: Abbr.
9 Avifauna
10 Famed diarist
11 Hesperus's undoing
12 He, in Genoa
13 Withdrawn at Belmont
14 Thief of Baghdad, e.g.
15 Costume
16 Sol or ela
17 She, in Marseille
18 High schooler
19 Rand's "____ Shrugged"
20 Like a $3 bill
21 River to the Moselle
24 March
29 ____ gamut (ranged)
31 Group of 100
36 Elmer of the comics
37 N.C.O.
38 Hit show: Slang
39 Stern
40 Bleat
41 Showery mo.
42 Elect
44 Saturate
46 Vowels or whirlwinds
47 Stowe novel
48 Unaccompanied
49 "Woe," to Caesar
50 Slowly, in music
51 Where Sucre is
52 More farinaceous
53 Helmet of old
54 Bull: Prefix
55 Frown
60 Irish seaport
61 Wife of Thor
63 Pilotless aircraft
65 Line fluffs in "All's Well"
66 Famed suffragist
69 Owns
70 Syringe amts.
72 Tragacanths
73 Pay dirt
75 Luster
78 Grog
79 Conductor Leinsdorf
80 Broadway hit
81 Sevilla's land
84 Late: Sp.
89 River of Orange Free State
91 Very pale
92 Opinion
93 Dope
96 "____ art's sake"
98 Shrub of beet family
99 ____ fashion (haphazardly)
101 Corn unit
103 Caesar's conquest
104 Trinidad's loc.
105 Inlet
106 Doctrine
107 Tea, in Toulon
108 Six-pointers: Abbr.
111 Riding whip
115 Roof covering
116 Jai alai ball
117 Hebrew letters
119 Bottom lines
120 Recess for holding vestments
121 Confuse
122 Groves on prairies
123 Sign symbol
124 Rivaled Niobe
125 Suspicious
128 Caspian feeder
129 "Lord, ____ I?": Matt. 26:22
130 In proximity
131 Recipe amts.
132 Protagonist
134 Which or who
135 Utah's lily
139 Thai river
140 Itch

81. Tall Titles by Maura B. Jacobson

ACROSS

1 Eden fugitive
5 Plays the horses
9 Genoese statesman
14 Critical comment
18 "M*A*S*H" star
19 Friend of Aramis
21 Wielding
22 "Rubáiyát" author
23 Meadow medley
24 ESP almanac
27 Life sign
29 Italian fabric
30 Probed
31 Clay, today
33 Aids for acquiring lore
35 Vane reading
36 First-aid manual
41 Fez ornament
46 Female ruff
47 Honkers
48 Juliette Low's org.
50 Western resort
51 Blue dyes
54 Bakery buys
56 Cacophonies
57 Less usual
58 Phone cut-in
61 Bread spreads
62 Slip-up
63 Landlord's paper work
65 An Athenian and a constellation
67 "____ a Nightingale"
69 Work unit
70 Cultists tell all
73 U.S. law group
76 Moslem ruler
78 Bogart role
79 Author Zweig
81 Tower site
83 "Of Thee ____"
85 Sellout sign
87 Homophone for wood
88 Refluxes
89 Jai alai item
90 Engines
92 Helps along
94 Exist
95 Laborite Ernest
98 Card game
99 Vaughan and Caldwell
101 Guide to nude beaches
106 Roulette bet
108 Partner of fits
109 Suffix with outrage and umbrage
110 Stances
115 Stem covering
116 Supply with funds
120 Handbook for careful pilots
124 Greek hero
125 Met basso Flagello
126 "Rights of Man" author
127 Engraved pillar
128 Emulate Petruchio
129 Ennis and Crandall
130 Saint ____ fire
131 Jacob's twin
132 Mesozoic and Cenozoic

DOWN

1 Bivouac
2 Matty of baseball
3 Adored one
4 Bahamian capital
5 Pipistrelle
6 Biblical verb ending
7 Lloyd C. Douglas opus
8 In ____ (to the extent that)
9 Chaperon
10 Donovan's gp.
11 Social reformer
12 "Bus Stop" author and kin
13 Amazed
14 Pear
15 Delhi nanny
16 Tantrum
17 Flat nail
20 Well-groomed
25 Map line
26 Pick up the tab
28 O'Neill tree
32 Othello's aide
34 Sets upon
36 Meadowlark's relative
37 Body-shop problem
38 Memoirs of a gossip columnist
39 Vespiary, e.g.
40 This, in Toledo
42 Cairo bigwig
43 Tale of a tanker
44 Ages and ages
45 ____-majesté
49 Org.
52 Plural ending
53 Humperdinck heroine
54 "She Stoops ____" (tall dancer's bio)
55 On high
59 Aide to a C.O.
60 They give their word
62 "____ forget"
64 Haggard title
66 Having: Fr.
68 Skid row affliction
71 Jong
72 Always, in poems
74 "Cat ____"
75 "Dombey ____"
77 Perle
80 Dawn goddess
81 Arthur and Lillie
82 Eban of Israel
84 Nish native
86 Host at Valhalla
91 "____ the valley of Death . . ."
93 Landscaper's buy
95 Yogi's family
96 Cold-war antidote
97 Countenances
100 Ruana's kin
102 Makes up for
103 Taylor, for short
104 Czech reformer
105 Squire's domain
107 Paste-on
110 Supplicated
111 Marsh or bog
112 Besmirch
113 Ring victories
114 Read cursorily
117 Not fully closed
118 The Hindu Cupid
119 Former mates
121 Mythical princess
122 Neighbor of Ga.
123 L.A. pitcher: 1972–79

82. Fire and Ice by Kenneth Haxton

ACROSS

1 Rid of frost
6 English draft horses
12 U.S.-U.S.S.R. negotiations
16 Gardenia, for one
20 Boredom
21 Straightforward
22 Layer of the iris
23 Mideastern citizen
24 Snub
26 What firemen do
28 Word of regret
29 Booted one
30 Protection
32 Stick to
33 Time of light
34 Type of jury
35 Kidded
36 Broadway hit
37 Where Orpheus almost triumphed
38 Hock and sack
39 The Fourth Estate
40 Where Mrs. Stowe lived
43 Pulitzer Prize poet: 1924
45 Hijack
48 No longer immaculate
49 Tanned, in a way
50 Like Bo Peep's sheep
51 Mexican's wherewithal
52 Like U.S.A.F. messages
53 Followed one's trade
54 Gather
56 One of the media
57 "____ tale's best for winter": Shak.
58 Breakfast fiber
59 High dudgeon
60 TV newsman
61 Flavius's foot
62 Oscar winner in 1975
66 Top dogs in college
67 Close
69 Thesmothete
70 Tap
71 Equine ophthalmia
73 Cordial greeting
75 Peck role, for short
78 Eric Blair's pen name
79 Goatlike creature
80 "Trinity" author
81 "Nor iron bars a ____"
82 Indian princes
83 Ballet ____
84 Lithuanian port: Ger.
86 Luce subject
87 Siouan Indians
88 Wrongful act
89 Evangelist McPherson
90 Voiced
91 Beak
92 White elephant of a sort
95 Certifies
96 Region, to Shelley
97 Gravelly ridge
98 Maverick
99 Three-base hits
101 Afghan V.I.P.
102 Tacitus's tongue
103 Cartoonist Gardner
106 "The Count of Monte ____"
107 Massage
108 Town retaken by Joan of Arc: 1430
109 Cheats
110 Bushmen's kin
112 "To ____ let virtue be as wax": Hamlet
115 Had the misery
116 Heckelphone's cousin
117 Wife abandoned by Paris
118 Tidal flood
119 Legal equal
120 Pigs' abodes
121 Former capital of Brittany
122 Dutch genre painter

DOWN

1 Ten
2 Suburb of Harrisburg
3 Tooth adjunct
4 Rechewable items
5 Cold cubes in Köln
6 U.S. marathon runner
7 Moslem maidens in Paradise
8 Bayou
9 Mr. Foxx
10 Native: Suffix
11 Under great tension
12 Intimate
13 Eschew
14 Porter's "____ Do It"
15 The way, in China
16 Kin of the Poncas
17 Stuns
18 Burden, in Bologna
19 Upturn
23 Adjective for Methuselah
25 Paid attention
27 Least furnished
31 At all
34 Did road work
35 Agreed
36 Coarse
37 Sank a putt
38 Was clad in
39 Bacon's forte
40 Songwriters' org.
41 Slipknot
42 Flimflammed with flattery
43 Regretful
44 Gonfalons
45 Tucker and predecessors
46 American dogwood
47 Louts
49 Wine-honey-spice drink
51 Cookout spot
53 Lunar
54 Hood's missile
55 Shelly, the drummer
56 Buffalo's home
58 Semiprecious stone
60 Champagne center
62 Scottish highlanders
63 "His hands were hairy, as his brother ____ hands": Gen. 27:23
64 Carried along
65 Einstein's birthplace
66 Damage
68 Trojan hero: Var.
70 Rock debris
71 Oligophrenic
72 Speak floridly
73 Squander
74 "The Pawnbroker" director
76 Facient
77 Piggy-bank fillers
79 Fodder plant
81 Little chief hare
83 Hostelry sign
84 Marner, for one
85 Legendary Irish beauty
86 Wagnerian god
88 Salamander
89 "You ____ It" (former TV show)
90 Sequence
92 Grooved
93 Avengers
94 Out of port
95 Brings into harmony
96 English fruit hawker
98 Brackish
99 Italian philosopher
100 Agile
101 Composer Bruckner
102 Bad buy
103 Maquillage item
104 ____ nous
105 Pale
106 Fellow
107 Honshu port
108 "Buddenbrooks" author
109 Blazer
111 Zenith
113 Golfer Trevino
114 Truckler's reply

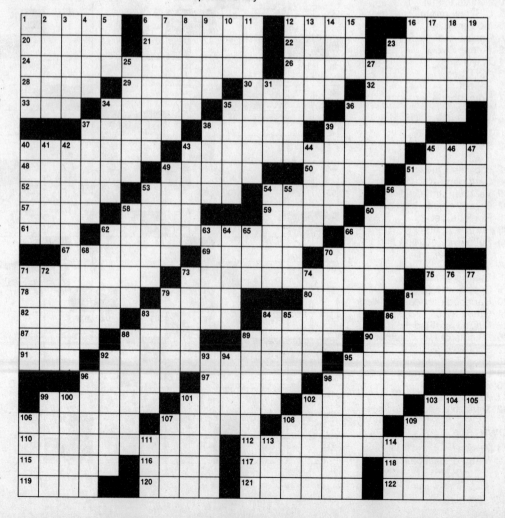

83. Alphabetical Acrobatics by Alfio Micci

ACROSS

1 Frolic
5 Flat cap
10 Certification
15 Like some cellars
19 Sioux
20 Famed Polish soprano
21 Norse pantheon gods
22 Great Lake
23 Crèche figures
25 Question for Brother John
27 Portable stove
28 Gold Coast republic
30 Oozes
31 Goes astray
32 Color of natural wool
33 Except
34 Perfumed bag
37 Ancient: Comb. form
38 Coastal dweller
43 Musketeer
44 Start of a famed soliloquy
46 Wrath
47 Believe, old style
48 Rational
49 Waistcoat
50 Landing craft
51 Evergreen
52 American novelist
56 Attack
57 Certain tires
60 Persian sprite
61 Slants
62 Ponderous
63 Happened
64 Wined and dined
65 "Wreck of the Mary ____"
66 Adjective ending
67 Touching
70 "Papa" of music
71 Blowguns
73 Abode: Abbr.
74 Regarding
75 Nigerian people
77 Familiar and cozy
78 Obnoxious one
79 Coin of old
80 Exam category
84 Form of croquet
85 Canine specialists
87 Actress Ellen
88 Clergymen's digs
89 P.I. native
90 Razor clam
91 Gasp for breath
92 A.R.C. founder
95 Horrify
96 S.A. dances
100 Certain testifiers
102 English ritual
104 Carter's Attorney General
105 Mideast hot spot
106 Scandinavians
107 ____ bene
108 Trifling
109 Derision
110 Administered medicine
111 Tore

DOWN

1 Philip or Lillian
2 Roman emperor: A.D. 69
3 Comedian Sahl
4 Raree

5 "Thanatopsis" poet
6 Bridge positions
7 Hoar
8 Compass reading
9 Citrus hybrid
10 Model
11 See former classmates
12 Greek peak
13 OPEC's concern
14 Plunder
15 Send with authority
16 Saharan
17 Sayers's "The ____ Tailors"
18 Beer containers
24 Faure and Wiesel
26 Region beyond city limits
29 Yesterday, in Paris
32 Din
34 Goatish god
35 Up ____ (at a disadvantage)
36 Line re a certain threesome
37 Hollow ringing sounds
38 Mulligan, for one

39 Alts.
40 Had lapses onstage
41 Soviet cooperative
42 Cozy retreats
44 Actress Jessica
45 Egglike
48 Bondsman
50 Embankment
53 Beat ____ to (make for hastily)
54 Tragicomic, for short
55 El or José
56 One of the "Little Women"
58 Novelist Charles ____: 1814–84
59 Merit
61 Ross or Palmer
63 Famed actress, Mrs. ____
64 Acreage
65 Reel
67 Garden bloomer
68 Offspring
69 Whales
70 Went in haste
71 Papal name

72 Prickle
75 Casual unconcern
76 Often: Abbr.
78 Boats used as bridge supports
80 Repress
81 Visits briefly
82 Tissue
83 Milesian's country
84 Arrested
86 Spill the beans
88 Spoiled
90 Asparagus unit
91 Country, in Calabria
92 Actress Andersson
93 Struck with wonder
94 Streamlet
95 Donkey, in Durango
96 Hubs: Abbr.
97 Hen's domain
98 Feed the kitty
99 African village
101 Abélard's "____ et Non"
103 ____ yong (Chinese omelet)

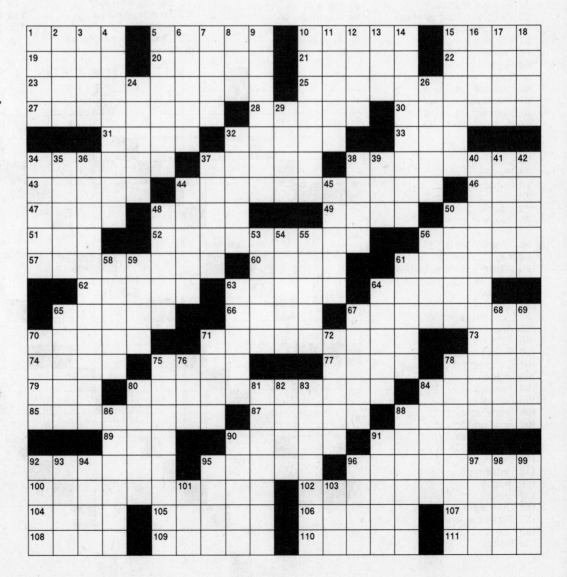

84. Fore! by William Lutwiniak

ACROSS

1 Man: Comb. form
6 Tumbler
11 Moth's bête noire
16 Settled
21 Crazy Horse, e.g.
22 Fortification
23 Mountain ash
24 Neighbor of Sverige
25 Woods
29 English horn's cousin
30 Organic compound
31 Distrustful
32 Traffic circle
33 Thrice, in prescriptions
34 Scriven
35 Prom queen
36 Bring down the house
37 Nephew of Daedalus
38 Cabbage or spinach
39 Overlord
43 Shuts in
46 Perplexed
47 "Great!"
48 Between L and P
49 Traps
52 Illicit gains
53 Being, to Juan
54 Window feature
55 Word with land or water
56 Seine feeder
57 Echidna's meal
58 Lower
60 Rural crossover
62 Erose
63 Allen or Ott
64 Arabic letter
65 Former U.N. head
66 "___ siamo," Verdi aria
67 Irons
75 Footnote abbr.
76 Carts
77 Hustles
78 Unhackneyed
79 Got an eyeful
82 Sizable
83 Between
85 Libertine
86 Kitchen utensil
87 Alpaca's habitat
88 Where poteen is distilled
89 River of Czechoslovakia
90 Retired
91 Links
97 ___ tee (exactly)
98 African ferryboats
99 Asch book
100 Sylvan tracts
101 Campus group
103 Infiltrators
104 Tangled
105 Barrett or Jaffe
106 Implacable
107 Folic and formic
108 Unprocessed
111 Be ambitious
114 Lamina
115 Protuberance
116 Ankles
117 Eagles
121 Overcost for tribute
122 Tureen adjunct
123 "Le ___ d'Arthur"
124 Reform
125 Sample
126 Schussed
127 Fall fabric
128 Untidy

DOWN

1 "___ in the Dark"
2 Classical weeper
3 Sad state
4 Straightedge
5 Chemical prefix
6 Elegantly: Mus. dir.
7 Dormice
8 Confuse
9 Nestorian
10 Older: Abbr.
11 Sponge
12 Desolate
13 On to
14 Plurality
15 Pass-catcher
16 Sleepyhead
17 Be unstable
18 Ionian Sea inlet
19 Stravinsky
20 Gainsay
26 Section of N.Y.C.
27 Field hockey team
28 Amok
34 Cautious
35 ___ metabolism
36 Amritsar money
37 TV repairman's stock
38 Memorial pillar
39 Glove material
40 In with
41 Hole-___
42 Remarked
43 Construction members
44 Originator of Eur. Common Market
45 Blotch
46 In statu quo
47 Refuse
50 Service acad.
51 Overcharge
52 Straight thinking
56 Gridiron units
58 Cold
59 Flicker, e.g.
60 Coruscated
61 Greek letters
62 Actress Leigh
64 Caution light
65 Orderly
66 Rue de la ___
68 Broadcast
69 Overshadows
70 Why, in Bonn
71 Object
72 Battery terminals
73 French pointillist
74 Pinches
79 Obsolescent footwear
80 Proscribed
81 In the back
82 Southpaw
83 Prosecutes
84 Takes the cake
85 Spur adjunct
87 ___ Arenas, Chilean port
88 Ruhr city
91 Invented
92 Drove
93 Reception
94 Swore
95 Tickle the keys idly
96 Joanne et al.
98 Divide proportionately
102 East
103 Unvarying
104 Sharpened
106 Old Italian money
107 Pianist-composer Previn
108 Sprints
109 Alda and King
110 Bombastic
111 Didion's "Play It ___ Lays"
112 Humane org.
113 J.E.C.
114 Immerse
115 "Never send to ___ . . ."
116 Occasion
118 Metric units: Abbr.
119 Danish district
120 L.A. athlete

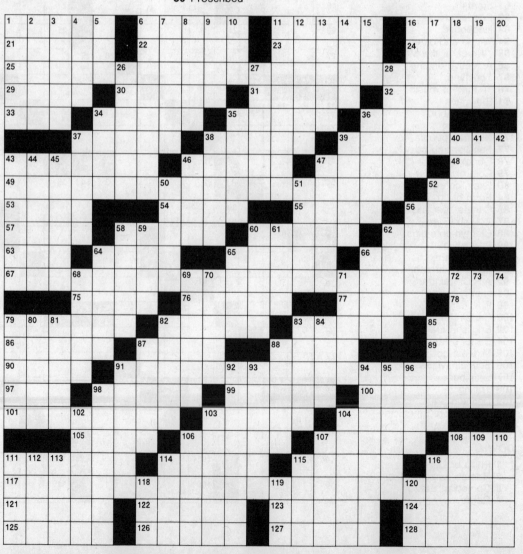

85. Palm Reading by Tap Osborn

ACROSS

1 Wherewithal
5 Fifth wheel
10 Wonder drug
14 D-day craft
18 Italian harps
19 Debussy's "____"
20 Seaver's bailiwick
21 State or city in Brazil
22 Palm
24 Palmate
26 Veranda in Oahu
27 "Rule Britannia" composer
28 Palm part
29 Upper crust
30 Wellington, to Napoleon
31 "____ the ramparts . . ."
32 Run-of-the-mill
33 But, to Brutus
34 Baum marten
35 Indy "500"
37 Sneak attack
41 For shame!
43 Family member
44 Pavlov
45 Al of films
47 Battle site: 1862
50 Blacksmiths, at times
52 Tooth: Comb. form
53 Part of A.E.C.
54 Get ____ of oneself
55 Member of a certain college
56 Peace or Marine
57 Statue garment
58 Dwindle
60 "____ Perpetua," Idaho motto
61 Palmer is one
63 "How like ____ . . .": Shak.
67 Kind of blind
69 Balbo
70 Part of a mart
71 Raised aloft
74 Madras, e.g.
75 Lark
76 "Riders to ____," Synge play
77 Poorly done
79 Letterpress worker
80 Feminist, colloquially
81 Father-in-law of Esau
82 Truth, Chinese style
83 Guileful
84 Composer Speaks
85 Pure and simple
86 Part of H.R.H.
87 Nabokov title
89 Middle-age spread
93 Timetable abbr.
94 Morsel for Seattle Slew
95 N.C.O.'s
98 Palmistry
102 Indira's gown
103 Ho Chi Minh's capital
104 Apparel made from palm-like plants
105 Palmy
107 Quibble
108 ____ Hopkins, Continental Navy leader
109 Dispur is its capital
110 Pandora's escapees
111 Origin
112 Sturdy boat
113 Salad days
114 Vortex

DOWN

1 Kind of stitch
2 Of space
3 Palma
4 Underworld goddess
5 Road sign
6 Candle sealer
7 In love
8 Conductor from Hungary
9 Contemporary of Dashiell
10 ____ maple, or box elder
11 Pullman
12 N.C. neighbor
13 Place guarded by Cerberus
14 Palm
15 Matador's cloak
16 Tare's partner
17 Marquis de ____
21 Tribal heads: Abbr.
23 Scurried
25 ____ Canals
31 Palmer
36 Letters
38 Solecism
39 Divider's word
40 Spot for a slot
41 Footprint
42 Two Roman statesmen
43 Micmac's cousin
45 Salk's target
46 Gulf of ____
48 Palms off
49 Prefix with prove or solve
50 Ben, the artist
51 Shoshonean
54 U.N. leader in 1948
55 Sic
57 Stowe novel
58 Grayish
59 Boggs or Irwin
61 Hindmost
62 Eskimo town near Thule
64 Palmer
65 Bay window
66 Criticize severely
68 Algonquian
70 Hit-show sign
71 Town on the Vire
72 Harris or Silvers
73 Goddess of youth
74 Sight on a clear night
75 To's partner
77 Socko!
78 Short play
79 Zealous advocate
82 Garden favorite
86 Throaty
87 Wimbledon champ: 1975
88 Sweetie pie
90 Capital of Togo
91 Physicians' org.
92 Exclaimed one's disdain
96 Elliot or Jay
97 Timid one
98 Auditors: Abbr.
99 One of the leporids
100 "Picnic" author
101 Ovid
102 Young oyster
106 Heath and Eden: Abbr.

86. Flowery Speech by A. J. Santora

ACROSS

1 Iniquity
5 Shaded walk
12 "There is ____ in the affairs . . ."
17 Kind of scale or test
18 Seats of taste
19 Pansy
23 Yellow violet
25 Forget-me-not
26 Others, to Dante
27 "A wither'd violet is her ____"
28 Rice dish
30 White ____ ("youthful innocence")
31 Fishline sinker
32 Reedlike grass
33 Pinchfist
34 Hubby's
35 Affirmative vote
36 Andy's partner
38 ____ bag (pitching aid)
39 "Pure and lovely," if red
43 His emblem is the thistle flower
44 Part of "A Loss of Roses"
46 Inclination
48 Yoko from Tokyo
49 Japanese city
52 Printshop worker
53 Dam
54 Agitated state
55 Signet
56 Deep red rose
60 He succeeded Nasser
61 White chrysanthemum
63 Bicycle part
64 Items of interest
65 Petulant
66 Easter oval
67 Love affair
69 Leeds's river
72 Seabee motto
73 Doe, in Düren
74 Thornless rose
78 The G-men
81 Like old jokes
83 Kind of tide
84 Pour ____ dire (so to speak): Fr.
85 Youngster
86 Worcester and York
88 Health resort
90 Pollute
92 Lasso
94 Soft, as a sound
95 Blue violet or heliotrope
99 Sheep genus
100 Réunion and Corse
101 Billboard
102 Inventor Pliny ____
103 Phase
105 High railways
106 Key dice throw
107 Regions
108 Crops
109 Cockade
111 After, in Arles
113 In this place
114 Troublesome
117 O.T. book
118 Rabbit tails
119 Sheepskin clutcher

121 "Adonais" is one
123 Hoofed animal
126 Max and Buddy
127 Garment for Gandhi
128 Man-____
129 Blue crocus
131 Peach blossom
134 French marigold or yellow rose
135 Italian port
136 Celebrate Alumni Day
137 Perfume ingredient
138 Leavened
139 Instance

DOWN

1 Green mint
2 Walking arm ____
3 Bachelor's button
4 Numerical ending
5 "Temptation" is their word
6 Rabbit fur
7 Tilting, as a ship
8 Fortifies
9 Fleur season
10 Contemnors
11 Town of St. Francis
12 Rose oil
13 Done, for short
14 Gambling note
15 Swordsman
16 Notre Dame de Paris, e.g.
17 Ruffian
20 Londoner's day off
21 Tenn. power project
22 Part of a min.
23 ____ Nui (Easter Island)
24 Monastery head
29 Photographer
33 Commercial alloy
34 Sharpen
37 Biblical land
38 Adjust
39 Recherché
40 Yellow honeysuckle
41 Eastern Catholic
42 Tetched
43 Dregs
44 Starlike
45 Barroom
47 Dalai ____
49 "Variety" is its word
50 Suit fabric
51 Yellow sunflower
54 Uttered
57 "____ to the wise . . ."
58 Synagogue
59 Hic, ____, hoc
60 Submitted
62 Inheritor, in law
65 Rooters
68 Daisy and Winnie
70 Give ____ try
71 Ecstasies
72 Piggy-bank money
75 Med. school subject
76 Army base in Alaska
77 Colliery
79 Irreducible
80 That is: Lat.
82 "Message" is its message

86 More cunning
87 Greeting
88 "Domestic virtue" is its phrase
89 Ship's boat
91 ____ breve
93 Apologetic exclamation
95 ____-fingered ivy
96 "Kind ____ more than coronets"
97 Bus riders
98 European coal basin
101 Clockmaker Thomas
104 It speaks of "delicate pleasures"
106 Recording systems
108 Doc
110 Quarantine
112 White lily
113 Basil
114 Four-leaf clover
115 Century plant
116 Unit of force
118 Butterfly
119 Poltergeist
120 Way
122 It signifies "eloquence"
123 ____ Mahal
124 Ribicoff
125 ____ hemp
126 Make ground tests
127 Hennas
130 Pecan
132 Miss Farrow
133 Curve

87. First Sign by Richard Silvestri

ACROSS

1 Milk, in Metz
5 Precinct
9 Hope
12 Cleopatra's craft
17 Recoil
18 Mineral made into jewelry
20 Deli offering
21 Go-betweens
23 Parnassian regions
24 Roman Helios
25 Lord's domain
26 Touched down
27 York or Dark
28 Krypton is one
30 Relative of a pompano
31 Pershing's command
32 Dried up
33 Group honored in April
39 Descartes's conclusion
42 Calendar abbr.
43 Foray
44 "How now! ____?": Hamlet
45 Flesh: Comb. form
46 A.M.A. members
47 Pod inhabitants
49 Break off
51 ____ Hari
52 Likely to collapse
55 Arrive
56 Indy entry
59 Bien-____ (Fr. darling)
60 Oregon or Santa Fe
61 Ill will
62 Sweet potato
64 Like a cliché
65 Dueler's choice
66 Maximally
67 Rental contract
68 David or Edwards
69 Clear
70 Money in Moscow
71 Spies
73 Bellow
74 "Ashcan" painter
76 Trap material
77 C.P.A.'s record
80 Osprey's cousin
81 Serb or Sorb
82 "Great Commoner"
84 Rebuff
86 "The Big Apple"
87 Minute vessels
91 Polish
92 Singing syllable
94 Fish dish
95 Rigby of songdom
97 Ranks
99 Geyserite
100 Filleted
102 The horned horse
103 Ought to
104 Roman Catholic tribunals
107 Makes happen
108 Lion, to impala
109 Taut
110 Atlas extra
111 Gas: Comb. form
112 On one's guard
113 Ham's companion

DOWN

1 Floor covering
2 Like a deer
3 Hockey milieu
4 Called
5 Ten-percenters
6 Renovate
7 Arabian prince
8 ____ rule (usually)
9 "We ____ different de-grees": Emerson
10 Geographic hub of N.Y.
11 Met basso
12 Balloonist's need
13 Animate
14 Offshoot
15 F.B.I. employees
16 Herr's word for 3 Down
17 Most like Solomon
19 Outlined
20 ____ Fell Pike (England's highest point)
22 Game counter
29 Military meal
30 ____ Lanka (Ceylon)
34 Clear the board
35 Ready money
36 Tangle or disentangle
37 Anger
38 Where the stapes is
40 Magazine piece
41 Least magnanimous
47 Makeup
48 Lazarus or Eames
49 Emulates Hamill
50 Nobelist Metchnikoff
51 Go soft
52 Employee's delight
53 "Take the ____," 1941 song
54 Stand used for shaping tiles
55 Sounds of surprise
56 Make vulgar
57 Statistician of a kind
58 Rude and boisterous
61 Acted the buffoon
63 Croissant
64 Melodic subject
65 Travail
67 Pope in 928
68 Rickety airplane
72 Wine city
74 Suburb of Rabat
75 Wash against the shore
77 The Somalis
78 Kind of vine
79 Nun's relative
81 Rutgers' ____ Knights
82 Wan
83 Tax agcy.
85 Read carefully
88 Balzac's "____ Goriot"
89 Near-perfect horseshoe pitch
90 Soldier on watch
91 Composed
93 Employ again
96 Garland
97 Comparative word
98 Campus org. active in the 60's
99 Czech stream: Ger. spelling
100 Letter on a key
101 ____ about
103 Biol. or chem.
105 Shooter
106 Between lge. and sml.

88. Aviary by Christopher Busch

ACROSS

1 N.Y.C. skyline letters
4 Berry-bearing
11 St. Louis Cardinal
18 Corvine sound
21 Fish-eating flier
22 A.L. team
23 Adm. Byrd was one
24 Castilian rah
25 Owners of 21 merit badges
27 Horripilation symptom
29 Villain's trademark
30 Auk genus
31 Nelsons
32 In high spirits
33 Like a snipefish
34 Seed for a plot
35 Purplish color
36 Lord or vassal
37 Rise high
38 Beatrice's idolater
39 Acct.
42 Stowe novel
43 Aquatint specialists
47 High ____
48 Hug
50 Fetters
51 Pseudo-esthetic
52 March style
56 Fra ____ Lippi
57 Kokomo product
59 Delays
60 Potter's clay
62 Author Eliav
63 Ornamental plume
65 Emergency funds
67 Eagles' objectives
68 Concoct
69 Play by Noyes: 1915
71 Busy
72 Clerical degree
74 What one has at the top
79 ____ volente
80 Northern
82 Rational
83 Algerian seaport
84 Certain articles
86 Curved pipe
89 Nags
92 Aleutian island
93 Broadway hit
94 Selassie
96 Literally, that is
97 Leader after Pericles
98 Coloraturas
100 Agitated state
101 Round Table knight
102 ____ Peak, U.S.S.R.
103 Blanc and Cenis
104 Jack Dempsey's birthplace
105 Hacks
109 Bath, for one
110 Sudanese group
111 Chore
112 Christmastides
114 Fountain drinks
115 Carefree adventure
116 Timberlane of fiction
120 Ground down
122 Hall of Fame pitcher
123 Dispatched
124 Lone Ranger's sidekick
125 Carroll and Orwell
127 Pride or envy
129 Palindromic word
130 Egg part
131 Gov. Babbitt's bailiwick
132 ". . . and Memories of ____": Poe
133 Small boy
134 Homesteaders
135 In a vile manner
136 Female ruff

DOWN

1 Warbler from Detroit
2 Rubberneck
3 Financial backer
4 Transvaal settler
5 Horace's "____ Poetica"
6 Winged insects
7 Office fixture
8 Bastard wing
9 Brains, in Brest
10 Curve
11 Stews
12 Unfold
13 Electron tube
14 Ramfis, in "Aïda"
15 Ending with graph and cord
16 Lanyard
17 Military exercise
18 Whirlybird
19 State without proof
20 Pulled out the spurry
26 Rocketry expert
28 "Downstairs" character
31 Tear drier, for short
34 Endings with court and front
35 Bird's back, wings, etc.
37 Slots spot
38 More calamitous
39 Joker
40 Outmoded
41 Chemical suffix
43 Brilliance
44 Falcons' concerns
45 Bird site in California
46 Wrestling throw
47 German riflemen
48 Bill's follower
49 Precollege exams: Abbr.
52 Bird of prey
53 Road gripper
54 Whirlybirds
55 Walks with heels turned out
57 VW competitor
58 Maori figurine
59 Prop up
61 London bourse: Abbr.
64 Made of wood
66 Cut
68 Gander or drake
70 Stilts' kin
73 ____-Liétard, Fr. mining town
75 Arlene and Roald
76 Koko's weapon
77 Annoys
78 Cardinal point
80 Org. for 25 Across
81 Lay ____ (fail)
85 Isles in Malay Archipelago
87 Bird sound
88 Destiny
90 Feathers
91 Archie's "dingbat"
92 Alan or Robert
95 Courtroom vow
97 Knock out
99 ____-relief
100 Gannet
101 Domino
103 Toledo team
104 Cocktail
105 Young swan
106 Dawn
107 Found fault with
108 Hardens, as cement
110 Frothy wave
111 Two-seated carriage
113 City on the Meuse
114 Mass of fine bubbles
115 Writer Jones
116 Mountain pass
117 Goose genus
118 Rural crossing
119 Weatherman's device
121 Cancel
122 Slovenly woman
123 Satiric comedian
124 Order or arrangement: Suffix
126 Romantic poet's monogram
127 Hdqrs.
128 Goose egg

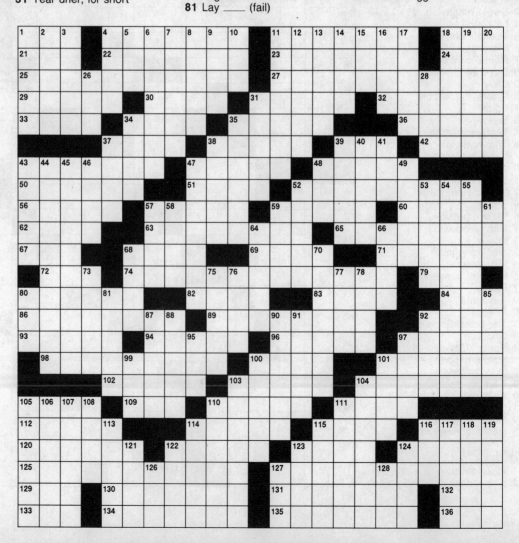

89. Circles in the Square by Jeanette K. Brill

(The circled squares from left to right, starting at the top, contain a quotation.)

ACROSS

1 Indian princes
6 Deficiency
10 Cockles
15 Cordon bleu
19 Father of Shamgar
20 Dust bowl fugitive
21 Raven's cry
22 Gounod contemporary
23 Person to whom quotation is attributed
25 Metric measure
27 Ancient ascetics
28 California city east of L.A.
30 Like some currents
31 Will subject
33 Hebrew months
35 Sites of knights' fights
36 Top gallant
38 ____ soul (contract with Satan)
41 Soft mineral
43 Commercials
44 Confine
45 Carnival lure
49 Cacophony
51 Detect
52 Former German coin
54 Wine: Comb. form
55 Teem
57 Brahmin
59 Candid
60 Layer
61 Long-shot odds
63 ". . . swift ____ radiant ends": Watson
65 Baghdad's country: Var.
66 Aspen or alder
67 Famed ex-jockey
68 Yorkshireman: Var.
70 Valenciennes, e.g.
73 Pitched woo
75 Fountain drinks
79 African cypress pine
80 Notch made by a saw
81 Allowance for waste
83 Easter shrub
84 Sow's home
85 Hanging jar at Navidad
87 Greek letters
89 Falling short of
90 Clinic clientele
92 Quotation source
95 Violinist ____ Bull
96 Strike hard
97 Arm armor
98 Dirk of yore
99 "Lonesome George"
102 Resort, for short
104 Formosa
106 Accrues
108 Keats and Sappho
111 Cargo carrier's charge
114 Passed bills
116 Of kinship
118 Gershwin's "____, Lucille"
119 Moving force
120 Osmund, for one
121 Clare and Henry
122 British machine gun
123 ____ Alegre, Brazil
124 Hang fire
125 Carved stone pillar

DOWN

1 Form by carving
2 Table-talk items
3 Impromptu jazz performance
4 Relaxing
5 Negative contraction
6 Seafood delicacies
7 Hawaiian fish
8 Diam. × 3.1416
9 Game akin to lotto
10 The West
11 Spheres of action
12 Sub detector
13 Use a shuttle
14 Mishap on ice
15 Synod attendees
16 Execrates
17 Choose
18 Dix and Knox
24 Beer ingredient
26 Author of 92 Across
29 Spire attachment
32 Pass
34 Slender dagger
36 ____-arms (soldier)
37 Sun-dried brick
39 Matinee idol
40 Upholstered footstool
42 Pharyngeal tissues
44 Madrileño
45 Enervates
46 Beneficiary
47 Draft status
48 Employment
50 Gold Rush name
53 Fine oilstone
56 Soft leather gloves
58 Author of "John Brown's Body"
60 Haberdashery item
62 Potion to dull sorrow
64 Formal speech
67 Kindhearted
69 Utterly defeated
70 Finn's neighbor
71 Field
72 Jargon
74 Domesday Book money
75 "____ Mater"
76 Decree
77 Elizabethan dramatist
78 Hindu garment
82 Numerical suffixes
85 Norman Vincent and Rembrandt
86 "____ Dream," 1937 song
88 Stately court dance
91 Basque's possible ancestor
93 Smith and Fleming
94 Dostoyevsky novel with "The"
97 Two-pronged weapon
98 Stayed to the end
99 Fish organs
100 ____ a time (singly)
101 G.I.'s "alarm clock"
103 Campaign target
105 Ululates
107 Affront
109 Jaunt
110 Arid
112 Author Greene
113 "Born Free" heroine
115 Short follower of long
117 Chaney or Nol

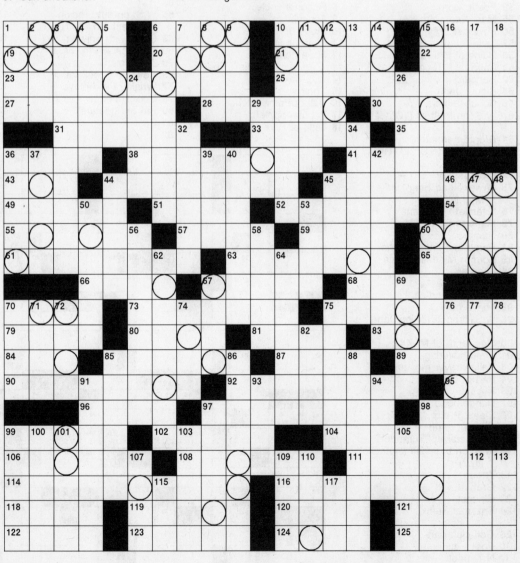

90. Shakespeare on Sports by Bert Rosenfield

ACROSS

1 Deep sleep
6 Awful, in Apulia
12 Remarkable variable star
16 Seer of a sort
21 Sandblaster's target
22 Eloquent speaker
23 Military miscreant
24 Trimmed, as upholstery
25 Mortise's companion
26 Drag through mud
27 Caesura
28 Highest of the Pyrenees
29 W.S. on hockey ("A Midsummer-Night's Dream" II, 1)
33 Belfry denizens
34 Alack's partner
35 Gaza or Sunset
36 U.S.N.A. graduate
37 Musical key
39 Northern constellation
40 Armstrong's "Perfect!"
42 Dog star
46 Cockchafers: Var.
47 W.S. on bowling ("The Tempest" I, 1)
53 Poetic word
55 Mae West role
56 Physicist Bohr
57 Latin I verb
58 Rains of film fame
61 Cairn _____ (Scottish peak)
62 Haggard
64 Singer John
66 Seoul soldiers
67 W.S. on football ("Othello" V, 2)
71 Brontë heroine
72 "_____ for the Czar" (Glinka opera)
74 Flying spray
75 "Awake and Sing" playwright
76 "Hamlet" segment
78 Marine mammal
80 Numero _____
81 Some ex-Princetonians
85 Former Mideast initials
86 Lean as _____
89 Hind's mate
92 _____ and end-all
93 Leave port
96 W.S. on golf ("King John" IV, 1)
100 One-tenth of MLXX
101 Seed covering
103 Yellow-fever mosquito
104 Part of Q.E.D.
105 Keys
107 Dunderhead
108 Sleep: Prefix
110 Cabinet dept.
111 Character in "Turandot"
112 W.S. on baseball ("Othello" III, 3)
118 Thong
122 Graf _____
123 Clangor
124 Enzyme: Suffix
125 Renounce
128 Golf-club part
130 Poet's concern
132 N.T. book
133 Part of Excalibur
134 W.S. on basketball ("Henry V" III, Prologue)
139 Dungeon sound
141 Litter Lilliputian
142 Fourth of a famous five
143 In the van
145 Ex _____
146 Arab chieftain
147 Salt marsh
148 Intrinsically
149 Hewers
150 Game in a Reno casino
151 Hamlet's "_____ and arrows"
152 Long legs, in Leghorn

DOWN

1 Rank above cpl.
2 Seasoning for pizza
3 Cold-remedy component
4 W.S. on tennis ("3 Henry VI" III, 2)
5 Budget item
6 Old Assyrian city
7 "Hard as _____ of ploughman": W.S.
8 Fictional uncle
9 Auricular
10 Stops up
11 In an upright manner
12 Scott hero
13 "_____ for Adonais": Shelley
14 _____ ha-Shanah
15 Choir voices
16 Hall of Fame pitcher
17 Popular apple
18 Little or Frye
19 Where Sills' trills gave thrills
20 Courtroom vow
30 Domestic deity
31 Mountain: Comb. form
32 "Mene, mene, _____, upharsin"
33 Troublesome
38 No longer new
40 "_____ going to St. Ives . . ."
41 Buck or Jesse
43 Having a grayish cast
44 Part of the Malay Archipelago
45 In accord
48 Root or Yale
49 Unyielding
50 Skeleton role
51 Slow; dull
52 Compass point
54 C.S.A. general's monogram
58 Stuff
59 Mascagni's temptress
60 Sib
61 Useful catchall
62 Fuddy-duddy
63 Hwy.
65 W.S. on auto racing ("Macbeth" II, 1)
68 Suffix with Taiwan
69 Composition for nine
70 _____ volatile
73 Seventh Greek letter
77 Wrigley Field player
79 Energy unit
80 Kin of "geetars"
81 Past
82 Hub
83 Dismounted
84 Cantabs' rivals
86 Oat protein
87 Decorated afresh
88 Soul, in Sedan
89 Where lint may glint
90 Papal crown
91 Dramaturgy is one
93 Nautical ropes
94 Fabulous fabulist
95 Progeny
97 Opposites of trochees
98 Race segment
99 Zilch
102 Thus, in Toledo
106 Alfonso's affirmative
109 More unusual
113 Diplomatic word
114 Mehta or Ozawa
115 Tallinn native
116 Second-sighted woman
117 Crested plover
119 Scolds
120 In any event
121 Ill humor
126 Black teas
127 601, Roman style
129 Like some buckets
130 Kingsley's "_____ White"
131 Pertaining to fissures
132 Spent
134 Mischief
135 Arduous journey
136 Actor Cronyn
137 Chookasian of the Met
138 Dummkopfs
139 Bus. consultant
140 Easygoing
144 Sandra or Ruby

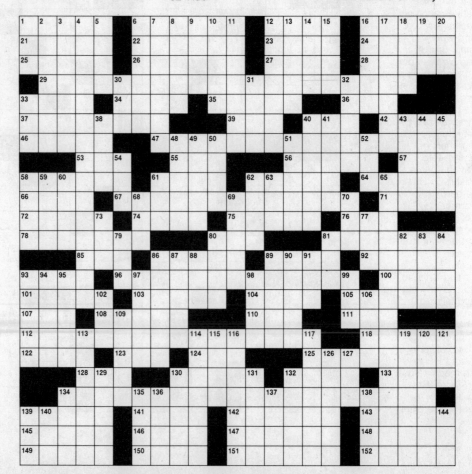

91. No More Diminutives by Bert H. Kruse

ACROSS

1 Diamond fragment
5 Stop ____
12 Millay's "Aria ____"
16 Singlehandedly
17 Sound at a door
18 "____ to Hold Your Hand"
20 Baked-apple dessert
22 Bribes
24 Mechanical repetition
25 Juridic
26 Pip-pip
28 Malayan archipelago
29 Suffix with boy or girl
30 Call it a day
31 Mexican gentleman
32 City in Kansas
33 Simpletons
35 Unit
36 More dreadful
37 Young cod
38 City southeast of Lima
40 Famed N.Y.C. hospital
42 Where to buy croissants
43 Predicament
46 Very unpopular
47 Bird's crop
48 Short tale: Abbr.
49 Attitudinize
51 Chem., geol., etc.
52 Tyrants
56 Boat covering, for short
58 Coarse linen cloth
60 Victory: Ger.
61 Punkie
62 Lake in Ireland
63 John Silver, for instance
65 Bismarck
66 Not jaggy
67 Little or Frye
68 Coquette
69 Girl in an old song
70 Did some sleuthing
72 Attys.' group
73 ____ mater
76 Camb. campus
77 Recent
78 Ledge
80 Cheyenne's foe
82 "In Cold Blood" author
85 Honors
87 West
88 Saltated
89 Doesn't own
90 Siouan
92 Links area
96 Anent
97 Exploded
98 Exchanged
100 Originally known as
101 Butte's relative
102 Spore sacs in fungi
103 Philosopher of the Absolute
104 Pre-Lenin ruler
105 Lake of ____, Switzerland
107 Medicine, osteopathy, etc.
111 Restrain
112 Intrinsic nature
113 Calcars
114 Overcasts
115 Cocktail
116 Yin's companion

DOWN

1 Endue
2 Foe of Washington
3 Caravansary
4 Elizabethan dramatist
5 Sources
6 Christ's childhood home
7 "And thereby hangs ____"
8 Flatfish
9 Resident: Suffix
10 Was important
11 Natural gas components
12 Castro's companion
13 Disciple's emotion
14 Police conveyance
15 Kind of wind or current
16 Started
19 Savile Row businessman
20 Two-master
21 Apollo's mother
23 Truckler
27 Rocky peak
30 Tire
31 Twist's persecutor
34 Chaplin's title
36 Hair style
37 European mining center
39 Army address
41 "And every ____ queen": Kingsley
42 C.S.A. general
43 Go without food
44 Trumpet's relative
45 Gone con
47 Solacer's advice
48 Mount
50 Goofed
52 Nappy
53 Punctual
54 "Panama ____"
55 Ermine in brown
57 Poker game
59 Dept. in the Cabinet
60 Cardinals' insignia
63 Dull finish
64 Equal, as a Parisienne
71 Noted suffragette
72 On a safari
74 Namath in 1977
75 Edgar or Emmy
78 Most impudent
79 Dental ____
81 Modernist
82 Conquer Everest
83 Epic in 12 books
84 Fire worshipers
85 Tamaracks
86 Reel
89 Czech martyr
91 Old Greek theaters
93 Like many heroes
94 Car parts
95 Linen marking
97 Boxing brothers
98 Object
99 "Crazy Legs" Hirsch
104 At that moment
106 Just out
108 "____ live and breathe!"
109 Bernstein nickname
110 Govt. power project

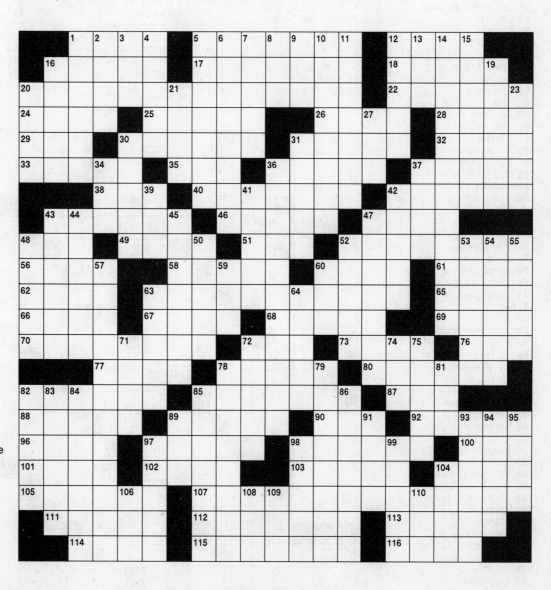

92. Run for the Roses by Anthony B. Canning

ACROSS

1 Shade of brown
7 Produce
12 Unit of power
16 Bernie of baseball fame
21 Conakry is its capital
22 "Fidelio" is one
23 Mingle-mangle
24 "You're ____ Smoothie," 1932 song
25 Ridder of rats in 1918?
27 Wilted immature flower of 1914?
29 Ruby or Sandra
30 Horsy flicks
31 Dillydally
33 Little or Frye
34 Mtg.
35 Author of "The Green Hat"
36 Years, to Claudius
37 Calloway
40 "Flee, feline!"
41 Tod ____, great jockey
42 General's host
46 Threatening
48 Solar year excess
49 Lagniappe
50 Lizard
51 Jaw teeth
52 Poet recalled in 1917?
54 Kind of story
55 Prefix for fold or graph
56 Endure
57 N.M. neighbor
58 Smelting mixture
60 Faulkner character
61 Nimble in 1905?
62 Where to get tired
64 Limoges item
65 Direction: Abbr.
66 Herb of 1909?
68 World's greatest coffee port
69 Papal capes
71 Poetic contraction
72 Infrequently
73 Della and Peewee
74 Road ridden in 1960?
78 Mary Quant's style
81 Order back
82 Apportioned
83 Bobbin
84 Japanese ship
85 M.O.M.A. display
86 "Bugs," the writer
87 Menu entree
88 Thrasher
89 Seoul soldier
90 U.N. Group of 1973?
93 Test eggs
94 Suffix with Siam
95 Choir group
96 Model
97 Size
98 Of noon in 1911?
100 Locale for Rosalind
101 Jazzman Fountain
102 Thing, in law
103 Placebos
104 Skedaddles
105 Entertainer Falana
106 Milan's subway
108 Brightness
109 SAC members

111 ____ Canals
114 Courteous Reynard of 1930?
116 Theme of this puzzle
119 Embassy worker
120 Sea or salt: Comb. form
121 Take over forcibly
122 Forecaster
123 Horse, e.g.
124 Former spouses
125 Specks
126 Loire seaport

DOWN

1 Well along
2 Elegance
3 Bit
4 ____-horse town
5 Fiddler or pianist
6 Capital of Syria
7 Aboveboard
8 Armadillos
9 Hanoi holidays
10 ____-Magnon man
11 Kind of miner
12 Fabric from yarn
13 Historian Nevins
14 Shipshape
15 Rocky peak
16 Enclosing frames
17 Lack of pep
18 Home wear
19 Indistinctness
20 Bizarre
26 Willows
28 Whatnot
32 Israeli port
35 Nose part
36 Desi or Lucie
37 Quotation marks
38 Aggregate
39 Charge a cobbler?
40 Fern spores
41 Disk harrow
42 Cézanne's "____ a Red Vest"
43 Saharan leader in 1970?
44 Overplays
45 Side arm
47 Thurmond of N.B.A. fame
48 Zola
49 Author of "Don Juan"
52 Final notices
53 Rhine feeder
56 Choreographer de Mille
58 Berlin song
59 Durant or Kissel
61 Felt out of sorts
62 Slender as ____
63 British dukedom
64 Western shrub
66 ". . . man who ____ there"
67 Little or Wilder
68 Attach, as a button
70 Perform a pesade
72 High-hat
73 Rest
74 Yaws
75 To be, to Bardot

76 Of a Hebrew prophet
77 Shock
79 Threatening term
80 Constraint
81 Ned ____, U.S. composer
82 City on the Ocmulgee
84 Thomas or Horace
86 Certain rays
87 Hudson Bay Indians
88 Zoo structure
90 Pullover
91 Hebrides island
92 Supplement
93 Award of 1948?
95 Loving
97 In Hades
99 Fibers for cordage
100 Czar-to-be, slain in 1918
101 Sea anemones
104 Violin aperture
105 Cuba ____, rum drink
106 Cob or drake
107 Lamb
108 Tunisian seaport
109 River into the Danube
110 Mrs., in Portugal
111 Denomination
112 Shield border
113 Sugars
114 Certain "gift"
115 ____ Four Horsemen
117 That, in Taxco
118 Merriman of opera

93. Mom's Remonstrance by Frances Hansen

ACROSS

1 Accept eagerly
6 Soprano Anna
11 Killer whale
15 Island attacked Dec. 7, 1941
19 Persian
20 ". . . upon ____ in Darien"
21 Kind of music or lore
22 Germany's largest dam
23 Tale or crayon
24 Throb
25 Take to the hills
26 Stone or Pound
27 Start of a verse
31 Waiter's burden
32 Sweet girl of song
33 Bk. of the Bible
34 "You ____ My Sunshine"
35 Dobbin's morsel
37 Writer Anaïs
39 Hen pen
42 ____ vu
45 More of the verse
51 Dip bait lightly
52 Little, in Lille
53 Bikini part
54 Rip
55 Business letter abbr.
56 Lamb
58 "Bonheur de Vivre" painter
61 Take ____ (relax)
63 Nonplus
65 Penpoint
66 Vast amount
68 Between L and P
69 More of the verse
77 Single
78 "Why ____ Love You?"
79 Self: Prefix
80 Popular steak cut
81 Lively Latin dance
85 Visited a warren
88 Prefix for chord
89 Girlfriend of 95 Across
90 ____ Ridge, famed horse
94 Naval off.
95 Alley of comics
97 Indian mulberry
98 More of the verse
103 Like a day in June
104 Cambodian money
105 Building wing
106 Kith's partner
107 Sort
109 Wild goat
111 New Guinea seaport
113 Computer input
117 End of the verse
124 Like a bump on ____
125 Siamese
126 Highway stopover
127 Hungarian farm dogs
128 Loll about
129 Mountain lake
130 Pilasters
131 Subside
132 Former spouses
133 Festoon
134 Approaches
135 Traveller or Rosinante

DOWN

1 Lawful
2 Bellowing
3 Zoo star
4 "For ____ is born this day . . .": Luke 2:11
5 Jetty
6 N.Z. tree
7 Rich
8 Cut down trees
9 Snaps, e.g.
10 Slangy assents
11 Outgrowth
12 Function
13 Musical symbol
14 Kipling's wolf
15 "And this little pig cried ____ . . ."
16 Carpenter's tool
17 Walter, Jean or Deborah
18 Time periods
28 Regard highly
29 Engrave
30 Church calendar
36 Cleo's way out
38 Had a few drinks
40 Corrida cry
41 Princess-prodder
43 Napoleon triumphed here: 1806
44 Rainbows
45 Conference site: 1945
46 Sherlock Holmes's drug
47 Subtle shading
48 Yuletide celebrant
49 ". . . ____ me a beaker of wine"
50 Sneaky
51 Arnaz
57 Pt. or qt.
59 Initials for a royal couple
60 Poet's word
62 Race-track figure
64 Winnie of fiction
67 "____ with a dulcimer . . ."
68 Shooting star
70 Deprive of weapons
71 ____ Passos
72 Kind of steer
73 Nigerian tribe
74 Making all stops
75 Inward: Anat.
76 New or raw
81 Male swan
82 H or witching
83 Can. province
84 Gigs and cabriolets
86 Like a rare steak
87 Court list
91 Comparative suffix
92 Gen. Marshall's alma mater
93 In on the crime
96 Letter on a key
99 Slippery
100 Susa's kingdom
101 "Open ____" (resort boast)
102 Hesitating
108 St. ____, Leeward island
110 Kaplan of fiction
112 Attachments for anges
114 Huge halls
115 Commonplace
116 Requested
117 A likely story
118 Evergreen genus
119 "The decent docent doesn't ____"
120 Sir Broadfoot Basham's creator
121 Honshu city
122 "____ boy!"
123 Health resorts

94. Playmates by Elaine D. Schorr

ACROSS

1 Bam!
6 Participant
12 Nape drape
17 Grover's Corners
21 Robin of ballad fame
22 Nobelist poet: 1913
23 Plotters or plot
24 "The Great" of Muscovy
25 "A Farewell to Arms"
28 Bingo device
29 Readies the presses
30 Of doves, hawks, etc.
31 ___ den Linden
32 Balt. or N.Y.C.
34 Good points
36 Pole's neighbor
37 British statesman
40 Preconceives
42 Siamese
44 Bob or Tiny Tim
47 Painful peregrinations
48 Equal shares for a trio
50 Wolf or Ranger
51 Suffix with Japan or Nippon
52 Attack
53 "A Majority of One"
56 Apportion
57 Highest of Pyrenees
58 Calla lilies
59 Inning sextet
60 Dovetail wedge
61 More fastidious
62 Dry, cold wind
63 Kind of fund
65 Larder
66 One of five in "Hamlet"
67 "Lady Be Good"
69 "The Hoosier Poet"
70 Venus's venous fluid
73 Vintage car
74 Reason for a D.S.C.
75 Serve the purpose
76 "The Sound of Music"
82 Filer's aid
85 Things to be done
86 Not watertight
87 Mauritanian
88 Floor, in France
90 Thespian Janis
91 Pointed arch
92 Turkey tot
93 Bulwer-Lytton novel
94 Catalonian cat
95 "The Cat and the Canary"
98 Christie and Ivanovna
99 Princess who became a goddess
100 Deserve
101 Part of H.S.H.
102 That is, to Tacitus
103 Discarded
105 Suffragette Carrie
106 Near ringers
109 High home
110 Who or Which
112 Not so short
113 Elec. currents
114 City in N.H.
115 Ade book: 1896
116 "Now hear ___!"
120 Choose greedily
123 "Ah, Wilderness!"
127 Tilden of tennis
128 Stormed
129 Pass, as time
130 Mucilage
131 Thenar
132 Sycophants' replies
133 Russian river
134 Salts or Downs

DOWN

1 Munro's pen name
2 One-eyed god
3 Firkin
4 "Command Performance"
5 Spot's scrap
6 Wonder of songdom
7 Items discarded by some nuns
8 Struggles
9 Town near Amiens
10 Forage plant
11 Varsity
12 "The Border Minstrel"
13 Sandhurst student
14 What 32 Across is
15 Bottom fish
16 Mauriac's "___ Blood"
17 ___-toe
18 Female gametes
19 Prankster
20 Dir. from Pisa to Verona
26 Cardinals' QB
27 Geographical hub of N.Y.
33 Jazzman Fountain
35 ". . . if ___ west/The Phoenix builds": Carew
38 "The Song and Dance Man"
39 Beard's field
40 Conciliatory
41 "Sleuth"
42 Musial, for short
43 Shakes a leg
44 Array
45 Altercations
46 Like Tom Thumb
47 Ethiopian lake
48 Neighbor of Provincetown
49 Beard boy
53 Small drum
54 Danube feeder
55 Corrosive coating
56 Park for T.A.E.
60 Manx's missing part
63 Sly guy
64 Author Uris
65 Say grace
67 Where Augustus died
68 Milanese music maker
71 "Pagliacci" showman
72 Hair's companion
74 Green, in Grenoble
75 At ___ (immediately)
76 The rear
77 Former Congolese prime minister
78 Essentials
79 Sum
80 Jeweler's eyepiece
81 Take life easy
83 ". . . through ___, darkly": I Cor. 13:12
84 Aesop character
85 Protection
88 Galahad's mother
89 "Luv," with "The"
91 River in Bavaria
92 Meter man
95 Hang-up of a sort
96 Get ready to serve wine
97 Like parts of the moon
100 "Beowulf" is one
104 Fit for tilling
106 Gossip's interest
107 Apocopates
108 Hebrew letter: Var.
110 Plains abode
111 Takes advice
112 Rubbish
114 Pub vessels
115 Rembrandt's "Lady with ___"
117 Dame Myra
118 "It ___ laugh": Pinero
119 Arrest
120 Fabian's monogram
121 Branco or Bravo
122 Hog's desire
124 "Some ___ meat . . .": Burns
125 U.N. labor body
126 Unclose: Poetic

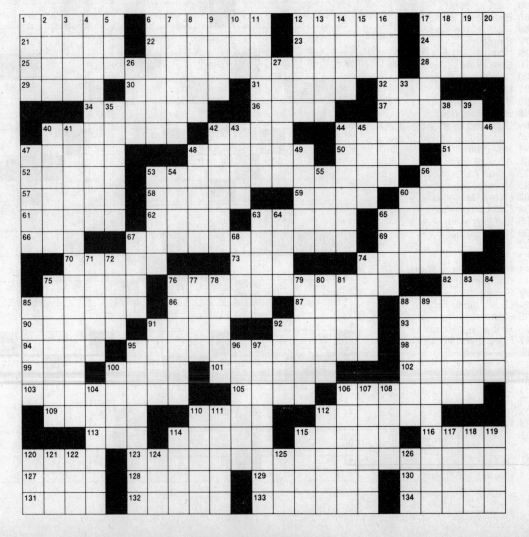

95. Omnium-Gatherum by Henry Hook

ACROSS

1 Author of "America"
6 First Bishop of Rome
13 Hashish source
17 Asian capital
18 Electronic musical instrument
20 Batten down
22 A Shaw
23 Macbeth's crime
24 For the time being
25 Baltic seaport
26 Kind of rail or plane
27 Bond film, "Live and ____"
29 Viper
30 Perpetually, poetically
31 "All systems go!"
32 Double agent
34 Malefic; baleful
36 Valentines
40 Tooth tissue
41 "Saturday night special"
42 Marker of a sort
43 Alphabetic trio
45 Putrefies
46 Singer John
47 Shaped like a tepee
48 Satisfy edacity
49 Littler and Wilder
50 A ____ Able
51 Hanging on for dear life
53 Let
54 Jockey Turcotte
55 Arm of a starfish
56 Cartoonist's choice
58 Albion
60 Yoga squat
62 Dupe
66 Famed Swiss conductor
68 Pique at its peak
69 Yeast nucleic acid: Abbr.
70 Simon's colleague
72 Low-heeled sandals
76 Grove on a prairie
77 Revenue, in Rennes
78 Fabius's foot
79 Lazy one
80 Doc
81 Sybarite's delight
82 Native of: Suffix
83 Seaver's home
84 1972 Summer Olympics site
85 Hayes or Taylor
88 "How swift the moments fly!"
90 Force into service
92 Loser to R.M.N.: 1972
93 Ship-shaped napkin holder
94 G.I.'s letter drop
95 "To thine ____ self . . ."
96 Enmity
98 In, in a way
100 Hammer part
101 Under
103 This may have charms
106 Scriven
107 Recognize rank
108 J.F.K.'s Defense Sec.
109 ____ Noster
110 Saloon orders
111 Shows up
112 Bottomless pit

DOWN

1 Writer of at least 154 sonnets
2 "My Friend Irma" star
3 "Ver-r-ry ____!"
4 Trouble's mate
5 Get a move on
6 Drive or putt
7 Subsequently
8 "____ My Heart"
9 Silkworm
10 Gumshoe
11 Girl in "Our Town"
12 Hitchhiker's quest
13 Follower of "enclosed"
14 Habitat: Prefix
15 Sports of sorts
16 Dais personage
19 N.J. five
20 Bookbinder's item
21 Josephine, e.g.
26 Hugo von ____, noted 19th-century botanist
28 "She ____ Say Yes"
31 Like ____ of bricks
32 Impassive
33 Alfred Adler et al.
35 Veins or strains
37 Jacket type
38 Leigh Hunt hero
39 Poor poker hand
43 ____ hand (aid)
44 Crèche trio
47 Walt Frazier
49 People, in Padua
51 "Mend when thou ____": Lear
52 Boniface's place
53 Mendacious men
55 Punjab princess
57 Quaker gray
59 Diogenes' burden
60 Divert
61 Carson subject
63 Spendthrift's problem
64 Foretastes
65 Lookouts
67 Art of literary comp.
70 Cabana items
71 P.D.Q.
73 Father of 38 Down
74 Radio sportscaster McCarthy
75 Car that's gone too far
76 Carte
77 Ratiocinates
78 Galileo was one
80 Fielding error
84 One 60-thousandth of a min.
86 Plume suppliers
87 Purchase on Wall St.
89 Erstwhile Colt star
91 Missile, for short
92 Julia Dent's bridegroom: 1848
97 1977 disaster film
98 Close-knit group
99 Pack of camels
100 Fiddler on the reef
102 Tincture
104 Small sailboat
105 Scottish uncle
106 New Deal agcy.

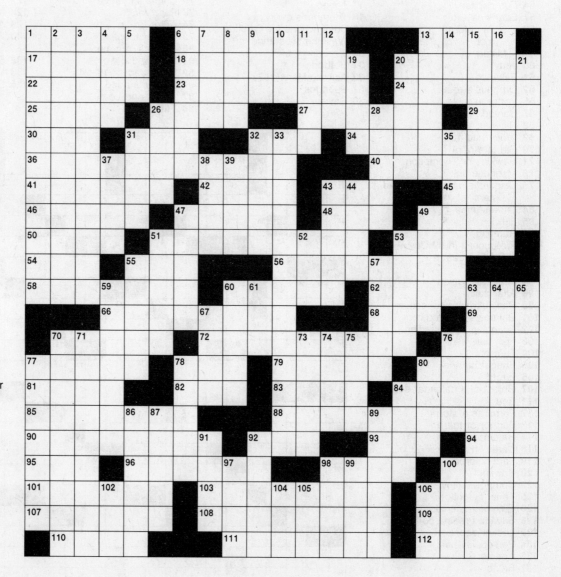

96. Flim Flam by Chet Currier

ACROSS

1 Black Hawk's tribe
5 Took on fuel
11 Discomfit
16 Kind of fish or cake
21 Tupelo, e.g.
22 Chemical weapon
23 Beta's follower
24 Lafitte's prize
25 Recorded proceedings
26 Relative of "We'll see"
27 Alaska native
28 Cordial herb
29 Cool cat
32 Don
34 Suffix for cash
35 Latin laborer
36 Unpleasant look
37 Prometheus's theft
38 Rel. of national income
41 Sharp scarps
43 Lemons
45 White-tailed bird
46 Love in León
47 Coffee and tea
53 Private chambers
54 Eur. capital
57 Czar's say-so
58 ____ in (inform)
59 ". . . riches ____ hell":
   Milton
60 Jetty
61 Essence
62 Orpheus's route
65 Potter, e.g.
67 Curved
68 Nigerian V.I.P.
69 Argus had 100
70 Girl in a pool
71 Hawkins or Thompson
73 Magnetic unit
75 Cinderella, stepmother and
   sisters
84 Threesomes
85 Link
86 Rampage
87 Protagonist in 89 Down
91 U.S.A.F. weapon
92 Savior-____
94 Firenze's region
96 Altar pair
99 Revolutionary statesman
101 Galatea's beloved
102 Founding or grounding
103 Fish bait
104 Turn out
105 Budget burden
106 Wroth
107 Object of a calendar search
111 Beaks
112 Form, as a storm
113 Partner of there
114 Hammerstein
118 Cards' insignia
119 Parti-colored
120 Bowsprit
122 Composer Novello
125 Tenn. neighbor
126 Etching materials
128 Savage-breast soother
132 Locker décor
134 Personality part
136 Specter
137 Baste

138 "I give up!"
139 Zodiac sign
140 Shrug off
141 Busy as ____
142 Trounces
143 Erstwhile car
144 Less jumbled
145 Biblical verb

DOWN

1 Radio problem
2 Toxophilite
3 Et ____
4 Closure
5 Hiawatha's transportation
6 Maine college town
7 Patty Duke ____
8 Highlands waterfall
9 Sufficient, old style
10 Actor Brandon
11 Chalcedony
12 Farm machine
13 Continental abbr.
14 Dallas campus
15 Swamp plants
16 Taper off
17 Taboo
18 Thumber's query
19 Conjunctions for Catullus
20 Washing substance
30 ____ dixit
31 Hotbed
33 Actress Mary: 1933–75
37 Sponges
39 Review

40 Didoes
42 Ecdysiast's final finery
43 Slap's partner
44 Pueblo's foe
45 Jewish month
46 Playa clay
48 Stage before imago
49 Consanguineous
50 Kind of race or line
51 Long
52 Sapped
53 Suffix with dull
54 "Many a woman has ____":
   Wilde
55 Hilarity
56 Mediterranean craft
59 Grind together
62 River feeder: Abbr.
63 S. Pacific area
64 Touch upon
66 Sandblaster's target
67 Fruit punch
71 Put up with
72 Cries of surprise
73 Wildebeest
74 Meeting: Abbr.
76 Chimp's relative
77 Pair: Var.
78 Actor Bruce
79 Timber toppler
80 Starters in rummy
81 Preprandial words
82 Red head: 1918–24
83 Brewer's need
87 Itzhak and Leah
88 Turkish inn

89 White House, to Fidel
90 Does cable stitching
92 Diamond call
93 Certain matériel, for short
94 Go like clockwork
95 Bone: Prefix
97 Dijon donkey
98 Sigh of relief
99 Calcar
100 Foulard
104 Cote mother
107 Braced framework
108 R.R. stops
109 End play in bridge
110 Conformist's concern
112 Enjoin
115 Melon
116 "____ Restaurant"
117 Charivari
119 Pan's music makers
120 Draft horse
121 Floral feature
122 Kind of TV board or card
123 Your, to Camus
124 ". . . fairest ____ daughters
   Eve": Milton
127 Group of devotees
128 Keep ____ on
129 Advocate
130 Zola novel
131 Nevada neighbor
132 Soho social spot
133 Made of: Suffix
135 Disencumber

97. Silly Syllabus by Stanley Glass

ACROSS

1 Sacrificial area
6 Mince-pie ingredient
10 Clumsy one
13 Early shipbuilder
17 Author of "Games People Play"
18 Killer whale
19 Robin Hood's drink
20 Does intensive research
22 Respond to a stimulus
23 She wrote "Seductio ad Absurdum"
24 Relatives
25 Type of tire
26 Study that Edith Bunker dug
29 Concept
31 Own
32 Rages
33 An 1898 discovery
35 Like some guesses
37 Defendants, in law
38 Trunk
39 Study of corrections
40 Study of Caesar's shapes and forms
45 Article much in use
46 Bullring cry
47 Jutting rock
48 Sequential notes
49 Impressionist master
51 "Have you ____ wool?"
52 Beloved, in Bordeaux
53 Puts in office
56 Emphatic refusal
58 Chanticleer's domain
60 Fodder storage
62 Angels of mercy
66 Statampere, for instance: Abbr.
67 Land mass south of Eur.
69 Rain check
70 Alt.
71 Use a Mason jar
72 Hungarian-born conductor
74 Glacial fissure
78 Malice
80 Russell of the N.B.A.
82 "I ____ arrow into the air"
84 Samoan port
85 Exist
87 Transvaal police
89 Italian terrorists' victim
90 Join
91 Beast of Barbary
92 Greedy one
93 Trotsky's private course in fossils
97 Study of snakes' evolution
100 Water nymph
101 ____ Nor, lake in Sinkiang
102 Hawaiian volcano
103 Ballet subject
104 Golf ball ingredient
107 ____ Pater (almanac)
108 European capital
110 Study of trash
113 Pool activity
115 Shoshonean
117 Outer portion of the earth
118 Exhausts
119 Blossom of the silents
120 Fem. group
121 Eight: Comb. form
122 French spa
123 Method: Abbr.
124 Command to oxen
125 Bridge positions: Abbr.
126 Feel

DOWN

1 Canyon mouth
2 Looks maliciously
3 Mather product
4 Moorings
5 Called it a day
6 Areas in London and N.Y.C.
7 Russian river
8 Science studied by yodelers
9 Noli me ____
10 Charter ____ of Hartford fame
11 Et ____
12 Wheel guard
13 Educational org.
14 Passé
15 The Wrights' delight
16 Celestial
20 Course for artful bartenders
21 Type of hammer
27 Expatriate
28 Former U.S. ambassador to U.N.
30 Did newsroom work
34 Average
36 Guevara
38 "Good-will ____": Longfellow
40 Chicken
41 Melodious
42 Dorothy from New Orleans
43 Sniggler for wrigglers
44 Cry of the wild goose
50 Italian for 13 Across
51 Atmosphere: Prefix
54 Canute's proof of his limitations
55 Eastern Europeans
57 Reduces
59 Informal farewell
61 Eastern nana
63 Hannibal's adversary
64 Gourmet's pleasure
65 Furtive
68 Science of carbonation
70 Author Lafcadio
73 Star pitcher
74 Round: Abbr.
75 Corded fabric
76 Study of certain high jinks
77 Put up with
79 Soothing
81 Iranian range
83 "O shed ____!": Keats
85 Honey factories
86 Inspect again
88 ____ souci
91 Names of several Turkish sultans
92 Sch. affiliate
94 Small boat
95 Affair of the heart
96 Monastery residents
98 Slow movers
99 Yangtze feeder
104 "Look out ____!"
105 Home of Fiat and Lancia
106 Sections or sectors
109 Nebraska City's county
111 London museum
112 Medieval drudge
114 Gain
116 Ram's dam

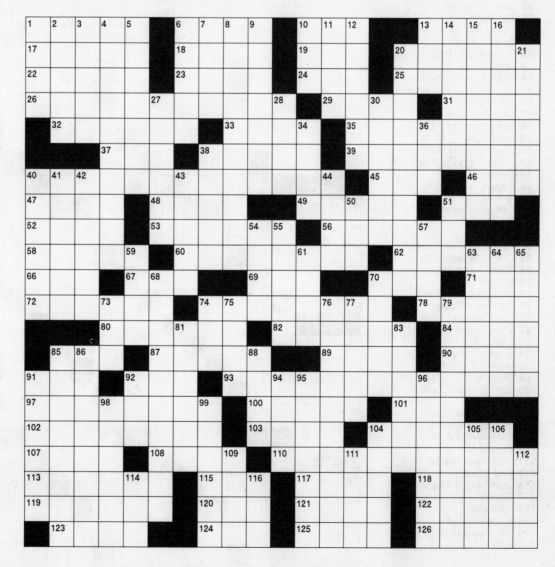

98. Dad's Due by Tap Osborn

ACROSS

1 Sizable
6 ____ oil
11 Strident
16 Photograph
21 ". . . sadly ____": S. Foster
22 Vichyssoise, for one
23 Flirty one
24 Dismiss
25 Start of a four-line verse
29 Performed with subtlety
30 Slow-witted
31 Cash in
32 Word with Simon
33 Pale blue
34 Spiny-finned fish
35 Multifaceted
36 Row
37 Obscure
38 Nicene ____
39 Torn ligament
43 Optician's product
44 Four-time homer king
45 Oopak or hyson
48 Second line of verse
55 Calm
56 "____ on Sunday"
57 Miscalculated
58 Gain an edge
59 Carriage
60 Sitting rooms
61 Fountain order
62 Downstairs person
63 Legume
64 Mother Hubbard, e.g.
65 Like some I.R.S. returns
66 Snakebirds
67 Fish, in a way
68 Dipsy doodle
69 Auto race
70 Did some tailoring
73 Victor from Denmark
74 Goren, at times
75 Expert
78 Horrify
79 Like a séance
80 Now
81 Off pitch
82 Pierre's "That does it!"
83 One of a famed trio
84 "Jean" and "Marie"
85 Square
86 Third line of verse
90 Alkaline solution
91 Buck heroine
92 White-tailed eagle
93 Rising high
94 Shaw's "Superman"
96 Ready to hit the hay
98 Dominion
100 Salt-covered plains
103 Flip
104 Anjou or Kieffer
105 James or Chanel
109 Protein-rich dish
110 Soupçon
111 Thistlelike plants
113 End of verse
116 Sign before Taurus
117 Devour
118 Walkway
119 Rugged ridge
120 Famous jockey of yore
121 Earrings
122 Plied with potions
123 Light amplification of a kind

DOWN

1 "Peanuts" character
2 Battleground
3 Street tough
4 Says "Aaah"
5 Moslem V.I.P.
6 Coined money
7 Stag bagger
8 Whirling
9 Prurient
10 Poet's "forever"
11 Moses or Morse
12 Realtor's bailiwick
13 Flounder
14 Maman's man
15 Kin of mos. and wks.
16 Raglan feature
17 Ran the show
18 Minklike swimmer
19 S-curves
20 "The Velvet Fog"
26 Expectant father's activity
27 Texas city
28 Most perverse
34 Undernourished sheep
35 Eurydice was one
36 Antimacassar
37 Tragedy by Euripides
38 Future officer
39 Engulf
40 Salk's target
41 Like legal pads
42 Arkin or Bates
43 Dungarees' kin
44 Bathtub-murder victim
45 Item on a marquee
46 Granddad
47 Then, in Vienne
49 Contemplate
50 Chapter's partner
51 Go over one's yesterdays
52 Pilotless plane
53 Every 3,600 seconds
54 Like many dirt roads
60 Maurois's biography of Shelley
61 Smith's place
62 "Bananas"
64 Rooster's wattle
65 Law expert
66 Firm, lustrous fabric
67 Author of "A Lonely Rage"
68 Barbizon painter
69 Dickens's "Barnaby ____"
70 Tangle or disentangle
71 Modern adhesive
72 Anise or mace
73 The "Borstal Boy"
74 One on the receiving end
75 Where Fisk crouches
76 He brings down the house
77 Eared seal
79 Allen or Frome
80 Local yokel
81 Defect
83 Globe-trotter's aid
84 Rueful
85 Stratagem
87 Salad item
88 Equivocate
89 Dieter's concern
94 Took four balls
95 Danish seaport
96 Cleansing process
97 Bars legally
98 Decide
99 Stayed for
100 Refreshments
101 Lucine of Met fame
102 Did an usher's job
103 Took care of
104 Basketball tactic
105 Menace in India
106 Steinbeck subjects
107 Gael, to Giscard
108 Famed Canadian physician
110 Peter I or Paul I
111 Money-changing discount
112 Cure
114 Unite
115 Dad, once

99. Free Associations by Louis Baron

ACROSS

1 Astronaut's find
5 Global supporter
10 Mugger on the boards
13 Texas farmer's land
18 Word with wise
19 Third-rate stuff
20 Soda jerk's tap
21 Have a crush on
22 Temple of Vesta
25 Like truth, sometimes
26 Gaslight ___
27 Bombay bigwig
28 Hits the books
29 Fifth word of "The Raven"
30 Leftover
32 Pippin piercer
33 Hair: Comb. form
34 It's east of Ill.
35 ___ game (shutout)
36 On the wagon
39 Base for a pedestal
42 Dead-letter office
44 Osprey's cousin
45 Tennis ace
46 Good taste
47 Cries of surprise
48 Colliery entrance
49 ___ rule
50 Hackneyed commercial
54 "Gypsy Love" composer
55 Oriole's cheer
58 Goodman
59 Word of honor
60 Columbus's hometown
61 The woes of toes
62 Slew
63 Kind of card
65 Task for Figaro
66 Sally Rand dance
69 Hot spot
70 Doubleheader
72 Scot. neighbor
73 "Play ___ It Lays": Didion
74 Adonis' killer
76 Great Asian river
77 Twin
78 Quaint clock
79 Roman relative
83 Specialty
84 Graffiti artist
87 Medicine's Sir William
88 Juan or Marquis
89 Height for a kite
90 Thompson's "___ a Stranger"
91 Nourish
95 Arrays on one side
97 Gone up
98 Hopper medium
99 Half of sex-
100 Sweater size
101 "Send me $50," etc.
104 "The ___ cast!"
105 Horatian creations
106 Vimy or Oak
107 "___ soit . . ."
108 First phase
109 Rocky pinnacle
110 Caucasian
111 Thrift-shop word

DOWN

1 Black snake
2 Yellowish pigment
3 Elite
4 Prefix for plop or choo
5 Within reach
6 "Last Case" sleuth
7 Minnelli
8 Calendar abbr.
9 New Bedford is one
10 He painted "The Life Line"
11 Baksheesh
12 A West from the East
13 Fungus
14 Ivanhoe's bride
15 Legit romance
16 Unsmiling
17 Airport near Paris
20 Melville's "Benito ___"
23 Derrick
24 Tribunal
29 Mites
31 Luxor's river
32 Brava or Rica
33 Ball of yarn
35 Some are proper
36 Pygmy
37 Affliction
38 ___ nous
39 ___ Basin
40 Bones, to a zoologist
41 Gold digger's fee
42 Lecterns
43 "___ Daughter," 1971 film
46 French dance tune
48 Sector of Mars
51 Lusitania undoer
52 Match opener
53 Nine: Comb. form
54 Alan, Diane or Cheryl
56 Yellow-fever vector
57 Cuckoos
59 Anemic sheep
61 Frenchman's fare
62 Fact
63 Spode, e.g.
64 Honey badger
65 Balance: Comb. form
66 Longest bone
67 Punkie
68 Give the eye to
71 "___ of Hoffmann"
74 Groundwork
75 Formerly
77 "___ tread on me"
80 Promotes
81 Glyceride
82 Pampas cowboy
83 Anat. cavity
85 Jackson or Smith
86 Conductor Ansermet
88 Melodious
90 Chilean export
91 Sitdown operation
92 D'Artagnan ami
93 Musical of 1919
94 Glossy
95 Ray of movies
96 Homophone for lane
97 Change the décor
98 Handicap
101 Parking place
102 Sonny's sibling
103 China's ___ Teh

100. American Song Bag by Anne Fox

ACROSS

1 Desserts
5 ". . . _____ bursting in air"
10 Task
15 Parts of refrains
21 Useless: Slang
22 Masefield novel
23 Harden
24 In a weird way
25 Words by S. F. Smith
29 Knock
30 A Robinson
31 Victim of anoia
32 Scoreboard entry
33 Chink
34 Chekhov
36 Disney's "World's Greatest Athlete"
37 Clean
38 "There is _____ . . ."
39 Words by Howe
45 The Reds' Rose, once
48 Virginia _____
49 Kind of stove
50 A.F.L. affiliate
51 Propeller
52 Andrea _____
54 Stop
57 Soft mineral
62 Key words
66 Concerning
67 Kind of preview
68 Once, once
69 Leeward island
70 Poker holding
71 Tabula _____
74 Sitology topic
76 Prefix with active or grade
79 Dolce _____ niente
80 Song c. 1780, with "For"
87 "Oedipus _____"
88 Recent Oscar winner
89 Takes a bath
90 Farm building
91 Hep
93 "Woe is me!"
95 Jeune fille
97 Miss Massey
101 _____ about
102 "God _____" (words by Bates)
107 Pitti, for one
109 La-di-da
110 Shade of green
111 Comparative suffix
112 _____ Vic
114 Virgil epic: Abbr.
115 Miss Arthur
116 Old fogy
117 Words by Norman H. Hall
127 Brink
128 Sal et al.
129 Hebrew lyre
130 Zoo animal
134 Olive, to Ovid
135 Red Sox slugger
136 Jacques, e.g.
137 Baronet's title
139 Kid
140 What Yankee Doodle did
145 "You bet!"
146 Roman spirits
147 Type of dye
148 Kirman and Kurdistan
149 "Gil Blas" author
150 Tête-_____
151 Irish dramatist
152 Slaughter

DOWN

1 Within: Prefix
2 "Over There" composer
3 Locale of "Aïda"
4 Plant
5 Clodhopper
6 Probability
7 Atlas abbr.
8 Sheep talk
9 Espadrille
10 Words by Hopkinson
11 Swiss-French author
12 Kind of steer
13 Annie, for one
14 Enjoy
15 Spreads hay
16 Doe, in Dessau
17 Best: Comb. form
18 Harry _____ Crosby
19 "_____ Is Dream of You"
20 Formulated theory
26 Prefix with bus or present
27 Martin, to friends
28 Moral principle
35 Part of i.o.u.
37 _____ an owl
38 "_____ Named Sue"
40 God of thunder
41 Cantab's school
42 French girlfriend
43 Tall tale
44 Emulate Gwinnett
45 Boston _____
46 Work for
47 Liberty _____
52 Baron _____ of '76
53 Hoosier humorist
54 Court statistic
55 Beatle with a beat
56 Lama land
58 Dilly
59 Blooey
60 Asian wild sheep
61 Joyous
63 Puppeteer
64 Pakistani language
65 Formal affirmations
72 Trifle
73 "_____ Wanna," 1906 tune
75 West Indies island
77 Capet, e.g.
78 Out _____ (askew)
80 Company
81 Kind of rinse
82 Eulogize
83 Waterway
84 Bold, in Barcelona
85 U.N. member
86 Shock
92 _____ pro nobis
94 Navigation hazards
96 U.S.A.F. group
98 Birthplace of seven Presidents
99 Lack
100 Of planes
102 Dispose of
103 Graceful tree
104 Philippine port
105 River to the Fulda
106 Spoken
108 Innermost part
113 Number
116 Ike
117 Open declaration
118 Moon goddess
119 Leanings
120 First name in mysteries
121 Washington port
122 Assailed
123 Not new
124 Persian water wheels
125 Mania
126 Pound
131 Columnist Heywood
132 See 55 Down
133 Vast chasm
135 Poet laureate: 1715–18
136 Cark
137 Anthem
138 Arrow poison
141 Dress (up)
142 Compass point
143 Schnapps
144 Before: Prefix

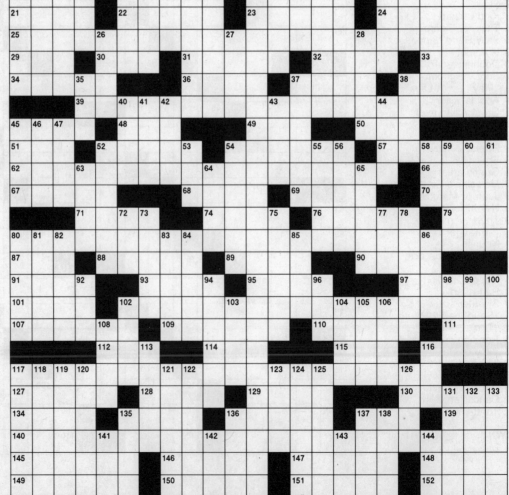

101. Puzzled Pariahs by Frances Hansen

ACROSS

1 Cicero's waters
6 Conform
11 Kind of car or stitch
16 Nile bird
20 Mandalay locale
21 Fog or mist
22 G sharp
23 "Mack the Knife" singer
25 Laughter, in Latium
26 Widened at the top
27 Nottingham's river
28 Chemical suffix
29 Start of a verse
33 Lyon lass: Abbr.
34 Waste maker
35 Oneness
36 A Barrymore
37 Heather's home
39 Slender nail
40 One of the Chases
41 "Abou Ben ____"
44 Trochee's opposite
48 Alamo hero
50 Airship, for short
53 More of the verse
58 "And we ____ home till morning"
59 N.C.O.'s
60 Al from N.Y.C.
61 O.W.I. successor
62 Nitrogenous: Comb. form
63 More qualified
65 Buddhist on cloud nine
66 Humming with activity
67 Millstone bar
69 Sometimes it's sinister
70 Smirch
72 Memory lapse
74 More of the verse
78 Province of eastern Cuba
81 City in western France
82 A famous Dean. for short
83 Coarse hominy
87 Full of zest
88 Loosened a knot
89 Dancer Gaynor
91 Jumble
92 Egyptian month
93 A son of Odin: Var.
95 Absalom's slayer
97 Donny or Marie
99 More of the verse
103 Miller or Sheridan
104 Licorice-liqueur plant
105 Pleased
106 One kind of path
107 Miss Adams
108 Equipment
110 Debatable
112 Sartre play
115 "The Destroyer," to Hindus
117 Grayish-brown
120 "Dies ____"
124 End of the verse
128 Canine, e.g.
129 She's Reddy to sing
130 Fairway gouge
131 Defame
132 Shaded walk
133 Town north of Saigon
134 Triangular wooden frame
135 Dye for wood or wool
136 N, S, E and W
137 Not a soul
138 ____ up (excited)
139 Passover repast

DOWN

1 James ____ Garfield
2 Ball point's ancestor
3 Bearish
4 Puzzle purpose, possibly
5 Shrine Bowl team
6 Gounod favorite
7 Coveted court cup
8 "I like . . . women who have ____": Wilde
9 Bad guys' pursuers
10 Waste allowance
11 Chain
12 Tremulous
13 Mixt
14 Singer Ross
15 Caesarean rebuke
16 "____ little bit of butter . . .": Milne
17 "South Sea" discoverer
18 Of an eye part
19 Move edgewise
24 Actress Gwyn
30 "Eureka!"
31 "Back Street" author
32 "____ Is Dream of You"
38 The last word
39 Hot cross and honey
40 "Heads ____, . . ."
41 Sadat
42 Pip; lulu
43 Where Kaifeng is
45 Declare
46 Churchman: Abbr.
47 Patronize a bookie
48 "Applause" actress
49 Final notice
50 Pitts et al.
51 Queen of Eng.: 1558–1603
52 Simon's "____ Suite"
54 Tolkien's Frodo, for one
55 Hubbub
56 Masters, in Mysore
57 Potatoes, e.g.
64 Behind schedule
65 Invited
66 Collection
68 Resort in northwest France
70 Bandage, as a wound
71 Circled
72 Colliery access
73 Some singers, for short
75 Bend, in shipbuilding
76 "____ Down My Walking Cane"
77 Okay to swallow
78 Conductor Seiji
79 Mature
80 "My life ____ for his" (Damon's offer)
84 "I am ____ . . .": Yeats
85 Small change, in the agora
86 Peter, in Palencia
88 Small one: Suffix
89 Topgallant
90 "The world ____ much with us"
93 Mussolini
94 Rose lover
95 Day, in Dijon
96 Gallic agreement
98 Shroud in obscurities
100 Salad-bowl brighteners
101 Stern or Newton
102 Came clean
107 An Oxford college
108 Bible by a hotel bed
109 Show, as interest
111 Scull
112 ____ bene
113 "Whether it be new ____"
114 Salerno's neighbor
115 Word with graph or type
116 Greeting
117 Take potshots at
118 Diplomat
119 "Paul Pry" playwright
121 Hot on the subject
122 Coeur d' ____, Idaho
123 Aunt of "Oklahoma"
125 "Younger ____ Springtime"
126 Aleutian island
127 Greek group in W.W. II

102. Potboilers by Alex F. Black

ACROSS

1 Ami of Porthos
7 Dowdy ones
13 Piece of needlework
20 Most churlish
21 Battologize
22 Stein-line ending
23 "God sends meat ____": J. Taylor
26 Myerson
27 Fountain
28 Dagger of yore
29 Agreed upon
30 Electrical pioneer
31 Cold course, in Cannes
34 Start of a Synge title
37 Binaural systems
41 "The Forty Days of Musa ____"
42 Raced
43 "____ one is born a roaster of meat": Brillat-Savarin
48 Toast, in Tours
49 Rocky outcropping
50 Pat on the back
51 Sale stipulation
53 One of the Graces
55 Scale duo
58 High points
59 Darnel
60 Grayling
63 Hearth
65 Passover dinner
66 "Kissing ____": Meredith
70 Blockheads
72 Rival of A. J. Foyt
73 Ruhr city
74 Unyielding
75 Stage
76 Quite a bit
78 Mrs. Kowalski
83 Ponerology topic
84 Mother of Rome's twins
86 "Ecclesiam ____": Pope Paul VI
89 Oily liquid
90 "Oh, I am ____": Gilbert
95 Muscle
96 In any way
97 Long gone
98 Famed judge of Israel
101 Crepelike fabric
103 Involuntary wink
104 Hair fabric
105 Rodomontade
106 Pushers' pursuer
108 Blind as ____
112 "Ruling a big country is ____": Lao-tzu
119 Diaskeuasts
120 Laundered
121 Card game
122 Stimulus-response devices
123 Acclimates
124 Tiny grooves

DOWN

1 Steed for a caliph
2 Norse poem
3 Increases
4 Shea team
5 Kabibble
6 Crane of Spender
7 Guitar part
8 Dreams, in Dijon
9 News org.
10 Allen or Brooks
11 Excerpt
12 "The Red and the Black" author
13 Kind of kick or car
14 Jennet
15 Singer Davis
16 Anti's antonym
17 Unfettered
18 Glacial ridge
19 Caesurae
24 Returns to civvies
25 Society-page word
30 Ciceronian collection
32 Worship
33 Gangster's getaway
34 Crosses
35 Nettle
36 Reflected upon
37 Monkey wrench
38 Rossini hero
39 Col. neighbor
40 Like some wines
42 "Rugs"
43 Ursa. to Pedro
44 Show affection
45 Makes watertight
46 Threadbare, in Toledo
47 Flag
52 Indian weight
54 Total: Abbr.
56 Prefix with watt or wave
57 Mythical princess
61 Sabbath stricture
62 Foisted
64 Gets high
65 Having equal resonant frequency
66 Parthenon style
67 Wall St. quantities
68 Hill, to a Syrian
69 Object, in law
70 Fidel's former friend
71 Viscous destroyer
75 Compare
77 Rulers
79 Magdeburg's river
80 Spinks
81 Happy tune
82 Common connective
85 Capital of S. Australia
87 ____ glance
88 T.M. word or formula
91 Cry of surprise
92 City on the Rhone
93 These, in Thiers
94 Signs of winter
98 Soupy
99 Tolerate
100 Historic atoll
101 Rec. place
102 Follow
105 Ornament
107 Elec. units
108 Distant
109 Hindu's cheap cigarette
110 Dog star
111 Friends' pronoun
113 French connections
114 Bill's partner
115 Hockey superstar
116 Kokoon
117 Chalice veil
118 W.W. II craft

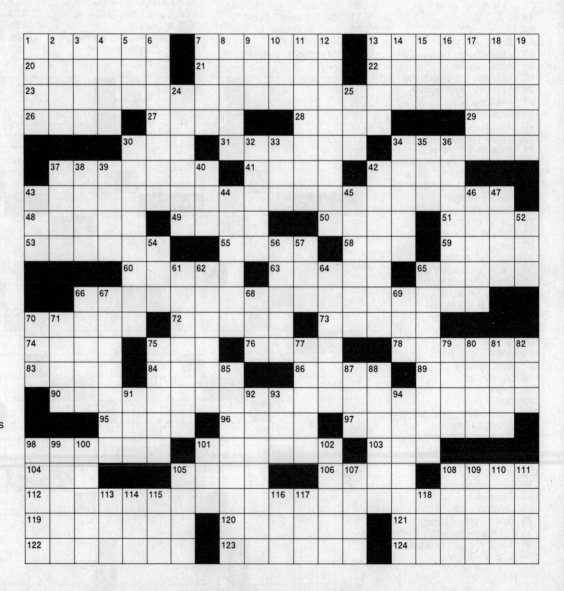

103. A Gaggle of Groups by Tap Osborn

ACROSS

1 Blueprint
5 Lusterless finish
10 Synthetic
16 Ottoman chiefs
20 Yokel
21 Thai, e.g.
22 Dinner party
23 Courage
24 Grunting group
27 Citified
28 Humdrum entree
29 Clerical group
31 Curmudgeon
32 Soul, to Descartes
33 Wide-shoe letters
34 Be fatuously fond
35 Heated
37 Canon cue sign
39 Zoroastrian's god
41 Grandson of Adam
42 Poised
43 Half a gaffe
44 Lose traction
46 Avant-gardist
48 Sandy's alert
49 Religious group
54 Minor, to a lawyer
58 Cover
59 Fashion
60 ____ fille
61 Serves as a mixologist
63 Dessert
64 Diamonds: Slang
65 Aug. 23–Sept. 22 person
66 La. name
67 ____ Pompilius
68 Old car
70 Threadlike structure: Comb. form
71 Mountain pool
72 United
73 Stage profession: Abbr.
75 Criminal group
79 A-F connection
80 Retreat
81 Language of some N.M. Indians
82 Ear benders
83 Window part
85 ____ facto
86 Norman Thomas bloc: Abbr.
87 Tremble with fear
88 Erwin
89 Sphere
92 Win a debate
94 Book size
95 Effete
96 Charge
97 Sadat's predecessor
98 Mendacious group
101 Strive in rivalry
102 Item for a dory
103 March, to Pompey's men
104 Kind of wind or omen
105 Autograph
106 Music guide mark
109 Confound
112 Pedestal part
115 "Scarlet Letter" name
117 Mary's follower
118 Homophone for neigh
119 Parking place
120 Kind of house or ship
121 Stroking group
127 Cagliari's locale
130 Sinclair
131 Very strict group
133 Vaticinators
134 Chitchat, British style
135 Pliny ____, U.S. inventor
136 Developed
137 Slips
138 Author of "The Potting Shed"
139 British golf cup
140 Girl in a Salinger tale

DOWN

1 Hyde Park vehicle
2 Magazine founder
3 Pair pulling for each other
4 Unallied
5 Father Prout, humorist
6 Dripping wet
7 Quarrel
8 Shooter for Junior
9 Craze
10 Sum, ____, fui . . .
11 Campus drill org.
12 Paduasoy material
13 Mars: Comb. form
14 Desert fruit
15 Made more savory
16 Hoity-toity group
17 Henry or Althea
18 Red dyestuff: Var.
19 Sight and taste
23 Eat
25 Ambitious bid
26 Poetic masterwork
30 Lambing
32 Asteroid
35 Cosmetic transplant area
36 Shinto temple gateway
37 Affectation
38 Arena gathering
39 Apery expert
40 Nabokov heroine
43 Ordered
45 City in Nigeria
47 Pass receiver
49 "One Fat Englishman" author
50 Coffee blend
51 Algonquian language
52 Iron: Comb. form
53 Attacks
55 Oenological group
56 "A Boy ____ Sue"
57 Hansa's purpose
62 Nine: Prefix
65 What belvederes afford
66 Afterward
69 Rude, clumsy group
70 "My Friend ____"
71 Grow bored with
73 "In like ____ . . ."
74 Neighbor of Naples
76 Classroom for Zeno
77 "____ Succeed . . ."
78 Spectral body
84 Penguins' cousins
86 Shoshonean
87 Recent: Comb. form
88 Endangered mammal
90 Prevail
91 Fashion's Geoffrey
93 Kind of jacket
94 Position
95 Subterfuge
99 Small, in Dogpatch
100 Merry song
105 Otologist's device
106 Section of a contract
107 Kitten, at times
108 Theatrical one
110 Neutralize a cobra
111 East Indian cedar
113 Spread of a sort
114 Deliberate
115 O. Henry
116 Joe ____ of baseball
120 Frankie, the pianist
122 Rural ways: Abbr.
123 A Johnson
124 Use of memory
125 Explorer Hedin
126 Simple
127 Corsican's neighbor
128 Grist for a list
129 "____ forgive those . . ."
132 Author Sarton

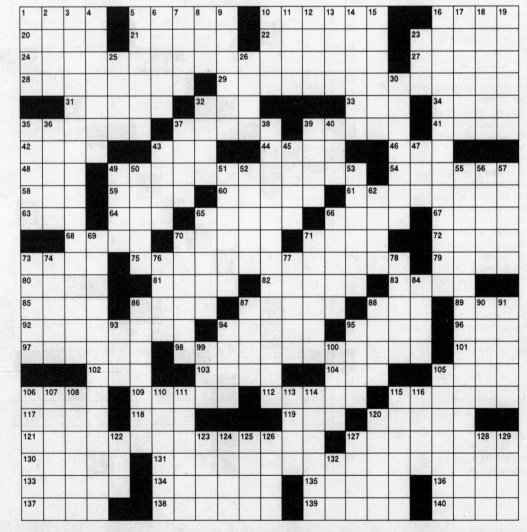

104. Who's Who by Virginia P. Abelson

ACROSS

1 Shade of brown
6 Mixer
10 On a cruise
14 Salk contemporary
19 Taro, for one
20 Church areas
22 Grimalkin
23 Maria Magdalena von Losch
25 Vast number
26 Osaka outcast
27 Butcher's merchandise
28 Wash out
29 Wickerwork willow
30 Kind of pin or stone
32 Decree
33 Troubles
34 M. Lupin
35 Arthur Stanley Jefferson
39 Keystone comic
42 Feudal lord
43 Twinge
44 Cliques
45 Divers information
46 Treaty gp. formed in 1948
47 Twirled
49 Trap
51 Fox or Rabbit
52 Nathan Birnbaum
55 Showy plant
56 Numbers man: Abbr.
59 Track units
60 One of the Pequod's owners
61 Resembling dice
62 Buildings at O'Hare
64 Price and Moffo
65 Tallest quadruped
66 Actor Edward and family
67 Haired like a mare
68 Between few and many
69 G-man
70 Inscribed pillar
71 Natasha Gurdin
73 Bench warmers
74 West Coast shrub
75 Direct a helmsman
76 Friend, in Aberdeen
79 Novelist Levin
80 Nobelist name: 1947
81 Essex or Nash
83 Factory
85 D.C. V.I.P.
86 Roy Fitzgerald
89 Want
90 A D-day target
92 "___, you noblest English!"
93 Ant
94 Callas
96 Island in Firth of Clyde
98 Colombian poncho
100 ___ Palmas
101 Inge's "___ of Roses"
102 Ruby Stevens
105 Springfield, e.g.
106 Certain stocks
107 One of a Hindu weaver class
108 Blasé
109 Marquis de ___
110 MacDonald's co-star
111 Ruhr city

DOWN

1 Of judicial chambers
2 "Christmas" or "Easter"
3 Battle scene: May, 1942
4 "Black gold"
5 Harmony lass
6 Cartoonist William ___
7 Artillery: Abbr.
8 Platform
9 Dunce, in Dijon
10 Roof adjunct
11 Push, in Pisa
12 Useful catchalls
13 Wimbledon winner in 1975
14 B. of E. concern
15 Faulkner's "___ for Emily"
16 William Henry Pratt
17 Shade of blue
18 ___-do-well
21 Sequence
24 Zilch
31 Shanks' mare
32 Rooter
33 Dampens
35 They jingle, jangle, jingle
36 Coarse seaweed
37 Treating shabbily
38 Kin: Abbr.
40 "___ to Live," TV program
41 Flaunted
47 Burns
48 Boston ___
49 Lake trout
50 Miners' finds
51 Rum cake
52 Glower
53 City on the Moselle
54 Chamfer
55 Salted
56 Frame
57 Lea
58 Anna Maria Italiano
61 Athenian commander
63 Sets
64 Computer fodder
65 Hatchet man
67 Russian diplomat
68 Faint
71 Undercover cop
72 Outer: Prefix
74 Forthwith
76 Actor Jack ___
77 Maxwell, Miller and Monroe
78 Musical interval
80 Wrinkled
81 God: Heb.
82 Waves' org.
83 Heavily: Mus. dir.
84 Wilder's "___ of Our Teeth"
87 Nasty
88 Helpless
89 Actress Merrill
91 Passageway
93 Fall guy
94 Red planet
95 Inter ___
96 "Us on ___," old song
97 Pro ___ (proportionally)
98 Foray
99 Worn
103 Turnpike: Abbr.
104 Existed

105. Capital Phrases by William Lutwiniak

ACROSS

1 Pickets
6 Propounded
11 ___ Pradesh, India
16 Robe for Cornelia
21 Swarming
22 Fanon
23 Pulitzer Prize author: 1918
24 Citified
25 Milkweed extract
26 Of apples
27 Medieval guild
28 Irish goblin
29 Rome
33 Conservative
34 Boundary
35 Les girls
36 Italian article
37 Sinuous shape
38 Crook in a branch
39 Relative of Sèvres
40 Video production
45 Troop group
46 Arkansas toothpick
47 Walt Kelly creation
48 U.S.S.R. river
49 Berlin
57 Glissade
58 W.W. II org.
59 Land of the Cymry
60 Cather's "___ Ours"
61 Asian evergreen
62 Shearer of ballet
64 Not live
65 Lovable
66 Hit letters
67 Disciplinarian
68 Singer Sumac
69 Black Sea resort
70 Panama
78 Part of U.S.N.A.
79 Salt Lake City athlete
80 Siouan Sooners
81 Fishpond occupant
82 Flounder
85 Walk daintily
87 Last of the Mohicans
88 Amphora handle
89 At ___ (confused)
90 Herd of seals
91 Poetic time
92 Till now
93 Vienna
99 SHAEF area
100 Venetians' resort
101 Budget item
102 ___ Gev, Israeli settlement
103 Identical
106 Sparling
108 Habilimented
110 G-man
113 Make known
114 Ho's partner
115 QE2 berth
116 Jungle sound
117 Copenhagen
123 Noxious substance
124 "___ Rookh"
125 Kid
126 Is a party to
127 Beautify
128 Made slick
129 Join
130 Theater seats
131 Backs
132 Resplendence
133 Cooper role
134 Conte

DOWN

1 Intellectual relish
2 Cottonwoods
3 Petrol units
4 Companion of each
5 Numerical prefix
6 Brilliantine
7 Temple or mandarin
8 Palliate
9 "Roast Pig" essayist
10 Rundown
11 Supported
12 Precisely
13 Show biz awards
14 To boot
15 Reduce sail
16 Limber
17 Capricorn, e.g.
18 Agora coin
19 Placid or Como
20 Boswellian collection
30 Thurify
31 "The Man ___"
32 Radiant
38 Cheat on a check
39 Wild sheep
40 ___ down (muted)
41 ___ Benedict
42 Portrayed
43 Hebrew Hades
44 Resembling peat
45 Nobelist in Literature: 1947
46 ___ David
47 Wroclaw man
49 Extreme
50 Native of Khartoum
51 Star-crossed
52 Agnew
53 Pundit
54 Spider monkey
55 Directs
56 Ink or rubber
57 Window part
62 Title for a chairperson
63 Supplement
64 Melville novel
65 Kin of cabbages
67 Bigot
69 Heathen: It.
71 Wetland
72 Pruritic
73 ___ as a pin
74 Took measured steps
75 Plastic for records
76 LTD's extinct relative
77 Ottoman
82 Men
83 Upper crust
84 "Dead Souls" author
85 Actress Adams
86 "Wishing Will Make ___"
88 Garland's "___ of the Middle Border"
90 Decorous
92 Gobilike
94 Cigar
95 Short: Prefix
96 Let up
97 Tolkien creature
98 Gets the benefit
104 Moslem mendicants
105 Raw pigment
106 Bear of a sort
107 Arthritis, e.g.
108 Shut
109 Hard-hit balls
110 Precede
111 Island annexed by Chile
112 Chichi
114 Cry of surprise
115 Aver
116 Golem, for one
117 Mossback
118 Nero's or Caesar's wife
119 Whip
120 Lament
121 Kelly or Tunney
122 Dutch painter
123 Urchin

106. Mute Musicale by Bert H. Kruse

ACROSS

1 C.S.A. general
6 "The Destroyer," to Hindus
10 ____ Alaska
15 More acidic
16 Flu symptoms
17 Region of simple pleasure
19 Capote work
21 Aquatic herbs
23 ". . . reck the ____": Burns
24 Presupposes
25 Mirador
26 Lupulus
27 Last word
28 Publications for employees
30 Virginia's Virginia
31 Cultivation of land
33 Grand Central: Abbr.
34 Auto pioneer
35 Nodded
36 Bond rating
37 Pointed arch
39 Melville book
41 Forest clearing
42 Othello's people
43 Tint
44 Japanese art medium
45 Kin of olés
47 Dull fellows
50 Snack
54 Boxed
55 Miss Negri
56 Came down
57 Dome
58 Suggestions
59 Additional
60 Force
61 Like certain organs
62 "The Gloomy Dean"
63 Indefinite number
64 Leonardo lady
65 Rely
66 Equal
67 Pentagon V.I.P.'s
69 Alter ego, e.g.
70 Danube tributary
72 "I Like ____"
73 Items in the fire
74 Bend over
76 Put by
78 Slangy denial
79 Cote sound
82 Seal
83 Marquette, for one
84 Dep.
85 Mild oaths
87 Sally ____ (tea cake)
88 Hearing aids
92 Discordia, to Greeks
93 Headache relief: Pharm.
94 Spanish rooms
95 Bradley U. site
96 Trig term
97 Dangerous dwelling
99 Symbol of dependence
101 U.S.-U.S.S.R. breather
102 Italian statesman
103 Sings atop 42 Down
104 Use a divining rod
105 Hunter's quarry
106 Della or ex-Dodger

DOWN

1 Vagabond's world
2 ____ Paix
3 Silvery
4 Land south of Den.
5 Ending for poly or tele
6 Dichotomy
7 "____ war": F.D.R.
8 Left-hand page
9 Viper
10 U.C.L.A. team
11 Sheridan character
12 Malden or Marx
13 Nigerian city
14 Stubborn one
15 Layers
16 Promises
17 Chafe
18 Renee of silents
20 Chimney sweeps
22 Tore
25 Coquet
29 Captured a dogie
30 Water carriers
32 Smiths' concerns
35 Slippery ____
38 Virtuous
39 Remote goal
40 Arizona city
41 Squall
42 Swiss-Italian peak
44 Hit, old style
45 Pickling solution
46 Kitchen appliance
47 Biblical mountain
48 Claude of cinema
49 Cubitus
51 Made of a grain
52 Endure
53 Ziegfeld's first wife
54 Amy's big brother
55 Vainglory
59 Place in space
60 Gave medicine to
61 Striated
63 Discontinue
64 Construct
65 Mail receiver
68 Charles or James
69 Book illustration, for short
71 White or Wilkins
73 Medic
74 Obtuse
75 Norman Crusade leader
76 Monterrey blanket
77 Liberal ____
79 Leathernecks
80 Ecstatic
81 Tax
82 Elgar's "King ____"
83 Sense of taste
84 Foolish
86 Dwell
88 Merits
89 Train bed
90 Ancient Ethiopian capital
91 Butterfly
94 Lobscouse
98 W.W. II arena
99 See 42 Down
100 Cervine creature

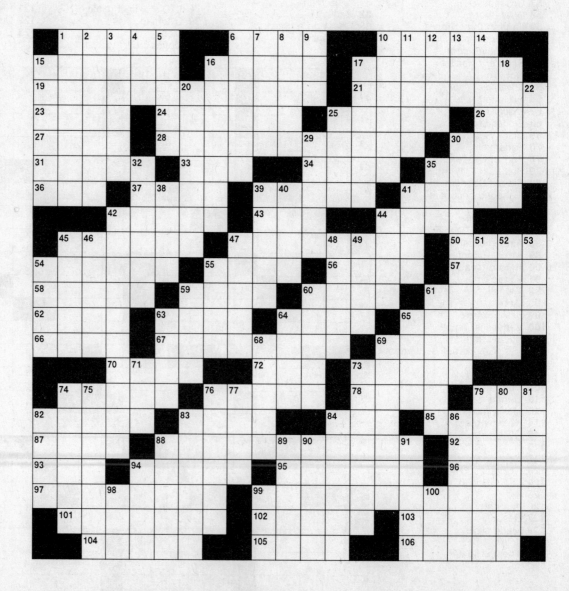

107. Urban Sound Waves by A. J. Santora

ACROSS

1 Union general
6 Maggie's mate
11 Army reserve gp.
15 Spoof
20 Modify
21 Page's trip
23 Precinct
24 Cinched
25 Where Michiganders might gander
27 Equal
28 Short novel
29 Relative of alpha
30 Common contraction
31 Woven fabric
33 H.G. Wells's "____ Bungay"
35 Needlefish
36 Retreats
38 Burrows
39 Notre Dame receiver
42 Landlord, in Livorno
43 Road shoulders
46 Noted U.S. physicist
47 "A ____ the wise . . ."
48 In any way
50 Dresses
52 Lhasa ____ (terrier)
53 Piles up
55 Fertilizer
56 Go it alone
58 Bryophyte
62 Color: Poetic
63 Stunning woman
64 Seattle basketeer
66 Disavowing
69 Trial lawyer Bailey
70 "____ fine lady . . ."
71 Zoological ending
72 Cockle
73 Neutral hue
75 Valley of grapes
77 N.C.O.
78 Little League baseball
83 Rowan
86 Devilism is one
87 Bohr subject
88 Swami
89 Flanged beam
93 Willful damage
95 Fairy-tale heavy
97 Decorator's color
99 Kind of wine
101 Musket balls, in India
103 Central rooms
104 Printing directive
105 ____ Minor
106 A Hollywood King
107 Wrote
109 Weather satellite
111 Most conceited
113 Ph.D. topic
114 Amoretto
117 Guttural
118 Think piece
120 Ref. books
123 Hula-dancing dazzler
125 Skill
126 Beehive
127 Chalice
128 Mil. medals
129 Mere: Comb. form
131 He rode Champion
133 Certain cover-up
134 Pilfer
136 Farm unit
138 It rivals Ozone Park ozone
141 Did he root for Yale?
142 Brad or spad
143 Mantle was one
144 Wash out
145 Golfing cup
146 Conjunctives
147 Turf
148 Gathered leaves

DOWN

1 Improvise, in a way
2 Gladdens
3 Theatrical group in Ga.?
4 Minerva, e.g.
5 Writer Bombeck
6 Wicked women
7 Mangle
8 Cave
9 Atlas rel.
10 Brumal blanket
11 Ecstasy
12 Pay dirt
13 Cut cuspids
14 St.-John's-bread
15 Kittatinny neighbors
16 Numero ____
17 Sounded a bell
18 Astronaut's instrument
19 ____-well
22 Soft leather gloves
26 Fit for planting
32 ____ clock (friarbird)
34 R.I. red wine?
37 Tightening device
40 Network
41 Athenian course for foo-traces
44 Shade of purple
45 Duped
49 Movie dog
51 Sigma follower
52 Ginger drink
53 Bell town
54 Free waters
57 Appearance
59 Purse fillers
60 Teutonic triumph
61 Avaunt!
63 Pop-in people
64 Nasty remark
65 Fly high
67 Ohio vehicle
68 Improbable
69 Out of
73 Ferrara family name
74 Sharkey of TV
76 Little, e.g.
79 Baker's aide
80 Contrary girl
81 Casual wear
82 Behind ____ (not "with it")
83 Singer Ed
84 Shaker filler
85 ____ Park
90 Place for Carson's checks?
91 Cambodge is here
92 Peruse
94 Kind of doxy
96 Driveway material
97 Come together
98 Singular
100 Paleozoic ____
101 Card game
102 Horatian creation
106 Small bottles
107 Surprised
108 Xanthippe's crock
110 Yellowish butterfly
112 Lab pots
114 Variety of beetle
115 Sermon
116 Eelgrass, e.g.
117 God on Mt. Etna
119 Limoges item
121 Cherry red
122 Was clement
124 Rain-forest plant
130 Provided that
131 Alaskan island
132 Scotch terrier's growl
135 Cuban hero
137 Disencumber
139 Opp. of SSE
140 Creek

108. Woof! by Sam Bellotto, Jr.

ACROSS

1 Smart follower
6 White House monogram: 1881–85
9 Legatee
13 Bundles: Abbr.
16 Ring around Rover
18 Cantor lass
20 Erstwhile
21 Chemical suffix
22 Part of B.L.T.
23 Prefix with action or figure
24 Put one's foot down
25 Shooting, in Savoie
26 Baudelaire, e.g.
28 It comes in scales
30 Name for a field dog
33 Midwestern rodents
35 "____ Tu," 1932 pop song
36 Purposive
38 Army org.
39 Stone or dog's
40 Peaks: Abbr.
41 Father of the Titans
43 Updike's "A Month of ____"
47 Canine coat
48 Of mixed origin
50 Waste away
51 Obligations
54 Fido's favorite food
56 Acted, in Arles
57 Table of ____
59 Detestable
63 Telephone word
65 Egg-shaped
66 Hound or line
67 More strange, to Alice
69 Gwyn and others
70 Adhered
71 "Here's looking ____!"
72 Polk was one
74 Page corners, turned down
76 Kitchen meas.
78 Letter after yodh
79 Apologetic interjection
80 Bugs and Buddy
82 Geological time period
87 Compass pt.
88 Hair stylist Vidal
90 Pompey's booty
91 R.R. depots
93 ____-de-sac
94 Antlered ruminant
96 Certain lingerie
97 ____ impasse
98 Incisor's neighbor
103 Cockle
104 Utterly exhausted
106 Galoshes
108 Pothouse potion
109 El ____
110 Emmett song: 1859
111 Viola's bridegroom
115 "Delta of Venus" author
116 Pulled thread
117 ____-Unis
118 Big-A "dog"
119 Inexplicable
120 Endings with musket and cannon
121 One or another
122 Cause jubilance

DOWN

1 Dog ____, in vaudeville
2 Old card game
3 Relative of a dogwood
4 Gripping
5 Girl in a 1918 song
6 Scribe's flourish
7 Light ____ (weightless)
8 Thus, in Tours
9 Showoffish athletes
10 Madden
11 Images
12 Foxx
13 Ringed planet
14 Stabs
15 Villeins, to lords
17 Caper
18 Ermines
19 Italian princely family
27 Sibling: Abbr.
29 Dogged tennis player
30 Unfermented grape juice
31 Edible submarine
32 Spirit
34 First New World printer
37 Crusty old codgers
40 Grant growth
42 Clairvoyant
44 New Deal org.
45 Toolsheds
46 Farewell
47 Merriment
49 Indian sailors
51 Sometime dog-walker
52 ____ Gay (bomber)
53 Limicoline bird
55 Ger. tribesmen
57 No. 4 wood
58 Radical coll. group
59 Permit
60 Coryza symptom
61 Sympathetic
62 Thirsty
64 Hallucinogenic chem.
66 A-E connection
68 Jots
73 Uncloses, in poetry
75 Dog ____ (baboon)
77 Con neutralizer
80 Romantic isle
81 Campus clique
83 Huge
84 Kazan
85 Light bites
86 Orient
88 Parhelia
89 Wild West "neckwear"
91 Impassive
92 Tail
93 Latin II "teaser"
95 Ordinal suffix
97 Hersey town
98 Davit
99 Protuberance
100 A Peron
101 Dale Evans, e.g.
102 Cask part
105 ____ dixit
107 Writer Gardner
112 Call ____ day
113 Catch sardines
114 Miner's find

109. Command Performance by James and Phyllis Barrick

ACROSS

1 Chagall
5 Throat-clearing sound
9 Bam!
14 Quick bread
19 Stair post
20 "Olympia" painter
22 Do a gardening job
23 Weight unit
24 Former mil. educ. program
25 Ruhr city
26 Histrion
27 Cant
28 With 30 Across, sports fan's imperative
30 See 28 Across
33 Albanians' neighbors
34 Thread: Comb. form
35 Check
36 Aphrodite's beloved
37 Stone paving block
39 Exploit
41 Voltaire was one
44 Spotlight
47 Part of speech
49 Yellow water flag
51 Tough alloy
53 Heart
56 Enjoin
57 "Camino ____"
58 Child in a casa
59 Dry, as wine
60 Sidestep
62 Chip's sister
63 Org. formed in 1844
64 Valuable shell
66 Skinks and geckos
68 Moslem leader
70 Formerly formerly
72 Bridge expert
74 Famed choreographer
75 W.W. II initials
76 Fir or pine board
77 Geometer's term
78 Oxford measure
79 What the Dr. ordered
80 Condition
83 Greek colonnade
85 "____ that touch liquor . . ."
87 Madrileño's coin
89 Score standard
90 Recent: Comb. form
92 Relative
94 Dueling blade
96 For, to Fabius
97 Left undone
99 Foch of films
100 Formal wear
101 Keddah
103 Brought to light
105 Twilled fabric
107 Noun suffix
109 Looked for clams
111 Fragrant resin
112 Use a straw
114 Instigate
115 Build
116 Macaw of Brazil
117 Neighbor of Isr.
118 Kind of drip
120 Australian parrot
121 Game piece
122 Ferrer or Allen
123 Starchy foodstuff
125 Melville opus
127 Couple
129 Property
134 Hardy heroine
136 Vessel for an adm.
138 Kitchen item
141 With 145 Across, bride's imperative
145 See 141 Across
147 Essence
148 Rose: Comb. form
149 Exchange premiums
151 Himalayan apparitions
152 Card game
153 Rod of baseball
154 Very soft and liquid
155 What spread-eagleists do
156 Room for jugs, linens, etc.
157 Mme. de ____
158 Indigency
159 Applies

DOWN

1 Western scenery
2 Vigilant
3 Alludes
4 Cragsman's imperative
5 Soul, in Savoie
6 Wears
7 Occurred as a consequence
8 Cardinals' imperative
9 Outburst
10 Prom flower
11 Kitten's quality
12 Peak
13 ". . . ____ perfumed sea": Poe
14 Cooking direction
15 Lading
16 Harmonium
17 Ruth's mother-in-law
18 Diminutive suffixes
19 Acorn
21 Potent compound
29 Value
31 Certain numbers
32 Advanced
38 Went over carefully
40 Sevareid
42 Road of yore
43 Withdraw
44 Arab garment
45 Branches
46 Dust bowler's imperative
48 Tantaras
50 Fabric with a lustrous finish
52 Hostess's imperative
53 Queen's imperative
54 Short poem
55 Mignonette
61 Clock numerals
65 WAC colonel's imperative
67 Coop sound
69 Counselor: Abbr.
71 Archfiend
73 One of the Marx Brothers
80 Ascus contents
81 In a docile way
82 Blind, in falconry
84 Toughen
86 Peninsula in Alaska
88 Patriotic org.
91 Black Sea port
93 Moslem's hat
95 Thalia, Clio et al.
98 Pro ____
102 Unadulterated
104 Watch part
106 Microbe
108 Celebrated tenor
110 Colleen, colloquially
113 Excess
119 Helper: Abbr.
124 River in the Carolinas
126 Songbird
128 Inhibits
129 Wide open
130 Goat antelope
131 Feed a fire
132 Hard red wheat
133 Pathetic
135 Glower
137 Gave light
139 Plutarch work, for short
140 Sends forth
142 Grampuses
143 Demonstrative
144 Former Mideast initials
146 Compass pt.
150 One of the Chaplins

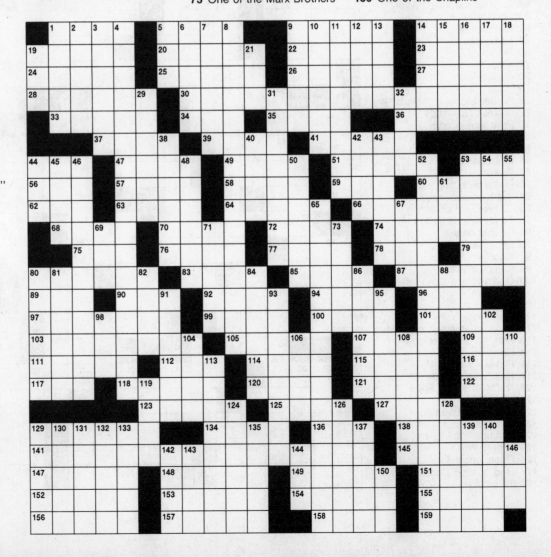

110. Rhyme Scheme by Maura B. Jacobson

ACROSS

1 Highlander
5 Masterson
8 Common contraction
12 State without proof
18 ". . . God ___ joined together"
19 Cuckoo
20 Talk-show hostess
22 Not so taut
23 Wings for Amor
24 Neptune's domain
25 Quicker
27 Munich Mr.
28 Tbilisi's river
30 Harpsichordist Landowska
31 Georgia ___ Clark
32 Sticker
36 ___ pearl
37 Son of Ramses I
38 Corn unit
39 Bouillon ingredient
41 Study: Suffix
44 Jeanne d'___
45 Trick, in Toledo
48 Chaplinesque figures
52 Alone
54 Slicker
57 Type of tent
58 Suffix for Paul or Bernard
59 Russian stream
60 Spectral
61 City in Cebu
62 St. Paul's writings: Abbr.
64 Sproutings
66 Shade tree
67 Fainéants
69 Pricker
70 Irate
72 Badger
74 Issue
76 Author Stone, to friends
77 Actress Rowlands
80 Puts fringes on
82 Electrical units
83 Would-be flower
85 More balanced
87 Ticker
90 Bird's breathing aid
91 "I'll take ___ road"
92 Convex, as a molding
93 Trafalgar and Times: Abbr.
94 Ordinal ending
95 ___ the finish
97 Mouths
98 Calendar abbr.
100 Galsworthy's "___ of Devon"
103 Flicker
110 Lieder
112 "___ of Roses," Inge play
113 Can.'s Yukon, for one
114 Disfigure
116 Picker
119 Healer at Valhalla
120 N.K.V.D. predecessor
121 Melodious
122 Quondam rulers
123 Caucho
124 Yuletide
125 Flag
126 Once, once
127 Mud or clay: Comb. form
128 To be: Lat.

DOWN

1 Pahlevi
2 Dickens's Plummer
3 Hokkaido city
4 Units of heat
5 Wicker
6 Lacking nervous energy
7 Coronet
8 Doctrine
9 Sprayed
10 Stars that blaze and fade
11 Triplets
12 Landon
13 Bank deal
14 Is humiliated
15 Cosmetician Lauder
16 Honkers
17 Made a gaffe
21 Within: Prefix
26 Togs
29 Vinegary mixture
33 Artist Rembrandt
34 Chili con ___
35 Himalayan apparition
40 Borgnine
41 "The bird ___ the Wing"
42 Hip joint
43 Snicker
46 Round robin: Abbr.
47 Hairdo
49 Thicker
50 Sandbox sight
51 Goblet part
53 Mild oath
54 "___ Boys Goodbye"
55 Untanned pelt
56 Do a tailoring job
63 Previous
64 Game for two
65 Bicker
68 Unit of instruction
69 Position, in Pisa
71 Hungarian city
72 Salamander
73 ___ Isaacs Menken of stage fame
75 "___ a Californian . . .": Frost
78 Without a chaser
79 Ogee, e.g.
81 "Mood Indigo" co-composer
83 Ayr child
84 Directed skyward
86 Held firmly
88 "___ brillig . . ."
89 Knickers
93 Aseptic
96 Spring phenomenon
99 Signoret
100 Musical org.
101 English sculptor
102 She wrote "The Promised Land"
104 Seine sight
105 Vikings
106 Ridge, in geology: Var.
107 Start a golf game
108 Nigerian capital
109 Cries of pain
111 Mediocre
115 Kicker
117 ___ sequitur
118 Q-U connection

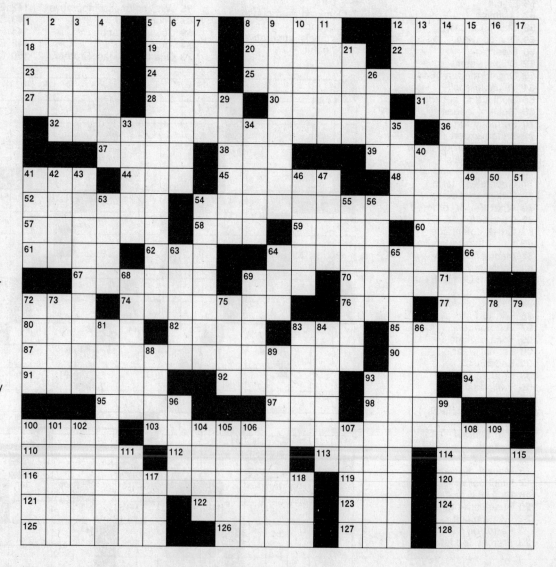

111. Atten—shun! by Arnold Moss

ACROSS

1 F-clef man
6 Kind of paper
11 African republic
15 Former defense pact
20 Rubinstein
21 Western jamboree
22 Kindled anew
24 Playwright Rice
25 Bagpipe's sound
26 Perform
27 G.M. Cohan's ancestors
28 Like Galahad
29 Locales for the Montessori method
31 1976, e.g.
33 Young onions
34 Euripides drama
35 Lisper's block
38 In the year before Christ: Abbr.
39 Bergland's dept.
40 Words on a new invention
48 Forest near London
52 Cabin cruisers
53 Facility
54 Skirt feature
55 Author Heyerdahl
57 Fanatical
58 Year in Severus's reign
59 Step above shavetail
63 Falstaff's title
64 Odalisque's quarters
65 Sides in cricket
66 "____ perfumed sea": Poe
67 Fair share
68 Ohs' partners
69 Amazed tourists
70 Hwys.
72 French brandy
74 Poland Chinas
76 Peon's pittance
77 KO finale
80 Municipal employee
85 Cry at Cork
86 Stage platform
88 Filipino chief
89 His name "led all the rest"
90 Skiing turns
93 Little brother of TNT
94 Chinese pagoda
96 Unfeigned
98 Inst. at Sandhurst
99 Mexican's cloak
100 Law, in Lille
101 Eisenstein's "Ten ____ the World"
104 Encore!
105 Moon crater
107 "Simon ____"
108 Crow of a kind
109 Film-maker Clair
110 "The light militia ____ sky": Pope
113 One of the steeplejacks
114 Fitzgerald opus
116 Sloth is one
117 Road sign
118 Pirandello's "____ Personaggi . . ."
119 Golfer Crenshaw
120 Music halls
124 Part of T.L.C.
131 Talent peddlers
135 Blender reading
136 French spa
138 Ghostly
139 Globe-carrier
140 "____ Give You Anything . . ."
141 Arrested
142 Raised Cain
143 Fraternal order
144 Cozy places
145 Chit
146 Ensile
147 ____ Tages (one day): Ger.

DOWN

1 Sunbathes
2 Okie's cousin
3 Pinch pennies
4 Voiceless consonants
5 Heraldry device
6 Piatigorsky
7 Legendary king of Ireland
8 Jewish month
9 Scallop
10 Very uncomfortable situation
11 Dernier ____
12 Jacob's ladder, e.g.
13 Hawaiian royalty
14 Kind of jockey
15 Judge's decision
16 He wrote "The Israelis"
17 Both: Prefix
18 Membrane
19 City on the Oka
23 Ara
30 Actress Diana
32 River nymph
36 Note-taker, for short
37 Swagger
39 Highest of the Pyrenees
40 Bode
41 Case in Lat. grammar
42 Shard
43 City once called Lutetia
44 Shrimps, crabs, etc.
45 Savoir-____
46 Willow
47 Champagne center
48 Strenuous try
49 Pedestal part
50 Fire worshiper
51 U.S. publicans
52 Soft, in Sedan
55 Capital of Albania
56 Core
58 Discipline
60 Monkeylike mammals
61 Their Jane gained fame
62 Just out
68 Anthology
69 Publish
71 Less plentiful
73 Road along a cliff
75 "____ the Lord . . ."
76 Greek port or gulf
78 Harmonium
79 In shape
81 Crosby's widow
82 "A Tramp ____": Twain
83 "Weep ____, . . ."
84 Richard or Sophie
87 Greek vowel
90 Spruce up
91 Engaged in
92 Fatuous
93 One of 12
95 Money in the bank
97 Ruhr city
100 Surplus or vestige
101 Fleur-____
102 Salt
103 Inflation result: Abbr.
106 Author Kesey
110 Olav's capital
111 Haitian hero
112 Certain shoe polishes
113 Sangria base
115 Keys
116 Leave a group
119 Pipe
120 H.R.E. founder
121 Actor Alain
122 Delete
123 Onagers
124 Bowling item
125 Führer's ally
126 Cycles
127 Fissure
128 Gogol hero
129 Señora's boy
130 Canter, e.g.
132 Fuel in Galway
133 "Tantum ____"
134 "____ That Tune!"
137 Compass point

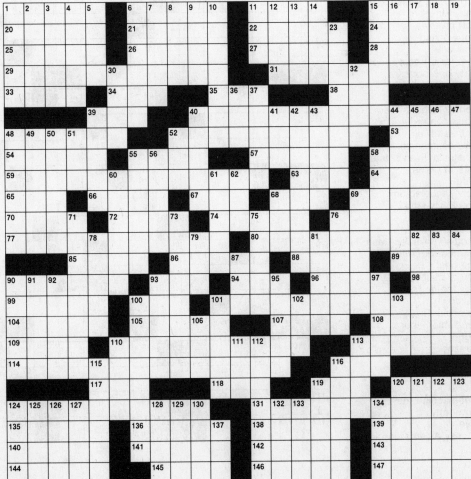

112. Expansion Teams by David J. Pohl and John M. Samson

ACROSS

1 Toy gun ammo
5 Put to ____ (printed)
8 Lava's cousin
13 Pythias' pal
18 Pepper
19 Scull
20 Eaglewood
21 Toughen
22 Old movie
23 New York debating team
26 "____ bragh!"
28 Maia or Electra
29 Negligent
30 Kind of show or warm-up
32 Performs
33 Pedestal part
34 Lebanese pit team
37 Hebrew letter
38 Space agcy.
42 Authors Mary and John
43 Scrambling Russian team
45 Lyric drama by Giordano
49 Run ____ (encounter)
51 Guarnieri's master
52 Witticism
53 Idolize
54 Org. formed in 1860–61
55 Dante's "____ Nuova"
57 Maria of tennis fame
59 Middle Eastern ecdysiast team
62 Kitchen gadget
64 Tips for tecs
65 "Exodus" hero
66 Other, to Odette
67 Refuse
70 Leg-pulling Welsh team
75 Poet Ginsberg
76 Soft breeze
77 Not working
78 Until now
79 Org. for a troop troupe
80 Kelly or Moore
83 Knot
85 Contemptuous
86 Henley Regatta team
88 Inquisition order
90 U.S. satellite
91 Dit's companion
92 Emotional French team
98 Wife of Osiris
100 Judge
101 Holy candelabrum
102 Greek city-state
105 Author Wouk
107 Meager
108 Scottish phys. ed. team noted for coolness
112 The best
113 Throat malady
114 Dog tag, for short
115 Razorbill
116 To scold: Sp.
117 "Endymion" poet
118 Blend
119 Garland
120 Machine carbine

DOWN

1 Slot-machine fruit
2 More lofty
3 Dive
4 Clumsy Asian skiing team
5 Fishing float
6 Mark or muff
7 Descent
8 ____ break (crucial)
9 Winners in 1918
10 Prado display
11 Heal
12 Botanist Gray
13 Cut into cubes
14 Windflower
15 Mr. Weisenfreund
16 Scraps
17 Loch ____
18 Moved stealthily
24 Firstborn
25 Necktie
27 Birthplace of G.R.F.
31 Greek letter
33 Arp's art
35 Turning point
36 Goblet for Henry VIII
37 Melodic subject
39 ____ forces
40 Pit
41 Famed son of a Waldorf butcher
43 Phooey!
44 African water polo team
45 Become weary
46 Author LeShan
47 Egg-case no.
48 Delos consultant
50 Defeated soundly
54 Amerind
56 Lilylike plant
58 Disquiet
60 Wine cask
61 Jack the quipper
62 Polish
63 Companion of thdr.
66 Influence
67 Braised meat stew
68 "____ Dream," Wagner aria
69 Becomes lumpy
70 Snooker sticks
71 Antibes antiseptics
72 U.S. humorist
73 ____ Borch, Dutch painter
74 Swine's confines
76 A protein, for short
81 Unit of angular measure
82 Cry said with a sigh
84 Mesabi miner
85 Homophone for sneeze
87 "Flattop" is one
89 Father of Isaac: Abbr.
92 Danish explorer
93 Aloof
94 Grooming process
95 Fur for Ferdinand
96 ____ thought (engrossed)
97 More reserved
99 Organ knobs
100 Check
102 Loot
103 This stack'll crackle
104 Venezuelan copper center
105 Cover up
106 Patricia from Ky.
109 Obscure
110 Repent
111 Long runner

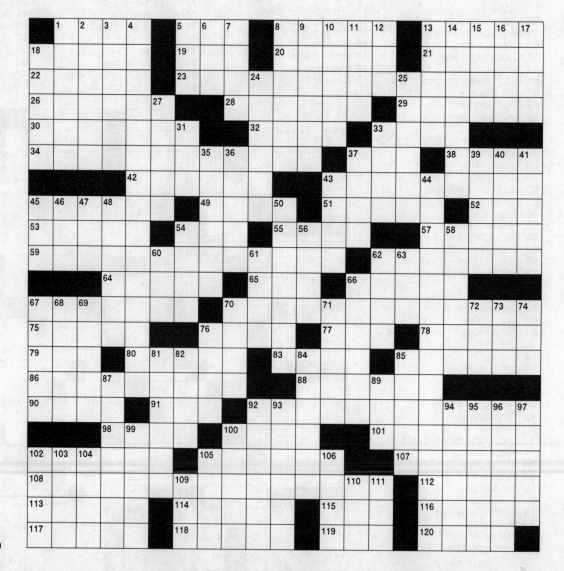

113. Pound Foolish by Henry Hook

ACROSS

1 Televiewer's problem
7 Bronx cheer
11 MacMurray
15 Shelter for cows
19 Like Jenny Lind, e.g.
20 Robert ____
21 Prentiss
22 Ending with court or right
23 Upstart
24 Zaftig
27 Begin's land: Abbr.
28 Scotch cocktails
30 Sodden
31 Parlor, in Puebla
32 Jacket or collar
34 Compete in a roleo
35 "Applause" actress
38 Impenetrable
41 Trevi throwaways
42 Ibsen hero
43 Scottish ruler: 1437–60
44 "The Kiss" sculptor
45 Fish or sailboat
47 Heywood proverb, with "The"
49 "The corn is ____. . ."
50 Leeds's river
51 Together: Mus. dir.
52 Dock wkr.
53 Bygone toiler
55 123-45-6789 org.
58 Party garb, at times
64 Lasses
66 Algerian port
69 Astronaut
70 TV ad
73 Pod plant
74 British and Roman
77 Approach to a pew
78 A title since 1882
83 Tatum O'Neal's Oscar role
84 Inserts new ammo
85 "____ Yar," Yevtushenko poem
86 Still
87 Connections
89 Iodine source
90 Bargain hunter's time
93 Cruel people
95 Kept a tryst
97 To join, in Dijon
98 Judicial garb
101 Author of "The Alteration"
104 "____ Cassius . . ."
106 "Was ____?" (Berliner's query)
108 College V.I.P.
115 Agua ____ (race track)
117 Frost's "____ Will"
118 Bishop's staff
119 Tim or Alice
120 Wagtail's cousin
121 Doesn't stay put
122 Mother's whistler
123 Snorting sound
124 High-hat
125 Pioneer in Hollywood
127 Horseplay
128 Field tent for G.W.
131 Ripen
132 Eddy song
137 Woody Allen film
139 Argot
140 Needlework case: Var.
141 Hoarfrost
142 Sudden great profit
143 Hefner or Downs
144 Elihu of Boston
145 Caesar's wife
146 Words "in your eyes," musically

DOWN

1 Third Reich emblems
2 Modern maniac
3 Part of speech: Abbr.
4 Level
5 "Money ____ object"
6 Twister from Philly
7 Homework assignment
8 Chemical radical
9 Kin of omegas
10 Colombian statesman
11 Disney classic
12 Indian drugget, e.g.
13 Extension
14 "Seven ____ in May"
15 ____ Georgia, succulent peach
16 We
17 Jamican export
18 Occult ability
19 Pitches
21 "Five Easy ____"
25 Pundit
26 Chaplain
29 Canadien's milieu
33 Cohan, to Uncle Sam
35 College in Maine
36 Peter ____ Hayes
37 Became cheerful
39 Letter man
40 180° from WSW
42 Wisecrack
43 Crock
46 Jazzman's jargon
47 Cries from the Dane
48 Repair
50 "The way of ____ in the air": Prov. 30:19
54 Horror-film sound
56 Last year's frosh
57 Tune for a Horne
59 Folk singer Baez
60 Rara ____
61 Reticulated
62 Reynolds or Sherman
63 Caught forty
65 Women's org.
67 Symbol of mourning
68 Native of Katmandu
70 Powwows
71 Radio, TV, etc.
72 Took cargo aboard
74 Warehouse or march
75 Played host
76 Malamute's look-alike
79 Numbers for a corpulent Henry
80 Desires
81 Oak or island
82 Suffix with aster
88 Ollie's pal
90 Basks
91 Freshman course
92 Sings fancily
94 Garret garb
96 Melville book
99 Fruity dessert
100 Female hormones
102 Concerning
103 Clear
105 "____ Town"
107 Tricky
108 Ingot
109 Nigerian tribe
110 Concur
111 "Shut ____!"
112 Plus quality
113 Shrewd
114 Pooh's creator
115 After quatre
116 Anita of films
119 C.I.A. head
123 Blood: Prefix
126 Morsel for Muffet
128 Cato's 2209
129 Newsman Abel
130 Grown-up grigs
132 Acad.
133 Saint Anthony's cross
134 Pariah, Japanese style
135 Piercing tool
136 Actress Joanne
138 City in Nevada

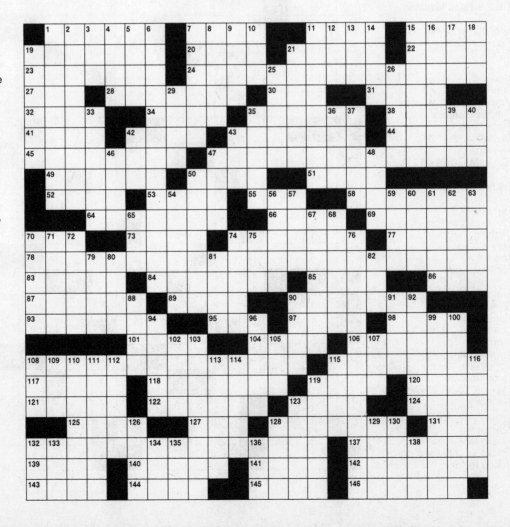

114. Remark from Mark by Caroline G. Fitzgerald

ACROSS

1 Bi plus one
4 Automobile trim
10 One-third of a film title
14 Founder of Dadaism
17 Little Red ____
18 Nomad
19 Author quoted below
20 Agua or bufo
22 Bad ____, German spa
23 Start of a quotation
25 Easy gait
26 Bore into
27 Sports event
28 Sulky
29 Stationer's item
31 Scintilla
33 Avalon, e.g.
34 Kind of voter
36 Stock certificate
38 Sonny
40 Poet Teasdale
42 Printer's mark
43 Quotation: Part II
47 Agenda entries
48 Suffix with sonnet
49 Indian sheep
50 Cobblers' blocks
52 Muse
55 Where 19 Across is buried
60 Silvers role
61 Danton's colleague
63 Word with man or mat
65 ____ marché (cheaply)
66 Quotation: Part III
70 Pulitzer Prize historian: 1934
71 April 13, to Caesar
72 Fiber for suits
73 Babble
74 Proven
76 Meager
78 Cup lips
79 Morrow from the Bronx
81 Tolkien creature
82 From head ____
84 Quotation: Part IV
93 Anserine call
94 City in Malaysia
95 Column base
96 Fusty
97 Shields
99 Turkish V.I.P.
101 Palette shape
102 Dashing
103 Wife of Osiris
104 Too
108 Japanese bay
109 ____ plaisir
110 End of quotation
114 Giant at 16
115 Nothing but
116 Champagne center
117 Stranger
118 Twisted tale
119 Soviet unit: Abbr.
120 Large lexicon
121 Fleming from Hollywood
122 Sci. suffix

DOWN

1 Asiatic lands
2 Spinks vs. Ali: Sept. 1978
3 Ready for use
4 Study hard
5 R.I. motto
6 Beef order
7 Skip
8 Ferrer or Tillis
9 Discoverer of Vinland
10 Taunt
11 Western pact gp.
12 Venetian canals
13 Handles, in Le Havre
14 Home of the Flames
15 Chanticleer
16 Society Islands capital
19 Beat the wheat
21 Streeter's "____ Mable"
24 Former chess champ
30 Close an opened envelope
32 Apparel item
33 Mythical princess
34 Leaping light
35 Disdainful cries
37 "Iron Pants"
38 Kind of rap or steer
39 Mother of Ceres
41 Wire-haired terrier
44 Part of a reply to Virginia
45 Thomas ____, Earl of Strafford
46 ". . . ____ all thy beauty lies": Shak.
50 Feudal vassal
51 Egyptian dancing girls
52 Ariel's master
53 Yokel
54 Pictorial presswork
56 "____ immortal verse": Milton
57 Steeplejack's item
58 Haley opus
59 Biographer Edwards
60 Jackanapes
61 Certain grad. school
62 Fruity drinks
64 Confess
67 "I ____ My Way"
68 A wk. has 168
69 Downstage areas
75 Conjures up
77 Full bloom
78 Heat meas.
80 I.o.u.
82 Arabic word for hill
83 Cry of amused surprise
84 Units of 24 sheaves
85 Clergymen Richard and Thomas
86 Siren
87 N.T. writings
88 "Ralph ____ Doister"
89 Lapse
90 Trattoria dish
91 Springy
92 Expunges
97 Southampton stroller
98 Pie ____
100 Tom of silents
103 "Woe ____!"
104 Hairdo
105 Kind of roast
106 Wooed
107 Odd, in Dundee
111 Modernist
112 Indistinct
113 Opposite of nope

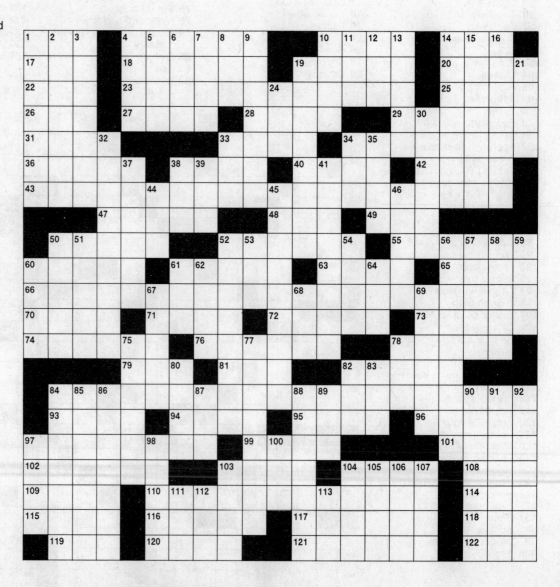

115. A Taxing Situation by Alfio Micci

ACROSS

1 Allay
6 Pivotal
11 Epic containing 24 books
16 _____-à-dire
20 Beset
21 P.D.Q.
22 Dipper
23 Polo
24 Start of a verse
28 Rodomontade
29 Douze mois
30 Napoleon: 1814
31 Chant
32 Diocletian and Julian
33 Painter Jan van der _____
34 Ryan of L.A.
35 Party man
36 Absquatulated
37 Pastry shell
38 Desert transport
39 Mutism
43 Verbal lumps for umps
44 Water buffalo
45 Caesar's X
48 Note
49 Bread, in Brest
50 Foreigner
52 Subtle emanations
54 Second line of verse
58 Regretful one, in songdom
59 Beldams
60 Gets better
61 Dunne and Rich
62 Fez color
63 Abounding with clay
65 Intrinsically
66 Tasks
67 Brazilian port
68 El Greco's homeland
69 Larceny
70 Practice the horn
72 Fulcrum for an oar
73 Courage
74 Brazier
77 Third-largest island
78 Breathe hard
79 Scriptorium item
80 Stupefy
81 Third line of verse
86 Take the helm
87 Hornswoggles
88 Marchioness
89 Varnish bases
90 Opposite of vert.
91 Courteous bloke
92 That: Fr.
93 Heir's windfall
94 Native of Yugoslavia
96 Brilliance
98 Dickens's Betsey _____
100 Miserly
103 Pub offering
104 British measure for herring
105 Title for Hess or Evans
109 Danish seaport
110 Disdain
111 Inclination
112 Greek group in W.W. II
113 End of verse
117 Crime laid to Nero
118 Sky over Seville
119 Chinese province
120 Skirt
121 Erect
122 Eve of films
123 Surpass
124 Plant substance

DOWN

1 Land's end
2 "Gypsy Love" composer
3 Iowa church society
4 Black Watch garb
5 Queen before Sofia
6 Okla. city or county
7 Thought
8 Mañana
9 Charley horse
10 Cousin of 6 Down
11 Hollies
12 Roper's item
13 Pastoral poem
14 Berlin graybeard
15 _____ volente
16 Monopoly
17 Baseball statistic
18 High-tea tidbit
19 London landmark
23 Casino game
25 Author of the verse
26 Target of the Pioneer
27 Southern resort
34 U. of Maine town
35 Tropical plant
36 Pulp sources
37 Coconut fibers
38 Salad ingredient
39 Garb for Gawain
40 One of the Philippines
41 "The way of a man with
    _____"
42 Jeune fille
43 Like old trousers
44 Two on the _____
45 Helen of soap operas
46 Makes simpler
47 Loch _____
49 Sacred song
50 Parisian's air-raid alarm
51 Tenant's contract
52 Loose, as a boat
53 Suffix with fraud or flat
55 What "baby makes"
56 V.P.: 1877–81
57 Chilean export
63 Shooting star
64 Concede
65 Radical European youths
66 Military headdress
67 French maid
68 Abrade
69 Waspish
70 Scout's rider
71 Bid
72 Emulate Circe
73 Ibsen woman
74 Toscanini's birthplace
75 Without life
76 Paperboy
77 Southampton shindig
78 Favorite resort
79 Started a card game
80 Vestige
82 Utopian
83 Ground gripper
84 "Johnny _____," 1948 film
85 Cassini
91 Legendary robot
92 Emulated a limpet
94 Cato's title in 184 B.C.
95 Cassock's relative
96 Principal dancer
97 _____ the cob
98 Sought a victim
99 Estancia
100 Until now
101 Dote on
102 Vice follower
103 Timetable, for short
104 Moved on all fours
105 Probe
106 A.k.a.
107 _____ Gras
108 German city
110 Cooking direction
111 Biblical pronoun
114 Government agcy.:
     1948–51
115 However, for short
116 Celtic Neptune

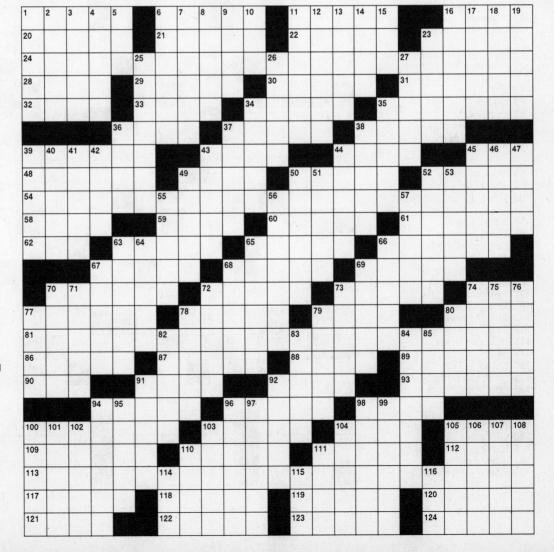

116. Happy Easter! by Frances Hansen

ACROSS

1 Caesar, for one
6 Very swank
10 The "Athens of Italy"
15 Neighbor of Miss.
18 Soap plant
19 Concerning
20 "Why Haven't ___ You?"
21 Guy's sweetie
23 Ah Sin's creator
24 Thick slice
25 Rock bottom
26 Ionian Sea gulf
27 Start of a verse
31 Sen. Birch of Ind.
32 What some put on
33 Head the cast
34 "Chances Are" singer
35 Prefix with pod
37 Lima or Orson
38 Kentucky bluegrass
39 Zodiac sign
42 "It Ain't Gonna Rain ___"
45 Olympic Games site: 1964
49 Existed
52 More of verse
57 Sacs that may get attacks
58 Italian beachhead: 1944
59 Perfect, in rocketry
60 Like a day in June
61 N.Y. or Rio
62 Western salt pan
64 Gov. Ella of Conn.
66 Writer Wister
67 Seaweed
68 Ceylonese monkeys
70 BB or FF
72 Mine, in Marseille
75 Adjective for St. Augustine, Fla.
77 Clip a merino
79 Choler
82 Finished
83 War assets org.
84 Miss Dinsmore
86 "Ye cannot serve God and ___"
88 More of verse
92 Jo's older sister
93 "Doe, ___, a female . . ."
94 "In ___ veritas"
95 Maine town
96 Capek classic
98 Beloved of Radamés
101 John Dickson or Vikki
103 Kate's younger sister
106 K-P connection
107 Twirled
109 Site of Frogner Park
113 End of verse
117 Descartes
118 Bingo's cousin
119 Slips
120 Lasso
121 Chemical compound
122 "Body all ___ and racked . . ."
123 Writer James: 1909–55
124 He corrects poor dyes
125 Labor org.
126 Electra, to Menelaus
127 Actor Foxx
128 Ecstasy's partner

DOWN

1 Sir, in India
2 Macapá is its capital (in Brazil)
3 London truck
4 Cornets' cousins
5 Consider
6 Intense desires
7 Canadian physician
8 Corset features
9 Bindle stiff
10 Mexican festival jar
11 Three golden apples undid her
12 "Every ___ staff of empire . . .": Bacon
13 Twice DXXVII
14 To the point
15 ". . . ___ search for God": Carman
16 William Joyce's title in W.W. II
17 Russian territory
22 Old poems
28 "Ten thousand saw ___ a glance": Wordsworth
29 Employ
30 In the ___ luxury
36 Party tidbit
37 Ruth's husband
39 M.I.T. rooms
40 "The jig ___!"
41 Lancaster
43 Slangy assent
44 "___ is Legion": Mark 5:9
46 Spanish Main waves
47 Dumplings, in Germantown
48 Honshu seaport
50 Swiss river
51 British gun
53 Like Miss Havisham's wedding dress
54 When Morpheus takes over
55 Tennyson poem
56 Dog, fox or turkey
63 "___ called Golgotha": Matt. 27:33
65 Home of St. Francis
67 Dying vat
69 Cruising
71 W. J. Bryan
72 First to take a ribbing
73 Sit about and brood
74 ". . . without ___ sense": Dryden
76 Appointment
78 Chopped down
79 "___ Tired," Beatles song
80 Reddish brown
81 Companion of Ares
85 Polynesian dance
87 Reflecting
89 Stuffed, as oysters
90 Vivid; striking
91 Tricked
97 Ailing
99 Recite monotonously
100 DeLuise of comedy
102 Picnic pest
103 He makes you yawn
104 Ireland, to Spenser
105 Poe's middle name
106 Oblivion
107 Worsted
108 Whittled
110 Bearskin's relative
111 Make tardy
112 Eared seal
114 Sites
115 Four seasons
116 Silkworm

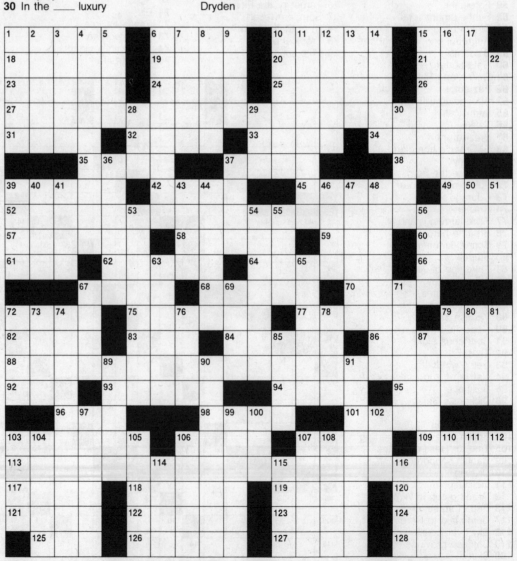

117. Name Stretching by Nancy W. Atkinson

ACROSS

1 Greet
7 Inundate
12 Lugubrious
15 Grazing land
18 Migs or mibs
19 Arachnids
21 Incised mark
23 Sport of a sort
24 Colossal
25 Imitate a ballerina
26 Successive scores for two Johanns
29 Check
30 Rowan
31 S.C. river
32 Shade of green
33 Persian: Comb. form
34 Assignations
35 Rates highly
38 Shankar plays it
39 ____ au rhum
42 Jennet
43 Famous Mohican
44 Pittsburgh product
45 Comedienne Coca
47 Intensity
48 Wine cup
51 Bands of bad guys
52 Tap
54 The life of ____
55 Eight: Comb. form
59 ____ van Holland, Neth.
60 On one's toes
61 Finished
62 Poky person
63 Hedge plant
66 Schedule
68 Infiltrated
70 Cameleer's robe
72 Rushed to see Arthur
76 Homophone for air
77 Smith's group
79 David or John
80 Having streaks
82 Titles
83 Gusto
85 Wild dog of Asia
88 Memorable couturier
90 British gun
91 Gent
92 Rubes
94 Opportunely
96 European border river
98 "L'Organiste" composer
99 Ranch expanse
101 Dumas adventurer
103 Sac
104 Roman or Persian
105 Wise ____ owl
106 Of bees
107 Warning for 101 Across
110 Ultimate goal
112 Small barracudas
113 Pill container
114 Edition of the classics
115 Dallas campus
118 Type
119 Composer's adornments
124 Piece of mischief
126 Sunrise greeter
127 Fantasize
128 Adolescent
129 Saint Andrew's cross
130 Anne Sullivan's pupil
131 Militant campus org.
132 Topper
133 Dental ____
134 Buries

DOWN

1 Dance of Brasilia
2 Large toads
3 Gate fastening
4 Senator Garn's state
5 Drying frame
6 Language course for Orlando
7 Mace and sage
8 Slender twig
9 A wife of Esau
10 Dialogue of Plato
11 Stiffly neat
12 Tea cakes
13 Olympian hawk
14 Performed
15 See 80 Across
16 Oak grove
17 Brave Trojan warrior
19 Kickoffs
20 Hotheads' creations
21 Mine entrance
22 Voice for James
27 Office V.I.P.'s
28 Meadow barley
33 That cad, to Caesar
34 Baseman, at times
35 Bandleader named on a check
36 Joplin's police force
37 Do road work
39 Brother or Bertha
40 Chinese nurse
41 Role for Sonny
43 Prod along
44 Furtive
46 Greenland group
47 Feel discomfort
48 Prone (to)
49 Ramón's rah
50 Deprived
53 Liver dish
54 René's roast
56 Dances at a governor's ball
57 Stadium area
58 Ye ____ Tea Shoppe
62 Harsh, shrill noise
64 Popular vehicle
65 Lincolns' late cousins
67 Pub
69 Conjunction
70 Author of "The Green Man"
71 Mukluk
73 "____, O north wind . . ."
74 Ruin
75 Bonn beast
78 Cocktail named for an educator
81 Cone-shaped
84 Banos or Gatos
86 Pods for soups
87 Trevino
89 Wrinkle, to an M.D.
91 Twice
93 Capital of ancient Lydia
95 Suffix with velvet
97 Ages upon ages
98 Chinchilla, e.g.
100 Raft for James
101 Put side by side
102 Casks
103 Plantation machines
104 Countenance
106 Collateral
107 Got around
108 Forty-____
109 Wander about
110 Fudd and Davis
111 Sluggish
114 "Ars gratia ____"
115 Fine-grained rock
116 Time machine
117 Consumers
119 Sacred: Prefix
120 Play the goldbricker
121 Weevil's delight
122 Anent
123 Native of Cardiff
125 Crony

118. Typecasting by Richard Silvestri

ACROSS

1 Hakenkreuzler
5 Outlets for admen
10 Variable star
14 Certain votes
18 Prayer response
19 "___ as good as a wink": Scott
21 Footnote abbr.
22 Gone to Davy Jones's locker
23 ___ avis
24 Star of "The Subject Was Roses"?
26 Stratagem
27 St. Vitus' dance
29 "___ with Love"
30 Qualified
32 Emulate Electra
34 In a frenzy
36 Belle of the Old West
37 Singer's quick way to Scotland
39 Strings
41 Corset
43 Job for Poirot
44 Kiowa's cousin
46 Fritz ___, film director
48 Heaters
50 Tiresome routines
52 Thomas and Condé
54 Positive
55 Within: Comb. form
56 Basis for a patent
57 "Gypsy Love" composer
59 Radio tube
62 Sound receiver
63 Titian's teacher
66 Wear away
68 "___ vincitor!" (Verdi aria)
70 Suit to ___
71 President of Texas: 1838–41
72 Kind of hand or rags
73 Workbench item
76 "___ piece of work . . . !": Hamlet
77 Oval
81 Fuss
82 Kitchen emanation
84 Simon and Diamond
86 Fort ___, Okla.
87 Rubber trees
89 Feed-bag fare
91 Show contempt
93 River duck
94 Thomas Moore's "___ Rookh"
96 Bant
97 Pundit
98 Creek
99 "___ like Water . . .": FitzGerald
101 Treat a wound
104 Islamic month or fast
107 Like bighorns
109 ___ on (deferred)
111 City near Peoria
112 Overcast
115 Stella ___
117 Jackson or Smith
120 Winged
121 Star of "Kiss Me, Kate"?
124 Duration

125 Dam's partner
126 Short foot, in prosody
127 Long seat
128 Part of 61 Down
129 Former Jets' QB
130 Charity
131 Repeated, old style
132 Essence

DOWN

1 Undercover cop
2 Oriental nurse
3 Star of "much Ado About Nothing"?
4 Consecutively
5 Coconut cookie
6 Photographer's abbr.
7 Love too fondly: Var.
8 Regional dialect
9 Bird's breathing apparatus
10 Zip or zilch
11 Shawn's descendant
12 Kin of 39 Across
13 Lets on
14 Sound the "H"
15 Star of "A Christmas Carol"?
16 Organic compound
17 Type of terrier
20 Fishing net
25 European flatfish
28 Area north of Afr.
31 The take
33 Star of "The Petrified Forest"?
35 Star of "Stormy Weather"?
37 Summa cum
38 Medicinal amount
40 Letters at Calvary
42 Old Scratch
43 Plagiarize
45 Star of "Run Silent, Run Deep"?
47 Star of "The Birds"?
49 Carolina rail
51 Something to toss
53 Abraham's wife
58 Co-star with Caesar?
60 Herb used for flavoring
61 Relative of etc.
64 "___ boy!"
65 At hand
67 Shipment from Baghdad
69 Horace, e.g.
73 What teamsters do
74 Loser to Dwight

75 Star of "Who's Afraid of Virginia Woolf?"?
78 Star of "On the Waterfront"?
79 Done in
80 Grasso
83 Downstairs person
85 Man behind the Bunkers
88 Drooled
90 Sailor's patron
92 Observed casually
95 Kabul nabob
100 Russia, to Churchill
102 ___ Tower, world's tallest building
103 More agile
105 Borg specialty
106 G.I. ID
108 Matriculate
110 From ___ toe
112 In the cellar
113 Medley
114 Bud or seed
116 Stone paving block
118 Hera's messenger
119 Give off
122 Highway sign
123 Bee follower

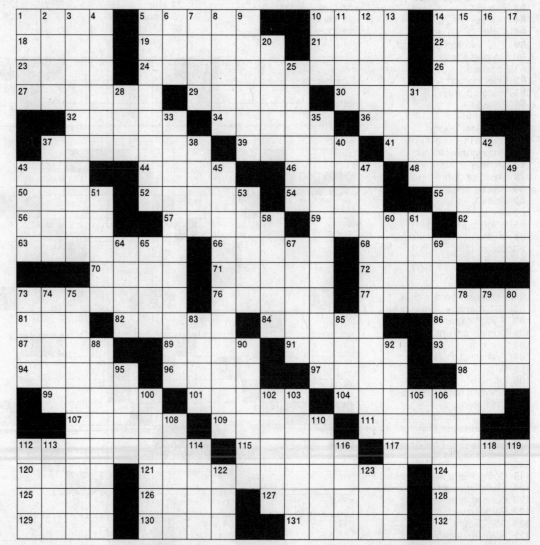

119. Good Mixers by Anthony B. Canning

ACROSS

1 Edmonton's locale
8 Jury
13 Topic in the tropics
17 Letter
20 Keep in office
21 Twine
23 Progress
24 Mauna ____
25 Held, Hale, Gide, Uncle
27 Appreciative
29 Nightclubs
30 Descendant of Esau
31 Dilute
32 Hwy.
33 Cohan's "Little ____ Kelly"
34 Buttons
35 Bet
39 Vintage cars
40 Example
41 Shame
43 Rib
44 Furthermore
45 Seine sight
46 Overshoe
48 Shrew
49 N.Z. bird that cries "More pork!"
51 Showed the way
52 Sidetrack
53 Inlet
54 West role
55 Münster men
57 Minuit, Seton, nobleman, Foster
60 Nostrils
61 MOMA display
62 Hiawatha carrier
63 Library list
65 Distort a report
66 Fishwife
68 Nordland native
72 Gateway to Finger Lakes
73 Latin bombshell
74 Cache
75 Malign
76 Seaweed eaten in Japan
77 Like hamsters' tails
78 Courage
79 Like wasps' nests
80 Up and around
82 Jousting
83 Fauntleroy
84 Balboa, Porter, lover, Gardner
88 Frank, e.g.
91 Shahn or Vereen
92 Gallic go-ahead
93 Hermes' herbs
94 Drone
95 Polynesian cloth
96 Say yea
98 Hinge
99 Peruvian plant
100 Zoot Sims plays it
101 Comedian Martin
102 Not so coarse
103 "Delphine" author
105 Title Nehru held
106 Charter
107 True grit
108 Slow up
110 Pipe joint
111 Garner name
113 Glossy coatings
115 Everest porter
118 Peale product
121 Webster, Roosevelt, Cousins
123 Goat's-hair fabric
124 Cartoonist Gross
125 Jot
126 Bernstein
127 Infra ____ (undignified)
128 Term at sea
129 Also-ran
130 Battle scene: 1571

DOWN

1 Nejd native
2 Poe girl, Irv of baseball, Zola girl
3 Axis name, Stout name
4 Happifies
5 Neural network
6 Exclamations of vexation
7 One ____ time
8 Hawk
9 Sign up
10 Oleoresin used as incense
11 Chinese fiber plant
12 Hare's tail
13 Bunk
14 Infuriate
15 Type of type
16 Lug
17 Nixie or pixie
18 Trifle
19 Girl of songdom
22 Compass point
26 Requisite
28 Fluff or muff
33 At least
34 Costume jewelry
36 Carpet fiber
37 Paint-shop offering
38 Malden or Marx
39 Spellbound
40 Met baritone
41 Red follower
42 "____ Free": Adamson
43 ____ Grande, Brazilian city
46 Male gypsy
47 Prevent
48 Pollster's study
50 Earaches
52 Take off
53 "And thereby hangs ____"
56 Mountain: Comb. form
57 Pivotal
58 Berate
59 One use for a high roof
63 Great weight
64 ____ Jima
65 Snipe's habitat
66 Quarry of "reve-nooers"
67 Brief story
69 Shepherd, Howe, Arthur, general
70 Part of r.p.m.
71 Thickness
73 Goat pepper
74 Tapering to a point
75 Pasternak heroine
77 Robust
78 Toast vessel
79 First in time
81 Treat at teatime
82 Kurt, Larry or Luther
83 Reasoned out
84 "____ la giubba"
85 Goose genus
86 Improve
87 Slangy declination
89 Replacement item
90 Kind of stand
91 Soho shindig
94 Raucous
97 Olympics attraction
98 Space off a kitchen
102 Easy
103 Isaac Bickerstaff
104 More farfetched
105 Breastbones
107 Escargot
108 Totaled, as a bill
109 Gives voice to
112 "Aeneid" opener
113 Timetable abbr.
114 Brad or spad
115 Old dirk
116 Dr. J.'s target
117 B. ____ Railroad
118 Expand
119 Sash for Yum-Yum
120 Joplin offering
122 Kit and caboodle

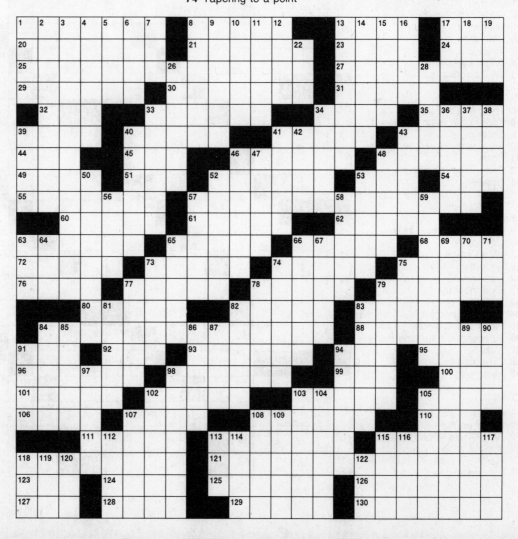

120. Memo to Dad by Tap Osborn

ACROSS

1 Fast-food shop
5 Ballerina's knee bend
9 Towel fabric
14 Scenic view
19 Buck heroine
20 Norman or Edward
21 Word of surprise
22 Lucubrated
23 Start of a verse
27 Romberg's forte
28 Insect: Comb. form
29 Repetitive recital
30 R & R spots
31 Aspect
32 Schnapps
33 Finger sign
34 Was homesick
35 Cellaret
40 Like an impala
43 Yarborough, e.g.
44 Chan's expression
45 Knucklehead
46 Second line of verse
51 Overlook
52 Say grace
53 Avant-garde
54 Stuck
55 Hood's weapon
56 Tall story
57 Actress Jeanne
58 Guarantee
59 Impugn
60 Space pioneer
61 Chigger
62 Construction workers
65 Winged
66 Cold wind in Peru
67 Intelligence
70 Bright-eyed
71 Kit Carson was one
72 Soil layers
73 Princess, in Punjab
74 Third line of verse
78 Year in the reign of Sweyn I
79 Encourage
80 Pittypat in "G.W.T.W."
81 Posh
82 Given to a false show
84 Needle
86 Marsh
87 "Ben ____"
88 Eruption
89 Poem by Shelley: 1816
93 Openness
97 Banks of baseball
98 Sedentary
99 Last line of verse
102 Elbe tributary
103 Shoelace tip
104 Hammett heroine
105 Pictorial presswork
106 Tippecanoe's running mate
107 Abzug
108 "Too bad!"
109 TV talking horse

DOWN

1 Carnegie was one
2 Marry on the run
3 Sing Sing's famed warden
4 Typical Woody Allen role
5 North ____, Neb.
6 Lithuanians' kin
7 "____ Dancer," Nureyev film
8 Age
9 Lottery ticket
10 Took life easy
11 Apportion
12 Svelte
13 Fireplace ledge
14 Dash
15 Criterion for a show dog
16 Ionian gulf
17 Nail remover
18 Author of "No and Yes"
24 "From ____ Eternity"
25 "____ Me," 1929 song
26 Writer Wylie
31 Suspect
32 Scenic peninsula
34 Korean port
35 Irritant
36 Esteem
37 River into Bay of Biscay
38 Overthrow
39 Unkempt
40 Batrachian
41 British Open winner: 1964
42 Rewrite, in a way
43 Item to be picked
44 "The Promised Land" author
47 Teams of horses
48 Actress Young
49 Boxer Bobick
50 Kyushu port
56 Gossip, Yiddish style
57 Kringle
58 Moses' mountain
59 Far ahead in a golf match
60 Revel in a victory
61 Swindle or fine
62 Puzo subject
63 Like a loner
64 Stroke on a letter
65 Suffered
66 Meaning
67 Power unit
68 Columnist Robb
69 Antimacassar
71 Cavalry weapon
72 Dwarf
73 Shower
75 Develop
76 Mal de mer
77 Emulate Sunday
83 String of pearls
84 Holland, for one
85 Loser at Palo Alto: 1846
86 ____ a pancake
88 Turbot
89 Sinuses
90 One of the Lesser Sundas
91 Egg-shaped
92 Doctor a lawn
93 Found
94 Putting position
95 Patricia of films
96 Excise
97 Advantage
98 Chemical suffix
100 Collar
101 Frost's "____ Vale"

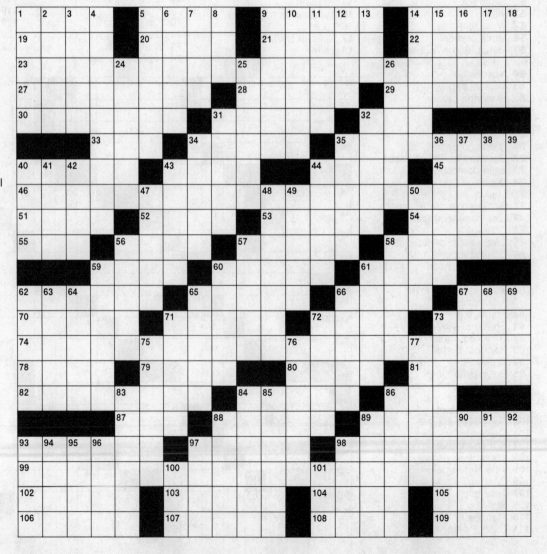

121. Whodunit? by Elaine D. Schorr

ACROSS

1 Barflies
9 Navigational systems
15 Butternut squash
21 Pangolin
22 Needlelike
24 Sound sight
25 Mrs. O'Leary did it
28 He used his lip
29 Affirmed sound
30 Inhibit
31 Laurel
32 Street runner
35 When Brutus did it
36 Part of L.C.D.
38 Day divs.
39 Steinbeck character
40 Bright
42 Schmo
44 D.D.E.
46 Diller's surgeon did it
49 Like some boas
50 Carl, Fritz or Rob
53 Prefix with fix
54 Split
55 Stewpots
56 Nobelist for Peace: 1931
57 One of the cattlemen
59 Censor a telecast
60 Anent
62 Devotee of an art
63 Apparition
64 Scatters
66 Select, as a jury
68 Musical direction
69 Solecist's word
70 Piece for Pavarotti
71 Decamp for romance
74 Luminescence
75 Armistead did it at McHenry
78 Peninsula in the news
79 Emulated Hero
80 To ___ (exactly)
81 Univ. course
82 ___ the arm (boost)
83 He wrote "Praise of Folly"
85 Traversely
87 Groundwork for plastering
88 Heliologist's topic
90 Lovely lake southeast of Rome
91 Proboscis
92 Danish city named for a god
94 Summer flounder
96 Legendary labyrinth builder
97 Swung round
98 Shebang
101 Portions for certain agents
102 Wall attachment
103 The Oysters did it for the Walrus
105 ___ volente
106 Swiss city on the Rhine
107 A.M. trumpet calls
109 "If I only ___ Heart"
110 Star pitcher
112 N.Y.S.E. category
114 Palpitate
115 Intensity
116 Causerie
118 Queue
120 Abalone

122 Arabic name meaning "father"
123 Simple Simon might have done it
130 Take turns
131 Necessitates
132 O.K.
133 Hole under a grate
134 "Lucia . . ." showstopper
135 Flint's cache

DOWN

1 Marble shooter
2 Singleton
3 Stop on a R.R.
4 Fishing gear
5 Eucharistic plate
6 Roman emperor: A.D. 69
7 ___ Borch, Dutch artist
8 Hit signs
9 ___ Como, Italian resort
10 Used a yellowish pigment
11 Fissures
12 Uris hero
13 Soothing substance
14 N.F.L. team
15 U.S.N. bigwigs
16 Douglas Fraser's org.
17 Kin of Mmes.
18 The village blacksmith did it
19 Lend ___ (hearken)
20 Admonishes
23 Truck stop
26 How we stand

27 ___ tide
32 Breathe laboriously
33 North African pine
34 Atlas did it when he sneezed
37 Blackbeard did it
40 Hub
41 Workers on layers
42 San Joaquin River plants
43 Cloakroom item
45 Coogan role
47 Bligh did it
48 "Hawaii ___"
49 Chanticleer did it
50 Pro ___
51 Town in West Germany
52 Alphabetical trio
55 Odorous
58 Rod for a cannoneer
59 Honeymooner
60 Aqaba noble
61 Light splash
63 City in Manche
65 Contes
66 Restraining items
67 George and T.S.
68 C.I.O. partner
70 In progress
72 Country: Sp.
73 German article
75 Village where Patton is buried
76 Case for trivia
77 Grayish yellows
82 Unctuous

84 Gets the point
85 Countermand
86 Publicist
88 N.Y.C. is one
89 Caucho
91 ___ qua non
93 Twosomes
95 Suffix with Adam or Edom
96 Assignments
97 ___ Island
99 Hair style
100 Pre-Lenin ruler
102 Blenheim, for one
104 Fencing actions
106 Creeper or roller
107 Thrust at repeatedly
108 Farthest from the surface
110 Capital of Ghana
111 Utter confusion
113 Red as ___
114 Presuppose
115 Fiber for rope
117 Springe
119 Tidbit from Iraq
121 Labor Day blessing
122 Youth's problem
124 "Lord is ___?": Matt. 26:22
125 Negligent
126 Kind of club or path
127 Teutonic sky god
128 Relative of "Lawd"
129 Chemical suffix

122. One for the Book by Jack Luzzatto

ACROSS

1 Protracted poems
6 Festive exhibitions
11 Negligent
17 "We ___ amused"
18 Able to pay bills
20 "Better ___ fool . . .": Shak.
21 Bookworm
23 Lebanon trees
24 Clue
25 Way to go
26 Feebler, as excuses
28 Tosspot
29 Aloof
30 Adm. Byrd book
31 Long John
33 Tall Asiatic tree
34 Martinet's activity
36 Meddled or muddled
37 "A ___ of Life"
38 Trouble en masse
39 Places for opinions
40 Lawful
42 Madagascar mammal
44 "___ Jimmy Valentine"
46 Beats all hollow
49 Catches flies
50 Hurdle
53 Embarrassments in print
55 "Ecstasy" name
56 Escapee from a witch
57 Trusted friends
59 Away
60 Jabberwocky
62 Dramaturgy is one
63 Bibliophile's possible acquirement
65 Underwater concrete depositor
66 Autocrat
67 Widow
68 Seattle transport
70 Wheat: Sp.
71 Good Book heroine
73 Commune near La Coruña
74 Of sea gulls
76 Wood joiner
78 The lowdown
79 Christie was one
80 Church pulpits
83 Conservatives
85 Critiqued a new book
89 "Stars" partner
90 Blows on the beak
91 Neighbor of Ethiopia
92 A nucleic acid
93 Bunyan blade
94 Adriatic northers
95 Clan chief: Var.
96 "The ___ of the Four"
97 "Ecce Homo" painter
99 Henry James was one
103 Strangely beautiful
104 Perkins, Greeley et al.
105 Tertiary epoch
106 Where Stone meets Gravel
107 Wax dramatic
108 Cubic meter

DOWN

1 Rostov book: 1977
2 Kin of shilling shockers
3 U.S.C. or U.C.L.A.
4 Fingerstall
5 Blue zircon
6 Specialty
7 Wind-shielded
8 Marsh elder
9 Sinclair Lewis's nickname
10 Fishhook lines
11 Foyt or Unser
12 Pitcher
13 "___ pleasures and palaces . . .": Payne
14 A Mississippi source
15 Take a walk
16 Method
17 ___ off the old block
18 Suddenly smarting
19 Emulate Gulliver
22 Koestler's "Darkness at ___"
27 Doc
30 French exclamation
31 Novel installment plans
32 Nobelist Singer
33 Popeyed
35 Drab and dismal
36 Heated; glowing
37 M. Cardin
39 Attach firmly
41 Malay dagger
42 "Land of ___"
43 French horns
45 Insect in bondage
47 Periodical author
48 Computer memory
49 Smith for horses
51 Twiggy broom
52 Resin for lacquer
54 Houston player
56 Obtained
58 Warble
60 Recesses
61 Fluffs
64 Duplicates
66 Thriller theme
69 Lowest point
70 Transportation for Theroux
72 Copter blade
75 Prepayments to authors
77 Register recording
80 Slacks off
81 Relative of 88 Down
82 Rennes native
84 Dwell
85 Sorry ones
86 Nervous
87 Donkey, e.g.
88 Guaracha or samba
90 Present occasion
91 Royalty, to an author
94 Chum, for one
95 Easy gait
96 Six, on a die
98 Spanish diminutive
100 Christmas boy
101 Eur. war theater
102 Piffle

123. Synthetic Synonyms by Bert H. Kruse

ACROSS

1 Dutch cheeses
6 Attacks
13 Demure
16 Nincompoop
19 Beverage
20 Boston square
21 Past
22 Berlin avenue
24 Author of "Hiawatha"
26 New Yorkers
28 Poetry
29 Porky's plaint
30 Storehouse
32 Colors
33 Customs
34 Decelerates
35 Let
36 Removes from office
40 Ahab's quarry
41 Soccer great
42 G.I. Jane
45 Stritch and May
46 Easy, vulnerable target
48 Trapper's trophy
49 Inn guest
50 Scenic view
51 Trilby on a Londoner
52 Dealt sparingly
53 Galore
54 Push
55 Debt memo
57 Treelike cactus
58 Desires
59 Growing out
60 Tore
61 A bit more tetched
62 Tupolev-144, e.g.
63 L.A. team
66 Rooks
67 More content
70 Bravo, in Barcelona
71 Memorable chief
72 Draws back
73 Dinner entree
75 Women's service org.
78 Beavers
79 Shanty
80 Aunt in "Oklahoma!"
81 Stowe transport
82 Dress
83 Buzzes
84 "___ needs a good memory"
85 Menace in India
86 Garlic unit
87 Frivolous girl
88 ___ nothing
89 Eddied
90 Honey site
91 G. & S. ship
94 Cat variety
95 Compass dir.
96 Bridge coup
97 Like a certain range
98 Props
99 Hoax
100 Erect
101 Actress Shire
102 Eastern incarnation
105 Asian inn
106 Perdition
107 Skin
111 A view from Cleveland

113 City northwest of Roma
117 Stranger
118 Spenserian hag
119 Circe, e.g.
120 Crime increasing in our time
121 Stop
122 Crop
123 Money in ancient Greece
124 Difficult years

DOWN

1 She loved Narcissus
2 Elwood, in "Harvey"
3 Throb
4 Avril et mai, e.g.
5 Lose pep
6 Is ambitious
7 Rich biscuits
8 Hose
9 Turpentine resin
10 ___ de France
11 Kind of TV show
12 Heart contraction
13 A cartoonist and cartoon hero
14 Flirt visually
15 "Te" in "Te amo"
16 Without help
17 Garden pest
18 Dry
22 Burning
23 Kind of curve
25 Western dam
27 Quiet
31 Greatly impressed
33 Actor from N.Y.C.: 1939–76
34 Condition
35 Field trial event
36 Holds up
37 R.I.P. speeches
38 Deer-antelope playground
39 King bested him
40 Makes cloth
41 Solid fuel
42 Famous jockey
43 Astaire's sister et al.
44 Tree on Lebanon's flag
46 Sea duck
47 Like many a model
48 P.R. man's forte
50 Oil-producing rocks
52 Garb for Gandhi
54 Escargots
55 Maskegons' kin
56 Chance
57 Tandy, to Cronyn
59 British, for one
61 Emerson contemporary
64 Owls' sounds
65 Musical high note
66 Nab
68 On the go
69 U.S. painter: 1859–1940
71 Peak in Thessaly
72 Rope-ladder step
73 Kind of punch

74 Tattle
76 Most unusual
77 Manual arts
78 Hide
79 Cordell
81 Wrong, in Roma
83 Injure
84 He crowned William the Conqueror
85 Mea ___
87 Realm of Rama I
88 Applicable, old style
89 "Storia di Cristo" author
91 Bright light
92 Lizard: Comb. form
93 Other names
94 ___ puisne
96 Dancer Ted
98 Small pike perch
99 Equine
100 Moisten
101 Vestige
102 Ga. neighbor
103 Galba's good-bye
104 Sib
105 Sp. lass
107 Reduce
108 If not
109 One in social demand
110 Browns
112 "___ Woman"
114 Hagen
115 Create a lap
116 Produce lace

124. Plaint Speaking by Maura B. Jacobson

ACROSS

1 Cut short
6 Landed
10 Qualified
14 Mother of Perseus
19 Prince de ____
20 Inside stuff
21 Crucifix
22 Typewriter type
23 Motorist's lament
27 Claudius's 502
28 "____ my Annie . . ."
29 Soft, in music
30 Branch of baseball
31 Jones's conquest
33 Up-tight
34 Meadowlands event
35 Tiriac of tennis
36 Six, on a die
37 Ominous
41 Dangerfield's lament
47 Shakespearean title word
48 Orgs.
49 Sees the cashier
50 Amalgamate
51 Seed covering
52 Mercer or Koehler
55 Guitar ridges
56 Elliptical
57 Nog
58 Mine, in Monaco
59 Memorable "Bugs"
60 Court coup
61 Tardy one's lament
69 Gorilla
70 Kind of code
71 O'Neill heroine
72 Father of Abner
73 Novel start
76 Besom material
78 Cephalalgia
80 Cyma recta
81 Duvalier's land
82 Braid
84 Bell the cat
85 Hematite, e.g.
86 Phony dieter's lament
90 Musical minim
92 Mouthward
93 Auberge
94 Outside: Comb. form
95 Dickens's Mr. Drood
97 Word with wood
101 Pulitzer play of 1953
104 Perfume source
105 Chemical compound
106 Spanish bear
107 Closet cleaner's lament
111 Martinique volcano
112 Call's partner
113 Christie's "____ Under the Sun"
114 Koussevitzky
115 Yule paste-ons
116 Start the pot
117 Miami's county
118 German iron

DOWN

1 Alkalis' opposites
2 Knife name
3 Walk ____ (be elated)
4 Map abbrs.
5 Fin's double
6 Altar sites
7 Pitchers' parts
8 Suffix with Jersey
9 Grey's "West of ____"
10 Former president of Pan-ama
11 ____ bouche (delicacy)
12 Ad design
13 Tokyo, once
14 Shortage
15 "____ Restaurant"
16 One of the Garters
17 Fit to
18 Hair-raising
24 "The play's the ____ . . ."
25 Teamster's oasis
26 Pen name of Jacques Thi-bault
32 Thus: Fr.
33 Microscopic
34 Mondrian namesakes
36 Airwaves nuisance
37 Barbecue need
38 Scarlett's home
39 Blue-pencil
40 Actor's quest
41 Muezzin's faith
42 ____ Carte
43 Stem covering
44 British spa
45 Archimedes' cry
46 Bergen dummy
51 Declare
53 S.A. vine
54 Nagy of Hungary
55 Eve's triad
56 Group of eight
59 Lucrezia or Cesare
60 Grandma Moses
62 Word for Apley
63 Nonclerics
64 Under control
65 Brigitte's regimen
66 Pizarro victim
67 Indira's father
68 Say hello
73 Milne bear
74 Pearl Mosque site
75 Virginia ____
76 Allegro non ____
77 Trick
79 Hersey town
81 Bathtub gin
82 Became extinct
83 Bank deal
86 Fires up
87 Namely
88 Sky chief
89 Fence in
91 Salad herb
95 Upright
96 Golden Hind captain
97 Point of view
98 Field hands
99 Kind of orange
100 Oscar winner: 1961
101 Knight's colleagues
102 ____ fixe
103 Tonic extract
104 Calcar
105 Bagnold
108 Bedouin robe
109 Yellow bugle
110 Chinese dynasty or river

125. DADAisms by A. J. Santora

ACROSS

1 POP, in a way
5 He was PAPA Tiger
9 Ht., as above the PAcific
13 Skeletal PArts
19 My DAD George
21 PArt of a shoe
22 Kin of amPERES
23 PAPPY
24 Dweller near Gulf of PAria
26 Word with FATHER
27 Played a PArt
29 Florentine poet exPAtriated in 1302
30 "____ your fore-FATHERS!": J. Q. Adams
33 PAsture breed
35 PAPPY Boyington's PAls
36 PAPAS of a sort
37 ____ la (PArt song)
39 Mountain PAsture
40 ____-snee (sPArring with knives)
43 PArent-teacher org.
44 Field where "POPpies grow"
47 Kin of PAprikas and PArsley
50 Eight-PArt group
53 HisPAnic name
54 UnPArallel, as tracks
57 Like a wing-shaped PArt
58 PAtrimony
60 How PAderewski played?
61 PAmpéan relative
62 Spouting PAp or oil
63 Dirt in PA., etc.
65 PAPA bear in PAnama
66 PArrot's relative
69 PAinful memories
71 Was a crossPAtch
73 Word PArt meaning shoulder
74 Group recently PAst 12
76 Thin as ____ (sPAre-set)
77 PAsture disease
79 PArnassian southeast wind
80 "The ____ of America" (PAperback title)
83 PAste-on
84 PAstry
85 ____ grass (PAsturage)
86 Time sPAce
88 PAssional
90 Kin of PArrs
93 PAssage in Roma
94 Suck a lolliPOP again and again
97 ____ PArisienne
98 Below-PAr mark
99 Cub Scout PAcks
100 PArt of R.S.V.P.
102 Six-PAck items
105 PAsses away
107 PAncake for PAncho
110 PAstoral canine
112 PAnzer
113 PAPA Bear
115 PATERnosters
119 DADDY Warbucks's girl et al.
120 Soft, in PAlermo
121 Fore-FATHERS
122 Was apPArently true
123 Actor PArker
124 PAss over quickly
125 Vessel similar to a dePAs

DOWN

1 DADS of jrs.
2 Tepid, in the PAlatinate
3 Harden against PAin, etc.
4 Kin of PAra nuts
5 Hesitate to PArticiPAte
6 PAy dirt
7 West Point's counterPArt: Abbr.
8 SamPAn's cousin
9 Actress PArsons
10 "Our FATHER"
11 "The Cocktail PArty" author
12 Places for juristic PAnels
13 UnPOPular fellow
14 PArt of the O.T.
15 POP
16 DooDAD
17 PAPA Andrea's violin
18 Slaves of the PAst
20 ____ PAPA, Sioux tribe
25 PAssage plan: Abbr.
28 Bufos, sPAdefoots, e.g.
30 NewsPAper fluff
31 PAssage between decks
32 POP off
34 Egg of a PArasitic insect
38 What a PArody might induce
41 PADRES
42 PAss-catcher Rote
45 VATER's refusal
46 Vehicles with PAir-runners
48 Remove, as PAint
49 PArticular ____ (council)
51 ABOU Ben Adhem, e.g.
52 POPdock derivative
55 American PAct org.
56 SIREd
59 PAludal plant
60 ". . . putty, ____, an' PAint": Kipling
64 Dies ____ (PAnegyrical hymn)
66 SePArately distinct lettering
67 PAsha's PAl
68 Puzo's "GodFATHER"
69 Becomes PArched
70 CrawDADS
72 Radar PAnel line
75 RaPA ____ (Easter Island)
76 PAcking guns
78 Gallery featuring Turner PAintings
80 PArtner of guy
81 "You'll ____," POP song
82 A sPArkling brightness
85 Kind of PA
87 POPsy or POPpins
89 PAPA swan
91 PAsses
92 PArboiled
95 Old PAlestinian letter
96 PArt
99 CamPAigner of 1858
100 Tales of the PAst
101 Actress PAPAS
103 U.S. Grant counterPArt
104 They go with grandFATHER chairs
106 ComPADRES
108 Kind of rose PAth?
109 FATHER of one of David's mighty men
111 AddlePAted guy
114 PArt of the Apocrypha: Abbr.
116 Univ. dePArtment
117 PAlindromic word
118 Where the SIRET flows: Abbr.

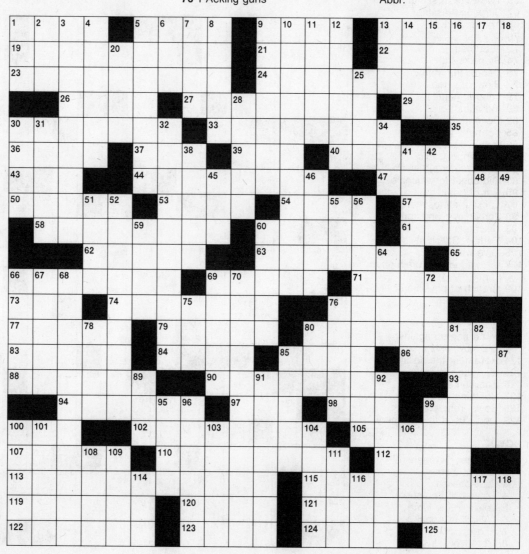

126. Hacked Saws by Caroline G. Fitzgerald

ACROSS

1 Where the Yukon rises
7 Sculptor Lorado
11 Part of a slip
16 Vinegary
17 Nondependent
19 "I'm in ____ for Love"
22 Offense
25 Silken
26 Floating zoo
27 Brace
28 Advice to a loner
29 Reason for a D.S.C.
33 Greek dialect
35 Cave man of comics
36 Studio spinner
40 Trash
43 Stamen parts
45 Triclinium meal
46 Herring barrel
47 Principled
48 Eureka!
49 Electrical unit
52 Mallorca or Menorca
56 Poor devil
60 "____ the truth!"
62 Factor in Mendel's law
64 Kind of shark
65 Two English saints
67 Surgeons' assts.
68 Ann or Andy
70 "By my ____!": Shak.
72 "Let them ____"
74 Stone or Iron
75 Dennis the Menace
77 Blow ____ top
79 Looped handle
80 Individual
82 Decorator's activity
85 Formerly formerly
86 Haw's opposite
87 Pop singer Janis
88 Tiny creature in warm seas
91 Old chest for valuables
95 Cut of beef
97 Lacking atmosphere
99 Jonathan Livingston
103 Discordia
104 Parties, British style
106 Give way
107 ____ aqueduct, brain channel
109 Branch of physical science
111 Antediluvian
113 River islet
114 Elèves' milieu
119 Put a nag up against a Derby winner
124 Hot under the collar
125 ____ time (singly)
126 Englishman
127 Soothing word
128 Soviet refusal
129 Liquid used in perfumery

DOWN

1 Clowder members
2 Charley horse
3 ____-do-well
4 To you, in Toulouse
5 Leave in the lurch
6 "Alas!" in Anhalt
7 Part of TNT
8 Moreover
9 Lambs or spondees
10 Dogtail, e.g.
11 Norm: Abbr.
12 Subjects of discourses
13 Highbred
14 Sanction
15 Orangutans
17 Little Lord Fauntleroy
18 Henderson, with his metronome
20 Locale of Frogner Park
21 Benchley's "The ____"
23 H.L. members
24 Former Pirate
30 Lug of a jug
31 Gallagher's partner
32 Subject of a Pope essay
34 Favorite word of Anna's king
36 Rain check, at times
37 Wife of Athamas
38 Sandburg's "Always the Young ____"
39 Irritated
41 Most subdued
42 Saddler's product
44 Hophni's father
48 Nabokov heroine
50 Indy trailer
51 Turkish chamber
53 Tree or fig
54 Player milieu
55 Uncertain
57 Terry or Drew
58 Steelers' coach
59 Nemo, to Nero
60 ". . . of folly": Addison
61 "How ____ with me . . .?": Macbeth
62 Oenology symbol
63 Gung-ho
66 Sordor
69 Taunting word
71 Herrick or Service
73 Venezia sight
76 Gamb
78 "Delta of Venus" author
81 Sudden pain
83 English swabbie
84 Neighbor of Syr.
89 "____ Love You"
90 Numbskull
92 Chest wall
93 Knockout
94 Say more
96 Vocalized pauses
97 Santa ____ race track
98 Mt. near Troy
99 Suddenly
100 Sikorsky
101 Wrestling hold
102 Teresa de ____
104 Handout
105 Hit Broadway
108 Amazon tributary
110 Town on the Niger
112 Refuse
115 Yak or jaw
116 Teutonic king
117 Trotsky
118 Former lightweight champ
120 Ronsard product
121 Whence Pate drives
122 Pilcorn
123 Where, in prescriptions

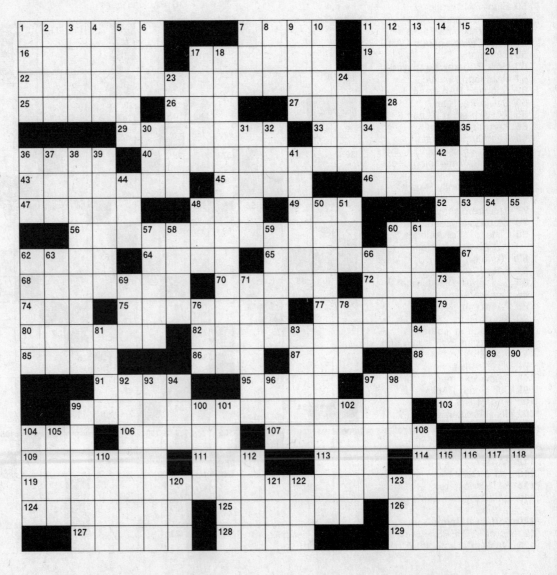

127. All-American Verses by Anne Fox

ACROSS

1 Speaks gruffly
6 Essays
11 Low bow
17 Literature Nobelist: 1925
21 Moslem prince
22 Droll
23 Spanish stew
24 Sheltered place
25 Poem for June 17, 1775
28 Turgenev's birthplace
29 Apple thrower of myth
30 Not seldom
31 Bakery aide
32 Bombard
34 Tennis great René
36 Chinese-American architect
37 That is to say
39 Poem for Aug. 6, 1777
48 Jelly fruit
52 ____ incognita
53 Asian tree
54 Sun: Comb. form
55 City on the Chemung
57 Kind of cross
58 Balancing
61 Pull
62 Poem for Dec. 26, 1776–
     Jan. 3, 1777
66 Heel's companion
67 "____ semper tyrannis"
68 Emulate Killy
69 Celt
70 Story from the past
72 U.S. satellite
74 Progenitor
77 Graduated
80 Poem for July 16, 1779
88 Moved along an apron
89 Chubby
90 Word with bank or ball
91 Magnificent
94 Over: Fr.
95 Western org.
98 First-rate
99 Daughter of Cadmus
100 Poem for May 12, 1780
108 Forbidding
110 Some speakers
111 Yangtze feeder
112 Show off
113 Memorable impresario
115 Réunion et al.
116 Overcast
118 Surround
119 Poem for Oct. 19, 1781
124 "The Bells of St. ____"
125 Promissory note
126 Pinched with a jerk
131 Past
134 Swirl
136 Teacher of Stradivari
139 ____ bene
140 U.S. island
141 Poem for April 30, 1789
146 Bed part
147 Mexican state
148 ____ the Riveter
149 Chan portrayer
150 First name in clocks
151 Comet man
152 Asian range
153 In disorder

DOWN

1 Biblical tower
2 Opera star Lucine
3 Esteemed object
4 Great horse of the 60's
5 Relative of Mme.
6 Goodly part of a yard
7 Breach
8 "Let ____," Beatles song
9 Vingt-____
10 With: Prefix
11 Money in coin
12 River to the Rhine
13 Long oven
14 Hero of a Sheed book
15 Every
16 African republic
17 U.S. poet Francis
18 Israeli dance
19 ____ plaisir
20 "Champagne music" man
26 "How ____ the little busy
     . . ."
27 German port
33 Rinehart character
35 Jumps
36 School group
37 Comedienne Fields
38 Praying figure
40 Greek letter
41 Island off Ireland
42 Swimming stroke
43 Ruler of the Aesir
44 Exchequer
45 Winged
46 Sheer fabric
47 Joined
48 "Ready, ____, go!"
49 Zwingli's first name
50 Actor Don from Kenosha
51 Médoc, for one
56 Astronaut's "perfect"
58 First president of the
     Transvaal
59 Fuel in the news
60 "Gee whiz!"
63 Unless before: Lat. abbr.
64 Throe
65 One of the tides
71 ____ point (lace)
73 Bone: Comb. form
75 Spirit of St. Louis
76 Free of
77 Erwin of films
78 Against
79 Contract phrase
81 Salts
82 "The ____ Incident," 1943
     movie
83 Baptismal basin
84 Thorn, for one
85 "Three men ____"
86 Texas town
87 Jackson's bill
91 Kind of seer
92 Loser to Reagan: 1970
93 French fruit
94 Pro
96 Loser to F.D.R.: 1936
97 Moon goddess
101 Strident
102 Plays the Doral
103 Southwest wind
104 Amador's delight
105 Dove's opposite
106 "He hath spread ____. . ."
107 Avuncular name
109 Battle site: June 28, 1778
114 Great English actor
116 Trifle
117 Be precise
120 Despicable one
121 Part of a fair
122 Toy
123 James Jones book: 1975
127 Fish
128 Bantu-speaking people
129 Collars
130 "Just great!"
131 Tweed, e.g.
132 ____ blue
133 Mountain pass, in India
134 Bad
135 Capitol feature
136 Truant G.I.
137 Topgallant
138 Land mass
142 "____-Binh," 1970 film
143 Annex
144 Lippo Lippi
145 ____ de guerre

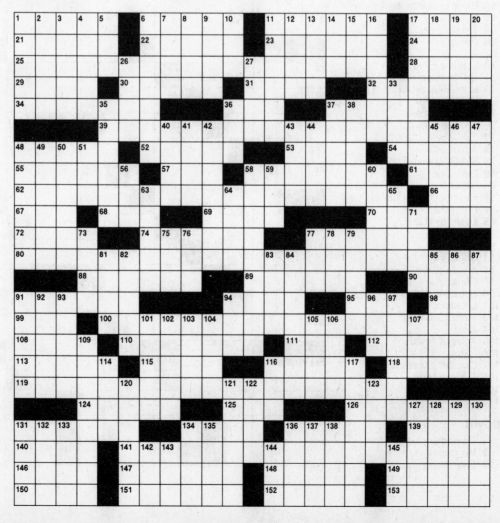

128. Fractured English by William Lutwiniak

ACROSS

1 Popular flavoring
5 Where the Tagus flows
10 Unfailing
14 Po tributary
18 Algerian port
19 Author of "Aminta"
20 Publish
22 Tolstoy et al.
23 Auto loans
25 Batters bird feather
27 Island or breed of cattle
28 A Brontë
30 British craft
31 Vonnegut's "____ Cradle"
32 Newspaper items
33 Coiffure pad
34 Nawab and dey
37 Krait, e.g.
38 Muskogean Indians
43 Aftersong
44 Old-time vehicle hit with force
46 Pastureland
47 Yacht haven
48 Maison head
49 Unsavory
50 Appease temporarily
51 Jackass, to Jacques
52 What U.M.W. pickets do
56 Brodie
57 Declined
59 "Golden Boy" author
60 Participant
61 Spring beauty
62 River of northeast Italy
63 Reject
64 Treelike cactus
66 Dayan
67 Want
70 Lends an ear
71 Sleep discourse
73 Numerical prefix
74 Unimproved
75 Cornmeal cake
76 Spirited tune
77 ____-Carlo Menotti
78 Adherent
79 Bases soundly
83 Disposed
84 Remedies
86 Escoffier's condiment
87 Blemishes
88 Loser to D.D.E.
89 Punish
90 Sennit
91 Specifies
94 In ____ (briefly)
95 Cads
99 Separate wales
101 Gleeful circle
103 Plant feature
104 Auto
105 Actress Anouk
106 "Step ____!"
107 Coastal phenomenon
108 Understands
109 Brants
110 Rorem and Calmer

DOWN

1 Comedienne Imogene
2 Nuncupative
3 Shortening
4 Come before
5 Tours de force
6 Sets the stride
7 Pallid
8 Honshu bay
9 Kelso feeder
10 Ariel et al.
11 U.S.S.R. range
12 Frosted
13 Nav. rank
14 "Little Men" author
15 Ten: Prefix
16 Lamebrain
17 Enzymes
21 Gibraltar
24 "____ Ben Jonson!"
26 To the rear
29 M.C.'s prop
32 Walking ____ (elated)
34 Summary
35 "Once ____ time . . ."
36 Goes for conservatives
37 ____ throat
38 Common swifts: Scot.
39 Put up drapes
40 Change state
41 Move waveringly
42 Word with sooth and nay
44 Paid attention
45 Hackneyed
48 Press and radio
50 Kick off
52 Valleys
53 Dewy
54 Ezra Pound's home state
55 At no time
56 Clipped
58 Miffed state
60 Skedaddle
62 Poznán, to a Berliner
63 Pitchman's stooge
64 Kind of reaction
65 Must
66 Waiters' handouts
67 Country crossover
68 Acknowledge
69 ____ Tages (one day): Ger.
71 Solarium, e.g.
72 Smart ____
75 ____ acid
77 N.F.L. milieu
79 Garson
80 Testifies
81 Go a round
82 Blatherskite
83 "Ici on ____ . . ."
85 Blab
87 Chewink
89 Cleaned (up)
90 Enclosures
91 Lovers' quarrel
92 Prepare to take off
93 Saharan
94 Malarial symptom
95 Cuba libre ingredient
96 Minute
97 Bagnold
98 N.C.O.'s
100 Saluki or dingo
102 Taradiddle

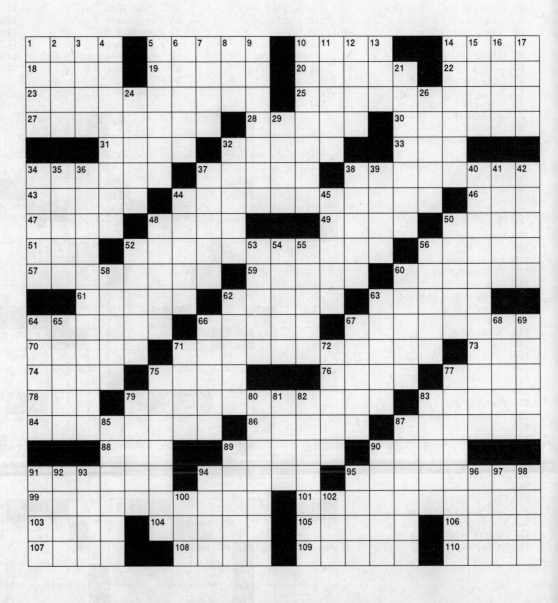

129. Conventional Places by Bert H. Kruse

ACROSS

1 "17," for one
7 Memorable coloratura
12 Thin coat of watercolor
16 Espionage name
20 Balfe heroine
21 Taurus's eastern neighbor
22 Prefix with chamber
23 Philippine island
24 Credit Managers Assn. site
26 Distillers of America site
28 Goddess of dawn
29 Rental papers
30 Macho type
32 Is impertinent
33 Made tracks
34 Vends
35 Eye trouble
36 Chiropteran
39 "___ ever so humble . . ."
40 Raven
41 Beecham or Beerbohm
42 Some are tight
46 Geology topic
48 Wool-gather
50 Layer of tissue
51 Judge
52 McPherson
53 Site for Clockmakers Unlimited
57 Depression initials
58 Clothing
60 Bartok and Gabor
61 Releases
62 Securities' nominal value
63 Initials since 1922
64 Stiff
66 Flat failure
67 Singles-bar rara avis
69 Biggin
70 Calder Society site
75 Frangipane
76 Pushkin gallant
78 Third of Field's trio
79 Ark landing place
81 Bills
82 Furniture Mfrs. Assn. site
87 Scot's negative
90 Mountain crests
92 "The stag at ___ . . ."
93 Synthetic fabric
94 Ferrer and Brooks
95 "Angela ___"
96 Pleasure cart
99 To ___ (exactly)
100 Shoulder warmers
102 Ingot
103 Trampoline Enthusiasts, Inc. site
107 Celebrated bovine
108 Bagnold
110 Soft palates
111 Gremio and Grumio
112 Perk up
114 Level
115 Suffix with journal
116 Fille's mother
117 Big first for baby
118 "The College Widow" author
121 "Mend when thou ___": Lear
122 Egyptian queen of the gods
123 On ___ of (for)
126 Soup
127 Defective
129 Adherent
132 Gourmands of America, N. Dak. site
134 U.S. Soc. of Sculptors site
137 Weapon handles
138 Cry of contempt
139 Not together
140 Rouge ___
141 Produces lace
142 Chipper
143 Memoranda
144 Playgoers' mecca

DOWN

1 "Quién ___?"
2 Musical group
3 "___ Well . . ."
4 Like a Dogpatch hero
5 Indigo
6 Mendel Soc. site
7 Hot drink
8 Ready for conflict
9 They have sobrinos and sobrinas
10 Ship-size unit
11 Naked
12 With affection
13 Author Seton et al.
14 Tommy's Tommy gun
15 Plymouth Rock
16 Rube
17 Stagg
18 Steak order
19 Annoys
23 Rule
25 Dehiscent
27 Alienate
31 Oleoresin
34 Sir Patrick of balladry
35 Storages for forages
36 Support
37 Melodious
38 Natl. Funeral Directors site
39 Follower of muy or très
41 Religious group
43 American Press Assn. site
44 Take off
45 Chichi
47 Esau's land
48 Old Nick
49 Peg Woffington's creator
50 Silent vamp
54 Saskatchewan's capital
55 Soda variety
56 Cosa ___
59 Liquor drink
65 Footnote abbr.
66 Baseboard
68 Presidential monogram: 1881–85
70 Grandson of Noah
71 Olympics contestant: 1976
72 Truncate
73 He wrote "The Fight"
74 "Indeed!" in Ireland
77 Trouter's need
80 Plant beards
81 Epithet for Elizabeth I
83 Hornet, e.g.
84 In any way
85 Historic Bantu empire
86 Corp. official
88 Part of SHAPE
89 Early ascetic
90 Relative of topaz
91 "Scram!"
94 Bamako is its capital
97 Bomb trial
98 Man or skye
99 Shoelace tag
101 "10-33!" in CB lingo
104 A Forsyte wife
105 Viking
106 Ma or Pa
109 Pours
113 Start of a P.O. motto
116 Paludal
117 River rapids
120 Automotive pioneer
121 "Born Yesterday" director: 1950
122 Buffalo pro on ice
123 Opp. of sold
124 Silkworm
125 Military command
126 Stay
127 Campus group
128 "Abominable" one
129 Admired one
130 Hit, old style
131 Starchy food
133 Saturn's consort
135 Post post letters
136 Follower of Santa

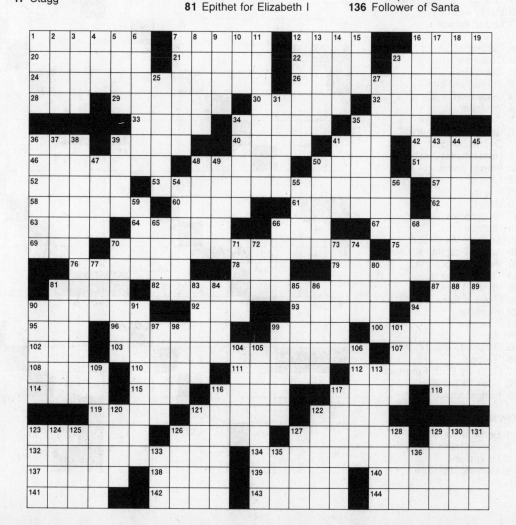

130. Easy Writers, Inc. by Alfio Micci

ACROSS

1 Principal
5 Altar's neighbor
9 Oriental weights
14 Lobster feature
18 Capri, for one
19 Composer Manuel de ____
21 Lowest deck
22 Bait
23 Certain travelers?
25 Indiscretions by two?
27 Young plant
28 Works on shoes
30 Ansermet
31 Muffler manglers
32 Learner
33 Coyote State: Abbr.
34 Fabric
36 Violinist Mischa
37 Procures the release of
41 Where a kanone glides
42 Pittsburgh sights?
44 Canals of Venice
45 Gumshoes
46 Attempt
47 Palm leaf: Var.
48 Warbled
49 Acorn sprouter
50 Valuable deer?
54 Feed the kitty
55 Wields the gavel
57 Ointments
58 Sofia native
60 Provisional document
61 One of the Philippines
62 Hindu wear
63 Lower in rank
65 Rife
66 Partner of saved
69 Colleen's land
70 Glares?
72 Three-toed bird
73 Deceased
74 Whimper
75 Cather's "One of ____"
76 Same, to Stéphanie
77 Ordinal suffix
78 Horticulturist's milieu?
82 Pianist Jorge
83 Files
85 Frenzy
86 Belief
87 Automotive pioneer
88 Buenos ____
89 Change the décor
90 Ancient capital of Laconia
93 Pain: Comb. form
94 Titian was one
98 Pennsylvanian?
100 Gives a false alarm?
102 Rainbow
103 Presume
104 Vex
105 River into the Tiber
106 Flatboat
107 Book by D. S. Freeman
108 Took to the hills
109 Famed fabler: Var.

DOWN

1 Serpent sound
2 Noted Italian family
3 Drug plant
4 Morning moisture
5 "'Tis not the dying for ____ that's so hard . . .": Thackeray
6 Chess pieces
7 Metallic residue
8 Cathedral city
9 Pulling cable
10 "Tempest" sprite
11 Building additions
12 City of Israel
13 Apace
14 Chain sounds
15 Pandurina
16 "Scourge of mortals": Homer
17 Bridge position
20 Undertake
24 Wash out
26 Postgraduate's concern
29 Gem
32 West Pointer
33 Menu item
34 Weather forecast
35 Key men?
36 ____-Unis
37 Wallet items
38 Marmalade base?
39 Shoshonean
40 Puma's relative
41 Telegram word
42 Throat ailment, for short
43 Glum
46 Miss Thompson
48 Site of Willamette U.
50 Trumpeter Al
51 Walking ____ (elated)
52 Papal cape
53 Use a shredder
56 Tea tidbit
58 Kennel sounds
59 Author Leon
61 Adorn oneself
62 Orchestrate
63 Crossed out
64 Muse of lyric poetry
65 Tamarisks
66 "March King"
67 Irish patriot: 1778–1803
68 Mimi-Rodolfo number
70 Court figures
71 Name for French kings
74 One who plunders
76 Unmusical one
78 False glitters
79 D.P.
80 Espionage name
81 Like O'Neill's "Ile"
82 Wet down
84 Most tender
86 Stiffened
88 Coeur d' ____, Idaho city
89 Pee Wee or Della
90 Omit
91 Alpaca's habitat
92 Hebrew letter
93 Indigo
94 Medicine holder
95 Réunion and de la Cité
96 Hair style
97 Tide type
99 Unseal, poetically
101 Whistler, for short

131. Gourmet Meal by Reginald L. Johnson

ACROSS

1 "Marching as ___"
6 Spartan magistrate
11 Heroic story
15 Kind of seaman
19 Have ___ (be prudent)
20 English author of 19th century
21 Yule-tree ornament
24 Coward
25 Banquet appetizer choice
29 Disgruntled
30 Resort near Lisbon
31 "Faster!"
32 Duchess of ___, Goya's friend
34 Coyote St.
36 Food store, for short
37 Bowler or dicer
40 Managed
42 One of the Johnsons
45 Nondisputable thing
48 Word with cap or gold
50 Banquet second-course choice
57 On one's toes
58 Afghan prince
59 On the briny
60 Vail equipment
61 Judge
62 Loman
65 Ready for reaping
67 "Get out!"
70 "___ My Shadow"
71 Trespass
75 Start-off trio
78 Gazetteer data
81 U. of Florida player
83 Subtle emanations
84 Banquet fish course
90 Gardner et al.
91 Suffix with sect
92 Civil War admiral
93 Performed
94 American historian
97 DeSoto and Hudson
100 Court ace
102 P.G.A. members
103 ___ of nature (nude)
106 ___ Scotia
110 Greek wine pitcher
113 Argentine actor
116 Airs
117 Mansard extensions
118 Banquet meat-course choice
123 Twain's pauper
124 Tooth: Comb. form
125 "___, you noblest English!"
126 "Tusitala" monogram
127 Friend of Pierre
128 Somewhat, in music
131 Goddess of discord
134 Predicate word
136 Superior violins
140 Complain
144 Dismounted
147 Banquet dessert-course choice
151 First place
152 Depended
153 Fencers' needs
154 Let down
155 Bustle
156 Crowlike birds
157 Polite blokes
158 Kind of circle

DOWN

1 Soviet agency
2 ___ Rios, Jamaica
3 Recipient of a guarantee
4 Prospero's servant
5 Ad ___ (pertinent)
6 Desire
7 Saucy
8 Saint's headgear
9 Perfumes
10 Bridge ploy
11 Command to Fido
12 Service scores
13 Equip or encircle
14 Those who give in
15 Prefix for dote or freeze
16 Mooring device
17 Waikiki wreath
18 Building extension
22 Easy gait
23 Sci. in the news
26 Teardrop or dewdrop
27 List of candidates
28 Coutel
33 Torment
35 Neighbor of Neb.
38 His, in Caen
39 Tableware: Abbr.
40 Artery
41 Chassis part
43 Heated and browned
44 Author Bombeck
46 "We ___ our guns all day": G. & S.
47 Pharaoh, for short
49 Bony
51 Venus de Milo's lack
52 Semisolid material
53 Wild ox, in the Bible
54 Gaelic
55 Gull's cousin
56 Secular
63 Purplish red
64 Med. study
66 Orison
68 Latin II teaser
69 Part of "to be"
71 Consequently
72 ". . . there shall come forth ___": Isa. 11:1
73 City in Colombia
74 Pay attention
75 "Wait ___!"
76 Weight: Comb. form
77 Refuse coal screenings
79 Distant
80 Bors or Modred
82 Having a holiday
85 Commotion
86 Close bond
87 Potter's net
88 He once played Othello
89 W.W. II area
95 Forty-niner's quest
96 A son of Isaac
98 Italian innkeeper
99 Daze
101 Midge
104 Witch bird
105 Eastern Uganda group
107 Past full bloom
108 Kind of cutlet
109 Inquires
110 Killer whale
111 Good earth
112 Affected with terror
114 Steel union's former boss
115 N.Z. tree
117 Slave of yore
119 Pounded the keys
120 Hwy.
121 Constellation
122 Austen product
129 Khayyám
130 Cabbage
132 Like some verbs: Abbr.
133 Composer Franz von ___
135 Novarro of films
137 Some ties end here
138 Where Laos is
139 Twist
141 Bearing
142 Chard
143 Bonnie bairn
145 ___ fixe
146 Virgin Islands, to U.S.
147 Stake
148 Foofaraw
149 Plugs
150 MacGraw

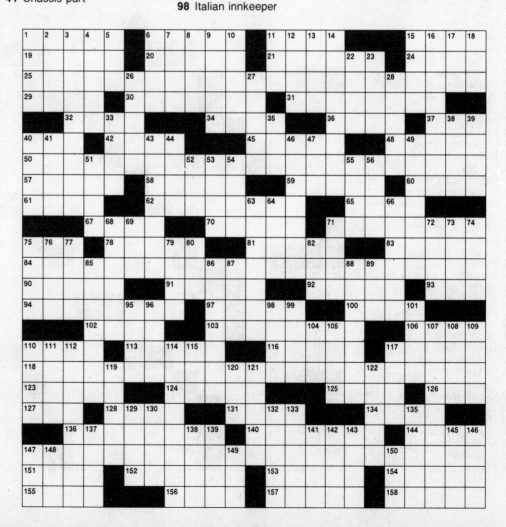

132. Entertaining Ideas by Tap Osborn

ACROSS

1 Style
5 Hokum
9 Sell hot tickets
14 Old Irish alphabet
19 Uzbek's irrigation source
20 He "planted" a handker-chief
21 "Santa ____," Italian song
22 Apollo 14 astronaut
23 Fan of Maria and Maximil-ian
26 Literary archipelago
27 Rescued from ruin
28 Poet Conrad
29 Still
30 Houdini's forte
31 "Hernani" playwright
32 "Saturday night special"
35 Blind impulse
36 Sonny, once
40 Lose one's cool
41 Type of cement
43 Coat
44 Entitled to putt first
45 Swedish port
46 Item for Muffet
47 Tune once sung by Anna May
50 Lap, perhaps
51 Panay people
52 "De Profundis" author
53 Kingdom loser
54 Dash, in radio code
56 Trail Blazers' league
57 "You're ____ Need"
58 Kind of flick
59 All thumbs
62 Close
64 Jacques of songdom
65 Kind of play
67 Little casino, if a spade
68 Wretched
69 Histrio's need
70 High's partner
71 Shrink
72 Rocky eminence
73 Drain
74 Colloid
75 Diplomacy's foundation
78 Premiere for James
80 Thin; watery: Comb. form
81 Hamitic language
82 Kind of food or brother
83 Arabian V.I.P.
84 Victorian blackout
85 Brake
86 One-nighters for Jo Anne
89 Wine: Comb. form
90 Flight feather
92 Former French coins
93 Casual wear
96 "Sunnybrook," e.g.
97 Griddle cake
99 Tall one's need
101 "Lizzie Borden took ____ . . ."
103 Clip of Maisie at the beach
105 Carl or Mark Van ____
106 Russian co-op
107 Sights at Aosta
108 German author of ghost stories
109 Pyknic
110 They make a mesh
111 Trudge
112 River duck

DOWN

1 Billiards shot
2 Killer whales
3 Stage presence, to Arlene
4 Noble
5 Ship's area
6 Valenciennes
7 "How like ____. . .": Hamlet
8 Relative of a vac.
9 Pung
10 Bananas
11 Part of a Racine work
12 Simba
13 Watson's 3, 4 or 5
14 Harmonium
15 Advance prints of Elliott's scenes
16 Celeste's acting career
17 Crazy ____ loon
18 Slick, with or without pix
24 Revers
25 Bacall
29 Grant
31 Lessen a risk
32 Get wind of
33 Eye part
34 Precise
36 Columnist Knickerbocker
37 India's official language
38 Changeable
39 Resided
41 Inadequate
42 Offer top dollar
47 Mount ____, in N.H.
48 Experience
49 Baseball's ____ Wills
52 Vigil
54 Ringer of a sort
55 Goose genus
58 Scottish island
60 Walter's transportation
61 "Moment-of-truth" man
63 Bite on director John's earnings
64 Last words of Pledge of Al-legiance
65 Mala or Stefanie
66 Chute material
68 Scottie's battle memento
69 Make a gaffe at bridge
73 Certain trailers, for short
75 Weightiest U.S. President
76 Pulitzer Prize novelist: 1958
77 Material for Vikki's songs
78 Like some cats
79 Westbrook
80 Curses
82 Took a dip
84 Former Italian coin
87 O.T. book
88 Hayseeds
91 Dunne
93 Toothsome
94 Oriental peninsula
95 Detect, in a way
97 Erudition
98 Sweetsop
99 Perdition
100 Olympic Stadium athlete
101 Foofaraw
102 British swell
103 Decline
104 Baize feature

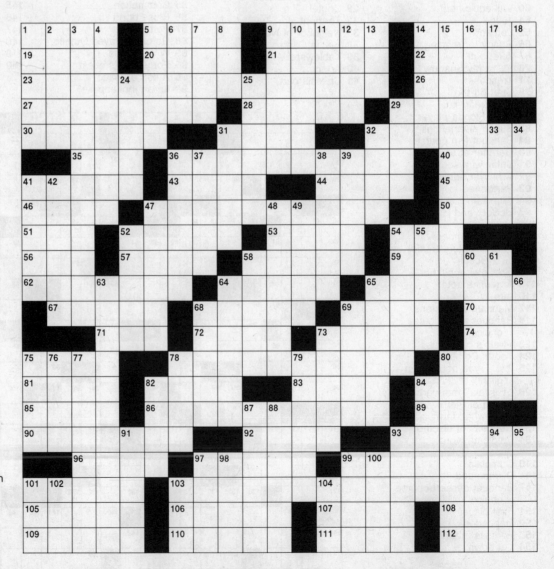

133. Turning Phrases by Jordan S. Lasher

ACROSS

1 Exhausted
6 Short golf shots
11 City in western India
17 "Heaven make thee free
___!": Shak.
21 River to Pamlico Sound
22 Charged
23 Marches or storehouses
24 State tree of Ark.
25 Cobbler's motto?
28 This, in Taxco
29 Moroccan range
30 Scatter
31 A.F.T. rival
32 Huntley
33 Subjoin
36 Conquers Everest
40 Blunder
41 "Yea, team!"
42 Kind of banana or dog
44 Row
45 Very unusual
46 Narrow channel
48 News agcy.
49 Clavicor, e.g.
51 Bawl
52 Balaam's beast
53 Jinx
54 Unit indicating loudness
55 Of a Great Lake
57 Suffix with harp or violin
58 Costa ___
59 Tumultuous
61 Uses pastels
67 Small whale
68 Develops
69 Unsews
70 ___ Miss, rival of 'Bama
72 Embellish
74 Baphomet, e.g.
75 Hamlet and Borge
77 Tunisian seaport
78 Mapmaking sci.
79 Workaholic's drive
82 Shrewd maneuverer
83 Old English letters
84 Gets one's dander up
85 Antiseptic: Comb. form
86 Glassware ovens
87 Author of "The Wall Street
Gang"
88 Actress Merrill
89 Cordage grass
92 Parabasis
93 Columbia River, e.g.
97 Jai alai basket
100 Chick
101 Ezra Pound work
102 U.S.S.R. moon probe
104 Female lobster
105 He has a sponsor
107 Singer Tillis
108 Afternoon hrs.
111 "King Lear" role
112 Pilcorn
113 "Half ___ is . . ."
114 Lateen or Jamie Green
115 Constance or Louise
117 "Be still!"
118 Dir. to Blarney from
Killarney
119 Jiffy

120 Go gaga over the roller
coaster
124 Past and perfect
126 Boone and Hingle
128 Once named
129 Walton's "The Compleat
___"
130 Fortas
131 Steel ingredient
132 "Her typewriter was broken!"
139 Dido died on one
140 Show plainly
141 Musical flourish
142 Ending of a Kilmer poem
143 Existence
144 Zone
145 Roofing tile
146 Some errata

DOWN

1 Aesop's "The ___ and the
Dove"
2 Ornament for Don Ho
3 Abner's radio partner
4 Rhone feeder
5 Like an amateur boxer
6 French vineyard
7 Help
8 Accuse
9 N.J. city or river
10 Office gadget
11 Tintinnabula
12 Any N.F.L. player
13 Actress Charlotte

14 Keys or jacks
15 Strike out
16 Very, in music
17 Oil cartel
18 Reputation earned by inept
rodster
19 Meanwhile
20 Refreshment server
26 Out-___ (alfresco)
27 Distrustful
33 Island for reclining and re-
fining
34 Document
35 Hippocratic oath, in a way
37 Warhol movie
38 Rapidity
39 Words of contempt
43 Light refractor
47 Kipling's Rikki-tikki-___
50 Okinawa's capital
53 Under ___ (perdu)
56 Hardy's returner
57 Part of T.G.I.F.
58 Pipe
60 Defunct Houston hockey
team
62 Dandies
63 Slangy suffix with sock
64 Dissocial
65 Fleming heavy
66 Egg white
71 Reno leavers
72 ". . . ___ o'clock scholar"
73 Twelve: Prefix
75 Tree of India
76 Away from the mouth

77 Napped leather
79 Cosmetic
80 Norway's patron saint
81 Run easily
82 Measure pulses
84 Up
88 Deprive a plant of water
89 Ordinal ending
90 Caroline Islands group
91 Battle site northeast of Verdun: 1916
94 Bear in the air
95 "___ by land . . ."
96 Author May
98 Hector
99 Feeds the kitty
103 Bestud
105 Fuel line
106 Mrs. ___ cow
107 Evil
108 Sycamore
109 Fonteyn and Kidder
110 Adroit: Var.
114 Raglan, e.g.
116 Early center of Christianity
121 Titicaca's milieu
122 Demolition man
123 Vertical
125 Reticular
127 Snick and ___
133 Suffix with differ or defer
134 Sgt. or cpl.
135 Guevara
136 French painter-sculptor
137 Antique car
138 Ja or da

134. Strip Tees by Ronald Friedman

ACROSS

1 Type of post
7 Former Yankee pitcher
11 African lake or republic
15 Convenes
18 Yield to gluttony
19 Hawaii and Alaska in 1958: Abbr.
20 Addiction
21 Poetry of people
23 David Frost's "TW3" of TV
26 Main artery
27 Kefauver
28 Rouses
29 Wild and excited
31 Fifty forming one
34 Stumble
36 Doctrines
37 Advances slowly
38 Milano, e.g.
39 Eye-opener
42 Serve food for a banquet
43 Landon
44 Pleaded
45 Moon's age on Jan. 1
47 She-bear, in Granada
50 Basketball targets
52 Ragged
56 Debases
58 Turtles
61 Playground item
63 _____ Benedict
64 Pule or mewl
65 Maris or Williams
66 City on the Merrimack
68 Inoculation or jigger
70 Quote
71 Pigs' kin
72 Suffix for gang or team
73 Pronoun
74 Pagan
76 Reese
77 Fool's gold
79 High schooler's problem
80 Heckled
82 Musical passages
85 Enjoyed oneself
87 Flow
89 Greet
90 Meat dish
91 Writing pad
92 Small amount
95 Floor piece
96 Honolulu is here
98 Poe tale, with "The"
103 Throw stones at
104 Stop for gas
106 New Rochelle college
107 Separate carefully
108 Cash or charm
109 Obsolete
111 Slide
112 Deep cut
114 Houston athlete
115 Bikini adjectives
122 Decayed
123 Margarine
124 Land west of Wales
125 One who samples oolong
126 Boy
127 Floating or swimming
128 Rent payer
129 Provides funds for

DOWN

1 Something to pledge
2 Gardner
3 Morning moisture
4 Most wrathful
5 Nutcrackers' suites
6 One who collects
7 Actor Ayres
8 Pulled apart
9 Gift
10 Soliciting
11 Dance step
12 Melt
13 To the stern
14 Perry's adversaries
15 Spiritualists' meeting
16 Tim's tune
17 Sally
22 Black Hawk's tribe
24 Trying
25 Number of Bears or Pigs
30 Makes into law
31 Criticize severely
32 He tries to suit the customer
33 Popular refrain
35 Michelangelo works
39 Omen
40 Keats work
41 Announce formally
46 Prefix for fix
48 Musician's transition
49 Analyze ore
51 Track
53 Shoots dice anew
54 Nondrinker
55 Lower in rank
57 Dead heats
59 Ringing of bells
60 Born: Fr.
62 Remainder
67 Policeman, at times
68 Former Iranian rulers
69 Six-armed Greek goddess
71 Board's partner
72 Detect
75 Degree of warmth
76 Cross out
78 Actress Louise
81 Swiss hero
82 Metalworkers
83 Electrical needs
84 Addison's colleague
86 Used the tub
88 Biblical weed
93 Pretend
94 Continental army volunteer
97 Basically, in Nice
99 Site of the Teatro São Carlos
100 Norse god of mischief
101 Sweet liqueur
102 _____-waiting
104 Crowd sound
105 Antiseptic
108 Leading
110 American inventor
113 Cygnet
116 Affirmative vote
117 Part of Q.E.D.
118 Harold of comics
119 This, in Valencia
120 Salamander
121 Time periods: Abbr.

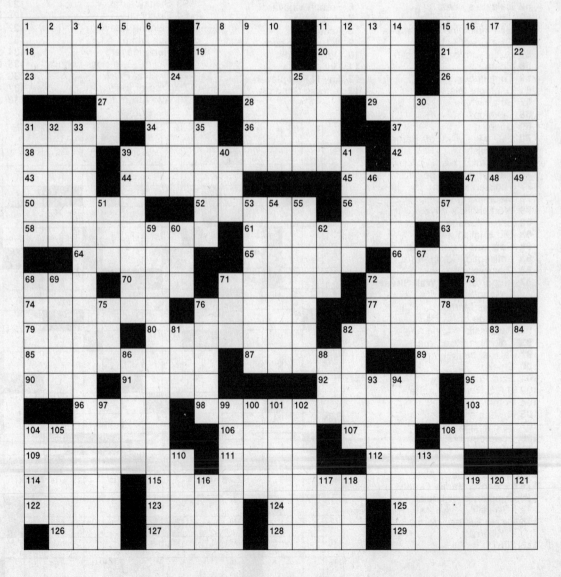

135. Electricks by David J. Pohl and John M. Samson

ACROSS

1 Kidded
7 "Phèdre" playwright
13 Heroic
17 Ready money
21 Quivering
22 Antagonism
23 Teacher
24 Concerning
25 Department store device
27 Snarl
28 Michael Romanov was one
29 "Captain" and Michael
30 National park in Utah
31 Strigine sound
33 Preserve
35 Blueprint, for short
36 One of the bills
37 U.S. violinist
39 Isolate
40 Canadian physician: 1849–1919
43 Nominees
44 Revoke
45 Unstable
48 Tower top
49 Cream of the crop
50 One and one-third drams: Abbr.
53 "Song of the Earth" composer
54 Court aide
55 Kind of rule
56 Nurse shark
57 Chemical suffix
58 High tension area
61 Springlike
63 Fig basket
65 Applause
66 Sly glance
67 Omits
68 College or collar
69 Barber's concern
70 Supply service
72 Without feeling
73 Radar antenna covering
75 Group of trout
76 Air Pump constellation
78 Grant
80 Drew a bead on
81 Freudian concerns
82 Raison d'____
85 Concert cry
86 ____ spumante
87 Premed subject
88 Russian co-op
89 Building stone
90 Vivid hue
94 Pitching stat.
95 Trumpet adjunct
96 One to pay
98 American lizard
99 Biblical berth
101 Big Board's "big brother"
102 Kierkegaard
103 Earth mover
104 Soothing
105 Phantom: Var.
107 Solitary
108 Ten C-notes
109 Topographic topic
111 Stroke of luck
112 French vineyard
113 Band of Zulu warriors

117 Save
118 Clayey soil
119 Damascene
120 Baseball's Rusty
121 Scantling
122 Sacred bird
124 Tourists' togs
128 School subj.
129 Penalty
130 Internal tax
131 Cause to sparkle
132 Eucalypt
133 Brat's rebuttal
134 Elocutionist, at times
135 Home of the Flyers

DOWN

1 Children's game
2 "Sail on, ____ of State!"
3 Screen
4 Anthracite
5 Heart testers, for short
6 Fourth in a series
7 More piquant
8 Elbow
9 Grafting shoot
10 Oahu baking pit
11 Type of buoy
12 Art lover
13 Incite
14 Fourth-down play
15 Belfast gp.
16 Headline material
17 Jerseys

18 Blotter entry
19 Solemn
20 Met star
26 Montezuma, e.g.
32 Pitchblende
34 Behold, to Pilate
37 David's weapon
38 Fortunetelling card
39 Suez port
41 Frets
42 Turkish coin
43 Use up
44 Sharp sound
45 Vestment
46 Nasser's successor
47 Entertainment outlet
48 Gig for Severinsen
49 Presbyter
51 Madame de ____
52 Friendly: Slang
54 Quota
55 Gibe
56 Not so clean
59 Pretense
60 Chose
62 Twelfth Jewish month
64 France of France
69 "Might-makes-right" game
70 Laugh-getter
71 "____ atque vale!"
74 Copperfield's first wife
75 With 118 Down, random
76 Wide-open
77 Response to the Little Red Hen

78 Rays
79 Result
80 Wan
81 "The Word of Love" poet
83 Aired again
84 Gladden
86 High resort
87 One of the poles
88 Radial city
91 Pillow padding
92 Pointless
93 Zola novel
97 Wedge, e.g.
100 Making an increase
102 TV hit
103 Doze
104 West Indian island
106 Harbor enhancer
107 Kit and caboodle
108 Sorting machine
109 Cross
110 Mob-scene actor
111 Pre-Easter customs
112 Jug
114 Danton colleague
115 ____ shame (rout in a bout)
116 "Brand" playwright
118 See 75 Down
119 Surrounded by
120 It seats 55,300
123 Stole
125 English river
126 N.Y.C. building
127 Lugubrious

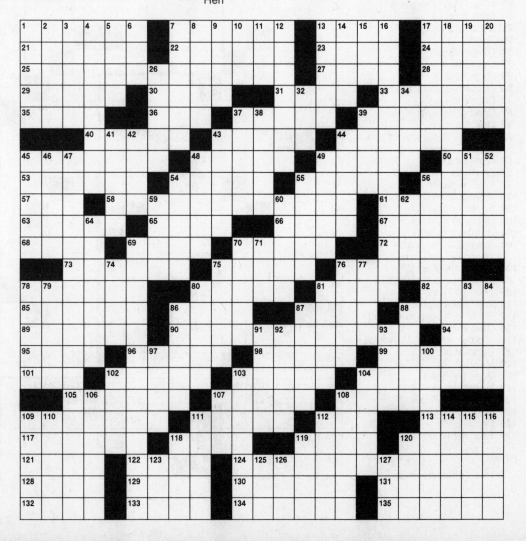

136. Stepquote by Eugene T. Maleska

ACROSS

1 Start of Stepquote
7 Prufrock's creator
14 What "you gotta have"
19 The Moor, to Verdi
20 Exposure to air
22 Ford succeeded him
23 Footpad
24 Stepquote author
25 Stepquote receiver
26 G.P.'s group
27 Scenic peninsula
29 A lot
31 Pawnee's cousin
32 The take
34 Stepquote: Part III
37 Nutriment
38 Outlet
39 Elève's milieu
41 Temper
43 Tibetan beasts
45 F.B.I. documents
47 Famed miler
49 Fitzgerald forte
50 Deadfall
51 Catch in a blunder
53 Stand for Cecil Beaton
57 Heavenly headgear
60 Done in by Livia
62 Old-womanish
63 Where to put your dough
64 Start of a Wolfe title
66 Sailor absent for 73 hours
68 Seaver, once
69 "Oom Paul" was one
70 Soak flax
72 Sybarite's delight
73 Form a lap
74 Diagnostician
77 Calories
79 Slots spot
80 ____ Rosita, city in Mexico
81 Cocky fellows
83 Used a mangle
85 One that rules
87 Bistro
88 Upper Thames or goddess
89 Can. air arm
91 Erudition
92 Kind of saber
96 What a litterbug ignores
100 Soprano Azuma
102 Delusion's partner
103 Grinder's relative
104 Japanese statesman and family
106 Stepquote: Part V
108 Epithet for a Sikh deity
109 That, in Taxco
110 Tall clown's props
112 Suffix with rend and vend
114 Guidonian note
115 Middle name of 25 Across
117 Brine or pickle
120 Meal
122 Book by Read
123 Disney employee
124 Home of a Rose
125 Van Doren's "Jane ____"
126 Dry
127 End of Stepquote

DOWN

1 Hunted for provender
2 Venezuelan aborigine
3 Supports for ruffs
4 Law deg.
5 Shake ____ (hie)
6 Stepquote: Part II
7 Two-headed drumsticks
8 Discriminate
9 R.A.F. underling, informally
10 Chou En-____
11 "Pay ____ mind"
12 ____ wintergreen
13 Short piece of bar steel
14 Dutch master
15 Psyche component
16 Doria or del Sarto
17 Governor
18 Birdy babble
21 Hose
28 Piano key
30 Inference
33 Howard of baseball
35 Schnauzer
36 Stepquote: Part IV
38 November activity
40 Name on a green stamp
42 Wolf, to Rocco
44 Kind of sale
46 Lafayette is here
48 Carmelites
51 Tugboat service
52 ____ pence (tax)
54 Bohemian brewery base
55 Liquid part of fat
56 Mann's "____ in Venedig"
57 Kind of pigeon
58 Lexington or Park
59 Stepquote source: 1900
60 Word with chair or sales
61 Three scruples
65 Testator's choice
67 Neighbor of Perugia
69 Ramus or Rickey
71 Saint ____ of Avila
75 To a great degree
76 Labor
78 Ending with crock or quack
79 Heroine helped by Figaro
82 Zeno's "classroom"
84 Flanges
86 Implicit
88 Twenty: Comb. form
90 Bluebeard's last wife
92 Fleming and Hamill
93 "Winner ____"
94 Russian body of water
95 Narrator
96 River behind King's College
97 Used-car deal
98 Koran language
99 Jeanette and Lloyd
101 Estados ____ Mexicanos
105 Threadlike groove
107 Stepquote: Part VI
110 Ship's prow
111 Birdbrain
113 Claudius's successor
116 Ab ____ (from the start)
118 Giant reed of India
119 Gormandized
121 Buddy

137. On a First-Name Basis by A. J. Santora

ACROSS

1 Has a meal
5 X
10 Recorded proceedings
14 Minimum
19 Step _____ (go fast)
20 Jael's victim: Judg. 4:5
21 Put on alert
22 Buyer, in law
24 Harangue a "silents" star
27 None
28 Expiating
29 Search after
30 Lace edging
32 Burnsian refusal
33 Fistfight
34 Toupee: Slang
37 More in want
39 Pastoral verse
41 Source of a beverage
44 Govt. advisory board
45 Approximately
47 Make Ben Casey a believer
52 Kind of assembly
55 Where Castro's revolt began
56 Quartet voice
57 Yachting
58 Gardner
59 Cajole
60 Sharp-edged
62 Hollywood award
65 Some cadets
67 Evaluated
70 Beside one another
72 Followers of hip and tip
73 Fowl feature
75 Dam on the Nile
76 Self-reproach
78 Moll or doll
81 Zero
82 Anything bow-shaped
84 Dijon donkey
85 Upon: Prefix
86 Five and _____
87 Comparison
89 Hayseed
91 "Star Wars" figures
94 Dead duck
95 Inhuman
97 Airplane maneuver
101 Wading bird
103 Gossip, Yiddish style
104 Sans _____ (nonpareil)
106 Forearm bone
107 Opposite of ecto
108 Prong
110 Santo _____ (Cape Verde island)
112 Beautiful girls
115 Having teeth
117 Sheepish singer
120 Mail
121 Good wood for oars
122 Kibitz
123 Mercutio's friend
125 Warsaw's river
128 Spade or Browne
129 Guitry of theater
134 Second person
135 Limerick, e.g.
137 Dickens girl
139 Cold wind of France
141 Edict

143 Abstruse news analyst
147 Available
148 Air
149 Gridiron official
150 Man is one
151 Former Indian soldier
152 Mimic
153 Approaches
154 Egyptian solar disk

DOWN

1 Daybeds' kin
2 Conjoin
3 Helmsman
4 Task
5 Shame the "Country Girl"
6 Triple this for a wine
7 Bee chaser
8 Goes wrong
9 Bite a dog
10 Stir up a tennis star
11 Panther or sailboat
12 Torrid Zone region
13 Broadway musical
14 Marquisette
15 Impassioned "Happy Warrior"
16 Appropriate
17 Obdurate court champ of 1953
18 Of sound quality
20 Bask
23 Stagger
25 Vitamin H
26 Shoe-width size
31 Rocky cliffs
35 Peak in Colorado
36 Diving bird
38 Pater
40 Payable
42 Ending for differ
43 Irish saint
46 Horn sound
47 Imogene
48 Spanish card suit
49 Neighbor of Sumatra
50 Annoyed
51 Lyres of yore
53 Reluctant
54 Cascades peak
57 Dance is one
61 Writer LeShan
63 "Godfather" actor
64 "Lou Grant" actor
66 W.W. II theater
68 "West Side Story" star, to Puerto Ricans
69 Drink from a flask
71 Attack an actor from N.Y.C.
74 Check beneficiary
76 Dun former man-in-blue
77 Heroic work
78 Silenced
79 ". . . in _____ of Light": FitzGerald
80 Light upon a film Bell
83 Reddish horse

88 Writer Wallace
90 Eagle-rider of myth
92 Two _____ kind
93 German bomber
95 Tournament draw
96 Pine
98 Turkish standard
99 Concerning
100 Colleen
102 Belgrade name
105 Nanny and billy
109 Brash
111 Test
113 Eng. lexicon
114 Port on the Black Sea
116 Three, in Rome
117 Abates
118 Denver's time
119 Mrs., in Madrid
123 Fix over
124 Dutch and brick
126 "_____ man with seven . . ."
127 Golfer Elder
130 Central halls
131 Alpinist's goal
132 Selassie
133 Stand-in for Standish
136 Lamarr
138 Gelatine flavor
140 "_____ Got a Secret"
142 Knock
144 Single
145 Acct.
146 Title Chaplin held

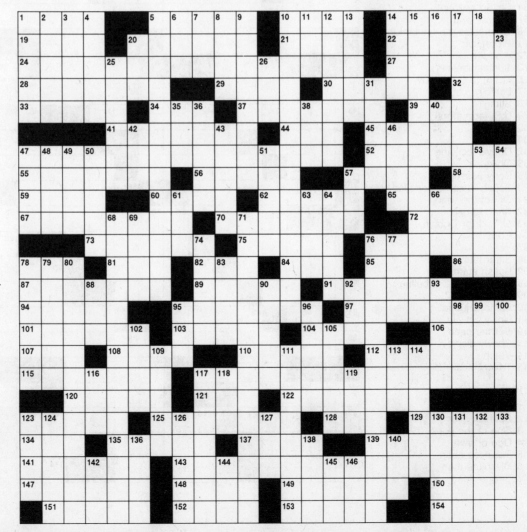

138. Backup Men by Herb L. Risteen

ACROSS

1 Marshy tract
4 Vivacity
8 Admitted fact
13 Cacholong
17 Actor Vigoda
18 Resort in Ontario
20 Bay near Nagasaki
21 Do office work
22 Austrian composer
26 Function
27 Overlook
28 Made slick
29 ____ canto
30 "____ Dimittis" (hymn)
31 Troubles
33 Crusading monarch
43 Suffix with sect
44 Western capital
45 King in Kings
46 Collection
47 Parts of pots
48 ____ de combat
49 She wrote "A Certain Smile"
51 Dixie tree
52 Dessert
53 Amiens's river
54 Heavy, gaseous element
55 Bridge expert
56 Condense, in a way
58 ____ energy
59 Blood-bank supporters
60 French author
64 Call to account
67 Partner of true
68 Assembles, as equipment
71 Protection
72 Wooden
73 Companionless
75 Truth, to Confucius
77 Loblolly
78 Stimuli
79 U.S. legislators
80 Apex
81 United
82 Denver building
83 Obliquely
85 Body passage
86 Scandinavian storyteller
91 Out of the wind
92 Bring to ruin
93 Morsel for Dobbin
94 Corrupt
97 Per ____
98 Bitter taunt
102 British statesman
108 Status quo ____ bellum
109 On a cruise
110 Famous judge
111 Noisy activity
112 Set the pace
113 Showy display
114 Vetch
115 Tavern item

DOWN

1 Rotund
2 Spanish river
3 One of the tides
4 Doe or ewe
5 Business abbr.
6 Dissolute man
7 Sooner than
8 Old master
9 Three on ____
10 Harbor craft
11 Receptacle
12 Barnyard noise
13 Aloof
14 Unpleasant person
15 Tub plant
16 Indecent
18 Native of Pusan
19 Male "dreamboat"
23 Horses' cousins
24 Stubborn as ____
25 ____ Heights
31 Account exec
32 Smooth out
33 Surrealist
34 Evergreen shrub
35 ____ over (helped along)
36 Powerful projectiles
37 Standard
38 Seine feeder
39 Great Hindu poet
40 City in Illinois
41 Prefix with lace and weave
42 A memorable Claude
48 "____ Lyricae," Watts poem
49 Fruit ____
50 London's "Before ____"
51 Hammer's companions
53 Lieder
54 City northwest of Paris
55 Swindle
57 Striped textile design
58 Hale and Hari
59 "I am ____, Egypt . . ."
61 Social classes
62 Cézanne's "Boy in ____ Vest"
63 Monotonous talker
64 Table fowl
65 German poet
66 Miss Moorehead
69 Driver's maneuver
70 Food in Firenze
72 One thousand kilograms
73 Galatea's beloved
74 Napoleon won here in 1796
76 Colorful fish
78 He wrote "The Counterfeiters"
80 Of the ribs
82 Disintegrates
83 ____ by verdict
84 Mouthlike openings
85 Landscaper's shrub
87 Rodomontaded
88 Jogged
89 Loos and Louise
90 Roman poet
94 River duck
95 "Green Gables" girl
96 Greek vowel
98 Therapeutic agents
99 Moslem lord
100 Scoria
101 Southern France
103 Hammarskjöld
104 ____ loss
105 Dixie sch.
106 G.B.S. was one
107 Achieved

139. Printer's Deviltry by Maura B. Jacobson

ACROSS

1 Hubs
5 Miller's material
10 Prima donna
14 Stanford
20 "Hardly ____ is now alive . . ."
21 Vietnamese capital
22 A
24 Writer Wylie
♪ 25 Au^{to}
27
29 ____ Gay
30 Two N.L. players
32 Spanish pipe
33 World's tallest building, for short
x
40 Is a consumer
41 S. African village
42 Silkworm
43 "Sore labour's bath"
45 Nabokov title
48 "Zebras" on a gridiron
51 ____ nous
54 Streisand song

58 8 A.M. surgeons
63 Curl the lip
64 Writer known as Artemus Ward
65 Nigerian staple
66 Neurons' juncture point
69 One of the Speakers
70 Concurred
71 Penn Station builder
73 Iktcs
75 Yule paste-on
76 Wingless
80 ____-pain (Parisian bread-winner)
81 Champagne's flavor and body
83 # 20/20
86 Immortal hawk
89 A sister of Thalia
91 Trig ratios
92 That girl, to Gaius
94 — — — — — — —
99 Poke fun at
100 More lethargic
102 With, in Aix
103 Part of B.T.U.
106 U.S. press org.
108 Depth bomb, to a gob
109 Hollers
111 A/C V.P.
114 Horse-opera setting
116 Novelist Lagerlöf
117 Denomination
118 T
119 Come ____ (confess)
122 Endings with aster and planet
124 River isles
127 Lone Ranger's prop
130 ✔ ✔
138 Delhi nannies
140 Whom Seth begat
141 Horse or antelope
142 Peep show
143 2nd   2nd
147 $1,000 "Manon"

150 Sour brew
151 Fencers' gear
152 Ade book: 1896
153 Caliph's title
154 Kidney: Prefix
155 Arboret, e.g.
156 Kremlin refusals
157 Acquires

DOWN

1 Gem feature
2 Muscat native
3 Ricochet
4 Hearths
5 F---J
6 Was a candidate
7 Fort Knox item
8 S.
9 Pussyfoot
10 Aswan, e.g.
11 Call ____ day
12 Artistic quality
13 Biblical tree
14 Pastoral place
15 LL
16 /
17 Celebes oxen
18 Part of N.D.
19 Boutique buy
23 Beau ____, Goldsmith character
26 Tobacco kiln
28 Wouk hero
31 On more solid ground
35 Became friendly

36 ____ fixe
37 Turner and Louise
38 Cooper hero
39 Corded fabric
44 Some M.I.T. grads
45 Uncle of Mohammed
46 Laments
47 Greek forums
49 Vaudeville name
50 Leonidas' city
52 Nessen and Ziegler
53 Part of Q.E.D.
55 Persian sprite
56 Ericsson
57 Formerly, formerly

Noon

59
60 Feminine ending
61 Kuwaiti ruler
62 Tap
67 Glances over
68 Heart exam
72 Dada display
74 Snow, in Scotland
76 On the move
77 Sound: Suffix
78 Short way
79 French ____, Ind. spa
82 Sea bird
84 Superdome athlete
85 The ____ (cruise destination)
87 Draw out
88 Filament of silk
90 Clerical garb

93 Wild buffalo
94 Milland and Eberle
95 Eye area
96 Dickens girl
97 Catchall abbrs.
98 Six, on a die
100 Of milk
101 Columbus campus initials
104 Nomothetes
105 Of organic matter
107 Chopping tool
110 Hurok
112 Consumers' advocate
113 Modified organism
115 Flimsy material
120 Bide ____
121 Kind of word
123 Rallying cry
125 "Comin' ____ the Rye"
126 Porpoise
127 Korean port
128 Adequate
129 Orchid byproduct
131 Vote in
132 Lou Grant on TV
133 Actor Hagman
134 Growing out
135 ____ de menthe
136 Horn: Prefix
137 Sutures
139 *
144 Sellout sign
145 D
146 Opposite of NNW
148 Kind of pick or wit
149 ____ Moines

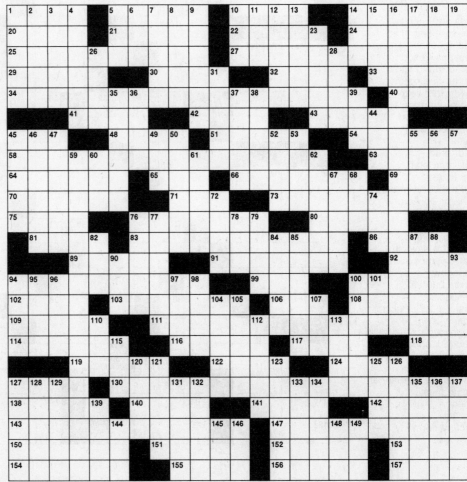

140. Echoes by Jack L. Steinhardt

ACROSS

1 Rum-soaked cakes
6 Name in espionage
10 Securely attached
14 Raddle
18 Siouan Indian
19 Over, in Offenbach
20 Wakefield churchman
21 Tops
22 Heliacal
23 Carolina rail
24 Courage, to Carlos
25 Cubitus
26 Musical sign
29 Glum activist
31 Firm denials
32 Iconoscopes, for short
34 Parisian's property
35 In toto
39 Inconsiderable
40 Unfamiliar
41 Calloway
44 Players' social group
46 Belgian river
48 Distinction
50 It's served at Sing Sing
51 Targets of a Wylie book
53 Stave unit
55 Claudia ____ Johnson
56 October beverages
57 Examination of records
58 Norwegian fjord
59 Hungarian sheep dogs
60 To boot
61 Heraldic band
63 Campaign verb
65 Of a secret order
69 Beg
70 Goats and rabbits
71 Lady's waiting maid
72 Gnostic power
73 Venetians' resort
74 Conrad of old films
75 Gain as due return
77 Shower footwear
79 Type of thermometer
83 Former court star
84 Coadjutors: Abbr.
85 Apiece
86 Fixed route
87 Prepare to start
89 Little foxes
91 Zasu's theater areas
94 Suffix for 20 Across
95 Sol. Gen.
97 Ballyhoos
99 Mahogany trees
100 Snout of a sawfish
102 What eleemosynars give
103 Hoosegow
104 Canvas bargain
107 Kapellmeister
113 "Vissi d'____": Puccini
114 Mooring chain
116 Hindu weight
117 Cathode's opposite
118 Russia's "Mother of Cities"
119 Retinue
120 One-man performances
121 Solemn music
122 Moderate
123 True grit
124 Formerly, formerly
125 Unctuous

DOWN

1 Anjou's cousin
2 Far East seaport
3 Aromatic resin
4 Husband of Jezebel
5 Name of three lakes in N.Y.
6 Bivalves' brawn
7 Frost's "____ Will"
8 Polk had one
9 Semitic language
10 Half a sawbuck
11 Type of test
12 South Pacific native
13 Medieval poet
14 ____ Arabia
15 Tint picker
16 Maxwell Anderson heroine
17 Tower
20 Roman emperor's drapery
27 Falana
28 Acceptable
30 Baseball's "Schoolboy"
33 Girded one's loins
35 Numerical prefix
36 Colorado ski resort
37 Salinger girl
38 1, 9, 66: Abbr.
39 Trailer type, for short
42 Greek region
43 Crude, coarse cads
45 Brouhaha
47 B.&O., etc.
49 São ____, Brazil
52 Lifted loaves
54 Direct passage
57 Et ____ (and others)
59 "____ My Heart"
60 Chem. process
62 Contemporary of a Stutz
64 Objectives
65 Get along
66 Demotes
67 Spots lots
68 Gulae
69 Musical suite
73 Places
76 Inquire
78 Folds over
79 Pitcher for Pericles
80 Complain bitterly
81 Prefix for chamber
82 Minus
84 Magnetizes
88 Teacup handles
90 Japanese ink
92 Shadow
93 Fancy meals
96 Peruvian seaport
98 Fly with an echo
101 Lofty, in Lourdes
103 Convinces
104 Benefit
105 See 113 Across
106 Middle East diplomat
108 Word with post or prize
109 Deep blue
110 Schary
111 Advantage
112 Malodor
115 Scuttle part

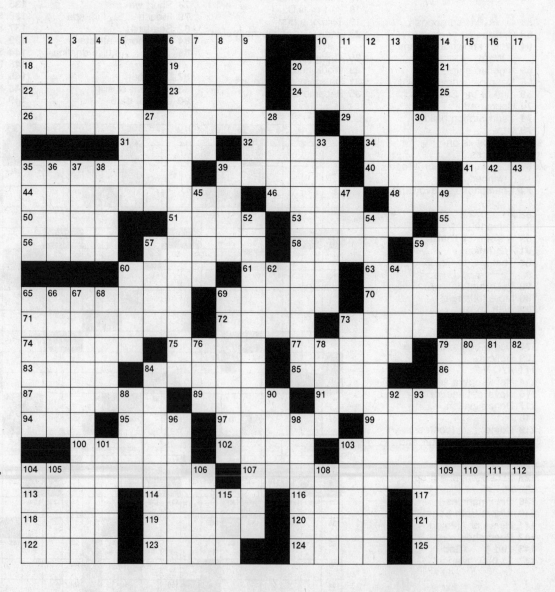

141. English Muffin' by Jordan S. Lasher

ACROSS

1 Merino's yield
5 West and Murray
9 Appetizer
13 Valuable N.Z. food fish
16 Eight times CCCXXV
20 "It's a true fact!"
23 Demented
24 When William II died
25 "I found my keys walking up the path"
27 Chinese unit of measure
28 Supermarket display
29 Countless years
30 Singer Brewer
31 Junior's Saturday evening post
32 Monogram of a Romantic poet
33 Old Faithful, e.g.
35 Scrap or scrape
38 "What Kind of Fool ____?"
41 Foulard
42 Andrea ____ Sarto
43 Dismounted
45 Suffix with velvet
46 Smith of Rhodesia
47 "I used to always go there"
53 Lennon's widow
54 Coffee variety
56 Insinuating
57 Parris Island dweller
58 ". . . for the gain of ____": Swift
59 Word susceptible to 17 Down
61 Mail ctrs.
62 River to the Adriatic
63 Obstacle
64 "La Douce"
66 It sometimes thickens
68 Formal mall
69 One of the Marianas
71 "Giddap!"
72 Muse
73 "I cannot tell ____"
74 Votes
75 Beast: Abbr.
76 Pusilanimous Pharaoh
80 Hold court
81 Setscrew receptacles
83 Roscoe of stuttering fame
84 Battery pole
85 Powerful initials
86 Gets into the act
87 Shaggy beast
89 Santa ____ (Holy See)
90 Rabbit or Fox
91 Office asst.
92 ____ earth (track down)
93 Father: Comb. form
95 Alliance acronym
97 Peon's pittance
98 One-thousandth of a millimeter
99 "My Name is ____ Lev"
101 February luminary
104 Word in the next clue
105 "One of us are wrong"
108 ____ polloi
109 Lookout, for one: Abbr.
110 Skewed
111 Novelist Levin
112 Morse signal
113 Denouement
114 Firework
116 Where Carey took care
120 Warp yarn
121 Tortoise's beak
122 Less exacting
124 Friend of 124 Down
126 ____ fatuus
131 Skin woe
132 "I only have two hands!" etc.
136 Cult
137 Opposite of WSW
138 "Keep this between you and I"
139 "____ Death"
140 Capek drama
141 "The Say-Hey Kid"
142 Be zetetic
143 Soprano from Cannes

DOWN

1 "____ Our Part," N.R.A. slogan
2 Viva voce
3 Caen's river
4 Trademark
5 An edile's 1002
6 Poe's Lee et al.
7 Bounds
8 African mahogany
9 Giotto was one: Abbr.
10 River isle
11 Hoity-____
12 Suffixes with refer and defer
13 One of the moods
14 "Laughing Cavalier" creator
15 Perceptual
16 Gloves, for Fisk
17 "Every dog has it's day"
18 "I don't have nobody"
19 Study
21 "Tusitala"
22 Has the means
26 Dander
32 Humdinger
33 Kelly and Tierney
34 Tolkien creature
36 Salt Lake City player
37 ". . . Paradise ____"
38 Intention
39 Chou's colleague
40 "If winter comes . . ."
41 Autocrat
42 Caper
44 What a tourist drops
48 Fort Knox treasure
49 A 1
50 Hints
51 Out at the plate
52 Dies ____
55 Successor to 39 Down
58 Dye herb
60 Parsley pieces
63 Mud volcano
64 "Oh! How ____ to Get Up . . ."
65 "I like this book, it's great!," etc.
67 Highland miss
68 "Bananas" star
69 Deject
70 Spectral type
72 Atlanta university
73 City near Johnstown, Pa.
74 Actor Crawford
77 "____ Eden"
78 "This ____ noblest Roman . . ."
79 Unit dosage of radiation
82 Art ____
87 Horse of the Year: 1966
88 Nested boxes
90 Heat meas.
92 Puerto ____
93 React to a thrust
94 On the briny
96 Arthritis drug
97 Vainglory
98 Landlubber's ailment
100 Crane's symbol of courage
102 Cyclotron item
103 Executed
105 Household god
106 Kind of rummy
107 Collar
115 Acts the accomplice
117 Back talk
118 Brazilian seaport
119 Palindromic bird
120 Unaided
123 Hokkaido native
124 After H.C.H.
125 Author Kingsley
126 "____ body . . ."
127 Ornamental fabric
128 Nautilus's skipper
129 OPEC member
130 Kazakh and Uzbek: Abbr.
131 Clean ____ whistle
133 Blubber
134 Dawn goddess
135 Nettle

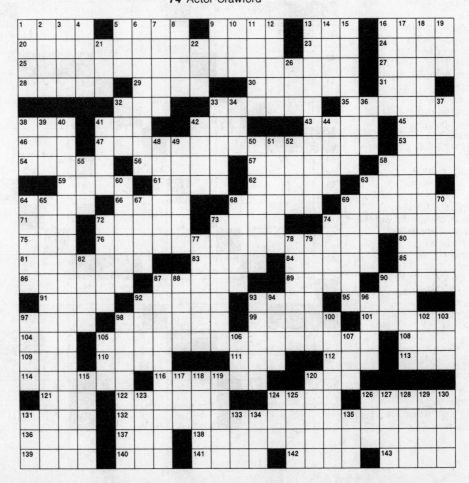

142. Parole Incrociate by Joseph La Fauci

ACROSS

1 Caracalla feature
5 Hazards for Columbus
10 Famous bovine
15 Pipe smoker's device
19 Lily plant
20 Medal presented by a doge
21 Leghorns' lodge
22 Kitchen staple
23 Brutus, to Antony
27 Stars, to Seneca
28 Michelangelo work
29 Marconi interest
30 What Cassius lacked
31 Thinly populated
33 Fen fuel
35 "Naughty Marietta" selection
42 Festivals, in Firenze
43 Rainbows
44 Neapolitan's naso
45 Orfeo's orecchio
47 Amor's wings
48 Galley word
49 Verdi opera
52 Salt, in Siena
53 Santo
54 Played glissandi
55 Fiori, in Fiesole
56 Plate for Pius
57 Verdon
58 Composed
59 Placid
60 Women's wear
64 Summer hat fabric
66 Fallible
67 Gone up
69 "The Bridges at ____-Ri"
70 Comedian Martin
71 Umbral
72 Red dye root: Var.
73 Ponchielli's "Cielo e ____!"
76 Relative of terrazzo
77 Frolicked
78 Annina, in "La Traviata"
79 Cavatina
80 Sly ____ fox
81 Irish island group
82 Hit the books
83 Absquatulate
84 Rivals for Silvia's hand
90 Gin pole
91 Ethically neutral
92 Altar in a chiesa
93 Key
96 "Don't ____ Lulu"
97 Came in on a radar screen
101 Amazing campanile
106 Etna has one
107 Gondolier
108 Romeo
109 Zest for life
110 Caldo, in Calabria
111 A diacritic
112 Sentient
113 Casanova

DOWN

1 Interdicts
2 Molto
3 Caesar's "esse"
4 "Inferno" sight
5 Acqua ____ (rose water)
6 Ferrara family
7 Poetic word
8 Broadway name
9 Chinese skiffs
10 Borgnine
11 Blackout villain
12 Upholstered item
13 Firm follower: Suffix
14 Anglo-Saxon letter
15 Source of a pasta sauce
16 "When I was ____ . . ."
17 Honey: Comb. form
18 Venetian globetrotter
24 Cause euphoria
25 Affectation
26 Sponge out
31 Begat
32 NATO is one
33 Kin of paesani
34 Although, to Antony
35 Word derived from "Caesar"
36 Aureola
37 Noted Alaskan
38 Via ____ (used by Hannibal)
39 Nail polish
40 Less like Oscar Madison
41 Chief ore of lead
46 Freshen
48 Dozed
49 "Memories of ____": Poe
50 Went far afield
51 ". . . and ye took me ____": Matt. 25:43
52 Andrea del ____
54 Spurners of pearls
55 Next to
56 Troublesome
57 Keats's is in Rome
58 Lost dogie
59 Hairnet
60 Basket, in Bologna
61 Titian was one
62 College course
63 Resort town in Mass.
65 "To Catch ____"
68 But, to Britannicus
71 Distort a report
72 Channing
73 Italian statesman
74 Arkin
75 City on the Tevere
77 R.W.R.
78 "____ Lisa"
79 Pugilist
81 Size of type
82 Trellis, Italian style
83 Calligraphy line
85 Fluffy fare
86 City in Kansas
87 Refugee
88 ____ Blanc
89 Soldato's courage
93 Hankering
94 Clog
95 Venetian's vigor
96 Invoice
97 Fox or Rabbit
98 Hair: Comb. form
99 Biblical twin
100 Hamlet
102 Likely
103 We, to Loren
104 "Mamma mia!"
105 Soprano Marton

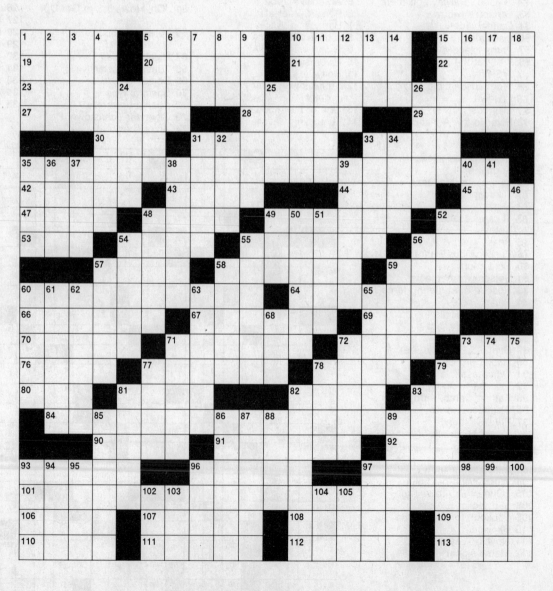

143. Putting on Airs by Louis Baron

ACROSS

1 Singer Vaughan
6 False god
10 Name for a lion
15 Harmony
21 Convex molding
22 Soprano Gluck
23 "Fledermaus" role
24 Sartre novel
25 Fissured
26 Captured, in poesy
27 Demeter, to the Romans
28 Indistinct
29 Burglar's song
33 ". . . cruell'st ____ alive": Shak.
34 Dos Passos trilogy
35 Draft a document
36 The g in Agamemnon
39 Trudge
41 Sounds of delight
43 Wagner's "____ Rheingold"
44 Nickname for Gulliver
47 Cook's song
50 Boring
52 Fabled deliverer
53 Islet
54 Fiddler's spot
55 Royal initials
56 Freshwater porpoise
57 Insomniac's song
62 CBS, for one
63 Clean the slate
64 Brynner
65 Paul Bunyan, e.g.
66 "____ Love You"
67 Wag
71 Tyke's marble
73 "A cottage in ____ . . .": Godley
74 Uncertain feminist's song
81 Mob's agenda
82 Loch in W. Scotland
83 Gelling agent
84 Turndowns
85 Girl's name meaning "esteem"
87 Miniver
89 Dearborn lemon
92 Smith and Jolson
95 Acrophobiac's song
102 It's on the watch
103 After noon
104 Mauritius casualty
105 Reine's mate
106 Fungi
107 "Man, ____ which makes bargains": Adam Smith
109 Ghost's song
112 Airport code for Saigon
113 Roman zilch
114 Augment
115 Stimulate
116 French factory
117 Construction crew
119 Marsh or Murray
120 Pindaric
121 Jalopy owner's song
131 Ruanda-____
132 An Alan of films
133 Shortly
134 Unlimited ages
135 Of boxing
136 Claude of film fame

137 Buzzard's cousin
138 Opera by Delibes
139 Trees aflutter
140 Irish dramatist
141 German dam
142 Paintings by a Swiss modernist

DOWN

1 Achy
2 Tel ____
3 Pinza's birthplace
4 Axillary
5 Cry of surprise
6 Take a dip
7 Kirghiz range
8 Sermon finale
9 Listless indolence
10 Actor-director Guitry
11 Angle
12 Talk-show name
13 Blackmails
14 Norse pantheon
15 Soup-can artist
16 Have a ball
17 Form a line
18 Glacial ridges
19 Radiation dosages
20 Period of power
30 Holier ____ thou
31 "The sun to me ____": Milton
32 Tormentor's hang-up

36 Barbarians
37 Author of "The Proper Bostonians"
38 Lakes or fens
39 Sleuth Vance
40 Spill the beans
41 Chariot race
42 Muscular
44 Fiction's "Studs"
45 Renowned
46 Inadequate, British style
47 F.D.R. follower
48 Tangible
49 We, in Perugia
50 Durocher
51 Infield hit
58 Kiln
59 Calabrian's chickpeas
60 Scottish philosopher
61 Ways
66 Wing: Prefix
68 One ____ time
69 Tackle
70 Geneticist's interest
72 Charity ball
74 "So we'll go no more ____": Byron
75 Telephone mechanic
76 "Cymbeline" heroine
77 Tower builder
78 Moody
79 Sediment
80 Lopez theme
81 Miss Rivera et al.

86 Bohr's science
88 Changed the décor
90 Lament
91 Hawley's colleague
92 Whodunit feature
93 Put the ____ (clamp down)
94 Mean and tricky
96 Parallel
97 Slangy earful
98 Amin
99 Not serving military aims
100 Blabbermouth's forte
101 Kind of blade
108 Bred without mixture
110 Fight promoter's interest
111 Bare: Prefix
114 Lost
117 Type of cape: Fr.
118 Approaches
119 Minister's house
120 Deed holder
121 Yellow flag
122 Tooth point
123 "Birthday suit"
124 Nobelist in Physics: 1976
125 Camelot lady
126 Show senility
127 Get better
128 Symbol of bondage
129 "This one is ____!"
130 Treats shabbily
131 City in the Urals

144. Bon Appétit! by Frances Hansen

ACROSS

1 Act that made history
6 Cousin of an I-bar
11 Sponsorship
15 Colorful fish
19 Hourly
20 Well-known Ike
21 P-U connection
22 Star of "Sin": 1915
23 Actress Verdugo
24 Adorned with long hair
25 Ubangi feeder
26 The "Hungarian Rome"
27 Start of a limerick
31 Rousseau classic
32 Hag in "The Faerie Queene"
33 Borrower on property
34 Set-in sleeve
37 Wooden pin
40 Alexander's group
41 Siouan tribesman
42 ____-Lautrec
45 Polka follower
46 Afternoon hrs.
49 More of limerick
54 Ben Adhem
55 Pate
56 Relative of a pkwy.
57 "Goodnight" girl
58 One of the Bears
61 Actor Davis
64 Mme. Swann, in Proust's books
65 More of limerick
71 Hilo hellos
72 Broadway hit
73 Oodles
74 Massenet opera
75 Kimono adjunct
76 Bellow
79 Island in a palindrome
83 More of limerick
89 One of the media: Abbr.
90 Loot
91 Fawning one
92 With "The," another Broadway hit
93 Church corner
95 It doesn't pay
96 Poser
98 Bradley U. site
101 City lines
102 Billiards shot
104 End of limerick
112 Donkey, in Durango
113 Stravinsky
114 Spry, in Dixie
115 Skipper's command
116 Simon or Diamond
117 Only
118 "La ____ è mobile"
119 Margins
120 Toward the mouth
121 French political unit
122 Günter Grass dwarf
123 "Tutu divine" painter

DOWN

1 Mets' home
2 Road fee
3 A code we live by
4 Leader slain by Vichy militia: 1944
5 Child's chum
6 Turkish porter
7 Mame's burden
8 Article for Goethe
9 Not up yet
10 "L'Après-____ d'un faune"
11 Regard as exactly alike
12 Diving bird
13 Capri, in song
14 Star-shaped
15 Followed orders
16 Missionary's concern
17 Rugged ridge
18 Ah Sin's creator
28 Boys of Barcelona
29 Hawthorne's birthplace
30 Race-track sign
34 Ponselle or Bonheur
35 "A Tale of ____": Swift
36 Kind of dancer
37 Fountain treat
38 Squelch; crush
39 Prefix for bar or gram
40 Scapula or fibula
43 Biblical name meaning "God helps"
44 Cobb or Trevino
45 Library device
46 Michelangelo masterpiece
47 Mind: Comb. form
48 Traveller or Rosinante
50 Private eye
51 New York canal
52 Dilate
53 Star's aide
59 City in Turkey
60 "The Second ____ Tanqueray"
62 Capuchin monkey
63 Breastbone
64 Cry of discovery
65 Truman's birthplace
66 African antelope
67 Circular painting
68 Bigwig
69 Do the cable stitch
70 Walk like a rooster
75 "____ you noblest English!"
77 Give the eye to
78 Arab wear
80 Salacious
81 Slammer springer
82 Cutting tool
84 Formal essay
85 Severe
86 March 15 in Napoli
87 Trunk
88 Got one's hackles up
93 Hap or Benedict
94 "O Sole ____"
95 Table wine
97 Mock
98 Upright, e.g.
99 Sedative, for one
100 "____ vincit amor"
101 ____ Gay, of W.W. II
102 Miss Loy
103 Rose essence
105 "____ Rhythm"
106 Hair style
107 Old cars
108 File's partner
109 Safecracker
110 Virginia willow
111 Flip a coin

145. Theydunit by Maura B. Jacobson

ACROSS

1 Thoreau vista
5 Ziegfeld
8 Watch the birdie
12 Certain lights
16 Campus shindig
20 Eye area
21 Mauna ____
22 Andes native
23 Hennery
24 Designer Gernreich
25 "Some Buried Caesar"
27 "Le Coup de lune"
30 Namesakes of 74 Across
31 Mlle. Signoret
32 Fabric design
33 Seine sight
34 On the stump
36 Curve intersector
37 "The Innocence of Father Brown"
41 Island near Sumatra
43 Do slaloms
44 Actress Prentiss
45 Spinks
46 Female adviser
48 Whodunit award
52 Pitch
53 Beggar's cry
54 "____ longa, vita brevis"
55 Kind of laugh
57 Pi-sigma connection
58 Tallinn native
59 Architect I. M. ____
60 Zilch
61 Ike's colleague in W.W. II
62 Mob scene
63 Assails
65 Brand of figs
67 Sine qua ____
68 Soprano Gluck
69 Tomato disease
70 River of Flanders
72 Italian port
74 "A Study in Scarlet"
76 ____ Marple
78 Locusts
80 Nard
81 "The Four of Hearts"
83 Defeated one
84 Reduce to carbon
86 Sheriff's group
90 Cousin's parent
91 Act the mime
93 Swamp plant
95 Contrite one
97 Cleavage
98 Southwest lariat
100 Signify assent
101 Peking idol
102 Art ____
103 Greek nickname
104 Thick
105 G-man or T-man
106 LaMotta of ring fame
107 Naval noncoms
108 Oblivion
110 Muscle
112 Marquis de ____
113 Lorelei's milieu
114 D.A.
116 Recipe direction
117 "Thank You, Mr. Moto"
119 Knight's cloak

122 Poirot
124 Keats subject
125 Insurance contracts
127 Norman Vincent's family
128 Over-the-line driver
132 "The Pale Horse"
134 "I, the Jury"
135 Appraise
136 Neighbor of Burma
137 "It is later ____ you think"
138 "McGraw's boy"
139 Leprechaun's land
140 Started, at golf
141 Coin receptacle
142 Thesaurus entries: Abbr.
143 Med. degree
144 Rio girl

DOWN

1 Aqua ____
2 Done with
3 Adjacent
4 "The Glass Key"
5 Small bloom
6 Gehrig and Costello
7 Stable staple
8 Crude metal
9 Kind of show
10 Skedaddle
11 I.R.S. interest
12 Tennis coup
13 "Drury Lane's Last Case"
14 Prices
15 Skyline sights
16 Settled up beforehand
17 Set-to
18 Tooth: Comb. form
19 Chinese dynasty
26 Oil city
28 Aladdin's mentor
29 See 134 Across
31 Spanish thickets
35 Cinema Camille
37 Made happen
38 Dash headlong
39 Namesakes of 81 Across
40 Negligent
42 Brown pigment
44 Small bird: Var.
46 "The Case of the Velvet Claws"
47 Choir member
49 Barbecue need
50 "Oh, give me ____ . . ."
51 Hurdy-gurdy
53 V-mail address
54 Be under the weather
56 ____ Bird Johnson
60 Portia's maid
61 Threatened
62 "The Big Sleep"
64 Sea inlet: Fr.
66 Neither sml. nor lge.
71 Andes echo
73 U.S.S.R. silk city
75 Ancient flask
77 Kind of drum
79 So-so grade
80 Wave coming ashore
81 Paper quantity
82 Not qualified
83 Charters
85 Drake's conquest
87 Intervene
88 "As is" item
89 Eaten away
90 Soviet sea
92 Pub measure
94 Olympus resident
96 "The Purloined Letter"
99 Extra inning
104 Disconnect
105 C.S.A. general and family
106 Bond of spydom
109 Garbed
111 Cesare of opera
112 Passions; emotions
113 Part of R.F.D.
115 Perry Mason's rituals
117 Bond of Georgia
118 Ring-toss game
119 Part of Caesar's wardrobe
120 Winged
121 Paste-on
123 Heathcliff's love
125 Role
126 Scram!
128 Said again: Abbr.
129 Spydom name
130 Step ____ (hurry)
131 Actress Rowlands
133 Q-U connection
134 Turf

146. Porcine Parade by Emanuel Berg

ACROSS

1 Like a crow's cry
7 Gnat or brat
11 Prefix with fix or fuse
16 Item unfit for a silk purse
17 Large toad
18 Asian goat antelopes
20 Footballs
21 Korean battle site
24 Chemical suffixes
25 Grieg's dancer
27 Best place for wurst
28 Decalogue mount
29 Oven for glass
31 Has sticky fingers
33 "____ and Marge"
35 One-year-old sheep
36 Ginglymoid joints
38 Opposite of yang
39 Summer drink
42 Sunshine St.
43 Evangeline's home
45 Wink
47 Strolls
49 Passover feasts
51 Untrue!
52 Babylonian Hades
53 A descendant of Noah
55 Shea player
56 Objects
59 In many instances
62 More reliable
64 He drew Joe Palooka
65 Czechoslovak measure
66 Donat role
67 "Bob, ____ Battle"
68 Wood sorrel
69 Kotter's plotters
72 Ulan ____
73 Baltic people
75 Practices endogamy
76 Hoover or Cougar
77 Sci-fi guy
79 Author of "Them"
80 Dormouse
82 Enlargers
86 Inculpates
88 Type of ungula
90 "We ____ amused"
91 Auricle
92 Fencing position
94 Hebrew letter
96 "King Olaf" composer
97 Small squall
99 Caroled
100 Little guys in sties
103 Wagnerian goddess
104 Old Irish script
106 Ritzy
108 Awn
110 Vedic sky serpent
111 Cuban battle site: 1961
114 Bring home ____
116 He created Bambi
117 Writer Leon
118 Delivery to a tavern
119 Raison ____
120 Italian river
121 Swirled

DOWN

1 Large barrel
2 Cries of pain
3 "____ silly question . . ."
4 Curbs
5 Soundness
6 French town on the Ill
7 ____ bull
8 Type of trip
9 Irrational number
10 "____ your leader"
11 Modern motto medium
12 Old car
13 Dadaist's display
14 Pitcher's dream game
15 Controversial inoculation
16 Library injunction
19 Louisiana town
20 Dances in 2/4 time
22 Bonnie's partner
23 Actress Kirk et al.
26 Arrested
30 Orangutan
32 Baby ____
34 Compose rapidly
37 Femme fatale
40 Trouter's specialty
41 Strad's relative
44 Afflict
46 Companion star
48 French grains
50 Procedures
52 Knight's attendant
54 Small eels
56 Dancer Valery
57 Georgia or Carnegie
58 Spanish Mmes.
59 Bone: Comb. form
60 Act the sycophant
61 Shakespearean tavern
63 Good times
64 Recently stolen
66 Gouda and feta
67 Where R.L.S. is buried
70 Syria, in the Bible
71 Nice noggins
72 Critic Clive
73 Finnish lake
74 Mother of Dionysus
76 Legal paper
78 Cartoonist Gardner
80 Arctic bird
81 Indonesian island
83 Endued with elegance
84 Selfish driver
85 Exert
86 Sired
87 Chortles
88 Like a ____ bricks
89 Beatles hit: 1972
93 Scarface Al
95 Reticulate
98 Postpone
101 Actress Signe
102 Pegasus, e.g.
105 Dillon
107 "This Gun for ____"
109 Hillside dugout
112 Ending with saw or law
113 The Cronyns' game
115 Forever, in Sydney

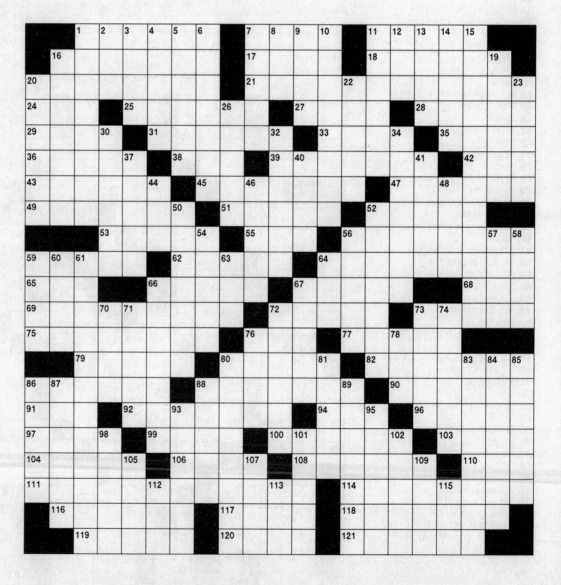

147. Reverse Versions by Alfio Micci

ACROSS

1 Quest of some scouts
7 Mess of cress
12 Trilby
16 Retired
20 Woman in Corneille's "Cinna"
21 "Philebus" author
22 Precipitate
23 Antitoxins
24 Worthy fellow?
27 Late?
29 Person on commission
30 Giant with a hundred eyes
32 Stupefy
33 Bustle
36 One at table
37 Lippizaner, e.g.
38 Anabaena
39 Sutherland, for one
41 Time span: Abbr.
42 Less cordial
43 Joe Doakes
47 Obtained vindication
49 Honorable racket game?
52 Resident of: Suffix
53 Wedded
54 Masters's river
56 "Hawaii Five-O" star
57 Kind of dive
58 Garden bloom
59 Steep declivity
60 Small role
62 Dance in a Brando film title
63 Most extreme
64 Ladd or King
65 Garage and yard events
66 Secrete
67 Half a fly
68 Dice game in the van?
71 Miscalculation
72 Where G.W. nestles with A.L.
74 Run off
75 Espadrille
77 Martinique volcano
78 Drawing near the index?
80 Time for a ser.
83 Respiratory sounds
84 Alaskan auk
85 Soprano Grist
86 Singing syllable
87 About 39 inches
88 Felicity
89 Utah city
91 Bravo or brava
93 Pale
94 Caterpillar's hair
95 Caesura
96 Prefix with nuclear or plastic
97 ___ Anne de Beaupré
98 Cause of disaster?
101 Man of Oman
102 Met tenor
104 Word of procrastination
105 Sixth-century date
106 Finish, in Frankfurt
107 Attic
108 Birds' morning song
109 Dating from birth
111 Understand
112 Malay mammals
115 Horse follower

116 Merciful
117 Unrealistic?
119 Large valise?
125 Decree
126 Gist
127 Discontinue
128 Work, in Milano
129 Russian news service
130 ". . . ere I saw ___"
131 Went after morays
132 Cleaned the blackboard

DOWN

1 Filer's aid
2 Doctors' org.
3 Wielded a baton
4 Tolkien creature
5 Zeus turned her into stone
6 Like some hillsides
7 Oral
8 Modify
9 Memorable comedian
10 P.I. native
11 Eleemosynar's gift
12 Humbug
13 Dolts
14 German direction
15 Stir ___ (excite)
16 Furnace worker
17 Lover
18 Water birds
19 Richest county in Fla.
25 Famous
26 Von Stroheim classic

28 She gave Lear the air
31 Seed
33 Unyielding
34 Strips
35 In good health?
37 Reporter's coup
38 Texas athlete
40 French seraph
42 Sikorsky
44 Uncovering sofas?
45 Old hand
46 Vinous prefix
48 Eur. country
50 Lake south of Leningrad
51 Certain votes
54 Limited
55 Gasp for air
57 ___ Romana Rota
59 ___ gin fizz
60 Coeds' milieux
61 Eaglewood
62 Late, in León
64 City on the Rhone
65 Williams' "Summer and ___"
66 Shelley's "The ___"
68 Mock
69 These make a mesh
70 Sister of Androclea
73 Tin Pan or Gasoline
75 "Jumblies" craft
76 Flying prefix
77 Quickly, maestro!
78 Pipe
79 Those in favor

81 "Marriages ___ in heaven": Lyly
82 English title
84 Kind of tenor
87 Not fem. or neut.
88 Suit
89 Priest's plate
90 Where Dortmund is
91 Rolled tea
92 Wife of Hercules
94 Identical
95 G. and S. operetta
96 Eternal or Bermuda
98 Eric of films
99 Dash
100 Island off China
101 Asian range
103 T.S. and George
105 Put a curse on
108 Famed Indian conductor
109 Nightingale, for one
110 Composer of "Vilia"
112 Clump
113 Samoan port
114 School orgs.
115 Awkward try
116 Get better
118 Electrical unit
120 Aberdeen's stream
121 Sen. Norris's pride
122 Cattle genus
123 Beatitudes verb
124 Jehovah

148. Who Has What? by Jordan S. Lasher

ACROSS

1 Iwo ____
5 Melted
10 "Wearin' ____ Green"
14 ____ crow flies
19 Neck projection
21 Brain part associated with speech
23 Talking animal in Numbers
24 Retinal layer
25 Smuts was one
26 Call's partner
27 Dawn goddess
28 Fugitive's haven
32 Former Cardinal star
34 Twisted: Comb. form
35 Lives
36 Perch
37 Nast's target
38 Staffers
39 Strawberry geranium
41 Consumer-protection agcy.
44 "Hinky Dinky Parlay ____"
45 Math course
46 Bireme gear
47 Prickle
48 Ann has two
49 Attraction in 1849
53 Spud
54 "Oh ____ is a gentle thing": Coleridge
56 Objects of veneration
57 Alone
58 Prate
59 In ____ way (vulnerable)
60 Mediterranean capital
61 Resistance quantity
62 Actress Taylor
63 Nymph or orchid
64 "If My Friends Could ____ Now"
65 Early name for Yellowstone Park
67 Letter addenda
69 Payment to a French estate owner
70 Disco dance
71 Numerous
72 Newt
73 Elev.
74 She should be above suspicion
78 Fixation
80 Bungle
81 Make one's day
82 Light-years, e.g.
83 Arrogant
85 Eocene or Neocene
86 Tan silks
87 Freeload
88 Qualified
89 Mitigate
90 Where the Hesperus was wrecked
92 Volcanic-glass drops
98 Three stars in a line
99 Fogbow
100 Tempi
101 One-time Mrs. Kovacs
102 Jet
103 Louver

DOWN

1 Poke

2 Tarbell
3 ____ de tête
4 Org. for Drs.
5 Renowned
6 Only horse to defeat Man o'War
7 Shadowbox
8 Subway branches
9 ____ Plaines
10 Demurs
11 Bannister's milieu
12 Pork cut
13 Household: Comb. form
14 Confident
15 Kind of cow
16 B.S.A. unit
17 Crux
18 "Do I dare to ____ peach?": T. S. Eliot
20 Wooden shoes
22 They reduce or moderate
26 Petty officer
28 Breathe hard
29 Fiery roller for Hera's suitor
30 Henry Purcell aria
31 Suffix with Siam or Annam
32 Danish comedian-pianist

33 Aussie creature
34 Grassy land
36 Singer-actor John
37 River ducks
39 Bandleader Shaw
40 Blessings
41 Contribution to the Vatican
42 Electrical storm phenomenon
43 Nut; kernel: Comb. form
45 N-____ (math term)
47 Orchid product
49 Marsh grass
50 All smiles
51 Fallen rocks
52 Pyle of TV
53 Hydrocarbon derivative
55 Cheeses
57 Rand or Struthers
58 Puccini heroine
59 Wife of Hagar the Horrible
60 Nearly, to Nero
62 Edd ____, Cooperstown name
63 Irritate
65 Battle site: 1346
66 Loser to Hoover

68 Tarries
70 Adds to the kitty
74 ____ Bluff, N.Y.C.
75 Abounding
76 ____ gin fizz
77 G.I. Jane
78 Impressionist's works
79 Neighbor of Uru.
80 Witticism
82 Anatomical cavities
83 Germ cell
84 Water wheel
85 "Christ Stopped at ____"
86 Metrical foot
87 Brahmin
88 Thunderstruck
89 Fitzgerald
91 Mariner's dir.
92 Litter member
93 Building wing
94 Vocal pauses
95 Be under the weather
96 Genetic molecule
97 N.C.O.

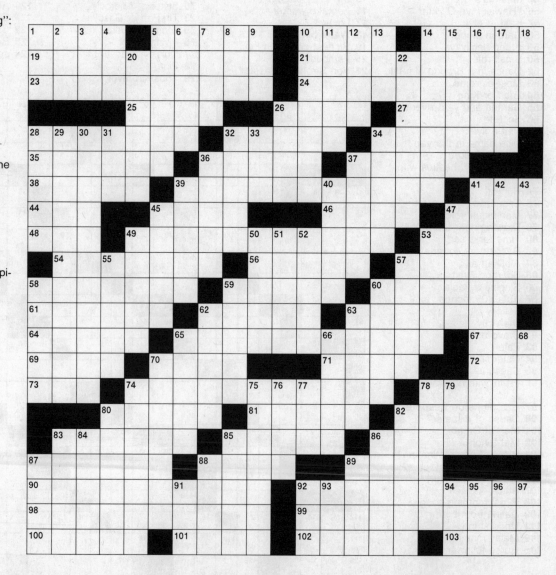

149. Rigged! by Hume R. Craft

ACROSS

1 Wheeler's partner
7 Sling mud
12 Nobelist for Chemistry: 1918
17 Where a mudder may get fodder
21 "Sirenize"
22 Dame's associate
23 Bouquet without color
24 Animal's coat
25 Iowa farmer's get-up?
27 Like a confirmed nudist?
29 Carlos or Juan
30 Gathering
31 Venetian family
33 "____ from an Old Manse"
34 French article
35 Singer Frankie
37 On the qui vive
39 Scotland's longest river
42 Action at the wire
44 Roman ways
46 Feeding the kitty
50 Greek matricide
52 Garb that can't be mentioned?
55 Avant-gardist
56 Stoned, but not squiffed
57 They were all about Eve
58 Chemical suffixes
59 Georgian group
60 Pivotal
61 First Oscar-winning film
62 He wrote "Night Music"
64 "____ are the snows . . .?"
65 N.C. college
66 Dravidian language
67 Panza's Dapple
68 Less partisan
69 In one's birthday suit
70 Wear for an atoll?
71 Throw at Vegas
72 Date for Calpurnia
73 In the slammer
75 Barbarians
77 Ebb
78 Douse the lights
80 Whale
81 Under the elms
83 Draft initials
86 What Croesus had
87 Castilian channels
88 "Golden-wedding day" destination
89 "Cómo ____ Vd.?"
90 Questioned
91 Beatrice's adorer
92 Used a strop
93 Tree yielding edible pulp
94 Residents: Suffix
95 Middling
96 Made corvine noises
97 Medicinal ointment
98 TV stage
99 Conventional robes?
102 Her hems were high
103 Trap
105 Trees of Morocco
106 Spot worn on a Hindu's brow
108 U.S.N.A. grad
109 Gimlet's relative
111 Quotes

113 May heroine
114 July 25 heroine
117 Incensed
119 Get news about
122 Baden-Baden, e.g.
125 Dressed like a dependent politician?
127 Headgear for Campbell or Moore?
130 Windigo
131 ____ prosequi
132 Hitchcockian
133 Dog-show measurement
134 Where she wore bells
135 Canasta pair
136 Pippins
137 Garb for a crop sprayer?

DOWN

1 Dips bait lightly
2 Grasso
3 Actor Alda
4 French pronoun
5 Sea fowl
6 Survived at Monte Carlo
7 Rhonchus creator
8 Speck
9 A Barrymore
10 "Blessed ____ the meek . . ."
11 Breaks
12 Canalboats
13 Cartoonist Peter
14 ____ nova
15 Australian bird
16 Garb worn in broken-down minarets?

17 "Be thou as ____ as ice . . ."
18 Ridges formed in knitting
19 Out of work
20 Karbis
26 He wants his blanket
28 Certain civil wrongs
32 Lalapalooza
36 General's staff
38 Roman tutelary gods
39 Hat for Cosmo?
40 Botanical space
41 Cowards' garb?
42 Suffix with song or mob
43 Retire
45 Kanonen
47 Cloak worn at a Scottish port?
48 Approximated
49 Their day is done
51 Laurel
53 Carelessly and diaphanously clothed?
54 Division word
57 Milquetoasty
59 Recoiled
61 Arouse
62 "That hurts!"
63 Give feathers a glossy finish?
64 Like corduroy
66 Mah-jongg pieces
67 Writer of "America the Beautiful"
68 One of the garment workers
70 Wheeled, in a way
72 Gave up, as lands

74 Flu symptoms
76 County in Nebraska
77 Jabbered
78 Cook slowly in fat
79 Start of a Longfellow poem
80 Judy from Jacksonville
82 Free from fraud
84 Richmond's island
85 She wrote "The Nine Tailors"
87 Suit follower
89 Frontier lawman
91 Recipient
92 Part of a ship's bow
93 Pikes
95 Top kick
96 Processions
97 Roared
99 John of ____
100 Shopping areas
101 Canter or trot
102 Plant life
104 First city of Brittany
107 Madison Ave. creations
110 Lunar valley
112 Kipling's ____ Khan
114 Kiltie
115 Lunch-counter phrase
116 Alpine stream
118 Bank (on)
120 Miss Markey
121 Wife, in Weimar
122 Vamoose!
123 British buttons
124 Rich Little, e.g.
126 Super ending
128 Traveller's rider
129 Jan.–Dec. periods

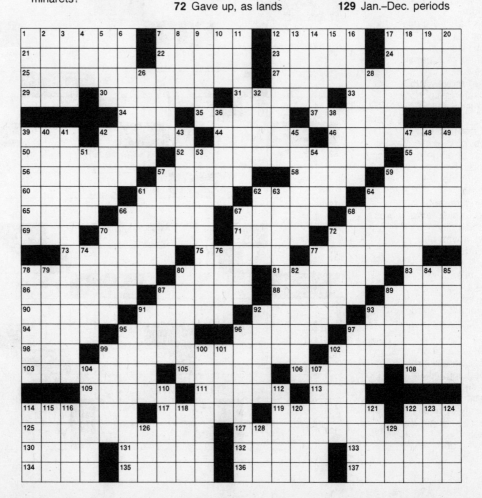

150. Seasonal Sequence by Anne Fox

ACROSS

1 Tennyson girl
5 Faint smell
10 Bluejoint, e.g.
15 City of Judah
19 ___ facto
20 Old-time comedian
21 Elvis ___ Presley
22 Pop
23 Old English carol words
27 Singer John
28 Actor Kruger
29 Famed nonagenarian of songdom
30 Play for time
33 Carousal
35 Dressy headdress
36 Words by Nahum Tate
43 Fortify
44 Used jointly
45 Word on a Canadian stop sign
46 Command to a husky
48 Jejune
49 Kind of bullet
52 Begone!
56 ___ Benedict
58 Consider
59 Deplete
61 Creek
62 English carol words
69 Roman emperor: A.D. 96–98
70 Portent
71 Head of hair
72 English carol words
77 Cuttlefish's output
78 Cooking abbr.
79 Wilder
80 Wins a card game
81 Spanish house
83 Pet
85 Period of expansion
87 Bulrush
91 Ladd movie: 1953
93 Cesare or Lucrezia
95 Buntline
96 French carol words (translated)
103 Sec. of War: 1829–31
104 Kind of angle or feather
105 Emissary
106 Having no key
108 Intend
109 Thingumabob
112 Old English carol words
119 Sicilian city
120 Twain was one
121 Florida city
122 Buck or drake
123 Females
124 Frets
125 Eased
126 Wagnerian goddess

DOWN

1 .001 of an inch
2 Bee: Comb. form
3 Seagoing initials
4 "Is that so?"
5 Habit
6 Saintly symbol
7 Sacred image: Var.
8 Sapin
9 Govt. agent
10 Spat
11 Carried on
12 Ship of myth
13 Help!
14 Social slight
15 Confines
16 Do-re-mi
17 Look up to
18 Bacchante
24 French word for 123 Across
25 Sage's accumulation
26 Clean, in Cannes
30 Did the butterfly
31 Word with way, in N.Y.
32 Sights
33 Cannonballed
34 High degree
37 Chases flies
38 Stern
39 Son of Gad
40 Indian of Iowa or Okla.
41 Take by force
42 Irish interjection
47 Cumbersome
49 Alley game
50 System of government
51 Italian astronomer: 1786–1863
53 Pitcher Swan
54 Oise feeder
55 Spud
57 Transplant, as skin
58 Tableware
60 Nut
62 Caper
63 Knot in rug weaving
64 Odysseys
65 Janis ___, pop singer
66 Elbow
67 English river
68 German painter Max
73 AMPAS award
74 "Up, ___ Away," 1967 song hit
75 To your heart's content
76 Giant of Norse myths
82 Since
84 Soak
85 Soup dish
86 Planet
88 Pitt or So. Cal.
89 Marquisette
90 Anxious
92 Lightweight silk
93 Arthur or Lillie
94 Wind: Comb. form
96 Annoys
97 Vietnamese town
98 Astonished: Fr.
99 Venerate
100 Glorifies
101 Barcelona boy
102 Lardner's "You ___ Al"
107 Cuts off
108 Soccer great
109 Midge
110 Northern home: Var.
111 Cinch
113 Wilde forte
114 Hurok
115 Dessert
116 Sound receiver
117 Betty Ford's honorary degree
118 Meadow

151. What's Whose? by Mary Virginia Orna

ACROSS

1 ____ by (saves)
5 Research ctrs.
9 Coil: Comb. form
14 Touchstone
18 It follows sieben
19 "____ a customer"
21 King or queen
22 Prefix for present
23 What Mark got stuck with?
26 Actress Patricia
27 Off-limits
28 "____ wise father . . ."
29 Right angle
30 Dry
31 Guernsey or Jersey
32 Greek shipping domain?
36 Dominique's donation
38 Booted feline
40 Gothic novelist Victoria
41 Stapes locale
42 Three-ring setting
44 Big cats
45 Copy
49 Rock song for Victorians?
53 Gallinaceous female
54 Angry; peeved
55 Lamb
56 Grand ____, Evangeline's home
58 Mt. Wilson glass
59 Ross or Andaman
61 Tupelo hero
63 Alpine feature
65 Ending with hex or malt
66 B'way sign
68 Cabinet appliance in 1867?
71 Rent
72 Chop off
73 Metal-bending tool
74 Ecole inhabitant
75 El ____, Spanish hero
77 Ripens
79 Storm part
80 Auricular
81 Tease
84 Textile dealer
86 Author Laura's decision?
91 Word with up or head
92 Brilliant unit
93 Emulates Marple
94 Personate
96 Expanse fed by the Amu Darya
97 Seraph's song: Var.
99 Sullivan and Wynn
100 Where George got free drinks?
106 Militant campus org.
108 A Waugh
109 A West
110 Circle parts
111 ____ miss (haphazardly)
114 Co-signer with Hancock
115 Wonderland tearoom?
119 Sheltered
120 Indian queens
121 Salts or Downs
122 Author Wiesel
123 Is employed in Valenciennes
124 Stewart or Joseph
125 Petrol-station accessory
126 Soaks flax

DOWN

1 NATO, e.g.
2 Bruins' campus
3 Did it cost three pennies?
4 Pigeon of a sort
5 Mauna ____
6 Clowns' specialties
7 Uppers and lowers
8 Part of a flight
9 Haggard novel
10 "The Tell-Tale Heart" author
11 Forms a new paragraph
12 Missouri campus town
13 Threatening alternative
14 Barber-ous?
15 Relative of a sheik
16 Watchdog's warning
17 Like many bathrooms
20 Bone: Prefix
24 "Chicago piano"
25 Preakness winner: 1955
33 The Taj Mahal, e.g.
34 Faulkner's "As ____ Dying"
35 Wimbledon winner: 1977
36 Recedes
37 Copter's cousin
39 Highs
43 "Friendly" pronoun
44 Tartan
46 "Little Women" sequel?
47 Future, e.g.
48 Town on Buzzards Bay
50 Elbowroom
51 Amount needed to fill a cask
52 Pound, in Paris
53 A companion of Falstaff
56 André or Dory
57 Strads' precursors
60 Balaam's "vehicle"
62 Compass dir.
63 Vinegar: Prefix
64 Title for a gov. or amb.
66 Bridge feats
67 Thesaurus name
69 Liquid container
70 Berlin's "When ____ You"
76 Chemical suffix
78 Horseplayers' concerns
82 Glacé
83 Hardy heroine
85 Emulate Hogarth
86 Mata ____
87 Dinars are spent here
88 Workers in cotton
89 Jeff Davis's org.
90 Osaka's island
92 Mine disasters
95 Spicy Italian mixture
97 Sissified
98 Ben Bradlee, e.g.
100 Corday's victim
101 Wing tip
102 Button for a bowler
103 West Coast shrub
104 Easily handled, as a ship
105 Skilled
107 More threatening
112 "You can bet ____!"
113 66, 95, etc.
116 A.F.L. affiliate
117 Psychic's métier
118 Soul, in Solesmes

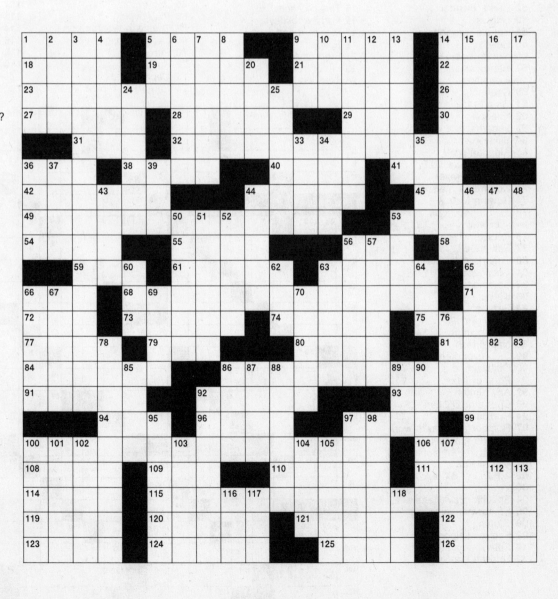

152. Old-Clues Ruse by George Rose Smith

ACROSS

1 Let up
7 Hebrew prophet
11 Lean-to
15 "Front porch"
19 Hard as nails, for one
20 Andrea ____
22 He sang "Start Movin'": 1957
24 Marquisette
25 Mineral springs
27 Building extensions
29 Bill
30 Showed mercy
31 Vetches
33 Plaid
34 Jorge of baseball
35 Desires
36 About
37 U.S. missile
40 Immaterial
41 "Common Sense" author
42 What déjeuners satisfy
46 Cloying or sticky
48 Mine entrance
50 Vein's glory
51 Strads' kin
52 Use a blender
53 Unguis
54 Koko's weapon
55 Heads
56 Not so noble
57 Happy as ____
59 Execution
60 Citole
61 Gas: Prefix
62 Sheep
63 Logomachize
64 Silkworm
65 Algerian port
68 Locker room V.I.P.
69 Morning Prayer
71 Room in a maison
72 Bowl in Miami
73 "____, one hope . . .": J. R. Lowell
75 Persian wheel
77 Felt shoe
80 Trigonometric term
81 Youngest son
82 Solemnity
83 Kernel
84 Sun hat
85 Shipworm
86 ____ couture
88 Napoli dish
89 ____ even keel
90 Quitclaim, e.g.
91 Pods of flax
92 Any human
93 Boone or O'Brien
94 Choice part
97 Romberg-Gershwin work
98 Imparts gradually
100 Month in Pamplona
101 Mar slightly
102 A.F.B. in Colorado
103 Vex
104 Specific-gravity scale
105 Somewhat, in music
106 Glutting
109 Fire worshiper
110 Fata morgana
112 Unseal: Poetic

115 Stone monument
117 Polish coins
120 Dash
121 Balzac's birthplace
122 Zenana
123 Halters
124 Help with the dishes
125 Harte
126 Oasis
127 Early cenobite

DOWN

1 Staff mem.
2 Fall for a gag
3 The last word
4 Sleeper
5 Cubits
6 Ravages
7 "Tobacco is ____ weed. I like it.": Hemminger
8 Peloponnesus
9 Toward the mouth
10 Part of R.S.V.P.
11 Spruce
12 Trapper's collection
13 Destinies
14 "Agnus ____"
15 Tiny blossom
16 Forty weekdays
17 Pier of a sort
18 Favor
21 Fred or Adele
23 In control
26 Turn aside

28 More intrepid
32 Part of A.D.
35 Cookie
36 Ghost
37 Wheat or cotton
38 Tommy of links fame
39 Table scraps
40 Galatea's beloved
41 Dido died on one
42 Set on a pedestal
43 Greek letter
44 XXX, to Pierre
45 Noted folk singer
47 Asian evergreen
48 Euterpe's sphere
49 Highland lord
52 "City of Light"
54 Best seller in 1924
56 Author of "Games People Play"
57 City NW of Madrid
58 Queues
59 Silas ____, U.S. diplomat
61 ". . . in ____ and Ten Cent Store"
62 Young hooter
63 Shade of green
65 In harmony
66 Play byplay
67 Gadfly in Washington
68 Lacking imagination
70 Peregrine
72 Public notices
73 Cephalopods
74 Earhart's co-pilot

75 Melville book
76 Word in a letter
78 Bring off
79 Alpine abode
81 Some Yalies
83 Belém
85 Companion of end-all
86 Viscount Templewood
87 Ray from Pen Argyl
88 Newel
90 Transport
91 Imperfection
92 Formed by one eruption
94 Detroit eleven
95 Least generous
96 Kokoons
97 Type of précis
99 Being three in one
101 Cabbage or kale
104 City in Vermont
105 Had deep longings
106 Merganser
107 Gudrun's spouse
108 Bunker
109 Stream
110 Star in the Whale
111 Biblical oldster
112 Its capital is Beauvais
113 Hammer part
114 Actual being
116 Rabble
118 Exclamation
119 Gogol tale

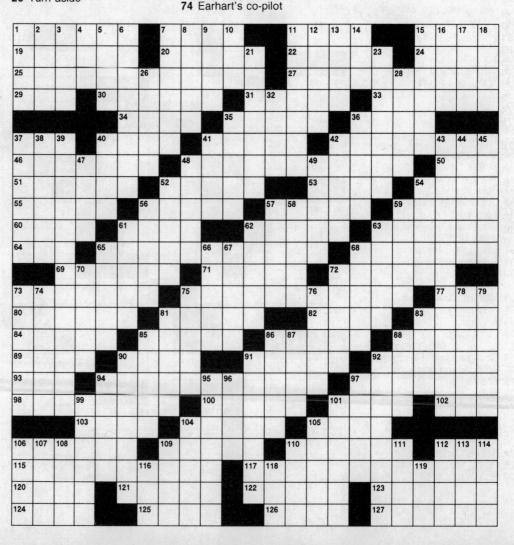

153. Numbers Magic by Timothy S. Lewis

ACROSS

1 Flatten
6 Little hooters
12 Italian dessert
19 Jouster's weapon
20 Marched en masse
21 Pedestrian bullfighters
22 Fur magnate
23 Impedes
24 "My cup ____ over"
25 V.P. after Hubert
26 Ransom
27 Obese one's nickname
28 Author of "Men of Iron"
29 Prefix with gram or type
30 Anne's 1,000
31 Place where jays prey
35 43,560 sq. ft.
37 Puts the lid back
41 Devil's walking stick, e.g.
42 Sapphira's co-conspirator
45 Rand and Struthers
46 Revealed
47 Horse exercise yard
48 Futile
49 Picked dandelions
50 Aussies' animals
51 Spat
53 Rate of speed: Abbr.
54 Indy cars lack these
55 ____ days, for prayer and fasting
57 Bug killer
58 Indeed
59 Bassoon's little cousin
60 "Jumblies" craft
61 Morse code signals
63 Liza or Mizar
65 I.C.C. concern
69 Within: Prefix
71 Inquisitive interjections
73 Abzug trademark
74 To the point
75 "Miniver Cheevy, ____ late . . ."
78 Misery
79 What Simon does
81 Simple
82 Certain daisies
83 Tranquilize
85 Wife jilted for Cleopatra
87 Irate
88 Hi-fi component, for short
89 Peak sometimes called Tacoma
90 Invention germ
91 Most uncivilized
92 Brothers in an abbey
93 Melampus or Mopsus
94 Certificate
95 Author Wiesel
97 Auditors
101 Pitiful
103 Eggnog additive
106 Verbal contraction
107 Off one's rocker
110 Lord High Everything Else
111 Dark grayish blue
112 Pressing
113 Car-door feature
114 Homophone for 22 Across
115 Behaves
116 Fermented dairy food: Var.
117 Manner

DOWN

1 Foulard fastener
2 Grating
3 "Wait ____ Dark"
"4 ____"
5 Idol
6 Mirador
7 ____
8 Word with star or stone
9 Inventor of a sign language
10 Type of paper
11 Radical org.
12 Pound prospects
13 Sulks
14 Ash holders
"15 ____"
16 Bauxite, e.g.
17 "To Have and Have ____"
18 Iffy suffix
"20 ____"
27 Like G. W.'s wooden teeth
29 Leaflet
"30 ____"
32 Disintegrate slowly
33 Dorcas was one
34 Minds
36 John L. Lewis's group in the 30's
38 "I earn that I ____": Shak.
39 Viscous
40 Decamps
42 After, to Marcel
43 Explorer Uemura
44 Pueblo material
46 Certain madrileña
49 Arachnid's work
52 Anti-saccharin agcy.
"54 ____"
56 Like prom suits
62 Drove away
64 Top rating for 94 Across
66 Roman fontana
67 Uncanny
68 Slander
70 Southampton shindigs
72 Caterpillars' hairs
75 Godunov or Badenov
76 Compound within rust
77 Book by D. S. Freeman
80 Panic
83 Thorny
84 Ship initials
86 Aunt, in Juárez
91 Betters
94 Arctic goose
96 Minimum
98 "Card ____," Stravinsky ballet
99 Photographer Adams
100 1,000,000 cc.
102 Kayo or lulu
103 Writer Ephron
104 Man, to Marcello
105 "Help Me Make It ____ the Night"
106 Springs
107 Oyster's home
108 Twibil
109 Tuck's partner
110 Word with roll or dirt

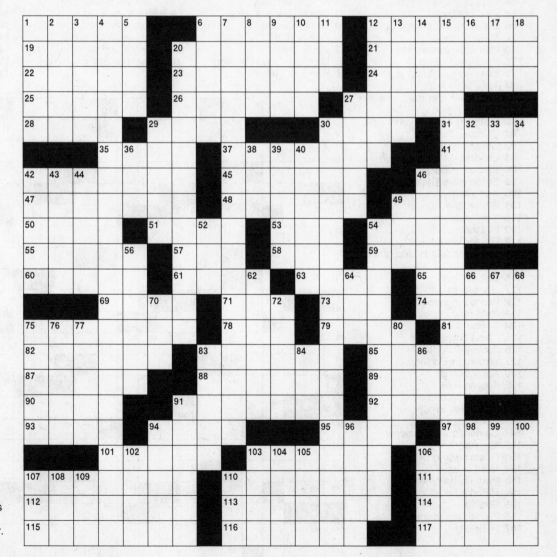

154. Common Proper Nouns by Reginald L. Johnson

ACROSS

1 Pepper picker
6 Flat
10 Furl a sail
14 Octagonal sign
18 Philadelphia's Spectrum
19 Not so green
20 "Voltaire" star: 1933
23 Part of the La. Purchase
24 Knitwear and footwear
28 Noun suffix
29 More frequently
30 Horatio et al.
31 Biographer of Henry James
33 Michael Romanov, e.g.
35 Arrow poison
36 M.I.T. degree
39 Hero of a Sheed book
41 Hoople's expletive
44 The Vistula, to Poles
47 Dais V.I.P.
49 Pendants and hairdos
56 Lulus or kayos
57 Blurbs
58 European blackbird
59 Neighbor of Minn.
60 N.Y.C. river
61 League or Legion
64 Kind of paper or box
66 Flue coating
69 Eleemosynar's largess
70 Make furrows
73 Half a Broadway title
76 Freshman cadet
79 Desi Arnaz's autobiography
81 Tiny Tim's verb
83 Headgear and frock coats
89 Inside: Prefix
90 Flatbush hero of yore
91 Of muscular vigor
92 Cellar player in '78
93 Loaded, as a cannon
96 Kind of editor or hall
98 Some were Dark
100 Accouterments
101 Attempting
105 Now's partner
109 Pilaster
112 Up and about
115 Like prophets Hosea, Joel et al.
116 Sub spotter
117 Signatures and life jackets
122 Pernod ingredient
123 Until now
124 Soprano Eames
125 Like Winkie
126 Jockey Turcotte
127 Wheat, in England
130 Apprehends
133 Talking bird
135 Took long steps
137 Humphrey in '68
141 Norwegian river
144 Carriages and rainwear
150 Neighborhood
151 Gasoline and Shubert
152 Mont ____
153 Parts of hammers
154 Hatching post
155 Seattle ____
156 French magazine
157 Ruhr city

DOWN

1 Part of R.I.P.
2 Khomeini's country
3 Sees
4 Over
5 Heyerdahl craft
6 Light shade
7 Cathedral projection
8 Intended
9 Piscivorous fliers
10 Use a crosscut
11 Due follower
12 Globular jar
13 Founder of Providence
14 Emulates Muffet
15 As well
16 Have
17 Ballerina's ____ seul
19 Battle of Brit. heroes
21 Omen
22 Old-time dirk
25 Nobelist in Medicine: 1906
26 Sketched
27 A cause of corruption
32 N.Z. tunas
34 Disencumber
36 Run before a gale
37 Wax: Sp.
38 Scriptorium item
39 Bitter, resinous juice
40 Singer Cantrell
42 Treats with CO_2
43 Small drink
45 Destroyer's gun platform
46 Brock or Gehrig
48 V.P.
50 Jujitsu and judo
51 First lady
52 To be: Sp.
53 Largest of seven
54 DDT target
55 Opposite of apteral
62 Bordeaux exports
63 Both: Comb. form
65 Izaak Walton's delight
67 Narcotic
68 "Viva!" relative
70 Orkney shed
71 Something to serve
72 Palazzo d'____, at Varese
73 Ugandan name
74 Retreats
75 Straight: Comb. form
77 Shakespeare
78 Ship's course
80 Fall mo.
82 Fast plane
84 Heavy shoes
85 Propriety
86 Greek letters
87 Unclose is one for counsel
88 Drop behind
94 Fictional plantation
95 Shamrock land
97 Hindu god
99 Old woman's home
102 Yang's partner
103 Neighbor of Ky.
104 Westernmost U.S. continental city
106 Wraps, as in bandages
107 Charge per unit
108 Gaelic
109 Discordant
110 What a censor deles
111 "The ____ Red Line," Jones book
113 Yellow-journalism tidbits
114 A daughter of Hyperion
116 Fluctuate
118 Hundred: Comb. form
119 Range of sight
120 Custer's finale
121 Ant
128 Odd, in Aberdeen
129 Ruffle
131 Frozen dessert
132 Narrow-minded
134 Things to count
135 Photocopy, for short
136 Donkey, in Bavaria
138 Suffix with iron or myth
139 Last of the teens
140 Letter abbr.
142 Pleven or Coty
143 Y.M.C.A. or N.A.A.C.P.
144 Forefront
145 Dander
146 These: Fr.
147 Certain vote
148 State in Austl.
149 Begin, in poesy

155. Inquire Practice by Maura B. Jacobson

ACROSS

1 Nasty remark
5 Senegal's capital
10 Cooperstown's Speaker
14 Chaliapin, e.g.
19 Sigmoid molding
20 Alamogordo's county
21 "To Sir, ____ Love"
22 Sadat
23 Query in a 1915 song
27 Conductor Caldwell
28 Del of baseball fame
29 Roof overhang
30 Pierce of "M*A*S*H"
31 French composer Erik
33 Finial
35 Bristle
37 Writer Deighton
38 Theologian's deg.
41 Disarrangement
42 Light-switch positions
44 Dancer Bambi
46 Biblical query
54 Thoroughgoing
55 M. Lupin
56 Once more
57 Lymph knot
58 Instiller of confidence
61 Gamp or Grundy
64 Part of Q.E.D.
65 Bit parts
67 "Fiddler" query
70 Behave
73 Choreographer Cunningham
74 "And be it moon, ____ . . .": Shak.
75 Dame's opposite
76 Costello's query
80 Customs
82 "____ Misbehavin'"
83 Lao-____
84 Maria ____, former queen
86 Sounds of discovery
90 Tonto's horse
92 Chair of state
94 Ancient galley
96 Nursery-rhyme query
101 Economize
102 Imaret, e.g.
103 Gives a leg up
104 Go-aheads
105 Prosecutors, for short
108 Body-shop problem
110 Actress Scala
112 Thomas and Condé
114 Film canine
116 Elegiac forms
118 Legislate
120 Astonish
124 Capulet query
128 Heller offering
129 Become ragged
130 Bits of gossip
131 "Roberta" composer
132 London broil
133 Kismet
134 Damned
135 Cain's nephew

DOWN

1 Salaams
2 Moslem bigwig
3 Van's antonym
4 Radioactive rays
5 Part of a colon
6 Nonbeliever
7 Most sharp
8 ____ for one's money
9 Miss O'Grady
10 Proverbial company
11 Abundant
12 "____ the best of times"
13 Diggers' needs
14 Cell feature
15 Novelist Seton
16 Slops
17 Ex-jockey of note
18 Kind of grinder
24 Medicine man
25 Advocated, as an idea
26 Neural networks
32 Will word
34 Below: Prefix
36 Singer Paul
38 Water bird
39 "Comin' ____ the Rye"
40 Polar explorer
43 Dombey's kin
45 Beersheba's locale
47 Hic, ____, hoc
48 Gayelord
49 Hockey great
50 Contrition
51 Nostrils
52 Home of the Dolphins
53 Stage direction
59 Bondsmen
60 ____ of Friends
62 Large Asiatic deer
63 Lazy ones
66 Opposite of "odi"
68 "____ Sweetheart"
69 Homophone for won
70 Floating
71 Prinze role, once
72 "Up ____," Al Smith's autobiography
77 Lonigan or Terkel
78 Laced, as a racket
79 More prickly
81 Puppeteer Tony
85 Brit.
87 Protagonist, usually
88 Berserk
89 Wields a needle
91 Frog's relative
93 ____ polloi
95 Adorn, in a way
97 "The ____ St. Agnes"
98 Bon-voyage party
99 Stock farmer
100 Certain algae
105 Begins to appear
106 "____ in the Dark"
107 McQueen or Martin
109 Land, in Roma
111 Caper
113 Combustion's companion
115 Length times width, often
117 Ticket assignment
119 Aleutian island
121 So be it
122 Zilch
123 Ages and ages
125 Lodge member
126 Pro vote
127 ____-Kamenogorsk, U.S.S.R. city

156. Letter-Perfect by David J. Pohl and John M. Samson

ACROSS

1 Mil: award
4 Menelaus' wife
9 Savoy dance
14 Lombard city
19 Wash
21 Glide along
22 Marine painter
23 "Pal Joey" author
24 i
27 State in NE India
28 Bring _____ (animate)
29 Twaddle
30 Lustrous black
32 _____-la-la
33 Card position
35 Slaughter
37 Turner's org.
38 PT or U-
39 Prefix with plasm
40 h
44 Crew member
47 Acme
48 Particular
49 _____ Palmas
50 Cardinal point
51 Locale
53 Invalidated
55 Swab
56 Excited
59 _____ Coeur, Parisian landmark
61 Den
62 Skipjack
64 Impoverished
65 Actor Alan
66 Pt. of speech
67 _____ es Salaam
68 Smear
70 Govt. agents
71 Adman's come-on
73 Antipathetic
76 Bric-a-_____
78 Undivided
79 Blunder
80 Quell
82 Refuse
84 Primate
86 Being, in Brest
88 Grooming
89 Tumultuous
91 Quiet
93 Alone
95 Its: Fr.
96 Past
98 Implicit
100 Deck
102 Crab's claw
104 Campus V.I.P.
105 Austrian neighbor
106 Practice quiz
108 Son of Odin
109 Arizona native
111 Scissors sound
112 Russian hemp
113 Painting
114 Ram's dam
115 _____ affaire flambée
117 _____ Paulo
118 o
123 Minus
125 Small songbird
126 Red Baron, e.g.
127 At no time: Poet.

128 Barked, in a way
131 Mass. cape
132 Pico de _____
134 Take down a peg
138 Memorable actress from Canada
140 Type of maid
142 c
145 Grenoble's river
146 Organic compound
147 Bias
148 Words on proofs
149 Narrow groove
150 Annoying
151 Bristles
152 June grads

DOWN

1 _____ Judgment
2 Stone monument
3 Selection
4 Royal letters
5 _____ out (got by)
6 City in Germany
7 Sewing case
8 e
9 Civil War battle site: 1862
10 Couperin's "Tic-_____-choc"
11 Jerusalem's Mosque of _____
12 Imperils
13 Conductor/composer
14 Lament
15 Letters on a chasuble

16 s
17 Turkey's highest point
18 Athlete/actor
19 Stake
20 Result
25 Münster man
26 Tear
31 Canvas support
34 p
36 Lawgiver
38 Actress Jacqueline
40 "El Libertador"
41 Oenochoe
42 Tasteless
43 Rural Roman god
44 Greek peak
45 Aside
46 f
52 Examination
54 Youth
55 Tasty tidbits
56 y
57 First place
58 Unit of force
60 Result
62 Fence
63 Flap
67 Trial witness, of a sort
69 Expose
72 Tritons
74 Legionnaire, e.g.
75 Stengel follower
77 Cholla and opuntia
81 Famished
83 Photocopies

84 Askew
85 Engine sound
87 Hebrew judge
90 Eyelashes
92 Emollient
94 Of vision
97 Tibetan gazelle
99 Steno's slip
101 Robert _____ Warren
103 Power tower
104 Pledge or risk
107 Portable chair
109 Almost a direct hit
110 "Anna Christie" playwright
113 Former
116 Discerns
118 Pundits
119 Composer Bloch
120 Glacial mass
121 Jumble
122 Seemann's milieu
124 Slapping sounds
129 Doyen
130 Fares
132 Range
133 Genus of 114 Across
135 Stare amorously
136 "Take _____!"
137 "Vulcan's chimney"
139 Forage plant
141 "_____ tu," Verdi aria
143 Squid's defense
144 _____ Anne de Beaupré

157. Elementary Substitutes by Jordan S. Lasher

ACROSS

1 Become raspy
8 Copycat
12 Name of 12 popes
16 Gas-electricity agcy.
19 Girl in "Great Expectations"
20 Like some fractions
22 NOW goal
23 Modern fuel
25 Second notes
26 Insurance transaction
27 Celeste from N.Y.C.
28 Air-strike warnings
30 Suffixes with convention and auction
31 "Red Roses for ___ Lady"
33 1973 Wimbledon champ
34 Snake oil, ostensibly
35 Words to "The William Tell Overture"
38 Abdicate
39 Maintains
42 Arabian Sea sultanate
43 Speech flaw
44 Capital of 42 Across
45 Motor fuels
47 Early Scandinavian
49 Relative of chocolat
50 Mite or tick
51 Place for Caesar's calceus
52 Founder of the Carmelite reform
55 City near Dayton
56 Kind of year
58 Grips for swashbucklers
59 Pop
62 Birthplace of Ceres
63 Pit vipers
65 Horse-collar part
66 Erwin from Squaw Valley
67 Nimbi
68 Roger Moore TV role
69 Rice style
70 Of minimum clarity
73 V.P. to F.D.R.
74 British Honduras, today
75 Like some horses
77 Med. subject
79 Oxidative
80 Maternal kin
81 Elusive
83 Utah's flower
84 Savings-account addn.
85 Hindu fire god: Var.
86 Showy embellishment
90 Twin
91 Crumbs: Sp.
92 Miller's salesman
93 Balanchine ballet
97 Braes
99 Teasdale
100 Cowboy flick
101 Building annex
102 Innermost orbiter
106 Wassail quaff
107 Hermetic device
108 Handout to the press
109 Dusk to dusk
110 Toils
111 Like "pie"
112 Protruding, as from water

DOWN

1 Therefore
2 "___ mio"
3 Stock-market term
4 Chutney, e.g.
5 Inner-city sight
6 Street name
7 Collar
8 U.S. Open golf champ: 1927
9 Stereotypical pirate
10 Cheese city
11 Country: Lat.
12 Amassed
13 Footnote word
14 Arm bones
15 Falconry verb
16 D.A.'s obstacle
17 Conference before a hearing
18 Tape holder
21 "Orphée" and "Le Repos"
24 Prussian lancer
29 Plant's adaptation to a new milieu
31 Memorable Turkish chief
32 Feathery scarves
33 Clothing category
36 Asia Minor region
37 Opposite of ut
38 Truro sight
39 Put-ons
40 Brogue, for one
41 Whence many a tune has come
44 Emporia
46 Met highlight
47 Dadaism and Cubism
48 He sold his birthright
49 African grassland
51 Cocoon dwellers
53 One of the believers
54 Pitcher Luis
56 Ghastly
57 "6 ___ Riv Vu"
60 Like Casey's Mets
61 Recall reason
63 Vegetables, for short
64 Amused expression
65 Hawaiian port
67 City on the Rhone
69 Big name in Argentina
71 Before such time
72 Ankle
74 Israeli chief
75 Nonpaying passenger
76 Leeward island
78 Soldier in "King Henry V"
79 Bataan native
81 Ionesco and Ormandy
82 Utensil on a pencil
83 Neighbor of Leyte
86 Furnishing help
87 Dry lakes
88 Dignified
89 Not so sunny
91 Heffalump's creator
94 Other women, in Mexico
95 Liège's river
96 Fortified
98 Washer cycle
99 La Guardia's neighbor
100 Oeillade
103 Lao-___, famed Taoist
104 Live
105 Ad ___ (pertinent)

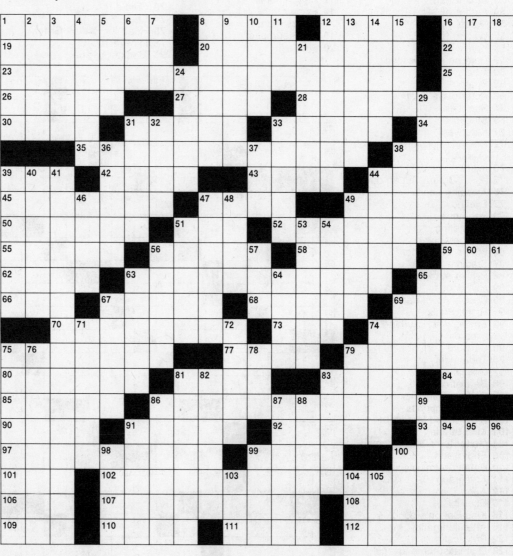

158. Dual Roles by William Lutwiniak

ACROSS

1 "He ____ me to lie down . . ."
7 Projecting edges
12 Kind of tense
16 Principal
21 Ballet duet
22 Cantina offering
23 To ____ (just so)
24 Sweetsop or soursop
25 Actor plays Fischer
28 Dog tag
29 City on the Oka
30 Nonpayer
31 Change: Mus. dir.
32 Yacht facilities
34 Rhone feeder
35 Glacial phenomena
37 German textile center
38 "The Chairman" turns rubbish collector
45 Sharif
48 Newspapers
49 Yens
50 Charge it
51 Nuchal area
52 Sam and Tom
53 Athanasian, for one
54 Author of "The Titans"
56 Notes
57 Waters
58 York's river
59 Dam on the Missouri
60 Titter
62 Spare
63 Actor plays Saarinen
68 Sun. talk
69 Stockpile
71 Kefauver
72 Antenna housings on aircraft
73 Injury
75 "____ Dream," in an opera
76 Albanian capital
77 Exalted
79 Peregrine
80 Staggering
81 Recipe abbr.
84 Writer turns actor
87 Stadium feature
88 Billiard stroke
89 Be curious
90 Cooperstown name
91 Right: Prefix
92 Ending with Paul and Bernard
93 Caesura
95 Legal right
97 Cranial feature
98 Be distressed
100 Debussy heroine
101 Vowel sequence
102 Final sound in a word
103 Kind of tide
104 Golfer turns businessman
108 Engrossed
110 Battery terminals
111 Autograph
112 Aged
115 Equalize
116 King Cotton's bundles
118 Attention-getter
122 Practical
123 Dramatist turns apiarist

127 Picardy bloomers
128 Obstacle
129 Accrue
130 Shoe feature
131 St. ____, W. Indies isle
132 Singer Stevens
133 He sang "Mack the Knife"
134 Vex

DOWN

1 Trumpeter perch
2 Swiss statesman: 1845–1928
3 Welles role
4 Alike, in Arles
5 Conway
6 Cornmeal goodies
7 Sea urchins
8 Interrupter's sound
9 Workbench adjunct
10 Greco and Cid
11 Fermented
12 Spaghetti and ravioli
13 Tie on
14 Grasp
15 Duration
16 Ville V.I.P.
17 Hearth item
18 Ex-quarterback turns numbers man
19 Choreographer White
20 Phooey!

26 Wooden stand
27 Nimbi
33 Copperfield's second wife
35 Safekeeping: Abbr.
36 Misocapnist's menace
38 Cousin of bonkers
39 Actor plays Gauguin
40 Poet Ginsberg
41 French marshal of 19th century
42 Adm. Condor's group
43 Slender as ____
44 Great respect
46 Each
47 Alley buttons
48 Macho matches
53 Malediction
54 Madison or Monroe
55 Melodrama cries
58 "Rock ____"
59 Gas-pump word
60 Kind of bore
61 Billed cap
64 Experience again
65 Japanese-American
66 News broadcasters
67 Great Plains denizen
69 Church vestment
70 Cradle rocker
74 Eheu!
75 Head for Gretna Green
76 Idiosyncrasy
77 Monkey or ape

78 Interest
79 Amo, ____, amat
80 Entrance court
82 Display
83 Figured fabric
85 Large lizard
86 Bar accommodation
87 Contemporary of Edison
91 Incautious
93 China piece
94 Make known
95 Was contingent
96 Inlets
97 Horse or leather
99 Uniform feature
101 Snake
102 Female water buffalo
105 Street sign
106 Potherb
107 Soprano Farrell
109 Basketball defense
112 Fog
113 Thine, to Thérèse
114 Secretary
116 Mackle
117 Sedan shelter
118 Varmint
119 Espy
120 Betray
121 Ceiba or ipil
124 Genetic letters
125 Memorabilia
126 Vane reading

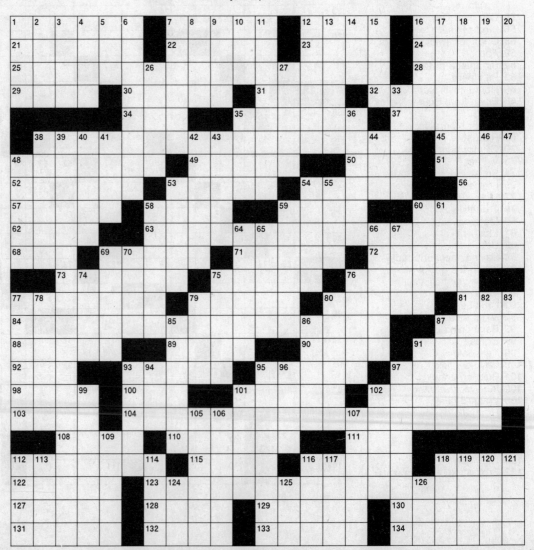

159. Stating It Briefly by Tap Osborn

ACROSS

1 Suit feature
6 Peaked
11 Chassé, e.g.
15 "Quiet!"
19 Actress Massey
20 Circus employee
21 "Vissi d'____," aria
22 Freshwater mussel
23 Foster classic
25 A 1932 hit song
27 Charlemagne's doughty dozen
28 TV spoof
30 It converts trash to ash
31 Communion is one
32 Court champ: 1963
34 Afghan city
35 Aphorisms
38 War cry in 1898
42 Outdistance
43 Clement one
45 Tympanum's locale
46 Zodiac symbol
47 Bob Burns
50 On guard
51 Pack of pachyderms
52 Port, for short
53 Ukrainian legislatures
54 Postprandial offering
55 The O'Grady girl
56 Taskmaster
58 One of the Feds
60 Mollusk or atomic particle
61 Historic painting
65 Diva Amara
68 Scene of a strike
69 Japanese emperor
73 Humble
74 Kind of glass
76 Wood joint
77 Droop
78 ____ Blanc
79 Gainer, e.g.
80 Volunteer from Bristol
83 Squash implement
84 Braun or Le Gallienne
85 Blossom of silents
86 Venerable, of yore
87 Song hit of 1934
91 Hoopster Bill
93 Greek letters
94 Vestibule
95 One of the Marxes
96 City captured by the French in 1859
98 Great: Comb. form
99 Joined securely
103 Fly that falls safely
105 Jolson-De Sylva-Meyer hit: 1924
108 Danish measure
109 Diminutive ending
110 Rain-forest plant
111 Done in
112 Outdo
113 Quitclaim, for one
114 First name of 115 Across
115 Memorable actress

DOWN

1 Flaccid
2 Star in The Serpent
3 Business combo
4 Optical projector
5 Glaswegian boy
6 Songwriter Jule
7 Cries of surprise
8 Latin I verb
9 Radiation dosage
10 Impertinent one
11 Eastern obeisance
12 Light carriage
13 Part of Afr.
14 Coffeebush
15 "The Last ____"
16 Drab condition
17 Join forces with
18 Gardener, at times
24 Little foxes
26 Mongolian tent
29 Unique thing
32 Certain tests
33 Parched
34 Suit card
35 Storm warning
36 Andrea ____
37 Famed fur trader
39 Source of protein
40 Andretti or Puzo
41 German port
43 Feast day for some
44 Socrates pupil
48 Corneille tragedy
49 Cyrus or Philo
50 Add-on
51 Peking's province
54 Long, thick locks
55 Having a new décor
57 Plot feature
58 Autocrat
59 Gump's wife
60 Playwright Jones
62 Veer
63 Half a comforting phrase
64 Mule's cousin
65 Charles and Mary
66 Lusitania's undoer
67 Melodious passages
70 Tennyson heroine
71 Slow: Mus.
72 City in Utah
74 Garners
75 Horse course
76 Savalas
79 Neutralized an asp
80 Feeler
81 ____ miss
82 Small cavity
85 Sailor's chantey
88 King's proxy
89 Early porch
90 Ogled like an ogre
91 China follower
92 Lely or Klee
95 Imam's text
96 Use a dirk
97 Spindle on a cart
98 Apportion
99 Word on a wall
100 Go gliding
101 Bedouin chief
102 Withhold
104 Shoshonean
106 Suffer
107 Linden or March

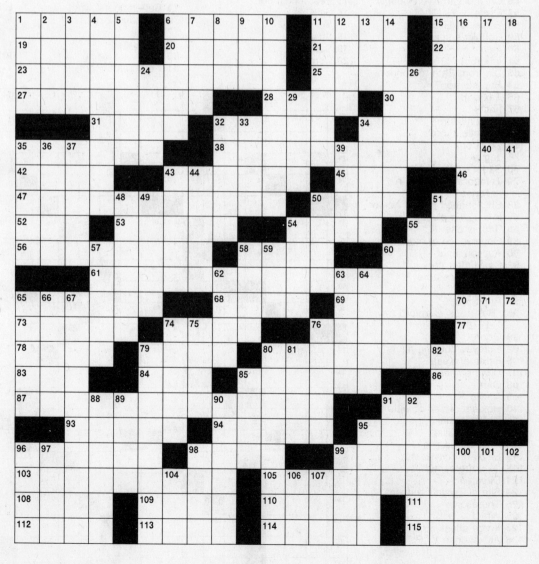

160. Linguistricks by William J. Yskamp

ACROSS

1 Hacks
7 Wild goat
11 Social classes
17 Appointment
21 Small pit
22 Dad, in Damascus
23 Contribute
24 Ardor
25 Darius, to his spouse?
27 Makes merry
28 Firm or quick
29 Snake eyes at Vegas
30 Poet Lizette
31 Had the misery
32 Gambling game
34 Writer Hentoff
35 Cardiff dog-track figure?
37 This often runneth over
38 Old name for a Swiss city
39 Hall of Fame surgeon
40 Part of O.D.
41 That that is
44 This, to a torero
46 Sigurd's steed
47 "___ Mir Bist . . ."
50 Blotter item
51 Peking supermarket group?
55 Chief city in Avon County
57 Owns
58 Ladies of Lisbon
59 Cobbler's sparable
60 Flee
61 Interrupt
63 Dir. from Bath to London
64 Rap session?
66 Tax org.
67 Facts
69 Party mixture
71 Aristotle irked?
74 Cruel one
76 Jaguar
78 Sadat's namesakes
79 Temporary teacher in Torino?
83 Ship-shaped napkin holder
85 In ___ (in place)
86 Bath is one
89 Observance of moral law
90 Auction input
92 Prowl after prey
94 Caesar was here
95 Leak
96 Rundown
98 "Bel ___," Burnford novel: 1978
99 Goon
102 Nureyev donning tights?
106 Feats of Keats
107 Dead ember
108 Oafs
109 Newts
110 Holders of salt or wine
111 Kipling's Kim
112 107, to Gaius
114 Rival of Martina
115 Emulate ecdysiasts
118 "A votre santé!"
121 Directed
124 Site of Twain's remains
125 Threesome
126 Weird
127 Force afloat
128 Alexandrian V.I.P.

129 Glum
131 Oriental desire
133 Cytologist's interest
134 Carol opener
135 Wicked
136 H.W.L. subject
137 Tosca's "Vissi d' ___"
138 Wise elder
139 Mack and Lewis
140 Fits' partner

DOWN

1 Gallinaceous entree
2 Omni or Kemper
3 Groucho wore one
4 Bryophyte
5 Whitney
6 ". . . I am ___ the gods": Socrates
7 Author Gay
8 Discomfit
9 Marine painter
10 Chafe
11 French dramatist: 1791–1861
12 Keep ___ on
13 Fastener
14 Impersonated
15 East Indian herb
16 Silly
17 Slander
18 Startle
19 Sample
20 Come in

26 Giant petrel
31 ". . . not worth ___"
33 Oppidan
35 Oft watched line
36 Like a Tate display
37 Lets off hot air
38 Beatified
40 Killer whale
41 Ben Ezra
42 Mistake
43 Seed coverings
44 She loved Narcissus
45 Pottery fragment
46 Major divisions in biology
47 Relative of bingo
48 Sevareid and Blore
49 British ___
52 Nigerian town
53 Porter opus
54 Burls on trunks
56 Old tongue
62 Fish or voice
64 Three-handed card game
65 Color
67 Platform
68 He took a ribbing
70 Roast or roaster
72 Start of Mass. motto
73 Adlai ___ Stevenson
74 Butterfingers' word
75 Potatoes, e.g.
77 Great!
79 Hindu god
80 Convex molding
81 Certain Mennonites

82 Stay
84 Indistinct
86 Sauce for pasta
87 He pours out whines
88 "I loved ___": Wither
91 Lalo's "Le Roi ___"
93 Weary Willies
94 Little women
96 Zzzzzzz
97 Norse saga
100 Foremen
101 Kindled again
103 Ethereal fluid
104 Dixie dweller
105 Le Havre's river
110 Network
111 Bird or player
112 Papini subject
113 Superficial polish
114 Anthozoans
115 Br. navigation aid
116 Danube feeder
117 Sparling
118 Robert or David
119 Labor; struggle
120 Hypothermal
121 Hen
122 Turn outward
123 Work units
125 ___ bien
127 Shade of green
130 Horatian gem
131 747
132 Bridge reversal

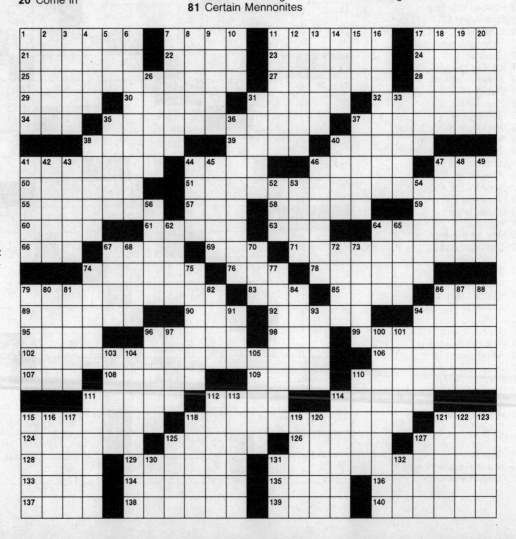

161. Pun Fun by Alex F. Black

ACROSS

1 Does the floor
5 Different
9 Belief
14 Scarlett's mansion
18 Jack's giant, e.g.
19 Held
20 Missouri feeder
21 Slithy creatures
22 Dressing rooms
25 List parts
26 Quintet plus two
27 Sheds
28 Panache
30 Never, in Neustadt
31 Pasty
32 A charge at the butcher's
36 Energy unit
37 Relative of "Pow!"
40 Econ. or ecol.
41 Like a galley
42 Sgt.'s superiors
43 Henry Miller novel
45 Mott St. hors d'oeuvre
48 Black or Red
49 Like an Abu Dhabi dance
51 Recedes
55 Jailbird
56 Bobolink
57 Filling for shells
58 Before, to poets
59 Modernize
61 Untidy
63 Continental subdivision
67 Wan
68 Rode the wind
70 Entrance
71 Remonstrates
74 Gaulish garb
76 Copter propulsion
77 Asner and McMahon
78 Korean G.I.
80 "___ not forgotten"
82 Polynesian fruit
83 Go up
85 Prague exile
87 Vintner's 252 gallons
88 Ancient Adriatic area
90 Reply to "Sez who?"
91 Cries of surprise
92 Condor's roost
94 Lippo Lippi's title
96 Ubiquitous bean
97 Chemical suffix
98 Cupid's collections
102 Clark's companion
105 Charge
106 On the ocean
107 Forest, in France
110 La ___, Spanish seaport
111 Northern highway
113 Roget and Webster
117 Tycoon J. Paul
118 Sandy ridge
119 Singer Cantrell
120 Former D.C. agency
121 "___ est percipi"
122 Takes a break
123 Former spouses
124 Reprieve

DOWN

1 Arabian coffee
2 Eyes amorously
3 Seer's ledger statement
4 Hunter's helpers
5 Just managed, with "out"
6 A Brown of renown
7 Abbr. on a Roman standard
8 Small case
9 Trunks
10 Superlative suffix
11 Scottish turndown
12 Pond denizen
13 Electrician-inventor
14 Short drink in a pub
15 Approach
16 Jog the memory
17 Cash or charm
21 Borax once imported from Tibet
23 Suspend
24 Descriptive wd.
29 "Oh, I am ___ . . ."
33 Readies champagne
34 "___ Must Fall," 1963 film
35 Escutcheon border
37 Sugar source
38 Truism
39 Igloo footgear
42 Italian poet: 1798–1837
43 Makes strips
44 Quiescence
46 Chromosome component
47 Singer Coolidge
48 Deck opening
49 Fool's play of yore
50 In the spotlight
52 Top dog
53 Multihanded giant
54 Caps or cans
60 Hgt.
62 "___ and little fishes!"
64 Trim
65 Nail's partner
66 Carney or Tatum
69 Certain cap wearers
72 Homer's one-horse town
73 Tart
75 Half, in Messina
79 "Mack the ___"
81 "___ valentine"
84 Land of Brian Boru
85 Sanctify
86 Dear, on the Via Condotti
89 Monotonous recital
91 Troublesome
92 Poplars
93 Throws out
95 Shady places
97 Antonym of aloft
98 Come ___ (mature)
99 Discourage
100 Hole for an anchor cable
101 In addition
103 Home of a Brahman
104 Fresh
108 Run in neutral gear
109 Tunisian port
110 Tomorrow, to Tiberius
112 Eroded
114 Gives the go-ahead
115 Catch
116 Homophone for won

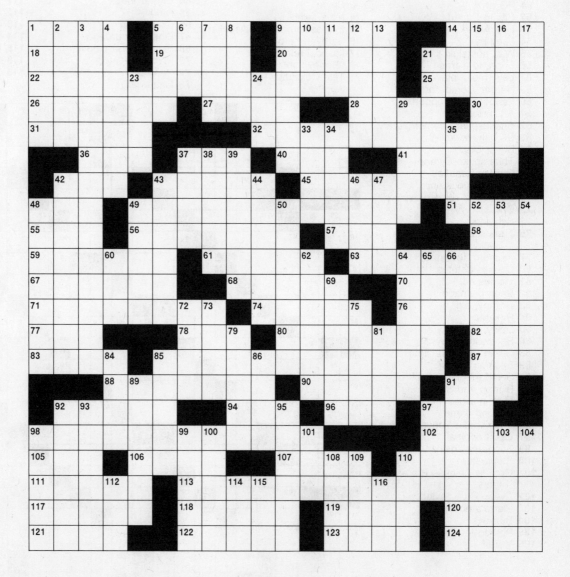

162. On Speaking Terms by George Rose Smith

ACROSS

1 Smokes
7 "Gil ___"
11 Platter
15 Soprano Clamma ___
19 Historic peak
20 Sorceress
22 Kind of committee
24 Nuncupative
25 Thus spake Arthur Guinness
27 Thus spake Edgar Bergen, with "in"
29 Chem. suffix
30 Porcupine's protection
31 Symbolized
33 Tomato blights
34 Heave
35 Utmost extent
36 Spinnaker
37 Sty occupant
40 Like Maine woodlands
41 Day or Duke
42 Currents caused by cars
46 Poseidon's weapon
48 Thus spake peace conferees
50 Initials in the 30's
51 PG or X
52 City in Canada
53 Like Albee's Alice
54 Land map
55 Was nostalgic
56 Soph, to a frosh
57 Low, moist place
59 Nature: Comb. form
60 Pandora's escapees
61 Art gallery
62 Shakespeare contemporary
63 Be half-awake
64 Boxer Cruz
65 Thus spake Cyrano
68 Garden beauties
69 Querimonious child
71 Sugar-and-spice group
72 China
73 Scholars
75 Thus spake Thackeray's Becky
77 Pinafore, for one
80 Causes detritus
81 Vicious eel
82 Shed plumage
83 Granny, e.g.
84 Reliable
85 Dewy, in poetry
86 Entertainer Rivera
88 Girl in "Twelfth Night"
89 Spasms
90 Seine tributary
91 Bishop and Sexton
92 Man in a box
93 Second name
94 Thus spake Venus de Milo
97 Least original
98 Suppress again
100 Studio item
101 God, to Chinese Protestants
102 Aves. 'kin
103 Pierre's notion
104 Burrows
105 Portico for Pericles
106 Visual

109 Kind of larceny
110 Gets a hint of
112 Adage
115 Thus spake the forgetful one at the grocery
117 Thus spake the umpire
120 To ___ (exactly)
121 Prevent legally
122 Squelched
123 Apollo 7 astronaut
124 Desideratum
125 Underling of yore
126 Hutches
127 Floral organ

DOWN

1 Bistro
2 Mashie, for one
3 ___ du Nord, Paris
4 Newspaper department
5 Fall calls
6 Kind of stone
7 Small, tapering fish
8 Tie on a boot
9 O.T. book
10 Wodehouse title
11 Tzara's cult
12 "___ Care," 1905 song
13 Close
14 Male swan
15 Expression of mild disbelief
16 Saroyan hero
17 Musical refrain
18 "Benevolent" ones
21 Title Columbus held

23 Thus spake the optimistic meterologist
26 Bright
28 Uplift
32 Turkish V.I.P.
35 Schlimazel
36 Actress Hasso
37 Narrow passage
38 Wise answer
39 Thus spake Gray's herd
40 Hang fire
41 Fatal
42 Like a crone
43 Thus spake Beverly Sills
44 Hogfish
45 French composer and kin
47 Seeker of subversives: 1938–44
48 "Dirty" group of 1967
49 Where Leghorn is
52 Butterfly
54 Bell ringer, for short
56 Leporine group
57 Tongue-twister verb
58 Cheat the bookie
59 Commonplace
61 Omar's production
62 Stravinsky's "Card ___"
63 Did business
65 Ivied
66 Israeli coin
67 Fiber for cordage
68 Flounces on blouses
70 Pluto, to Plato
72 Ponies
73 Game dog

74 Achieve success
75 Peloponnesus
76 Accord
78 Ill-treat
79 Fits' partner
81 Dayan
83 Eartha
85 Garand or M-1
86 Systems of signals
87 War, to Sherman
88 Futile
90 Recipient of a bid
91 Money in Madrid
92 Inspires
94 Resembling: Suffix
95 Biological specimen replacing the original
96 Salvador from Spain
97 Strip of leather
99 Sloped
101 Toby's cousins
104 Extra dividend
105 Already, in Anhalt
106 Buck heroine
107 Bring into court
108 Beneficiary: Law
109 Signals for silence
110 Satisfy
111 Patio gear
112 Ski turn
113 Tall Asiatic tree
114 Reporter's query
116 Dir. of L.A. from Reno
118 Faucet
119 "The law ___ ass": Dickens

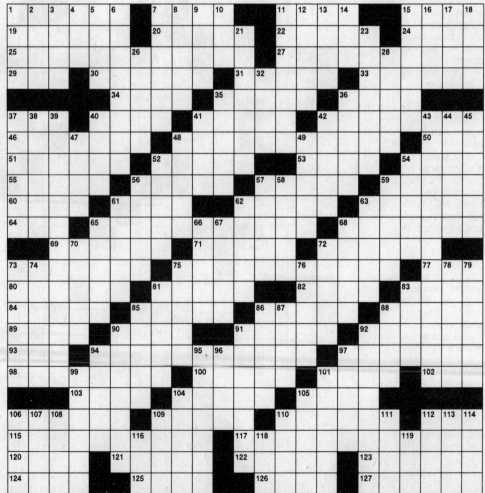

163. Light Housekeeping by Lynn Gilbert Lempel

ACROSS

1 HUD relative
4 Nautical dir.
7 Cape Town's famous son
12 Pilot's residence
17 Revel noisily
19 Dieter's snack
21 "Wolsey" author: 1930
23 Raids
24 Iroquoian group
25 "___ Butterfly"
26 ___ land
27 Poet McKuen
28 Flatfish
30 Yoga posture
31 Night watchman's residence
35 Golden-rule word
36 Sea sight
37 Jack London hero
38 Dead heat
39 RR terminal
40 Egyptian deity
41 ". . . ___ saw Elba"
42 With it
43 Corrigendum
45 Gulfs
47 Syrian statesman
50 Crimean resort
52 Former TV host
53 Star: Comb. form
55 Surly, churly chap
57 Their, in Tours
59 Desert region
60 Exigency
61 Eighth-century Chinese poet
62 Penned
64 Smooth musical passage
67 Gave consent
69 Harden
70 Physicist from Hungary
71 Item sought by 4 Down
72 Inca territory
74 Jasmine, e.g.
75 Check
76 Wapiti
77 Plunder
78 Drover's concern
79 Organ knobs
82 Permission
85 Bits
87 Ménage à ___
89 Irritate
90 Oates novel
91 Synagogue
94 N.L. arbiter
95 Otto ___ Bismarck
96 Alta. or Ont.
97 Org. for boys
100 Assuage
101 Outcast's residence
105 Dishonest gain
107 Hussein's queen
108 Sullivan and Wynn
109 Vibration
110 Symbol
112 Dallies
114 Cleft
115 Connect
116 Greet
117 Gladdens
118 Turn aside
119 Kingly
120 Loser to D.D.E.
121 Book by Bry: 1976

DOWN

1 Type of benefit
2 Lovelace's first love
3 U.S.A.F. member
4 Straphangers
5 Doctor's residence
6 Forage plant
7 Reporter's coup
8 Orders
9 Suffix for cult or strict
10 "Valse ___": Sibelius
11 Sin City
12 Mil. weapon
13 Pastures
14 Numismatist's residence
15 Be brazen
16 Marinara ingredient
18 Fly high
20 "Honor Thy Father" author
22 Start of a Williams title
27 Operated
29 Kind of blank
32 German-Polish border river
33 Rushes headlong
34 "G.W.T.W." estate
41 Item to be lent
42 Overaggressive salesman's residence
44 Hacienda pots
45 Calling
46 Bargains
48 Niacin is one
49 Con artist's residence
51 Looked at the books
52 Hunter's souvenir
54 What hairdressers do
56 Roundup
58 Alludes
61 "___ It Be," Beatles hit
62 Juvenile delinquent's residence
63 Couple
65 Second-rate singer's residence
66 Robert Nagy is one
68 Kind of walk
73 Pulpits
78 Haw's partner
80 Serve drinks
81 What he says goes
83 Rugby's river
84 Feud
86 Misfortunes
88 Jests
91 Bob ___, pop singer
92 Was destructive
93 Convenient
95 Masculine
96 Monogram of the "Ozymandias" poet
97 Stupefy
98 Nighttime disturbances
99 Relaxed
102 Bicuspid's neighbor
103 Lemon on wheels
104 Western hill
106 Place for a chapeau
111 Debussy subject
113 Proverbial dirt hider
114 "Conning Tower" columnist

164. Through the Looking-Glass by Michael Priestley

ACROSS

1 Silvers from Brooklyn
5 Mashes grapes
11 Metric weight
15 Sermon's preface
19 Beans
21 Imitation gold
22 ____ de boeuf
23 Baker's assistant
24 Yawning
25 Adviser to Odysseus
26 Age
27 Turner
28 Pale hero
30 "Nat Turner" author
31 Parachutist's descent
32 Sub detector
33 Short distance
35 Seeds
37 Liz or Robert
42 The law's reach
43 "Follow me ____!": Kipling
44 Neighbor of Mex.
47 Roman moralist
50 Radamès's beloved
51 Egg, to Nero
53 Iroquoian
55 Richard Arlen role: 1933
58 Cartoonist's light bulb
60 Consequence
61 Discordant
62 Prunes
63 Flagpole rope
66 Oscillate
67 Tender
68 Boxer's stat
69 Rosie's fastener
70 Cygnet's sire
72 These, to René
73 Uses a letter opener
75 Distant: Prefix
76 Flick foretaste
79 Look-alikes
88 Finesse
89 Uproot
90 Witch's town
91 Actress Charlotte
94 Dernier ____
95 Hebrew A
97 Ling. unit
100 Preserve
101 Dole out
104 Go gaga over
106 Pad of sorts
107 Prefix with chord or meter
108 Glassy
110 Aesir, e.g.
111 Edna May Oliver role: 1933
114 In high dudgeon
116 Computer's sustenance
118 Llama's habitat
119 Hindus' sacred books
120 Rumanian coin
121 Yale name
122 Torme
123 Neighbor of Perugia
125 Flourish
128 Perry's creator
130 What "duco" means
134 Dillydallier
136 Population statistic
138 Gibberish
144 Andean native
145 Desirable thing
146 Like Verdi's music
147 "____ Sensational," 1956 song
148 Soviet sea
149 Phalanges' locales
150 "Ecce homo" man
151 Comforts
152 Wife: Law
153 Long ago, long ago
154 Annual incomes, in Arles
155 Angel Clare's bride

DOWN

1 Surveyor's map
2 Anticyclones
3 Adult insect
4 Rabbit fur
5 "____ Like It Hot"
6 Weight allowance
7 Atlanta's civic center
8 Lepidopteran
9 Snow removers
10 California's Big ____
11 Western novelist
12 Leonine outbursts
13 One of the Fates
14 Use of a wrong name
15 Diacritical mark
16 Pre-election competition
17 Kind of phobia
18 Golfer's obstacle
20 Byrd or Hart
26 Egghead
29 Isthmus or monkey
30 Abject
34 Lao-tse's way
36 Freshen
38 Brute
39 Speech imperfections
40 Tributary verses
41 Bowl call
45 Unguent
46 Pays the pot
47 Wheedle
48 Mite or tick
49 Cylindrical
52 ____ culpa
54 That, in Toledo
55 Armor part
56 Kind
57 Piaget subject
59 Discharged light
64 Vindicates
65 Symbol of peace
69 Possible creator of some Easter bonnets
71 News acct.
74 Highway sign
75 Doubly: Prefix
77 Catch-22, perhaps
78 Town in Gelderland
80 French noble
81 Being, to Sartre
82 Part of A.E.S.
83 Land unit, in Canada
84 Ovation's demand
85 Reasoned out
86 Not ____ red cent
87 Pick up the tab
91 "La Valse" composer
92 Type of skirt
93 Kind of soup
96 Fine shines
97 Vilipends
98 Sonora Indian
99 Inc., in London
102 Sixty minutes, in Siena
103 Blake's model of symmetry
105 Mann's "Der ____ in Venedig"
106 Doctor's bills
109 Vow taker
112 D.C. ecology group
113 Bad-luck glance
115 Quotient factor
117 "____ in the Family"
124 Dubbed one
126 Pant
127 Gaels
129 Craggy nest
131 Armed vessel, British style
132 Revile
133 ____ Salaam
134 Late chanteuse
135 Between dix and douze
137 Criterion
139 Ceramist's need
140 Layer
141 Bone: Prefix
142 Troubles
143 Falconer's strap
146 Mar. follower

165. Yule Collection by Anne Fox

ACROSS

1 Commander of David's army
5 Sound seeking attention
9 Mexican sandwich
13 The other woman, Roman style
19 Chaplet for Galahad
20 Long skirt, for short
21 Ebro y Tajo
22 Creator of Dr. Fu Manchu
23 Glove leather
24 Buck heroine
25 Evergreens
26 Let ____ (bettor's expression)
27 Story by Queen Marie of Rumania
30 Pieces of pottery
31 Former Eastern rulers
32 "Land of Cockaigne" author
33 Part of U.S.A.
35 Actress Hagen
37 Part of a bottle
38 Petroleum
42 Words by Faith Baldwin
49 Ad ____
50 Elusive one
51 Bad ____ (German spa)
52 "Rap session"
53 Bungling
55 Actor Vigoda
56 Sways
59 Abysses
60 Trolls
61 Maugham character
63 Type of roof
64 A Cantor
65 Cal. ____
66 Words by Clement Moore
72 Largest of seven
73 F.D.R. measure
74 Tolkien creature
75 Nebraskan Indians
77 Liliaceous plant
80 Frustrate
81 Letter stroke
83 ____ de tête
84 Speaker of the House: 1801–07
85 Trees or nuts
87 Elec. unit
88 Dec. 24
89 Kind of shadow
90 "It was told ____" (words by Janet Knox)
95 Celebration at Yuletide
97 Hurried
98 Patriotic org.
99 Puzzle word
102 Mild expletives
104 Intrigue
108 Eddies
111 O. Henry story ending
114 Two-seated carriage
115 Deserve
116 ____ fixe
117 Guthrie
118 Freshen, as a room
119 ____ Major
120 Piano piece
121 Religious image
122 Sailor's jumper
123 Rabin's predecessor
124 Midge
125 Corvine calls

DOWN

1 Dr. Salk
2 Plant resembling spinach
3 Beginning
4 Tight squeeze
5 Bible book
6 Discontinues
7 Critical studies
8 Moslem tower
9 Christmas thought from Dickens
10 Suburb of Honolulu
11 Monks' wear
12 Caucasian native
13 Bristles
14 Words by John Bowring
15 Beat
16 Bedouin chief
17 Foxx
18 War god
28 Title of an editorial by Francis Church: 1897
29 Meistersinger Hans: 1494–1576
34 Item on Pierre's Yule tree
36 Air: Comb. form
39 Book by Oates
40 Faith follower
41 Bible book
42 Arthur and Lillie
43 Middle Eastern fiddle
44 ____ Diable
45 Italian island
46 California Indian
47 Red star in Scorpius
48 Cartoonists' org.
54 ____ game
57 Relations
58 Dutch philosopher: 1632–77
60 Set
62 Aviator Balbo
65 Shoe type
67 Cake ____
68 Ram on high
69 Chemical suffix
70 Pyle of TV
71 Throw with effort
76 Gift for a moppet
77 Merganser
78 Yucatec
79 Desserts
80 Falstaffian
82 Puckerels
85 Circle of light
86 Siberian antelope
91 Shaggy
92 Bringing up
93 Appended
94 Semitic language
96 "La Tosca" dramatist
100 Fiddle with a uke
101 N.Y.S.E. unit
103 Stone monument
105 Hannibal's family name
106 Lit up
107 Service group
108 Thick slice
109 Lament
110 Obi accessory
112 Though, to Tacitus
113 Fervor

166. With Best Wishes . . . by Eugene T. Maleska

ACROSS

1 "Happy ____!"
8 Communication
15 In Hades
20 Sudden inclination
21 Epical
22 Apocopates
24 *Start of a greeting to solvers*
28 Biblical verb suffix
29 Año nuevo celebrant
30 Hebrew letter
31 Encumbrance
32 Attic promenade
33 Iago's forte
35 Interdict
37 Extremities of cold, etc.
39 Peppery
40 Catfish's lookalike
42 "The Sun Also ____"
44 "I am ____ a man": Shak.
46 Ballerina's leap
47 "He wasted both toil ____": Cicero
49 Word with horn or string
50 "____, There," 1954 song
51 Cynical
53 Three, in Toledo
55 Court defense
57 *Greeting: Part II*
58 Neighbor of Perugia
61 Pullulate
62 Golden-rule preposition
66 Mazuma
69 Writer Bontemps
70 Girl in "Le Nozze di Figaro"
72 Grudge
74 Daube
76 Tropical climber
78 Man of the soil
80 Attends Choate, e.g.
82 Links gadget
83 Song-____ man
85 Nabokov novel
86 Native of Asmara
88 Panay inhabitant
89 Where Chanticleer rules
91 Greek phonetician
94 One hundred make a gridiron
95 Exec's note
97 Between: Prefix
99 Voiceless sound in German
101 Bundle of cotton
102 Lessee's payment
104 Unit of loudness
105 Turkish weight units
106 Rose or nomad
108 *Greeting: Part III*
110 Ocean greyhound
112 Musketeer's foil
113 Old hand
116 Washington V.I.P.
117 Fasces items
120 Assails
124 Type of dive or song
125 Geometer's straight line
127 "____ the Rose," Young novel
129 Sailing vessel
130 Sigma follower
131 ____ peanuts
133 Innsbruck is here

135 Dreary, in Dundee
136 "____ boy!"
138 Assent in Acapulco
139 Negation in Nürnberg
141 Pram pushers
143 From ____ Z
144 *End of greeting*
149 Main course in U.S.
150 Refined
151 Osmium or uranium
152 Begat
153 N.H.L. team
154 Calls it a day

DOWN

1 Genus of stoneworts
2 Fear or hate, e.g.
3 Harry Hopkins: 1935–38
4 Actor Brynner
5 Building wings
6 Interrogated
7 Carl, Fritz or Rob
8 Jewish religious exposition
9 "A right jolly old ____"
10 Thailand, once
11 More lucid
12 Madison Ave. copywriters
13 Adjustable piece in a machine
14 Bionomics
15 Commands
16 Esau's father-in-law
17 Adjective for Abner
18 Bookie's concern
19 Everybody's concern
23 Supercilious
25 Ora pro ____
26 Word with flat or spare
27 Appointment
34 Mary Stuart's realm
36 Begins anew
38 Rises
41 Charter
43 Swain's song
45 Raggedy doll
46 Peridot, e.g.
48 Inviting word
52 Brain scan, for short
54 Bits or hints
56 Efflux
58 Moslem's greeting
59 Caxton or Zenger
60 Stop ____
61 Oriental shrine
63 Knot in cotton
64 Mother ____, Nobelist for Peace
65 Puccini prelude
67 Football play
68 Lever on a loom
71 Takes care of
73 Spire ornament
75 Not so sparse
77 Rhine feeder
79 They follow an animal's trail
81 Swine's confines

84 We, to Luciano
87 Formed a joint, in carpentry
90 Half a score
92 Type of cigar
93 "____ ne passeront pas"
96 Pope's "Essay ____"
98 Let up
100 Campers' curfew
103 The "it" game
107 Proverbial heirs
109 Affirmation
111 One with a plan
113 Wrap in bandages
114 Stretches tightly
115 Dwelt
116 Organ stop
118 "____ me only . . ."
119 Eastern inn
121 Vagabond
122 Paint solvent
123 On ____ (at variance)
124 E.R.A. or R.B.I.
126 Instance
128 Companion of Blitzen
132 Muralist Rivera
134 Soup scoop
137 Oppositionist
138 Popeye's ____ Pea
140 Abba of Israel
142 Galley word
145 Bobble the ball
146 Cicero's "I maintain"
147 Tolkien creature
148 Chinese peak

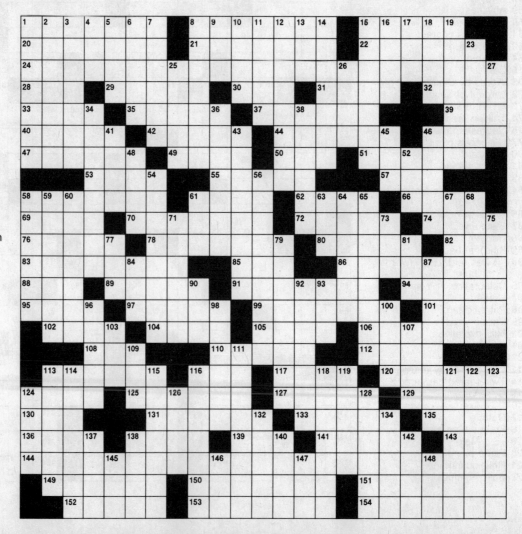

167. Postcards to the Snowbound by Frances Hansen

ACROSS

1 Mo or Stu
6 Tender
11 Tinge
15 Portly U.S. President
19 Pastoral people of Kenya
20 Relative of Yoo-hoo
21 Western Indian
22 Winglike
23 Swedish actress May
24 Super!
25 Disagreeable one
26 Yuletide guests
27 Clare and Whiting's card
31 Eat away
32 Clique
33 Upper House
34 Diva Geraldine
37 Change
40 Yearn
41 Old English letter
42 Precedent-setter, in court
45 Thor's wife
46 Much-puzzled bird
49 Hershey and Swander's card
54 Aspersion
55 Flying prefix
56 Many eras
57 Burning
58 Catkins
61 ____ Heights
64 Kind of titmouse
65 Harold Rome's card
69 Napkin material
72 Red as ____
73 Having no key
76 Reach by radio
77 O.T. book
78 Wrestling needs
81 Club assessments
83 Kahn, Eliscu and You-mans's card
89 Princess-prodder
90 Former Arab org.
91 The Emerald Isle
92 Smith or Fleming
93 Escritoire
95 Hunter or Kelly
96 Glycerides
98 Gobi or Negev
101 Bill's partner
102 ____ the good
104 Hammerstein and Rod-gers's card
112 Swank
113 Frontier lawman
114 Type of pansy
115 Peripheral
116 Top of an abbé
117 "Judith" composer
118 Opposite of 115 Across
119 Place to schuss
120 Olympian hawk
121 Decorticate
122 Lascivious looks
123 Silverweed

DOWN

1 Boss on a shield
2 Junior's imprecation
3 ____ were (so to speak)
4 Foam
5 Learned lot
6 George Burns film
7 Denmark's ____ Islands
8 Absquatulated
9 Greek resistance org. of W.W. II
10 "Goodbye, Columbus" author
11 Penny, in Soho
12 On a slant
13 Pas seul
14 Rebukes severely
15 Petruchio's activity
16 Confirmation slap
17 Bundle of twigs
18 Worthless writing
28 Bridge expert
29 "____ hand you cannot see": Tickell
30 Author Deighton
34 G-men, e.g.
35 Writer St. John
36 Catarrh
37 Maple genus
38 French naval battle area: 1692
39 Monogram of Prufrock's creator
40 Simba
43 Stow away
44 "On ____ Riviera": Sylvia Fine's card
45 Lewis or Ezra
46 Parkway sign
47 Former filly
48 Secondhand
50 Laundry cycle
51 Bring up
52 Bull: Comb. form
53 Turkish title of respect
59 Japanese-American
60 Tut!
62 Have creditors
63 "____ a little kinder": Guest
64 Asian holiday
66 P.L.O.'s Arafat
67 Scottish resort
68 Wears
69 Bead
70 Swiss river
71 Isinglass
74 March of fiction
75 "Merry Widow" composer
77 Author Dinesen
79 Choir response
80 Rocky peak
82 RR stops
84 Rubbish pile
85 Hurl
86 Make tracks
87 Physicist Bohr
88 British taps signal
93 Frees from frost
94 C.G.S. unit
95 Evangel
97 Yeastlike fungus
98 Judicial assertions
99 BBC realm
100 Hit heavily
101 French film director
102 More qualified
103 A king and a poet
105 Darnel
106 Malefic
107 Postcard note
108 Like an anchoret
109 Lay ____ (flatter)
110 Clusters of fibers
111 Jane or Zane

168. All-Year Hit Parade by Tap Osborn

ACROSS

1 Irreligious
6 Note, to Key
12 Serape
17 Largest natural lake in Wales
21 In harmony
22 Trilling or Hampton
23 TV morning show
24 Tiant
25 January 1 beauty queen's plea
28 Octave of a feast
29 Rubber tree
30 Docket
31 Take a flier
32 Show up for the 25th
33 Code word
35 Dirs.
36 Material for 36 keys
38 Item near a tub
40 One with pressing duties
42 Jolo's archipelago
43 Aug. 4, 1892, crime name
44 Lack
46 June gardener's Elvis-style lament
49 Former Met diva
52 Impious
53 Word with cork or thumb
55 Part of R.W.E.
56 Purdah prop
57 Quotidian
58 Wild plum
59 Yule-tree hanger
61 Diplomat Silas
62 Bonn article
63 Stone landmark
64 Spiffily togged out
65 Curving out
66 Deadlocked
67 Potpourri: Abbr.
68 Tetra minus one
69 "____ tu," Verdi aria
70 Travel hazard
73 April sound for bird watchers
77 Help call
78 Spare rib, once
79 Mouths
80 Grafted: Her.
81 Gift of gab
82 Establishes
84 Kind of bulb
86 Fall quencher
87 Sibilant aside
91 Sing lustily
92 "Micah ____," Doyle novel
93 Listless
94 Speed: Comb. form
95 Together, at the Met
96 Feudal V.I.P.
97 "I ____ the Songs"
99 Master of love ballads
100 Viaud's pen name
101 July farm-journal entry
103 K and C
104 Wolves, often
106 In the past
107 Ranch animal
108 Extempore
110 Vulgar
112 Anjou's cousin
113 Additionally
116 Take a second shot at
117 Rank
118 Gordon or Irish
120 Result of many a "lost weekend"
121 Thine: Fr.
122 December dorm notice
127 Prurient
128 "Paper Moon" name
129 Usurer, for one
130 "The Friends of Eddie ____"
131 Toiler of yore
132 Art category
133 Domain
134 Assault

DOWN

1 "Kiss Me, Kate" locale
2 Coral reef
3 Closed-shop sign in May
4 Colony denizen
5 Tiber tributary
6 Property receiver
7 "Born again" candidate
8 Street toughs
9 Soprano Moffo
10 Ad ____ (pertinent)
11 Wield
12 Coloring agent
13 Oversized
14 Aleutian isle
15 Bundle
16 Caustic
17 October victory for Yale
18 November headache
19 Tropical vine
20 Desirable thing
26 Means
27 English musician: 1835–1909
32 Sent back: Abbr.
34 Tiny space
36 "Bravo," Greek style
37 March shopper's woe
38 Parisian's plug
39 Ex-constellation
41 "____ a Rose"
42 Squad-car item
43 Domineer
44 Carcassonne's river
45 ____ B'rith
47 Kind of hitter
48 Savoir-faire
50 Moola
51 Actress Smith
53 Cast
54 Welsh-bred dog
58 Health spa feature
60 Class distinction
61 Rub out
63 Nest noise
65 Muezzin
67 Byelorussian city
68 Judge for Dred Scott
70 Like a gala
71 Cook too long
72 Weatherman's August warning
73 "Body and ____"
74 Start of a hymn
75 Nobelist in Literature: 1948
76 Spine
83 Jingly February outing
84 Defects
85 Camera genius Edwin
86 Region, to Keats
87 Color change on old silver
88 They resume in September
89 Kind of plaster
90 Flip
92 Combo on the keys
94 Film maker Jacques
96 In that case
98 Hambletonian, e.g.
99 Grateau's wave
102 "____ Something to Me"
103 Put back in shape
105 Minstrel's song
107 Machree of songdom
108 Fanon
109 Celebrations
110 Net, in business
111 Jaeger's weapon
112 Fashion's Geoffrey
114 Panache
115 Central Caucasian
117 Augury
118 ____ Jahan
119 Petrocelli of baseball
122 Duroc
123 Romberg's "____ Alone"
124 Literary monogram
125 Porter's "You're the ____"
126 Giovanni or José

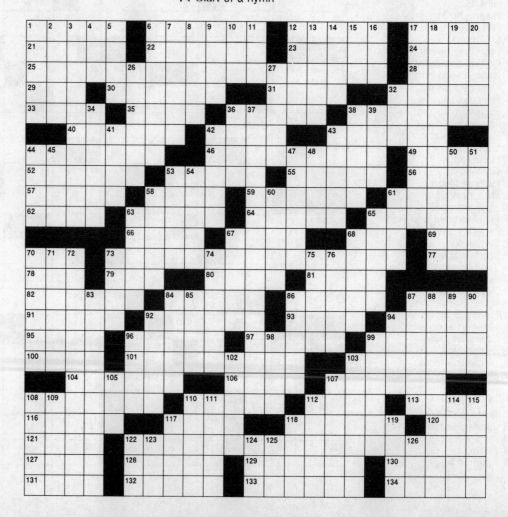

169. Atticisms by Alfio Micci

ACROSS

1 Greeks' ligneous ruse
6 Plied with potions
11 Turn left
14 Hit, old style
18 Mythical Greek hunter
19 Apocopate
20 Harem room
21 Singer Cantrell
22 Some disks
25 "____ on her toes"
26 "What ____ is new?"
27 Bellow work
28 Certain shoe sizes
30 Caner's material
32 Louis XIV and XVI
33 Algonquian
34 Conclamation
37 Oboist's concern
38 "Masterpiece" on wheels
39 G.I. fare
44 Do a sailor's job
45 Rye beard
48 Devilkin
49 Ballerina Alicia
50 Olive shade
52 Cravat
53 Eskimo craft
54 Ruminant
55 Sheer fabric
56 Bare
58 Used a mangle
60 Ornamental stud
61 Former draft org.
62 Dakar is its capital
64 Public Health agcy.
65 Prefix with gram or meter
68 Top floors
69 Stained
74 Of an eye part
75 Sticky substances
76 Netherlands city
78 Race the motor
79 To-do
81 Legendary magician
82 Pasture sound
83 Kin of secs. and mins.
84 Partner of void
85 Vintage car
88 French cleric
89 A one
90 Laconic
91 Ultra
94 Table d'____
95 Bed item
99 Kind of house
101 Fable ending
102 Bridge position
106 Swift
107 Frederick Knott melodrama
110 Granular snow
111 Frequently, to poets
112 Silly
113 Bambino's parent
114 Certain votes
115 ____ Paulo
116 Lament
117 Food portion

DOWN

1 Burrow
2 Buccal
3 Fellies
4 Recover from a wassail
5 Fragment
6 Warehouse
7 Tony of A.L. fame
8 Lorelei
9 Pulitzer Prize biographer
10 Nov. follower
11 Frightful
12 ____ Ababa
13 Vespid
14 Like a hibernal glaze
15 Gozo's neighbor
16 Family member
17 Tax, in Torino
23 Pismire
24 Siouan Indians
25 Air rifle
29 Buddhist monk, free from karma
31 One ____ time
32 Gambling mecca
34 Vaudeville offerings
35 ____ up (emote)
36 "Happy Hooligan" cartoonist
37 "La Cenerentola" composer and family
38 Excalibur
40 Highway features
41 "I cannot tell ____"
42 Poisonous mushroom
43 Sign
44 Bethlehem sight
45 Seed covering
46 Weave wickerwork
47 Red refusal
50 The Seine, to Spaniards
51 "The Overcoat" author
53 W.W. II menace
54 Arctic transport
57 Eastern religion
59 Kind of room, for short
63 Harrow's rival
64 Part of an opera
65 Start of a Shakespearean title
66 Novello
67 Moon vehicles
68 Lively
70 Mine entrance
71 Arthurian wear
72 Lacerates
73 Dodge
77 ". . . ____ I saw Elba"
80 Like a ____ lard
81 Be gloomy
85 Roadside sign
86 Western lizard
87 Kind of case
88 Georgia city
89 Part of b.l.t.
91 Molasses confection
92 Stan's partner
93 ____ buffa
94 City on the Bay of Acre
95 To date
96 Antler tip
97 Peep show
98 Shade giver
100 TV predecessors: Abbr.
101 Actor who played Zola
103 Egyptian skink
104 Painter José María
105 Family lineage
108 Word with rib or riff
109 Fenway Pk. figure

170. Against Regulations by Bert Beaman

ACROSS

1 Hidden stores
7 Occult system
13 Traveller's rider
16 German count
20 Handy
21 Part of Spain
22 Mandarin
24 *Start of a Berton Braley verse*
26 Fragrance
27 Coll. degree
28 Border water
29 Soprano Lucine
31 Generate
32 Piece for Price
34 Coverings at marinas
37 Unyielding
38 Gangland group
40 Annoy
42 *Verse continued*
47 U. of Md. athlete
49 Uncloses: Poet.
50 Man, e.g.
51 Greek music halls
52 Pitcher Swan
55 Evangelist's advice
57 Dwindles
58 Interpret
59 Actress Crabtree: 1847–1924
60 Tennis name
61 Prefix with rail or tone
63 Worldwide relief org.
64 *Verse continued*
69 Convened
70 ____ off (repel)
71 First ____
72 Leavings
73 French menu item
75 Milestone for mountain climbers
77 Gard's capital
79 Purim is one
83 Flesh: Prefix
84 Walden, for one
85 Hosp. employees
86 Vidal
87 Plant
90 *Verse continued*
96 Kind of steamer
98 Words of understanding
99 Expenditure
100 Gallery
101 Roast, in Reims
102 Sapins
104 Lime's cousin
105 Tartan wearers
106 Chemical suffixes
107 Zoo favorite
109 Amphora adjunct
110 A mild cheese
112 *Verse continued*
116 Obliterated
120 Standish
121 Switchblade: Slang
122 Expert
124 Historic ship
125 Have ____ (beware)
127 Monster: Prefix
129 Snooker sticks
131 More, in Madrid
132 Lawyer's concern
136 *End of verse*

140 Bring together at a focal point
141 Lower
142 Irish city
143 Neighbor of Hung.
144 Actor's last line
145 ____ de corps
146 Accent

DOWN

1 Agile burglar
2 Cleave
3 Kind of card
4 Road ____
5 Gaels' land
6 Track employee
7 Japanese export
8 Football first name
9 Tribunal
10 Moslem title
11 Like the best topsoil
12 He played Cochise on TV
13 New Guinean city
14 Remnant
15 Kind of trip
16 Newcomer
17 Certain fight fans
18 Noun ending
19 Places for loafers
22 Wayfarers
23 Rush-hour weapon
25 Farrow

30 Lynda Bird ____
33 Ballerinas' poses
35 Drive
36 Tops: Abbr.
38 Middleweight champ: 1923–26
39 Bookie's concern
41 Juridic
43 ____ hand (helped)
44 Stroke on a violin
45 Brazilian state
46 Attacked
48 Election district
52 Memorable actor
53 Seaman in a gig
54 Agreed
56 Dodge
61 Encore plea
62 Inning sextet
63 Army group
65 Place selling "Jersey juice"
66 ____ plume
67 Kind of musical note
68 Italian physicist
74 Railroad employee
76 Light
77 Slangy negative
78 Concerning
79 Cold: Prefix
80 Parisian's "Eureka!"
81 Fire inspector's concern
82 Inclines
84 Stand the test

87 Fodder or bedding
88 Maine college town
89 Conduits
91 King of Tyre
92 Aim
93 Open ocean
94 Beach
95 Levant
97 Send the wrong way
102 Arctic sight
103 Founder of Troy
104 Louvre display
108 Wimbledon winner: 1975
111 Spots
113 Hydrocarbon type: Suffix
114 Diatribe
115 Seemly
117 Figure of speech
118 Mothers' relatives
119 Olympic events
123 Sometimes it's funny
125 Old brocade
126 Point of chief interest
128 Weatherman's abbr.
130 Spanish painter
133 Explosive
134 Greek letter
135 Trousers part
137 Grandfather of Saul
138 Pacific porgy
139 Hell, to Sherman

171. Uncommon Letters by Henry Hook

ACROSS

1 Flirtation
10 ____ vobiscum
13 Eliot called it cruellest
18 Chicago-born actress
20 Secretary between Day and Root
21 Succulent
22 Furniture on casters
23 Former Red Sox star
24 Shakespearean setting
25 "Grand Old Man of Football"
26 They're often exploded
28 Pay
29 One of Uranus's moons
31 In medias ____
32 Pen talk
35 Adjective aptly applied to Apley
36 Ozark "encore"
37 Grandiosity of a sort
41 Seaworthy
42 Resort in the Bahamas
43 Austrian contralto: 1803–77
44 Mrs. Warner's nickname
47 Shetland chapeau
48 He once was Bud's buddy
49 Ictus
51 Irish county
53 Conforming
55 Passover wafer
57 Store-window sign
58 Exculpate
60 Sides of cricket fields
64 Locale of a 1944 novel
65 Gym twist
69 Spreads nitrates
71 Excellent poker hand
72 "Darling, Je Vous ____ Beaucoup"
73 Beatle name
74 Tamiroff
75 Pippin
78 Insipid
82 Bumps on the skin
84 Hedda of fiction
87 Kramden's vehicle
88 "No way!"
89 Loser to H.C.H.: 1928
90 Search widely
92 Restrain with a chain
95 Pitchfork part
96 She was Tosca on TV in 1955
98 Mrs. Van Buren, née ____
99 Coin of Cuba
102 Sierra ____
103 Mardi Gras V.I.P.
104 Bloodhound's clue
106 Product for overseas sale
108 Callas or Tallchief
110 Vowel sequence
112 Ante
113 Desert coat
115 Principle of minimized hypotheses
119 True's partner
120 Grackle
121 Hawkish
122 "____ of Iwo Jima"
123 Persian unit of length
124 After-dinner drink

DOWN

1 The fourth Musketeer
2 Piscine pens
3 Fencer's maneuver
4 Sill
5 "Well, ____ be!"
6 Word with some or struck
7 Beak
8 Renowned Missourian
9 She grins and bares it
10 Mr. America's source of pride
11 Drivers' org.
12 Talleyrand's "Affair"
13 Character in the "Iliad"
14 Like Burgess's cow
15 "____ cockhorse . . ."
16 ____ sale
17 Dorothea ____ Dix
18 Wall St. abbr.
19 Winner over T.E.D.
27 After yoo or boo
28 Thrall of puzzledom
30 K-S connection
31 Grid linemen
33 Convent dwellers
34 Delivery to a pub
36 ____ spumante
38 N.C.A.A.'s rival
39 Noted U.S. entomologist: 1879–1943
40 D.C. group protecting minorities
44 Calif. pearl-fishing center
45 Mrs. Vernon Castle
46 Two Greek philosophers
48 "____ d'Or," 1909 opera
50 Mansard
52 Home of over 25,000 Garden Staters
54 Japanese straw mat
55 XVII times LIX
56 N.R.C. concern
59 Actress Hagen
61 Hew a yew
62 Manumit
63 R R depot
64 Shade of green
65 Southern African fox
66 Jack of old films: 1903–78
67 Catches red-handed
68 Actress Patricia
70 Damages
76 Rose, for one
77 Set costs of articles before retailing
79 Emulates Gompers
80 12:51
81 Quintet in this puzzle
83 Enzyme
84 Used up
85 Detroit offering
86 College near Phila.
87 Bill, in Nice
91 Young zebra
93 Molasses
94 Variety headline word
95 ". . . to reach ____ of God": Wilde
96 What Lot's wife did
97 A.F.T. rival
99 Aphids
100 Paperboy's cry
101 Whence Cugat came
105 "I do not ____ farthing candle . . . for Handel": Lamb
107 Riverfront men
109 Hijack
111 Ust-____, U.S.S.R. plateau
113 Axlike tool
114 Ewe said it
116 Alpine pastureland
117 Year in the 11th century
118 N.C.O.

172. Addled Activists by Louis Baron

ACROSS

1 Paint on Sundays
5 Santa Anna won here
10 Keys' kin
15 Peeler's target
19 Fire: Prefix
20 "____ is an island"
21 'Tisn't's vulgar cousin
22 Freshwater mussel
23 Stage-door loser
26 Caen's neighbor
27 Domesday Book money
28 What Anne Hathaway hath
29 Alone, on the boards
30 Bacon slice
32 Dicer's lucky throw
34 "Peanuts," e.g.
35 "Duino Elegies" author
36 He could build castles in Spain
37 Gotlander
38 Woodshed sessions
41 Goya duo, for short
44 Horne in the hurdles
46 Virgilian wrath
47 Alike, in Arles
48 Kind of flakes or snow
49 Flag maker's name
50 Leg: Prefix
51 Fox's relative
52 Rainier's daily activity
56 "____ alive!"
57 Magazine Mountain man
59 Mouthward
60 Marmalade tree
61 Corbeled window
62 Spot in Sherwood Forest
63 ". . . to come to the ____ the party"
64 Two points for any eleven
66 Punjab princess
67 Marine mollusks
70 First First Family of the 49th
71 Straphanger Boone
74 Gilbertian peeress
75 Slavonic sprite
76 Companion of spick
77 "Rome of Hungary"
78 Some Feds
79 Wing that can't fly
80 Eve's poor job
84 Hellhound
85 Chains heard from coast to coast
87 Cause euphoria
88 Juan or Salvador
89 Hogback
90 Dentist's advice
91 Retire
95 Top grade
97 Leinsdorf or Korngold
98 Feels blah
99 Outside: Prefix
100 It tans sans sun
101 Greenhouse calamity
105 Big Daddy portrayer
106 What "syne" means
107 Auriculate
108 Musette
109 Nudnik
110 Plains Amerinds
111 "____ Daughter," 1970 movie
112 One Tuesday

DOWN

1 City on the Ouche
2 Where to buy an amphora
3 Tip the derby
4 Storage place
5 Haphazardly
6 Kind of color
7 Seaport in southeast China
8 Mayan language
9 Ballroom oldie
10 Tchaikovsky's "Capriccio ____"
11 Took notice
12 Pure (or impure) fiction
13 Photog's offering
14 People of Graz
15 U.S.S.R. cape
16 Carter-cliffhanger phrase
17 El Bahr
18 Saloon swinger
24 Breathers' needs
25 "____ believe": Mark 9:24
31 Calgary's prov.
33 Orsk's river
34 He had a way with Proust
35 Della from Detroit
37 Finch
38 Certain birds of a feather
39 Say "Shalom"
40 Mudslinging fumarole
41 Flattop on land
42 Kanten
43 Busy unionizer
44 Far from faithless
45 A, B, C, D or F
48 Mudville fans' fanner
50 Flavor
52 Peaks of pique
53 ____ Heights
54 Ten C-notes
55 Spokes
56 He made a beginning with Begin
58 Washington's ____ Theater
60 Shankar plays it
62 Sigurd's steed
63 Atremble
64 See 32 Across
65 Like a tabby
67 Immie's mate
68 First place
69 Hourglass filler
71 Heel stepped on by women
72 Red news feeder
73 O'er's antithesis
76 Sea in an ocean
78 Marchetti of pro football
80 What a hobo rides
81 Guernsey lilies
82 "Alceste" composer
83 Receiver of checkout checks
84 Borgnine role
86 Solomonic to the nth degree
88 Cubes and pyramids
90 "Funny Girl" girl
91 Specified
92 Bathysphere man
93 Eulogize
94 Apportioned potions
95 Drop in the Vegas bucket
96 In the flesh
97 Pianist Balogh
98 Monument site in India
102 Skeet feat
103 Capitol Hill turndown
104 It's heard from a herd

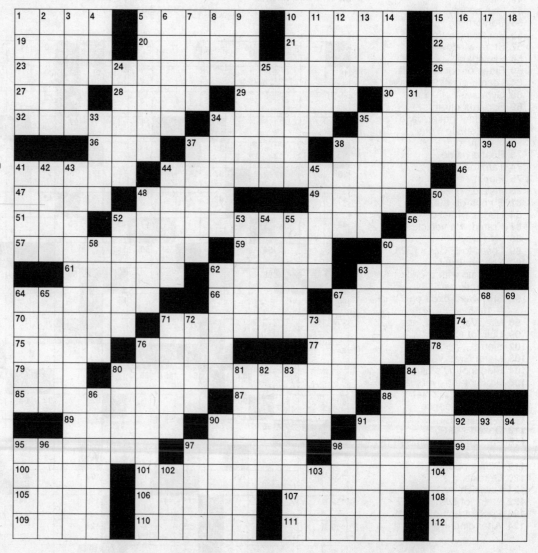

173. The Name of the Game by Jordan S. Lasher

ACROSS

1 Kind of rally
4 Asserts
9 Ocean
13 One of a Nixon sextet
19 Aramis, to Athos
20 City on the Seyhan
21 Hector Hugh Munro
22 Sojourn
23 Version of a game also called mill or merels
26 Shavers of the ring
27 City in Greece
28 Plaster the walls
29 Game played with burning brandy
31 Atlas contents
32 Greeting in Lod
34 Eins plus zwei
35 "Slippery" tree
36 From ___ Z
37 Irving's Bones
38 Astronaut Grissom
40 Courage; spirit
42 Catch
44 ". . . and two if ___"
46 Hairpiece for Sir Roger
49 Turn right
50 Seventh Greek letter
52 By all means: Slang
54 Actress Balin
55 Jacob's vision
57 Gave a hoot
58 Hurting
59 Amused expression
62 "Roberta" composer
63 Spud
64 Kind of ingenuity
66 Seat of Clearwater Co., Idaho
68 Seat of Essex Co., Mass.
69 Teases good-naturedly
70 Boston hockey team
71 Seats for judges
72 New Year's word
73 Lunar New Year in Asia
74 Tweed Ring's nemesis
75 Cabbage or kale
76 A son of Jacob and Leah
78 Suffix for Capri
79 Tall summer drink
81 Celestial sphere
82 Rip off
84 Laurel-derived spice
86 Disney's middle name
88 Doone and Luft
91 Solitudinarian
93 Boyd-___, Peace Prize winner: 1949
94 "Will be," in a Doris Day hit
95 Prescription abbrs.
97 Add up
98 "Country" Slaughter
100 Orchid derivatives
102 Sing like Ella
103 Game played for money in a hat
106 Brian ___, early Irish king
107 Lathered up
108 Famous Borgia
109 Card game also called Earl of Coventry
112 Antarctic coastal area
113 Out of work

114 Silas Marner's foundling
115 "The Greatest"
116 Bears from Waco
117 Opposite of da
118 Mother Goose entry
119 Inventor's monogram

DOWN

1 Jipijapa item
2 Moslem nobleman's bailiwick
3 Table game
4 Muggers on the boards
5 Author of "Fables in Slang"
6 Card game of the all fours family
7 Trouser line
8 Dravidian language
9 Tadzhik or Turkmen: Abbr.
10 Flivvers
11 Four of ___ (high poker hand)
12 Make friendly
13 Ascribed
14 Posterior
15 Eshkol or Eban
16 Cricket variation
17 Manner of speaking
18 "Has Anybody Here ___ Kelly?"
24 Dawn goddess
25 Branch of learning
30 Made a sound
32 Mrs., in Madrid
33 Elimination game
37 Train a tyro
39 Buildings in capital cities
41 Effort
43 ___ Aviv
44 Tennyson crossed it: 1892
45 To the point
47 Belong
48 Most lively
51 Big casino's spot
53 Suffix for musket or cannon
56 Nookeries
58 Crumb toter
59 Friendly chat
60 Textbook insert
61 British keno or lotto game
63 Citrus hybrid
64 U.S. locksmith
65 Pyrenees republic
67 In good shape
68 Pan-fry

69 Poorly played whist
71 Bloke
72 Ditty
75 Fix the boundaries of
76 Sparks's frantic message
77 Part of N.C.O.
79 Suffix with cash or cloth
80 Man on a tylopod
83 Game like chemin de fer
85 "___ the curtains": Cowper
87 Jidda natives
89 Conjunctions
90 Shoulder blade
92 Alarm bell
94 Heavenly being
96 Thwart
97 Gardner's "___ Calls It Murder"
99 Dennis or Duncan
101 See 91 Across
102 ___ Canals
103 Strikebreaker
104 Cold, in Cádiz
105 Rug surface
107 Old dagger
110 Nana, to Wendy
111 Actor Alastair

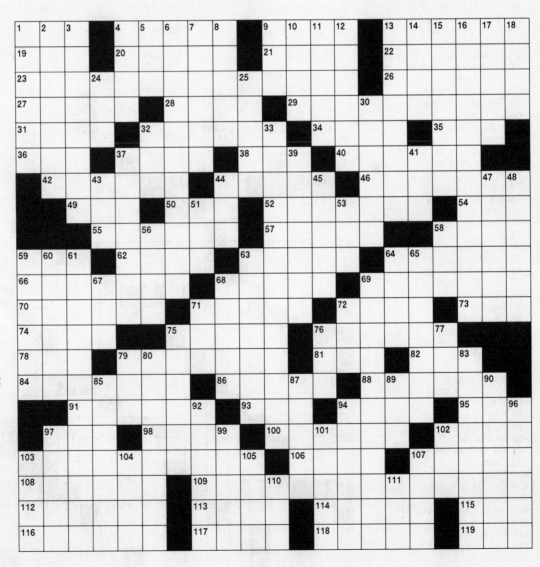

174. Hebdomadness by Jeanette K. Brill

ACROSS

1 Roman in charge of games
6 Aristophanes' "The ____"
11 Word with fettle
15 Masticate
19 Churchill's "enigma"
21 Dido
22 "____ Do This Sum"
24 Vatican tribunal
25 Travolta hit
28 Slayer of Castor
29 Nigerian native
30 Salt maker of sorts
31 Bizarre
32 Common Latin phrase
34 One of the Stooges
35 Canonical hour
36 Rarae ____
37 Power tool
42 Volcano on Martinique
43 One-eyed god
44 N.Y.S.E. item
47 Von Weber opera
48 Sandy Dennis stage vehicle
51 Pallid
52 Pundit
53 Meted out
54 Drudgery
55 ____-majesté
56 Burgoo and matelote
57 Winsor heroine
58 Posts
60 Duomo statue in Firenze
61 Followers of cannon and musket
62 Sand, to Chopin
63 Tureen accessory
64 Jousted
65 U.K. award
66 Female assistant
69 Notables
70 ". . . ditties of ____": Keats
73 Word with Costa or Puerto
74 Graft, as a plant
75 Classify
76 Ex-Dodger outfielder
78 Ossuary
81 Scale
82 ____ Square
83 Affected manner
84 Scottish hillside
85 Sudden thrust
86 Vacuous
87 Fusses
89 Olivia's clown
90 "Candy striper"
91 Fleuret's relative
92 Memento
93 Gross
94 Labor org.
95 "____ This Must Be Belgium"
98 Teach, for one
99 Aye neutralizer
100 Hair style
101 Sword handles
102 Calmed
103 Melville opus
104 First king of Egypt
105 Bacheller hero
106 "King Olaf" composer
108 Episperm
109 Medium's state
112 Saturn's consort

115 Cupid, in art
116 With 18 Down, erstwhile TV show
120 Hookah
121 Caravansary
122 Wear away
123 Rap session of sorts
124 Ilmenite and uraninite
125 Jupati
126 Eclipse cycle
127 "I ____ of Jeanie . . ."

DOWN

1 Gaelic
2 Pair
3 Ratio words
4 Baton Rouge inst.
5 Sometime name for Ireland
6 Singer Newton
7 British princess
8 The slammer
9 Poke occupant
10 Taught
11 XV
12 Champagne buckets
13 Hub
14 Compass dir.
15 "____ and Whispers"
16 Masons' burdens
17 Coup d'____
18 See 116 Across
20 Inflexible
23 Minuscule

26 Lined up
27 Brought into harmony
33 Disavow
35 More recent
36 ____ Ababa
37 Ordered around
38 Subsides
39 Melina Mercouri movie
40 Delineates
41 "____ and Lovers"
42 W.W. II journalist
43 "____ mio"
44 Steinbeck novel
45 Preferences
46 Work with the hands
48 Esteem highly
49 Swedish philanthropist
50 Poet Dickinson
55 Fragrant shrub
57 Make ____ (get rich)
58 "Call Me ____"
59 Joppolo's post
60 Kind of glass or table
62 Where oboli were spent
63 Laps up
64 Salvers
67 "Firefly" composer
68 Resembling a cereal grain
69 Growls
71 Siouan people
72 Reference book
74 Oligophrenia
75 Celestial Eagle
76 Gets one's goat

77 Comaneci
79 Ostrich or emu
80 Requisite
81 Done in
82 Attach
84 Yogi of baseball
86 "Dum ____, spero"
87 Rorschach, etc.
88 Auto pioneer
89 Discomfit
91 Struggles
92 Quitclaims
93 Joins
95 "____ Camera"
96 In ____ (socially active)
97 Range in Utah
102 "Judith" composer
103 Scarebabes
104 Bismuth, e.g.
105 V.P.: 1925–29
106 Kuwaiti chieftain
107 Gait like a canter
108 Fictional mansion
109 Air Force missile
110 Change the décor
111 Supplemented, with "out"
112 Without, in Weimar
113 S.A. rodent
114 Watch part
115 G.I.'s overseas address
117 Onto
118 Refrain syllable
119 Salt

175. Odd Jobs by Maura B. Jacobson

ACROSS

1 Set boundaries
6 Part of h.c.l.
10 Kind of cracker
14 Diamond's "____ Believer"
17 Head garland
19 Leister
20 Type of trial
21 Painter Ernst
22 Junkmen
25 Gird up
26 But, to Ceasar
27 March division
28 "____ Theme . . .": 1966
29 Camembert's cousin
30 Plumber
35 Costa ____
38 Semisweet liqueur
39 "____ Sympathy"
40 Unscrupulous realty agent
46 Mother Hubbard
49 "Rose ____ rose . . ."
50 ____ sequitur
51 Ennis and Crandall
52 Undercover org.
53 Out, in Edam
55 ____ volatile
56 Chooses
58 "____ was saying"
59 Piedmontese citizen
61 Demotic
64 Alcohol-like compound
66 Huguenot center
67 Absalom, to David
68 Florist
71 Printer's bodkin
72 What ecdysiasts do
74 Neural networks
75 Meets the challenge
77 Cape Cod abodes
79 Churchmen: Abbr.
81 Blind feature
82 Before sigma
85 Color or city
86 Free (of)
87 Kind of school
88 "One Day ____ Time"
89 Chiang ____-shek
90 Get in shape
92 Barbers
96 Souk
98 Cytoplasm substance, for short
99 Impulse
100 Butchers
108 W.W. II entente
109 Pick pockets
110 Ski lift
111 Cretan peak
114 Nabors
115 Art dealer
120 Violinist Bull
121 Word for Adenauer
122 Red dye
123 Ventilate thoroughly
124 Cherry or tomato
125 Jubilation
126 Have in tow
127 Nobelist Lagerlöf

DOWN

1 Chem. milieus
2 Anent
3 Tennyson heroine
4 Mar. 15, in Milano
5 Seed covering
6 Math is his forte
7 ". . . slowly ____ the lea"
8 In a mournful way
9 Foot the bill
10 Soothing one
11 Mohammed's favorite wife
12 Chemin de ____
13 Forage plant
14 Japanese porcelain ware
15 "West Side Story" song
16 Choppers
18 Griffin
19 Sea duck
23 Through: Prefix
24 High ridges
29 Alphabetic quartet
30 Resinous substance
31 Adult acorn
32 Wheel, in Avila
33 Zenith's opposite
34 "In thunder, lightning, or ____?": Shak.
35 Scorecard letters
36 Bergman role in "Casablanca"
37 Miner
41 Rounded ornament
42 Clearance
43 Like a moose or stag
44 Teacher's homework item
45 Root
47 Lawyer
48 Fiber for cordage
52 Side dish
54 Gumshoe
57 Appeases hunger
59 "No man is a hero ____ valet"
60 Without a chaser
62 "Step ____!"
63 Bandicoot
65 Dayan's land: Abbr.
67 Dark ale
69 Books of records
70 Gaucho's item
72 Place for a P.T.A.
73 Outcast
76 Pentacle
78 Tokyo's Broadway
80 Camilla of films
83 ____ fire (pend)
84 Beauvais's department
87 Zoroastrian
91 Basics
92 Hallstand
93 Serpent follower
94 Marat's colleague
95 Press for payment
97 Having a handle
100 Hoople or Barbara
101 Prospero, e.g.
102 Covered with frost
103 Worked in a regatta
104 Kind of board or walker
105 Nigerian native
106 Actress Thompson
107 Bird life
111 Teraph
112 "Te ____"
113 Canine of flicks
115 Shopper's need
116 Right angle
117 Former rural-credit org.
118 Captain's boat
119 Yorkshire river

176. Malaprop Pops Up Again! by Bert H. Kruse

ACROSS

1 Peridot
6 Poet Shapiro
10 E.r.a. or r.b.i.
14 "High ___ Windy Hill"
17 End of a Stein line
18 Roosevelt and Teasdale
19 Hemidemisemiquaver
20 Robert ___ Sherwood
22 Mail service, to M.
24 M.'s name for Athens's famous height
26 Sommer from Berlin
27 Final disposal
28 Fight
30 ___ of quinine
31 Polytheistic
32 Kind of pool
33 Salver
34 Undrafted mil. group
37 Mouths
38 Don't, in Dundee
40 German emperors
43 Treat under glass
46 M.'s considered opinions
49 Actress Hagen
51 Worsted
52 Life of Riley
54 Stew
55 ___ Penh
56 Harvested alfalfa, e.g.
57 Public-utility magnate of the 30's
59 Sailing problem
60 Iraqi port
61 Killer whales
62 Pyknic
63 "Ripeness ___": King Lear
65 Shipbuilder's strip of wood
66 Father ___, in a Wolff opera
67 M. identifies a certain law
69 Netherlandish
70 Film awards
72 S.A. port, for short
73 Pacify
74 Dahlias' kin
75 M.'s word for future generations
79 Wander idly
82 One not dry behind the ears
83 Skipper's order
84 City in Ohio
85 Except
86 Face with stone
87 Word to a dog
88 Caught lepidopterans
90 Santo ___, Philippine university
91 Lulu
92 Tenderhearted one
94 Banker's decision
95 U.S.S.R. monetary unit
96 Merry, in Metz
97 What M. learned
99 Secy. of the ___ (Cabinet post, to M.)
102 They use gins to get skins
105 "Half Mile Down" author
107 Measure of area
108 Blaster's need
109 Tiny chorine
110 These make some love N.Y.
112 Creator of the Moffats
114 Sugar, e.g.
117 Large barges
118 Aristocles
119 Shock
123 M. gets a medical checkup
125 M.'s sharp perceptions
127 Practical
128 Bore
129 Ex___ (one-sided)
130 Religious society of Iowa
131 British collation
132 Canasta item
133 More underhanded
134 Rhode Island Red

DOWN

1 Play tricks
2 Of an age
3 Solve, as a puzzle
4 Commune near Padua
5 Hawaiian wreath
6 Greek letter
7 Here and there
8 Wood file
9 W.W. II craft
10 Jam that's not sweet
11 "Rob Peter ___ Paul"
12 Surmounting
13 L.A.P.D. member
14 Insecticide, for short
15 Hatching post
16 Fit to ___
18 Madison Ave. product
20 Athenian's homeland
21 "Light of ___!": Herbert
23 Soprano Lucine
25 Tense for Thucydides
28 Transmit
29 Director René
31 Propounded
32 Genuflect
33 Late great jazz pianist
34 Outcome
35 Having an uneven gloss
36 M.'s singular vascular problem
39 Sends forth
40 Hillock
41 M. ranges from A to Z
42 Part of a London building
44 Jaques' septet
45 M.'s lessees
47 Portuguese colony off China
48 Parisienne's peer
50 Galsworthy's "___ of Devon"
53 Fox of southern Africa
57 Herd of seals
57 Building steel
58 Relationship
60 Lt. col.'s group
62 Kind of seal
64 Fret on a guitar
65 Channel markers
67 Gift for milady
68 Jog
69 Was foolishly fond
71 Filet mignon source
73 Cousins of satyrs
74 Punta ___, Chile
75 Buonarroti masterpiece
76 Holy Grail, e.g.
77 Inter
78 Singer Coolidge
80 King Arthur's final home
81 Painted ___, Ariz.
82 Tar's quaff
83 Ring blows
85 Off-key
87 Very old
89 Red ___ (southern African shrubs)
90 Last of a Hemingway title
92 Play start
93 Be rude in a crowd
98 Sources of archers' bows
100 Not so slovenly
101 Refrigerant
103 Dismay
104 Husband of Pocahontas
106 Where to catch congers
110 Squama
111 Buddy of rock fame
113 "A votre ___!"
114 Occlude
115 Poet laureate after Shadwell
116 Where Bhutan is
117 Cicatrix
118 Resound
119 Iwo ___
120 Singer Anita
121 Unaspirated
122 Winter Palace resident
124 N.Y.C. or Balt.
125 G.I. aides to cooks
126 Gal of songdom

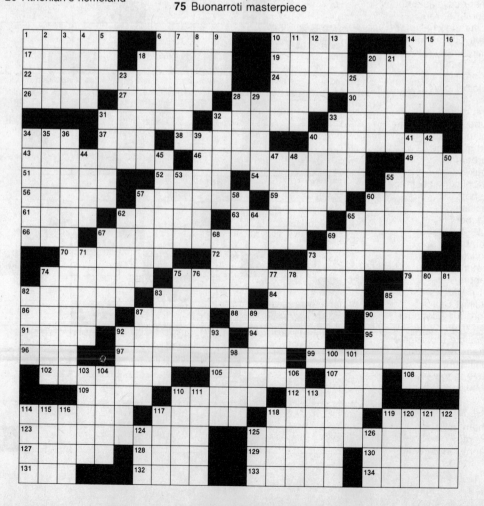

177. Old-Fashioned Challenger by C. J. Angio

ACROSS

1 Nudges
5 Steep slope
10 Thaumaturgy
15 Maguey center in Mexico
19 Moonfish
20 Relating to stakes
21 Japanese pottery center
22 Vendition
23 Prophesy
25 Gibberish
27 Londoner's lift
28 Plastics source
30 Habit; custom
31 Busy as ____
32 Buttons
33 Companionway
35 Character in "The Rivals"
37 Hagiologist's topic
39 Thespian
43 The clear sky
44 Bookworm
46 Desinence
47 Erudition
48 Summon
49 Cut down
50 Large number
51 Without limit
52 Linguists
56 Mezzo-soprano Marilyn
57 Fledgling
59 Oenochoes
60 Rush wildly
61 Mt. Ida maiden
62 French toast
63 City NE of Boston
64 Almondy drink
66 Japanese-American
67 Ineffectual
70 Largest asteroid
71 Science comparing computers with man's nervous system
74 Forty winks
75 Wellaway!
76 Like a quidnunc
77 Nurse shark
78 Asian evergreen
79 Embouchure
80 Giraffes
84 Growing out
85 Gain
87 Freshets
88 Integuments
89 Liberals in Canada
91 Football's Panthers, for short
92 Pillow cover
93 Ambling horse
96 Henry the sculptor
98 Most fuliginous
102 Scientific study of colors
104 Temperance
106 Autocrat
107 "Cosi fan ____"
108 Small combos
109 One of triplets
110 "____ Came Running": Jones
111 Weltanschauung
112 Due e cinque
113 Family branch

DOWN

1 Zeus, to Nero
2 Cacholong
3 Channel for molten metal
4 Noisy, mock serenade
5 Wrongs deliberately
6 Buckeye or piroque
7 Opposite of apteral
8 Bandicoot
9 Succeed
10 Type of dynamo
11 Not in
12 Annoys
13 "Lord, is ____?": Matt. 26:22
14 Madison Ave. drive
15 Suddenly
16 Rue de la ____
17 Jai ____
18 G.I. refectory
24 Pole in a Scottish sport
26 Rebel
29 Fire: Comb. form
32 Picasso or Casals
34 Unbends
35 In harmony
36 Write in letters of gold
37 Horizontal timber
38 Earth or baseball
40 Like dross
41 Vacant
42 More bizarre
43 Joie de vivre
44 TV pioneer
45 Linen marking
48 Thimblerig
50 City in Canada
52 Nul tiel records
53 Hire
54 One having legal title
55 Arrive
56 Forces to go to court
58 Robles and wicopies
60 First to stab Caesar
62 Sorceresses
63 Four for Goren
64 Silver Springs's neighbor
65 Vestige
66 Big Board initials
68 Preserves
69 Germany's Count von ____
71 Celestial streaker
72 Plume
73 Moppets
76 Direct a jet
78 To them, stones have souls
80 One of the Moluccas
81 Sets against
82 Match
83 Certifies
84 Muse for Sappho
86 Neglect
88 Cry from Richard III
90 Vulcan
92 Not ____ (mediocre)
93 Cuts for agts.
94 Chan's exclamation
95 Three scruples
97 Eight: Comb. form
98 Brochette
99 Brontë heroine
100 Minx
101 Yurt or marquee
103 Word of disapproval
105 Mispickel is one

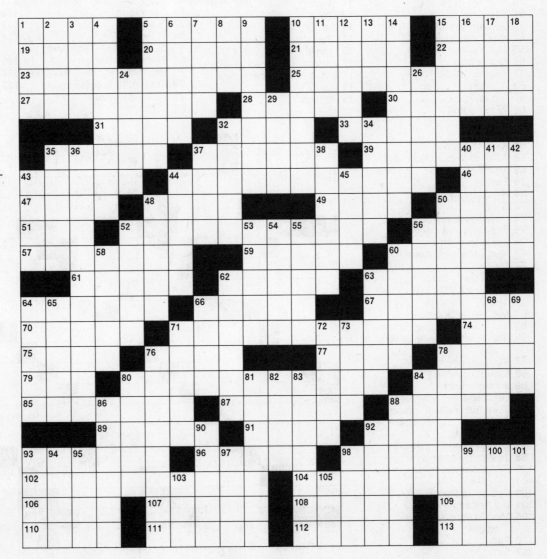

178. Literary Relativity by Hal R. Hollinger

ACROSS

1 Like Kate, as a wife
6 Son of Eric the Red
10 Moon crater
15 Coronet's cousin
20 Cat-quick
21 Brother of Brynhild
22 Reserved
23 Sitting pretty
24 Orwell prediction for 1984
26 Educe
27 Suffix for Rock
28 Fair to middling
29 "The ____," rock group
30 "In ____ are many mansions": John 14:2
33 Declines
35 Sessions for Borg
36 Take ____ the lam
37 Sch. for shavetails
40 Prefix with chance
41 Part of Caesar's trio
42 Sends back to the Hill
46 Like April, proverbially
48 Back of a leaf
49 Black-and-blue
50 Relative of H.I.M.
51 Hopeless cases
52 Sohrab, to Rustum
53 Make interesting
55 Much-wived Henry
56 Creil's river
57 Behave badly
59 Anatomical passage
60 Dig for data
61 Wood sorrel
62 Olga, Masha and Irina
66 Binge
67 Kind of mother
68 Actor in "Four Daughters"
69 Milieu of "Mother Courage"
70 Banish
71 Sleep lightly
73 Spile
74 Herodias's daughter
75 Provision in a contract
76 Made-to-order kin
77 Item for a high-stepper
78 Dir.
81 ____ l'oeil
82 She wrote "My Life's History"
84 Mrs. Weller's boy
85 Les Folies Bergère, for one
86 Sleuth with a "number one son"
87 Plaintive poem
88 Canton is here
89 Western team
90 Discipline
93 "Life with Father" name
94 Author of "Eight Cousins"
96 Telpher, e.g.
97 Mother Seton's mainstay
98 Jewish ceremonial dinner
100 Special article
101 Tangles
103 Castor, to Pollux
104 Adj. for some verbs
105 Mrs. Skelton's favorite color?
106 Fearful, in a way
107 Satisfy
108 Walking ____

110 Lear production
116 One of the Cole family
117 Uniform, in Paris
121 Furuncles
122 Lubricator
123 Ivan Petrovich Voinitsky
126 Montague's offspring
127 Swann's wife
128 Somersault
129 President: father or son
130 Inexorable
131 Wield a divining rod
132 One of 52
133 Mrs. Rochester's kin

DOWN

1 Sugar daddy pickups
2 Exchange premium
3 Russian planes
4 Ell
5 "____ Rosenkavalier"
6 Like some detergents
7 Group character
8 ____ du Diable
9 Company
10 Anagram for Oriental
11 Skips
12 Loads
13 Part of HOMES
14 Chesapeake Bay is one
15 Fragile footing
16 Perform Gregorian chants
17 Island in the Near group
18 Bambi's aunts
19 Recess

22 Purpose of the DEW line
25 Some of the haves
31 River to the North Sea
32 She wrote about Mrs. Reynolds
34 Little, e.g.
37 First U.S. Postmaster General
38 Option
39 Lawrence relationships
41 Mother of Aeneas
42 Cleaves
43 Time for Alice, Allegra and Edith
44 Hot-plate holder
45 Less gregarious
47 "My Wife's a Winsome ____ Thing": Burns
48 Has one's say in the U.S.A.
49 Quart in a London pub
52 Part of "I Remember Mama"
54 Belgian steel center
55 Viper's defense
57 Rebel
58 Car part
60 Storage places
62 Barnstorm
63 Bow neck
64 Tolerate
65 "____ Along," 1959 song
66 She has a ball at a ball
70 Mrs. Miller's naïve daughter
72 Branch, to a botanist
73 Edit subjectively
74 "El ropo"

75 King Minos was one
76 Evel Knievel upheaval
77 Vilification
79 To be born, in Brest
80 Overplayed
81 Cease-fire
82 Indian river landings
83 A Pilgrim Father
86 Time of your life
88 Mo. for hobgoblins
90 Proofreader's mark
91 Make a guess
92 Couturier's annual surprise
94 Charge with gas
95 Gulls, terns, etc.
97 Cringes and flatters
99 Pickle
100 At long last
102 User of spads and brads
107 Scientist's concern
108 Tante's husband
109 Rough's partner
110 Digests, for short
111 Corsair's quest
112 Thorny tree
113 Image: Comb. form
114 Took a Concorde
115 Mongol tent
118 Snarl
119 Contemporary French author
120 Bonnie bairn
124 Hide ____ hair
125 ____ victis

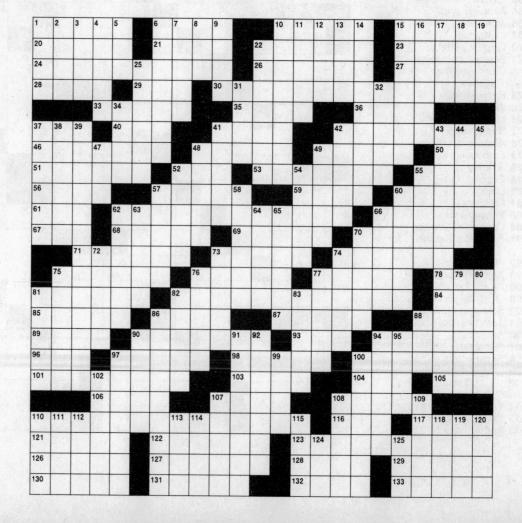

179. Charades by Alfio Micci

ACROSS

1 Humid
5 "Time ___ the essence"
9 Lecturer's aid
14 Rudiments
17 Notion
18 Sinuses
19 Logrolling contest
20 Emporium
22 Wardens
24 Averse to writing research papers
26 Circus people
27 Seabees' motto
29 Rock salt
30 TV appendage
31 Cant
32 Wild
33 Seine
34 Urgency
35 Cape hartebeest
36 Humane org.
39 Where a native will clue you in
41 Very softly: Mus. dir.
44 Your, in Hanover
45 Gugelhupf
46 Some, in Spain
47 Raja ___, Indian novelist
48 Philippine tree
49 A man's enunciation
53 Choreographer Kurt
55 Elec. unit
56 Hippolyte's sire
57 Racket
58 Ardor
59 Beam
61 Briefly brilliant stars
62 Curtain recently opened
63 Popular health food
64 Sourdough
65 Watson's cry
66 ___-la-la
68 Mites
69 Allotments in Cluny
71 Fleming or Smith
72 Trading place: Abbr.
73 Word on a door
74 Lyrical literature
75 Blockhead
76 Compass reading
77 Cutie Knievel guided
81 Tooth surface
82 Triangle
83 "Let's Make ___"
84 Holiday, for short
85 Becoming
87 City east of Erie
88 Some are à trois
92 "Rigoletto" setting
93 Cousin of a union
94 Steep in a pickling solution
95 Hinder nice blokes
97 Country without women
99 Natives of: Suffix
100 Finnish lake, to Swedes
101 Sheeplike
102 Lab burner
103 Tate offering
104 Shipment from Iraq
105 Wendy Darling's dog
106 Quiescence

DOWN

1 Pronouncements
2 Bedeck
3 Egyptian amulet
4 G. & S. heroine
5 Hindu god of thunder
6 Cécile and Jeanne
7 Retiree of hockey fame
8 Mussolini was one
9 Agriculturist
10 Sonata movement
11 Kind of saxophone
12 Architect I. M.
13 Fiery bosses
14 Menotti heroine
15 Washbowl
16 Minoan's home
18 Concerning
21 Mao ___-tung
23 Nine: Comb. form
25 Injures
28 Feed the kitty
31 Divided, as highways
32 Papal vestment
34 B.S.A. outings
35 Birchbark
36 Verdi opera
37 Fake jewelry
38 Shore up an entryway
39 Item spent in Praha
40 Rainer
41 Snead swing
42 Former Ph.D. tests
43 Luxurious
45 Insert mark
49 Kind of arch?
50 Hole-___
51 Shelter
52 Jeweled band
53 He wrote "What Maisie Knew"
54 Sphere
58 Cautions
60 Kolinsky, e.g.
61 Special position
62 Expressed dislike
63 Sweet potatoes
64 "Three Sisters" character
65 He overthrew Fulgencio
67 Broadway org.
69 Robust
70 Hydrocarbon
73 Tiresome person grew old
75 Wine bottle
77 Object
78 Gladstones' kin
79 Biographer of 53 Down
80 Entices
81 Craze
82 Execrate
84 Sci-fi pioneer
85 Andalusian song
86 Diarize
87 Bizarre
88 ___ cum laude
89 Offenbach's "___ Parisienne"
90 Short jackets
91 Body meeting in Paris
92 Year in Luther's time
93 Punkie
94 Conduit
96 Sofia's predecessor
98 Dam org.

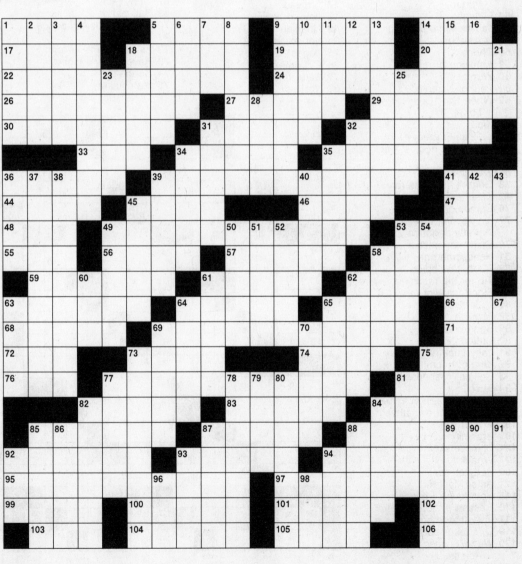

180. April Showers by Frances Hansen

ACROSS

1 Proxy
6 Not together
11 Vestment
16 Relative of rain
20 Possible Easter topper
21 Community character
22 April 5, in old Rome
23 Bogus
24 Dixon/Rose/Warren query
28 Botanist Gray
29 Did a prelaundry job
30 Oligophrenic
31 Stockholm gnome
32 Family-tree twigs: Abbr.
34 Rock group
35 Strength
36 Check
37 Part of speech
39 Gudrun's husband
40 Galosh
41 Kahal/Wheeler/Fain rainy-day advice
52 Remarque or Segal
53 Where to put your dough
54 City celebrated by Cole Porter
55 Fitting
56 Japanese verse form
57 Nectarous
58 Chose
59 Antelope or drum
60 Wonts
61 Paul or Nicholas
62 When Gary Coleman will be 34
63 Kibitz
64 ____ soup (heavy fog)
65 "____, you noblest English"
66 Wettish
67 Wedge-shaped
68 Gene Kelly exuberance
72 Easel adjunct
76 Carries on
77 ". . . spring time, the ____ pretty ring time": Shak.
78 Rainy-day prize
81 Handsome one
82 "Ooh, that hurts!"
83 Tie for the races
85 Flood follower
86 ____ incognita
87 Alighieri
89 Short-billed rail
90 Cotton cloth
91 Lady Luck reigns here
92 Kind of boom
93 Roll-call response
94 Bucolic
95 Como admission in 1946
101 Opposite of aweather
102 Abrupt
103 Brahmin
104 Chinese skiff
107 Whack
109 Petty officer
111 Actor Montand
115 Sourdough's concern
116 Rossetti's "____ Beatrix"
117 ____-than-thou
119 U.N. labor body
120 Wood/Fulmer reply to 24 Across
124 Cremona name

125 Emanations
126 Possible port in a storm
127 Scene of Dec.–March rains
128 Springy, in a way
129 Foam; froth
130 Jurymen
131 Side dishes

DOWN

1 Fighting
2 A Canadian transient
3 Part of E.R.A.
4 Not any, to the D.A.
5 Spreads hay
6 Cupids
7 Sulks
8 Provence city
9 "Spring Song" author
10 Tut's cousin
11 Portia saved his skin
12 He wrote "Esther Waters"
13 Under guidance
14 Actor in "The Rain People": 1969
15 Meek's partner in comics
16 Part of a ship's bow
17 "I loved ____ . . .": Wither
18 Holm or key
19 Albanian coin
23 Not so rainy
25 Dogpatch name
26 A Brontë
27 Garb formally
33 Noshes

35 Tax or dental compound
36 Sultan's son in "The Arabian Nights"
38 ____ Peak, N.M.
39 Red as ____
40 "You bet!"
41 Abate, as rain
42 Blot out
43 Skin ailment
44 Like Gray's herd
45 Square
46 Arrogant
47 Emu or ostrich
48 Chew the scenery
49 ____ hand (helped out)
50 On the up and up
51 Do penance
57 Rhone feeder
58 Leaves out
59 Easter ____
61 Fits of temper
62 "April is the cruellest . . ."
63 Erected
65 Old Rome's port
66 Popular pie
67 Tippy boat
69 Satirical
70 Sinuous Eastern dance
71 Cradle
72 Father: Comb. form
73 Revoke, as a legacy
74 Doone
75 Matriculate
78 "Aïda" debuted here

79 Attorney ____
80 Ding-a-ling things
83 "____ We All?"
84 Puppeteer Tony
85 Contemptible
87 Senior member
88 Faulkner hero
89 Sylvan spring sound
90 Ian Fleming character
92 Deli offering
96 Large deer
97 Most discerning
98 Singer Yma
99 Baseball plays
100 ____ tube
104 Rascal
105 "____ should have a good memory"
106 An Alou of baseball
107 Aquarium fish
108 Guffaws
109 Game akin to roulette
110 More mature
112 Banky of silents
113 Funny-bone locale
114 Oriental legumes
116 "____ Skies," Berlin prediction
117 Strop
118 Seamstress Betsy
120 Existed
121 Place
122 Sass
123 Shastri of India

181. Proper Nomenclature by Richard Silvestri

ACROSS

1 Due follower
4 Welfare
8 Alias
11 Assuage
17 Already, in Bonn
19 Lars Porsena was one
21 For example
22 Fields comedy classic
24 Dutch genre display
25 Arch in a vault
26 Sought coal
27 Summer coolers
28 Looie's aide
29 Sid's co-star
31 Where Perry triumphed
32 Dandy's partner
33 Piece of wisdom
34 A place for fins
39 Lugubrious
42 Gaelic
43 Petty quarrel
44 "Hard ___!"
45 City in Mo.
46 Woodland deity
48 King beater
49 Begat
51 Read a meter
52 Esthetic movement
56 Mulligrubs
57 Wood sorrel
60 Buffalo, for one
61 Leeds's river
62 Conditional release
63 Efface
65 Moffo and Pavlova
66 Certain steeplejack
67 Optimally
68 Title Mac held
69 Special
70 Pres. and prem.
71 Doctor
72 Urban noisemaker
74 Merit
75 Type of cigar
77 Hang loosely
78 First P.M. of India
83 Envelope abbr.
84 Type of deck
85 Powerful bloc
87 Grandmother of Timothy
88 N.B.A. whistler
89 Garb of young Sinatra's fans
93 Nard
94 Miasma
96 Easy: Scot.
97 Scoop, e.g.
99 Actor from Dublin
101 Chevet
102 Delays, to D.A.'s
104 Start of a hole
105 Oxidized
107 Ball-park fare
110 Acclivity
111 Circular diamond
112 Silkworms
113 Combinations for Serkin
114 Suffix with malt
115 Crucifix
116 Shivaree

DOWN

1 "___ of heraldry . . .": Gray
2 Rifle
3 Champlevé
4 ". . . ___ the worst too young!": Kipling
5 To be: Fr.
6 Desiccated
7 Director Jean-___ Godard
8 University in Nova Scotia
9 Hoopster Abdul-Jabbar
10 Connectives
11 Draft org.
12 External
13 Immense quantity
14 Bathrobe material
15 Knack
16 Actual being
17 Stars' companions
18 Foolish fancy
20 Omar from Alexandria
23 "Delta of Venus" author
30 Colour
31 Ouphe
32 Skedaddled
35 Restive
36 Place
37 Banking game
38 Violinist ___ Bull
40 Benefited
41 Graham's group
47 Bigot
48 A.B.A. member
49 Celestial being
50 Sherbets
51 Miffed
53 Fissure
54 This is often grande
55 City in NW France
56 Carlsbad attraction
57 Carousing
58 Cheap
59 One way to dine
62 Nap
64 Spare
65 Hebrew instrument
66 Inclined plane
69 Loose garment
72 Mock
73 Waugh or Templeton
75 Cordon bleu
76 Part of Borg's game
79 Verve
80 Breed of dairy cattle
81 Where the jet set may get wet
82 Democrats' adjective for Grant
84 Play a role
85 Belgian port
86 Cry of contempt
90 Copies, for short
91 Mild medicinal beverage
92 Rode the waves
93 Become enraged
95 Board
98 Greek letter
99 Bric-a-___
100 Cattail
101 Hairdo
102 Grain sorghum
103 European capital
106 Skid-row affliction
108 Waxlike: Comb. form
109 Part of TNT

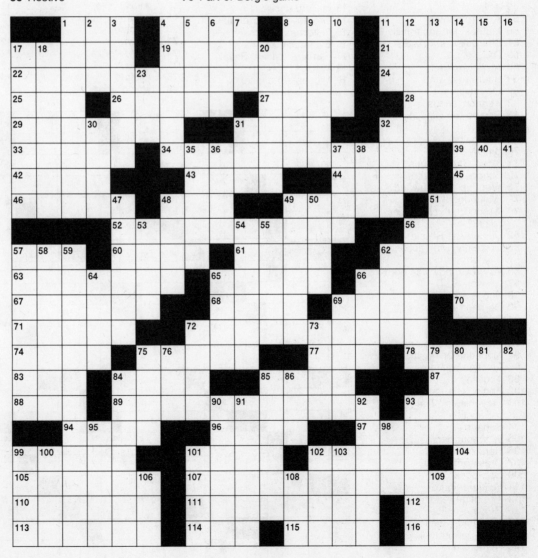

182. Globaloney by William Lutwiniak

ACROSS

1 Eschews food
6 Fitzgerald specialty
10 Cumulus
14 Balances
20 Active
21 Memorable hostess
22 Hep
23 Taxonomic categories
24 Thames Tugboat Co.'s slogan?
27 Abaft
28 Ending with myth or iron
29 Brier
30 Tumuli
32 Conceit
33 Caused turbulence
35 Pied-à-____
36 Tree-lined walk
39 One or more
40 Lackaday!
41 Not so
42 Daedalian
43 Norm: Abbr.
44 Cnemis or zygoma
45 Thrall
46 Used an ottoman
49 Jell
52 A votre santé!
56 Material for some mills
57 Sierra Nevada resort
59 Dau., e.g.
60 Arctic explorer
61 Southwest wind
62 On in years
63 Kennel sounds
65 Scrape the windshield
66 Former
68 Abrogated
70 Smithy
71 "____ Street Blues"
72 School threesome
73 Went up the Irrawaddy
77 Whiffenpoof word
80 "Angélique" composer: 1927
82 City on the Rhone
83 Cowardly, lyin', fictional fatso
85 When Grundy was born
87 Networks
88 Sends soaring
90 Do handwork
91 Prior (to)
92 Doughboy's ally
93 Prefix with form or cycle
94 Marianne or Thomas
95 Election winners
96 Tequila?
102 Ending with part or vint
103 Trevanian's "The ____ Sanction"
104 Sedans
105 Worn-out horses
106 Harp on
107 Dress ornament
109 O.T. book
111 Folklore figure
112 Tire-gage reading
115 Gross injustice
117 Held and Neagle
118 Rock-drilling tool
120 Número uno
121 Burgeon

123 Large white goose
124 ____ Field, Dallas airport
125 Luster
128 Subsidized housing in Riyadh?
131 Michener book
132 Pierrot's Pierrette, perhaps
133 Brusque
134 Undergoing vertigo
135 Abandon
136 Uses a shuttle
137 Viet ____
138 Hotbeds

DOWN

1 Bluebeard's last wife
2 Depth charge
3 Unshaken
4 Kind of deed
5 Sellout notice
6 Word on a dollar
7 Gators' cousins
8 Code word for A
9 ____ Aviv
10 Bridge assets
11 Undergo
12 Reconciled
13 Mallard's milieu
14 Org. for Trevino et al.
15 Followers of ens
16 Eventually
17 Farmers outside Beirut?
18 Misdid
19 Mideastern capital
21 Imbue
25 Opulence
26 Foo yong
31 Pay
34 Fritter
35 Sunbathes
37 "Hello, Dolly!" name
38 The birds
41 Paddock youngsters
42 Farrell's "Bernard ____"
44 Smuts, e.g.
45 Spread out
47 Martian: Comb. form
48 Duration
49 Brenda or Kay
50 Gung-ho
51 Cardiff memorabilia?
53 Traffic
54 Gluck's output
55 Put on
58 Parabasis
61 Trouble
63 Kudos
64 Triton
65 Crowns of furnaces
66 Stripes from strokes
67 Famed film official: 1879–1954
69 Environs
70 Collapse
71 Squawk
74 King of Persia
75 Warble
76 Subjoin
78 Flaming

79 Pursuing
81 Army unit: Abbr.
84 Ring windup
85 Letters
86 ____ account
87 "Dead Souls" author
88 Dollops
89 Persons
92 Flower features
94 ____ David
96 Recital
97 Maui dance
98 Elaborate
99 Smyrna export
100 Hybridize a shrub
101 Keel-shaped part
108 Regard highly
109 ____-all (smart aleck)
110 Hardens
111 Tea type
112 Inquiries
113 Muscovites' council
114 Paragons
115 Swift
116 Playa clay
117 Scent
118 Ship's officer
119 Iceblink
122 City map
123 Commune near Caen
126 Letter opener
127 Boater, e.g.
129 Media network
130 Managed

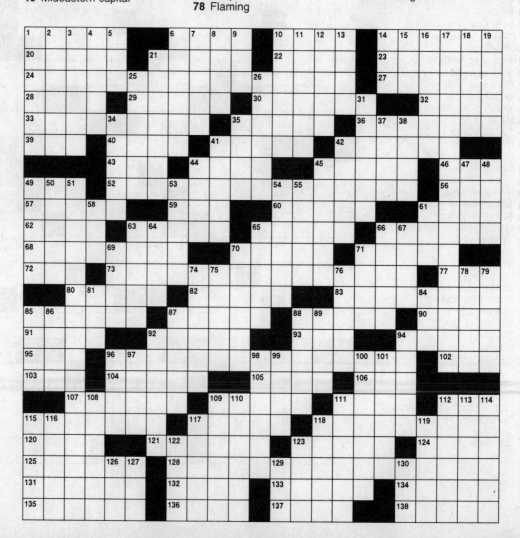

183. Human Nature by John M. Samson

ACROSS

1 Chicago club
5 Pilfer
10 Charitable gifts
14 Slightly open
18 Danny's histrionic daughter
19 Not ___ in the world
20 Tide type
21 Part
22 Inlet
24 Festival
25 Son of Judah
26 Work periods
27 Gale's biting force
30 Lake Victoria, e.g.
32 Strangers
33 Holding the bag at Shea
34 Browns
35 Make more suitable
40 Panamanian coins
44 Seneca, Cayuga, etc.
46 Afoot, in Quebec
47 Bully
51 Twain's grave site
52 Lurch
53 One-billionth: Prefix
54 Temple
57 Bedouin chief
58 Bergen
60 Useful quality
61 Doughnut-shaped
63 Calm spot amid turbulence
68 Rocky debris
69 Watson's 5's, 7's, etc.
70 Blanched
73 Was in the red
77 The best
78 Akin
79 ___ voce (orally)
80 Strike out
82 Gantry and Fudd
84 Gold, e.g.
85 Mojave plants
89 Ike's boyhood home
91 "Dum spiro, ___"
92 ". . . break ___ of steel": Chapman
93 Adorns
96 ___ BILLS (sign on a wall)
98 Pivotal areas
103 Neighborhood
108 Fixation
109 Strain
110 Age, of old
111 Calif. spot for Mr. America
113 Brake part
114 "B.C." character
115 "Set me as ___ upon thine heart"
116 Ant
117 Wail
118 Nine: Comb. form
119 Old Spanish coins
120 Clark's friend

DOWN

1 ___ blanche
2 Largest lake in Iran
3 Tow-colored
4 Pine, e.g.
5 Temp. type
6 Summer drink
7 Devices using light rays
8 Malayan dagger
9 Prelim race
10 Luandan
11 Foliating
12 Natives of Valletta
13 Hall-of-Famer Warren
14 In line
15 Singer Mitchell
16 Ladd or Mowbray
17 Split
18 TV hit
23 Ethiopian lake
28 ___ hand (humble)
29 "___ 'ot sand an' ginger . . .": Kipling
31 Cooking abbr.
36 Title Christie held
37 Tamiroff
38 Beautiful woman
39 Emperor
40 Undisguised
41 Mimicked
42 Feudal lord
43 Make fast, as a rope
44 View from a range
45 Holy Grail, e.g.
48 Podiatrist's concern
49 ___ in (withdraws)
50 Crook in a branch
54 Cause of a bong or dong
55 Pie fancier
56 "Trinity" author
59 ___ integra
60 Hair style
62 Zucchetto, e.g.
64 Group of eight
65 ___ and Thummim
66 Type of orange
67 Bon ton
71 John, in Wales
72 Peace ___, R.I.
73 Ends' friends
74 Emulate Niobe
75 Besides
76 Does
81 Kind of sphere or phyte
82 Curve into an arch
83 Mosel tributary
84 Designate falsely
86 Area between the fetlock and hoof
87 Joint
88 Ancestry
90 "___ Beautiful Sea," 1914 song
93 "___ Is Not a Home": Adler
94 Gulf of Suez neighbor
95 Spanky of "Our Gang," e.g.
97 Mature
99 Kind of scope or meter
100 African lake discovered by Livingstone
101 Leaders like Mussolini
102 Specific heat: Abbr.
103 "The Turtle" poet
104 Reverberate
105 Victuals
106 Ship's backbone
107 Khayyám
112 Certain notebooks: Abbr.

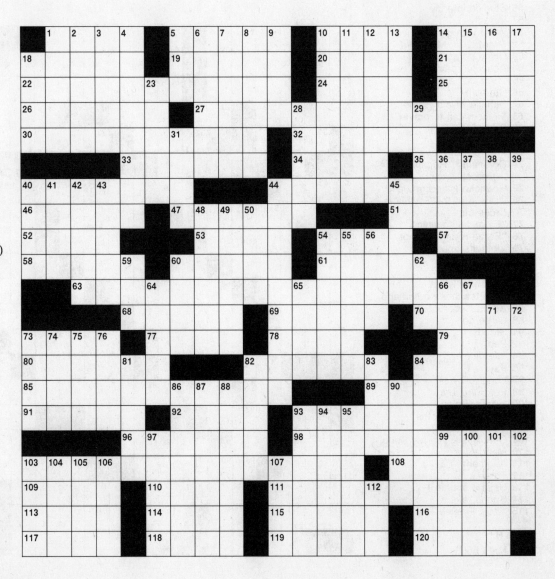

184. Informal Garden by Reginald L. Johnson

ACROSS

1 Chatter
7 Rank
13 Importunes
17 Kind of floor
18 Dana and Greeley
20 Johnny of N.F.L. fame
23 Sound system
24 Royal trimming
26 Comical Harold
27 Heavy hammers
29 Famed Florentine
30 Map abbr.
31 H.S.T., ____, J.F.K.
32 Bridle part
33 Kind of car
35 Early furrier
37 ". . . but as ____, it ain't": Carroll
40 Creek
41 Guide
42 Pelagic bird
44 Sugar Bill
49 Twosomes: Abbr.
50 Orderly
52 Garden need
53 Rely on
55 "G.W.T.W." character
56 Studied intently
57 In fact
61 Word with glass or ice
62 Great ____, Mont.
63 China item
64 Acapulco parrot
65 "Serpico" author
66 Cut away
67 Scholar of old Rome
68 Moslem call to prayer
69 Part of U.S.S.R.
70 A.k.a.
71 Preprandial prayer
72 Colonel in "Hogan's Heroes"
73 Roanoke Island group
75 Division of the Scythians
76 Cross out
77 "From ____ shining . . ."
78 "Battle Hymn" author
79 Vintner's apparatus
80 Arab's garb
82 King's O.K.
85 Measures of wt.
86 Latin teacher's command
88 Ad ____ (pertinent)
89 Large dog
91 Steed
92 Pop
94 Interdict
95 Paul
97 Long follower
98 Puccini opera
100 Mosconi ploy
102 She wrote "Moths"
104 Coop group
108 Chaplin's "____ My Song"
110 Mandatory
111 Augment
112 Forty-____
113 Uses a shuttle
114 Spring, e.g.
115 "____ Fideles"

DOWN

1 Main point
2 Fed the kitty
3 Sob sister
4 Battle site in Wars of the Roses
5 Palter
6 Biblical country
7 Compensate
8 Matured
9 Bows, e.g.
10 Inhabitant of: Suffix
11 Refusal, in Rennes
12 Book of religious chants
13 "La Bohème" highlight
14 Dislodge from office
15 Zero
16 One with a gun for a run
19 Kind of dragon
21 Mason and Plummer
22 Prognosticator
25 Wind dir.
28 Cartoonist Dean
33 Turning points
34 Squiffed
36 Partitions
38 Key
39 Control
41 Indecent
42 Dutch humanist
43 Tremble anew
45 Oarlocks
46 ____ Series
47 Type style
48 Esoteric
51 Cauchos
54 Petition
56 Item for Butterfly
58 Locks of sorts
59 Plantain, in Spain
60 Where to see standard-breds
62 ____ middling
63 Sycamores
66 Delectate
67 Kind of shrimp
68 "____ right with . . .": Browning
70 Stout
71 Forbidding
72 Ships, in poesy
74 Nicholas I and II
75 Former sultan of Turkey
76 Dogfall
79 Hindu foot soldiers
80 Farthest point
81 Title created by James I
83 Confers holy orders
84 Well-known quadrennial runner
87 Fishing device
90 Arthurian lady
91 Author of "Look Who's Talking!"
92 G.I.'s award
93 Suffer
94 Bench, in Bologna
96 Something to keep on
99 Track word
100 "____ sana . . ."
101 Smoky peak
103 To be, to Virgil
105 "Bleak House" heroine
106 "Voi ____ sapete"
107 Mowgli's python
109 Concealed

185. Memorable Mothers by Vincent L. Osborne

ACROSS

1 Cascades peak
7 In a dudgeon
12 Jazz artist Zoot
16 As ___ kite
18 Ruark's "Poor ___"
20 Portray
22 Tear gas, e.g.
24 Mother of Orestes
26 Diamond of song
27 Astral phenomena
29 Repeater requisite
30 Thummim's biblical companion
31 Sops
34 Smith or Jones, at times
35 Uvula
36 Egyptian killer
38 Cause of a suit
39 Condign
40 Ross and Macduff
42 Site of Marina City
44 Touch on
46 Everglades denizen
48 Drift
49 City on the Rio Grande
51 Conspicuous
55 Mawkishness
56 Grinding powder
57 Aggregate
59 Where Saul saw a witch
60 Black or red follower
61 Incite
63 Source of mohair
64 These: Fr.
67 Mother of Louis XIV
70 Mercator item
71 ___ razor (philosophic rule)
73 Assay again
74 Unit of resistance
75 Man from Shiraz
76 Ukr. or Lith.
77 Tureen's companion
79 Toil
84 Enesco's homeland
86 Where Frontenac governed
87 Tilled land
88 Catches
90 ___ even keel
91 City on the Volga
93 Predicament
96 Cowboy's sidekick
98 Chiang ___, Mao's widow
100 Charlemagne's domain: Abbr.
101 Wrapper
102 As free as ___
104 Pacific pinnipeds
106 Puts in reserve
107 Miracle site
108 Single pers.
109 Hindu caste
112 Mother of Marie Antoinette
115 Flotation device
118 Linda Lavin role
119 "___ 17"
120 U.S. research rocket
121 Cummerbund
122 Comes alive
123 Dickeys for clergymen

DOWN

1 Tibia's locale
2 Engage
3 Mother of Nero
4 Grifter's accomplice
5 Work on a doily
6 Third king of Judah
7 Machu Picchu residents
8 Lead, perhaps
9 Chip's sister
10 Bottom lines
11 Hermit
12 Diocese
13 Setting apart
14 A Mother's Day honoree
15 Skilled penman
17 Mother of Elizabeth I
19 Madame Bovary
21 Subdues a shrew
23 "___ or not . . ."
25 Cosa ___
28 Hit song of 1958
32 Cry wolf
33 Short smoke: Slang
34 Hudson or DeSoto
36 Treads the boards
37 Man on the Ark
39 Mother of Liza Minnelli
41 Mother of Constantine the Great
43 Heart
45 Deprived
47 Loser to R.M.N. in 1972
50 Desert potentates
52 Neighbor of old Palestine
53 Nick Charles's wife
54 Springe, e.g.
57 Plea at sea
58 Immeasurable
60 Metaphysical being
62 S.A. country
63 Scope
64 Cordage fiber
65 Color of raw silk
66 Con game
67 Mother of Mohammed
68 "___ the ramparts . . ."
69 Mother of Romulus and Remus
72 Aspirin, e.g.
76 Blue
78 Emulated Ted Shawn
79 Handel opus
80 Parseghian
81 Mother of Solomon
82 Scent
83 Laudatory review
85 Whole
86 Lanyard
89 Small harpsichords
92 Cuckoo
93 ___ facie
94 Certain trains
95 Where the Tagus flows
97 Reputed terminal peak
99 Ave!
103 Debunkers' words
104 Navigation hazards
105 Mogul
108 Munich's river
110 "___ a Song Go . . ."
111 Mailmen's tours: Abbr.
113 "Shropshire Lad" monogram
114 Wallach
116 Chemin de ___
117 Pitcher's stat

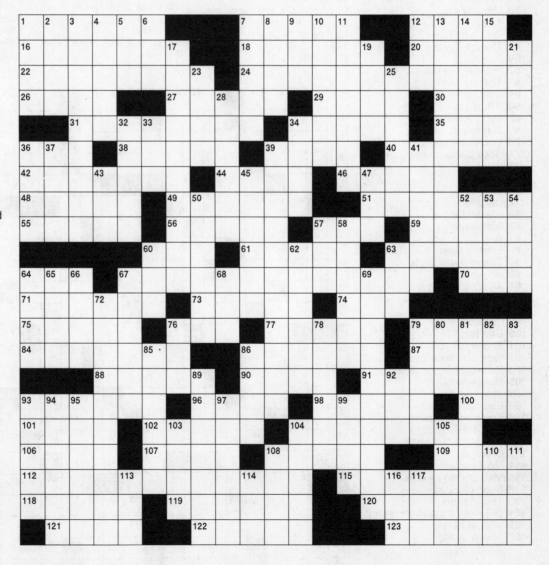

186. Nag, Nag, Nag by A. J. Santora

ACROSS

1 Blanched
6 Make a choice
9 Faucet
12 "City of the Kings"
16 Star in Ursa Major
20 Grocery, e.g.
21 Prefix for view
22 Greek letter
23 Kind of hygiene
24 Jackstay
25 Marx film shot at Eider Downs?
28 Advice to a pony-car owner?
30 Unseat
31 Allow to pass
32 Business abbr.
33 Three rivers in England
34 Cannes season
35 Make beloved
36 One with a blazing saddle?
39 Carved stones
41 Fortuneteller
44 Members of the "400"
47 Tenderly, in music
49 Antitoxins
50 Pinpoint
54 Favorite
55 Manservant
56 Keep
58 "We hold these ____ . . ."
59 That, in Sonora
60 Ready
62 Work at the bar
63 Thither
64 Everglades denizen
66 RR depot
67 Apportioned
69 Simpletons
70 Medieval dagger
71 Does some roofing
73 Bitter
74 Annoy
75 Lives
77 Dillon of TV
79 African tongue
82 Witnessed
83 Wag
87 Bren or Sten
88 Stockholm institute
90 Heyerdahl
94 Anoints, old style
95 Jargon
97 Cockloft
99 Canzone
100 Devilfish
101 Bridge cards
102 Nick and Nora's pooch
103 Buffalo team
105 Nero's pronoun
106 Knocked down
108 European capital
110 Tooth or tomato follower
111 Bo Derek's rating
112 Roman of Nebraska
113 Cross
114 Most banal
116 Man of many words
118 Short-barreled rifle
120 Threesomes
121 Old mare's throat problem?
125 Kind of circle
127 Sheep sound
130 Out of sorts
132 Understand
133 Rustlers' activity
136 Horseless carriage
137 "Equus"?
139 Dabbling in polo?
141 Alleviate
142 Fashion
143 Boo-boo kisser
144 Actuary's concern
145 Loosen
146 Flintstone
147 ____ Nostra
148 Huxtable
149 Rorem
150 Solvent

DOWN

1 ". . . lived in ____"
2 Thickset
3 Shut out the Texas Rangers?
4 Whilom
5 Once named
6 Public
7 Chatters
8 Aquarium fish
9 Pullulate
10 Bell town
11 Napoleons and Bismarcks
12 Valid reasoning
13 One of the Horae
14 Duplicate
15 Corolla part
16 He wrote "Swann's Way"
17 "Girl of the Golden West," etc.?
18 Altar area
19 Ruby and Sandra
26 Penalties
27 Era when people were old-fashioned and crazy?
29 Mr. Ed's words of wisdom?
35 Overacts
37 Hussein's stable?
38 Swearword
40 God on Olympus
42 Blue flag
43 Prohibit
45 Do a surgeon's job
46 Expresses
47 Skipper's "Cease!"
48 Neighbor of Gozo
49 Pilots
51 Galena and cuprite
52 Remedies
53 Snacked
57 To be: Fr.
61 Id est
63 Scray
65 Sparkle
68 Recorded proceedings
69 Goliath
70 White poplars
72 Food fish
76 Addict
78 What a ghost rider beats?
80 Pairs
81 Glazed
83 Revived
84 Catapult or ass
85 Three for the swayback?
86 British stoolies
89 Breakfast cereal
91 Whence tips come to a D.V.M.?
92 Lefty's creator
93 Cycling button
96 Miasma
98 Studio activity
101 Inst. at Fort Worth
102 Point ____ (equine term)
104 Subtract
107 Goes wrong
108 S.A. country
109 Like violins
115 ____ bell (register)
117 Flipped
119 Bronchospastic problem
120 Pricking
122 Dome-shaped abode
123 Approaches
124 Original forms of words
126 French spa
128 Palmer of gold
129 Krait
130 Cuisinier
131 Stadium sound
134 Canopy
135 "My Friend ____"
136 Source
138 First-class G.I.
140 Mourn

187. Silly Questions by Jean Reed

ACROSS

1 Questions
5 Arith. process
9 Fills a truck
14 L-Q connection
18 Elegance
19 Andretti of auto racing
20 ___ all (do oneself in)
21 Air: Comb. form
22 During Lent, does ___?
24 What drove ___?
26 Plant of the rose family
27 Net resembling tulle
29 Gatherings of geese
30 Coral reefs
32 Lat. case
33 River at Frankfurt
34 Loathed
37 In one ___ out the other
39 Singing sisters
42 Tree or residue
43 Maxims
45 Of cranial cavities
47 British cans
49 Fashion name
51 Whereness
53 Melchizedek's city
55 ___ the Lip
56 What interest does a ___ pay?
58 Incites
60 Court ___
62 Murphy's ___ bed
63 Alamogordo's county
64 Pigtails
65 Jacob, to Laban
68 Switzerland
70 Quivering trees
72 Name for a movie house
74 Frightened
77 Rent
78 Pernod ingredient
79 Moving stairs
81 Cuckoo
82 Color slightly
84 Start growing
86 He wrote "An Exchange of Eagles": 1977
87 Compos mentis
89 Show sudden interest
91 Removes a sheepshank
93 Permit: Abbr.
94 Looks after
96 O'Keeffe, e.g.
98 Roger's last name?
100 Picnic ham
101 Operating
102 Some votes
104 Gas stretcher
107 Competition
109 Disturbed the peace
113 What are a candidate's ___?
115 At whom did ___?
117 Cyma recta
118 County in Mont.
119 Error's mate
120 Computer fodder
121 Sordor
122 Rod used in basketry
123 Parabases
124 Once, once

DOWN

1 German exclamations
2 Tour the stores
3 Earthbound bird
4 Like hens' teeth
5 W.W. II fliers
6 Metric weight
7 Fell out
8 "Last but ___"
9 Brezhnev and some shooting stars
10 Start
11 Mil. man
12 Virgules or twills
13 Take both sides
14 Simenon's inspector
15 "Salvation ___"
16 Gen. Wingate: 1903–44
17 Jays' cousins
19 War planning date
23 "How to ___ Book": Adler
25 Bonn is its cap.
28 Auberge
31 Like Aphrodite or Nereids
34 Post-Mecca Moslem
35 Man from Manchuria
36 Did George III give ___?
38 Opposed, Dogpatch style
39 Schnitzler's idle worldling
40 What secrets did ___?
41 Golf great
44 Civil-rights writer
46 Grenoble's river
48 Plants seed
50 Fixes over
52 Sun ___-sen
54 What we all are
57 Shakespearean gem
59 Aphra of writing fame
61 "___ a star . . ."
63 Has creditors
64 Delay, old style
66 ". . . there I ___ be": H. Van Dyke
67 Balzac book: 1832
69 Emptiness
70 Wellaway!
71 French lawmakers
73 Latin diphthongs
75 Borne by the wind
76 Harsh lawmaker
78 Who turned ___?
79 What streams did ___?
80 Barflies
83 "He that ___ anger . . .": Prov. 16:32
85 ___ words (verbalizes)
88 Makes a cryptogram
90 Big cat
92 Young lover
95 Morse man's long ones
97 Capek play
99 Tristram's beloved
101 Rope fiber
103 Epochal
104 Over the hill
105 Theater box
106 Indian of Manitoba
108 Clinton's waterway
110 Snag
111 Highway sign
112 Mild cussword
114 Any of 18 named Louis
116 Mates of pas

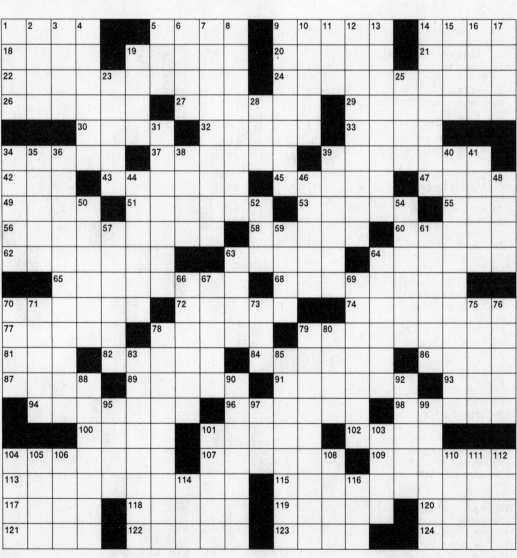

188. Long Runs by Threba Johnson

ACROSS

1 Religious executive
7 Small handbill
12 Diminished
18 Kind of sheet or press
19 Immediately
20 Amplifiers of electromagnetic waves
21 Senior citizens
22 Shames
24 Shining
25 Utter
26 N.A. Indians
28 Culprits, in Calabria
29 Region, to René
31 Fast long-run carrier
37 Living quarters: Abbr.
39 Ingredient of pepper pot
40 Cockle
41 Chinese pagoda
42 One of the Yugoslavs
44 Public
46 Bulfinch specialty
47 Long run on Broadway
48 Army missile
49 More competent
51 Bulgarian weight
53 Bone marrow
55 An Amerind
57 Assyrian war god
59 "Spirit of '76" musician
60 Vertexes
61 Humane soc.
62 Verve
63 Montemezzi's "L'Amore dei ___ Re"
66 Littler or Wilder
67 Kitchen meas.
69 Famed physicist: 1787–1854
70 Spacecraft unit
71 Ark passenger
72 Part of a joule
73 Ancient mariner
74 Perfect paradigm
76 Hinder
78 Feel
79 Desolate
80 Seculars
81 Highly agreeable
84 Compass pt.
85 Squirrels' nests
88 Brit. lexicon
89 Mine, in Marseille
90 Father, in Arabia
92 Nostrils
94 Froth
96 Contraction
97 Hogarth subject
98 Nudniks
100 Sputnik's bpl.
101 Long run in the North
107 With great tension
108 A follower
109 Press
110 Unpopular bill
113 "___ of Sundays": Updike
115 Radar device
118 Worse
120 Horn: Comb. form
121 Would-be frat member
122 Ultimate conclusion
123 King of Morocco
124 Dogie catcher
125 With profundity

DOWN

1 A good pair
2 Gaucho's weapon
3 Bad place for a long run
4 Augment, with "out"
5 Pancake topper
6 Part of a sonnet
7 D.C. bank group
8 Cub
9 Japanese immigrant
10 Moral principle
11 Coral of a lobster
12 Long run on TV
13 Authors L. Frank and Vicki
14 Tin Pan Alley acronym
15 Like the W.C.T.U.
16 Piscivorous bird
17 Summer time in N.Y.C.
19 Unresisting
23 Tern
27 Actor Flynn
30 Hardest part of a long run
32 Dos Passos trilogy
33 Teatro San Carlo offerings
34 "Mean ___," 1929 song
35 Marsh hen
36 St. Patrick's headquarters
37 Land area
38 Thrive
43 Subdue
45 Result of many a long run
47 Ben-___
50 Long run in April
52 Role for Hoffman or Streep
54 Unter ___ Linden
56 Sherbet
58 What the victor gets
59 Hew a yew
61 Court celebrity
63 Christie's record-breaking long run
64 Ransoms
65 Redactor
68 In which a long run leads to home
71 Snoop
73 Avant-gardist
75 Gromyko or Vishinsky
77 Cumulus
78 School subj.
81 Unit of power
82 Moslem noble
83 Card-file devices
84 Brings to court
86 Breathe
87 Tanglefoot
91 Approves
93 Adds
95 Jeu de mots
99 Like Jay Peak
102 Pushers in Hyde Park
103 Sermon of Buddha
104 Eucalyptus eater
105 Queen ___ lace
106 Hole-___
111 Efficiently
112 End of a Parisian's long run
113 Sigh in Stuttgart
114 ___ culpa
116 An N.C.O.
117 Self
119 Genethliacon, e.g.

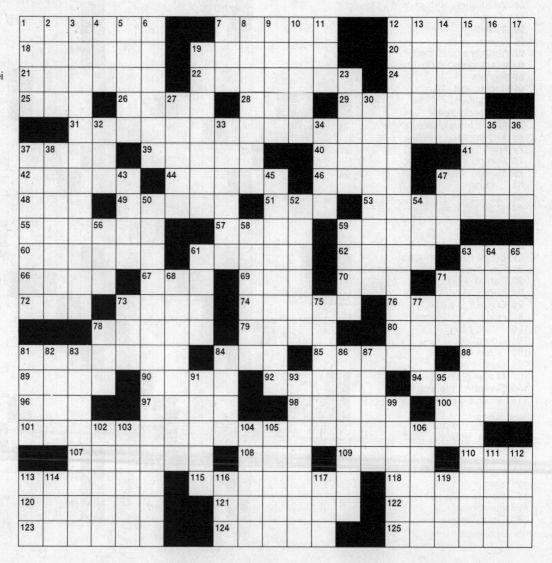

189. Diamond in the Rough by Walter Webb

ACROSS

1 Initials of the Wagner Act: 1935
5 An N.F.L. eleven
9 Attention-getter
13 To _____ (precisely)
17 Smoothed
20 Spread not fit for a bed
21 Pitch
23 Contemporary rendezvous
25 Logarithmic instrument
26 One-on-one gamble, usually
27 Riled
29 Irish peer
30 Trattoria treat
32 Men to be headed off at the pass
34 ". . . _____ to touch": Brooke
37 Prefix with meter and liter
40 Mac's nix
41 Brest beast
42 Distributor
44 Take
47 Coral islands
49 Dir. from Pisa to Verona
50 Horn leader
51 Versatile one
54 Garrison
55 Brut's relative
56 N.L. team
57 Consequently: Var.
59 Squeeze, in Savoie
61 Prank
63 U.S.N. or U.S.A.F.
64 His home has a dome
65 Guidry, Cey and Santo
66 Emulate Fisk
68 Word before stand or draw
69 Short surplice
71 Aves.
73 "_____ Spake Zarathustra"
75 Good vision, to an umpire
77 Rude
79 Journalism, for one
81 Kind of hen
83 Batters' stats
84 "Gulf Stream" painter
88 _____ word (briefly)
89 This, to Thérèse
90 Oil exporters
91 Fragmented, as food
93 Some have fallen
96 Gists
97 Plath's "The Bell _____"
98 Former darling of the Met set
99 Discard
100 All trailer
101 One with aspirations
104 How some runners pull up
106 Strike areas
108 CB O.K.
112 Zinc, e.g.
116 Military command
118 Put back in office
119 Sailing
120 Pals of Fran and Stan
121 Transactions
122 It's for the birds
123 Linen marking
124 Canonical hour

DOWN

1 Promontory
2 Half of CXIV
3 Sunder
4 Like putti
5 Coaching, e.g.
6 May who worked with a Mike
7 _____ alba (gypsum)
8 N.L. pitcher
9 Nominee endorser in Britain
10 McRae of baseball
11 Inventor Howe
12 Middle: Comb. form
13 Father of Agamemnon
14 Greek letter
15 Wing
16 Get by, with "out"
18 Exile island
19 Rivers in Scotland and Wales
22 Feudal underlings
24 Substitute
28 Thirty-two are a mouthful
31 Caught one's breath
33 Strike out
35 Average
36 Stimulus-response device
37 Org. units
38 American Indians
39 Musical standard
41 What Fred Lynn wields
42 That cad: Lat.
43 Kind of rocket
45 "A portion of the _____": Shelley
46 Gannets' kin
48 Comic Bert
52 Nonclerical group
53 Snorri Sturluson's summary
54 Vexers
58 Agriculturists
60 Printing processes, for short
62 Hall of Famer
63 Be quiet!
67 Plug
68 Dilute
69 About
70 European graylings
71 Ado
72 Flat occupant
74 Plant openings
76 _____ in (aware)
78 "There be fools alive, _____ . . .": Shak.
80 Ancient Semitic tongue
82 Art movement
85 Cried harshly
86 Sept. 23–Oct. 22 baby
87 W.W. II group
92 Sharp reprimands
94 City once called Last Chance
95 Dutch cheeses
97 Fool
100 Bristles
101 Compact
102 Change the interior
103 Organic compound
105 World Series winners: 1969
107 Early wildlife preserver
109 Stage prize
110 Eurasian shrub
111 Musical symbol
112 Undergarment
113 N.R.C. predecessor
114 Ride the bench
115 Consumed
117 Owns

190. Father's Day by Tap Osborn

ACROSS

1 Balk
6 Semblance
11 ____ Peak, N.M.
15 Diagonal spar
20 Sky: Comb. form
21 Like a rainbow
22 Changsha's province
23 Ecuador's capital
24 7:30 A.M.
27 Inferior
28 Infant's word
29 Correct
30 Incendiarism
31 Sunday best
32 Shoshoneans
33 Peaked
34 Like newly poured concrete
35 Bulwer-Lytton heroine
36 Artist Edouard
38 8 A.M.
45 Sign on the dotted line
47 Tax
48 Lounging slipper
49 Helm letters
50 "____ of Honey"
54 Author of "The Morning Watch"
55 Nabokov novel
56 Tendency
58 9 A.M.
64 "____ a Song Go . . ."
65 Tidal flood
66 "China" star: 1943
67 Catch red-handed
68 Dinner-party items
70 ". . . ____ of sympathy": Emerson
71 Tucker's partner
72 Balderdash!
73 British rank
74 9 A.M.–5 P.M.
84 Boniface's place
85 Cold sea
86 Luggage shade
87 "You can't pray ____": Twain
88 Long cloak
92 True grit
93 Row at the Met
95 California valley
96 Touch upon
97 5 P.M.
103 Street show
105 Fedora
106 Innisfail
107 Spalpeens of 106 Across
108 Dunderhead
109 Peau de ____
111 "____ 17"
114 Kind of shooter
115 5:30 P.M.
119 Ancient storyteller
124 Egyptian symbol
125 Palmer
126 100 square meters
128 Idle
129 Hit man's weapon
132 Suffix with sect
133 Neutralize
135 Field
136 Scandinavian Neptune
137 7 P.M.
140 Kashan man
141 Bantu group
142 Lunar trench
143 Concatenate
144 Mercer creation
145 Widgeon
146 Reflex sites
147 Jewish feast

DOWN

1 Soft-nosed bullet
2 Corrigenda
3 Inflame
4 Discomfort
5 Future swimmers
6 Riot-squad gear
7 Pressing
8 Religious replication
9 Do a farm job
10 Begley and Wynn
11 Magazine section
12 High-hats
13 Goldie
14 Lewis's "____ Vickers"
15 Peered, in a way
16 Waggish verbalist
17 Tease
18 Journey, to Ovid
19 He kept loyalty to royalty
22 Buckskins, e.g.
25 Condensation
26 Exotic dance
31 Paddock newcomer
34 Remove a dowel
35 Entomb
37 Josip Broz
39 Scrupulously exact
40 Improve
41 Moreno of baseball
42 Like a beldam
43 Deduce
44 Reticulate
46 Neoteric
50 Facing Seaver
51 Cleo's god of wisdom
52 Kite's site
53 Exorbitant
54 Some Semites
55 City on the Jumna
57 Torn or tear
59 Of Lamb's writings
60 Potentially
61 Gullible one
62 Plaice or dace
63 Kind of ring
69 Branch
71 Pulitzer Prize poet: 1929
73 Timid
75 Brightened
76 Solicited earnestly
77 Demoralize
78 Tallinn native
79 Dutch genre painter
80 Raccoon's Tibetan cousin
81 Tocsin
82 Stunt
83 Lambs
88 200 milligrams
89 Disconcert
90 "Big A" prize
91 Suffix with Capri
93 Pentateuch scroll
94 Architect Jones
98 Do a tire job
99 "Mother of Russian Cities"
100 Brawl
101 Enzyme
102 College sports org.
104 For the cognoscenti
110 Rara avis
111 Ear irrigator
112 Former Japanese P.M.
113 Distilling phase
114 Reads carefully
116 Prep-school freshman's subject
117 Rowing motion of yore
118 Conceal
120 Galahad's mother
121 Vile
122 ____ of quinine
123 Gary of golf
127 Mischievous moppet
129 Acclaim
130 Like a wax museum
131 Culture medium
132 Psst
133 Tennis term
134 Emil Ludwig subject
137 Fin. officers
138 Whence came Mork
139 Eur. country

191. Feminine Mystique by Vicki and Alex Black

ACROSS

1 Teeny or weeny
6 Yearns
11 Script girl
16 Dormant
18 Roman fountain
19 Is conscience-stricken
21 Nancy Drew
23 Instances of syncope
25 Tennis star
26 Deduce
27 Connives
28 King Cole
29 Soldat's weapon
30 U.N. translator
32 Bog
33 Endings for young and old
35 Much used article
36 Misses' antonym
37 Hymn
38 Theologian's degree
39 Faded
41 Networks on charts
43 Makes leather
44 Customs
45 Kind of pocket or brush
46 Web-footed one
48 Sinks
50 Columnist for the lovelorn
53 Soil
57 Nothing's alternative
58 Grey or McCrea
59 Paton or Hale
60 In a bad way
61 Gets one's goat
62 Swamplands
63 Smear
64 Greek physician
65 Where to find Moab
66 Regretted
67 Cultivates
68 Tincture for bruises
69 City in Arizona
70 Anchor woman
72 Minute quantities
73 Flower holder
75 Airline pilot's record
76 Syrian-Lebanese sect member
77 Stork's relative
79 The Hulk, e.g.
81 Many eras
82 IRT's running mate in N.Y.C.
85 "Oh, I am ____ . . .": Gilbert
86 Ancient Syria
87 Southwest Conf. member
88 Corpulent
90 Mister, in Munich
91 Jane Marple
95 Sundance Kid's girl
96 Top pilot
97 Dare not, in Dogpatch
98 Fine
99 Type of hog
100 Pestered
102 Woman behind the throne
104 Geese, ducks, etc.
105 Thimblerig
106 Brewer
107 Seamstress
108 Property rights
109 Unkempt

DOWN

1 Desperado of the 19th century
2 Postmistress
3 Startled
4 Account book
5 Money in Bulgaria
6 Ambassador's aides
7 He thanked God for Friday
8 Everglades denizen
9 Ties
10 Adele, to Fred
11 Fracases
12 Necks of land
13 Luck, in Limerick
14 Singular prefix
15 Shelley was one
17 Short wave
19 Contradicts
20 Shows teeth
22 Lies close
24 Halt
27 Saharan
31 Last stop before home
32 Leader of a women's group
34 Booty
37 Educational org.
40 Composer of "Judith"
41 Methane and butane
42 Coin for Khomeini
44 Emily Post
46 Despot
47 Poetic time
48 Piaf was here
49 Halls or large rooms
50 Tout le ____
51 Gentleman's gentleman
52 Son of Tros
54 Kukla's friend
55 Templeton and Waugh
56 Talkative starling
57 One of the timpani
58 Deride
62 Unite
63 Entertaining Dane
64 Eastern governor
66 "6 ____ Riv Vu"
67 Strigine sound
68 ____ for one's money
71 Pleasingly zaftig
72 Rout
74 Request
76 Bad marks
77 Arctic feature
78 Ennui
79 Snifter contents
80 Absorbed
82 ____ oneself (goes)
83 Coiffeuse
84 Salver for a certain service
85 Peck role
86 Aver
87 U.S. cardinal
89 Word of warning
91 Cuban writer-patriot: 1853–95
92 Hebrew scholar: 1040–1105
93 Carson role
94 Nimble
97 Heraldic symbol
101 Astronaut Grissom
102 Law degree
103 Hebrew letter

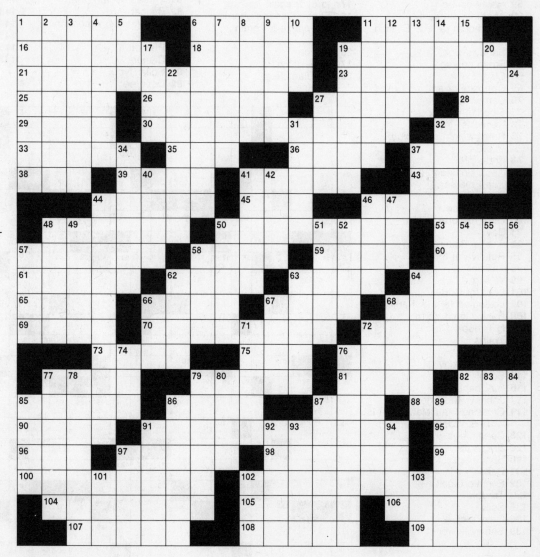

192. Historic Lines by Anne Fox

ACROSS

1 Pretext
5 Underwater gear
11 Act of 1765
16 Island off Venezuela
21 Acclaim
22 Hag in "Ivanhoe"
23 Of bodily tissue
24 Tutelary deities
25 Boston Tea Party (à la O. W. Holmes)
29 Daughter of Tantalus
30 Flavor
31 Dugout
32 Creek
33 Dr. Rhine's field
34 Cutting tool
36 Acacia or tulip
37 ___ bono
39 Meeting: Abbr.
43 Valley Forge (à la T. B. Read)
50 Devilkin
51 Vex
52 Ancient Syrian city
53 ___ Moines
54 Type of shoe, for short
56 Barristers, in Brest
59 Malay canoe
60 Appoint summarily
62 Monmouth (à la L. E. Richards)
66 Sandy's word
67 Frosh course
68 Clear
69 Opposite of ant.
70 Carried away
71 Siberian antelope
73 Desserts
76 Heavyweight champion: 1934
78 Press org.
80 "___ unfurled" (Concord, à la Emerson)
88 Cuckoo
89 Actor Frobe
90 Gobi explorer Hedin
91 Bay
92 B ___ Baker
95 Relative of Inc.
98 Fall call
99 Willing
101 Loot for Cortés
102 Lexington (à la J. Parker)
109 Back: Comb. form
110 N.T. book
111 Trains
112 Home: Abbr.
113 Call ___ day
114 Soubise, e.g.
116 S.A. cape
117 Johnny Reb's govt.
119 Crossing the Delaware (à la G. E. Woodberry)
128 Certain age
129 Singer Janis
130 Space agcy.
131 Baba
132 Female rabbit
133 Trouble
135 Sully
136 Navy recruit
139 Showy flower
141 Betsy's battle flag (à la M. Irving)
148 Canvas holder
149 Flabbergast
150 Barber's window sign
151 Sharpen
152 Penned
153 Softened
154 Mother ___
155 French window

DOWN

1 Earth, e.g.
2 Somewhat tardy
3 Grand Tour site
4 Star in Draco
5 Solicit
6 Cupboard
7 Turkish city
8 Take part in a roleo
9 Vinegar: Comb. form
10 Kind of sack
11 Soprano Eleanor
12 Insectivorous mammal
13 Jai ___
14 First name of 76 Across
15 Grand ___
16 Fire god
17 Go over again
18 "Faerie Queene" heroine
19 Receptacle for grain
20 Help
26 Obscure
27 Former filly
28 Blue flags, e.g.
35 Hocked
36 Affix, in a way
37 Portuguese poet: 1524–80
38 Restless
40 Phantoms
41 Advance
42 Six-line stanza
44 One of the Durants
45 Sexy literature or art
46 Affluent
47 Excoriate
48 Weird
49 City on the Brazos
54 Mount ___, Idaho
55 Caine role: 1966
57 Long watch
58 Basks
59 Soprano Roberta
61 Actor Pat
62 Topgallant
63 Long
64 Harvest
65 Slight
72 Colossi
74 Kind of roll
75 Ships' parts
77 Atlas abbr.
79 Nosed
81 Thread: Comb. form
82 Buccal
83 Foreign and American
84 Tangle
85 Run off
86 Ciphers
87 Collar type
92 Devotee
93 Placate
94 ___ form (at one's best)
96 Emotional shock
97 Region of India
100 Mexican liquor
103 Conductor Lukas
104 Salt Lake City team
105 Indistinct vowel sound
106 Indicate
107 Tribunals
108 Russian river
115 With lance in hand
118 Fluffs
120 Peevish
121 Nap
122 Caught red-handed
123 Where the Storting sits
124 Pilgrim ___
125 Martin-Preston vehicle
126 External world
127 Sporadic spouter
134 Man, for one
135 Ella's forte
136 ___ fide
137 What ___? (So?)
138 Honshu city
140 Squeezed (out)
141 ___ Gardens
142 Type of drum
143 Inner: Comb. form
144 Son of Noah
145 Ratite bird
146 Bull ___
147 Devon river

193. Noncandidates by Bert Rosenfield

ACROSS

1 Experienced afresh
8 City in the news: Nov. 1979
15 Ending for law or saw
18 Turkey portion
20 Pizza seasoner
21 Key letter
22 Have effect, pro or con
23 Part of western Texas
25 One gored by a boar
26 Like sachet
28 Ph.D. applicant
29 ____ 'acte
31 Taro or skunk cabbage
32 Heroine's word to a villain
33 Sweet lady of song
37 Pope John Paul II at baptism
39 "Summer and Smoke" heroine
40 A hermit is one
41 One of the Fords
43 St. Louis bridge
47 Gaucho's milieu
49 Foe's light vessel, British style
52 Ending for a cardinal point
53 Buffalo hockey player
54 Ribald
56 Silly
58 One more time
59 Hebrew letter
61 Words of enlightenment
62 Nome necessities
64 Radar sweep
68 Foreign Relations Committee chairman: 1941
71 Kitchen finisher
72 Moisten
74 Strip of shoe leather
75 Episcopacy
77 TV waitress
78 Mukluks and loafers
81 Rather plain plain
86 Violin parts
87 Spring mo.
88 Ambassador Howard et al.
90 Prospero was one
91 Office V.I.P.
92 Conn
94 Mosel tributary
96 Nicklaus has won it four times
97 Store up
99 Choleric movie comic
103 Arcane
106 Handle, in Hannover
107 Singer Adams
108 Athenian comic poet
109 Flatterer's forte
111 Will Rogers prop
115 Hall of Fame name
117 Without rancor
119 Large dam in Germany
120 Kind of cat or cross
121 Provide weapons
122 N.J. neighbor
123 Concurs
124 Lake Ontario feeder

DOWN

1 Name of seven Siamese kings
2 Camelot lady
3 Composer of "Le Roi d'Ys"
4 Circuit judge, e.g.
5 November activity
6 Resilient
7 Morse-code word
8 Corrida headliner
9 "Blood hath been shed ____": Macbeth
10 ____ pad
11 Incited, with "on"
12 Boer assembly
13 Gloucester's cape
14 Office of matins division
15 Gossipy woman
16 Dutch town
17 Illuminated
19 Loser to H.C.H.: 1928
21 Mediocre
24 Wine: Prefix
27 ____ acid (H₂CO₃)
30 Word for Ben Jonson
33 Beaufort scale word
34 Singer Logan
35 Great Persian poet
36 ____ au rhum
37 Core
38 Toughens
42 Welcome symbol
44 Sternward
45 Pollster's interest
46 Import
48 German physicist: 1787–1854
50 Classify
51 Of adolescents
53 Ervin
55 Annapurna denizen
57 French cathedral city
60 Family in Eleanor Estes books
63 Gypsy gentlemen
64 Met soprano
65 Mosquito genus
66 Liturgical vestment
67 Paperback detective
69 Nearsighted people
70 Water
73 Plaines or Moines
76 It starts in juin
79 Shipment to Kokomo
80 Tower
82 Absolve
83 Calumet, for one
84 Obtested
85 Start of a count-out
89 "Art for art's ____"
92 Hard-glazed Japanese pottery
93 Like the Philippines in W.W. II
95 Ground a jet
98 Sea, in Saxony
100 Most dismal
101 Op art and pop art
102 Pellagra victim's need
103 RR giveaway
104 Undermine
105 Tylopod
106 The nominees
109 Oil units: Abbr.
110 Dixie favorite
112 Egret's relative
113 ____ hemp
114 Newcastle's river
116 Initials at Pensacola
118 Assault or overact

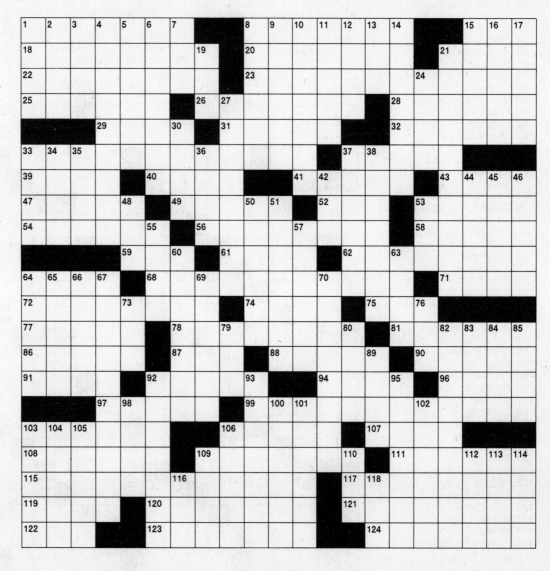

194. Triple Talk by William J. Yskamp

ACROSS

1 Era
7 Clean-cut
12 Poses
16 Possesses
19 Neighbor of Siberia
20 Of the air or ear
21 Asian sea
22 West Indian Indian
24 Marsupial in Washington zoo
27 Greek vowel
28 Koko's weapon
29 March of ____
30 Greenish blues
31 Degrades
32 Bond
34 "Oberto" composer
35 Cheese of Normandy
36 Frequently, to FitzGerald
39 Variegated
40 Ruth
41 Spectral type
42 Numbs
44 Mediocre women's club
47 Thickset horse
50 Astray
51 King Cyaxares' subjects
52 Christie's "____ at End House"
53 Letters
54 Flocks of mallards
55 Kind of talk or tax
56 Stairs to the Ganges
57 Unit of 1,000 kilograms
58 Spline
59 Mine roof prop
60 Flashy fowl
62 Atmosphere: Comb. form
63 Dance diagrams
65 Plague
66 Counter-balances
68 Barbarian
69 Made of a grain
70 Asian peninsula
72 Dessert makers' contests
78 Wheel tooth
81 Tuaregs' headgear
83 Book by D.S. Freeman
84 Pomander
85 Took steps
86 Korbut and Romanov
87 Brother of Moses
88 Dantean division
89 Guy
90 Beckett's absent character
91 Companionway
92 Floor finisher
93 Long time
94 "Farewell, polliwog"
96 Household chore
97 Brazilian port
98 Baksheesh
99 "Stop it!"
100 E.T.O. head
101 Santa Anna at the Alamo
104 Tern
106 Combed wool
108 Niobe's brother
109 Massenet opera
110 Italian poet: 1544-95
111 Domino, e.g.
115 Of a piece
116 Queues for canine meals
119 Diehard's cry
120 Swiss river
121 Type of type
122 Uncle's darlings
123 Bk. of the Bible
124 Stowe novel
125 Ruth St. ____
126 Placid

DOWN

1 Manhandles
2 Dash
3 Respiratory sound
4 British ____
5 Orel's river
6 Vacationer's nonactivity
7 Soothed
8 Archon
9 Cleo's co-attendant
10 Use a crosscut
11 Sugar pills
12 Caesar, e.g.
13 Man of Kerman
14 Keep ____ on
15 Stallone's sobriquet
16 Glockenspiel player's implement
17 Of a region
18 "In hoc ____ vinces"
22 Latin American dances
23 Fiber for ropes
25 Candy stripers
26 Trichords
31 "Wait ____ Dark"
33 Starts the bidding
34 Potiches
35 Neighbor of Perugia
36 Black Sea port
37 The hickory stick
38 Irascible Scot's garment
40 Grocery, in Granada
41 Bridge positions
43 ____ of Worms
44 Psalm word
45 Wealthy biblical city
46 Undergo chemical change
47 Shot of a dance
48 Sty talk
49 Sampler word
51 Crushed grape skins
53 Wavy pattern in fur
55 Bex and Dax
56 Cocoa-exporting land
57 "____ Amore," 1953 hit
59 Clip
60 Squawfish
61 Irritate
63 Bawled
64 Fireside ____
67 Cloister
69 W. Budapest, to Berliners
70 Demean
71 Right-hand page
72 Hag
73 Underworld tongue
74 Rossetti's "____ Beatrix"
75 African enclosures
76 Weird
77 Whistling swans, etc.
79 Belgian port
80 First name of 40 Across
82 Pele was one
84 Whining speech
87 Tiny particle
88 Social stratum
90 Ketch tippers
91 Made an ostentatious display
92 Preludes to night
94 What a hothead loses
95 Old Persian coin
96 Back: Comb. form
97 Out of order
99 Track events
101 Nine inches
102 Morse course: Abbr.
103 Popeye's friend
104 Part of S.P.
105 Made corvine sounds
106 Chollas
107 Varnish additive
109 The Indian Desert
110 Doppelgänger, to a live person
112 ____ and for all
113 "It might have ____"
114 Actual being
116 Heel
117 Cheer in Madrid
118 Golfer's concern

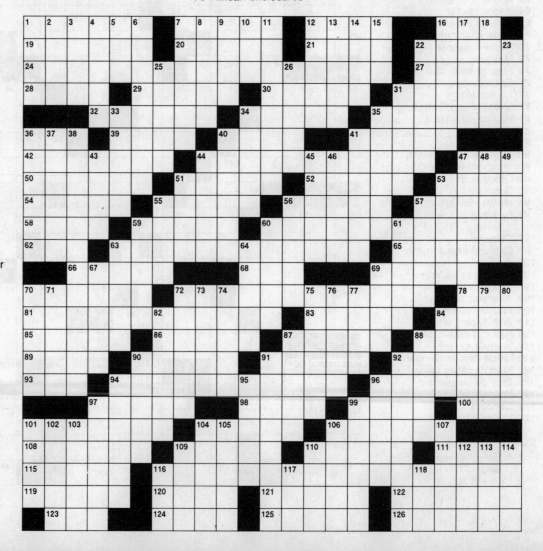

195. What in the World? by Mary Virginia Orna

ACROSS

1 Rara ____
5 Gaiter
9 Excluding
13 Flintstone
17 Hair: Comb. form
18 Saharan "ship"
20 Killer whale
21 Derby winner, ____ Ridge
22 "Lulu," e.g.
23 Marketplace
24 Institution at Reading
25 Writer Bagnold
26 Sturdy cloth
27 Hamilton baby's diaper?
30 N.E. cape
31 Down ____
33 Where the Gurgan flows
34 Orchestra section: Abbr.
35 N.A.A.C.P., for one
37 Dilly
38 "Adam and Eve and ____":
   Coppard
41 Pads
44 Minneapolis lipids?
47 Courtier in "Hamlet"
48 Shake a leg
50 Trap
51 London lane
52 Despoilment
54 Obstructs
56 Down
57 Coal size
58 Kojak
59 Yield
60 Presidential monogram
61 Hialeah arithmetic
63 Belfast beautician?
67 Concordes, e.g.
71 "____ Heldenleben":
   Strauss
73 Bonds
74 Native of Nejd
76 Bench for the masses
77 Age, to Agrippa
80 Enthralled
81 Popular conductor
83 Narrow openings
84 ____ José
85 Stout
86 Greek con man at Troy
87 Louisville lid?
92 Music for a poem
94 Hobson or Harper
95 Gas: Comb. form
96 Courts
97 Tullamore's land
98 Jason's command
99 Perceived
101 Possesses
104 Brabant babes?
109 Salten creation
111 Jazzman Hines
112 Denomination
113 Best and Purviance
114 One of Tirpitz's pack
115 Buster Brown's pooch
116 Alexis, e.g.
117 Fish-tank favorite
118 Wallechinsky's forte
119 Freshly
120 Bone: Comb. form
121 Sturdy boat
122 ____-majesté

DOWN

1 Canadian land unit
2 Schubert's schillings?
3 Crucifix inscription
4 Jainat jazzman?
5 Strikebreakers
6 English statesman:
   1505–63
7 Cupid, in art
8 Depots
9 Director of "Picnic"
10 Part of Q.E.D.
11 Catapult
12 Vital
13 Parisian picnics?
14 Echo
15 Pernicious
16 Miami's county
17 Musical ending
19 Miss Bacall
28 Repair, in a way
29 Like some courtyards
32 Hexapod
36 Skidded
37 Augury
38 Greek letters
39 Poem by Tennyson
40 Raison d'____
41 Log, in Livorno
42 ____ as a beet
43 More timorous
45 Snowy one
46 ____ Darya, Aral feeder
49 Year in the reign of Sweyn I
53 Attenuated
54 Threatened
55 Coolers
59 Block part
60 Mild oath
62 Mariners' lot?
64 Word with hand or grand
65 Afrikaans
66 Gannets' relatives
68 Señor Hart?
69 Mortise's partner
70 Playground feature
72 Bond circulators
75 Back Bay edict?
77 Query
78 Hgt.:
79 Actress Louise
80 Comedienne from Butte
81 Irish county
82 Middleweight Antuofermo
84 Describing some dogs
88 "____ the world . . .": Mark-
   ham
89 Holliday's friend
90 Rue
91 Worried
93 Ma that says "maa"
98 Hearth
99 Packers' coach
100 Try
102 Slacken
103 Forms a lap
104 Kind of ray
105 Word with coat or check
106 Prod
107 "Flee, feline!"
108 Toward: Poet.
110 "Agent" of cartoons

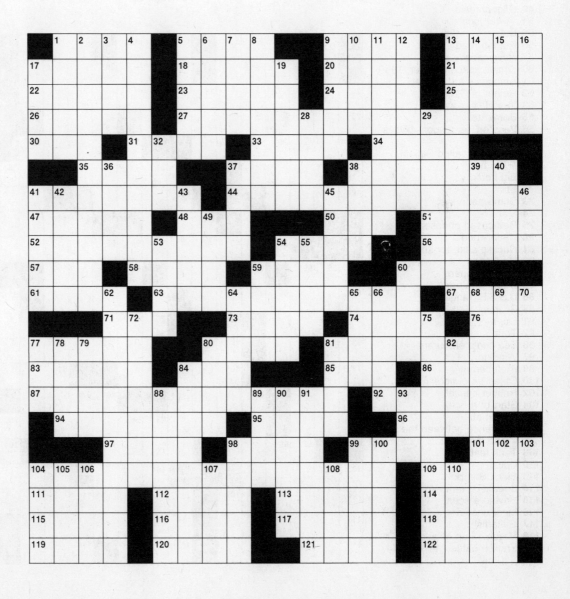

196. Polyglot by Richard Silvestri

ACROSS

1 Slabs of peat
6 W.W. II front
9 Say further
12 Tool for planting seeds
18 At the summit
19 ____ New York
21 Sports official
22 Alter
24 Principles of faith
25 Notable play of 1921
26 Gaggle group
27 "What ____, Life?": Mase-field
28 It's often hard to break
29 Hole enlargers
31 Monroe follower
33 Cowboy's chum
34 Computer fodder
35 Arena
39 April initials
42 Spotted
43 Con men
44 Toward the mouth
45 Hoop hanger
46 Driller's deg.
48 Hill dweller
49 Oligophrenic
51 Tower locale
52 Due
56 Roman road
57 Newspaper's logo
60 Simian space traveler: 1959
61 Amonasro's daughter
62 Reiner or Sagan
63 In a clumsy way
65 Bobwhite
66 Pass on, as responsibilities
69 Hair style
70 City once called College Farm
71 Big book
72 Still
73 Dumb performer
74 Mar
79 Red-cased cheese
80 Underworld
81 Nucleic acid, for short
82 Hindrance
84 Coin of Japan
85 Stony weather
86 U.S.S.R. range
88 Scarce
91 Ouph
92 Tout
96 Sea lion's entourage
97 Windigo
99 Protuberant
100 Objective outlook
102 Rubber capital
104 Start of a hole
105 Leo et al.
107 Difference between the ai and the unau
108 Tank feature
110 Court
113 Black Sea port
114 Speaker's concern
115 Having a scent
116 Most uncouth
117 Guitarfish
118 March 15, in Milano
119 English battle site: May 14, 1264

DOWN

1 Part of TNT
2 Like some statues
3 Map abbr.
4 Overlook
5 Screen in a British manor house
6 Roe
7 Monkey puzzle, e.g.
8 Done, to Donne
9 Cossack chief
10 Casual wear
11 Anhydrous
12 Summer in N.Y.C.
13 Where Fischer beat Spassky
14 Goof
15 Pane
16 Court calls
17 Gaelic
20 "____ of Gaul," medieval romance
22 Perfume base
23 Capone's nemesis
30 Sic transit gloria ____
31 Hoosier humorist
32 Big spender
33 Instrument for Serkin
36 Broadway heroine
37 ____ bene
38 In a line
40 Store or stock
41 Hollywood hopeful
47 Photocopy
48 Associate
49 In style
50 Algerian port
51 One-trillionth: Comb. form
53 Lat. case
54 Names meaning "sweet or pleasant"
55 Does clerical work
57 Thai
58 Non-Moslem, to Moslems
59 Rot
64 Skald's opus
65 Malacca
66 Tennyson heroine
67 German river
68 Change direction
71 Keynote
74 A source of oil
75 Water carrier
76 Off-the-cuff remark
77 Kukla's friend
78 Of the ear
83 Merrill or Milnes
85 Tackle
86 Silvery
87 Not of the cloth
89 Vichy et al.
90 Irish patriot
93 Beaverlike fur
94 Like cumulus clouds
95 "Cogito, ____ sum"
96 Fight
98 Juniper
101 Register
102 Noun suffix
103 African antelope
105 Wearing pumps
106 Former African province of Spain
109 Use a shuttle
110 Four-termer's monogram
111 Twice LI
112 Fell

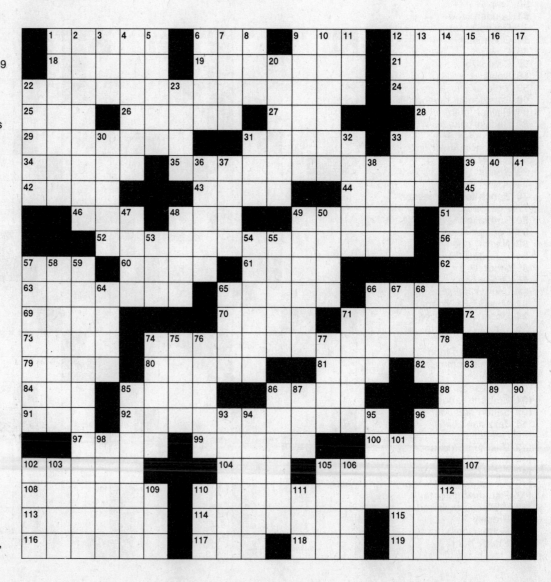

197. Titillating Tunes by Jordan S. Lasher

ACROSS

1 Right-angle extension
4 Ready
7 ___ as a ghost
13 Thespian
18 Architect I.M.
19 Soup green
21 "___, My God, to Thee"
22 Polynesian native
23 Suffix with editor or janitor
24 "Chanson d'Amour" sub-title
27 Como hit of 1947
29 Grenoble's river
30 Writer Christie
31 "___ Time": 1921
32 British parties
33 "___ Maria"
35 Rubberneck
38 A Siamese twin
39 Part of H.S.H.
40 Not windward
41 Roger and Madeline
42 Inflict
45 Part of a table setting
47 Steer's wild ancestor
48 Appearances
49 Sills specialty
50 Attorney's deg.
51 "Song of the South" song: 1946
54 Nessen or Ziegler
57 Sire of Osiris
58 Sharpshooter
59 Blackbird
60 One-time Mrs. Sinatra
61 Call ___ day
62 Song by Sayers: 1891
69 Gulliver, for short
70 Ezra Pound work
71 Tra followers
72 Comedian DeLuise
73 Natural resource
74 Zoo favorite
75 Berlin song: 1913
81 Pussycat's poetic partner
82 Dispossess
84 Vincent of chillers
85 Algonquian language
86 Pure
88 Trade-in candidate
89 Range between continents
90 Island feast
91 Kin of tri
92 Emulate Daedalus
93 Relieves
94 Speedometer rdg.
95 They, in Marseille
96 "___ Hear a Waltz?": 1965
97 Member of the sacerdocy
100 "Così fan ___"
102 Oscar-winning song of 1964
107 Como hit of 1950
109 Fire
110 Elephant of juveniles
111 "___ Kelly, I Love You": 1922
112 Dispatched
113 Peerce
114 Luce
115 Kind of fee
116 A.D.A. member's degree
117 Chip's sis

DOWN

1 "Beowulf," e.g.
2 Laban's daughter
3 "Hi-___, Hi-Lo": 1953
4 Broths
5 Greatest Mogul emperor of India: Var.
6 Minister to
7 "The Breeze ___": 1940
8 Shore or dune
9 Sumatran seaport
10 Berlin song: 1915
11 Mother of the Gemini
12 The Big Band ___
13 Pile up
14 Word in Gardner titles
15 An "Irish Lullaby": 1914
16 "It's Now ___": 1960
17 Tractor-trailer
20 St. Louis sight
25 "I caught you!"
26 Miniature scene
28 Heifers' habitats
32 Took out
34 "A mouse!"
35 Sneak's activity
36 Officer under Cornwallis
37 "Dig You Later" subtitle: 1945
38 Naturalness
39 Arlen or 67 Down
40 C.I.O.'s complement
42 Car attachment
43 U.S. cartoonist
44 Denouement
45 Williwaw
46 First note: Var.
48 Glistening mineral
51 "Iz ___ so!"
52 Surround
53 ___ volente
55 More than satisfactorily
56 Unknown
63 "Everybody Loves ___": 1958
64 Smoothed sand traps
65 Stout
66 Draw out
67 "Fanny" songwriter: 1954
68 Rheine's river
75 Full-house sign
76 In a pique
77 Warren or Joyce Carol
78 Grand Ole ___
79 Plural of os
80 Little fox
83 Chosen, in Cannes
85 Where the Minotaur menaced
86 Einstein's birthplace
87 Kind of vows
88 Welcome words to a hitch-hiker
89 Outcomes
92 Human frailty
93 Kind of base or fiddle
95 ". . . long before ___": Brooke
96 Ferocious dog of India
97 Prof, probably
98 Journalist Jacob
99 Plant deeply
101 Aspen transport
102 Betty Ford is one
103 Companies, in Caen
104 Delhi noble
105 Midterm or final
106 "___ Meeny Miney Mo": 1935
107 U.K. network
108 Gerund ending

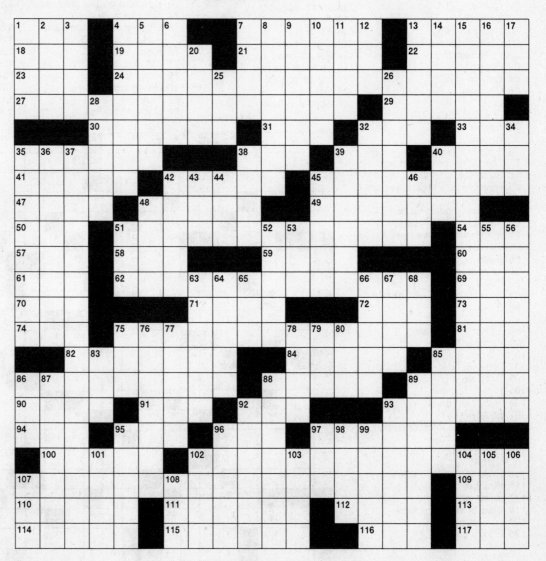

198. Play, Pen! by Marjorie Pedersen

ACROSS

1 Portable room
7 Thank-you-____ (bumps)
12 Money in Madras, once
17 P.G.A. star
21 Melodious
22 Follow
23 Culpability
24 Cupid
25 Arizona perfumes?
27 Thread
28 Free electrons
29 These oppose pros
30 Rialto sign
31 Chicken farmer's astonish-
   ing reward?
34 Jennets
36 "The ____'e knows . . .":
   Kipling
38 Summarize
39 Hessian river
40 Tommie ____, famed trumpeter
42 Intensity
44 Suffix with serpent
45 Korbut and Connolly
50 Baryshnikov's fall guys?
55 "Tristram Shandy" author
56 Gardner
57 Gibbet
58 Secreted
60 Housekeeping
61 Carriage drawn by oxen
62 ____ than thou
63 Potion
64 Century plants
65 Unequal
67 West
69 Ignoble
71 Before
72 Accent
73 Aisle not taken at a gallop?
77 Container for cymbidiums
78 Salambao
79 How the hirsute tortoise finished?
81 Vermouth designation
82 Kind of bean or dragon
84 Summer's noncreator
85 Twisted, e.g.
88 Bunk
89 ____ processing
90 Suffix with class or test
91 Semiarid Australian district
93 Pluto, to Cleo
95 Turn
98 Became very irate
100 Feminists' org.
101 Gorge
102 Itinerary hdg.
103 Decisive
105 British carbine
106 Lycée learners
107 Lovely loch?
110 Change a stone's position
111 Mineo
113 "Micrographia" author:
   1665
114 River to the North Sea
115 Pinafore
117 Baste or shirr
118 Kind of watch or sign
121 ____ apple
125 Chef's song?

131 Swiss canton
133 Wild plum
134 Gay blade
135 Pith helmet
136 Dollar Day melee?
139 Lenard's "Winnie ____ Pu"
140 Originate
141 City in western Wis.
142 Witch foiler
143 Be zetetic
144 Squelched
145 Olympic star in 1936
146 Dillon portrayer

DOWN

1 "Envious" stabber
2 Author of "Le Mal": 1916
3 Appearances
4 Soprano from Conn.
5 Erhard's therapy
6 First woman to govern a
   state
7 "Tea for two and ____ you"
8 One or another
9 ". . . notions about ____
   power": Swift
10 Loose gown
11 Crested spoons
12 Ornamental cord
13 Jour's opposite
14 Army hut
15 Refer
16 Cubic meter
17 Poker count
18 Mine, to Marie
19 Kin of oodles
20 Gaelic
26 Acapulco gold

32 Scholar's acquisition
33 Michelangelo, to Lorenzo
35 Hurok
37 Room in a pension
41 "____ and little fishes!"
43 Municipal agcy.
44 "Whatever ____ right":
   Pope
46 Leapin' ____
47 Beats in Gray's "Elegy
   . . ."?
48 French city on the Maine
49 Asiatic partridge
50 Impact
51 Options for changing the
   inhabitants?
52 Shakespearean hanger
53 Glissaded
54 Greek letter
55 Batter
56 Antony's faithful soldier
59 Exclude
62 "Hearken!"
63 Without listening
66 Small spring
67 Where eggbeaters hover
68 Gustaf ____, former Swedish king
70 "Faerie Queene" hag
73 Egyptian god of pleasure
74 Not processed
75 Monogram in the news:
   Nov. 22, 1963
76 Fido's offering
77 Slit in a jacket
79 Pismire
80 Ho's partner
81 True grit
82 Cooking utensil

83 Cash-register recording
84 Pleasant changes
85 Fought like D'Artagnan
86 C.A. trees
87 Cockcrow
89 Apartment area
91 Year in Henry II's reign
92 Norwegian monarch
94 Cleave
96 Bibliog. entry
97 Devour
98 What a plump steed does
   to an extent?
99 Double quartet
103 ". . . there are ____ be
   broke": Scott
104 "Kanthapura" author: 1938
105 Sowers
108 "Take ____ Train," 1941
   song
109 Teachers' org.
111 Mexican matron
112 Axilla
116 Letters for Y. A. Tittle?
117 Splendid raiment
119 Elves
120 Sawlike: Comb. form
122 Winged
123 Pouts
124 Markets
125 Speaker at Cooperstown
126 What a dibble makes
127 Kind of tide or log
128 Actor Donald: 1880–1946
129 Gypsum
130 Indian Ocean vessel
132 Actress Swenson
137 Spider
138 Wolfhound's warning

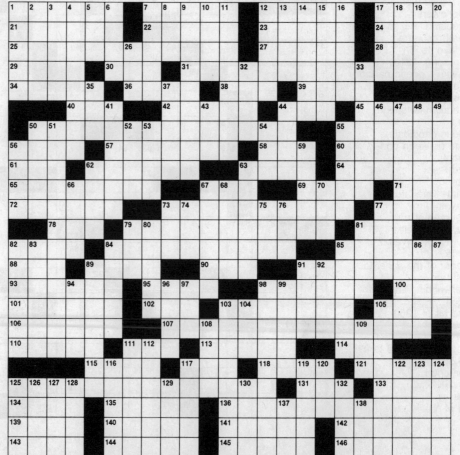

199. Fore! by Margaret Rigby

ACROSS

1 Nobelist Hahn
5 Chick chaser
9 The Beehive State
13 Louis from Louisiana
18 These are flaky
20 Somewhat, in music
21 He wrote "La Vie de Jésus": 1863
22 Jeans' partners
23 U.S. emblem
26 Metric unit
27 Of a piece
29 King of Mass.
30 ____ gestae
31 Dock
34 Like a chit
36 Biblical priest
37 Type of verse
39 Play the card
41 Despot
45 Aegean island
46 Event on June 17, 1775
50 Tapir
51 Citole and trichord
52 Prep sch.
53 Cay or holm
57 Wading bird
59 Electrical wave: Prefix
61 Scotch fiddles
63 Wife of le roi
65 Epic in 12 books
67 Persons easily swayed
68 Rochet's relative
69 Preeminently
73 Poet's palindrome
74 Fusty
76 Trinacria, today
77 Peak in NW Wash.
79 Arty parties
81 Character on a staff
82 Foundation
83 Suburb SE of Paris
84 Romance lang.
86 Harry or Henry
89 You, to a Quaker
92 The bends, to caisson workers
97 U.N. labor body
98 Title of honor
99 Hair conditioner
100 Oscar and family
103 Enzyme
104 Grand ____
107 Venturi
108 Lumber splitter
109 By way of
110 Flavoring for ouzo
112 Lizard, also called fringefoot
113 Classifies
116 Color shade
122 Pitiless
123 Actuality
124 Race-track pavilion
125 Kefauver
126 Refuges
127 Maxwell or Schiaparelli
128 Sketched

DOWN

1 East, in Essen
2 Hallux or dactyl
3 Menlo Park monogram
4 Rhea, to Romans
5 Talia from N.Y.C.
6 Personnel official
7 Choose
8 Pelion's supporter
9 Greek vowel
10 First sergeant
11 Area unit
12 Gardener's tool
13 Be successful
14 Pacific herb
15 "Odalisque" painter: 1814
16 Cob and buck
17 "____ of robins . . ."
19 Oratory
24 Patron saint of Catania
25 Coach Shula
28 "____ pray"
31 Spongy cake
32 Where Matrah is
33 Ruddy duck
35 President who weighed over 300 pounds
38 Barney Miller's colleagues
40 The world, to Jaques
42 Japanese seaport
43 Without hesitation
44 Penny ____
47 Queen of Italy in 1900
48 External
49 Ides, in Roma
54 Rope-shortening knot
55 ____-Rollin, French politician: 1807–74
56 Curvy letters
58 Mature
59 "____ by land"
60 Mistress Quickly
62 These beat deuces
63 Cow catcher
64 Place for a reredos
65 Vein, nerve or feather
66 "Behold!" to Brutus
70 Houdini feat
71 Inventor of dynamite
72 Affray
75 St. Ignatius of ____
78 Gaynor from Chicago
80 Incite to attack
85 Asian silkworm
86 Parisians' pleasures
87 Hill builder
88 The "Say Hey Kid"
90 Gaelic language
91 London hero
93 Escorts
94 Township in NE N.J.
95 Demands firmly
96 Former county of Northern Ireland
97 "____ Sixpence"
100 Small error
101 Departures
102 Lizzie's predecessor
105 Pips or pippins
106 Protozoan
110 Opposite of apterous
111 Ending for differ or refer
114 Suffix for ethyl
115 Birds ____ feather
117 "____ Be Seeing You": 1938
118 Curl or Funseth
119 Cont.
120 Compass pt.
121 Just out

200. Mix and Match by Judson G. Trent

ACROSS

1 Amiens's river
6 Donner or Khyber
10 Chrysalis
14 Southwestern art center
18 Nautical term
19 Krubi's kin
20 Pyromaniac's act
21 Reef
22 Importunate?
24 Enumeration?
26 Tay feeder
27 Common verbal contraction
28 Arizona flattops
29 Schools in Sedan
30 Ruby that sparkles onstage
31 Middle of a well-known Kipling trio
32 Welland is one
33 Groups of three
34 Dutch cheeses
35 Maestro Georg
36 Indian ranges
37 Falsifies, as evidence
40 Iridescent?
42 Links teacher
45 "All ____!"
46 Kind of artery or vein
47 As to
48 Uncompromising
49 Novelette
50 "Awake and Sing!" playwright
51 Springe
53 Female sandpiper
54 Myra or Rudolf
55 Blockhead
56 Article in Aachen
57 "Laura" lyricist
58 "____ was saying . . ."
59 Legislator?
63 Antenna connectors
64 TV hit show
67 Emanate
68 Sacking
69 L.A. eleven
71 Emendation?
73 Call ____ day
76 K.P. utensils
77 Cumulus
78 Nones follower
79 Expectant
80 He played Chan 16 times
81 Consecrate
82 Duties
84 Saw
85 "I ____ Song Go . . ."
86 Berlin's "He's ____ Picker"
87 Lawmaker
88 London critic
89 Nabokov's "The ____"
90 Coordinate?
93 Holy Land pilgrims
94 Like Bryce Canyon
96 Roman games official
97 Quest of running mates
98 Lacking
100 Word with time or room
101 Suspicious
102 Vichy is one
105 Flower or locust tree
106 Parts of tents
107 Trunk line, in a way
108 Actor Tamiroff
109 Oscillation?
111 Procreation?
113 Prompters
114 Coppers
115 Abstracted
116 Mickey Mouse, in Mexico
117 Wrongful act
118 Aglets
119 Raisin for Reynaldo
120 Mingle

DOWN

1 Flavorsome
2 Like Falstaff
3 Oberon from Tasmania
4 Pistol-packer of songdom
5 Cassowary's cousin
6 Plates for the Host
7 Adjective for a flared skirt
8 Letter drop
9 ____ Bernadino
10 Dull
11 Prevalent
12 Lily from France
13 Pismire
14 Joining pegs
15 An Astaire
16 Pointed arches
17 Sun. discourses
19 Ricochets
20 Catkins
21 Aboveboard
23 Geraint's tunic
25 Oxygenize
28 Derived from apples
31 Idolize
32 Musical denouements
33 "____ is a tide . . ."
34 Les ____-Unis
35 Pet
36 Art of Bruegel or Vermeer
37 Muscovite's villa
38 Shawm's descendants
39 Desecration?
40 ____ la Cité
41 Merry
42 Peripatetic?
43 Split
44 Measures in Judea
46 Teraphim
48 Frey's wife
50 Sevillian stewpots
51 Earthquake
52 Nipponese born in Napa
53 Kind of estate
55 Kon-Tiki's troubles
57 Ponds, in poesy
60 Celts
61 Battle scene: Feb. 24, 1916
62 Corcovado's city
63 Mandolins' kin
65 Detroit's Joe Louis ____
66 Daube
68 Black Forest site
69 Letter-shaped wagon tongue
70 "Roots" author
71 Muralist Rivera
72 Ford's predecessor
74 Subject of a Blake poem
75 Copyists
77 "Big A" bet
79 Inedible apple
81 Finistère port
82 ____ de Jouy (fabric)
83 Tub plant
84 Part of a tennis court
86 Lord or God, in Hebrew
87 Stimulates
88 Henchman
91 Victuals
92 Modifies
93 Berryman's bequest
94 Convoy
95 Saddlers' products
97 Home of Valentine and Proteus
98 Hearing: Comb. form
99 He packs cotton
100 First-aid contrivance
101 Western weeds, for short
102 What the Rangers do
103 Climber's spike
104 Improve
105 I.R.S. employee
106 Kind of market
107 Buffalo's cousin
108 Inland sea
110 Emulate Arnold Moss
111 Ketcham's Dennis, e.g.
112 Any planet

ANSWERS

1

```
JACOB   CHAP   SLAPS   POLES
OSAKA   LIMA   TOTAL   SALADE
SITAR   ELAM   AGORA   HIEMAL
HATSOFFTHE   ISPASSINGBY
        NUT    LSD    SHAPES
RUNSIN  AMAT   BOO    MSS   VEE
EVITA   ADE    OVERLAP      KINE
DUVAL   MOW    NARD   CLE   ISSY
   LER  SORI   ENGINEER     RICO
SANS    TRETS         EAT   ROSTER
PALO    HADUP  TAB    ATONE
   THATOUR   WASSTILLTHERE
   RANK  SAO   METOO  ARUN
SAIGAS  DNS    INARI        SHE
TIRL    RAISEDA       AHEM  SLUB
ALIE    ALA    VUGS   LOO   STALE
FEED    FLEECED        OF   QATAR
FDR     TAR    NNE    OAST  RUDEST
        LOVERS        TWR   MIA
   ISEWEDUN   GINGLYONTHAT
   WAVER  GAMUT   UXOR   TAXED
GIBEAT   BRASH   EINE   ALILA
SNEERS   YENTE   DIDY   GOLLY
```

2

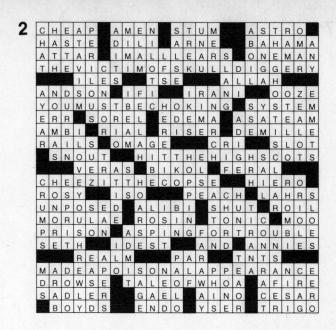

```
CHEAP   AMEN   STUM    ASTRO
HASTE   DILI   ARNE    BAHAMA
ATTAR   IMALLEARS      ONEMAN
THEVICTIMOFSKULLDIGGERY
        ILES   TSE     ALLAH
ANDSON  IFI    IRANI   OOZE
YOUMUSTBECHOKING       SYSTEM
ERR     SOREL  EDEMA   ASATEAM
AMBI    RIAL   RISER   DEMILLE
RAILS   OMAGE  CRI     SLOT
SNOUT   HITTHEHIGHSCOTS
        VERAS  BIKOL   FERAL
CHEEZITTHECOPSE        HIERO
ROSY    ISO    PEACH   LAHRS
UNPOSED ALIBI  SHUT    ROIL
MORULAE ROSIN  TONIC   MOO
PRISON  ASPINGFORTROUBLE
SETH    IDEST  AND     ANNIES
        REALM  PAR     TNTS
MADEAPOISONALAPPEARANCE
DROWSE  TALEOFWHOA     AFIRE
SADLER  GAEL   AINO    CESAR
BOYDS   ENDO   YSER    TRIGO
```

3

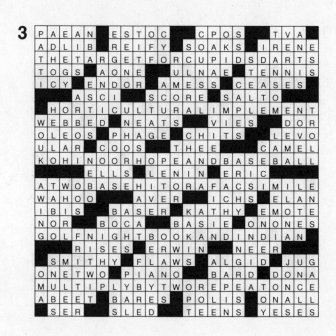

```
PAEAN   ESTOC  CPOS    TVA
ADLIB   REIFY  SOAKS   IRENE
THETARGETFORCUPIDSDARTS
TOGS    AONE   ULNAE   TENNIS
ICY     ENDOR  AMESS   CEASES
        ASCI   SCORE   SALTO
HORTICULTURALIMPLEMENT
WEBBED  NEATS  VIES    DOR
OLEOS   PHAGE  CHITS   LEVO
ULAR    COOS   THEE    CAMEL
KOHINOORHOPEANDBASEBALL
        ELLS   LENIN   ERIC
ATWOBASEHITORAFACSIMILE
WAHOO   AVER   ICHS    ELAN
IBIS    BASER  KATHY   EMOTE
NOR     BOCA   BASIE   ONONES
GOLFNIGHTBOOKANDINDIAN
        RISES  ERWIN   NEER
SMITHY  FLAWS  ALGID   JUG
ONETWO  PIANO  BARD    DONA
MULTIPLYBYTWOREPEATONCE
ABEET   BARES  POLIS   ONALL
SER     SLED   TEENS   YESES
```

4

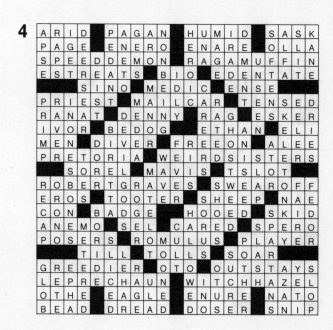

```
ARID    PAGAN  HUMID   SASK
PAGE    ENERO  ENARE   OLLA
SPEEDDEMON     RAGAMUFFIN
ESTREATS       BIO   EDENTATE
        SINO   MEDIC   ENSE
PRIEST  MAILCAR        TENSED
RANAT   DENNY  RAG     ESKER
IVOR    BEDOG  ETHAN   ELI
MEN     DIVER  FREEON  ALEE
PRETORIA       WEIRDSISTERS
SOREL   MAVIS  TSLOT
ROBERTGRAVES   SWEAROFF
EROS    TOOTER SHEEP   NAE
CON     BADGE  HOOED   SKID
ANEMO   SEL    CARED   SPERO
POSERS  ROMULUS        PLAYER
        TILL   TOLLS   SOAR
GREEDIER       OTO   OUTSTAYS
LEPRECHAUN     WITCHHAZEL
OTHE    EAGLE  ENURE   NATO
BEAD    DREAD  DOSER   SNIP
```

5

```
CARAT   CODE   SARA    SIGNS
ANOLE   HARM   CHIN    CORAL
LEAVECAREBEHIND        ADOBE
MANANAS GREERS         SLAVED
SRS     ALEF   ALMAE   PETES
        GIRO   CEE     AIRER
ABODE   OVERREACTS     CRS
HOUR    BELA   DYES    GLUE
ANTA    AKEGOFBEER      GUEST
BADGERED       ROOMS   BRAVES
        OATER  MARIA   GLARE
STOWED  MONTS  CHANDLER
ARRAS   HITTHEROAD     IASO
RUBY    DONE   ANTE    ANNO
DEA     FINALFLING     ANDES
        RAREE  RON     EMEU
   ABRIM   DRIBS   SERS   BBC
GREETS  REJAIL         ONTARIO
ASCOT   LABORDAYWEEKEND
BOULE   AMAL   EVOE    RINGY
SNEER   BABE   REND    EASES
```

6

```
GUYS    AMISS  HEIR    PASTA
ANEW    TASTE  ORNE    ASPIC
IDLEGOSSIP     TATTLETALE
TOLERATORS     STORYLINES
        OTIS   PEST    POOL
ATWITTER       SCOW   SNAGGED
MAJESTIES      AVE     LODE
PROP    ORPHANED       GLEASON
ETUIS   ELAND  SOLECISMS
RAREE   ARTA   PETERI
ERN     SCANDALSHEETS   PTA
        APTEST MOOR    ISCHL
SALOONIST      OSKAR   SPORI
ERICSON RANOUTOF        ELAN
MASH    ALG    MINISCULE
INTENSE PEEL   CENTIMES
        OHNO   ARAL    EOAN
ARISTOCRAT     SOCIALLIFE
PECCADILLO     HAIRRAISER
ANEAR   NOIR   ECLAT   STAR
SORRY   ANDY   SHINS   TSTS
```

7

```
GIROS UTAH DRILLS CHEW
AGANA SIDE EONIAN FHOLE
FUZZYGUZZY TOOTSYWOOTSY
FAZE RAZES ESNES IRISES
ENL DELYS INTER ANGRY
AERIES ANTE ALTE TAB
DANK HUGGERMUGGER ONA
CLARES ABIES AROAR ITER
OOZED OLOR BLARE COSMO
LAZE DOLLALOLLA RUNYON
ATL POET MODES SOLI
SHEPHERD BEFIT NAUTCHES
RELS RENTE TOTE ORT
FILIAL ROWDYDOWDY LOGO
ABIND MAYAS DIOR TACOS
CELT SOFAR FUELS MIGHTS
TAL HUSTLEBUSTLE OKAY
AMY ANES ARES BRINKS
PADDY CARRS HAULS OKA
TRIUNE TAINO FARCE MOOT
MELLOWYELLOW RICKYTICKY
ECLAT ARLENE OLDE ACHIP
NUYS PRIDED MEET PAYEE
```

8

```
AWL SAP SPARTA ALCAN
BIO ERA AENEAS BAHIA
SELS ASCENDEDSTEADILY
ARLEDGE TESTATOR INES
IDI IONIA NEURONE
SAW ODER APA NICOSIA
ORAL ABBOTT DNA ETS
NEWINTHERACKET GLARES
MAIA ASKARI ANIME
REJOINS DEE VEEP AVON
ELU LEAVESTRANDED ENT
SESO ATON MEL ICEFREE
TATRA ITTOME THEE
ANITRA DOWNINTHEDUMPS
MOC EGG NIENTE DAIL
PRESEAR SYD ACID LEA
BOLDEST FRAME APT
SKYE INERTIAL MANIPLE
HARVARDNEWSPAPER REAR
ALOES ENSILE ARE ART
HENRI LASTED WAT STE
```

9

```
RIGA APARA SCOT PAWS
ITER PLACES ARAR ALLIES
GEORGEBURNS TOTIEFIELDS
ORR OREL TETEA BITE BAT
RAGED EFLATS TAURE SUNS
STEAL OILSA STERNER
ESSE ERNS RAISE ELMS
ATTENDS IDLE PROFILE
TIN ASS SANDE BREN LEA
ANDHAVE IRAE ERIA BLET
INSURE IRE DAVIDFROSTS
LASARRE BENEFIT
GERALDFORDS SON INTEND
ENOS RITA TEAR CRESTED
TUB MORE COVET COM HOT
ARERIPE SANA FORSAKE
ERAT HOMED SONE BILL
TRELLIS ERICV SEWON
LOBE AEROS RATHER ERASE
AMU TRAS OUSTS RAIN TES
MARSHAHUNTS TOMSMOTHERS
ANNIES TOTE ENDEAR ARTE
ISTO ELOD DEIST ISON
```

10

```
CAVORT CATER OPAH ALCAN
IBERIA OBESE NISI DIEGO
OCLOCKSHADOW DAYSWONDER
NSA HELOTS IMINE ALDER
HARE ORONO PYLE
POL MOTT SMITE BALANCES
EPITOME STINT SOLAR YAK
RETAPE THATGOTAWAY OLGA
UNTIE COEDS ATTU SWILL
SELL HOPEI RADIO DINNED
ERE MENONAHORSE CREEDS
ICUMEN ALP COUVRE
ANISES HILLSOFROME RRS
SUDDEN TOTES URALS AMAH
TRIES ROTC OTICS FLORA
ROAR LANEHIGHWAY MOSTEL
URN BAGEL NOSIR CABOOSE
MASTERED RESAT MARS RTS
HAIR DIPSY RAVI
SEERS TAPTI MATINS FIE
ONTHEAISLE POINTLANDING
SITAR DAIS ENSUE DUENNA
STETS ERST DEEPS EGGSON
```

11

```
MOANS WAAC KIDS BATCH
ACRID ICER UVEA OPHIO
THEGRATEFULDEAD NEEDS
TECH RCT EAU DIAS WET
ERAT GHOULS AERATE
MOOING HIGHSPIRITS
BEGAD NEON RUE IRAE
EARRING ICEMAN ANDRE
GRAECO DEMON DISMISS
ETV FAIT FEM COATI
THESPIRITOFSEVENTYSIX
YEAST UNI MIRO TRY
WARTHOG ENDOR REDEAL
CHRIS FRAISE SALERNO
TODA ALL GAMO BASIN
NASTYDEVILS LAUDED
HECATE ARGYLE BREW
CRI LOUS RIA PFC EAVE
RIFLE DEVILSFOODCAKES
ESTOP ENIN POLO STERE
WASNT SDAK SEED ASSYR
```

12

```
HIS SLUG MALLS SMU PAD
ANTIHERO ELAIO AIM JAVA
WROTEOUT DALEYANDBAILEY
NEWMANSCHUMANANDTRUMAN
EURE HOSE STREAK NUB
AMPS PARADED ARG ICEL
RIOTACT NEARED MEANEST
ILE CHASE SLOPE SIG
OLA RESCALE VERA DEBIT
SANDER ENABLE ISSUE EKE
ENDED ANDREI ACTON SLED
DBL KEELANDSTEELE ALA
ABEE ARROS OURARI HINNY
MIA STAIR ISLAND RECEDE
ALULA ENON UPDATER LPS
IRI SENDS BYAND LIT
OCARINA SEAMER MISTAKE
FAME IST FROLICS ANER
FRO ATOAST OUCH MAUD
WELLINGTONANDELLINGTON
GABLEANDGRABLE OUTTHERE
ASAD LEA AVOIR ENTITLES
SHE STY HESTS SAYS LOS
```

Crossword puzzles 13–18 (completed grids)

13

```
IRAN  LOP      BARE   GLUB
NEGEV IDEA  SWEDEN    RAVEL
PENOFPOETS    PODOFDIETERS
USE WINSIT ROO      NAHANT
TESS  NESTOFEGGHEADS  SES
       TESLA REI  AGREED
TENON    NILE  ESKAR  DEJA
SLICER   SOAR  EELER  WADE
PACKSOFSMOKERS   ETAL  NOX
STE   SLY   AETA    JUJUBE
ERA  SANE  ADLER    NOSES
    DROVESOFMOTORISTS
ABODE   TROUT  WANT   HSM
BOASTS  HAUS   PSI    TIM
BOS SOFA  CLIQUESOFHEELS
ALTS  LIBEL CUTE   FIXING
ASTI  REBEC EARS   LINER
    SNIPER ALE  HAETS
SEA  KNOTOFMARINERS  TOTE
UNBELT  LES  GIANTS   ZAP
PRIDEOFSNOBS  OFREALTORS
SODAS  ARROYO RTES  SANTO
  LEMS  GOAD     YDS   DEEM
```

14

```
SRACES    IMPS  THAW   OWL
ERRATUM   RIOT  RATE   NIE
NOTSEEIDENORAIROF    ODS
AMIE  CROON    EADSTONES
TOSS  SHOUT  ARNES   NENE
ETA  TOAST   LION    RISER
  ENCORES   HELEN   OOID
   HURL  FIDO   SPRANG
SMEARY   LEDTO   AIRSHIP
HAIRS  OHARA  RACES   OLE
ANNA  APPYOOLIGAN   ORLO
POR  ANISE   PESOS   OLSEN
ERICSON  DOPES   AULERS
  CRIMES  VERA    MUTE
  SHAD  PEERS   MONGREL
ATIME  TERR   TANTO   LAS
LAMP  LENOS  WORTS   PENN
AMMEREADS   KORDA   ECTO
MEL  COMEELLORIGHWATER
ONE  ANER   CEDE   EYESORE
SSR  FEDS  DEYS    STERNS
```

15

```
LINDA  SPIRALS   SCAN   QUA
AVERS  ALSATIA   OHIO   PUNY
MARYHADALITTLELAMB   HIDE
ANON LIN  LEANERS   TODOS
    ELIS  ZOE  ULM  ERN
BATSINTHEBELFRY   BRIEFER
ENISLE ONE OIE  MAO  BRAE
ATA  LOAD  RARE  OUTS  OERS
REJOINS  DOWNFORTHECOUNT
CAUSE  SAUNA   TATE   LTD
UTAS  PAWN  KOCH   REHIT
BEN  CHINESECHECKERS   AEC
RABID  ODAL   URNS   ONLY
 BUG  SEER   OIRAT  ANSER
CARLSBADCAVERNS   RIVOLTA
RIAL  URDU  IRON  MYNA  IAN
ASSN  NAY  SSS  ETO  ALEPPO
BESEECH  VICTORIACROSSES
   CRO  BEG   USE  RANT
ALIKE  ZERMATT   AUG   IRIS
JOKE  HERMAJESTYSSERVICE
ACED  ANTI  ALECOST   EAGER
XIS   LOAN  RETUNES   BLAST
```

16

```
PAT     ARM   BET   OLGA
ALAS  CLII  INRE  REALMS
ROKE  RIND  OTANNENBAUM
CHECKINGITTWICE    BSA
HAM  ABEL  RAINOR   AMAHL
 SECT  IDA  NED   CAMEL
  LEARNED  EEE   LARAS
SOME  BUGLE    ROTL
CRUMPLE   EPEES    ERS
RARELY  MISTLETOE   YOUR
ATANY  CAROLLERS   ASTRO
MELT  FRUITCAKE  GIGGED
 DSM  RAISE    ENTHUSE
   OBIT    AORTA   OTTO
 SPORT  TDS  IDEATES
SPIRE   REP  MAP   UTAH
TIGER  BECOME  APIE   NOW
ENS  EBENEZERSCROOGE
MAKINGALIST  ATEE   KITE
SLIVER  EVOE  DEUS   SNIP
  NEER    ERR  SED   TEY
```

17

```
ALES  FULAS   AQABA   ADAPT
RENT  OFARC   SUMUP   WARRED
IONE  RANCH   TOOTS   AMMONO
TRUANT  GHANA   TEAK   AVOW
HAILTHOUEVERBLESSEDMORN
  THEBES   STAY   PARE
ALPH  MAD  FTHENRY   WANTAD
VEL  LADOGA  ERNIE   ATTILA
ANURAN  CORNI   CASK   MEN
INVEIGH  DOORDIE   TEANECK
LOIS  EAVE  CPOS   AUGIE
 NOEARMAYHEARHISCOMING
  DROPS  ANTI  TACO  SORA
GIRAFFE  ANTHEMS   ODYSSEY
UNO  BREL  ISAAC   PRETER
SCATHE  GOLFS  ATELES  RTE
THROAT  GEORGEM  LOO  LASS
   RUHR   AOUT  ALEPPO
OLITTLEKINGINSTABLEBORN
RENO  EXAM   DAKAR  EGERIA
CALIPH  PATTI  ULAMA  LAGS
ADESTE  ORION  NAGEL  ILOT
 STEAM  KIANG  KNELL  AERY
```

18

```
CLAM    PRIM   APPTS   AGHA
LOGAN  LIMO   SELAH   SAON
URANO  ADAR   MRORR   SROS
BRINGINGMEWASYOURIDEA
SYNE  IKE  TIROS    BOGEY
   QUIT   ONAN      ANN
SHOUT  OBAD   APSES   SEX
NOWIMINAMAUDLINSTUPOR
ARENOT  WAYNE  TOO   RONA
PAD  SHALL  CARHOP   ITSY
  STOT   FILLE   THIS
ISAW  UNDINE  SOYAS   EBB
NENA  GOA  FADES   GOSLOW
GETMEHOMEORELSEILLBEA
AKH  ETNAS   SLAV   DEARY
   REL    OSLO    EPEE
LOVEA  STEAL  ARI    PANG
SUPERDUPERPARTYPOOPER
AZON  ORARE  TITO   PURGE
ROIL  BARIS  EGAN   STORE
ANDY  ELECT  DARE   SNIT
```

19

```
MARC  MORON  CLAM  BREAD
OMOO  ARULE  OARY  LUNGE
SOMMERANDWYNTER  UNION
TIPPLING  BATH  THEODDS
LIST  HOWE  ELF
ACHES  SERENE  TRAFFIC
SLAT  BOWANDDARROW  ALE
KORE  APER  GEAN  ASIA
EST  BLUEANDGRAY  ETTAS
WEARIEST  ARIEL  TIRADE
NOTE  SHIVS  EDEN
MADDEN  DOANE  AGREEDTO
ANSER  BULLANDBAER  LOU
CIAO  CARO  RIOT  WONT
ASH  ROBANDSTEELE  HOAR
WELCOME  GENIAL  AISLE
ATE  NOED  HALS
DEFLATE  CURB  SOLSTICE
EXALT  WILDEANDWOOLLEY
MARIE  ERIE  READE  ELBA
OMENS  RAPS  SEKOS  REUS
```

20

```
ACROSS  GROS  SSA  ARDEN
CREDIT  RETE  HUTS  PEELER
CUDDLY  OSTE  ONAS  PETITE
UCA  LEFTTORIGHT  ASSENTS
SENDS  ATE  STAIRS  ECOLE
ESSO  CROSSSTITCHES  TRET
WHIR  HERES  ITAL
CANNAS  OSIRIS  KNUTE  DAM
ASAPH  BOSNIA  DEEPINDEBT
ROMANCINGS  ARES  ADOBES
TREY  ANAT  PHREN  STEWS
MATES  DOUAI  CAIRN
BETHS  RICER  GARO  TRAP
POINTA  VASO  PALINDROME
BUTTERFISH  CAROLS  EOSIN
STS  STOOP  NOVELS  ELDEST
TIRL  TETES  ENID
APRS  CROSSSECTIONS  EDER
DREAM  ONEATA  NOD  ANODE
DIGGERS  GROUNDFLOOR  TIP
EMIGRE  MUIR  AERI  SEDATE
RENEGE  BENS  NEAT  SAIGON
DARED  ASA  APSE  ALPERT
```

21

```
ACTUP  LOCAL  APPLE
RESNAP  EXILED  PAIRER
CLAMMED  JETPROPULSION
STRIPER  ONES  DIG  TONE
XANADU  AGA  SORES
CAFES  PORPOISEFULLY
AROS  SER  HOOK  MOP
MSU  CHAMPIONSHIP  ALAR
PORTAE  SOC  AAA  CENT
INSOLE  CHAD  RLO  KATE
COLTBLOODEDMURDER
ROOM  SRI  LASH  TERNES
AURA  AMP  POB  HASSLE
WREN  SUPERBOWLWIN  HEV
YOU  SOLI  AAN  AONE
SCENESTEELERS  ASWAN
BATHS  RAY  RETINA
ALAI  AIM  AREA  EVEREST
RIDEEMCOWBOYS  DELUDER
ASIFTO  SOLARE  SELENE
STASH  KYNES  DENTS
```

22

```
CHAP  THUG  IDAS  IMAY  TLC
LISA  RONA  NOCT  MONA  HAH
EVER  ETAL  LUTE  AMOK  ERA
FEATHERSOFABIRD  EMS  MIS
OTHO  PHILO  OMNI  CAST
HALFSOLE  ADEN  NOTE  ORSE
UNIT  ULT  TORERO  ALCAN
BATHES  HAJJ  FATOF  POH
EXEC  SOU  TWO  TERROR
ABAFT  RAKED  HEATHS  OFA
PAHI  BIKE  GOER  RES  FIVE
TBAR  AMID  MOP  NASA  ADIG
SINS  NET  HEMI  ESPY  NENG
EDT  FOEMAN  ELIHU  NOSEY
RIPOFF  EST  COG  RANT
NAN  TONTO  ECHO  BEHELD
ASTRO  HOTOFF  APO  ELIA
BAHT  KEPI  EROS  FOURRIER
UREY  ESSO  RENTA  PTAH
SAB  SEC  NORETURNOFPOINT
ICI  PLED  LODI  LAVA  ROUE
VER  EENY  PROM  OPEC  SWIT
END  CREE  ESME  SERE  EATS
```

23

```
ABASED  DIPS  OBOL  BAWL
LENAPE  INRE  AURA  OLIO
BACKINANGER  SHADOWOFA
STEIG  THECRUEL  STEED
EUR  SLURS  ALTO
SATRAPY  TULE  ASIA  TPK
ENHALO  DAYAFTERNOON
AVIS  NANCE  NORI  OHRE
LISP  ANOA  DATA  NOTATE
ELF  MISSIONIM  DRIVEL
ODHAL  HARTS  CARNE
GARRET  ISGREENER  ASS
ALHIRT  LAOS  RINK  TNUT
FLIP  RILL  SALON  EDDO
FORTHESEESAW  ENSTAR
EWE  ASER  CRAW  ISOTONE
RISE  PARMA  CST
SURAL  PARADISE  DAZED
KNOWSBEST  NOFORCOMEDY
IDLE  OAST  GWEN  ANLAGE
MOLD  ARTY  ENDO  DEALER
```

24

```
BASS  SIDE  ULES  HEAPS
ALTA  EMUS  PILAR  ONTOP
TEAR  AMPS  ATOLL  SCOUR
HERDOFELEPHANTS  TANNA
SHORE  RINGO  ASPECT
ADE  MOS  MELIAN  POSSES
CORPSDEBALLET  LIF
TENS  AGA  SERENA  AMS
AGENCY  MYTH  DEN  NASAL
LIA  AIAS  STAGLINE
ALEXANDERSRAGTIMEBAND
COLOSSUS  TERR  LIL
CRASS  LEA  MGOS  ESCORT
TEN  REALMS  AUR  ARIA
ERR  BOYSCOUTTROOP
CLAQUE  GULASH  POA  STA
RERUNS  ALAMO  OSOLE
ENVOI  SWARMSOFLOCUSTS
WOETO  LANDE  SLOP  GAEA
ELLEN  VICAR  LOPE  ETAL
RASES  NEYS  OWEN  SEME
```

25

```
BASELESS   OBTAIN    AMALG
ASTRAEAN   SOONLY   MNESIA
THESHERIFFOFNOTTINGHAM
SEWER  API  MOAN  WLU  IRMA
     THEBELLMANOFLONDON
SAHARA      EEL   BOO  MESNE
THEMERCHANTOFVENICE
LOWED  AID  WIE  ELY  NADA
OMEN  ANTIC  ERR  MEOWER
   THEMASTEROFBALLANTRAE
   TOTI   DID   JOT  TAYRA
   THETHIEFOFBAGHDAD
ASPEN  EAR  ULA   RIVE
THEPIEDPIPEROFHAMELIN
MUSICA   SAL   TONED  SUMP
OLAV  CRO  RET  UNE  AERIE
     THEVICAROFWAKEFIELD
ATPAR  DIS   INF   FATSOS
THEBARBEROFSEVILLE
TELL  EAD  CIEL  SEA  TROIS
   THEMAYOROFCASTERBRIDGE
EATERS   MEETNO  DURATION
EMOLS   NESSES   SERPENTS
```

26

```
SATI   MITES   ATIME   RCAF
OLAN   INURE   PACES   EHRE
FIRSTSERGE   PRINCEVALI
APPURTEN   DIET   LATERON
      REED  ALDA  POPART
SAUGER   THEELBE   EGBERT
ALLEN   PIETA   LST   EERIE
LAYS   ROTAS   HEART   REMN
ELS   SALAD   BANDIED   DUD
MUSICMAN   GUYDEMAUPASS
      EARP   ARLES   CROC
RUSSIANEMIGR   FOURACTS
ANS   PRENAME   KAPPA   OAT
DRIP   TASTY   CRIES   RUNE
IRMAS   LEI   PAINS   LONGA
CAPRAS   ASPERSE   TOMTOM
   STREAM   ANDS   COPA
AVOIDER   ANNI   ARKANSAN
NONCONCORD   GATEATTEND
GIGI   TOONE   APLEY   YMCA
LERP   OTHER   NOELS   REEK
```

27

```
SLOPE   COSTA   VASE   AMID
PIVOT   ORLON   REMIT  INONE
ANENCLOSUREFORAPAINTING
CERT  ALONE  RUBS   SNORES
EST  BRINK  GATOS   SHINER
   CAVE   MACES   LEAN
MANANA   TWOBASEBALLGAMES
ORANGE   ROSES   RILL  FULA
TROTS  PAULS  BEARS  COROT
HOMO  ALINE  AUNTS  MIRAGE
SWINGSANDMISSES   LEVELED
   ITIS   SOT   ROME
STRIVED   HALFSIZEBOTTLES
TRACER  CADET  SAVES  HIKE
AUDEN  MINES  COPES  DAVIT
FRAN  TORO  SAPOR  CEMENT
FORTHEPRICEOFONE   ONEDGE
   ONEI   RULED   HATS
STOURS   EURUS   BLARE  MER
ATERRE   DIET   SLATS  HALE
DUPLICATESKEPTINRESERVE
IDEES  CANEA   OUNCE  URIEL
BYES   TOSS   ADDED   BRASS
```

28

```
WASHUP   AMAIN   ALMA   SPIT
IGNORE   BARCO   TEAR   SCENA
THEPEANUTMEGSTATE   URALS
SADE   NOSIER   LIVE   GRANET
   UPEND   PORED   REPUTE
BEAST  TED   CEPE   SATIT
ETHELS   RELAPSE   ATONCE
LEAPAT   LITANY   LAME  GRAB
ARROYO   OTARU   TIRED   AGE
INDY   YES   LATERON   SACRE
REP   TOWS   SPITES   HIKER
   ENSUE   ORDAINS   PAINE
OHARA   SHOOIN   LAPP   RTE
LUNAR   ALADDIN   ATE   ASEM
GNU   CALOR   BOOED   ASSURE
ATTA   OPEN   CONURE   NOTIME
   STRIPE   GALLING   UNITER
   ORNIS   ROTC   ALT   REDS
ARCADE   SITUS   DALIS
DARNED   TRET   PUNISH  AGUE
IMAGE   FROMSOUPTOPEANUTS
RACED   MINI   ARRET   LINNET
ELKS   SAYS   FRESH   LAISSE
```

29

```
 MEETS   AAA   PEI   AGON
GANOHI   SCRIBERS   NINE
ONTHEWATERFRONT   GAGES
TIE   FAIR   ATONAL   EMIRS
HARAR   MARSHA   ESNE
   MEASLE   EDDA   ATRAP
MALANG   DAYWAR   SLIVER
EVINCE   FOL   AMA   SECEDE
SELFHEAL   LAYIN   AMARES
ASSOC   RAGTIME   ORANTE
   ROOT   AHLEN   MINI
CRANNY   REELSIN   SNUGS
CHALNA   TOKYO   MISAPPLY
HAMLET   ANI   DIP   AGADIR
ENESCO   ANNOYS   ARROBA
SEETO   LEGS   ANDREI
   AITS   SHARER   ESTER
TASSO   ANIMAL   TASM   RNA
ORION   GONEWITHTHEWIND
STAN   AMENABLE   ENATES
HEMS   NEE   ISR   ATSEA
```

30

```
MALAY   SPLIT   STAFF   STEMS
AMOLE   PRADO   MYLAI   ORLON
RANGA   ROVES   UPTON   HELIO
IHEARDOFASEAGOINGROVERW
   ENNUI   TEX   SEA   ISAY
HAM   ATTU   DIANA   RTD
AHEMS   ENE   OREY   MAI  OSF
HOSAILEDFROMMANHATTANTO
STAGGER   INK   ONACLEAR
   INAN   TEACARTS   THAMIN
ARO   OSIS   ABORTS   TONE
DOVERHELEFTNEWYEARSEVEW
DUEL   SABLES   DRAW   EDS
STRIES   NOONTIME   TMEN
GETSLOST   CAD   REREDOS
ITHAFLASKUPHISSLEEVEAND
NOE   IFI   OMOO   TEE  ERICA
   NED   SPRIG   LAHR   LEK
APOS   GGS   SOI   TAUNT
GOTTHEREALITTLEHUNGOVER
ARTIE   ADIOS   HAVEN   ARALU
ITOLD   CAROM   AVERT   IAMBS
NASTY   ENEMY   MARYS   OLPAE
```

31

```
SHACKS . BOAT . COMFIT
SLURRED . PONCE . OLEARIA
MIMIINSTLOUIS . TENURES
SCOOTS . KITS . THE . TSARS
. ERSE . JOEL . MAE . SOT
. ORDO . RAJA . ATTRACTS
ADA . IOS . SCUR . RHO . IOOI
COTTAGE . ESCE . AMADEUS
URSA . CHASTEN . IAL . DRI
PIERS . AES . GAI . SCOT
. CARMENTHROUGHTHERYE
. YETI . CAD . MAH . SEEDS
WOE . LOO . ADULATE . ALGA
ARGALIS . NINO . KINDLED
ALAI . LES . CODA . NCO . SRA
COLDFEET . AVER . OARS
. ARS . ALL . SILT . TIAS
ANIMA . AGE . STAY . SHERPA
NINEPIN . MANONSUPERMAN
SCRAPED . OPINE . BARRETT
.EELERY . NOPE . INNATE
```

32

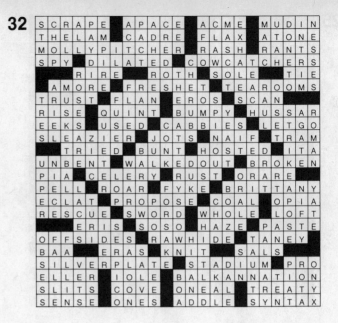

```
SCRAPE . APACE . ACME . MUDIN
THELAM . CADRE . FLAX . ATONE
MOLLYPITCHER . RASH . RANTS
SPY . DILATED . COWCATCHERS
. RIRE . ROTH . SOLE . TIE
AMORE . FRESHET . TEAROOMS
TRUST . FLAN . EROS . SCAN
RISE . QUINT . BUMPY . HUSSAR
EEKS . USED . CABBIES . LETGO
SLEAZIER . JOTS . NAIF . TRAM
. TRIED . BUNT . HOSTED . ITA
UNBENT . WALKEDOUT . BROKEN
PIA . CELERY . RUST . ORARE
PELL . ROAR . FYKE . BRITTANY
ECLAT . PROPOSE . COAL . OPIA
RESCUE . SWORD . WHOLE . LOFT
. ERIS . SOSO . HAZE . PASTE
OFFSIDES . RAWHIDE . TANEY
BAA . ERAS . KNIT . SALS
SILVERPLATE . STADIUM . PRO
ELLER . IOLE . BALKANNATION
SLITS . COVE . ONEAL . TREATY
SENSE . ONES . ADDLE . SYNTAX
```

33

```
SILAS . SCAD . ACE . SLAW
SONANT . ERIE . NUTS . PINA
ENTICE . TERM . NEAT . OMIT
WEARENOTAMUSED . ETOILE
SAK . REMARK . PRINTER
. RESIDER . IRANIANS
. INA . LETATCESTMOI
KINGSROW . DEBS . UREDO
ELEMENTARY . GLEANED
GOFAR . TYPOS . MCLI . MUSE
. THEWOMANILOVE
SRTA . ARES . LENOS . SPARE
LARGESS . ANDSOTOBED
ACORN . GOGO . SAWHORSE
VENIVIDIVICI . EEL
. ISOTONES . LOSRIOS
CORTEGE . ZANIER . RED
HAIRDO . IWANTTOBEALADY
OKAY . OKRA . BIST . BEATLE
PITS . DEMI . UTAH . BOLOED
SEAT . WAN . GATE . SNARY
```

34

```
AJAR . IVAN . OPTS . TALON
BATIK . MODE . GROUP . AGATE
MOSTPEOPLEWOULDBEGLADTO
ADO . EDNAS . SPIES . DOE . LEN
REND . GIL . IDA . ENTER
. IPECAC . ANENT . ASTI
PLEASE . ASSESSORS . SNAGS
BOOTS . ANTI . TEE . SPOT
ROVES . ANDEAN . DECALS . PAY
ABED . MINIM . AROSE . ATOLL
CAL . FUMED . STAT . SATIRE
THEIRTAXESWITHASMILEBUT
. TROTTA . EAVE . DIONE . URE
STONE . TORTE . DOORS . STIR
THE . DRAINS . STERNE . TATAR
WARN . POE . ELIS . ADELE
ANSER . ENTERTAIN . FAKIRS
. METS . OMERS . GLARES
SHOVE . ITA . ALA . TAMP
ETO . ERA . STAIR . OSAGE . BOO
GOVERNMENTINSISTSONCASH
GREET . PREEN . VALE . NOOSE
YELLS . SEED . PLOD . WOES
```

35

```
FORMAL . SALT . LOA . FLIP
ATEASE . AIRER . ABBELANE
TOPSPINDRIVE . WISEACRE
ESSE . ODES . EDITOR . EEK
ENPLANES . ESER . ADDS
IFFY . LEMS . ELL . RBIS
NOA . BASS . ANILS . SAMPS
DUSTINS . ALABAMA . MASON
ORTHO . AVID . SENT . RYME
SCOTS . LEVO . TATA . ACES
SQI . APACHE . ORRERY . HPS
OURS . ANOA . TWEE . PAROL
MACH . SEHR . REED . LOPAT
ARLEN . TORMENT . GRIMACE
EELER . LIONS . ROUE . TEC
. LOAM . MOD . SERF . AHSO
BAAS . MAYA . SLOTHFUL
OAK . APRONS . AURA . NICE
CAKEWALK . SUPREMECOURT
CARNEGIE . TRACE . NUTRIA
ISAE . END . SIZE . STOLEN
```

36

```
LIPPI . (O)BEDS . MOLAR . (O)DROP
OMARS . LIBYA . IDARE . SEIZE
OTTER . EPEES . NEGUS . HAMAN
THEEASTER(O)HUNTONTHELAWN
SENNET . DTS . METS . EIL . SAY
. SLOP . WILE . DELL
FIB . L(O)Y . ARAL . L(O)O . ALOP
AN(O)SWAYOFMAKINGANOTHER(O)
SPATE . SNOOT . IER . BIRDIE
TURRET . UNHAND . CIT . GOD
. TSE . IGOR . RIALTO . AMEN
. WALLSTREETLAYSAN(O)
. BRNS . UTHANT . REIN . RIO
PRE . TET . FEEBLE . (O)ROLLS
EOSTRE . ALT . (O)EDON . AWIDE
PUTSALLHIS(O)SINONEBASKET
ONEA . ESQ . ATNO . OVA . ERA
. RAGA . SNAG . ELSE
(O)SA . ORT . LODI . THI . SUNDAY
CANAN(O)HEADDRAWANEASTER(O)
UTILE . ENNEA . LOBAR . ARIAS
PUTS(O) . ROGER . L(O)ING . NEST
SPATS . SWEPT . OSTEO . BEMIS
```

37

```
URIS  OSSA  SODA  SPEAK
NENAS KEYSTONES COSTA
AITCHAITCHAITCH ASSAY
INO OBESE TRIKE LEPTO
RELIVES ITEM APSE
EDILE ARCEEEMPEE EPI
DINAR NOED ELOD CUR
NEY AUKS SATIN FERA
ENKAYVEEDEE LIEST
ADV VEES ORRIS FESCUE
DEEJAYS CLAIM JAYCEES
OLEINE SOUSA AINT EDT
RIEMS EMEMELEXVEE
ALFA ANODE LOES ARC
TAD ROOK UPON ENEAS
OHO ENWYEENWYE MATTE
URGE REDS PICKETS
ARBOR COELO GLARE MIT
VALVE ELBEEJAYSVEEPEE
ABEET SPURRIERS DREST
SEUSS TESS GLEE ARTS
```

38

```
CATA MAGI KEGS SCATS
ASUR IPIN TELLIT CHALET
STROLLINGTHROUGHTHEPARK
HANGINGAROUNDTHECORNER
MISUSE AWL STRAKE
ARIEL PITIED SERE OKRA
NEN EARLET ASNEAT PLIED
DOLS TYPEE WALLED
SAPONIFY AWAYFROMITALL
TRAPANS BLAT RETEST
OGRES COUNTS EACH HOB
WATCHEDANIGHTATTHEOPERA
ELY LONG SEETHE VADIS
GRIEFS REIS TAIPANS
GOINGFORAWALK SUNDAYGO
POETRY ONICE CANO
AGREE ALSINE DOLING CAR
TOSS CREE SLANTS ABONE
GUERRE ECT ELICIT
TAKEMEOUTTOTHEBALLGAME
WASONAFISHINGEXPEDITION
VIOLIN STEREO TORE ENSE
ALFIE SLED SEIR NEOS
```

39

```
HARTE SPLASH SLAV
BEMOANS ERASTUS POLIS
ALONGSTORYSHORT ANITA
SLEDS ANGES ODETS GIN
KIBO ANSER ALLTO SHAD
ESA ALTE ABIE GRITTY
THELIGHT FREER ERNES
IDEE KEEL SCENEI
MAHLER CONFER ATTENDS
ORALS TOSCA ALIAS GET
RIDE WASHELLBENT TBAR
ASA AERIE LAINE MAUNA
LEHAVRE RAGGED SINGED
ICIEST DUOS SULK
MATIN SWAYS UPINARMS
AGREES AIRS NOTE OAT
NEER HORNE ALINE MALI
INC MEDIC ARIAS CANON
ADORE ASHORTSTORYLONG
CARNE STEPOUT REMAKES
SDAK SSTARS DARES
```

40

```
DEMURS BALL ISOLDE OMSK
APOGEE ALEE SCREAM ROAN
MOTHERINLAWSTONGUE OTTO
ECH NIACIN KOTO TRY HIC
SHEITEL SERIOS TIGE EEK
RTES RED WHEELER
ASNER DUE COOKIE SLALOM
TEAM GYPSYMOTHER STOLA
BAT CANAPE HALOS ADAM
ERUDITE YAHOO DUENA ENA
SCRAG SAC PEGGED
THELASTOFTHEREDHOTMAMAS
ROONEY AUK ILONA
HEM SPACE UNTIL MORETON
ODOR DELIS NEGATE HIT
SITAR MOTHERGOOSE LENA
ETHNOS OUTAGE NOT CARTS
EARHART GIS TOUR
IHR ERNE RENNES SAWDUST
NOW MIG CERO ALIENS STU
TUES MOTHERGIVEMETHESUN
OSLO PRAISE DEEP RETIRE
WELD SAPPED ARTS ADDAMS
```

41

```
LET ARAM MALMO RAM
ASA CRIMEA ODEON AMIN
ITPROFFERSYOUASERVICE
RESIN RIPENESS HIRED
TEA IDEAS TYSON
SAFE RECANTED ODETTE
PRO LOA STA CRASHED
ARR TENNIS WIRES END
TIEPINS MADONNAS ADDS
ESSENE LAMER GITANAS
TNT WIMBLEDON CAV
CHASTEN ALLOT DAMIEN
MOIL ESTERASE HERESTO
ALL SATYR ESTATE CON
ILLNESS ADV HIE URE
MYSORE TRAPPERS SPOT
MELTS ELIOT TOE
GROAN REASONER DRAFT
BUTDEMANDSRETURNOFYOU
SETI EDDIE SITTER RUR
DOC TESTS CHET ELK
```

42

```
MATS DRIP TRIB CIA AJAR
ONIC REDA HAJI RNS TACO
SEPARATECHECKS ATTRACTS
TWODEGREESBELOWZERO KEY
SAGE STEW NOISOME
SAM MEAD SLAP NET MOFFO
CRIB DDAY LYON RAVENOUS
ATSEA RAH SOC TEL USS
RESTSBETWEENHALVES URSA
ETHEL LURE MAO TORT
DISALLOW RIPE STA UNHAT
ANN ATTHREEONTHEDOT QID
WOOER HEE STOW SELLOUTS
TASS ANT ILEX EDINA
BOHR PUTTHECARINREVERSE
ELI BUN SAX POE EATER
LANYARDS NEWT NAPS METS
ANGER EPI CARD TAPE RAT
SECRETE SIAM RENE
ALL SIGNONTHEDOTTEDLINE
BOYSTOOD TWOSECONDSFLAT
EDNA NNE ROUT KLEE ISON
TEXT SER ESTE SARD NASA
```

43

H	A	S	T	O		D	A	D	S		S	L	U	M			S	P	A	N
A	S	T	R	O		E	N	U	N	C	I	A	T	E			S	P	O	R	E
S	L	E	E	P	I	N	G	P	A	R	T	N	E	R			P	A	U	L	A
T	O	P	E		T	O	L	E	R	A	T	E	S			C	A	R	R	O	T
E	P	I		R	E	T	E		L	Y	E	S		S	O	R	T	S		
	E	N	C	O	R	E		D	I	O	R		S	C	R	E	A	M	E	R
	L	A	S		C	O	N	N		B	A	R	E	D		O	R	A		
A	I	M	E	D		R	A	N	G		B	O	N	E	R		S	N	I	P
S	N	O	W	G	O	O	S	E		C	R	U	D	E		T	E	E	N	S
E	I	N		A	D	A	H		S	O	U	N	D		J	U	R	Y		
	M	A	K	E	M	O	N	E	Y	H	A	N	D	O	V	E	R	F	I	S	T
	E	V	E	R		D	E	I	S	T		L	I	E	N		N	E	O	
K	A	Y	O	S		G	I	A	N	T		F	L	O	R	E	S	T	A	N
E	L	B	E		M	A	N	S	E		S	E	A	L		D	O	O	N	E
E	M	U		R	O	B	O	T		Y	E	A	R		S	O	U		
P	A	S	S	E	D	O	N		G	E	A	R		T	O	U	R	E	D
	I	C	I	E	R		S	L	O	B		S	H	U	T		N	O	G
T	E	N	O	N	S		A	T	O	M	I	S	T	I	C		S	A	N	E
A	L	E	N	E		I	F	I	W	E	R	E	A	R	I	C	H	M	A	N
R	I	S	E	R		C	A	L	E	N	D	A	R	S		A	R	E	T	E
T	A	S	S		A	R	E	D		S	T	E	T		P	I	L	O	T

44

S	C	A	T		M	E	A	T		T	A	M	P	A		A	G	I	T	A	T	E
C	O	L	A		U	R	T	H		O	K	I	E	S		P	O	L	A	R	I	S
O	R	A	L		G	R	E	E	N	G	I	A	N	T		S	L	I	P	O	N	S
P	A	R	K	A	S		A	B	E	A	M		E	K	E	D		E	S	N	E
E	L	M		C	H	A	R	L	I	E	B	R	O	W	N		F	O	R	A	Y	S
			A	T	O	M		U	N	D	O	E	R		I	S	I	S		
S	O	L	D		T	O	T	E			B	A	T	T	E	N	S		K	O	S
A	D	U	L	T		Y	A	K	S		P	I	N	E		A	G	A	I	N	S	T
G	E	N	E	R	A		U	N	P	A	I	D		A	G	E	E		S	O	S	O
A	S	T	R	A	L		T	I	R	Y	N	S		O	A	R		E	W	E	R
		I	D	O		G	E	E	K		C	R	A	G		A	R	E	T	E	
	L	A	S	T	O	F	T	H	E	R	E	D	H	O	T	L	O	V	E	R	S
F	I	N	E	S		F	I	T	S		R	I	O	S		E	G	O		
L	A	I	R		B	C	L		S	T	E	R	E	O		R	U	B	B	L	E
A	N	T	A		L	O	T	S		T	O	T	E	M	S		E	C	L	A	I	R
M	A	R	I	T	A	L		T	A	R	N		S	A	L	T		H	I	N	D	I
E	S	A		A	C	O	L	Y	T	E		R	O	S	A		N	E	O	N
			O	K	R	A		L	E	G	A	C	Y		A	M	O	K		
H	A	R	A	S	S		W	H	I	T	E	R	U	S	S	I	A	N		A	P	T
A	L	I	T		H	O	N	I		R	A	B	B	I		S	E	I	Z	E	R
T	A	L	L	I	E	D		G	R	A	Y	B	E	A	R	D	S		M	U	R	A
C	R	E	A	S	E	D		H	A	N	O	I		B	E	D	E		A	S	K	S
H	Y	S	S	O	P	S		S	E	N	N	A		Y	S	E	R		M	A	S	H

45

P	I	S	A		R	E	P	L	E	N	I	S	H			C	E	N	T	R	I
O	D	O	R		E	N	S	U	R	A	N	C	E			A	V	O	W	E	R
N	E	U	T	R	A	L	I	Z	A	T	I	O	N			G	E	N	E	V	E
S	E	R	I	E	S							T	R	E	E	N		N	E	L
			S	L	O		S	H	A	W		F	I	N	D		O	T	R	A
C	A	F	T	A	N		C	I	P	H	E	R	E	D		F	L	Y	I	N
A	V	I	A	T	E		A	E	R	A	T	E	S		F	O	O	T	E	D
T	E	R	S	E	R		W	R	I	T	H	E		T	O	U	G	H		
A	M	S					O	S	S			C	A	R	R	Y	I	N	G	
C	A	T		C	O	R	D	E	R	O		L	O	P	A	T		R	E	A
O	R	A		S	H	I	F	T	I	N	T	O	H	I	G	H		D	W	T
M	I	N		H	A	S	T	O		S	I	M	O	N	E	S		S	H	E
B	A	D	M	A	R	K	S		Y	E	T							T	A	L
	F	O	R	A	Y		S	O	C	A	G	E		R	E	P	A	V	E	
S	C	O	O	P	S		B	E	G	O	N	I	A		E	L	A	T	E	S
P	A	R	E	S		B	R	A	I	N	I	E	R		D	O	N	E	N	S
I	L	E	D		L	A	O	S		D	A	D	S		R	I	D		
N	O	M		S	A	R	A	H				I	S	E	U	L	T		
E	R	O	T	I	C		D	O	U	B	L	E	R	E	V	E	R	S	E	S
T	I	S	A	N	E		E	R	A	D	I	C	A	T	E		T	A	M	P
S	E	T	T	E	R		N	E	W	S	P	A	P	E	R		O	F	A	N

46

O	P	E	N	E	S	T		B	A	T	E	S		S	A	B	E	R		B	A	R
A	R	I	E	T	T	A		E	R	O	S	E		A	B	O	L	T		E	D	E
F	O	R	W	H	O	M	T	H	E	B	E	L	L	T	O	L	L	S		R	I	F
T	I	A		R	I	T	E		E	I	R	E						E	M	U
T	A	S	S	O		M	A	N	H	A	T	T	A	N	T	R	A	N	S	F	E	R
A	L	E		P	I	E		D	A	R	E	R		S	O	C	I	E	T	A	L
M	A	R	U		O	L	D			L	A	C	E		T	U	N			
P	R	I	S	O	N	E	R	O	F	S	E	C	O	N	D	A	V	E	N	U	E
A	M	O	U	R		E	A	R	L	E		T	O	T	O	S		A	R	R	Y
			A	D	A		F	L	A	T	S		T	E	M	P	E		S	A	N	E
T	H	E	L	A	S	T	T	Y	C	O	O	N		R	E	A	L	M		N	A	M
H	O	S		I	L	O		K	U	N	I	E		L	I	E		I	N	E
U	M	P		N	O	M	A	N		T	A	K	E	T	H	E	A	T	R	A	I	N
M	E	A	T		W	A	D	E	R		R	I	L	E	Y		S	R	O	
P	O	N	E		T	A	T	U	M		T	E	E	M	S		I	A	M	B	I
	F	A	R	F	R	O	M	T	H	E	M	A	D	D	I	N	G	C	R	O	W	D
			M	I	O		E	R	N	E			R	I	O		S	W	A	Y
S	P	E	E	D	W	A	Y		S	I	S	A	L		P	T	A		E	N	L
L	I	E	D	O	W	N	I	N	D	A	R	K	N	E	S	S		F	E	R	A	L
A	R	R		G	N	U	S		A	I	N	T					F	R	A	
T	A	I		T	R	E	A	D	M	I	L	L	T	O	O	B	L	I	V	I	O	N
E	T	E		M	I	L	N	E		C	E	D	A	R		L	U	C	E	R	N	E
D	E	R		S	P	A	D	S		H	E	S	S	E		Y	E	A	S	T	E	D

47

E	V	E	N		E	L	M	O		H	U	S	H		A	M	O	R
T	E	L	I		N	I	E	C	E		O	A	T	E	S		S	A	T	E
T	A	L	C		T	I	N	T	E	R	S	W	A	I	L		T	R	I	M
E	L	I	E	L	I		D	E	L	E	S		G	R	A	M	E	R	C	Y
	E	N	O	C	H		T	E	R	M	S		S	N	A	R	Y		
S	I	B	E	R	I	A	N		R	E	A	C	H		G	L	O	B	A	L
A	N	A		E	N	T	E	R		E	R	A	O	F		T	I	O	G	A
L	U	K	E		G	E	N	O	A		T	R	U	E	S		D	R	O	P
E	R	E	T	S		T	E	A	R	S		Y	R	E	K	A		E	R	P
M	E	S	H	A	C	H		R	E	C	A	P		T	E	R	E	S	A
		A	L	O	E		I	N	O	U	R		P	I	E	D		
	C	A	N	T	A	B		N	A	U	R	U		O	N	A	S	S	I	S
F	O	H		S	T	O	N	G		T	A	N	N	U		S	E	T	T	E
I	D	E	M		S	O	U	P	S		L	E	O	N	S		L	A	I	T
F	E	R	A	L		K	L	A	U	S		R	E	D	I	D		L	O	A
E	D	D	I	E	D		L	I	B	E	L		L	I	N	I	M	E	N	T
			I	N	T	R	A		N	U	D	E	S		N	A	T	C	H
C	O	N	S	T	A	N	T		R	E	N	E	W		T	A	C	O	M	A
A	N	T	A		W	O	R	D	B	O	T	C	H	E	R		O	N	U	S
L	E	H	I		L	I	A	N	A		S	T	O	L	A		Y	E	T	I
F	E	E	L		A	M	A	N		S	A	Y	S		S	S	T	S

48

O	T	S	E	G	O		P	A	R	C		H	I	L	T		C	A	R	P	A	L
S	H	A	M	U	S		A	B	E	L		A	C	O	R		O	T	O	O	L	E
S	A	M	U	E	L	C	H	A	S	E		J	O	S	E	P	H	H	E	W	E	S
A	I	L		S	O	U		I	R	W	I	N		N	O	N			E	P	I
	A	P	T		B	R	O	D	I	E		S	E	C	T		H	A	R	P	O
A	I	D	A		O	B	E	C	H	E		T	H	S	N	E	L	S	O	N
F	R	A	N	S	L	E	W	I	S		O	M	A	R		A	L	E		
A	R	M		T	A	R	A	S		O	L	I	V	E	R	W	O	L	C	O	T	T
R	A	S	P	U	T	I	N		A	N	D	R	E		U	R	S	A		O	H	O
	I	C	E	S		S	L	I	T	S		G	N	U		S	A	L	E	S
	L	A	N	C	E		P	O	O	H		I	R	O	N	Y		R	O	S	E
B	U	T	T	O	N	G	W	I	N	N	E	T	T	O	F	G	E	O	R	G	I	A
E	G	A	L		S	L	A	N	G		S	O	I	F			S	T	A	Y	S
L	O	B	E	S		E	Y	E		P	E	K	O	E		O	M	E	N	
O	S	A		A	L	A	N		T	I	T	A	N		C	O	A	L	T	A	R	S
W	I	L	L	I	A	M	E	L	L	E	R	Y		B	A	S	A	L		B	A	A
			A	D	M		E	C	R	U		R	O	B	T	M	O	R	R	I	S
W	M	W	H	I	P	P	L	E		S	T	M	A	L	O			B	A	N	K
H	E	A	R	T		E	A	S	E		H	A	T	E	T	H		T	I	C
E	L	D		T	A	U		M	U	S	I	C			H	R	H		L	U	I
R	O	D	N	E	Y	S	R	I	D	E		T	H	O	S	H	E	Y	W	A	R	D
E	V	E	N	E	R		E	V	E	L		R	E	N	O		A	M	O	R	A	L
S	E	R	E	N	E		L	A	N	E		E	T	E	S		M	E	E	K	L	Y

49

```
LIPPI  GCD   ELM  MALL
VINOUS ACRE  REA  ASEA
MANVSTHEELEMENTS  RIFT
OPCIT  DAVIDVSGOLIATH
LOOT ARI    EATONES
ERLE NET MANN    CACTI
NEEDS  EDS   UNWISHED
LIV YALEVSHARVARD  ALL
UNS ERASE  LIANA  TREE
REDOLENT GRIT  PSALM
EBOLI THERIVALS  IWEEP
RUDDY  BADE  AMORISTS
CIGS ARMED  SHERE  VET
HAL BRAINSVSBRAWN  SRS
ATALANTA   ITE  RESAW
RESOD  IHAD  TEL  SAGE
READILY    ERL   SLAT
ATHENSVSSPARTA  LICIT
DUAL MIRANDAVSARIZONA
ABLE ANE OOZE  COMETS
YETI DAD   SER  TOAST
```

50

```
ACACIA  BEAM  SALEM  RUBE
MULISH  ILLE  SIEVE  OLLA
ALLTHATGLISTERSISNOTAU
TEE BAS ETA  BSC   OMRI
JUG  THENACLOFTHEEARTH
AREAS AOK   EAR  OLD  HEE
VESPER TESS STEEPS  AONE
BEIT  SOLD  ELI   SUED
VONPAPEN DIESELS  COAST
ETUI ENID PLINY  ANNES
SHIP  ACED EVE  FARAD
TOTE SNHORNGAMBLER  OPEN
CHUTE AAA  YOUR  LUNA
ILIAD SMITE ABIE  DROP
SONGS STALEST  SEAMLESS
BANC  MAR  STIR   STOA
HIGH PINEAL EPIC  SOCCER
AAL WAN ETE  MAO  TEASE
THEMANINTHEFEMASK  CCC
GATE ONE CPA  TIA  TKO
AGBELLSANDCOCKLESHELLS
LEER AIMAT CREE  KOREAN
IDLY PRESS HOGS  STARRY
```

51

```
RIGHT  LEFT   PAS  ASCAP
AROSE  IDLE  AURA CARTA
CONTENTION  FRATERNITY
ENE  ETTES FEMALE  MAN
SERF OLES  SABINE  MERE
LINED  STIRS   ETO
FEATS  TORE   ERICA
TINGE  RAILED  SNAKES
INDOMITABLE SPINELESS
LIEN DRILLS  ABETS
LSD SEINES CURSES  RGT
AMATI  GENDER  ROLE
TURBULENT UNCONSCIOUS
ALERTS EDISON  LOSES
GETAT  LITE   TATTY
DYS ELGAR  SHAME
RAKE CASTER PEAK  DALE
AVA PAMPAS DENSE  MIL
JERRYBUILT UNSHAKABLE
ARMOR  SEES AGEE  OCEAN
STAKE  EDS  LESS  LORCA
```

52

```
CASTE  SCREE MASK  DOOMED
ASIAN  PRILL ARIA ENSILE
CHRISTIESMYSTERY  LESSON
HEEL ANTE SHIM ODE  ASPS
END CLEAT USE  IDA  GEE
THESNOWATSTOWE  SRI
STEER  OISE  MEG  TASTE
SORA STRAND AERO  ATHEE
ALIMB HODGEPODGE  SISAL
FALSE EWES  ERDA  GEMOF
ERL ARIEL ORNE AURA  ITS
SIS MIDLERSFIDDLERS  SRA
TAB ETES EMUS  ASSET HIC
YESES SLIM ERAS  ELDER
TAMED  TWICEPRICE  RAISE
WHIRR BRAC ARNESS  ISTS
OSSIE EER  ELSE  ELCHE
SEA TEMPLESDIMPLES
RAS MAE RAN  FOLDS  DAB
ERIA OLE OPTS IDEO  TOME
COLLAR THESONDHEIMRHYME
ASLANT COME  OCALA HELOT
PESETA HESS  BIDED OMENS
```

53

```
RAH  COAT  MAJA  BADGER
MORO ARCH  ATOM  AMALFI
PUTOFFTHYSHOESFROMOFF
SESTETS  FOLLY  RELAPSE
CTA SEMEE  CUBES
NOTHINGWEARS LIAS  JAW
AHOYS  AET  ROTC  SEGO
DAH HAME  FAIT  KATHIE
IRA LIT BIRCH  RERUNS
RAVELLED  AGLEE  ICE
SEVEN  ISBLISS  DIAGS
AVA SABES  BREAKOUT
DIKDIK OLLAS UAR   DME
CHEESE REEF  TBSP  IMA
CANS  DODS  VMI  ROVES
IDO ETRE  COMEASYOUARE
ERROR ACORN  APT
PRONOUN ICENI  SWEPTUP
TAKEITOFFTAKEITALLOFF
APEACH ANUN SLAT  APOD
HANSAS MISS TOGA  YES
```

54

```
MAKOS  INARUT  DAMP  REDS
ALINE  NEROLI  EMIR VENOM
KATZENJAMMER CACOMISTLE
ETTE  AUTOS ERASE ADOREE
REY HIRER FLAGS  SNARED
BALER  SEENO  AHALT
ARCADES CATSANDDOGS  PAR
BEHEAD LOVES RIPE  SULU
AVERT PULED CLOTS SUSIE
TESS GOGO  RIOS  POISED
ETH RESERVEFUND  SALTINE
IRONER ICOME  SPLEEN
STRIPED CELEBRITIES  BOB
ARETES  VIDA  WAND  SORE
LACED BEGET CRETE LEONE
OCAS LANA  CHERE  SORTOF
NET AELUROPHOBE  SADISTS
BRAKE ULEMA  ALLEN
STEADY STUMP FLEAS  SST
STELMO NAOMI GELID CUTE
HOTTINROOF COLLEGECHEER
ALOES ANNI AWEIGH BADEN
WEND  POET LENSES STEPS
```

61.

```
. T O R E . D E T E R . C A S S . O S A
E R R O L . A M O R E . A L U M . N L F
M I S S I N G P E R S O N S B U R E A U
B O S K Y . A G E S . P R I O R . U N K S
U T E . A P E R . R I A S . A G G I E S
S E C R E T A R Y B I R D . S C R A G
S T E N O . R O E . H E A T H E R
. P E L L . S A D . D O E . N E T T Y
T A C O . L O U N G E L I Z A R D . S H E
A N A S . S N A G . I L O . A M A T I
A D M I R E . S K I . N U N . P A L A C E
O P T E D . E E N . E T E S . G N A R
A R A . F O R E I G N D E S K S . I D L E
F R I A R . I N N . O R D . Y O R E
L A G G A R D . G P O . A I R E D
N A M E S . S N A P P Y D R E S S E R
P A C T E S . O P A L . L O U S . T V A
A C H E . I N L A W . B A U M . A W A I T
P R E S I D E N T I A L C A B I N E T S
A E S . S E R E . N A D I R . D O N E E
S S T . T R O Y . G A R D E . A N T S
```

62.

```
T O S C A . F A R A D S . A B L E . C A W E D
A T E A R . O M E L E T . C R A W . A S H E S
W H A T M A K E S A B E B E A M E . S M O L T
N E T S . M I N T S . E R I C A . S H A M
Y R S . S A N D S . L O N E . T A R A S
. U S E S . G A B S . S E R E N A D E
F A W K E S . A L I A S . R O A D . E S S
A S H E R . W A S A N N E F R A N K . C O S T
L I O N S . A B A S E D . I O T A . B A S I E
S A M S . L I E N S . A L S O . M O S C O W
E N D . I S R A Y N O B L E . I N C A N
. I W A N T . A R I . P R Y O R
A D A G E . W A S B E N B L U E . W I G
D U C K E D . H A L T . A R I L S . F I N O
U S H E R . A I D E . A N N U L S . M I L N E
A S E S . I S R I C H L I T T L E . O L D E R
L I V . A N T E . E M C E E . H O M E R S
E Y E G L A S S . R A H S . S C A R
S C R E E . E L A N . S T A R E . C H E
H I L T . S C A L D . T H I R D . M O O R
S H A V E . W H O M D I D M O L L Y P I C O N
M E S A S . H O N E . N E A R T O . F L O P S
A M E N S . O D D S . E R N E S T . C O A S T
```

63.

```
G O B S . I A T R O . S E C . S W A T
A B E T . B R I E F . U R U . S T O L I D
H A R R Y S R E A S O N E R . T R O I K A
E N G I N E E R . M E R V S G R I F F I N
. D E N T . P A S O . R A V E
D A M E S . D E L E O N . I T E R A T E
A M I N . E T H E L S M E R M A N . V A S
T A K T . P O O L . G O E L . C A S T
E T E . N O E L S C O W A R D . H A S T E
D I S P E N S E . A M I T Y . S E R G E S
. H A R Y . S N A R E . T W O A
S H A L O M . S T A R E . P U R E B R E D
E A M E S . P A U L S D R A P E R . D N A
I S M S . H E L P . O L G A . G N A W
S T E . C A P T A I N S C O O K . R E T E
M O R D A N T . S N A C K S . T O R E S
. O G G I . A B O Y . G R O W
E D D I E S C A N T O R . S E A P L A N E
C U A N D O . N O R B E R T S W I E N E R
O R I G I N . O V A . R O U T E . R O S S
. A S S N . N A P . S O B E R . S A T E
```

64.

```
. L I S P . O R S O . S I T . S E P A L S
. D A N T E . P O E T . A L O E . P L A C E T
J U N G A T H E A R T . F O D D E R I M A G E
E N D O R . A N D R E . E N D I V E . D I R
S N I T . C H E . A R D . A L B E E . C I O N
T A N . H O A R D . U S S E L . P L A N E
E G G M A N . S T E R E O . D E N D R I
R E S U L T S . S T E L M O . S T E E P L E S
. T E R N S . C E P E D A . H I S T O R Y
R E S T R A I N S . L E N D S . S T O R E D
A R I E S . P I T . R E E K S . T O M E
U S N R . O E D I P U S W R E C K S . A T M Y
. A C I D . E N E R O . R E L . U N T I E
A T T O R E . G R A N T . S N I P P I E S T
P E R M I T S . S A L A A M . T E R R A
T R A P D O O R . K I L M E R . G I O C A R E
. L E A S E D . T I P T O P . M O S L E M
W A R E S . B I D E T . C A R E T . G A B
I L E X . S A U N A . Y A W . T A R . M E S A
N B A . E N I G M A . L A P I N . W A R O N
G I L T F E E L I N G . T H I N K S H R I N K
E N T R A P . D E E R . A O N E . H A L A S
D O Y E N S . S R O . R O K S . E T O N
```

65.

```
S H E A . M A D C A P . O R E S T E S
W A L L A . B A R R A G E . C A P T I V E
A L I E N . I N S E V E N T H H E A V E N
M E T E O R O L O G Y . C A R E E R
I R E . M A T I N S . T I M E D . S A G E
. A N I L S . P A L E D . L I V E N
N A S A L I T Y . S L I E R . S O N A N T
O U T S I D E . S T A N D . L I V O N I A
C R A K E S . R I A N T . P A T E N T E D
K A T E S . E E R I E . T O R O S E
S L E D . U N D E R T H E S U N . S W A T
. F A N T A N . A E R I E . S E A L E
B A R O N I E S . B R A N T . T A Y L O R
I N O R D E R . S O I L S . C O T E D O R
N A N T E S . C L A U S . M O S E S O N A
A M A H S . C H A R M . P A N E L
L E S E . C H A P S . S O R R E L . L E A
. M O L A R S . S C U B A D I V I N G
O N T O P O F T H E W O R L D . T O T A L
R E H O U S E . O T A R I E S . E L U T E
S P E N S E R . T E N E T S . S P E T
```

66.

```
G R I M E . E V A D E . R I P E N . T R A S H
R E L A X . M O P E D . E N U R E . R O L L O
A P O L I T I C A L H A C K D I D B E W A I L
S E N A T E R A C E . S I E G E . R E A R E D
P L A Y . R A L E . A S T R E . B U R N E R S
. W E T . A T E E . A R T A
H I S F A T E I N S E N D I N G O U T M A I L
A S T A R E . M O I S T . N O N O S . C E R O
M A R R Y . S P R A T . T U N E D . O C T A D
L I A R . S L O A N . B O R E S . T U L A N E
E A T . S T A R . O R A N G . S E T I
T H A T C O N T A I N E D S O M E A D V I C E
. W A N T . R A I N Y . A G R O . L O P
L A Z I L Y . S A M O S . T O K A Y . A L S O
A B U S E . R U B I N . B A L E R . C R I M P
M E L T . P O P I N . S A L A D . G O O N I E
P L U S S O M E C A S H T O V O T E T W I C E
. P T A S . C O O N . E T E
A L S O R A N . C R O O N . D E N S . K I T E
N E A T A S . M A O R I . S O L U T I O N A L
T O D A Y H E S R U N N I N G F R O M J A I L
I R A T E . S T A T E . R A M I E . P A N N E
C A T E R . P A T E R . S P A N S . S K E E N
```

67

```
BRAD OTTO MABEL THUD
AARE REINS ALAMO ROTO
THEPRINCEANDTHEPAUPER
SALOONS RODE DAISY
ELL DOOR SHAN
BATTLEOFKINGSMOUNTAIN
ALOES LOESS OLEO IRE
KITS GEAL TODAY SMEW
EVE TRAMP MITER PEENE
DEMERIT MATIN SEEDER
JAMESEARLCARTER
FLEECY ALINE AIRSACS
LANCE CLONE FINNS VOE
ERAT SATIE LOTT SAAR
ECT FUME STONE CESTA
THEQUEENOFTHEADRIATIC
UNDO TARE ADS
SCRAG IRON ESSENCE
THECOUNTOFMONTECRISTO
LANK SOUSA NORMA POOR
ODDS AMBER NEIL ESNE
```

68

```
ALOHAS THEWEB LOX SPRAT
MARINA HABANA IDI TROVE
IVLETTERWORDS VISHOOTER
RAY SCREEN GIVEN INTERN
HIND TALES ISEE
SAL DECI EMIT TNT STOP
TRIPOLI LANES SILO TRUE
ARSON IIIMUSKETEERS AST
TITLES BLIP RESTIN UTA
EVEL ISLAS AIR CARMEL
DEN ITOUCHOFVENUS REARS
EVERS TRI NAMED
PATNA THEIIISTOOGES CCC
ATHAND STS OLPES BLAH
NOR ORBITS WADE STRATA
ANE VIIDEADLYSINS RARER
MEAL NEER RENTE TSETUNG
ASTI KRA JOAN LATE SAE
BASE MOONS SETA
ALLYOU PABLO STAIRS BOY
VYEARPLAN IVLEAFCLOVERS
ICENT ART NETTLE ELAINE
DORSA PTA GRATED TENTER
```

69

```
CESTAS APISH EGO¢RIC
SALTINE LETHE VALUATE
¢RALLYLOCATED EMERGES
ENTO FLOC EGG SOY
DEE IN¢IVE READ SPAT
RELIEVE ¢ERBET LURE
NOTRE IRS SAR AGED
TRAINEE ENATE DONNISH
HAGGARD ENL AC¢UATES
ITEM ROC RHETT
MAGNIFI¢AMBERSONS
RESEE SOO OATS
DEBACLES TUB TOLITES
TURISTA THINS EDISONS
ONE¢ AMI ANT MNEME
MEDE RIDING BAPTISM
SENT CORD ARREST OFF
NOM LEV SOIR ARLO
BASINET FORTWO¢SPLAIN
AVIATOR UTURN EPAULET
HARLOWE LENOS RAMMER
```

70

```
ROASTS SCUFF SHIFT NUB
INBLUE MOTEL TANEY NEVE
ACUATE OVERABARREL OXEA
LET UNITES BARREL ATTAR
SUSU ODE LEI FIGHT
PUPATE SAWYERS APRIORI
SOPOR SAPPIER DISANNUL
INONE WREST SWINE GONE
TAN ASTAIRE SCENT TEX
SHIRT SHALE SOPH
COBB UNDERSHIRT NUTTIER
OPERANTS OHARA MONTANAN
DESERTS ABOVEBOARD SGTS
IRIS PRUNE BOARD
NAD PULSE HAIRDYE BAG
OLEO LEROT HAITI PHYLE
ELONGATE HARDEST TOTAL
LINEATE ADOPTER UHHUHS
ESTER EIN GNU REUS
DOSES NORMAL OSIERS HIP
ABEL BELOWNORMAL OTIOSE
WOLF ORIBI BEARD NONUSE
NEF GODET SYRIA SPARED
```

71

```
FASTENS ELLIS ADMIT
APPOINT REACH AUROCHS
THATLEANANDHUNGRYLOOK
SIREE MISSIONER TENSA
ODE ETIVE ESTEE OSSET
TANANA ESE DECA
AMIS RALLY OLDAS CPA
TARTAN SETTLE PTBOAT
AREAR CRUSHES LATE
OBOE INERTE ECCE
PUTWORDSINONESMOUTH
SOME BEDLAM CASS
PLIE AMATEUR ARENA
CLANGS PIANOS PRIZES
AOK AKRON SPICE DROP
VIOL BFS RHONDA
MASSE TIARA LIANE PAC
OSAKA UTTERMOST ADORE
THROWONESWEIGHTAROUND
HEADAND EERIE ESTONIA
SHAYS ARSIS REORDER
```

72

```
RABI OHARE STASI WAG
PRENSA NOBIS CHALKS RYE
CANCAN ERUPT HELLESPONT
BOULDERSTREETMCMAHON
STRAIN ASOLD ENERGY
DROP ALI SONS KNEE
MEADOWLAIRELIOT MEETS
LENTAN ASCI EOLIC ARSIS
LAITY ATHENA NOSE LASSO
ASSISTS GUT SLAG
MULL RIATA SCAPA EYERS
AREA ANTEBOSHMARCH HAWN
ESSAY AMATI ALCOA ODEA
CUSS TER PRIVIES
TAROT IRIS SEETHE DEATH
ODETO BASIC CLEO PELTAE
SEPTS VICHYASTOTEASES
SLUM RTES IOU KEEL
ELATER BULBS ALSOPS
SSRCAPITALKETTLEPART
BOISEIDAHO OIDEI ROTORS
REV STELAE SNORE STEVIE
ARE SERED EGGER ROPE
```

73

```
ANON . DINER . . PEGS . SALK
LEVY . OCOTES . UTAH . EVEL
SWEETNIGHTINGALEAWAKE
AET . AWLS . INEE . PRAISE
BLARNEY . INGOT . WHIRL .
. IAN . BRUIN . HIE . DAFT
TUFA . OBRIEN . VOTRE . BEA
OREL . WEED . GHAT . DUPLEX
AIM . POLA . OPAL . ISRAELI
SAMSHU . SPHERE . SCAT
THELORDTOEARTHHASCOME
. ANGE . INCISE . MIHIEL
CASPIAN . TRES . RHEA . LUV
OCASEY . YOYO . AMAT . LESE
DEC . SAJOU . NONEGO . ODES
ADAR . POM . CENAS . SKI
. JUMPY . WRACK . PEANUTS
CRANIA . HURL . BAER . SHA
HOWFARITISTOBETHLEHEM
OLEO . EROS . HUMERI . GERM
WEAR . LOOK . DENIM . GREY
```

74

```
LACES . RECAP . ROTAS . ADAPT
OSAGE . ALULA . IMUST . MOXIE
COLON . PISAN . TORSO . INEPT
OFFTOWASHINGTONIWENT
. IRONS . NILE . OSSA . SERA
AVES . DUAD . KORBUT . TEACUP
LITTLEI . ABIB . ETON . LYRES
MARION . ARENEAR . ROWE . USE
ALECS . LUNE . BAY . TACT
. THISISWHATIHADTOSAY
CANS . APPT . HELENA . ESTATE
OBOE . ROI . IDO . ITS . ELLA
TRIPOD . CARMEN . FREI . MEIR
SIRIFIWEREPRESIDENT
. AFER . ADE . PEON . OCTET
HIS . IRAQ . ARTLESS . SCHIZO
EDWIN . PUTS . OAST . SCOOTER
FLANGE . ISAJOY . APIA . ROLY
TENN . SAXE . ETAL . ADLAI
. IDABOLISHNEWYEARSDAY
BWANA . ATILT . EVENS . UTILE
BONGS . BIOME . GENET . BEVEL
SWISH . ACTOR . GESSO . AREAL
```

75

```
BLIMP . CADI . SAGE . SOFAS
AURAL . UPON . HOOP . ECOLE
GLOBALTENSIONWILLEASE
SUNSCALD . HAVEN . AVALON
. ATE . RAGE . AMAN .
ATBOTHTHEPOLARREGIONS
ROUSE . USES . DETRE . SOP
INRI . SOME . ONE . ACTI
AIRPOLLUTIONWILLABATE
SOO . NIPS . RUING . INURED
. WIDE . ITT . GONG .
MALICE . WASTE . CONE . PTS
ASENERGYSHORTAGESGROW
GATE . ONT . RIOT . RAKE
IDO . CLONE . FAIR . CODED
CONGRESSWILLTOILASONE
. RITE . SALE . NAT .
SMOOTH . POLIO . UNDERFED
TOVOTEITSELFAPAYRAISE
OLIVE . SALT . MEAT . ELENA
WADER . MHOS . ERSE . REFER
```

76

```
RASP . LAMB . . BONED . ARM
ANTI . PIPEUP . VICEROY . PEA
WEREHAVINGAHEATWAVE . RAP
IMARET . NESTORS . STEMMERS
SIT . FISC . CPT . . CEES
HAILTOTHECHIEF . PHONEMES
. ESSA . MAYS . IDIOT . OAT
BATS . BLAS . PLEDGE . DIDO
ABEL . FAIRHARVARD . OLIO
SEMI . ETE . MEET . ILUS . REED
REPEAL . ARD . DESKPAD .
ATE . SINGININTHERAIN . EIS
. SEAPORT . OUI . ISOLDE
ETTA . ERIC . USNR . BIN . RULE
RIIS . PHILEASFOGG . IGET
RANT . TAMEST . ULAN . EERO
ORA . OKADA . LETI . OMAN
RATTIGAN . WHITECHRISTMAS
. EIDE . ETC . EENY . AST
GRANITAS . ALTHEAS . IOLITE
LAP . OHWHATABEAUTIFULDAY
ORO . MERESES . SCREWY . BERN
WAT . RYDER . HARA . SNEE
```

77

```
JEST . CROP . SID . ASES
IDEA . HORA . ETSI . LINKS
BEATGENERATION . ENDEAR
ENTERED . POPLAR . GULLS
. AROMAS . PARADEREST
ARIAS . ISEULT . CARET
WILDPITCH . SEEDER . OSH
LOLA . SERENE . IRE . INCA
. MALTOSE . SPA . SMOKER
. TONER . LETIN . ANENT
ADO . STAFFSERGEANT . YES
CIRCE . LEONA . MITTS
EXTORT . OWN . DEFENSE
RIIS . IER . HAMLET . ROSA
BEL . GRASSO . BARHARBOR
. LEBEN . QUIVER . SAINT
MEASURESUP . IDEALS
GIFTS . SOAPED . COASTAL
RELATE . PROMISSORYNOTE
. RATER . PERU . HORN . AGON
. TERA . YST . EDNA . GAMS
```

78

```
DADE . APT . PAVED . NIP . POT
ALAN . CUI . BETIDE . ECOTYPE
LECTERNS . ELECTRACOMPLEX
ACCRUED . RAVES . OUTS . KENT
ISAAC . IRANI . AGLAIA
. PLATONICAFFAIR . ROAST
PASSIM . UKE . BAITS . LINGUA
ARM . DARTS . GENRE . COSINES
SAO . EINE . MIDGE . BLOTTERS
TROJANS . NOR . ERATO . SSE
EATEN . GOATS . SPINETS
. THEGLORYTHATWASGREECE
. PEONIES . CRACK . LEHUA
ACT . OVENS . ENT . SAILING
DREAMERS . HADES . ROMA . DIN
DANCERS . AEGIS . NEVIN . ECU
EVENTS . SCARE . SUB . SLIDES
DETER . SOCRATICMETHOD
. YELLED . NIECE . GESSO
PACA . LEON . OATEN . AVIATED
ACHILLESTENDON . TRACTILE
THEDEEP . EXTENT . RUN . ELMO
SEW . ANY . DOONE . APE . SEAN
```

79

BACH · RELIC · ▓ · HAPS · OTIS
OSHA · EXILE · ROBOT · FETE
STUM · FAMILIARITY · STEW
COMMERCE · ERINGO · PAEAN
MINET · ASIDE · FALLA
SPEEDS · ANTAE · AGLITTER
OLDS · HANDANDGLOVE · EYE
NEWTS · DAYS · OLLA · ATRI
ANI · TROT · AIDED · CLEAN
RATTAIL · BABOON · CAL
HAILFELLOWWELLMET
PRE · LIBYAN · BEDEWED
YIPES · SAGAS · CAFE · OSO
ETAS · LITH · PARR · NASTY
GAL · TOGETHERNESS · UCAL
GLADHAND · ELENA · TAGORE
RHODA · OASTS · SERUM
SPOOR · TERRET · STAYSPUT
ELUL · BUDDYSYSTEM · TARE
GONE · ARNEE · UTILE · ANGE
ODDS · GEAR · PARER · NYES

80

ATTAR · CRAB · PRE · SIGNET
ATHOME · PHARISEES · CREOLE
THEWRATHOFGRAPES · RATTLE
LEL · ADROIT · DAYFORAQUEEN
ANIS · ONCE · SRS · ATIP
SAFE · FOYERS · BANC · MAO
ENDUP · GODSOFTHELAPP
BOARD · MATTEROFTHEHEART
LOFTED · ERA · SELF · EDEN
OLSEN · CAMUS · DOOM · UTES
WIT · CHOLERIC · AGO · ORTS
EVA · HABITOFCREATURE · RAH
RIFT · SHE · SURNAMES · ONE
AFAR · RAVI · MINDS · PARTE
RIGA · SINE · CIO · GARSON
BRIDEOFTHEFATHER · ANTON
WISETOTHEWORD · QUAFF
IAM · SEEN · STPAUL · OCTA
AMER · AWL · HELI · ROOM
KINDOFATHREE · ALERTS · MTB
USEDTO · SERPENTOFTHEYEAR
RIALTO · PROTRACTS · AGEDLY
ATREST · SOW · YMHA · TONYS

81

CAIN · BETS · DORIA · BARB
ALDA · ATHOS · USING · OMAR
MOOS · THEFORESIGHTSAGA
PULSE · RAION · SEARCHED
ALI · ORGANA · SSE
OFHUMANBANDAGE · TASSEL
REE · GEESE · GSA · TAHOE
INDIGOS · TARTS · DINS
ODDER · TAP · OLEOS · LAPSE
LEASES · DRACOS · ODETO
ERG · THEJOYOFSECTS · FBA
AMEER · MANTEE · STEFAN
BABEL · ISING · SRO · WOULD
EBBS · CESTA · DIESELS
ABETS · ARE · BEVIN · LOO
SARAHS · BRAZENINTHESUN
RED · STARTS · OUS
POSTURES · OCREA · STAKE
LOOKBACKINHANGAR · AJAX
EZIO · PAINE · STELA · TAME
DELS · ELMOS · ESAU · ERAS

82

DEICE · SHIRES · SALT · ODOR
ENNUI · HONEST · UVEA · OMANI
COLDSHOULDER · GOTOBLAZES
ALAS · ERRED · AEGIS · ADHERE
DAY · PETIT · JIVED · GREASE
HADES · WINES · PRESS
ANDOVER · ROBERTFROST · ROB
SOILED · CURED · LOST · PESO
CODED · PLIED · AMASS · RADIO
ASAD · BRAN · RAGE · RATHER
PES · GEORGEBURNS · SENIORS
NEARBY · SOLON · SPIGOT
MOONEYE · WARMWELCOME · MAC
ORWELL · FAUN · URIS · CAGE
RAJAS · RUSSE · MEMEL · WOMEN
OTOS · TORT · AIMEE · SONANT
NEB · FROZENASSET · ATTESTS
CLIME · ESKER · STRAY
CLOUTS · AMEER · LATIN · REA
CRISTO · KNEAD · MELUN · CONS
HOTTENTOTS · FLAMINGYOUTH
ACHED · OBOE · OENONE · EAGRE
PEER · PENS · RENNES · STEEN

83

ROMP · BERET · PROOF · DANK
OTOE · RAISA · AESIR · ERIE
THREEYSMEN · RUSLEEPING
HOTPLATE · GHANA · EXUDES
SINS · BEIGE · BUT
SACHET · PALEO · SHOREMAN
ATHOS · TOBORNOTTOB · IRE
TROW · SANE · VEST · LSTS
YEW · LNGLASGOW · BESET
RETREADS · PERI · BEVELS
HEAVY · FARED · FETED
DEARE · ITIC · PATHETIC
HAYDN · PSHOOTERS · HSE
INRE · EFIK · HOMY · PEST
ECU · SAQUESTIONS · ROQUE
DENTISTS · TERRY · MANSES
ATI · SOLEN · PANT
BARTON · APPAL · CARIOCAS
IWITNESSES · AFTERNOONT
BELL · SINAI · NORSE · NOTA
IDLE · SCORN · DOSED · SPED

84

ANDRO · GLASS · FLAME · STAID
SIOUX · REDAN · ROWAN · NORGE
HOLLYHARDGREENANDCOTTON
OBOE · AZOLE · LEERY · ROTARY
TER · WRITE · BELLE · RAZE
TALOS · SAVOY · SUZERAIN
IMMURES · ATSEA · SUPER · MNO
BOOBYMOUSEANDSPEED · LOOT
ENTE · SILL · TIDE · YONNE
ANTS · ABASE · STILE · JAGGED
MEL · ALIF · THANT · PARI
STFAMGRIDWROUGHTANDCAST
IBID · WAINS · HIES · NEW
STARED · LARGE · TWIXT · ROUE
PARER · PERU · ERIN · ODRA
ABED · CUFFMISSINGANDWEAK
TOA · PONTS · MOSES · FORESTS
SORORITY · SPIES · AFOUL
RONA · STERN · ACIDS · RAW
ASPIRE · SCALE · KNURL · TALI
SPREADDOUBLEANDAMERICAN
ICENT · LADLE · MORTE · AMEND
TASTE · SKIED · TWEED · MESSY

85

```
CASH  SPARE  ACTH   LCTS
ARPE  LAMER  SHEA   CEARA
BEACHOROIL   HANDSHAPED
LANAI  ARNE  LINEOFFATE
ELITE  FOE  OER   SOSO
   SED  FUR  RACE   RAID
TCH  SIS   IVAN   PACINO
RAPIDAN  SHOERS  ODONTO
ATOMIC  AHOLD  ELECTOR
CORPS  DRAPE   SHRINK
ESTO  ARCHIPELAGO  AGOD
   SCREEN  ITALO  STORE
SPHERED  STATE   FROLIC
THESEA  BOTCHY  PROOFER
LIBBER  ANAH   TAO   SLY
OLEY   MERE   HER   ADA
   FLAB  ARR   OAT  SERGS
CHIROMANCY   SARI  HANOI
PANAMAHATS   PROSPEROUS
ARGUE  ESEK  ASSAM  ILLS
SEED   DORY  TEENS  EDDY
```

86

```
   VICE  ALAMEDA  ATIDE
BINET  PALATES  THOUGHTS
RURALHAPPINESS  TRUELOVE
ALTRI  BLISS  PILAU  LILAC
PLUMB  BENT  MISER   HIS
AYE  AMOS  ROSIN  ROSEBUD
   SCOT  SCENE  SLANT  ONO
ASHIYA  PAGER  MARE  SNIT
SEAL  BASHFULSHAME  SADAT
TRUTH  WHEEL  ANA  FEISTY
EGG  AMOUR  AIRE   CANDO
REH  EARLYATTACHMENT  FBI
   TIRED  NEAP  AINSI  LAD
SHIRES  SPA   TAINT  NOOSE
LENIS  FAITHFULNESS  OVIS
ILES  SIGN  EARLE  ASPECT
ELS  SEVEN  AREAS  MAWS
ROSETTE  APRES   HERE  BAD
   NEH  SCUTS  GRAD  ELEGY
TAPIR  BAERS  DHOTI  TOMAN
ABUSENOT  IAMYOURCAPTIVE
JEALOUSY  TRIESTE  REUNE
   ESTER  YEASTED  CASE
```

87

```
LAIT   AREA   BOB   BARGE
WINCE  GEMSTONE  SALAMI
INTERMEDIARIES  CLIMES
SOL  MANOR  ALIT   ALVIN
ELEMENT   SCAD   AEF
SERED  SECRETARIES   IAM
TUES   RAID   ARAT   CRE
MDS  PEAS  SEVER   MATA
   RAMSHACKLE   GETIN
CAR  AIME  TRAIL  MALICE
OCARINA  TRITE  PISTOLS
ATMOST  LEASE  CAMP   NET
RUBLE   EMISSARIES
SAUL  SLOAN   SAND   ACC
ERN   SLAV   PITT   SLAP
NYC  CAPILLARIES  SHINE
   TRA   EELS   ELEANOR
TIERS  OPAL  BONED   GNU
SHOULD  PENITENTIARIES
CAUSES  PREDATOR  TENSE
INSET   AER   WARY   EGGS
```

88

```
RCA  BACCATE  REDBIRD  CAW
ERN  ORIOLES  AVIATOR  OLE
EAGLESCOUTS  GOOSEPIMPLE
SNEER  ALLE  HOLDS  ELATED
EELY  IDEA  MAUVE   LIEGE
   REAR  DANTE  CPA   DRED
ETCHERS  JINKS   CLASP
CHAINS   ARTY  GOOSESTEP
LIPPO  STEEL  SLOWS  ARGIL
ARIE  AIGRETTE  NESTEGGS
TDS  MAKE  RADA   ASABEE
DTH  ABIRDSEYEVIEW   DEO
BOREAL  SANE  ORAN   ANS
SWANNECK  HENPECKS  ATTU
ANNIE  HAILE  IDEST  CLEON
SONGBIRDS  SNIT   MODRED
   GARMO  MONTS  MANASSA
CABS  SPA  FULAH   TASK
YULES   SODAS  LARK  CASS
GRATED  SPAHN  SENT  TONTO
NOMSDEPLUME  CARDINALSIN
ERE  ALBUMEN  PHOENIX  ELD
TAD  NESTERS  SLIMILY  REE
```

89

```
RAJAS  LACK  OASTS  CHEF
ANATH  OKIE  CROAK  LALO
SAMRAYBURN  CENTIMETER
ESSENES  COVINA  DIRECT
   ESTATE  ADARS  LISTS
MAST  SELLONES   TALC
ADS  STRAITEN  SIDESHOW
NOISE  SPOT  THALER  ENO
ABOUND  SNOB  OPEN  TIER
TENTOONE  MEANSTO  IRAK
   TREE  SANDE   TIKE
LACE  SPOONED  SODAPOPS
ARAR  KERF   TRET  SPIREA
PEN  PINATA  ETAS  UNDER
PATIENTS  FISHBAIT  OLE
   BASH  BRASSARD  SNEE
GOBEL  EVIAN   TAIWAN
INURES  ODISTS  BOATAGE
LEGISLATED  RELATIONAL
LALA  AGENT  IRON  LUCES
STEN  PORTO  PEND  STELA
```

90

```
SOPOR  ATROCE  MIRA  SWAMI
GRIME  RHETOR  AWOL  PIPED
TENON  BEMIRE  REST  ANETO
GENTLEPUCKCOMEHITHER
BATS  ALAS  STRIP   ENS
ANATURAL  LEO  AOK   ASTA
DORRS  MERCYONUSWESPLIT
OER  LIL   NIELS   AMO
CLAUDE  EIGE  DRAWN  ELTON
ROKS  LETHIMNOTPASS  EYRE
ALIFE  SCUD  ODETS   ACT
MANATEE  UNO   ALUMNAE
UAR  ARAKE  STAG   BEALL
SAIL  GIVEMETHEIRON  CVII
TESTA  AEDES  ERAT  ISLETS
ASS  SOMNI  AGR   LIU
YOUDIDBIDMESTEAL  STRAP
SPEE  DIN  ASE   ABDICATE
   TOE  METER  APOC  HILT
HEARTHESHRILLWHISTLE
CLANK  RUNT  EMILIE  AHEAD
PARTE  EMIR  SALINA  PERSE
AXMEN  KENO  SLINGS  SESTE
```

91

CHIP · ONADIME · CAPO
ALONE · RATATAT · IWANT
BROWNELIZABETH · GETSAT
ROTE · LEGAL · TATA · RHIO
ISH · RETIRE · SENOR · IOLA
GEESE · ONE · DIRER · SCROD
ICA · STLUKES · BAKERY
SCRAPE · HATED · CRAW
STO · POSE · SCS · PHARAOHS
TARP · CRASH · SIEG · GNAT
ERNE · MARGARETLEG · OTTO
EVEN · APER · OGLER · NITA
DETECTED · ABA · DURA · MIT
LATE · SHELF · PAWNEE
CAPOTE · LAURELS · MAE
LEAPT · HASNT · OTO · ROUGH
INRE · BURST · TRADED · NEE
MESA · ASCI · HEGEL · TSAR
BIENNE · HEALINGARTHURS
DETER · ESSENCE · OVENS
SEWS · STINGER · YANG

92

ALMOND · HATCH · WATT · CARBO
GUINEA · OPERA · OLIO · ANOLD
EXTERMINATOR · OLDROSEBUD
DEE · OATERS · DELAY · MIMER
SESS · ARLEN · ANNI
CAB · SCAT · SLOAN · BRIGADES
OMINOUS · EPACT · BONUS · UMA
MOLARS · OMARKHAYYAM · SOB
MULTI · ABIDE · ARIZ · MATTE
ANSE · AGILE · AKRON · SAUCER
STH · WINTERGREEN · SANTOS
ORALES · EEN · SELDOM
REESES · VENETIANWAY · MOD
REMAND · METED · SPOOL · MARU
OPART · BAER · CAPON · CANER
ROK · SECRETARIAT · CANDLE
ESE · ALTOS · IDEAL · BIGNESS
MERIDIAN · ARDEN · PETE · RES
SOPS · FLEES · LOLA
METRO · SHEEN · PILOTS · SOO
GALLANTFOX · DERBYWINNERS
ALIEN · HALI · USURP · ORACLE
BEAST · EXES · MOTES · NANTES

93

LAPUP · MOFFO · ORCA · WAKE
IRANI · APEAK · FOLK · EDER
CONTE · PULSE · FLEE · EZRA
IADOREALLTHESEFLOWERS
TRAY · SUE · ESTH · ARE
OAT · NIN · COOP · DEJA
YOUSENTMEWHOLEBOWERS
DAP · PEU · BRA · TEAR · ENCL
ELIA · MATISSE · ITEASY
STUMP · NIB · SEA · MNO
IAMTOUCHEDANDBEGUILED
ONE · DOI · AUT · TBONE
CHACHA · SLUMMED · OCTA
OOLA · RIVA · ENS · OOP · AAL
BUTREMEMBERDEARCHILD
RARE · RIEL · ELL · KIN
ILK · TAHR · LAE · DATA
TODAYISNTMYDAYITSOURS
ALOG · THAI · MOTEL · PULIK
LAZE · TARN · ANTAE · ABATE
EXES · SWAG · NEARS · STEED

94

SOCKO · SHARER · SCARF · TOWN
ADAIR · TAGORE · CABAL · IVAN
KISSTHEBOYSGOODBYE · CAGE
INKS · AVINE · UNTER · SPT
MERITS · LETT · HEATH
IDEATES · THAI · CRATCHIT
TREKS · THIRDS · LONE · ESE
SETAT · THREESACROWD · METE
ANETO · ARUMS · OUTS · TENON
NICER · BORA · SLUSH · PANTRY
ACT · NONONANETTE · RILEY
ICHOR · REO · VALOR
AVAIL · TINPANALLEY · TAB
AGENDA · ALEAK · MOOR · ETAGE
ELSIE · OGEE · POULT · LEILA
GATO · THEODDCOUPLE · ANNAS
INO · EARN · SERENE · IDEST
SCRAPPED · CATT · LEANERS
EYRIE · THAT · TALLER
ACS · KEENE · ARTIE · THIS
GRAB · THEPETRIFIEDFOREST
BILL · RAGED · ELAPSE · PASTE
SOLE · YESES · DONETS · EPSOM

95

SMITH · STPETER · HEMP
HANOI · THEREMIN · SECURE
ARTIE · REGICIDE · PROTEM
KIEL · MONO · LETDIE · ASP
EER · AOK · SPY · SINISTER
SWEETHEARTS · DENTINE
PISTOL · BUOY · LMN · ROTS
ELTON · CONIC · EAT · GENES
ASIN · CLUTCHING · LEASE
RON · RAY · INDIAINK
ENGLAND · ASANA · CATSPAW
ANSERMET · IRE · RNA
BINET · HUARACHES · MOTT
RENTE · PES · IDLER · MEDIC
EASE · ITE · SHEA · MUNICH
ACTRESS · TEMPUSFUGIT
SHANGHAI · GSM · NEF · APO
OWN · RANCOR · CHIC · CLAW
NETHER · BRACELET · WRITE
SALUTE · MCNAMARA · PATER
RYES · ATTENDS · ABYSS

96

SACS · COALED · ABASH · ANGEL
TREE · ARSINE · GAMMA · BOOTY
AOTA · NOTNOW · ALEUT · ANISE
THELIONINWINTER · PUTON
IER · PEON · LEER · FIRE · GNP
CRAGS · DUDS · ERNE · AMOR
SEPARATETABLES · ADYTA
AMST · UKASE · CLUE · GROWIN
PIER · PITH · TOHELLANDBACK
ARTISAN · ARCED · OBA · EYES
STENO · SADIE · GAUSS
THEGOODTHEBADANDTHEUGLY
TRIOS · NEXUS · SPREE
RICK · AAM · FAIRE · TOSCANA
AMANANDAWOMAN · OTIS · ACIS
BASING · CHUM · EVICT · RENT
IRATE · THELOSTWEEKEND
WEBS · BREW · THEN · OSCAR
STL · PIED · SPAR · IVOR · ALA
ACIDS · THESOUNDOFMUSIC
PINUP · TRAIT · WRAITH · TACK
UNCLE · LIBRA · IGNORE · ABEE
BEATS · EDSEL · NEATER · HAST

97

```
ALTAR  SUET   OAF   NOAH
BERNE  ORCA   ALE   DELVES
REACT  HAHN   KIN   RADIAL
ARCHIEOLOGY   IDEA  HAVE
 STORMS  NEON  EDUCATED
   REI  TORSO  RIGHTING
SALADGEOMETRY  THE  OLE
CRAG  REMI   MANET  ANY
AIME  ELECTS   NODICE
ROOST  ENSILAGE  NURSES
ESU  AFR  DAM  HGT  CAN
DORATI  CREVASSE  SPITE
   CAZZIE  SHOTAN  APIA
ARE  ZARPS   MORO  LINK
APE  PIG  PAYLEONTOLOGY
HISSTORY   NAIAD  EBI
MAUNALOA  SWAN  BALATA
ERRA  OSLO  LITTERATURE
DIVING  UTE  SIAL  TIRES
SEELEY  NOW  OCTO  EVIAN
 SYST  GEE  NSEW  SENSE
```

98

```
LARGE  SHALE  RASPY  SHOOT
IROAM  PUREE  OGLER  LETGO
NEWPIPENEWROBEORSWEATER
UNDERACTED  DENSE  REDEEM
SAYS  CIEL  PERCH  DIVERSE
   TIER  MISTY  CREED
SPRAIN  LENS  MAYS   TEA
WOULDGIVEDEARDADATHRILL
ALLAY  NEVER  ERRED  OUTDO
MIEN  ATRIA  FLOAT  BUTLER
POD  DRESS  JOINT  DARTERS
   SEINE  CURVE  RALLY
RESEWED  BORGE  DUMMY  PRO
APPALL  EERIE  TODAY  FLAT
VOILA  ATHOS  SONGS  PLAZA
EXCEPTTHATTWOWEEKSLATER
LYE  OLAN  ERNE  TOWERY
   WOMAN  WEARY  SWAY
SALADAS  SASSY  PEAR  COCO
OMELET  TASTE  ARTICHOKES
DADKNOWSWHOLLGETTHEBILL
ARIES  EATUP  AISLE  ARETE
SANDE  DROPS  DOSED  LASER
```

99

```
ROCK  ATLAS   HAM  ARADO
ACRE  TRIPE  COLA  GOFOR
CHERCHEZLAFEMME   AWFUL
ERA  RANA  PORES  DREARY
REMNANT  CORER  CRINI
 IND  NORUN  ALACARTE
SOCLE  POSTMORTEM  ERN
ASHE  GOUT  YOWS  ADIT
ASA  ADNAUSEAM  LEHAR
RARAAVIS  BENNY  PAROLE
 GENOA  CORNS  DIDIN
CREDIT  SHAVE  FANDANGO
HADES  TETEATETE  ENG
ITAS  BOAR  AMUR  DUAL
NEF  ANTEBELLUM  FORTE
ALFRESCO  OSLER  DON
 AERIE  NOTAS  SUSTAIN
ALIGNS  RISEN  OILS  TRI
LARGE  LETTRESDECACHET
DIEIS  ODES  RIDGE  HONI
ONSET  TOR  OSSET  USED
```

100

```
ICES  BOMBS  LABOR  TRALAS
NOGO  ODTAA  ENURE  EERILY
THYWOODSANDTEMPLEDHILLS
RAP  MRS  IDIOT  HITS  SLIT
ANTON  NANU  WASH  ATIDE
 WITHAGLORYINHISBOSOM
PETE  HAM   GAS   CIO
OAR  DORIA  ARREST  GYPSUM
PRESERVEDUSANATION  INRE
SNEAK  ERST  SABA  PAIR
RASA  DIET  RETRO  FAR
THEGLORIOUSFOURTHOFJULY
REX  BURNS  TUBS  SILO
ONTO  ALAS  LASS  ILONA
ONOR  SHEDHISGRACEONTHEE
PALACE  TOOTOO  CEDRE  IER
 OLD   AEN   BEA  DODO
ASTARLITFLAGUNFURLED
VERGE  GALS  ASOR  ZEBRA
OLEA  RICE  FRERE  SIR  RIB
WENTTOTOWNRIDINGONAPONY
ANDHOW  MANES  AZINE  RUGS
LESAGE  ATETE  SYNGE  ENOS
```

101

```
AQUAE  ADAPT  CABLE  IBIS
BURMA  VAPOR  AFLAT  DARIN
RISUS  EVASE  TRENT  OLIDE
ALASTOMISSTHEANNUALBALL
MLLE  HASTE  UNITY  LIONEL
 MOOR  BRAD  ILKA
ADHEM  IAMBUS  BOWIE  ZEP
NOONEHASSENTUSABIDATALL
WONTGO  SGTS  PACINO  USIA
AZA  ABLER  ARHAT  ABUZZ
RYND  BAR  BESOIL  AMNESIA
 ISITTHINKABLEDEAR
ORIENTE  ANGERS  DIZ  SAMP
ZIPPY  UNDID  MITZI  PIE
APAP  BALDUR  JOAB  OSMOND
WEWEREBUMPTIOUSLASTYEAR
ANN  ANISE  SUITED  OSTEO
 EDIE  GEAR   MOOT
NOEXIT  SHIVA  SEPIA  IRAE
ORBESOTTEDICANNOTRECALL
TOOTH  HELEN  DIVOT  LIBEL
ALLEE  ANLOC  APOLE  AZINE
 DIRS  NOONE  KEYED  SEDER
```

102

```
ARAMIS  FRUMPS  SAMPLER
RUDEST  REPEAT  ISAROSE
ANDTHEDEVILSENDSCOOKS
BESS  PETE  SNEE   SET
 OHM  SALADE  RIDERS
STEREOS  DAGH  TORE
ONECANBECOMEACOOKBUT
SALUT  SCAR  LAUD  ASIS
AGLAIA  REMI  UPS  TARE
 OMBRE  INGLE  SEDER
DONTLASTCOOKERYDO
CLODS  UNSER  ESSEN
HARD  LEG  LOTS  STELLA
EVIL  ILIA  SUAM  OLEIN
ACOOKANDACAPTAINBOLD
THEW  EVER  ANCIENT
SAMSON  PLISSE  TIC
ABA  BRAG  NARC  ABAT
LIKECOOKINGASMALLFISH
EDITORS  DONEUP  ECARTE
SENSORS  ENURES  STRIAE
```

103

```
PLAN  MATTE  ERSATZ  AGAS
RUBE  ASIAN  SOIREE  SPINE
ACRUSHOFWRESTLERS  URBAN
MEATLOAF  APECKOFTYPISTS
   CRANK  EGO      EEE  DOTE
STEAMY  PRESA  MAZDA  ENOS
COOL   BOO   SKID    NEO
ARF  AMASSOFLAMAS  INFANT
LID  MODE  JEUNE  TENDSBAR
PIE ICE VIRGO LONG  NUMA
   NASH  FIBRO  TARN  ONED
ACTG  ASLEWOFHITMEN  BCDE
LAIR  TIWA  BORES  SASH
IPSO SOCS COWER STU  ORB
OUTSPEAK SEXTO WEAK  FEE
NASSER  ALINEOFLIARS  VIE
   OAR  ITER   ILL   SIGN
CLEF ADDLE SOCLE  PRYNNE
LAMB  NEE  LOT  COURT
APOOLOFOARSMEN  SARDINIA
UPTON  ADROVEOFMARTINETS
SEERS  NATTER  EARLE  GREW
ERRS  GREENE  RYDER  ESME
```

104

```
COCOA  SODA  ASEA  SABIN
AROID  TRANSEPTS  CRONE
MARLENEDIETRICH  HORDE
ETA  LOINS  RINSE  OSIER
ROLLING    FIAT    WOES
ARSENE  STANLAUREL  KOP
LIEGE  PANG  SETS  ANA
OAS  SPUN  TOILS  BRER
   GEORGEBURNS  CALLA
CPA  LAPS  PELEG  CUBOID
HANGARS  DIVAS  GIRAFFE
ASNERS  MANED  SOME  FED
STELE  NATALIEWOOD
SUBS  SALAL  CONN  EME
IRA  CORI  AUTO  PLANT
SEN  ROCKHUDSON  DEARTH
   CAEN  ONON  PISMIRE
MARIA  ARRAN  RUANA  LAS
ALOSS  BARBARASTANWYCK
RIFLE  UTILITIES  TANTI
SATED  SADE  EDDY  ESSEN
```

105

```
PALES  POSED  UTTAR  STOLA
ALIVE  ORALE  POOLE  URBAN
LATEX  MALIC  HANSE  POOKA
AMERICANVARIETYOFAPPLE
TORY  EDGE  ELLES    GLI
ESS  KNEE  SPODE  TELECAST
   GIS  SHIV   POGO   CHU
UNITEDSTATESSONGWRITER
SLIDE  OPA   WALES  ONEOF
ATLE  MOIRA  TAPED  CUDDLY
SRO  RAMROD  YMA   POTI
HATMADEOFJIPIJAPALEAVES
   ACAD  UTE  OSAGES  IDE
MEGRIM  MINCE  UNCAS  ANSA
ALOSS  PATCH   EEN  ASYET
LIGHTCRUSTYBREADORROLL
ETO  LIDO   RENT    EIN
SELFSAME  SMELT  CLAD  FED
   AIR  HEAVE  SLIP  ROAR
DUKEOFWELLINGTONSHORSE
TOXIN  LALLA  TEASE  ABETS
ADORN  OILED  ENTER  LOGES
DORSA  GLORY  DEEDS  STORY
```

106

```
   BRAGG    SIVA    BAKED
SOURER  ACHES  ARCADIA
THEGRASSHARP  BURREEDS
REDE   POSITS  ORIEL  HOP
AMEN  HOUSEORGANS  DARE
TILTH  TRM    OLDS  ERRED
AAA  OGEE  TYPEE  GLADE
   MOORS  HUE   SUMI
BRAVOS  HUMDRUMS  NOSH
CRATED  POLA  ALIT  PATE
HINTS  MORE  DINT  VITAL
INGE  SOME  MONA  DEPEND
PEER  TOPBRASS  FRIEND
   HRON   IKE   IRONS
STOOP  SAVED  NOPE  MAA
OTARY  PERE  STN  DRATS
LUNN  EARTRUMPETS  ERIS
APC  SALAS  PEORIA  SINE
FIRETRAP  APRONSTRINGS
DETENTE  LEONE  YODELS
DOWSE   PREY   REESE
```

107

```
MEADE  JIGGS  ROTC  PUTON
ALTER  ERRAND  AREA  ONICE
KALAMAZOOZOO  PEER  CONTE
ETA  ARENT  WEFT  TONO  GAR
DENS  ABE  SOUTHBENDEND
OSTE  BERMS  KURIE  WORDTO
   ATALL  ATTIRES  APSO
AMASSES  GUANO  SOLO  MOSS
TINCT  VENUS  SUPERSONIC
RETRACTING  FLEE  TOSEEA
INAE  OAST  ECRU  NAPA  SGT
   WILLIAMSPORTSPORT
ASH  CULT  ATOM  SEER  HBAR
MAYHEM  OGRE  CHARTREUSE
ELDERBERRY  GOLIS  ATRIA
STET  URSA  VIDOR  SCRIBED
   ESSA  VAINEST  THEMA
CHERUB  VELAR  ESSAY  ENCS
HONOLULULULU   ART  SKEP
AMA  PSIL  DSMS  AUTRY  BRA
FILCH  ACRE  MONTCLAIRAIR
ELIHU  NAIL  YANKEE  RINSE
RYDER  ANDS  SWARD  RAKED
```

108

```
ALECK    CAA   HEIR   SKS
COLLAR  SUSIE  ONCE  ANE
TOMATO  TRANS  TROD  TIR
   SYMBOLIST  DANDRUFF
SHEP  PRAIRIEDOGS  ERES
TELIC  OTC   AGE   MTNS
URANUS  SUNDAYS   FUR
MONGREL  ERODE  DUTIES
   MEAT  AGI  CONTENTS
ACCURSED  HELLO  OVOID
BLOOD  CURIOUSER  NELLS
CLUNG  ATYOU  DEMOCRAT
DOGSEARS   TSP   KAPH
WHOOPS  BAERS  NEOCENE
NNE  SASSOON  SPOLIA
STAS  CUL   ROE  SLIPS
ATAN  CANINETOOTH  OAST
DOGTIRED  OVERSHOES
ALE  PASO  DIXIE  ORSINO
NIN  SNAG  ETATS  PLATER
ODD  EERS   ANY   ELATE
```

109

```
MARC  AHEM   SOCKO   SCONE
NEWEL MANET  PRUNE   CARAT
USAFI ESSEN  ACTOR   ARGOT
TAKEME OUTTOTHEBALLGAME
 SERBS  NEM  REIN   ADONIS
   SETT  DEED  DEIST
ARC  VERB  IRIS  STEEL  COR
BAR  REAL  NINO  SEC  EVADE
AMY  YMCA  SCALA  REPTILES
 IMAN  ERST  LENZ  DEMILLE
 ETO  DEAL  SINE  EEE  MED
STATUS  STOA  LIPS  PESETA
PAR  NEO  AUNT  EPEE  NAM
OMITTED  NINA  GOWN  TRAP
REVEALED  SERGE  ANCE  DUG
ELEMI  SIP  ABET  REAR  ARA
SYR  NASAL  LORY  DART  MEL
   SALEP  OMOO  DUAD
ASSETS  TESS  USS  SIEVE
GETMETOTHECHURCH  ONTIME
AROMA  RHODO  AGIOS  YETIS
POKER  CAREW  RUNNY  ORATE
EWERY  STAEL  NEED  USES
```

110

```
SCOT  BAT  ISNT  ALLEGE
HATH  ANI  SHORE  LOOSER
ALAE  SEA  MOVINGFASTER
HERR  KURA  WANDA  NEESE
 BUMPERACCESSORY  SEED
  SETI  EAR  BEEF
ICS  ARC  TRETA  TRAMPS
SOLELY  KINDOFRAINCOAT
OXYGEN  INE  URAL  EERIE
NAGA  EPS  GROWTHS  ELM
 IDLERS  PIN  HEATED
NAG  EDITION  IRV  GENA
EDGES  OHMS  BUD  EVENER
WALLSTREETTAPE  AIRSAC
THELOW  TORIC  SQS  ETH
 INAT  ORA  TUES
AMAN  SHINEUNSTEADILY
SONGS  ALOSS  TERR  MAIM
COTTONWORKER  EIR  OGPU
ARIOSO  TSARS  ULE  NOEL
PENNON  ERST  PEL  ESSE
```

111

```
BASSO  GRAPH  CHAD  SEATO
ARTUR  RODEO  RELIT  ELMER
SKIRL  ENACT  IRISH  NOBLE
KINDERGAR10S  BICEN10NIAL
SETS  ION  ESS  AAC
  AGR  PA10TAPPLIEDFOR
EPPING  MOTORBOATS  EASE
FLARE  THOR  ULTRA  CCIIII
FIRSTLIEU10ANT  SIR  HAREM
ONS  OERA  DUE  AHS  GAPERS
RTES  MARC  SWINE  PESO
THECOUNTOF10  PARKAT10DANT
 ARRA  RISER  DATO  ABOU
SWINGS  MNT  TAA  TRUE  RMC
MANTA  LOI  DAYSTHATSHOOK
AGAIN  ENCKE  SAYS  SCARE
RENE  OFTHELOWER  WELDER
10DERISTHENIGHT  SIN
  SLO  SEI  BEN  ODEA
10DERLOVING  10PERCENTERS
PUREE  EVIAN  EERIE  ATLAS
ICANT  RANIN  RAGED  MOOSE
NESTS  NOTE  STORE  EINES
```

112

```
CAPS  BED  MAGMA  DAMON
CHILI  OAR  ALOES  INURE
RERUN  BROOKLYNACCENTS
ERINGO  PLEIAD  REMISS
PREGAME  DOES  DADO
TYREPATCHERS  TAV  NASA
 OHARAS  REDALERTS
FEDORA  INTO  AMATI  MOT
ADORE  CSA  VITA  BUENO
GAZASTRIPPERS  BLENDER
 CLUES  ARI  AUTRE
DECLINE  CARDIFFGIANTS
ALLEN  AURA  OFF  ASYET
USO  GRACE  NODE  SNEERY
BATHSALTS  RECANT
ESSA  DAH  BRESTBEATERS
 ISIS  DEEM  MENORAH
SPARTA  HERMAN  SKIMPY
AYRCONDITIONERS  ELITE
CROUP  IDENT  AUK  RENIR
KEATS  MERGE  LEI  STEN
```

113

```
STATIC  RAZZ  FRED  BYRE
SWEDISH  ELEE  PAULA  EOUS
PARVENU  PLEASINGLYPLUMP
ISR  ROBROYS  WET  SALA
ETON  BIRL  BACALL  DENSE
LIRE  GYNT  JAMESII  RODIN
SKIPJACK  FATISINTHEFIRE
 ASHIGH  AIRE  ADUE
STEV  ESNE  SSA  PAJAMAS
 WENCHES  ORAN  LOVELL
CML  OKRA  EMPIRES  AISLE
HEAVYWEIGHTCHAMPIONSHIP
ADDIE  RELOADS  BABI  YET
TIEINS  KELP  SALEDAY
SADISTS  MET  UNIR  ROBE
  AMIS  YOND  ISTDAS
BIGMANONCAMPUS  CALIENTE
ABOYS  CROSIER  TINY  LARK
ROAMS  KETTLE  HUNH  SNOB
 LOEW  FUN  MARQUEE  AGE
STOUTHEARTEDMEN  SLEEPER
CANT  ETWEE  RIME  KILLING
HUGH  YALE  UXOR  YESYES
```

114

```
TRI  CHROME  TORA  ARP
HEN  ROAMER  TWAIN  TOAD
EMS  APRILITHISIS  LOPE
EAT  MEET  CART  ERASER
ATOM  ISLE  ABSENTEE
SCRIP  BONO  SARA  STET
THEDAYUPONWHICHWEARE
 ITEMS  EER  SHA
 LASTS  PONDER  ELMIRA
BILKO  MARAT  DOOR  ABON
REMINDEDOFWHATWEAREON
AGAR  IDES  ORLON  PRATE
TESTED  SPARSE  BRIMS
  VIC  ENT  TOTOE
THEOTHERTHREEHUNDRED
HONK  IPOH  ORLO  STALE
PROTECTS  EMIR  OVAL
RAKISH  ISIS  ALSO  ISE
AVEC  ANDSIXTYFOUR  OTT
MERE  REIMS  EERIER  LIE
SSR  TOME  RHONDA  ICS
```

115

```
S L A K E   P O L A R   I L I A D   C E S T
H E M I N   A P A C E   L A D L E   M A R C O
O H A L A S W I T H E V E R Y T O M O R R O W
R A N T   A N N E E   E X I L E   I N T O N E
E R A S   M E E R   O N E A L   C A T E R E R
        F L E D   C R U S T   C A M E L
A L A L I A   B O O S   A R N I   T E N
R E M A R K   P A I N   A L I E N   A U R A E
M Y A S S E T S G R O W L E S S A N D L E S S
O T I S   H A G S   H E A L S   I R E N E S
R E D   M A R L Y   P E R S E   S T I N T S
      B E L E M   C R E T E   T H E F T
T O O T L E   T H O L E   H E A R T   P A N
B O R N E O   H E A V E   D E S K   D A Z E
A N D N O W I A M F O R C E D T O B O R R O W
S T E E R   D U P E S   L A D Y   E L E M I S
H O R   G E N T   C E L A   L E G A C Y
      C R O A T   E C L A T   P R I G
S A V E A L L   S T O U T   C R A N   D A M E
O D E N S E   S C O R N   T R E N D   E L A S
F O R S O M E T H I N G T H E Y C A L L I R S
A R S O N   C I E L O   H O P E H   E V A D E
R E A R   A R D E N   O U T D O   R E S I N
```

116

```
S A L A D   P O S H   P A R M A   A L A
A M O L E   A S T O   I T O L D   D O L L
H A R T E   S L A B   N A D I R   A R T A
I P R O M I S E Y O U A L O V E L Y D A Y
B A Y H   A I R S   S T A R   M A T H I S
      O C T O   B E A N   P O A
L I B R A   N O M O   T O K Y O   W A S
A S U N N Y S K Y A N D A L L O F T H A T
B U R S A E   A N Z I O   A O K   R A R E
S P T   P L A Y A   G R A S S O   O W E N
      K E L P   M A H A S   S H O T
A M O I   O L D E S T   S H E A R   I R E
D O N E   W A A   E L S I E   M A M M O N
A P E R F E C T D A Y I S W H A T I S A Y
M E G   A D E E R   V I N O   O R O N O
      R U R   A I D A   C A R R
B I A N C A   L M N O   S P U N   O S L O
O R I W I L L E A T M Y E A S T E R H A T
R E N E   L O T T O   E R R S   R I A T A
E N O L   A C H I N   A G E E   I N K E R
      A F L   N I E C E   R E D D   A G O N Y
```

117

```
S A L U T E   S W A M P   S A D   L E A
A G A T E S   S P I D E R S   S C R I B I N G
M U T A N T   T I T A N I C   T O E D A N C E
B A C H T O B A C H H O M E R U N S   R E I N
A S H   E N O R E E   N I L E   I R A N O
      T R Y S T S   E S T E E M S   S I T A R
B A B A   A S S   U N C A S   S T E E L
I M O G E N E   A R D O R   G O B L E T
G A N G S   S P I G O T   R I L E Y   O C T O
H O E K   A L E R T   O V E R   S N A I L
      P R I V E T   S L A T E   E N T E R E D
A B A   M A D E A B E A L I N E F O R   E R E
M O R M O N S   W A Y N E   S T R I P Y
I O T A S   E L A N   D H O L E   D I O R
S T E N   B L O K E   Y O K E L S   O N C U E
      N E I S S E   F A U R E   A C R E A G E
A T H O S   B U R S A   E R A   A S A N
A P I A N   E N G A R D E   E N D A L L
S P E T S   V I A L   A L D I N E   S M U
S O R T   H A N D E L B A R M U S T A C H E S
E S C A P A D E   R O O S T E R   I D E A T E
T E E N A G E R   S A L T I R E   K E L L E R
S D S   L I D   F L O S S   I N T E R S
```

118

```
N A Z I   M E D I A   N O V A   A Y E S
A M E N   A N O D I S   I B I D   S U N K
R A R A   C L A I R E B L O O M   P L O Y
C H O R E A   T O S I R   E L I G I B L E
      M O U R N   M A N I C   S T A R R
      L O W R O A D   C E L L I   S T A Y S
C A S   O T O E   L A N G   E T N A S
R U T S   N A S T S   S U R E   E N T O
I D E A   L E H A R   D I O D E   E A R
B E L L I N I   E R O D E   R I T O R N A
      A T E E   L A M A R   G L A D
H A N D S A W   W H A T A   E L L I P S E
A D O   A R O M A   N E I L S   S I L L
U L E S   O A T S   S N E E R   T E A L
L A L L A   D I E T   S A G E   R I A
      I C A M E   D R E S S   R A M A D A N
      O V I N E   S L E P T   L A C O N
L O W E R I N G   M A R I S   R E G G I E
A L A R   G R E G O R Y P E C K   T E R M
S I R E   M O R A   S E T T E E   A L I I I
T O D D   A L M S   R O T E D   G I S T
```

119

```
A L B E R T A   P E E R S   H E A T   E S S
R E E L E C T   E N L A C E   O N G O   L O A
A N N A T H A N D R E M U S   G R A T E F U L
B O I T E S   E D O M I T E   W A T E R
R T E   N E L L I E   P A G E   R I S K
R E O S   M O D E L   A B A S E   C O S T A
A N D   I L E   G A L O S H   T A R T A R
P E H O   L E D   D I V E R T   A R M   L I L
T E U T O N S   P E T E R N E S T E P H E N
      N A R E S   O P A R T   C A N O E
T I T L E S   S L A N T   S C O L D   L A P P
O W E G O   C H A R O   S T O R E   L I B E L
N O R I   S H O R T   S P I N E   P A P E R Y
      A S T I R   A T I L T   E R R O L
V A S C O L E A N D E R L E   D I A R I S T
B E N   O U I   M O L I E S   H U M   T A P A
A S S E N T   D E P E N D   O C A   S A X
S T E V E   F I N E R   S T A E L   S H R I
H I R E   S A N D   R E T A R D   T E E
      N A N C E   E N A M E L S   S H E R P A
P O R T R A I T   D A N I E L E A N O R M A N
A B A   M I L T   T I T T L E   L E O N A R D
D I G   A L E E   L O S E R   L E P A N T O
```

120

```
D E L I   P L I E   C R A S H   S C A P E
O L A N   L E A R   H E L L O   P O R E D
N O W T H A T M A M A S L I B E R A T E D
O P E R E T T A   E N T O M   L I T A N Y
R E S O R T S   F A C E T   G I N
      V E E   P I N E D   T A N T A L U S
F L E E T   B U S T   A H S O   D O P E
R E D R O S E S H O L D N O P R O M I S E
O M I T   P R A Y   O U T R E   M I R E D
G A T   Y A R N   C R A I N   S U R E T Y
      D E N Y   G L E N N   M I T E
M A S O N S   A L A T E   P U N A   W I T
A L E R T   S C O U T   S O L A   R A N I
F O R M A M A H A S A N T I C I P A T E D
I O I I   A B E T   A U N T   R I T Z Y
A F F E C T E D   T A U N T   F E N
      H U R   B U R S T   A L A S T O R
C A N D O R   E R N I E   I N A C T I V E
A W E E K E N D I N S A I N T T H O M A S
S A A L E   A G L E T   N O R A   R O T O
T Y L E R   B E L L A   A L A S   M R E D
```

121

```
T O S S P O T S   L O R A N S     C U S H A W
A N T E A T E R   A C E R A T E   M A R I N A
W E N T T H R O U G H F I R E A N D W A T E R
    L E O   S N O R T   D E T E R   S T A N
G A M I N   I D E S   L E A S T   H R S
A L O N   N I T I D   T W E R P   I K E
S A V E D F A C E   F U R R Y   R E I N E R
P I E   R I V E D   O L L A S   A D D A M S
    D R O V E R   B L E E P   A S T O   I S T
S H A P E   S T R E W S   I M P A N E L
A T E M P O   A I N T   A R I A   E L O P E
F L A M E   H E L D T H E F O R T   S I N A I
L O V E D   A T E E   E C O N   S H O T I N
    E R A S M U S   A C R O S S   L A T H S
S U N   N E M I   S N O U T   O D E N S E
P L A I C E   M I N O S   S L U E D   H U T
T E N T H S   P I N U P   T O O K S T E P S
    D E O   B A S E L   D I A N S   H A D A
A C E   R A I L S   P A N T   A R D O R
C H A T   B R A I D   O R M E R   A B U
C A R R I E D C O A L S T O N E W C A S T L E
R O T A T E   E N T A I L S   S A N C T I O N
A S H P I T   S E X T E T   T R E A S U R E
```

122

```
E P I C S     F A I R S     R E M I S S
A R E N O T   S O L V E N T   A W I T T Y
C O N S T A N T R E A D E R   C E D A R S
H I N T   R O U T E   L A M E R   S O T
I C Y   A L O N E   S I L V E R   A C L E
P A D D L I N G   M E S S E D   P S A L M
    R I O T   F O R A   L I C I T
T E N R E C   A L I A S   C R E A M S
S H A G S   O B S T A C L E   E R R A T A
H E D Y   G R E T E L   A L T E R E G O S
O F F   N O N S E N S E V E R S E   A R T
E R U D I T I O N   T R E M I E   C Z A R
R E L I C T   M O N O R A I L   T R I G O
    E S T H E R   N A R O N   L A R I N E
    T E N O N   D I R T   D A M E
A M B O S   T O R I E S   R E V I E W E D
B A R S   N O S E R S   S U D A N   R N A
A X E   B O R A S   T H E G N   S I G N
T I T I A N   L I T E R A R Y C R I T I C
E X O T I C   E D I T O R S   E O C E N E
S E N A T E   E M O T E   S T E R E
```

123

```
E D A M S   A S S A I L S   C O Y   A S S
C O C O A   S C O L L A Y   A G O   A L L E E
H W H I G H P O C K E T S   P L U S F O U R S
O D E S   O I N K   E T A P E   T I N G E S
    M O R E S   S L O W S   H I R E
D E P R I V E S   W H A L E   P E L E   W A C
E L A I N E S   S E A T E D T E A L   H I D E
L O D G E R   S C A P E   H A T   D O L E D
A G O G O   S H O V E   C H I T   C H O L L A
Y E N S   E N A T E   R A N   L O O P I E R
S S T   M A L E S H E E P   C A S T L E S
    H A P P I E R   O L E   P O N T I A C
    R E C O I L S   R O A S T E L I A   O R T
C A S T O R S   H U T   E L L E R   T B A R
A T T I R E   H U M S   A L I A R   C O B R A
C L O V E   S A L   A L L O R   P U R L E D
H I V E   G I R L S A P R O N   M A L T E S E
E N E   S L A M   A L P E N   S U P P O R T S
    S H A M   B U I L D   T A L I A
A V A T A R   S E R A I   R U I N   P E L T
L A K E W E I R D   S A U S A G E I T A L I A
A L I E N   A T E   E N T I C E R   A R S O N
    E N D   M A W   S T A T E R S   T E E N S
```

124

```
A B O R T   A L I T   A B L E   D A N A E
C O N D E   P I T H   R O O D   E L I T E
I W A S N T S P E E D I N G O F F I C E R
D I I   S H E S   P I A N O   R I C K E Y
S E R A P I S   T E N S E   P A C E
    I O N   S I C E   S I N I S T E R
I D O N T G E T N O R E S P E C T   A D O
S O C S   P A Y S   U N I T E   A R I L
L Y R I C I S T   F R E T S   O V A T E
A L E   A M O I   B A E R   A C E
M Y A L A R M C L O C K D I D N T R I N G
    A P E   A R E A   N I N A   N E R
P A R T I   T W I G S   H E A D A C H E
O G E E   H A I T I   P L A T   D A R E
O R E   I O N L Y A T E O N E P E A N U T
H A L F N O T E   O R A D   I N N
    E C T O   E D W I N   A L C O H O L
P I C N I C   O R R I S   E N O L   O S O
I D O N T H A V E A T H I N G T O W E A R
P E L E E   B E C K   E V I L   S E R G E
S E A L S   A N T E   D A D E   E I S E N
```

125

```
S L A P   H O U K   E L E V   C O S T A E
R A C E H O R S E   S O L E   A B O H M S
S U C C U L E N T   T R I N I D A D I A N
    L A N D   A C T E D O U T   D A N T E
T H I N K O F   H O L S T E I N   G I S
Y A M S   F A L   A L P   S N I C K A
P T A   F L A N D E R S   T H Y M E S
O C T A D   L U I S   A L O P   A L A R Y
    H E R I T A G E   B Y E A R   P E B A N
    A G U S H   R E D S O I L   O S O
R E D B I L L   S C A R S   C R A B B E D
O M O   T E E N E R S   A R A I L
N E N T A   E U R U S   G R E E N I N G
D E C A L   P I E S   G A M A   S P E L L
E R O T I C   S T E R L E T S   V I A
    R E S O R B   A L A   D E E   D E N S
S I L   B E E R C A N S   D E P A R T S
A R E P A   S H E E P D O G   T A N K
G E O R G E H A L A S   F I S H L I N E S
A N N I E S   L E N E   A N C E S T O R S
S E E M E D   F E S S   S K I D   E W E R
```

126

```
C A N A D A     T A F T   S T R A P
A C E T I C   E A R N E R   T H E M O O D
T H E O T H E R S I D E O F D E F E N S E
S E R I C   A R K   T W O   M I N G L E
    H E R O I S M   E L E A N   O O P
D I S C   A L L T H A T L I T T E R S
A N T H E R S   C E N A   C A D E
M O R A L   A H A   M H O   I S L A
    A F I E N D I N N E E D   A I N T I T
G E N E   L O A N   O S W A L D S   R N S
R A G D O L L   T R O T H   E A T C A K E
A G E   H E L L I O N   O N E S   A N S A
P E R S O N   E M B E L L I S H I N G
E R S T   G E E   I A N   S A L P A
    A R C A   R U M P   A I R L E S S
    A B I R D I N T H E S A N D   E R I S
D O S   B U D G E   S Y L V I A N
O P T I C S   O L D   A I T   E C O L E
L E A D A H O R S E T O S L A U G H T E R
E N R A G E D   O N E A T A   B R I T O N
    T H E R E   N Y E T   I O N O N E
```

127

```
BARKS   TRIES  SALAAM   SHAW
AMEER   WITTY  PAELLA   COVE
BALLADOFBUNKERHILL      OREL
ERIS   OFTEN  ICER     ATTACK
LACOSTE      PEI       TOWIT
     THEBATTLEOFORISKANY
GUAVA   TERRA   DITA   HELIO
ELMIRA  TAU  POISING   YANK
TRENTONANDPRINCETON     TOE
SIC  SKI   GAEL      LEGEND
ECHO   PARENT    SCALAR
THESTORMINGOFSTONYPOINT
     TAXIED   ROTUND   SNOW
SUPERB   FINI    OAS    ACE
INO  SONGABOUTCHARLESTON
GRIM  WOOFERS   KAN   FLAUNT
HUROK   ILES   SEWED   EMBAY
THENEWSFROMYORKTOWN
     MARYS   IOU   TWEAKED
BYGONE   EDDY  AMATI   NOTA
OAHU  THEVOWOFWASHINGTON
SLAT  COLIMA   ROSIE   OLAND
SETH  HALLEY   ALTAI   MESSY
```

128

```
COLA   SPAIN   SURE    ADDA
ORAN   TASSO   PRINT   LEOS
CARTOUCHES    RAMSHACKLE
ALDERNEY  EMILY   EBOATS
     CATS   OBITS    RAT
RULERS  SNAKE   CHOCTAWS
EPODE  STAGESTRUCK   LEA
COVE  MARI    RANK    STAY
ANE  DETERMINING   STEVE
PASSEDUP  ODETS   SHARER
     TULIP   PIAVE   SCORN
CHOLLA  MOSHE   SHORTAGE
HARKS  RESTORATION   TRI
ASIS   PONE    LILT    GIAN
ITE  GROUNDSWELL   PRONE
NOSTRUMS  EPICE   TAINTS
     AES   SPANK    CORD
STATES  AWORD   LOWLIFES
PARTRIDGES    BLITHERING
AXIL   COUPE   AIMEE   ONIT
TIDE   GETS    GEESE   NEDS
```

129

```
STALAG   PATTI   WASH   HARI
ARLINE   ORION   ANTE   SAMAR
BILLINGSMONT   RYENEWYORK
EOS  LEASES   HEMAN   SASSES
     SPED   SELLS   STYE
BAT  BEIT  PREY  SIR   ENDS
EROSION  DREAM   TELA   DEEM
AIMEE  GREENWICHCONN   WPA
ROBING  EVAS   LETSGO   PAR
USSR   RIGID   DUD   ESCORT
POT  MOBILEALABAMA   TART
     ONEGIN   NOD   ARARAT
ONES  DAVENPORTIOWA   NAE
ARETES  EVE   ORLON   MELS
MIA  CHAISE   ATEE   SHAWLS
BAR  HOTSPRINGSARK   ELSIE
ENID  VELA   ROLES   ENLIVEN
RAZE  ESE  MERE  STEP   ADE
     COOT   CANST   SATI
BEHALF  PUREE   FAULTY   IST
GRANDFORKS   MARBLEHEADMA
HILTS  POOH   APART   ETNOIR
TATS   SPRY   NOTES   RIALTO
```

130

```
HEAD   APSE   TAELS   CLAW
ISLE   FALLA   ORLOP   LURE
STOWEAWAYS   WILDEOATES
SEEDLING  SOLES   ERNEST
     RUTS   PUPIL   SDAK
CLOTH  ELMAN   BAILSOUT
SLOPE  STEELEMILLS   RII
TECS   STAB   OLAY   SANG
OAK  HARTEOFGOLD   ANTE
PRESIDES  NARDS   BULGAR
     SCRIP   PANAY   SAREE
DEMOTE  ARIOT   SCRIMPED
ERIN  STERNELOOKS   EMU
LATE  PULE   OURS   MEME
ETH  GREENEHOUSE   BOLET
DOSSIERS  MANIA   TENET
     OLDS   AIRES   REDO
SPARTA  ALGIA   VENETIAN
KEYESTONER   CRIESWOLFE
IRIS   OPINE   TEASE   NERA
PUNT   RELEE   FLED   ESOP
```

131

```
TOWAR   EPHOR   SAGA   ABLE
ACARE   READE   ICICLE  NOEL
SHRIMPORLOBSTERCOCKTAIL
SORE   ESTORIL   STEPONIT
     ALBA   SDAK  DELI  HAT
RAN  ARTE   TASTE   FOOLS
OXTAILORGREENTURTLESOUP
ALERT  AMEER   ATSEA   SKIS
DEEM  SALESMAN   RIPE
     SCAT   MEAND   ENCROACH
ABC  AREAS   GATOR   AURAE
SAUTEEDFILLETOFGREYSOLE
ERLES  ARIAN   FOOTE   DID
COMMAGER  AUTOS   BORG
     PROS   INASTATE   NOVA
OLPE  LAMAS   TUNES   EAVES
ROASTDUCKORVENISONSTEAK
CANTY   DENTI   ONON   RLS
AMI  POCO   ERIS   VERB
     CREMONAS  GRUMBLE  ALIT
BAKEDALASKAORPIEALAMODE
EDEN  RELIED   EPEES   LOWER
TODO   DAWS   GENTS   INNER
```

132

```
MODE   BLAH   SCALP   OGHAM
ARAL   IAGO   LUCIA   ROOSA
SCHELLCOLLECTOR   GULAG
SALVAGED  AIKEN   CALM
ESCAPE   HUGO   HANDGUN
     ATE   CHERHOLDER   RAVE
SOREL  HIDE   AWAY   UMEA
CURD  WONGNUMBER   SEAT
ATI  WILDE   NAIL   DAH
NBA  ALLI   ADULT   INEPT
TIGHTLY  FRERE   PASSION
     DEUCE   SORRY  ROLE  DRY
     SHY  CRAG   SEWER   GEL
TACT  CAANOPENER   SERO
AGAO  SOUL   EMIR   SWOON
FERN  WORLEYGIGS   OEN
TERTIAL  SOLS   SLACKS
     FARM   LATKE   HEADROOM
ANAXE  SOTHERNEXPOSURE
DOREN  ARTEL   ALPI   APEL
OBESE  GEARS   PLOD   TEAL
```

133

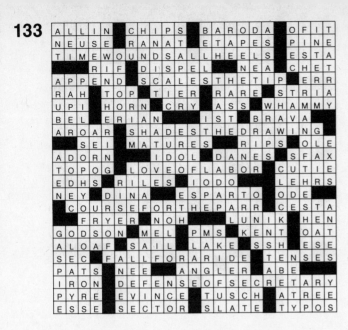

| A L L I N | CHIPS | BARODA | OFIT |

Row by row (across):
- ALLIN · CHIPS · BARODA · OFIT
- NEUSE · RANAT · ETAPES · PINE
- TIMEWOUNDSALLHEELS · ESTA
- RIF · DISPEL · NEA · CHET
- APPEND · SCALESTHETIP · ERR
- RAH · TOP · TIER · RARE · STRIA
- UPI · HORN · CRY · ASS · WHAMMY
- BEL · ERIAN · IST · BRAVA
- AROAR · SHADESTHEDRAWING
- SEI · MATURES · RIPS · OLE
- ADORN · IDOL · DANES · SFAX
- TOPOG · LOVEOFLABOR · CUTIE
- EDHS · RILES · IODO · LEHRS
- NEY · DINA · ESPARTO · ODE
- COURSEFORTHEPARR · CESTA
- FRYER · NOH · LUNIK · HEN
- GODSON · MEL · PMS · KENT · OAT
- ALOAF · SAIL · LAKE · SSH · ESE
- SEC · FALLFORARIDE · TENSES
- PATS · NEE · ANGLER · ABE
- IRON · DEFENSEOFSECRETARY
- PYRE · EVINCE · TUSCH · ATREE
- ESSE · SECTOR · SLATE · TYPOS

134

Row by row (across):
- RADING · LOPA · CHAD · SIS
- OVEREA · ERRS · HABI · EPOS
- HAWASHEWEEKHAWAS · AORA
- ESES · SIRS · FRENEIC
- SAES · RIP · ENES · INCHES
- CIA · AENIONGEER · CAER
- ALF · URGED · EPAC · OSA
- HOOPS · AERED · PROSIUES
- ERRAPINS · EEEROER · EGGS
- WHINE · ROGER · NASHUA
- SHO · CIE · BOARS · SER · HEY
- HEAHEN · DELLA · PYRIE
- ACNE · NEEDLED · SOSENUOS
- HADABALL · SREAM · SALUE
- SEW · ABLE · RIFLE · ILE
- OAHU · ELLALEHEAR · PEL
- REFUEL · IONA · SIF · ASSE
- OUOFDAE · SKID · GASH
- ASRO · ISYBISYEENYWEENY
- ROEN · OLEO · EIRE · EAASER
- LAD · NAAN · ENAN · ENDOWS

135

Row by row (across):
- JOSHED · RACINE · EPIC · CASH
- ASHAKE · ANIMUS · GURU · ASTO
- CHARGEACCOUNT · GNAR · TSAR
- KIDDS · ZION · HOOT · RETAIN
- SPEC · TEN · STERN · SECLUDE
- OSLER · SLATE · CANCEL
- ASTATIC · SPIRE · ELITE · TSP
- MAHLER · STENO · SLIDE · GATA
- IDE · WASHINGTONDC · VERNAL
- CABAS · HAND · PEEK · ELIDES
- ETON · PART · CATER · NUMBLY
- RADOME · HOVER · ANTLIA
- BESTOW · AIMED · EGOS · ETRE
- ENCORE · ASTI · ANAT · ARTEL
- ASHLAR · SHOCKINGPINK · ERA
- MUTE · PIPER · ANOLE · ARARAT
- SEC · SOREN · SPADE · ANODYNE
- IDOLON · ALONE · GRAND
- TERRAIN · FLUKE · CRU · IMPI
- EXCEPT · MALM · ARAB · STAUB
- STUD · IBIS · BERMUDASHORTS
- TRIG · COST · EXCISE · AERATE
- YATE · SASS · READER · DAYTON

136

Row by row (across):
- FORLAB · TSELIOT · HEART
- OTELLO · AERATION · AGNEW
- ROBBER · MCKINLEY · LODGE
- AMA · GASPE · OODLES · REE
- GATE · SHORTD · FOOD · VENT
- ECOLE · ANNEAL · GNUGOATS
- DOSSIERS · RYUN · SCAT
- TRAP · TRIPUP · TRIPOD
- HALOES · POISONED · ANILE
- OVEN · THEWEB · STRAGGLER
- MET · BOER · RET · EASE · SIT
- INTERNIST · THERMS · RENO
- NUEVA · ROOSTERS · IRONED
- GERENT · NITERY · ISIS
- RCAF · LORE · SCIMITAR
- TRASHCAN · ATSUKO · SNARE
- HERO · ITOS · HANASH · AKAL
- ESA · STILTS · ITION · ELA
- CABOT · MARINADE · REPAST
- ALIVE · ANIMATOR · TRALEE
- MECOM · SAPLESS · DOLLAR

137

Row by row (across):
- SUPS · DECEM · ACTA · LEAST
- ONIT · SISERA · WARN · EMPTOR
- FILIBUSTERKEATON · NOTONE
- ATONING · SEEK · PICOT · NAE
- SETTO · RUG · NEEDIER · IDYLL
- TEATREE · NAC · ABOUT
- CONVINCEEDWARDS · GENERAL
- ORIENTE · BASSO · ASEA · AVA
- COAX · KEEN · OSCAR · PLEBES
- ASSESSED · ABREAST · STERS
- DEWLAP · ASWAN · REMORSE
- GAL · NIL · ARC · ANE · EPI · TEN
- ANALOGY · YOKEL · ROBOTS
- GONER · BEASTLY · FISHTAIL
- GODWIT · YENTA · EGAL · ULNA
- ESO · TINE · ANTAO · LOOKERS
- DENTATE · EMBARRASSEDAMES
- ARMOR · ASH · INTRUDE
- ROMEO · VISTULA · SAM · SACHA
- EVE · RHYME · NELL · MISTRAL
- DECREE · ESOTERICSEVAREID
- ONHAND · TUNE · UMPIRE · ISLE
- SEPOY · APER · NEARS · ATEN

138

Row by row (across):
- FEN · FIRE · DATUM · OPAL
- ABE · KENORA · OMURA · FILE
- TRAZOMSUEDAMAGNAGFLOW
- OPERATE · OMIT · OILED
- BEL · NUNC · AILS
- DETRAEHNOILEHTDRAHCIR
- ARIAN · BOISE · AMON · ANA
- LIDS · HORS · SAGAN · TITI
- ICE · SOMME · RADON · GOREN
- ADSORB · SOLAR · DONORS
- TNASSAPUAMEDYUG
- CHARGE · TRIED · RIGSUP
- AEGIS · TREEN · ALONE · TAO
- PINE · GOADS · CONG · CUSP
- ONE · MINT · ASIDE · AORTA
- NESREDNANAITSIRHCSNAH
- ALEE · UNDO · OAT
- TAINT · DIEM · SARCASM
- ENOTSDALGTRAWEMAILLIW
- ANTE · ATSEA · SIRICA · ADO
- LEAD · GAUDS · TARE · GIN

139

```
FOCI  GRIST  DIVA    LELAND
AMAN  HANOI  ATILT   ELINOR
CARGOINGUP    MARGINALNOTE
ENOLA  OTTS   TUBO    SEARS
TIMESWITHOUTNUMBER    USES
    STAD   ERIA    SLEEP
ADA   REFS   ENTRE   PEOPLE
BIGTIMEOPERATORS     SNEER
BROWNE  YAM  SYNAPSE  TRIS
AGREED  REA    STICKSHIFT
SEAL   APTERAL    GAGNE
SEVE  SHARPVISION   ARES
ERATO   SECANTS     ILLA
RUNONLINES   KID   LOGIER
AVEC  BRITISH  NIA  ASHCAN
YELLS   ACCOUNTEXECUTIVE
SALOON   SELMA   SECT  TEE
    CLEAN   OIDS    AITS
MASK  TWOCANCELLEDCHECKS
AMAHS  ENOS   ROAN   RAREE
SPLITSECONDS  GRANDOPERA
ALEGAR  EPEES  ARTIE  IMAM
NEPHRO  TREE   NYETS  GETS
```

140

```
BABAS  MATA    FAST    SCAR
OMAHA  UBER   VICAR   AONE
SOLAR  SORA   ANIMO   ULNA
CYMBALSYMBOL   DOURDOER
     NOES   IKES   AVOIR
OVERALL  SCANT  NEW   CAB
CASTCASTE   YSER  REPUTE
TIME   MOMS   VERSE   ALTA
ALES  AUDIT   ALST  PULIS
    ALSO  ORLE   REELECT
MASONIC  PLEAD  ANGORAS
ABIGAIL  AEON   LIDO
NAGEL  EARN   CLOGS  ORAL
ASHE  ASSTS   EACH   LANE
GETSET  KITS  PITTSPITS
ESS  ATT  TOUTS  SAPELES
    SERRA  ALMS   STIR
SAILSALE   LIEDERLEADER
ARTE  CABLE   TOLA  ANODE
KIEV  TRAIN   SOLI  DIRGE
EASE  SAND    ERST  SLEEK
```

141

```
WOOL  MAES  PATE   IHI  MMDC
ERRORINDICTION  MAD  IIOO
DANGLINGPARTICIPLE  TSUN
OLEOS  AEON   TERESA   TUB
     PBS   GEYSER  TUSSLE
AMI  TIE  DEL   ALIT   EEN
IAN  SPLITINFINITIVE  ONO
MOCHA  SNIDE  MARINE  AFEW
OURS   GPOS   PIAVE   SNAG
IRMA  PLOT   ALLEE  SAIPAN
HUP  ERATO  ALIE  BALLOTS
ANL  MISSPELLEDWORDS  SIT
TOEDOGS  ATES  ANODE  TVA
ENTERS  BISON  SEDE  BRER
SECY   RUNTO   PATR  NATO
PESO  MICRON  ASHER  CUPID
ONE  LACKOFAGREEMENT  HOI
MTN  ALOP   IRA   DAH   END
PETARD  ALBANY    ABB
NEB  EASIER   FALA  IGNIS
ACNE  MISPLACEDMODIFIERS
SECT  ENE  ERRORINGRAMMAR
ASES  RUR  MAYS  SEEK  PONS
```

142

```
BATH   REEFS   ELSIE   TAMP
ALOE   OSELA   ROOST   OLEO
NOBLESTROMANOFTHEMALL
STELLAE    PIETA    RADIO
    FAT  SPARSE   PEAT
THEITALIANSTREETSONG
SAGRE   ARCS    NOSE   EAR
ALAE  STET   ERNANI   SALE
RON  SLID   BLOOMS  PATEN
    GWEN  SEDATE  SERENE
CAPRIPANTS   MILANSTRAW
ERRANT  ARISEN   TOKO
STEVE  SHADED   CHOY   MAR
TILE  PLAYED   MAID   SOLO
ASA  ARAN    PORE   SCRAM
TWOGENTLEMENOFVERONA
    MAST   AMORAL   ARA
ISLET   BRING   BLIPPED
THELEANINGTOWEROFPISA
CONE  POLER   LOVER   ELAN
HEAT  TILDE   AWARE   ROUE
```

143

```
SARAH  BAAL  SIMBA   ACCORD
OVOLO  ALMA  ADELE   NAUSEA
RIMAL  TAEN  CERES   DREAMY
EVERYTHINGIHAVEISYOURS
     SHE   USA    DRAWUP
GAMMA  PLOD  AHS  DAS  LEM
HOMEONTHERANGE  TIRESOME
STORK  AIT   ROOF  HSH INIA
THREEOCLOCKINTHEMORNING
SYS  ATONE   YUL   LOGGER
PSI   CARD   MIB   ALANE
ALITTLEBITINDEPENDENT
CRIME   EIL  AGAR   NOS
HONORA  FUR   EDSEL   ALS
IVEGOTAFEELINGIMFALLING
TIME  ONE  DODO  ROI  OIDIA
ANANIMAL  IAINTGOTNOBODY
SGN  NIL  ADD  WHET  USINE
    MASONS   MAE    ODE
ICANTGETSTARTEDWITHYOU
URUNDI  ARKIN  ANON  AEONS
FISTIC  RAINS  KITE  LAKME
ASPENS  SYNGE  EDER  KLEES
```

144

```
STAMP   HBEAM   EGIS   OPAH
HORAL   ALIBI   QRST   BARA
ELENA   MANED   UELE   EGER
ALADYNAMEDISABELWYATT
   EMILE    ATE   LIENEE
RAGLAN    SPILE    BAND
OTO  TOULOUSE   DOT   PMS
SUGGESTEDTOMEANEWDIET
ABOU   HEAD    RTE   IRENE
    MAMA    OSSIE  ODETTE
IFTSDRINKWATERSHESAID
ALOHAS   ANNIE    TONS
MANON  OBI   ROAR   ELBA
ANDEATNOTHINGBUTBREAD
RDO   ROB  ADULATOR  WIZ
    AMEN   CRIME   RIDDLE
PEORIA   ELS    MASSE
IAMNOTINAHURRYTOTRYIT
ASNO  IGOR  PEART   LIETO
NEIL  SOLE  DONNA   EDGES
ORAD  ETAT  OSKAR   DEGAS
```

145

```
POND FLO  POSE ARCS  PROM
UVEA LOA  INCA COOP  RUDI
REXSTOUT  GEORGESSIMENON
ARTHURS SIMONE STRIPING
   ILE ORATING SECANT
CHESTERTON NIAS SKI
PAULA LEON EGERIA EDGAR
HURL ALMS ARS BELLY RHO
ESTH PEI NIL MONTY RIOT
BELABORS ELEME NON ALMA
EDEMA YSER GENOA DOYLE
MISS CICADAS BALM
QUEEN LOSER CHAR POSSE
AUNT APE SEDGE REPENTER
RIFT RIATA NOD MAO DECO
ARI DENSE FED JAKE CPOS
LETHE TENSOR SADE RHINE
ATT STIR JPMARQUAND
TABARD HERCULE URN
POLICIES PEALES ROADHOG
AGATHACHRISTIE SPILLANE
RATE LAOS THAN OTT ERIN
TEED SLOT SYNS DDS RITA
```

146

```
HOARSE PEST TRANS
SOWSEAR AGUA SEROWS
PIGSKINS PORKCHOPHILL
OLS ANITRA DELI SINAI
LEHR STEALS MYRT TEGS
KNEES YIN ICEPTEA FLA
ACADIA NICTATE AMBLES
SEDARIM NOTSO ARALU
PELEG MET PROTESTS
OFTEN TRUER HAMFISHER
SAH CHIPS SONOF OCA
SWEATHOGS BATOR ESTHS
INBREEDS DAM VERNE
OATES LEROT REAMERS
BLAMES TOENAIL ARENOT
EAR SECONDE MEM ELGAR
GUST SANG SHOTES ERDA
OGHAM POSH ARISTA AHI
THEBAYOFPIGS THEBACON
SALTEN URIS BEERKEG
DETRE RENO EDDIED
```

147

```
TALENT SALAD FOOT ABED
AMELIE PLATO RASH SERA
BADFORNOTHING AFTERHAND
BROKER ARGUS BEMUSE
ADO EATER STEED ALGA
DIVA CEN ICIER SOANDSO
AVENGED GOODMINTON OTE
MERGED SPOON LORD SWAN
ASTER SCARP CAMEO TANGO
NTH ALAN SALES CACHE
TSE FRONTGAMMON ERROR
WALLET ELOPE SANDAL
PELEE BACKISPIECE SAB
RALES ARRIE RERI TRA
METER BLISS PROVO CHEER
ASHY SETA PAUSE THERMO
STE BEFOREMATH ARABIAN
CORELLI LATER DLI ENDE
LOFT MATIN NATAL GET
TAPIRS SENSE HUMANE
UPTOEARTH UNDERNIGHTBAG
FIAT MEAT CEASE LAVORO
TASS ELBA EELED ERASED
```

148

```
JIMA FUSED OTHE ASTHE
ADAMSAPPLE BROCASAREA
BALAAMSASS JACOBSCOAT
BOER BECK AURORA
HIDEOUT BROCK STREPT
EXISTS ROOST TWEED
AIDES AARONSBEARD PSC
VOO TRIG OARS SETA
ENS SUTTERSGOLD TATER
SLEEPIT ICONS SOLELY
TWADDLE HARMS PALERMO
OHMAGE RENEE CALYPSO
SEEME COLTERSHELL PSS
CENS FRUG MANY EFT
ALT CAESARSWIFE MANIA
BOTCH ELATE FARCRY
SNOOTY EPOCH PONGEES
SPONGE ABLE EASE
NORMANSWOE PELESTEARS
ORIONSBELT ULLOASRING
BEATS EDIE PLANE SLAT
```

149

```
DEALER SMEAR HABER CRIB
ALLURE NOTRE AROMA HIDE
PLAINCLOTHES UNSUITABLE
SAN SOIREE POLOS MOSSES
UNE LAINE ALERT
TAY SPURT ITERS ANTEING
ORESTES UNDERSKIRTS NEO
PELTED TREES INES SVAN
POLAR WINGS ODETS WHERE
ELON TAMIL BURRO FAIRER
RAW BIKINI ACES CALENDS
JAILED GOTHS RECEDE
BLACKEN CETE SHADED SSS
RICHES CANOS DOVER ESTA
ASKED DANTE HONED PACAY
ITES SOSO CAWED CERATE
SET GENEVAGOWNS FLAPPER
ENSNARE ARARS TILAK ENS
AUGER CITES MOM
STANNE IRATE HEAROF SPA
COATTAILED GLENGARRYCAP
OGRE NOLLE EERIE EARAGE
TOES TREYS SEEDS DUSTER
```

150

```
MAUD WHIFF GRASS AMAM
IPSO OAKIE AARON SODA
LISTENLORDLINGSUNTOME
ELTON OTTO BERLIN
STALL SPREE TIARA
WHILESHEPHERDSWATCHED
ARM SHARED ARRET
MUSH ARID TRACER SCAT
EGGS DEEM SAP RIA
ASTARSHININGINTHEEAST
NERVA AUSPICE CRINE
THEYFOUNDHIMINAMANGER
INK TSP GENE GINS
CASA CARESS BOOM TULE
SHANE BORGIA NED
THELORDTHENEWBORNKING
EATON AXIAL ENVOY
ATONAL PLAN GISMO
SINGNOWELLOSINGNOWELL
ENNA PILOT OCALA MALE
SHES STEWS LETUP ERDA
```

151

PUTS・LABS・SPIRO・TEST
ACHT・ONETO・HONOR・OMNI
CLEOPATRASNEEDLE・NEAL
TABOO・ITISA・ELL・SERE
・ELM・CHRISTINASWORLD・
EGG・PUSS・HOLT・EAR・・
BIGTOP・・PUMAS・・DITTO
BRAHMSLULLABY・PEAHEN
SORE・ELIA・・PRE・LENS
・SEA・ELVIS・ARETE・OSE
SRO・SEWARDSICEBOX・LET
LOP・SWAGE・ELEVE・CID
AGES・EYE・OTIC・TWIT・
MERCER・HOBSONSCHOICE
START・・CARAT・SOLVES
・ACT・ARAL・PEAN・EDS・
MARTHASVINEYARD・SDS・
ALEC・MAE・RADII・HITOR
RUSH・ALICESRESTAURANT
ALEE・RANIS・EPSOM・ELIE
TATS・ALSOP・TYRE・RETS

152

ABATED・AMOS・SHED・FLAB
SIMILE・DORIA・MINEO・LENO
STEELSPIRALS・ADDINGONTO
TEN・SPARED・TARES・TARTAN
・・ORTA・WANTS・SOME・・
SAM・AIRY・PAINE・APPETITS
TREACLY・MYFRONTDOOR・ORE
AMATIS・PUREE・HOOF・SNEE
POLLS・BASER・ALARK・DOING
LUTE・AERI・OVINE・DEBATE
ERI・AFRICANWINE・TRAINER
・MATINS・SALLE・ORANGE・
ONELOVE・MIDEASTBIKE・PAC
COSINE・CADET・RITE・PITH
TOPEE・BORER・HAUTE・PASTA
ONAN・DEED・BOLLS・MORTAL
PAT・LEADINGLADY・ROSALIE
INSTILLS・ENERO・DENT・ENT
・ROIL・BAUME・POCO・・
SATING・PARSI・MIRAGE・OPE
MTRUSHMORE・SHINEPENNIES
ELAN・TOURS・HAREM・NOOSES
WIPE・BRET・WADI・ESSENE

153

CRUSH・OWLETS・SPUMONI
LANCE・TROOPED・TOREROS
ASTOR・HINDERS・RUNNETH
SPIRO・REDEEM・FATSO
PYLE・TELE・・DAYS・NEST
・ACRE・RESEALS・TREE
ANANIAS・SALLYS・SHOWN
PADDOCK・OTIOSE・WEEDED
ROOS・TIFF・MPH・FENDERS
EMBER・DDT・YEA・OBOE
SIEVE・DAHS・STAR・RATES
・ENDO・EHS・HAT・ADREM
BORNTOO・WOE・SAYS・MERE
OXEYES・SOOTHE・OCTAVIA
RILED・PREAMP・RAINIER
IDEA・WILDEST・FRAS
SEER・BOND・ELIE・CPAS
・SORRY・NUTMEG・SHANT
BANANAS・POOHBAH・PERSE
EXIGENT・ARMREST・ASTER
DEPORTS・YAOURT・STYLE

154

PIPER・TAME・STOW・STOP
ARENA・RIPER・ARLISS・IOWA
CARDIGANSANDWELLINGTONS
ENCE・OFTENER・ALGERS・・
・EDEL・TSAR・INEE・SCD
ALI・EGAD・WISLA・EMCEE
LAVALIERESANDPOMPADOURS
ONERS・RAVES・OUSEL・NDAK
EAST・AMERICAN・SAND・
・SOOT・ALMS・STRIATE
IDO・PLEBE・ABOOK・BLESS
DERBIESANDPRINCEALBERTS
INTRA・REESE・TONAL・MET
SHOTTED・CITY・AGES・
・GEAR・ESSAYING・HERE
ANTA・RISEN・MINOR・SONAR
JOHNHANCOCKSANDMAEWESTS
ANISE・ASYET・EMMA・WEE
RON・CORN・NABS・MYNA・
・STRODE・NOMINEE・OTRA
VICTORIASANDMACINTOSHES
AREA・ALLEYS・BLANC・PEENS
NEST・SLEW・ELLE・ESSEN

155

BARB・DAKAR・TRIS・BASSO
OGEE・OTERO・WITH・ANWAR
WHATSTHEUSEOFWORRYING
SARAH・ENNIS・EAVE・ALDA
・SATIE・EPI・SETA・LEN
STB・MESS・ONS・LINN・
WHYHASTTHOUFORSAKENME
ARRANT・ARSENE・AGAIN
NODE・ASSURER・MRS・ERAT
・CAMEOS・DOYOULOVEME
ACT・MERCE・ORSUN・SIR
WHOSONFIRST・USAGES・
AINT・TSE・THERESA・AHAS
SCOUT・THRONE・BIREME
HOWDOESYOURGARDENGROW
・SAVE・INN・AIDS・OKS・
DAS・DENT・GIA・NASTS・
ASTA・ODES・ENACT・AMAZE
WHEREFOREARTTHOUROMEO
NOVEL・FRAY・ITEMS・KERN
STEAK・FATE・CURST・ENOS

156

DSC・HELEN・STOMP・MILAN
BATHE・SKATE・HOMER・OHARA
EYEOFTHEHURRICANE・ASSAM
TOLIFE・DRIVEL・RAVEN・TRA
FACEUP・ENOS・CIA・BOAT
・ECTO・BEETHOVENSFIFTH
OAR・TOP・OWN・LAS・EAST
SPOT・NULLED・MOP・FLUSHED
SACRE・LAIR・BONITO・NEEDY
ARKIN・ADV・DAR・DAUB・TMEN
TEASER・AVERSE・BRAC・ONE
・FLUFF・REPRESS・TRASH
APE・ETRE・TOILET・HECTIC
LULL・SOLO・SES・AGO・TACIT
ORLOP・NIPPER・PROF・ITALY
PRETEST・TYR・NAVAJO・SNIP
・RINE・OIL・EWE・UNE・SAO
SECONDINCOMMAND・LESS
WREN・ACE・NEER・YIPPED
ANN・ANETO・DEMOTE・LILLIE
METER・CIVILRIGHTSLEADER
ISERE・AMINE・SLANT・STETS
STRIA・PESKY・SETAE・SRS

157

```
HOARSEN ▪ APER ▪ PIUS ▪ FPC
ESTELLA ▪ REDUCIBLE ▪ ERA
NOPLUMBUMGASOLINE ▪ RES
CLAIM ▪ ▪ HOLM ▪ REDALERTS
EERS ▪ ABLUE ▪ KODES ▪ CURE
▪ ▪ HIHOARGENTUM ▪ DEMIT
HAS ▪ OMAN ▪ LISP ▪ MUSCAT
OCTANES ▪ GEAT ▪ VANILLE
ACARID ▪ PES ▪ STTERESA
XENIA ▪ LUNAR ▪ HILTS ▪ DAD
ENNA ▪ CUPRUMHEADS ▪ HAME
STU ▪ AURAE ▪ SAINT ▪ PILAF
▪ MURKIEST ▪ HST ▪ BELIZE
DAPPLED ▪ ANAT ▪ AEROBIC
ENATES ▪ EELY ▪ SEGO ▪ INT
AGNIS ▪ AURUMPLATING ▪
DUAL ▪ MIGAS ▪ LOMAN ▪ ROMA
HILLSIDES ▪ SARA ▪ OATER
ELL ▪ PLANETHYDRARGYRUM
ALE ▪ INNERSEAL ▪ RELEASE
DAY ▪ NETS ▪ EASY ▪ EMERSED
```

158

```
MAKETH ▪ EAVES ▪ PAST ▪ MAJOR
ADAGIO ▪ CHILI ▪ ATEE ▪ ANONA
DONAMECHESSMASTER ▪ IDENT
OREL ▪ CRIME ▪ MUTA ▪ MARINAS
▪ ▪ AIN ▪ SERACS ▪ GERA ▪
FRANKSINATRASHMAN ▪ OMAR
DAILIES ▪ URGES ▪ OWE ▪ NAPE
UNCLES ▪ CREED ▪ JAKES ▪ TIS
ETHEL ▪ OUSE ▪ OAHE ▪ TEHEE
LEAN ▪ FREDRICMARCHITECT
SER ▪ AMASS ▪ ESTES ▪ RADOMES
▪ DAMAGE ▪ ELSAS ▪ TIRANA
SUBLIME ▪ ALIEN ▪ AREEL ▪ TSP
ISAACASIMOVIESTAR ▪ TIER
MASSE ▪ GAPE ▪ TRIS ▪ RECTI
INE ▪ PAUSE ▪ DROIT ▪ BASION
ACHE ▪ LIA ▪ AEIOU ▪ AUSLAUT
NEAP ▪ ARNOLDPALMERCHANT
▪ RAPT ▪ ANODES ▪ INK ▪
MATURED ▪ EVEN ▪ BALES ▪ PSST
UTILE ▪ EDWARDALBEEKEEPER
ROSES ▪ SNAG ▪ ENURE ▪ INSOLE
KITTS ▪ KAYE ▪ DARIN ▪ NETTLE
```

159

```
LAPEL ▪ SHARP ▪ STEP ▪ HUSH
ILONA ▪ TAMER ▪ ARTE ▪ UNIO
MYOLDKYHOME ▪ LAHAYRIDE
PALADINS ▪ SOAP ▪ BURNER
▪ RITE ▪ OSUNA ▪ HERAT ▪
ADAGES ▪ REMEMBERTHEME
LOSE ▪ SPARER ▪ EAR ▪ RAM
ARTRAVELLER ▪ WARY ▪ HERD
RIO ▪ RADAS ▪ MINT ▪ ROSIE
MARTINET ▪ TMAN ▪ LEPTON
▪ WACROSSINGTHEDE ▪
LUCINE ▪ LANE ▪ HIROHITO
ABASE ▪ HOUR ▪ TENON ▪ SAG
MONT ▪ DIVE ▪ TNERNIEFORD
BAT ▪ EVA ▪ SEELEY ▪ OLDE
STARSFELLONAL ▪ WALTON
▪ BETAS ▪ ENTRY ▪ KARL ▪
SAIGON ▪ MEGA ▪ MORTISED
TXLEAGUER ▪ CAHEREICOME
ALEN ▪ ETTE ▪ LIANA ▪ SLAIN
BEST ▪ DEED ▪ ELLEN ▪ TERRY
```

160

```
CABMEN ▪ TAHR ▪ STRATA ▪ DATE
AREOLE ▪ ABOU ▪ CHIPIN ▪ ELAN
PERSIANLAMB ▪ REVELS ▪ FAST
ONES ▪ REESE ▪ AILED ▪ ECARTE
NAT ▪ WELSHRABBIT ▪ BRIMMER
▪ BASLE ▪ REED ▪ OLIVE ▪
REALITY ▪ ESTA ▪ GRANI ▪ BEI
ARREST ▪ CHINESECHECKERS
BRISTOL ▪ HAS ▪ DONAS ▪ NAIL
BOLT ▪ ABORT ▪ ENE ▪ SEANCE
IRS ▪ DATA ▪ DIP ▪ GREEKCROSS
▪ SADIST ▪ CAT ▪ ANWARS ▪
ITALIANSUB ▪ NEF ▪ SITU ▪ SPA
NOMISM ▪ BID ▪ RAVEN ▪ GAUL
DRIP ▪ SEEDY ▪ RIA ▪ GORILLA
RUSSIANDRESSING ▪ VERSES
ASH ▪ CLODS ▪ EFTS ▪ CELLARS
▪ OHARA ▪ CVII ▪ CHRIS ▪
DISROBE ▪ FRENCHTOAST ▪ LED
ELMIRA ▪ TRINE ▪ EERIE ▪ NAVY
CLEO ▪ MOROSE ▪ JAPANESEYEN
CELL ▪ ADESTE ▪ EVIL ▪ REVERE
ARTE ▪ NESTOR ▪ TEDS ▪ STARTS
```

161

```
MOPS ▪ ELSE ▪ TENET ▪ TARA
OGRE ▪ KEPT ▪ OSAGE ▪ TOVES
CLOTHESQUARTERS ▪ ITEMS
HEPTAD ▪ RIDS ▪ ELAN ▪ NIE
ASHEN ▪ ▪ JOINTACCOUNT
▪ ERG ▪ BAM ▪ SCI ▪ OARED
▪ LTS ▪ SEXUS ▪ EGGROLL
SEA ▪ SHEIKTOSHEIK ▪ EBBS
CON ▪ ORTOLAN ▪ TNT ▪ ERE
UPDATE ▪ MUSSY ▪ EASTASIA
PALLID ▪ KITED ▪ PORTAL
PROTESTS ▪ SAGUM ▪ ROTORS
EDS ▪ ROK ▪ GONEBUT ▪ FEI
RISE ▪ BOUNCEDCZECH ▪ TUN
▪ ILLYRIA ▪ SEZME ▪ OHS
▪ AERIE ▪ FRA ▪ SOY ▪ ANE
OBJETSDHEART ▪ ▪ LEWIS
FEE ▪ ASEA ▪ BOIS ▪ CORUNA
ALCAN ▪ TWOGOODFORWORDS
GETTY ▪ ESKER ▪ LANA ▪ USIS
ESSE ▪ RESTS ▪ EXES ▪ STAY
```

162

```
CIGARS ▪ BLAS ▪ DISC ▪ DALE
ARARAT ▪ LAMIA ▪ ADHOC ▪ ORAL
FORTHERECORD ▪ DOUBLETALK
ENE ▪ SPINES ▪ MEANT ▪ EDEMAS
▪ PANT ▪ LIMIT ▪ SAIL ▪
SOW ▪ PINY ▪ DORIS ▪ AIRFLOWS
TRIDENT ▪ DISARMINGLY ▪ NRA
RATING ▪ SOREL ▪ TINY ▪ PLAT
ACHED ▪ HAZER ▪ SWALE ▪ PHYSI
ILLS ▪ TATE ▪ PEELE ▪ DROWSE
TEO ▪ VERYNASALLY ▪ PEONIES
▪ WHINER ▪ GIRLS ▪ TEASET ▪
SAVANTS ▪ MOSTSHARPLY ▪ HMS
ERODES ▪ MORAY ▪ MOLT ▪ KNOT
TRIED ▪ RORAL ▪ CHITA ▪ VIOLA
TICS ▪ OISE ▪ POETS ▪ BATTER
EVE ▪ OFFHANDEDLY ▪ TRITEST
RESTIFLE ▪ EASEL ▪ SHEN ▪ STS
▪ IDEE ▪ MOLES ▪ STOA ▪
OCULAR ▪ PETIT ▪ SCENTS ▪ SAW
LISTLESSLY ▪ ATAHIGHPITCH
ATEE ▪ ESTOP ▪ SATON ▪ EISELE
NEED ▪ ESNE ▪ PENS ▪ STAMEN
```

163

```
FHA . SBE . SMUTS . ALOFT .
ROISTER . CARROT . BELLOC
INROADS . ONEIDA . MADAMA
NOMANS . ROD . SOLE . SQUAT
GUARDINAPARTMENT . UNTO
ERN . EDEN . TIE . STA . ATON
. EREI . HEP . ERROR .
. CHASMS . ASSAD . YALTA .
PAAR . ASTR . CUR . LEUR
ERG . NEED . LIPO . YARDED
LEGATO . ACCEDED . OSSIFY
TELLER . SEAT . PERU . TEA
. REIN . ELK . LOOT . HERD
. STOPS . LEAVE . SHREDS .
. TROIS . VEX . THEM .
SHUL . UMP . VON . PROV . BSA
EASE . ROOMINDEBASEMENT
GRAFT . NOOR . EDS . TREMOR
EMBLEM . FLIRTS . FISSURE
RELATE . SALUTE . PLEASES
. DETER . REGAL . AES . EST
```

164

```
PHIL . STOMPS . GRAM . TEXT
LIMAS . ORMOLU . ROTI . ICER
AGAPE . MENTOR . YEARS . LANA
THGINKETIHW . STYRON . DROP
. SONAR . STEP . SPORES .
. TAYLOR . ARM . OME . USA
CATO . AIDA . OVUM . SENECAN
TACERIHSEHC . IDEA . RESULT
AJAR . LOPS . HALYARD . WEAVE
SORE . KOS . RIVET . COB . CES
SLITS . TELE . PREVUE .
EEDELDEEWTDNAMUDELDEEWT
. OUTWIT . GRUB . ENDOR
RAE . CRI . ALEPH . SYL . CURE
ALLOT . ENTHUSE . FLAT . OCTA
VITRIC . GODS . NEEUQDEREHT
ENRAGED . DATA . PERU . VEDA
LEU . ELI . MEL . ASSISI .
. THRIVE . ERLE . ILEAD
POKE . BIRTHS . YKCOWREBBAJ
INCA . ASSET . ARIOSO . YOURE
AZOV . TOES . PILATE . EASES
FEME . ERST . RENTES . TESS
```

165

```
JOAB . AHEM . TACO . ALTERA
ORLE . MAXI . RIOS . ROHMER
NAPA . OLAN . YEWS . ITRIDE
ACHRISTMASTALE . SHARDS
SHAHS . SERAO . STATES .
. UTA . NECK . NAPHTHA
BRIGHTISTHEMANGER . HOC
EEL . EMS . SEANCE . INEPT
ABE . ROCKS . PITS . GNOMES
SADIE . HIP . IDA . TECH .
. BUTAMINIATURESLEIGH
. ASIA . NRA . ENT . OTOES
SMILAX . FOIL . SERIF . MAL
MACON . HAZELS . AMP . EVE
EYE . THATASTARAPPEARED
WASSAIL . HIED . SAR .
. ACROSS . EGADS . CABAL
SWIRLS . THEYARETHEMAGI
LANDAU . RATE . IDEE . ARLO
AIROUT . URSA . NOLA . ICON
BLOUSE . MEIR . GNAT . CAWS
```

166

```
NEWYEAR . MESSAGE . BELOW
IMPULSE . ILIADIC . ELIDES
TOALLKINDFANSBOTHOLDAND
ETH . SENOR . MEM . LIEN . STOA
LIES . DEBAR . RIGORS . HOT
LOACH . RISES . TOGETA . JETE
ANDOIL . SHOE . HEY . SNEERY
. TRES . PRESS . NEW
SPOLETO . TEEM . UNTO . GELT
ARNA . SUSANNA . PEEVE . LARD
LIANA . PEASANT . PREPS . TEE
ANDDANCE . DAR . ERITREAN
ATI . ROOST . ETACIST . YARDS
MEMO . INTER . ICHLAUT . BALE
RENT . SONE . OKES . RAMBLER
. MAY . LINER . EPEE .
STAGER . SEN . RODS . SETSAT
SWAN . SECANT . SORED . KETCH
TAU . SALTED . TIROL . DREE
ATTA . SISI . NIE . NANAS . ATO
THENEWDECADEBEKINDTOYOU
. ENTREE . ELEGANT . ELEMENT
. SIRED . TORONTO . RETIRES
```

167

```
UDALL . OFFER . CAST . TAFT
MASAI . HALLO . OTOE . ALAR
BRITT . GREAT . PILL . MAGI
ONTHEGOODSHIPLOLLIPOP
. ERODE . SET . SENATE
FARRAR . ALTER . LONG .
EDH . TESTCASE . SIF . EMU
DEEPINTHEHEARTOFTEXAS
SLUR . AERO . EON . AFIRE
. AMENTS . GOLAN . TUFTED
. WISHYOUWEREHERE
DAMASK . ABEET . ATONAL
RAISE . ISA . MATS . DUES
ORCHIDSINTHEMOONLIGHT
PEA . UAR . HIBERNIA . IAN
. DESK . GREEN . ESTERS
DESERT . COO . ALLTO
ITMIGHTASWELLBESPRING
CHIC . EARP . VIOLA . OUTER
TETE . ARNE . INNER . SLOPE
ARES . PEEL . LEERS . TANSY
```

168

```
PAGAN . ASHARP . SHAWL . BALA
ATONE . LIONEL . TODAY . LUIS
DONTRAINONMYPARADE . UTAS
ULE . AGENDA . RISK . REUNE
ALFA . ENES . EBONY . BATHMAT
. IRONER . SULU . BORDEN .
ABSENCE . IGOTSTUNG . ALDA
UNHOLY . SCREW . WALDO . VEIL
DAILY . SLOE . ICICLE . DEANE
EINE . CAIRN . NATTY . CONVEX
. HUNG . MISC . TRI . ERI
FOG . SINGININTHERAIN . SOS
EVE . ORA . ENTE . LINE .
SETSUP . FLASH . CIDER . PSST
TROLL . CLARKE . LOGY . TACHO
ADUE . THANE . WRITE . MATHIS
LOTI . HOWDRYIAM . RATIONS
. OGLERS . ONCE . MERINO .
OFFHAND . CRUDE . BOSC . ALSO
RETRY . OLID . SETTER . DTS
ATOI . HOMEFORTHEHOLIDAYS
LEWD . ONEAL . LOANER . COYLE
ESNE . GENRE . SPHERE . ONSET
```

169

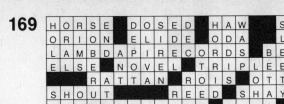

H	O	R	S	E		D	O	S	E	D		H	A	W		S	M	I	T
O	R	I	O	N		E	L	I	D	E		O	D	A			L	A	N	A
L	A	M	B	D	A	P	I	R	E	C	O	R	D	S		B	E	L	L	S
E	L	S	E		N	O	V	E	L		T	R	I	P	L	E	E	T	A	S
	R	A	T	T	A	N		R	O	I	S		O	T	T	A	W	A
S	H	O	U	T			R	E	E	D		S	H	A	Y
K	A	P	P	A	R	A	T	I	O	N	S		S	W	A	B		A	W	N
I	M	P		A	L	O	N	S	O		S	T	O	N	E	G	R	A	Y
T	I	E		U	M	I	A	K	S		D	E	E	R		T	O	I	L	E
S	T	R	I	P	P	E	D		I	R	O	N	E	D		A	G	L	E	T
	S	S	S		S	E	N	E	G	A	L		S	G	O
M	I	L	L	I		A	T	T	I	C	S		M	A	C	U	L	A	T	E
U	V	E	A	L		G	O	O	S		L	E	I	D	E	N		R	E	V
C	O	M	M	O	T	I	O	N		M	E	R	L	I	N		M	A	A
H	R	S		N	U	L	L		M	O	D	E	L	T	A	U	F	O	R	D
	A	B	B	E		T	O	P	S			T	E	R	S	E
T	O	O	T	O	O		H	O	T	E		S	P	R	E	A	D
A	L	P	H	A	F	R	A	M	E		M	Q	R	A	L		E	A	S	T
F	L	E	E	T		D	I	A	L	M	U	F	O	R	M	U	R	D	E	R
F	I	R	N		O	F	T		I	N	A	N	E		M	A	D	R	E
Y	E	A	S		S	A	O		D	I	R	G	E		P	L	A	T	E

170

C	A	C	H	E	S		C	A	B	A	L	A		L	E	E		G	R	A	F
A	D	R	O	I	T		A	R	A	G	O	N		T	A	N	G	E	R	I	N	E
T	H	E	G	R	A	M	M	A	R	H	A	S		R	E	D	O	L	E	N	C	E
M	E	D		E	R	I	E		A	M	A	R	A		B	E	G	E	T
A	R	I	A		T	A	R	P	S		I	R	O	N		G	O	O	N	S
N	E	T	T	L	E		A	R	U	L	E	A	B	S	U	R	D	W	H	I	C	H
	T	E	R	P		O	P	E	S		B	I	P	E	D		O	D	E	A
C	R	A	I	G		R	E	P	E	N	T		E	B	B	S		R	E	A	D
L	O	T	T	A		E	V	E	R	T		M	O	N	O		U	N	R	R	A
I	W	O	U	L	D	C	A	L	L	A	N	O	U	T	W	O	R	N		S	A	T
F	E	N	D		A	I	D		O	R	T	S		P	O	I	S
T	R	E	E	L	I	N	E		N	I	M	E	S		F	E	S	T	I	V	A	L
	S	A	R	C		P	O	N	D		R	N	S		G	O	R	E
S	O	W		M	Y	T	H	A	P	R	E	P	O	S	I	T	I	O	N	I	S	A
T	R	A	M	P		I	S	E	E		O	U	T	G	O		S	A	L	O	N
R	O	T	I		F	I	R	S		C	I	T	R	O	N		C	L	A	N	S
A	N	E	S		L	L	A	M	A		A	N	S	A		E	D	A	M
W	O	R	D	Y	O	U	M	U	S	T	N	T	E	N	D		E	R	A	S	E	D
	M	I	L	E	S		S	H	I	V		A	D	E	P	T		N	I	N	A
A	C	A	R	E		T	E	R	A	T		C	U	E	S		M	A	S
C	L	I	E	N	T	E	L	E		A	S	E	N	T	E	N	C	E	W	I	T	H
C	O	N	C	E	N	T	E	R		D	E	M	E	A	N		T	R	A	L	E	E
A	U	S	T		T	A	G		E	S	P	R	I	T		S	T	R	E	S	S

171

	D	A	L	L	I	A	N	C	E		P	A	X		A	P	R	I	L
R	A	Q	U	E	L	W	E	L	C	H		H	A	Y		J	U	I	C	Y
T	R	U	N	D	L	E	B	E	D	S		Y	A	Z		A	R	D	E	N
S	T	A	G	G		M	Y	T	H	S		E	X	P	E	N	D
	A	R	I	E	L		R	E	S		O	I	N	K	S		L	A	T	E
A	G	I	N		M	A	G	N	I	L	O	Q	U	E	N	C	E
S	N	U	G		N	A	S	S	A	U		U	N	G	E	R		L	I	Z
T	A	M		L	O	U		S	T	R	E	S	S		C	L	A	R	E
I	N	S	T	E	P		M	A	T	Z	O			O	P	E	N
	A	C	Q	U	I	T		O	F	F	S		A	D	A	N	O
C	O	N	T	O	R	T	I	O	N		F	E	R	T	I	L	I	Z	E	S
A	A	A	A	Q		A	I	M	E		L	E	N	N	O	N
A	K	I	M			A	P	P	L	E		J	E	J	U	N	E
M	I	L	I	A		G	A	B	L	E	R		B	U	S		N	I	X
A	E	S		S	C	O	U	R		T	E	T	H	E	R		T	I	N	E
	L	E	O	N	T	Y	N	E	P	R	I	C	E		H	O	E	S
P	E	S	O		L	E	O	N	E		R	E	X		S	C	E	N	T
E	X	P	O	R	T		M	A	R	I	A		A	E	I	O	U
S	T	A	K	E		A	B	A		O	C	C	A	M	S	R	A	Z	O	R
T	R	I	E	D		D	A	W		B	E	L	L	I	G	E	R	E	N	T
S	A	N	D	S		Z	A	R		D	E	M	I	T	A	S	S	E

172

D	A	U	B		A	L	A	M	O		I	S	L	E	S		R	I	N	D
I	G	N	I		N	O	M	A	N		T	A	I	N	T		U	N	I	O
J	O	H	N	N	Y	C	O	M	E	L	A	T	E	L	Y		S	T	L	O
O	R	A		A	W	A	Y		S	O	L	U	S		R	A	S	H	E	R
N	A	T	U	R	A	L		S	T	R	I	P		R	I	L	K	E
	R	E	Y		S	W	E	D	E		B	E	A	T	I	N	G	S
M	A	J	A	S		L	E	A	P	I	N	G	L	E	N	A		I	R	A
E	G	A	L		C	O	R	N		R	O	S	S		S	C	E	L
S	A	C		S	A	Y	I	N	G	G	R	A	C	E		S	A	K	E	S
A	R	K	A	N	S	A	N		O	R	A	D		S	A	P	O	T	E
	O	R	I	E	L		G	L	A	D	E		A	I	D	O	F
S	A	F	E	T	Y		R	A	N	I		A	S	T	A	R	T	E	S
E	G	A	N	S		S	T	A	N	D	I	N	G	P	A	T		I	D	A
V	I	L	A		S	P	A	N		E	G	E	R		G	M	E	N
E	L	L		R	A	I	S	I	N	G	C	A	I	N		F	I	E	N	D
N	E	T	W	O	R	K	S		E	L	A	T	E		S	A	N
	R	I	D	G	E		B	R	U	S	H		G	O	T	O	B	E	D
C	L	A	S	S	A		E	R	I	C	H		A	I	L	S		E	X	O
H	I	D	E		S	H	R	I	N	K	I	N	G	V	I	O	L	E	T	S
I	V	E	S		S	I	N	C	E		E	A	R	E	D		O	B	O	E
P	E	S	T		O	T	O	E	S		R	Y	A	N	S		W	E	L	D

173

P	E	P		H	A	S	I	T		S	C	A	D		C	R	I	S	I	S
A	M	I		A	D	A	N	A		S	A	K	I		R	E	S	I	D	E
N	I	N	E	M	E	N	S	M	O	R	R	I	S		E	A	R	N	I	E
A	R	G	O	S		C	E	I	L		S	N	A	P	D	R	A	G	O	N
M	A	P	S		S	H	A	L	O	M		D	R	E	I		E	L	M
A	T	O		B	R	O	M		G	U	S		M	E	T	T	L	E
	E	N	T	R	A	P		B	Y	S	E	A		P	E	R	I	W	I	G
	G	E	E		E	T	A		I	N	D	E	E	D	Y		I	N	A
	L	A	D	D	E	R		C	A	R	E	D		A	C	H	Y
H	E	H		K	E	R	N		T	A	T	E	R		Y	A	N	K	E	E
O	R	O	F	I	N	O		S	A	L	E	M		B	A	N	T	E	R	S
B	R	U	I	N	S		B	A	N	C	S		A	U	L	D		T	E	T
N	A	S	T		D	O	U	G	H		S	I	M	E	O	N
O	T	E		I	C	E	D	T	E	A		O	R	B		R	O	B
B	A	Y	L	E	A	F		E	L	I	A	S		L	O	R	N	A	S
	H	E	R	M	I	T		O	R	R		S	E	R	A		C	C	S
	T	O	T		E	N	O	S		S	A	L	E	P	S		S	C	A	T
S	H	U	F	F	L	E	C	A	P		B	O	R	U		S	O	A	P	Y
C	E	S	A	R	E		S	N	I	P	S	N	A	P	S	N	O	R	U	M
A	D	E	L	I	E		I	D	L	E		E	P	P	I	E		A	L	I
B	A	Y	L	O	R		N	Y	E	T		R	H	Y	M	E		T	A	E

174

E	D	I	L	E		W	A	S	P	S		F	I	N	E		C	H	E	W
R	U	S	S	I	A		A	N	T	I	C		I	C	A	N	T		R	O	T	A
S	A	T	U	R	D	A	Y	N	I	G	H	T	F	E	V	E	R		I	D	A	S
E	D	O		E	A	R	N	E	R		O	U	T	R	E		I	D	E	S	T
	M	O	E		N	O	N	E	S		A	V	E	S
B	A	N	D	S	A	W		P	E	L	E	E		O	D	I	N		S	T	K
O	B	E	R	O	N		A	N	Y	W	E	D	N	E	S	D	A	Y		W	A	N
S	A	V	A	N	T		D	O	L	E	D		M	O	I	L		L	E	S	E
S	T	E	W	S		A	M	B	E	R		M	A	I	L	S		P	I	E	T	A
E	E	R	S		A	M	I	E		L	A	D	L	E		T	I	L	T	E	D
D	S	O		G	I	R	L	F	R	I	D	A	Y		G	R	E	A	T	S
	N	O	T	O	N	E		R	I	C	A	N		I	N	A	R	C	H
	A	S	S	O	R	T		R	I	C	K	M	O	N	D	A	Y		U	R	N
S	Q	U	A	M	A		T	I	M	E	S		A	I	R	S		B	R	A	E
L	U	N	G	E		S	I	L	L	Y		T	O	D	O	S		F	E	S	T	E
A	I	D	E		E	P	E	E		R	E	L	I	C		S	O	R	D	I	D
I	L	A		I	F	I	T	S	T	U	E	S	D	A	Y		P	I	R	A	T	E
N	A	Y		A	F	R	O		H	I	L	T	S		A	L	L	A	Y	E	D
	O	M	O	O		M	E	N	E	S		D	R	I
	E	L	G	A	R		T	E	S	T	A		T	R	A	N	C	E		O	P	S
A	M	O	R		T	H	A	T	W	A	S	T	H	E	W	E	E	K	T	H	A	T
P	I	P	E		S	E	R	A	I		E	R	O	D	E		S	E	A	N	C	E
O	R	E	S		P	A	L	M		S	A	R	O	S		D	R	E	A	M

175

```
LIMIT.COST.SAFE.IMA
ANADEM.SPEAR.OYER.MAX
BRUISEDCARDEALERS.ARM
SED.TRIO.LARAS.BRIE
.LAVATORYTECHNICIAN.
RICA.EAU.TEAAND.
BLOCKMARKETEER.DRESS
ISA.NON.DELS.CIA.UIT
SAL.OPTS.ASI.TORINESE
.POPULAR.THIOL.NERAC
.SON.PETALPUSHER.AWL
STRIP.RETIA.RISESTO
COTTAGES.BPS.SLAT.RHO
HUE.RID.PREP.ATA.KAI
.TRAIN.HAIRAIDWARDENS
.BAZAAR.RNA.URGE
MERCHANTSOFVENISON
AXIS.STEAL.TBAR.IDA
JIM.BEAREROFGOODNUDES
OLE.ALTE.EOSIN.AIROUT
RED.GLEE.DRAG.SELMA
```

176

```
JEWEL.KARL.STAT.ONA
AROSE.SARAS.NOTE.EMMET
PARTIALPOST.APOCALYPSE
ELKE.MOPUP.SCRAP.OLEATE
.PAGAN.KELLY.TRAY
USV.ORA.DINNA.KAISERS
PHEASANT.SEDIMENTS.UTA
SERGE.EASE.RAGOUT.PNOM
HAYED.INSULL.CALM.BASRA
ORCS.OBESE.ISALL.BATTEN
TYL.STATESTATUE.DUTCHY
.OSCARS.RIO.SOOTHE
.ASTERS.PROSPERITY.GAD
GREENY.LIETO.NILES.SAVE
REVET.HEEL.NETTED.TOMAS
ONER.SOFTIE.LOAN.RUBLE
GAI.CATACLYSM.INFERIOR
.SNARERS.BEEBE.ARE.TNT
.PONY.SHOWS.ESTES
STAPLE.SCOWS.PLATO.JOLT
HASAFISCAL.KEENINSIDES
UTILE.PALL.PARTE.AMANA
TEA.TREY.SLYER.LAYER
```

177

```
JOGS.SCARP.MAGIC.APAM
OPAH.PALAR.AWATA.SALE
VATICINATE.GALIMATIAS
ELEVATOR.VINYL.PRAXIS
.ABEE.PAGE.STAIR.
.ACRES.SAINTS.HISTRIO
ETHER.BIBLIOPHAGE.END
LORE.CALL.HEWN.SCAD
ANY.PHILOLOGERS.HORNE
NESTLER.EWERS.CAREER
.OREAD.SANTE.SALEM
ORGEAT.NISEI.USELESS
CERES.CYBERNETICS.NAP
ALAS.NOSY.GATA.ATLE
LIP.CAMELOPARDS.ENATE
ACHIEVE.SPATES.ARILS
.GRITS.PITT.SHAM.
PADNAG.MOORE.SOOTIEST
CHROMATICS.SOPHROSYNE
TSAR.TUTTE.TRIOS.TRIN
SOME.ETHOS.SETTE.SEPT
```

178

```
TAMED.LEIF.ROMER.TIARA
AGILE.ATLI.DEMURE.ONTOP
BIGBROTHER.ELICIT.ETTES
SOSO.WHO.MYFATHERSHOUSE
.WANES.SETS.ITON.
OCS.PER.VENI.REELECTS
SHOWERY.VERSO.LIVID.HRH
GONERS.SON.ENLIVEN.VIII
OISE.ACTUP.ITER.DELVE
OCA.THREESISTERS.BENDER
DEN.RAINS.STAGE.DEPORT
.DROWSE.STAKE.SALOME.
.CLAUSE.CLONE.STILT.NNE
TROMPE.GRANDMAMOSES.SAM
REVUE.CHAN.ELEGY.OHIO
UTES.CHASTEN.DAY.ALCOTT
CAR.FAITH.SEDER.FEATURE
ENSNARLS.TWIN.IRR.RED
.AWED.FILL.ONAIR.
ALLINTHEFAMILY.NAT.EGAL
BOILS.OILCAN.UNCLEVANYA
ROMEO.ODETTE.ROLL.ADAMS
STERN.DOWSE.TREY.EYRES
```

179

```
DAMP.ISOF.GRAPH.ABC
IDEA.ANTRA.ROLEO.MART
CONTENDERS.ANTITHESES
TRAINERS.CANDO.HALITE
ANTENNA.LINGO.FERINE
.NET.HASTE.CAAMA.
ASPCA.HINTERLANDS.PPP
IHRE.CAKE.UNOS.RAO
DAO.MALEDICTION.JOOSS
AMP.ARES.NOISE.WARMTH
.RAFTER.NOVAE.BAMBOO.
YOGURT.MINER.FORE.TRA
ACARI.LACERATIONS.IAN
MKT.PUSH.ODES.DOLT
SSE.DISHEVELLED.MENSA
.DELTA.ADEAL.VAC.
.SEEMLY.OLEAN.MENAGES
MANTUA.GUILD.MARINATE
DETERGENTS.STAGNATION
ITES.ENARE.OVINE.ETNA
ART.DATES.NANA.REST
```

180

```
AGENT.APART.AMICE.WAIL
TOQUE.MORES.NONAE.FALSE
WOULDYOULIKETOTAKEAWALK
ASA.SORTED.MORON.NISSE
RELS.KISS.SINEW.ARREST
.NOUN.ATLI.SHOE.
LETASMILEBEYOURUMBRELLA
ERICH.OVEN.PAREE.MEET
TANKA.SWEET.OPTED.BONGO
USES.SAINT.MMII.BUTTIN
PEA.ONON.MOIST.CUNEATE
.SINGININTHERAIN.
PALETTE.RANTS.ONLY.CAB
ADONIS.OUCH.ASCOT.GATE
TERRA.DANTE.CRAKE.DRILL
RENO.SONIC.HERE.RURAL
IMALWAYSCHASINGRAINBOWS
.ALEE.CURT.SNOB.
SAMPAN.THUMP.BOSN.YVES
CLAIM.BEATA.HOLIER.ILO
WAITTILLTHECLOUDSROLLBY
AMATI.AURAS.INLET.SAMOA
SPRY.YEAST.PEERS.SLAWS
```

181

182

183

184

185

186

187

```
ASKS   ADDN  LOADS  MNOP
CHIC  MARIO  ENDIT  AERI
HOWARDFAST   OSCARWILDE
SPIREA MALINE GAGGLES
      CAYS  GENIT  ODER
HATED EARAND ANDREWS
ASH  ADAGES SINAL  TINS
DIOR UBIETY SALEM  LEO
JAMESBOND  ABETS  OFLAW
INADOOR    OTERO  BRAIDS
     SONINLAW  HELVETIA
ASPENS ODEON  ALARMED
LEASE ANISE ESCALATOR
ANI  TINGE SPROUT  SELA
SANE SITUP UNTIES  LIC
   TENDSTO ARTIST WILCO
     CALA  INUSE  YEAS
ALCOHOL STRIFE RIOTED
WORDSWORTH  NORMANLEAR
OGEE  TOOLE TRIAL  DATA
LEES  OSIER ODES   ERST
```

188

```
ABBESS    FLIER    ABATED
COOKIE   PRESTO   LASERS
ELDERS  ABASHES   LUCENT
SAY  UTES   REI   CLIMAT
    SUPERSONICTRANSPORT
APTS  TRIPE    OAST   TAA
CROAT  OVERT  MYTH  HAIR
ROC  ABLER  OKE  MEDULLA
ESKIMO    ASUR    FIFER
APICES  ASPCA  ELAN  TRE
GENE  TBS  OHM  LEM  SHEM
ERG  NOAH  IDEAL  IMPEDE
     SENSE  LORN  LAYMEN
WELCOME  SSW  DRAYS  OED
AMOI  ABOU  NARES  SPUME
TIC  RAKE    PESTS   USSR
 TRANSALASKAPIPELINE
    TAUTLY  ONE  IRON TWO
AMONTH  SCANNER   POORER
CERATO  PLEDGE    ENDALL
HASSAN   LASSO    DEEPLY
```

189

```
NLRA     JETS   AHEM  ATEE
EVENED   OLEO   SALESTALK
SINGLESBARS   SLIDERULE
SIDEBET  IRATE   AIRE
    LASAGNA   ENDS   FURS
DECI  NAE  BETE  ISSUER
PROCEEDS   ATOLLS    NNE
TIN  TRIPLETHREAT  POST
SEC  ENNEAD   THEREFOR
SERRE  DIDO  SER  ASTRO
RONS   CATCH    WITH
COTTA  STS  THUS  ASSET
IMPOLITE    ESTATE  MUD
RBIS  WINSLOWHOMER  INA
CET  IRAQIS   MORSELED
ARCHES  NUBS  JAR  ALDA
  SHED  STAR  DESIRER
   LAME  LANES  TENFOUR
BASEMETAL   ONTHEDOUBLE
REINSTATE  ASEA  OLLIES
ACTA  SEED  HERS   SEXT
```

190

```
DEMUR  GUISE    OSHA  SPRIT
URANO  ARCED  HUNAN  QUITO
MRDEEDSGOESTOTOWN
DADA  EMEND  ARSON  FINERY
UTES  WAN  UNSET   IONE
MANET STRANGERSONATRAIN
   INK  IMPOST  MULE   NNE
ATASTE  AGEE   DAR  DRIFT
THETOWERINGINFERNO  ILET
BORE  LADD  NAIL   NAPERY
ATIE  BIB   PISH    SIR
THEPLEASUREOFHISCOMPANY
   INN  ROSS   TAN  ALIE
CAPOTE  GUTS  TIER   NAPA
ABUT  TAKETHEMONEYANDRUN
RAREE  LID   ERIN  SCAMPS
ASS  SOIE  STALAG   PEA
THELONGVOYAGEHOME  AESOP
ATEN  ARNIE   ARE   LOLL
HEATER  ARIAN  ANNUL  AREA
AEGIR  THANKGODITSFRIDAY
IRANI  REGGA  RILLE  UNITE
LYRIC  SMEE   KNEES  SEDER
```

191

```
SMALL     ACHES    MSCUE
ASLEEP    TREVI   REPENTS
MSADVENTURES   ELISIONS
BORG   REASON  ABETS  NAT
ARME  MSCONSTRUES   MIRE
STERS   THE    HITS  PSALM
SSD  PALE  GRIDS    TANS
   MORES   AIR    TEAL
 BASINS   MSADVISE   LOAM
DOUBLE  JOEL  ALAN   ILLY
RILES  FENS  BLUR   GALEN
UTAH  RUED  HOES   ARNICA
MESA  MSREPORT   TRACES
   VASE   LOG   DRUSE
IBIS  BRUTE  EONS    BMT
ACOOK  ARAM  SMU   OBESE
HERR  MSAPPREHEND   ETTA
ACE  DASNT  AMERCE  WART
BADGERED   MSCHIEFMAKER
 POULTRY  CHEAT  TERESA
  MSFIT   LIENS   MESSY
```

192

```
PLEA  SCUBAS   STAMP  ARUBA
LAUD  ULRICA   TELAR  GENII
ATRIBEOFREDMENAXEINHAND
NIOBE  SALT   ABRI    RIA
ESP  DIE   TREE  CUI   SESS
THEWINTERFIERCEANDWHITE
   IMP  RILE   EMESA   DES
BAL  AVOCATS  PROA  COOPT
MOLLYWITHYOUREYESSOBLUE
ARF  ENGI    NET   SYN  RAPT
SAIGA  ICES   BAER    UPI
THEIRFLAGTOAPRILSBREEZE
ANI   GERT   SVEN   INLET
ASIN  LTD  RAH  GAME   ORO
DONTFIREUNLESSFIREDUPON
DORSO  ACTS  SCHOOLS   RES
ITA  SAUCE    HORN    CSA
CHRISTMASSNOWWASFALLING
TEEN  IAN  NASA   ALI  DOE
   AIL   SOIL   BOOT  PEONY
KEEPSTHECOLOROFTHESKIES
EASEL  AMAZE  UNISEX  EDGE
WROTE  MUTED  NATURE  DOOR
```

193

```
RELIVED  ▓ TEHERAN  ▓ YER
ANATOLIA OREGANO ▓ BETA
MILITATE REAGANCOUNTY
ADONIS ▓ SCENTED ▓ TESTEE
▓ ENTR AROID ▓ UNHAND
GEORGIABROWN ▓ KAROL ▓
ALMA ▓ CRAB ▓ GLENN ▓ EADS
LLANO ▓ EBOAT ▓ ERN ▓ SABRE
EARTHY ▓ ANSERINE ▓ AGAIN
▓ MEM ▓ ISEE ▓ EARMUFFS
SCAN ▓ TOMCONNALLY ▓ ETTE
HUMIDIFY ▓ RAND ▓ SEE
ALICE ▓ FOOTGEAR ▓ STEPPE
NECKS ▓ APR ▓ ESMES ▓ EXILE
EXEC ▓ STEER ▓ SAAR ▓ OPEN
▓ AMASS ▓ EDGARKENNEDY
SECRET ▓ STIEL ▓ EDIE ▓
CRATES ▓ BLARNEY ▓ LARIAT
HOMERUNBAKER ▓ AMICABLY
EDER ▓ MALTESE ▓ MUNITION
DEL ▓ ASSENTS ▓ GENESEE
```

194

```
PERIOD ▓ CRISP ▓ SITS ▓ HAS
ALASKA ▓ AURAL ▓ ARAL ▓ CARIB
WALLAWALLAWALLABY ▓ OMEGA
SNEE ▓ DIMES ▓ CYANS ▓ UNMANS
▓ SOLDER ▓ VERDI ▓ ANGELOT
OFT ▓ PIED ▓ BABE ▓ NSTAR
DEADENS ▓ SOSOSOROSIS ▓ COB
ERRING ▓ MEDES ▓ PERIL ▓ MAIL
SUTES ▓ SALES ▓ GHATS ▓ TONNE
SLAT ▓ SPRAG ▓ CHICHICHICKS
AER ▓ CHACHACHARTS ▓ HARASS
▓ TARES ▓ HUN ▓ OATEN ▓
ARABIA ▓ BABABAKEOFFS ▓ COG
BERBERBERETS ▓ RELEE ▓ CASE
ACTED ▓ OLGAS ▓ AARON ▓ CANTO
STAY ▓ GODOT ▓ STAIR ▓ SANDER
EON ▓ TATATADPOLE ▓ DUSTING
▓ BELEM ▓ ALMS ▓ DONT ▓ DDE
STORMER ▓ SCRAY ▓ CARDED
PELOPS ▓ THAIS ▓ TASSO ▓ ROBE
ALIKE ▓ CHOWCHOWCHOWLINES
NEVER ▓ AARE ▓ ELITE ▓ NIECES
▓ GEN ▓ DRED ▓ DENIS ▓ SERENE
```

195

```
▓ AVIS ▓ SPAT ▓ LESS ▓ FRED
CRINI ▓ CAMEL ▓ ORCA ▓ RIVA
OPERA ▓ AGORA ▓ GAOL ▓ ENID
DENIM ▓ BERMUDATRIANGLE
ANN ▓ EAST ▓ IRAN ▓ PERC ▓
▓ ASSN ▓ ONER ▓ PINCHME
TABLETS ▓ MINNESOTAFATS
OSRIC ▓ HIE ▓ GIN ▓ DRURY
PREDATION ▓ BARS ▓ EIDER
PEA ▓ THEO ▓ CEDE ▓ DDE
ODDS ▓ IRISHSETTER ▓ SSTS
▓ EIN ▓ TIES ▓ ARAB ▓ PEW
AETAS ▓ RAPT ▓ MANTOVANI
SLITS ▓ SAN ▓ ALE ▓ SINON
KENTUCKYDERBY ▓ SETTING
▓ VALERIE ▓ AERO ▓ WOOS ▓
▓ ERIN ▓ ARGO ▓ SEEN ▓ HAS
BRUSSELSSPROUTS ▓ BAMBI
EARL ▓ SECT ▓ EDNAS ▓ UBOAT
TIGE ▓ TSAR ▓ TETRA ▓ LISTS
ANEW ▓ OSTE ▓ DORY ▓ LESE
```

196

```
▓ TURFS ▓ ETO ▓ ADD ▓ DIBBLE
▓ ONTOP ▓ GREATER ▓ SCORER
OLDERINGERMANY ▓ TENETS
RUR ▓ GEESE ▓ AMI ▓ LEASE
REAMERS ▓ ADAMS ▓ PARD ▓
INPUT ▓ SANDINSPAIN ▓ IRS
SEEN ▓ NOES ▓ ORAD ▓ NET
▓ DDS ▓ ANT ▓ MORON ▓ PISA
▓ ITALIANFORTWO ▓ ITER
SIG ▓ ABLE ▓ AIDA ▓ CARL
INEPTLY ▓ COLIN ▓ DEVOLVE
AFRO ▓ AMES ▓ TOME ▓ YET
MIMI ▓ SPANISHFORSEA
EDAM ▓ HADES ▓ RNA ▓ RUB
SEN ▓ HAIL ▓ ALAI ▓ RARE
ELF ▓ ALLINFRANCE ▓ HAREM
▓ OGRE ▓ BULGY ▓ REALISM
AKRON ▓ TEE ▓ SIGNS ▓ TOE
TURRET ▓ FRENCHFORSHORT
ODESSA ▓ DICTION ▓ OLENT
RUDEST ▓ RAY ▓ IDI ▓ LEWES
```

197

```
ELL ▓ PAT ▓ ASPALE ▓ ACTOR
PEI ▓ OKRA ▓ NEARER ▓ MAORI
IAL ▓ THERADADADADADASONG
CHIBABACHIBABA ▓ ISERE
▓ AGATHA ▓ ANY ▓ DOS ▓ AVE
STARER ▓ ENG ▓ HER ▓ ALEE
KAHNS ▓ WREAK ▓ SALADFORK
URUS ▓ MIENS ▓ TREMOLO
LLB ▓ ZIPADEEDOODAH ▓ RON
KEB ▓ ACE ▓ MERL ▓ AVA
ITA ▓ TARARABOMDERE ▓ LEM
NOH ▓ LALA ▓ DOM ▓ ORE
GNU ▓ SNOOKEYOOKUMS ▓ OWL
▓ BEREAVE ▓ PRICE ▓ CREE
UNBLOTTED ▓ CRATE ▓ URALS
LUAU ▓ TER ▓ FLY ▓ SPELLS
MPH ▓ ILS ▓ DOI ▓ PRIEST
▓ TUTTE ▓ CHIMCHIMCHERES
BIBBIDIBOBBIDIBOO ▓ AXE
BABAR ▓ NELLIE ▓ SENT ▓ JAN
CLARE ▓ GREENS ▓ DDS ▓ AMY
```

198

```
CAMPER ▓ MAAMS ▓ ANNAS ▓ PATE
ARIOSO ▓ ENSUE ▓ GUILT ▓ AMOR
SCENTSOFYUMA ▓ LISLE ▓ IONS
CONS ▓ SRO ▓ PULLETSURPRISE
ASSES ▓ ORSE ▓ TOT ▓ EDER
▓ LOY ▓ ARDOR ▓ INE ▓ OLGAS
▓ BALLETSLIPPERS ▓ STERNE
ERLE ▓ GALLOWS ▓ HID ▓ MENAGE
RUT ▓ HOLIER ▓ DOSE ▓ AGAVES
ONESIDED ▓ MAE ▓ BASE ▓ ERE
STRESS ▓ BRIDALPATH ▓ VASE
▓ NET ▓ AHEADOFHARE ▓ SEC
SNAP ▓ ONESWALLOW ▓ DANCED
COT ▓ DATA ▓ IFY ▓ MOUNTEBA
OSIRIS ▓ VEER ▓ BOILED ▓ NOW
RAVINE ▓ ETA ▓ CRUCIAL ▓ STEN
ELEVES ▓ ATTRACTIVENESS ▓
RESET ▓ SAL ▓ HOOKE ▓ DEE
▓ TIER ▓ SEW ▓ STOP ▓ ADAMS
THYMEONMYHANDS ▓ URI ▓ SLOE
ROUE ▓ TOPEE ▓ SHOPPINGMAUL
ILLE ▓ ARISE ▓ TOMAH ▓ GRETEL
SEEK ▓ SATON ▓ OWENS ▓ ARNESS
```

199

```
OTTO  SHOO  UTAH    PRIMA
SOAPCHIPS  POCO   RENAN
TEESHIRTS  SPREADEAGLE
   ARE  ALIKE  GOV  RES
BOB  PERT  ELI   ANAPEST
AMUSE   AUTOCRAT  IOS
BATTLEOFBUNKERHILL
ANTA  LUTES   ACAD  ISLE
  EGRET    ONDA   ITCHES
LAREINE  AENEID   REEDS
ALB  PAREXCELLENCE  ERE
STALE  SICILY   OLYMPUS
SALONS  CLEF   BASIS
ORLY  ITAL   JAMES  THEE
  OCCUPATIONALHAZARD
 ILO  SERENITY   RINSE
LEVANTS   ASE  SLAM  KEN
AXE  VIA  ANISE  UMA
PIGEONHOLES  NILEGREEN
STONY   FACT  CLUBHOUSE
ESTES   ARKS  ELSA  DREW
```

200

```
SOMME  PASS   PUPA  TAOS
ABEAM  CALLA  ARSON  LEDGE
PERMUTATION  MOUNTAINEER
ISLA  ARENT  MESAS  ECOLES
DEE  ABONE  CANAL  TRINES
  EDAMS  SOLTI  GHATS
DOCTORS  INDISCREET  PRO
ABOARD  ILIAC  INRE  GRIM
CONTE  ODETS  SNARE  REEVE
HESS  CLOD   EINE  MERCER
ASI  ALLEGORIST  LEADINS
  DALLAS  ARISE  BURLAP
THERAMS  DENOMINATE  ITA
PARERS  PILE   IDES  ATIP
OLAND  BLESS  TAXES  ADAGE
LETA  ARAG  SOLON  SLATER
EYE  DECORATION  PALMERS
  EROSE  EDILE  VOTES
ABSENT  SPARE  LEERY  SPA
ACACIA  FLAPS  AORTA  AKIM
COLONIALIST  INCORPORATE
CUERS  CENTS  MOONY  RATON
TORT  TAGS   PASA  BLEND
```

RANDOM HOUSE CROSSWORD ORDER FORM

VOL.	ISBN	QUANT.	PRICE	TOTAL

New York Times Sunday Crosswords

New York Times Sunday Crossword Puzzles
Volume 22 • 978-0-8129-3645-2 ____ $8.95 ____

New York Times Sunday Crossword Puzzles
Volume 23 • 978-0-8129-3646-9 ____ $8.95 ____

New York Times Sunday Crossword Puzzles
Volume 24 • 978-0-8129-3647-6 ____ $8.95 ____

New York Times Sunday Crossword Puzzles
Volume 25 • 978-0-8129-3648-3 ____ $8.95 ____

New York Times Sunday Crossword Puzzles
Volume 26 • 978-0-8129-3649-0 ____ $8.95 ____

New York Times Toughest Crossword Puzzles
Volume 7 • 978-0-8129-3650-6 ____ $8.95 ____

New York Times Toughest Crossword Puzzles
Volume 8 • 978-0-8129-3651-3 ____ $8.95 ____

New York Times Crossword Tribute to Eugene T.
Maleska • 978-0-8129-3384-0 ____ $13.95 ____

Los Angeles Times Sunday Crosswords

Los Angeles Times Sunday Crossword Omnibus
Volume 5 • 978-0-8129-3683-4 ____ $12.95 ____

Los Angeles Times Sunday Crossword Omnibus
Volume 6 • 978-0-375-72248-6 ____ $12.98 ____

Los Angeles Times Sunday Crossword Puzzles
Volume 25 • 978-0-375-72156-4 ____ $9.95 ____

Los Angeles Times Sunday Crossword Puzzles
Volume 26 • 978-0-375-72174-8 ____ $9.95 ____

Los Angeles Times Sunday Crossword Puzzles
Volume 27 • 978-0-375-72175-5 ____ $9.95 ____

Los Angeles Times Sunday Crossword Puzzles
Volume 28 • 978-0-375-72176-2 ____ $9.99 ____

Washington Post Sunday Crosswords

Washington Post Sunday Crossword Omnibus
Volume 3 • 978-0-375-72187-8 ____ $12.95 ____

Washington Post Sunday Crossword Puzzles
Volume 14 • 978-0-8129-3491-5 ____ $9.95 ____

Washington Post Sunday Crossword Puzzles
Volume 15 • 978-0-8129-3492-2 ____ $9.95 ____

Washington Post Sunday Crossword Puzzles
Volume 15 • 978-0-8129-3488-5 ____ $9.95 ____

Boston Globe Sunday Crosswords

Boston Globe Sunday Crossword Omnibus
Volume 3 • 978-0-375-72186-1 ____ $12.95 ____

Boston Globe Sunday Crossword Puzzles
Volume 14 • 978-0-8129-3487-8 ____ $9.95 ____

New York Magazine Crosswords

New York Magazine Crossword Puzzles
Volume 6 • 978-0-8129-3526-4 ____ $9.95 ____

New York Magazine Crossword Puzzles
Volume 7 • 978-0-8129-3684-1 ____ $9.95 ____

New York Magazine Crossword Omnibus
Volume 1 • 978-0-375-72153-3 ____ $12.95 ____

Chicago Tribune Crosswords

Chicago Tribune Daily Crossword Omnibus
978-0-375-72219-6 ____ $12.95 ____

Chicago Tribune Daily Crossword Puzzles
Volume 5 • 978-0-8129-3560-8 ____ $9.95 ____

Chicago Tribune Daily Crossword Puzzles
Volume 6 • 978-0-8129-3561-5 ____ $9.95 ____

Chicago Tribune Sunday Crossword Omnibus
978-0-375-72209-7 ____ $12.95 ____

Chicago Tribune Sunday Crossword Puzzles
Volume 5 • 978-0-8129-3563-9 ____ $9.95 ____

Random House Vacation Crosswords

Random House All Weather Crossword Omnibus
978-0-375-72200-4 ____ $12.95 ____

Random House Endless Summer Crosswords
978-0-8129-3624-7 ____ $6.95 ____

Random House Harvest Moon Crosswords
978-0-8129-3628-5 ____ $6.95 ____

Random House Springtime Crosswords
978-0-8129-3626-1 ____ $6.95 ____

Random House Summer Nights Crosswords
978-0-8129-3627-8 ____ $6.95 ____

Random House Winter Treat Crosswords
978-0-8129-3623-0 ____ $6.95 ____

Random House Year Round Crossword Omnibus
978-0-375-72201-1 ____ $12.95 ____

Random House Crosswords

Random House Casual Crossword Omnibus
978-0-375-72244-8 ____ $12.95 ____

Random House Casual Crosswords
Volume 3 • 978-0-8129-3666-7 ____ $9.95 ____

Random House Casual Crosswords
Volume 4 • 978-0-8129-3673-5 ____ $9.95 ____

Random House Casual Crosswords
Volume 5 • 978-0-8129-3674-2 ____ $9.95 ____

Random House Crosswords
Volume 5 • 978-0-8129-3501-1 ____ $9.95 ____

Random House Casual Crosswords
Volume 6 • 978-0-8129-3675-9 ____ $9.95 ____

Random House Casual Crosswords
Volume 7 • 978-0-375-72331-5 ____ $9.99 ____

Wall Street Journal Crosswords

Wall Street Journal Crossword Puzzle Omnibus
978-0-375-72210-3 ____ $12.95 ____

Wall Street Journal Crossword Puzzles
Volume 4 • 978-0-8129-3640-7 ____ $9.95 ____

Wall Street Journal Crossword Puzzles
Volume 5 • 978-0-375-72154-0 ____ $9.95 ____

Specialty Crosswords and Puzzle Reference

Mel's Weekend Crosswords
Volume 1 • 978-0-8129-3502-8 ____ $9.95 ____

Mel's Weekend Crosswords
Volume 2 • 978-0-8129-3503-5 ____ $9.95 ____

Random House Webster's Crossword Puzzle Dictionary
4th Edition 978-0-375-72131-1 ____ $18.95 ____

Random House Webster's Large Print
Crossword Puzzle Dictionary
978-0-375-72220-2 ____ $24.95 ____

Stanley Newman's Crosswords Shortcuts
978-0-375-72306-3 ____ $12.95 ____

Stanley Newman's Movie Mania Crosswords
978-0-8129-3468-7 ____ $7.95 ____

The Puzzlemaster Presents: Will Shortz's Best
Puzzles from NPR
978-0-8129-3515-8 ____ $13.95 ____

15,003 Answers: The Ultimate Trivia Encyclopedia
978-0-375-72237-0 ____ $24.95 ____

To place your order, fill out this coupon and return to:
RANDOM HOUSE, INC., 400 HAHN ROAD, WESTMINSTER, MD 21157
ATTENTION: ORDER PROCESSING
☐ Enclosed is my check or money order payable to Random House
☐ Charge my credit card (circle type): AMEX Visa Mastercard

Credit Card Number

NAME   SIGNATURE

ADDRESS   CITY   STATE   ZIP

To order, call toll-free 1-800-733-3000

Postage & Handling	
CARRIER	ADD
USPS	$5.50
UPS	$7.50

Total Books ____
Total Dollars $ ____
Sales Tax * $ ____
Postage & Handling $ ____
Total Enclosed $ ____

* Please calculate according to your state sales tax rate